To Brom Vermeulen

Audrey Clark

MIKE FIVE EIGHT
Air War Over Cambodia

By
Rocky Raab

Copyright © 2006 by Rocky Raab

All rights reserved under Pan-American and
International Copyright Conventions.
Printed in the United States of America. No part of this publication may
be reproduced in any way or by any means, or stored in any information
retrieval system of any kind, without the prior permission in writing from
the author, except in the case of brief quotations embodied in critical
articles and reviews.

This book is completely fictional. Any resemblance to people,
places or events is purely coincidental.

ISBN : 978-1-4303-0062-5
Published by: Lulu Press, Inc
Morrisville, NC
Printed in the United States of America

*To the men of what is now
an extinct form of aerial combat:*

Forward Air Controllers

PROLOGUE

"Sorry, Lieutenant Naille, there is no mistake. The needs of the Air Force come first."

"But, Sergeant... I was promised."

"By whom, sir? Someone here at Military Personnel Center?"

"Well, no; by my former commander. Back in Vietnam."

"Again, sir, I'm sorry. But no one outside MPC has authority to make assignments. According to your records, you are a qualified Forward Air Controller in the O-2A aircraft. You did not complete your original overseas assignment in that capacity due to a non-combat injury, and you have now been returned to flight status by the flight surgeon. Is all of that correct, sir?"

"Yes," Rusty said, his shoulders sagging as he mentally foretold the rest of the conversation.

"Then I have no choice but to assign you back to your unit in Vietnam, effective immediately. The assignment orders you received are correct. Sir," the voice on the phone added, signaling the end of the discussion. The line clicked.

Rusty turned to Mary Beth, disappointment and resignation clouding his face. "It wasn't a mistake. No OV-10. I'm going back to 'Nam in the O-2."

"When," she asked, the date her husband would be leaving far more important to her than what he'd be flying.

He waved the papers he'd been clutching. "Tomorrow, just like this says."

"Oh, not so soon! I haven't had you here long enough!"

"Long enough for some things," Rusty grinned, sliding his hand up and over her breast. "Even with that cast on my arm and all..." His face slumped just a trifle as he added, "I really had my heart set on that OV-10 Bronco, though."

"But you said you liked the O-2."

"I like the FAC job more than the plane, actually. The Oscar Duck is kind of a pig."

"A duck is a pig? Forward Air Control pilots have an odd sense of biology."

His grin sprang back. "O-2, Oscar Deuce, Ruptured Duck, Sky Pig...it's all the same plane. Not anywhere near as sexy as the OV-10 Bronco, no matter what you call it."

"Sexier than I am?" She pressed her hand over the one that cupped her.

"Oh, no. After all, I wanted to trade in the O-2. I'm keeping you."

"It brought you home once, though. It will again. And it's only eight months this time, not a full year. Promise me you *will* come home, Rusty. Promise."

"With all my heart, Mary Beth. I promise. And I always keep a promise."

Her eyes welled up suddenly, betraying the fear that lurked behind her brave words. It had been hard enough on her when Rusty went off to combat the first time, when they were freshly married. It was brutal this second time. She hoped that he wouldn't sense how terrified she really was.

He had seen the tears, though, and he turned back to his printed orders to cover the catch in his throat. "I guess I'd better start packing."

That night, they lay next to each other, fingers entwined. Neither of them spoke or made an overture to do more. It was as if, by unspoken mutual consent, neither wanted to make love one last time – for fear that it really might be the last time.

MIKE FIVE EIGHT

CHAPTER ONE

I f possible, the 20-hour trip in the tubular torture chamber otherwise known as a stretched DC-8 belonging to Flying Tiger Airlines was even more gruesome the second time around. The food and the forced smiles on the cabin crew were even more plastic. It seemed to Rusty that the fug of nearly 300 men cramped into that tube seemed even stronger, the fetid tang of fear even more pervasive, the miasma of futility and frustrated anger even thicker now.

But even that unwholesome air seemed like the lilac-scented zephyrs of spring when the cabin doors opened at Cam Rahn Bay. Someone ahead of him exclaimed, "What the hell is that?" It was precisely what Rusty had said when he'd arrived here half a year ago. The reek of dead fish, diesel exhaust, human feces, smoke and other unidentifiable horrors hadn't improved.

"It's just Vietnam," Rusty said. "You won't get used to it." It was precisely what someone behind him had replied. Rusty shook his head, enjoying the irony if not the experience that allowed it.

Experience has its benefits, though. While the work crew at the Aerial Port Squadron unloaded the plane, Rusty bypassed the milling throng awaiting their bags and went through the in-processing line and then found a phone. "Twenty-first TASS? I'm Lt Naille. I'm at the Aerial Port and need a jeep so I can report."

"Yessir. I have your orders right here. One jeep coming up, no sweat. You know where to go?"

"Oh yeah. Not my first time in Paradise."

"Uh huh. I copy that. You got your bags?"

"I will have by the time you get here. I'll be at the flightline door, north end."

"Won't be me, but no sweat. You're our only arrival today."

Twenty minutes later, Rusty was standing outside the corrugated metal building, duffel bag at his feet and sweat already running down inside his shirt. A jeep pulled up and stopped, a two-striper enlisted man at the wheel. He neither saluted nor got out. "You the FAC? Hop in."

The nonchalant, almost irreverent tone didn't shock or anger Rusty like it had the first time he'd arrived in Vietnam. Few enlisted people volunteered for Vietnam, and being here was already the worst punishment most of them could suffer. Disrespect for superiors, especially for junior officers, was rampant. And, Rusty knew, it became even more pervasive as a man's year-long tour drew to a close.

"Yup," Rusty replied. He glanced at the man's nametag. "How short are you, Mandeville?"

The man's eyebrows shot up. "Two-digit midget. Fifty-six and a wakeup. Sir," he appended, half heartedly. "How'd you know?"

"Doesn't take a Sherlock. Your uniform is shot and your mustache is out of limits, but the big clue is that your 'give a shit' meter is off the scale low."

"You gonna give me a ration of shit for it?" Mandeville said, a hard edge creeping into his voice.

"Nope, no point to it. Wouldn't help you or me. You're clearly not a lifer. I could give you a lecture about how respect for your superiors is in your best interest whether you're military or civilian, but that's a lesson you'll learn on your own, or won't learn at all. Either way, it's no skin off my nose."

The man merely grunted his disinterest in this junior lieutenant's pontificating. He popped the clutch the moment Naille's butt hit the seat.

Rusty reported in to a Major Pennington, who told him he'd probably be at Cam Rahn for a week or two. He'd have to be re-qualified in the airplane and as a FAC due to his months of ground duty while recuperating from his broken arm. He assigned Rusty to a room in the temporary quarters used by officers of the 21st Tactical Air Support Squadron.

"Settle in, get unpacked and try to get some sleep, Naille. Report back here anytime tomorrow and you can pick up your flight manuals and equipment. I'll schedule your first re-qual flight for day after tomorrow."

"Yessir. I can hardly wait to get back to it. Any idea where I might be assigned?"

Pennington looked at him, a slightly bemused expression on his face. "Uh, let's not go into that until you're back up to speed. For now, just go hit the rack until you acclimate to the change of a dozen or so time zones. You look blasted, as usual for somebody just off the plane."

"Um, yeah...sir. I guess I am at that. See you tomorrow." Rusty saluted and went back out to the jeep. This time, Airman Mandeville was silent as he drove off the flightline and up the hill to Rusty's quarters.

Rusty found his second-floor room, threw down his duffel and collapsed onto the bed. He had a chance to marvel that the room was air-conditioned before he drifted off, but that was all.

Rusty awoke in pitch blackness to a series of loud but distant booms, followed by piercing sirens and the sound of running footsteps in the hallway outside his door. Rocket attack, he thought to himself, before nonchalantly rolling over and going back to sleep. When he woke again, daylight filtered in through the heavily draped window.

One down and about two hundred forty to go, Rusty thought to himself, almost automatically. Well, it's better than three sixty four. His previous tour had been cut short when he'd fallen off a roof, shattering his left arm. After seven hours of surgery, he'd been hustled out of the pig-sty called Landing Zone Emerald and back to the US for more surgery and physical therapy. All told, he'd been in Vietnam for about four months that first time, and the Air Force was now extracting the other two-thirds of his pound of flesh.

He showered, shaved, dressed in fatigues and walked to the nearby mess hall for breakfast. When he got back, he called and got a ride back to the 21st TASS headquarters.

"Lieutenant Naille, reporting for duty, sir."

Major Pennington, as it turned out, would be not only his checkout and re-qualification instructor but his personnel officer as well. "Everybody here wears two hats now, Naille, if not three. What with the drawdown and all. Things change every day. Hell, we're even serving as an in-country O-2 transition school now. Got two former O-1 drivers in just the other day. Their original units and bases closed, and the decision was made to upgrade them to the O-2 to finish their tours. Here comes one of them in from a training flight now."

Rusty looked out the window and saw a slight, almost thin man, now drenched in sweat but clearly possessed of off-blond hair with mustache to match. He was walking next to a captain, who gesticulated in time with his unheard words. They rounded a corner of the building and passed from sight.

"His name's Hubert. He arrived in-country about four months ago, got assigned to a tiny little Forward Operating Post with the Army and promptly made a helluva name for himself as a promising FAC. Then the Army closed the FOP and Hubert had no place to go. He was among the last of the replacement Bird Dog pilots, and there simply wasn't an assignment open for him. So we're upgrading him to the O-2 here. He's about done with that."

As Pennington spoke, he ruffled through Rusty's paperwork. "I see you were making quite a name for yourself, too. How'd this injury happen?"

"It's a bit embarrassing, sir. They were closing LZ Emerald, too, and on our last night there, I was lighting a gas-fired water heater we had installed on the roof of the FAC Shack for hot showers. It blew up, and I fell off the roof. I guess I landed on my arm. I don't actually remember much after the thing went kablooie, though."

"You're pulling my leg."

"No, sir. I wish I weren't. I'd be flying an OV-10 now if it weren't for that stupid heater." Rusty felt an edge of anger, frustration and resentment creep into the last sentence, and tried to correct for it. "No disrespect intended, sir. I do love being a FAC, but I had fairly lusted for an OV-10."

"Hmmm. Well, we can't always have what we want, Naille. The O-2 is good enough for the rest of us, it ought to be good enough for you."

Knowing he would not be able to dig himself out of the disastrous first impression he'd just given, Rusty just said, "Yessir. Indeed it is, sir."

Well, that about screws that pooch, Rusty thought to himself. Pennington is my new instructor *and* my personnel officer. Wonder what absolute hellhole I'll be assigned to now?

For the rest of the day, Rusty drew equipment and was assigned to a flight schedule. He'd essentially fly once a day, working up through a curriculum of basic aircraft maneuvers through combat maneuvers and culminating with at least one airstrike. Academic work would include aircraft systems, the current Rules of Engagement, weapons characteristics and the current US/Vietnamese chain of command. He thought that the flying part of it would come back to him quickly, but he soon learned that the politically-regulated Rules of Engagement varied almost daily, dictated by civilians in Washington and having little or no bearing in reality.

With his newly-issued flight gear stowed in a locker near the flightline, his Colt CAR-15 carbine and Smith & Wesson .38 revolver locked in the squadron armory and a briefcase of books, manuals, maps and schedules under his arm, Rusty was driven back to his quarters. He napped, still trying to accommodate himself to the massive shift in his bodily rhythms, but woke in time for the evening meal.

Afterwards, he was stretched out in a chair in the dayroom of his quarters, sorting through the manuals, when he saw that same blondish pilot walk in and sit down. "Hi, I'm Rusty Naille. Major Pennington says your name is Hubert, right?"

"Uh, yeah," the man said, apparently shaken that a stranger knew his name. "Sandy. Sandy Hubert. Did you say Rusty Nail? Are you putting me on?"

"Yes and no, in that order," Rusty said, rising to shake his hand. "It's a childhood nickname, but it's all I've gone by for most of my life."

"Well, there is kind of a reddish tint to your hair…sorta," Hubert said. "That's where I got my moniker." He tapped his hair, which, now that it had dried, was almost exactly the color of beach sand, matched by his mustache. "What's your real first name?"

"Um, you first, Sandy."

Hubert smiled back, his face opening into a wide, toothy grin that bespoke intelligence and wit. "Ah, you too? Well, then – how about if we just leave it at Sandy and Rusty, huh?"

"I like you already, Sandy. Deal." They shook hands again, chuckling.

They chatted well into the night, comparing experiences of their first assignments. Sandy had worked a number of very hot troops-in-contact situations, taking numerous non-lethal but scary bullet hits in the process. He actually had been forced down once, but managed to land on a paved road and be rescued minutes later by an Army helicopter. But Hubert sat wide-eyed and open-mouthed when Rusty described his final mission. During that flight, Rusty had been forced to use himself as a decoy – no, a target - so that a team of Army Rangers (Rusty was careful not to mention that it had been a covert Special Operations team) could escape from a large force of NVA. In the process, Rusty's plane had taken dozens and dozens of bullet hits, virtually wrecking the plane. He'd managed to nurse it back to LZ Emerald, without radios or electrical power, his right-seater wounded and his engines moments from failure.

"Damn," Sandy said. "But you didn't get hit?"

"Not quite. They found a bullet wedged in that tiny square of Kevlar plate in the pan of my seat. Right underneath my…" He pointed shyly at his groin.

"Damn," Sandy said again. Then he grinned suggestively, "Or should it be double damn?"

"And me a newly married man, too," Rusty joined him in a long laugh.

They traded war stories as only young pilots can do until late that night. Finally, Sandy said, "I don't know about you, but I have to fly tomorrow, and I need my beauty sleep."

"Oh, yeah, sorry. I guess I'm still operating in some other time zone because I'm not sleepy yet."

"Better hit the rack and try, though. The sooner you get over your jet lag, the better."

"Yeah. I have a flight tomorrow, too. Boy, it sure will feel strange after all these months. Any tips about Pennington as an IP?"

"No, not really. He's pretty straight forward, not like some of the rear echelon pricks walking the halls here."

"Good to hear. The jerk I had the first time here was a notorious knuckle knocker. If you weren't an Academy grad, you were nothing. He's the so-and-so who assigned me to LZ Emerald out of spite. I hope I haven't gotten off on the wrong foot with Pennington already. I kinda gave the impression that I'd really rather have gotten an OV-10 like I was promised at Emerald, and Pennington went a bit cold towards me."

"Ah. Well, who wouldn't rather have a Bronco than a Ruptured Duck? At least you didn't grouse about being a FAC and not a fighter jock." Sandy said, raising his eyebrows suggestively.

"Why is that?"

"Oh, that's Pennington's peeve. He got an F-100 assignment to Luke, but when he got there, they told him 'Sorry, all Hun assignments have been changed to FACs.' He'd fought tooth and nail to get a fighter, and had that rug jerked out from under him before he'd even walked on it. So he knows how you feel…in spades."

"I'll try to remember not to talk glowingly about Huns, then," Rusty winked. "But enough. I'm keeping you up again. 'Night, Sandy."

"Good night."

Over the next week, Rusty found that flying is like bicycle riding: you really don't forget how. He had to brush up a bit on some of the procedures – especially those that had changed in the past few months- but the nuts and bolts of the relatively simple airplane, and its easy to master pusher-puller engine arrangement came back to him as though he'd never had a four-month break. He could fly it as though on muscle memory, which in fact it was. Even the fairly complex tasks like firing rockets, communicating on several radios simultaneously and reading large-scale topographic maps proved to be unlost skills.

"Well, I don't see anything that you haven't mastered, Naille," Pennington told him during his most recent post-flight debrief. "But then you don't exactly fall into the usual run of replacement FACs straight out of training, either. The only thing you haven't done again is to work an actual airstrike. I have absolutely no doubt you would excel at that, also. Not that it'll matter."

"Uh, excuse, me, sir. Why wouldn't it matter if I can work airstrikes?"

"Oh, it'll become clear. Would you rather dink around here another week waiting for an airstrike checkride or would you prefer me to waive the rest of your re-qualification flights and put you up for immediate assignment?"

"I'd very much like the latter, sir. I wouldn't ordinarily ask for special treatment, but as you say, I'm not exactly a virgin at this. Neither is Lieutenant Hubert," Rusty added, hoping to put in a plug for his new friend.

"Funny you should mention Hubert, because I want to talk to both of you together. Tell him to report here with you later this afternoon. Fifteen hundred sound okay to you?"

"Uh, yes. Yessir. I'll go look him up and we'll report back here then."

At 1500 hours both of them, in clean uniforms, were seated in Pennington's office, the door closed and locked behind them. "I'd like to talk about your assignments," Pennington said without preamble. "There's a need for two experienced, very capable and level-headed FACs. The job can't go to a new FAC, and it's a strictly volunteer arrangement. I think the two of you fill the bill perfectly, and I'd like you to consider volunteering for the mission."

"What mission is that?" Rusty said, barely beating Sandy to the question.

"I frankly do not know anything about the mission. But I do know that they've specifically requested you, Naille. By name. And they've seen your records and not objected to you, Hubert. Unless either of you object, you can consider yourself assigned."

"That's volunteering? Nice."

"Now, Hubert, don't go huffy on me. Believe me, this is a compliment to you. That's all I'm at liberty to say."

"And me?" Rusty asked.

"Well, they did ask for you specifically. Even before you arrived in country, as a matter of fact."

"So that's why you ducked my question about assignments when I reported in, huh? You already knew."

"Well, I did have to make sure that you were as good as your records claimed you to be. But, yes. I did know where you were headed, pending your successful re-qual. You passed that in spades, so…"

"So where is this assignment?" Sandy asked.

"It's called Ban Me Thuot. It's up in the Central Highlands. Nice and cool up there, they say. And that is positively all I know about it. You'll have to ask any other questions when you get there."

"Which would be when, sir?"

"Tomorrow morning. Pack your bags and enjoy Happy Hour at the Officers' Club, gents. Tonight'll be your last night in civilization."

Rusty and Sandy exchanged glances and read each other's thoughts: *This* is civilization? Compared to where we're going? Oh, no.

CHAPTER TWO

T hey stood on the ramp, duffel bags, carbines and flight gear at their feet, sweat already beginning to trickle down inside their flight suits despite the early hour. Before long, an O-2 taxied up and shut down; their ride had arrived. Rusty immediately noticed something unusual about it. Aside from the numbers 012 on the vertical tail and under the front propeller, the plane was unmarked. No huge black USAF letters, no blue and white star and bars, none of the regulation markings at all. When the pilot climbed out, he was wearing the usual sage-green Air Force flight suit, but it was also bare of markings. No rank, no name, no unit patch. Even odder, he wore a red bandanna around his neck, and sported a huge black handlebar mustache – one much larger than Air Force regulations allowed.

He had a deep tan, an almost Afro-like brush of kinky black hair, and wore a pistol belt with a .45 automatic slung in a holster, but no parachute or survival vest. All this was very, very strange indeed. He shook hands with Sandy and Rusty, and then introduced himself as Kit Rushing.

With no further ado, Kit had them throw their duffels into the back of the O-2 and strap in. They looked at each other in mutual doubt, but climbed in. Sandy took the tiny rear seat, saying he'd rather watch the scenery. Rusty climbed in last, into the right-hand seat. Before they'd finished buckling in, Kit had fired the engines up again and immediately taxied off.

Reinforcing the image of a cowboy pilot, Rushing didn't stop to do the normal end-of-runway checks before takeoff. He called for takeoff to the tower while he was still taxiing, and when he got clearance; he merely swung onto the runway and shoved the throttles to the stops. Weighed down by the three men plus bags, acceleration was hardly neck snapping, but they did manage to lift off and claw their way into the muggy, rank air. The O-2 sagged in its usual way as the gear doors opened, then recovered when they closed.

Rushing had no maps, at least none that Rusty saw. He just headed to the northwest and continued climbing. Soon, they were passing over the rough, bare mountaintops that formed Vietnam's spine. The black basalt upthrusts were still rough and sharp despite eons of weather and erosion. The tops looked like claws straining to rip the belly out of any plane rash enough to get too close. In poor weather, that was a common happening, especially if the unlucky pilot was under radar control of the lackadaisical – not to say completely incompetent – Vietnamese air traffic controllers. But today was a clear, delightful day and the mountains clawed ineffectually at them. So far, Rushing had said nothing since introducing himself. Rusty attempted to break the ice.

"So tell us a little bit about this volunteer mission, Kit. What is it and what's Ban Me Thuot like?"

"You'll hear all about the mission when the time comes. Until then, I can't talk about it. But Ban Me Thuot is an interesting place. We live at BMT East. There's a smaller Army airfield called BMT City. We're actually located at the civilian air terminal. The tower is Vietnamese-controlled, but they speak reasonably good English, as you'll soon see. The city is the Dar Lac provincial capital, the biggest city in the central highlands. As nice a place as you'll find, considering the war. Our compound is small. It used to be a lot bigger when there was an Army artillery battery attached, but that's closed now. There are five of us FACs, and you two will make it seven. We usually operate with anywhere from six to eight, but a couple are due to DEROS soon, so our village will still be short an idiot or two."

Rusty wondered why he couldn't talk about the mission, but other questions popped up in his mind. "Civilian air terminal? I didn't know there was a civilian airline in Vietnam."

"Oh yeah, there is. They fly DC-3s and such. Vietnamese people travel and visit relatives just like anybody else, ya know. Not that I'd get aboard one with all the chickens, ducks, goats and such they cart aboard with them. Not to mention the nuoc mam."

"The what?" Rusty said, revealing his complete ignorance.

Rushing turned to look at him. "How long've you been in Nam? You've never heard of nuoc mam?"

"Uh, I was here a few months the first time, working out of LZ Emerald up near the Bong Son on Highway One. I got hurt just as the place was closing and went home to heal up. Been back for a few weeks getting re-qualled. But I've never heard of nuoc mam, why? What is it?"

"How can anyone be among Vietnamese and not know about nuoc mam?" Rushing asked, incredulous.

Rusty opened his mouth to answer, but suddenly realized that so far, he'd never even met a Vietnamese person. He'd seen one or two at Cam Rahn, and watched some plant rice outside the wire at LZ Emerald, but he'd never actually met one. Rusty admitted as much, and Kit turned in his seat to eye him skeptically.

"Jesus H. Christ. You gotta be shitting me. You've been in-country for months to save the Vietnamese people and you've never met one Vietnamese? How's that possible?"

"Uh, I don't know, I just haven't. You know, until just now, I hadn't even realized that. The only people I've actually worked with have been GI's. I'm almost as surprised as you are," he added.

"Well, that will end soon, I promise you. And you'll learn about nuoc mam, too!" Kit grinned somewhat evilly. Rusty surmised that this nuoc mam thing wasn't a pleasant experience. A skin disease, maybe.

They flew on for a half hour or so, chatting about flying and their backgrounds until Kit pulled back the power and lowered the nose. "Well, there it is...Bang My Twat." Rusty peered over the glare shield, and Sandy leaned left to look out the window on that side. There, scraped out of the ubiquitous red dirt was an ugly square of barbed wire, metal planking and ramshackle-looking buildings. Next to it was a long asphalt runway. And next to that stood the only titty pink control tower Rusty had ever seen.

"A *PINK* control tower? Kit, what the heck is with that?" he asked as Kit entered the traffic pattern.

"Well, the story goes that someone told some local workers to paint the tower red and white. Whoever gave the order may have been thinking red and white checkerboard, but he didn't say that. So they painted it with red and white paint – mixed. What you see was the result. All it needs now is a giant condom!"

Both passengers convulsed with laughter.

Kit landed and taxied to the far eastern end of the runway, then carefully taxied down a strip of metal planking just barely wider than the main gear. It led to a wide barbed wire gate that slid open to receive them. The wire was hung with several hand grenades wired so that the pins would be pulled if the gate were opened incorrectly. Once through the gate, they taxied onto a football field-sized rectangle of metal planking. Kit stopped beside a row of eight or nine other O-2s. None of them had any national or service markings, only those three numbers on the nose and tail. A crew chief and another pilot waited for them to climb out.

Rusty was absorbed in getting himself and his duffel out of the plane and hadn't paid attention to the welcoming committee. When he ducked out from under the wing and stood up, he was staring straight into the face of Dave Sanderson, his flight school IP and FAC school schoolmate.

"Dave! What are you doing here?" Rusty blurted, too amazed to utter anything but the cliché.

"Waiting for you to finally come to heel, you pup! The last I saw you, you almost jettisoned an AT-33. How's your wife?" He pumped Rusty's hand firmly and enthusiastically. Dark and ruggedly handsome, Mary Beth had once said that Dave made her go gooey inside. Rusty could actually understand that – the man really was good looking.

"She's still got the hots for you. At least now I know she's safe!" Rusty quipped. They both laughed.

"Seriously, Rusty, I'm your direct boss here – or will be if you volunteer to stay. I just took over a few weeks ago so I'm still picking up the business here. It's different, but that's all I can say for now. And you must be Sandy Hubert," he turned and shook Sandy's hand. I've heard very good things about you… both of you. Or you wouldn't be here."

They threw the bags in the back of a jeep. It was only a hundred yards to the low buildings that turned out to be their barracks, and Kit drove the jeep while the rest walked. Dave gave them a rundown of the place as they did. "This compound is part of what was an Army heavy artillery base. What's left is a square only a bit more than three hundred meters on a side, but it's home. It's fairly comfortable. We have a small all-ranks club, a chow hall, a laundry and hot water showers, plus a dispensary and even a small canteen and barbershop. Maid service, even!"

"But that's about all I can tell you until you get the initial briefing. We'll leave your bags in the jeep until after that. Walk this way." Captain Sanderson led them to a narrow concrete stairway that descended into a massive underground bunker. The mounded roof of it was about waist-high and it was clear there was much more below ground than above. The three of them walked down and turned left through a massive steel door. Just inside was an interior door and a small fluorescent-lit briefing room. A dozen chairs were lined up to face a blackboard.

"Just have a seat. Somebody will be with you in a minute, and I'll see you afterwards to see what you decided," Dave said, closing the door and leaving.

"Decided? What does that mean?" Sandy said.

Rusty remembered a similar arrangement back at LZ Emerald, right down to the semi-buried bunker, when he'd been "invited" to take part in a Special Operations covert mission, but he played dumb with Sandy. "Beats me. I guess we'll find out. Did you notice all those Vietnamese troops out there? Not all of them were wearing regular uniforms. That's what's bugging me."

Sandy replied, "Uh huh, I did. I don't know what the regular uniform for Vietnamese is, but some of them were..."

Before he could finish, the door opened again. With a whirl of deja vu Rusty watched as a tall, lean and very hard-looking man walked in and deliberately locked the door behind him. Except for his unusual fatigues, camouflaged in a bold wavy pattern of deep black and two shades of green, he was a dead ringer for the anonymous agent who'd briefed Rusty at Emerald. He was bareheaded with brownish hair shaved almost to the scalp and had a chiseled, very soldierly face. He wore no rank or nametag. He strode to the blackboard, which was draped with an olive-green woolen Army blanket, and stood at parade rest with his hands behind his back. When he peered down at them, his eyes were like blue shards of glacial ice. Without introducing himself, he began.

"Gentleman, you have been brought here as potential volunteers for a covert mission. You are free to leave this room now and you will be returned to your former unit with no ramifications; but once I begin the formal briefing and lift this blanket, you may not leave and you may not decline the mission. Is that understood? Leave now if you choose, or you are committed to performing the mission, regardless."

"You mean if you tell us what the mission is, we can't decline?" Sandy said.

"Precisely. Decide now: stay or leave."

Rusty looked at Sandy. Sandy looked back. "Hell, Sandy, I don't know about you, but I just hafta know what's under that blanket, don't you?" Rusty was becoming more sure of what they were about to hear, but still didn't let on.

"I guess so. Brief away. I think we both volunteer," Sandy said to the imposing figure.

"Very well. Welcome aboard. What follows is classified Top Secret, and may not be revealed in any manner whatsoever except to similarly briefed individuals with the proper clearance and a confirmed need to know." He had them raise their hands and swear an oath of secrecy, then turned and lifted the blanket. Under it was a map of the eastern half of Cambodia and the southern end of Laos. "Gentlemen, the mission which you are now committed to perform is a combined action of Special Operations and Special Forces assets. As far as command structure is concerned, we are assigned to the Military

Assistance Command, Vietnam-Studies and Observation Group: MACV-SOG. That is a deliberately benign-sounding cover name for what are actually clandestine special operations. Our mission is to obtain covert intelligence of eastern Cambodia. As a covert mission, this entire operation is and must remain totally deniable. In short, neither the mission nor you exist in the usual way. We operate under a plausible cover story, which is all you may divulge, now or ever. If you are shot down, captured or otherwise discovered outside of the borders of Vietnam, the United States will disavow your existence. Do you have any questions so far?"

"Yeah, does the tape self-destruct in five seconds?" Rusty quipped, taken by the similarity to the hokey beginning of the "Mission Impossible" television show. Sandy snickered, obviously thinking the same thing.

The briefer stared balefully at them in turn. "This is *not* a joke, gentlemen. This is no shit, dead – and I mean absofuckinglutely *DEAD* – serious. Do you copy?"

They lost their smiles instantly. They squirmed a bit in their chairs as he stared down at them, seeming to swell menacingly as he did so.

"To continue then…your basic mission is to infiltrate small teams of indigenous personnel into areas of known enemy operations and then exfiltrate them after a suitable interval. We use volunteer personnel from a variety of sources, including mercenaries and chieu hoy resources. It will be your job to locate suitable infiltration sites, assist in the team's insertion, monitor their condition and then assist in their recovery either when planned or when it becomes necessary. Each of you may be given an additional mission that will be yours and yours alone. If you are assigned such a personal mission, you may not discuss that individual mission with anyone whatsoever, even among yourselves, but only with a designated debriefing officer. Is that clear?"

They nodded again. This was basically what Rusty had expected, but went far beyond what he'd done back at Emerald. He was already overwhelmed with questions, but sensed that they wouldn't be welcome – or answered.

The stone-faced briefer continued, "Finally, in the event that you are shot down anywhere outside Vietnam, the clandestine nature of your mission means that standard military search and rescue forces cannot be used to affect your recovery. If covert Special Operations assets cannot recover you, you will not *be* recovered. Is *that* clear?"

Sandy's eyes went even wider. Both men stared at him, too stunned to even nod.

"Very well. Welcome to Special Operations." He didn't smile. He didn't offer to shake their hands. He simply turned on his heel, walked straight to the door and left without another word.

"Uh, Sandy, what do you think? Are we just plain screwed, royally screwed or screwed six ways from Sunday?"

"Well, the part about inserting teams and then plucking them out didn't sound too bad, but that 'existence will be disavowed' and 'no rescue unless we rescue you' stuff scared me shitless. Are we spies now, or what?"

"I don't know either, let's go talk with Dave."

They rose and tried the door. It was unlocked now, and they stepped out. Captain Sanderson was in the hallway, and he ushered them out the exterior door and up the stairs. Rusty had the distinct feeling Sanderson didn't want them to explore the rest of the bunker.

"Well, welcome to the Mike FACs, guys. Good to have you aboard."

"How do you know we volunteered?" Rusty asked, stupidly.

Sanderson looked at them from the corner of his eye. "If you didn't come out after the first fifteen seconds, you volunteered. You're both Mike FACs now, and that's all you will be until you DEROS."

"What do you mean?" Sandy said.

"Once you get the Special Ops briefing, you are Special Ops, period. You won't and can't do anything else. I'm afraid that means your airstrike days are over. We don't run airstrikes outside of Vietnam, and Mike FACs don't work inside Vietnam. I know that's mainly what you're trained to do, and I know how much fun those can be, but airstrikes aren't part of the Mike mission."

"No airstrikes and no work inside Vietnam? I'm really beginning to feel like I got shafted here," Sandy said. He looked at bit disgruntled – even victimized. "And there's no way to back out of this now?"

"Nope, sorry," Dave said. "Special Ops is a one-way door. You can't see what's inside until you enter, and once you get in, it locks behind you. Look, how many times have you heard or been told that the US isn't in Cambodia or Laos? That's official national policy as far as you knew, right? Except that now you definitely know otherwise. Even knowing that little tiny bit, you can't be released to any other job."

"Like me," Rusty said, resignation clear in his voice.

"Huh? What do you mean?" Sandy said, now even more disoriented.

"Well, I got an introduction to Special Ops back at Emerald. Even my briefing was a lot the same. Not as drastic, but a lot alike. And I always suspected that having been exposed to Special Ops was why my OV-10 assignment got cancelled. Now I'm sure of it. Once In Special Ops, always in Special Ops, just like Dave said."

"No shit? What did you do before?" Sandy asked.

"Well, uh… Actually, I can't say, Sandy."

"Really?"

"That's right," Dave interrupted. "There's that 'need to know' angle, even for us. There are things going on here that you will learn when you need to, and things that you'll probably never learn about."

"Fill us in on what you can, please," Rusty said.

"Sure. The basic mission that we all do here is simple in concept. We are given general locations where a team needs to go. One FAC is designated as lead FAC for that team's mission. He has overall responsibility for that team and will find an appropriate infil site. He'll then help insert the team – that's done by Vietnamese helicopters, by the way. There's a squadron of H-34s here called Kingbees. Using them helps preserve the notion that we don't have any US people 'on the ground' in Cambodia. It's a quibble, I know, but it makes a huge difference politically. Anyway, to communicate with them, there's a little guy – we call them robins - who rides along with you. He does all direct contact with the team and translates to you if they need anything. When the mission is over, or when the team gets in trouble, you find a suitable site to pick them up. That's it in a nutshell."

"That hardly sounds like top secret stuff to me," Sandy said.

"It isn't your job to make that decision, Sandy. Just accept the fact that it is very, very secret stuff. Admittedly, it's a lot more cloak than dagger, but you are effectively an intelligence agent of sorts, as we all are."

"We *are* spies? You're shitting me. Do we carry cyanide capsules with us?" Rusty joked.

"No need. You'll wear a pistol for that," said Sanderson. Rusty looked at him with a half-grin, anticipating the laugh. But Dave wasn't smiling - not even a little. "Let's move on to more pleasant things. Now that you're officially Mike FACs, let's get you bunked up and meet your fellow Mikes."

Rusty's smirk died, and he almost tripped over his own feet. Wear pistols for…that? Holy shit. It took two quick steps to catch up. Sanderson was already naming the others.

"I'm your Ops Officer and go by Mike 52. Your ALO is Major Earl Esterhouse - Mike 51, but he spends a lot of time off-site coordinating with headquarters and other places, so you may not see him much. The other call signs rotate as guys DEROS out. Sandy, you replace a guy named Gary

Dickerson who went as Mike 57. Rusty, you'll be Mike 58, replacing Larry Green. The others here now are Flip Fillipini, Derlin Burman, Dave Bates and Richard Hrducik. You've already met Kit Rushing. We usually bunk two guys to a room. Sandy, we'll bunk you up with Batman — that's Dave Bates but Batman's his nickname. Rusty, you'll bunk with Richard. This hootch here is where you'll live." He pointed to the building they were approaching.

It was a long, light-green clapboard building with corrugated steel roofing held down with sandbags. Six or seven exterior doorways ran at intervals down the side. Between it and another identical building, there was a scraggly, grassy courtyard with two distressed-looking trees. A third, smaller building sat on the third side, and the result looked depressingly like a really seedy motel. The main differences were the sandbags that dotted these roofs and a row of dirt-filled 55-gallon drums serving as blast and shrapnel shields beside the narrow cement sidewalk outside the doorways.

"We all live on this side," Dave went on. "That's the shower and toilet building there in the middle, and our enlisted guys bunk in that building on the left. The back side of ours is where the Green Hornet guys stay."

"The Green Hornets? Who are they?" This time Sandy beat Rusty to it by a half-second.

"Oh, they're our helicopter support. They're part of the 20th Special Ops Group, and they fly those N-model Hueys you saw on the ramp. Some Cobras too, when we need them."

"I thought you said we used Vietnamese choppers," Rusty butted in.

"We use both. The Kingbees do all insertions with the indigenous troops, and the Hornets do…uh, let's just say 'other stuff' for now."

"Ah, I get it," Rusty said, putting his finger to his lips.

"You catch on fast, as usual. Sandy, remind me to tell you about Rusty's adventures in UPT sometime," Dave grinned now, deviously. Rusty bowed his head. Nothing like having a boss who knows which corner of your carpet hides the dirt. Dave went on, "That's my room here on the end. Door's always open, as they say. Rusty, that's yours next door, then the big room where Flip and Derlin live, then Kit's and finally Batman and yours, Sandy. They claim Kit snores, but that's not why he's alone. There's just a vacancy."

Rusty dropped his duffel into the indicated room and took a quick look around. It looked like a typical college dorm room, but about ten levels more primitive. The top bunk was made up with a camouflage poncho liner as blanket, and the lower had bedding folded atop its bare mattress. The furniture consisted of standing double lockers at each end of the room and a small desk and chair angled into the corner at the foot of the bunks. The walls and ceiling were made of plywood painted the same dirty green color as the exterior. A horizontal screened window near the top of the outer wall let in light and air. The wooden door was solid, but there was a handmade screen door as well. The room smelled a bit stale and dusty but not sour. Hardly a deluxe hotel room, but brighter and cleaner than the squalid FAC Shack at Emerald had been. It'd do.

They walked to the middle of the building's length, and Dave pushed open the door. "This is the big room. Hey, guys meet the new meat. This is Rusty Naille and this is Sandy Hubert. That's Flip Fillipini on the left and the other reprobate is Derlin Burman, our official short-timer. You already know Kit."

Flip was a friendly-looking guy with an open, smiling face holding a spray of freckles and a mustache just a bit redder than his light brown hair. Derlin was more striking. Rusty did a double take because the man before him was the absolute spitting image of Jim Croce the singer: kinky masses of dark brown hair, massive mustache, a broad and powerful nose, large teeth, skin a bit dark and pocked – and he was holding a guitar. It looked like he might break into 'Bad, Bad Leroy Brown' or something at any second, but all he did was put down the guitar and stand up to his full six feet-six. They shook hands all round.

"You'll meet Batman and Hrducik when they get down. They're up on missions right now. You two can unpack and settle in, then get better acquainted. I'll work up an orientation schedule to get you flying ASAP. I'll be in the TOC." With that, Dave left.

Rusty looked around. This room was almost twice the size of Rusty's assigned room; it looked as though it may once have been intended as a common room for the other tenants. Now, it housed two with a third bed and additional room to spare. It had individual steel cots and the same type of double lockers as the other rooms. But there were also tables, chairs and paperback-stuffed bookshelves made from the wooden crates that rocket and artillery rounds came packed in. Some of them looked well made, too. A carpenter or handy man lived here - or had.

"Either of you play?" Derlin asked as he picked up his guitar again.

"Only the radio, and I'm no expert at that," Rusty admitted. Sandy shook his head.

"Ah, well. Can't have everything," Derlin said. "It's good to have two new bodies, anyway. What'd you think of the Special Ops briefing?"

"I almost expected to hear the theme song from Mission Impossible, to tell the truth. I had no idea that people actually got that dumb opening speech about 'the secretary will disavow all knowledge' and stuff. Who'd a'thunk it," Rusty said.

"Me, too," Sandy added. "I almost laughed out loud, till he – and who *was* he, by the way? – came down on us like a ton of bricks."

"That's No-Name," Flip said, "or at least nobody ever uses his name if they know it. Spook First-Class No-Name would be his rank and name. The Company, obviously."

"What company?" Sandy asked.

"*THE* company. The three-letter company that starts with 'C' and ends with 'A'? Like Cyclops, with one "I" in the middle? But don't ever *say* those letters together," Flip cautioned. "They aren't really here. And those guys with the black baseball caps aren't Green Berets, either. There are no Green Berets in Vietnam anymore. Just like they say in the news. Black baseball caps, sure, but no green beanies." Flip winked broadly.

"Ah. I see," Sandy said, smiling. "Another see no evil, hear no evil, speak no evil deal, huh?"

"Guys, nothing here is what it seems, nothing that happens here happens and nobody who's here is here. And the sooner you realize that, the better. That's why we're all so clean-shaven," Derlin said, twirling his massively bushy handlebars. "Cuz stashes are against Air Force regs."

Flip looked at his Seiko watch. "Hey Derlin, jeetjet?

"Nojew?"

"Yungry?"

"Mungry. Sqweet!"

The three of them stood up and moved towards the door. Sandy and Rusty stared at each other, mystified.

"That was 'mikespeak' for 'it's lunchtime'," Flip grinned conspiratorially. "Chow hall's this way."

They all walked out and turned down a smooth dirt street. Also walking the same direction were pairs of Vietnamese men, all dressed in the same aggressive-looking camo fatigues that No-Name had worn. And some were holding hands. Rusty stared openly.

"Rusty, a word," Kit said, tugging at his sleeve. "It's considered extremely rude to stare. Meaning 'knife in your gut' rude."

"Oh, uh, sorry, I guess. But like I told you, those are the first Vietnamese I've ever seen up close, and they're holding hands. I was just taken aback." He could see that Flip and Derlin were about to have the same incredulous response that Kit had had, so he held up a hand. "Yeah, I know. It's weird that I haven't met a Vietnamese. But the sight of two men holding hands is weird, too."

"Only at first. It's normal in their culture. We do things that they think are weird, too," Derlin agreed. "Like eating dairy products, for example. Just different cultures."

Flip sidled over to Derlin and took his hand, then lisped, "Besides, it's *sooo* sweet to have friends." The pilots all laughed, and two nearby Vietnamese men pointed at them and joined in the laughter.

The chow hall looked almost like a regular military one, with rows of steel tables and attached bench seats. Everyone went through a cafeteria serving line in an adjacent room, sliding plastic trays down a railing and selecting dishes from hot or cold serving trays. The fare itself was like nothing Stateside, though. A cultural hodgepodge of cold rice balls, what looked like dried fish, sandwiches, carrot and celery strips, small bowls of lettuce salad, and a kettle of hot soup formed the lunch offerings.

Rusty took a couple sandwiches, some raw vegetables and a cup of the soup, but when he picked up a bowl of salad, Flip said, "Oops, you probably shouldn't eat any of the lettuce, Rusty. That's for the locals."

"Huh? Why?"

"Well, the carrots and celery are trucked in, so they're okay, but the lettuce is locally grown, and they fertilize the fields with human waste. Unless you want a jolly case of worms, parasites and other intestinal nasties, stick to cooked or peeled and washed veggies."

Rusty looked at the lettuce, imagining what might be clinging to it, and put the bowl back. Then he wondered if the same hands that filled the lettuce bowls also peeled the carrots, but didn't say anything.

As they ate, he looked around, trying not to stare long enough to be insulting. There seemed to be at least three different groups of Vietnamese, all sitting at separate tables. Rusty asked Derlin quietly about it.

"Well, you're right," Derlin said. "The little guys in the Tiger Stripe cammies are Vietnamese. The ones in the plain green fatigues or in the mixed dress are either 'yards or Cambode 'yards."

Rusty looked blank. Derlin nodded, and continued. He leaned close, so that the kitchen staff couldn't overhear him. "It's related to the job, Rusty. That's all I'll say here, but I'll tell you more later."

Back in the big room, they all sat down. Derlin, as the most experienced FAC at BMT, naturally assumed the job of teacher. "I keep forgetting. I've been here long enough to take lots of things for granted. Let's go to the basics. We use teams of little people for our missions. Some of them are regular South Vietnamese, or Arvins. Some are members of either Vietnamese or Cambodian Montagnard tribes, and some of the little guys who ride with us are Chieu Hoys, former North Vietnamese Army regulars who came over to our side."

"Did you say *North* Vietnamese?" Rusty blurted, staring at him.

"And they ride with us? Why?" Sandy added.

"I'll get to that, but it's simple, really. We put teams of five to six guys on the ground along the Ho Chi Minh trail. Our guys dress in uniforms that match what trail-walkers wear, or they dress like indigenous folks in order not to arouse suspicion. They claim to be lost or separated from their own units, or they're from a nearby village. They mingle with the bad guys, chit-chat with them, and maybe even walk along with them for a day or two, then sneak off. After that, they may find another group or they sneak back to where they hid their radio and request pickup. But the key is that they have to blend in with either locals or the enemy. That's why you might see some very odd characters, and even stranger uniforms. We have to be able talk to the teams, so the robins…"

"Ah ha, now I get it," Sandy said.

"But some of them are actually North Vietnamese? We trust them?" Rusty asked, still dumbfounded.

"Yes and sort of would be the two best answers," Derlin went on. "Our side drops a bazillion Chieu Hoy leaflets along the DMZ and the trail. Those leaflets promise safe passage for any VC or NVA to come over to our side. A surprising number of them do come over. How many of them just want a hot meal, how many are genuine converts and how many are double agents is the sixty-four-dollar question."

"Yeah, that was my point," Rusty said.

"Only ones who positively prove themselves ever get used in sensitive missions like this one. Those are called Hoi Chanh. No system is perfect, though. We've lost several whole teams with Hoi Chanh as team members. Just disappeared. We even lost one O-2 and FAC where the most likely explanation was that the robin deliberately crashed the plane. That robin was a Hoi Chanh. The best advice is to never trust one completely."

"Except for Truong," Flip added.

"Yeah, except for Truong," Kit and Derlin both said at once.

"Who's that?" Rusty asked.

"Truong Lan Hoang was an NVA infantry Captain from Hanoi. He decided to chieu hoy, got thoroughly vetted, and is one of our best robins. He actually helped save a FAC here a couple of years ago. Seems the FAC mismanaged his fuel usage. He was on aux tanks and ran them both dry at the same time. That wouldn't have been a problem if he hadn't been at about ten feet altitude at the moment. Both engines quit and they instantly skidded in. Fortunately, they were over grass plains and not rocks or triple canopy jungle. The pilot whacked his head pretty good in the crash, and when he came to, he was lying in the shade of one wing. Truong was on the radio talking a Kingbee helicopter in to a landing. So we think we can trust Truong."

"I'll say," Rusty said. "But what the hell was the FAC doing at ten feet altitude?"

"Oh, we sometimes climb that high," Kit deadpanned, "although we'd rather fly down low."

Rusty just stared at him. He'd already stopped assuming that any wild-ass thing said around here was a joke. Kit was smiling, but not much.

Derlin nodded, "Well, we do prefer to take it right down on the deck when we're trying to get somewhere unobserved. The only safe altitudes are well above 1,500 feet or right in the weeds, you know. Anywhere between those two and you are a sitting duck. Up high and you're out of small arms range, and really low you go by too fast to be seen or shot at — especially if there are any trees at all."

Rusty thought about it. Derlin was right. Anybody looking up from the ground would clearly hear and see a plane at 500 feet or so, with plenty of time to react and shoot at it. But if that plane were only a few feet above the trees, a ground troop might not even hear it coming until it flashed overhead and was gone. Hmmm.

Derlin went on. "So when we do an infil, we get right down on the deck to lead the Kingbees in. It's not only safer for them and us, but it's easier to hide the operation. Exfils too, when we know the pickup point in advance. Not always possible, but nice to do."

Kit chimed in, "Hot exfils, where the team is fighting their way out, are like Chinese fire drills except less predictable. You just do what you gotta do."

"How often does that happen?" Sandy said.

Kit looked at Derlin. "Oh - maybe a third to half, that seem about right?" Derlin and Flip both nodded. "Sometimes the infil and the exfil happen together. The landing zone turns hot the minute the team hits dirt and you have to extract them ricky-tick. It can get interesting."

"Yeah, it can," Derlin went on. "If you pick a poor site, or if the bad guys move too near it just before the insertion, it can get hairy in a hurry. Sometimes it seems like the bad guys are so thick out there that there's no such things as safe insertion sites. A site that is safe is probably so far from anything of interest that the team couldn't walk to their objective before they ran out of supplies." He shrugged. "Like Kit says, you do what you gotta do."

"Guys, I have a lot to think about here. I'm going to go unpack and muse a bit," Rusty said. "How about you, Sandy?"

"I think that's a plan. Anything on the schedule for the rest of the day?"

"Not for you two," Flip said. "I'm set to take off in about an hour to relieve Batman, but that's it for the day. It's a bit slow right now."

"Relieve him? You mean like a troop cap? We're both used to those," Sandy asked.

"Uh huh, pretty much. We go up with a little guy and orbit at 5,000 feet or so a few miles from where the team is and just monitor their frequency. If the team is working normally, you might hear nothing at all for days. If they make a report, or if the shit hits the fan, they call the robin and speak in code. He translates to you and you do what you gotta. It's four and a half hours of boredom…"

"Punctuated by moments of sheer panic. Yeah, we know," Sandy finished the old pilot's adage for him. "Been there, done that. Rusty, too."

"Good war stories are always welcome," Derlin said, smiling.

"Well, mine maybe," Sandy said. "Rusty's got one that was no fun."

"Too hairy to talk about?" Derlin said, looking squarely into Rusty's eyes.

"Yeah, it was; for now at least. Maybe I'll let Sandy tell you – when I'm not around."

"Ouch. That bad, huh?" Kit said. "Well, we won't pump you for it. Batman might flush it out of you, though."

"How's that?" Rusty asked, glad for the diversion.

"Well, Batman is a Mormon, so he never drinks – not even coffee, for Christ's sake." He grinned to himself at the unintended joke. "But he insists on being our bartender so he won't miss out on the fun. Believe me, when Batman mixes, nobody even crawls home."

"Yeah, we party in the FAC hootch out on the flightline. It was a brand new Conex we converted to a slum," Flip laughed to himself. "The official Mike FAC drink is the frozen daiquiri, and Batman's been known to burn out an electric mixer a month makin'em. Brrr!" He shuddered in mixed delight and feigned horror.

"Frozen daiquiris? Hey this place might not be as dreadful as it looks!" Sandy said.

"Except for the hangovers," Rusty added.

The others continued to chat while Rusty and Sandy walked to their rooms to unpack. Rusty shoved his door open, but almost jumped back, startled to be looking at the bent over rear end of a young woman. She was dressed in baggy black silk trousers and a tight white silk blouse, and she immediately stood and spun around to face him. She shrieked, "Hey, you no come now! Go way! Clean now! Go way, go way!"

Rusty stopped dead in his tracks. His first direct contact with a Vietnamese, and it turned out to be a young girl screaming and waving a straw broom at him to chase him out of his own room. He stammered, "Huh? Who are you?"

She stared back at him, squinting at his face, then down to his nametag. "Who you? You new GI? How say you?"

Again, Rusty could only stammer. He heard what she said, but her aggressiveness and pidgin English stunned him. Before he could answer, she went on, "What matta you? You dinky dau! Numba ten GI!" Then she muttered something in Vietnamese, came closer and poked his nametag. "How say you?"

"Oh! Oh, I get it," Rusty said, the light finally flickering. "My name is Naille." She scrunched up her brow, silently moving her lips. She canted her head and said, "Na-oh?"

"Naille," he repeated, then again, slower, "Nay-uhl. Naille. Um, how say you?"

She giggled, and it struck him that she wasn't more than about 13 years old. She still had her baby-fat softness and silliness. She touched her chest where a nametag would be and said what sounded like "My-Yin."

He repeated it as best he could, "My-Yin" but she shook her head. "My-Yin. My-yin," she said. He thought he'd said it exactly the same as she'd said it, but he tried again, "My-Yin?" She shook her head again, but this time in frustration. "All GI..." and then she used a Vietnamese word. She giggled to herself.

He knew when he'd been called a name. Rusty laughed, too. She redoubled her laughter as she picked up her odd angular broom and edged past him out the door, singsonging that same word over and over amidst mounting giggles.

There were almost no signs of occupancy in the room except for a steel infantry helmet and flak vest hanging from one post of the bunk beds. But one locker was full and the upper bunk made, so Rusty clearly had a roommate. He stowed his clothes in the empty locker and made up the lower bunk with the bedclothes stacked on top of the mattress. While he worked, he looked around; but there were no photos, no books, and no personal items at all. Even the little desk was bare.

"Hi, I'm Richard."

Rusty almost jumped out of his boots. He hadn't heard anyone approach, but when he spun around there was a pilot standing in the doorway behind him. Rusty's first impression of the man was 'fireplug.' He stood about five feet six, shaped like a whiskey barrel. His large head was covered in a burr-cut fuzz of black hair. Except for a neat black mustache, he was clean-shaven, but his face held a whisker pattern like a blue-black birthmark. Coarse black hair curled out of his collar from his chest and seemed to go all the way around to his back.

"Jeez, you startled me. Uh, Hi. I'm Rusty. Rusty Naille. Glad to meet you." They shook hands. Richard's was sweaty, and tiny rivulets ran down from his scalp.

"Richard Herdic?" Rusty pronounced it the way he thought Dave had. "Anybody ever call you Hard Dick?"

"It's 'Herdacheck.' And no." His look clearly said Rusty had already ticked him off.

"Oh. Sorry, just making a joke. Won't happen again."

Hrducik leaned a collapsible-stocked CAR-15 carbine in the corner between his locker and the wall, then scrambled crab-like up into his bunk. After one pointedly silent glare at Rusty, he shut his eyes.

Rusty had wanted to ask him about the Vietnamese girl, but changed his mind and left again. He pulled the door shut behind him and went back into the big room. Sandy had also returned, and the others were still there, except for Flip. "You meet Richard?" Derlin asked.

"Sure did. Got off on the wrong foot with him, though. I asked him if anybody ever called him Hard Dick. It didn't go over well."

"Called him...? Oh, I get it. No, as far as I know nobody's ever called him that. He doesn't like to be called Dick or Rich, either. Always Richard."

"Well Hard Dick sure seemed to rub him the wrong way."

"Hard Dick? Rubbed the wrong way? Oh, that's good, Rusty. That's great," Kit said. "Sandy, does he come out with shit like that all the time?"

"Well, Rusty does seem to like puns and wordplay, if that's what you mean. Yeah, he does."

Derlin's face was split with a huge toothy grin, too. "Wait till Flip hears that one. He loves jokes and surprises."

"Hey, speaking of surprises, who was that young girl in my room?"

"Oh, your hootch maid? Ain't she cute?" Kit said. "There are three or four of them that make our beds, sweep the rooms and stuff. They come in every day. You couldn't have seen Mama-san or you wouldn't possibly have said young – or cute. Mama-san on her good days looks more like the wicked witch of the west."

"Girls did you say? How cute are they?" Sandy said, lewdly.

"Cute as a rice bug, most of them, Sandy," Derlin said, "If you happen to like pre-teens. But that's no block to a 'nooner' if you really want one – you'd certainly not be the first. Just ask some of the maintenance troops."

"You're kidding," Sandy said, the lascivious tone instantly gone from his voice.

"Unfortunately, I'm not," Derlin went on. "Mama-san tries to keep the girls in line, but there's no stopping young lust – on either side. Besides, some of our troops aren't much older than the girls, really." He shrugged. "It's not surprising."

"I think I'd have to be here a long time before it became irresistible," Sandy said. "But just to make sure, I think it's maybe a good idea to not be in my room while they clean."

"Sounds like a good idea for me, too," Rusty agreed. "I'm no pedophile, but…"

Derlin raised one eyebrow. "Got the hornies already, Rusty?"

"More like still having them. But at least they seem to be lessening. Maybe it's like fasting. They say that after a while, your stomach shrinks and you just don't feel hungry."

"So what's shrinking on you, Rusty?" Derlin quipped, and the others howled in glee.

Rusty laughed, too. "It can't shrink much more and still be there at all. It looks less like a dick and more like an egg in a nest already."

They all laughed again, even harder. Derlin picked up his guitar and started singing.

"Now listen my children, a story you'll hear.
A song I will sing you; 'twill fill you with cheer.

A charming young maiden was wed in the Fall.
She married a man who had no balls at all.
No balls at all. No balls at all.
She married a man who had no balls at all.
The night of the wedding she leaped into bed.
Her breasts were a-heaving; her legs were well spread.
She reached for his penis; his penis was small.
She reached for his balls; he had no balls at all."

Rusty managed to shout over the hooting and howling, "Very funny, Derlin. But didn't you say there's no such thing as a safe insertion site?"

Kit fell off his cot and Sandy slid down in his chair, both holding their sides in gleeful pain.

When it died down, Sandy wiped his eyes and asked, "But let's get back to what we were talking about when Rusty came back and so rudely interrupted us. You were saying that there are only about a hundred Americans here, but two or three times that many uh, what did you call them? Little people? What do they all do?"

Kit answered, "Well, lots of them are team members, either active or in training. Some are Kingbee crews and their maintenance troops. Some of the camp staff are local Vietnamese, like the cooks, the barber, the laundry people, the hootch maids and the guys who work in the motor pool. The gate and tower guards are little people, too, but different. They're local tribe members and we hire them as guards because they are never VC."

Sandy and Rusty both looked puzzled at that.

Derlin explained, "We hire local Montagnards as guards because they don't recognize the Vietnamese government at all. As far as they're concerned, what we call Vietnamese are all invaders. The Montagnard tribes just wish they could be left alone to live their lives the way they did before that invasion happened a thousand years ago. They'd be fighting the invaders with or without us, and they help us because we're fighting them, too. But the 'yards also wish we'd just wipe out the whole bunch – South and North Vietnamese alike. The 'yard tribes may squabble among themselves, but they absolutely hate the Vietnamese, and that means all Vietnamese. They consider any enemy of their enemy to be a friend, and right now that's us. When this is all over and we're long gone, the 'yards will still be fighting the Vietnamese, but both sides will have guns instead of crossbows and blowguns. It won't be pretty."

"You mean the way the Lakota Sioux, the Blackfeet and the other tribes sometimes fought each other, but teamed up to whup Custer's ass?" Rusty asked.

"Yeah, that's it exactly. The Algonquin and Hurons sided uneasily together with the French against us, too. In that fight, we invaders finally won, and the native tribes died. That's gonna happen here, too. The 'yards know nothing about America's past, but they suspect what's in their own future. You can see it in their eyes." Derlin paused a moment, then concluded, "If anybody asked me, I'd say I'm not fighting this war for the Vietnamese. I'm fighting it for the Montagnards."

They all sat there in silence, thoughts weighing each one down in varying degrees. Is this what they call white man's guilt, Rusty wondered? Or is it true that history is a drama endlessly performing the same script with different actors?

Derlin broke the silence. "So, Rusty...if you've never met a Vietnamese yet, how'd you like to go downtown and immerse yourself in the culture?"

"Downtown? You mean off the base? Is that allowed? We were forbidden to leave Cam Rahn or LZ Emerald. Isn't that true here?"

"Nope. We go downtown fairly often, in fact. Once in a while, we get a security alert and go to lockdown, but most of the time, we can just take a jeep and go downtown. There's a market there, a pretty decent hotel and restaurant, and an orphanage where we volunteer some muscle power at times. A few steam and cream places, too, but I'd steer clear of those if I were you."

"Steam and cream?"

"Massage parlors. You can get a steam bath, a rubdown and a blowjob. You can also just as easily get robbed and have your throat cut. The most notorious one is called the Bakery. For loafing around, apparently." He grinned.

Sandy guffawed and then asked, "No kidding, Derlin, we can go off base? I think I'd enjoy that myself. The other stuff, not the steam and cream."

"Well, no time like the present, then. You two have any civvies?"

They both nodded.

"Ok, then, after you get your stuff stowed, change into civvies and I'll sign for a jeep. We'll leave about six and have dinner downtown. Either of you picky eaters?"

Sandy shook his head. Rusty answered, "Picky eater? Not hardly. My motto is 'If it's slower than I am, it's lunch.'"

"Then you'll fit in well at BMT. Our chow is a bit non-standard – even on base."

"You mean like the lettuce?" Rusty asked.

"Yup. Like that. We get a good percentage of our food from the local economy. Some gets flown or trucked in, but we buy some downtown and some from the 'yards. Did you like the soup at lunch?"

"Yeah, why?"

"It was monkey noodle soup. We have it about three times a week."

"*MONKEY* noodle soup?" Sandy yelped. "You mean, with actual monkey meat?"

"Of course with actual monkey meat. Otherwise I'd have called it dog noodle soup or water buffalo noodle soup. We get those, too. We eat a lot of water buffalo, and some dog – especially when we eat off base. The 'yards love it. Dog's a delicacy with them, you know."

Sandy paled one shade, but Rusty said, "I thought the soup was actually pretty good. Monkey, huh? Tasted a lot like squirrel, mild and sweet. I liked it. I'm not sure what dog would be like, but I'm game to try it."

"You can order that tonight if you like, but if you let me do the ordering, you'll get a better idea of true Vietnamese cuisine," Derlin said.

"They have a cuisine?" Sandy said, sarcastically.

"Yeah, they certainly do. Think about it. Vietnam draws on the best parts of two of the world's finest cuisines: Chinese and French. Here on the western border, there are traces of Cambodian, Laotian and even Thai cooking as well. All in all, it's great stuff. But you'll see for yourselves."

Later, they all changed into blue jeans and polo shirts, and then piled into a jeep. Kit, Sandy and Rusty jumped into the passenger seats and Derlin drove out the west gate. The five or six miles between the East Field and the city were two-lane asphalt, in pretty good condition, Rusty thought. They bounced past slum-like hootches where toddlers ran around naked except for raggedy-edged tee shirts, roared between the deep green walls of a tea plantation, and slowed as they neared tiny businesses with garish signs. Here, traffic thickened, too: hundreds of bicycles mingled with tiny three-wheeled trucks powered by motor scooter engines. Regular motor scooters abounded, including one that caught Rusty's eye. Perched bolt upright on its seat was a stunningly beautiful young woman. Lithe, slender and with an a primly regal bearing, she wore shiny black silk pants and a long, flowing white silk top that was skin tight down to her waist, then was split at the sides to hang loosely to her knees. She was grace in motion with her shiny waist-length black hair streaming behind her. Rusty was smitten with her beauty.

Entering the city itself, the newcomers were amazed to see multi-story brick buildings designed in Western style. The streets became narrower and progressively more crowded until they were filled from curb to curb with luridly decorated pedi-cabs, scooters, bikes and pedestrians, all moving seemingly at random.

Derlin said, "Any time you're boxed in like this, keep your eyes open. It's rare, but even a cute little schoolgirl could sidle up and drop a grenade into the jeep. Anybody and everybody around you might be VC."

The comment made Rusty's vision of beauty on a scooter suddenly seem a bit less innocent. But what Derlin said was true. It was impossible to tell the enemy from the innocent.

"The ones to really watch are the cowboys. They're violent young men on motor scooters. Outlaws and gang members, they prey on people in the heaviest traffic. They can slit your pocket open and grab your wallet before you know it. Or slit your throat, for that matter."

Derlin pulled up in front of a stately white brick building, and a man in a garish red uniform immediately approached and waved him to an open parking slot. "That's the hotel doorman," Derlin said. "He'll watch the jeep. There'd be no place to park at all unless he kept this part of the block clear. Never leave the jeep unattended or it'll vanish before you turn the corner."

Rusty believed it. He'd been getting increasingly uneasy at the press of the crowd, the pall of blue exhaust fumes and the overwhelming sense of being watched by hostile eyes. But when they entered the hotel's lobby, his wariness suddenly disappeared in wonderment.

"This is the Thang Loi Hotel," Derlin said, gesturing broadly with one sweeping arm. "The French built it, but even though they're long gone, the Vietnamese keep that aura of French civility alive."

The lobby was filled with potted palms, dark woodwork and gilt fixtures, all lit by warm candlelight. A fountain tinkled softly in one corner. The odors of waxed wood and cool water mixed with an indefinable, library-like smell of... gentility. It might have been someplace in Paris but for the bowing and smiling Vietnamese facing them. He wore a black pinstriped suit and crisp white shirt. His silk tie and the carnation in his lapel were of the exact same brilliant red. Never showing more than the top of his slickly oiled and sharply parted head, he extended his right arm towards the other side of the lobby, where a wide spiral staircase beckoned.

As they climbed, new odors filled their nostrils. Food. The restaurant's décor matched that of the lobby, with dark wood furnishings, warm glowing candles and crisp white linen. Seated at a table for four, Rusty felt decidedly underdressed for such a place. Derlin took a menu from the bowing host and pointed to a number of items without consulting the others. The host grinned, bowed even deeper and departed.

"So, what did you order?" Sandy asked.

"A representative sample of the hotel's fare, my friend. Nothing exotic, or at least nothing bizarre. Don't fret, just enjoy."

The waiter first brought glasses and a bottle of red wine. Rusty felt as amazed as Sandy looked. Derlin explained that the wine was from the French influence. It turned out to be a musty, tart red, very rich in flavor both on the tongue and after. Very good, indeed. As Derlin refilled the glasses, a parade of servers approached. Along with a second bottle of wine, they rapidly spread almost a dozen different dishes around the flower centerpiece of the otherwise bare table.

Bowls of soup were placed in front of each man, as well as empty bowls and a pair of chopsticks. Closer to the center of the table were the main dishes. Derlin explained and pointed to each one.

"Those are cha goi and goi cuan: spring rolls. It's fish or meat with herbs and vegetables, wrapped in lettuce leaves or rice paper. You add from these bowls of shredded herbs if you want, and dip them in those cups of sauces. The skewered meats over rice are beef and chicken, charbroiled. The noodle dish has fish in it along with vegetables and onions. I can't pronounce those. Oh, and the soup is noodles in beef broth. It's what the locals usually eat for breakfast. They call it pho bo. Nothing is really spicy, so I think you'll enjoy it all. Dig in."

Everything was delicious, Rusty thought. The soup was light but flavorful, with a delicate onion undertone. He especially loved the unexpected combination of shrimp rolls with mint and basil leaves. Dipped in a peanut sauce, the flavors were complex and surprising. Other rolls were beef with basil and other herbs, and were to be dipped into a golden liquid he couldn't identify.

Rusty scooped some of the fish and noodle dish into a bowl with his chopsticks, and took a bite. The aroma coming from it as it passed under his nose was startlingly pungent, but the flavor was rich and wonderful. "Whoa! Derlin, what is this?"

"That's dried fish with carrots, green onion and basil, and the sauce is nuoc mam."

"Nuoc mam? This is nuoc mam, Kit? This is what you warned me about?"

"Sure is. Potent stuff, huh?"

"Potent, but also delicious. Why did I get the impression you were talking about something atrocious, like a disease?"

"Well, there's nuoc mam and then there's nuoc mam. This is prime stuff here in this sauce cup and in that noodle dish. It's graded something like olive oil. As they go lower, the grades edge downward from delicate past pungent and towards low tide at the wharf. The cheapest stuff would gag a skunk."

"What is it?" Rusty asked.

"It's a fish sauce," Derlin chimed in. "They put fish and salt in barrels or huge vats and let it ferment for a whole year in the sun. Well, ferment is highly charitable. The stuff rots, actually. After months, the fish parts settle to the bottom and what's left is an oily liquid. The top layer is a clear, fine amber, like this we're having. As it's drawn off, however, the lower stuff gets darker and more virulent as it goes. The last stuff out of the vat can be horribly strong, as Kit says. Hope I haven't put you off your feed bag."

"Who me? Nah. But I think Sandy may not be as immune." In fact, Sandy sat staring at Derlin, looking like he wasn't sure he believed what he was hearing.

"You're pulling my leg, right?" he said. "This stuff I've been dipping these rolls into is rotted fish? Tell me not."

"Uh, you won't turn green will you? Because if you might, then I'm not saying," Derlin cautioned him.

"Well, I'm not sure. It doesn't taste like spoiled fish – well, not much. More salty than fishy; but now that I think of it, it is fish, isn't it? Is it really made like you said?"

Derlin nodded. "Sure is. It's the major industry of several cities along the coast. It's the most common sauce in all of Asia, maybe more common even than soy sauce. And soy sauce is made the same way, by the way. Beans bunged up with brine and left to…um, ferment. Then bottled."

"I'll be damned," Sandy said. He dipped a finger into the small cup of dipping sauce, and tasted it cautiously. "I'll be double damned."

Rusty had already gone back to eating, but grunted his assent from a full mouth. "Um-hmm."

After servers cleared the nearly empty dishes, the waiter brought small cups of scalding hot, very strong coffee.

"Holy smoke that's strong!" Rusty exclaimed after taking a tiny sip. "I didn't know the Vietnamese drank coffee, just tea."

"Oh no, they love coffee, too. And in the French style. That's some of the finest mountain-grown espresso you'll ever have the pleasure to enjoy. Locally grown, by the way. The Central Highlands are perfect for it."

"I wish they had some of this back at Cam Rahn. What they drink there is the worst excuse for coffee in the world," Rusty said.

"Ain't that the truth," Kit added. "I think I'd prefer boiled, blue-label nuoc mam to that swill."

The bill came shortly after. Derlin looked at it and narrowed his eyes, calculating. Rusty braced himself to hear the total. "What do we owe, Derlin?"

"Uh, counting the tip, it comes to…oh…call it four bucks each."

Rusty sputtered, "Four dollars each? For all that? Including the wine? Are you kidding us? You must be. No fair you paying most of the bill, if that's what you're doing. Make it a straight four-way split, bud."

"I did. I was just making sure he converted piaster to dollars fairly. If I have the conversion right, it comes to about fourteen bucks. Sixteen with a very generous tip," Derlin said.

Rusty stared at him open-mouthed. All that gourmet food, in a place this elegant, and the bill comes to a measly fourteen dollars? Incredible.

He was musing about how well a man might live here in retirement as they walked out. At the hotel's front entrance, the first waft of Vietnam's pervasive half-garbage, half-charnel house smell popped that pleasant thought like a pin in a balloon. The shock was as sharp as if they'd materialized here from another universe. In a way, of course, they had.

The doorman must have gotten word they were coming down, somehow. He was standing at attention next to the jeep. As they approached, he bowed deeply. His ornately decorated outer coat fell slightly open and Rusty glimpsed leather and steel. A .45 automatic in a shoulder holster nestled under the man's left armpit. No wonder the jeep was safe under his watchful eye.

The trip back to the field was fortunately uneventful. Even espresso couldn't offset the effect of full stomachs and good wine, and they rode along in surfeited silence. Kit nodded a bit in the passenger seat, but the two tiny seats in back were less comfortable, keeping Sandy and Rusty at least half alert. Derlin drove faster than before, really lead-footing the treacherous little jeep. After a few minutes, he half-turned and yelled back over his shoulder.

"We need to push it before they lock the gates. After ten p.m., nobody gets in or out, no exceptions. And it's almost ten now. We may have lingered a bit too long over the espresso."

But when they passed the East Field civilian air terminal and turned the slight bend in the road, the main gates were standing open. Derlin slowed and doused the headlights as they approached. "Wouldn't want to get hosed as infiltrators," he explained.

He slowed and stopped at the gate, where a Montagnard guard shined a flashlight in their faces, each in turn, then looked carefully underneath the jeep and back down the road behind before he waved them through with a sly grin.

"What was that all about?" Sandy asked.

"He probably thought we'd been at the Bakery and might be trying to smuggle a good time girl back into camp with us. And also that we weren't being followed," Kit said. "The VC would love to sneak a truck full of sappers in here some night, and following a jeep full of legitimate guys through the gate would be one way to do it."

Derlin parked the jeep and returned the keys to the rack in the radio room. Sgt Young was on duty, as the radio room was manned 24 hours a day. He smiled. "How was the 'bread,' sir?"

"We didn't go to the Bakery, Young. Honest. We ate at the Trang Loi. Wanna smell my nuoc mam breath to see?" Derlin taunted him back.

"Uh, no sir. I do not. I believe you, sir. Really." Young held his hands out to fend off Derlin, who might have charged in and puffed in his face no matter what Young professed to believe.

"Well, I'm glad to be taken at my word, sergeant. After all, I am a gentleman," Derlin drew himself up and turned his head, nose high.

"And it took Congress to achieve it," Young quipped back in the usual rejoinder. Derlin laughed along.

"Anyone for a nightcap?" Kit asked when Derlin came out "The Club is still open."

"I think I'll hit the rack," Rusty said, the very thought triggering a huge yawn. "Thanks, Derlin. That was a magnificent dinner. I'd never have guessed such a thing existed here."

"I second that vote, and the thanks," Sandy added, Rusty's yawn proving contagious.

They went to their rooms. Rusty noted that his was empty and wondered where Richard might be. He undressed and slid into the lower bunk, and dropped off almost immediately.

KABOOM! BOOM!

Rusty leapt up, scraping his forehead on the springs of Richard's bunk.

BOOM! KABOOM!

Above him, Richard snored. Rusty lay there tensely, wondering if that had been incoming or outgoing. He squinted at the phosphorescent glow of his watch. Midnight. Nothing else happened, no running feet, no shouts, and no sirens. After two full minutes, he thought he heard four distant, dull booms. Outgoing.

At breakfast, he asked, "Hey Kit, what was that outgoing last night? I thought the artillery base was long gone."

"Oh, that's harassment fire. We have heavy mortars – those big four point two-inch bastards – and the crews launch a few rounds most nights."

"On what?"

"Oh, they target places where they think Charlie might be. They pick map coordinates from a list of possible enemy locations that Intel provides, and drop a few rounds in on a different one every night."

"Do they ever hit anything?"

"Who knows? But I bet it keeps Charlie guessing, huh? That's why they call it harassment."

CHAPTER THREE

"We try not to transmit actual map coordinates over the radio," Derlin said as he and Rusty flew northwestwards along the snaking Tonle Srepok river in Cambodia. "We call that right-angle bend in the river 'the elbow' for example. If we were to call back and give our position now, we'd just say we're at the elbow and the radio guys would know where we are. There's a whole set of maps there in the radio shack, and we label some of the better landmarks with nicknames. That way if they need to come find us, they know where to start looking, but the bad guys don't."

Rusty was struck by the beautiful deep green of the landscape. Much of it seemed to be gently rolling pastureland, grass-covered and simply begging for livestock. Irregular patches of thick jungle meandered through the grasslands, and here and there a half-dozen isolated grass-thatched hootches were huddled. From the air, it was gorgeous.

Elsewhere, the jungle was absolutely impenetrable to aerial inspection. True triple-canopy stuff, three separate layers of treetops huddled between earth and sky. Hardly a photon reached the ground with these trillions of energy-hungry leaves spread out above the earth. It made perfect cover if you wanted to drive trucks anywhere unseen. And there were tens of thousands of enemy troops down there determined to do exactly that. Only where those lush grasslands interrupted the jungle could one find traces of tracks. The infamous Ho Chi Minh Trail was not a single roadway, but a tracery of trails, tracks and paths used almost at random to avoid detection on any one of them. It was more like the body's pattern of tiny capillaries than a single massive artery. But this circulatory system pulsed with deadly cargo, not life-giving blood. Trucks, bicycles, elephants, oxen and even individual soldiers carried their burdens of ammunition, guns, food and the true sustenance of military action: paperwork. Forever moving north to south, from massive factories in China and Russia, through the rail and ship networks into North Vietnam, and then via this tenuous trailway to military units, soldiers and insurgents in the south. A long and dangerous path, and one that many, many people on our side were determined to interrupt. Stopping it was as impossible as controlling a swarm of ants, but with diligence, energy and the application of massive firepower, at least some of it could be stomped out. The craft of learning where to stomp was what Rusty was about to learn.

"If you ever have to transmit an actual map location, only do it on the crypto radio. Remember, we ain't supposed to be here," Derlin went on.

"I copy that. But when would I want to transmit map coordinates if we don't run airstrikes?"

"You'd only need to do it if your team gets into hot contact. Maybe I should say when instead of if, because they go hot almost half the time. When they do, they'll often be running to either a defensible spot or one where a chopper can land and extract them. Preferably a spot that's good for both. If they can hold out for a half hour or so, we can usually call in the Kingbees and extract them. You need to know that the Kingbees are much better than the usual Arvin fliers. They can crank and launch in just a few minutes. Count on it. If they were regular Arvin, you shouldn't count on them being able to launch at all – or be willing to."

"That bad?"

"Worse. The damn Arvin are cowards. They'll find a reason to avoid or pull out of a firefight on the least excuse, or none at all. Half the time I think they don't deserve to win this war. They don't seem like they want to win it."

Rusty shook his head in silence. It wasn't the first time he'd heard that comment. Coming from Derlin, who'd seen a whole year of the war and no longer had anything to gain by blind allegiance to authority, it carried extra weight.

"Besides, this war is essentially over anyway. Johnson fucked it up so bad by trying to micro-manage it that there's no way to win it now. The best we can do is to slink away and lick our wounds. Johnson and that fuckstick MacNamara and his whiz kids..." This time, Derlin shook his head and went silent.

They droned on at five thousand feet. Derlin was showing him the boundaries of the working area. Amazingly, unlike the hundred or so square miles he'd tried to learn around LZ Emerald, the Mike FAC area extended from the Vietnam border westwards to the Mekong River where it left Laos, then down that famous waterway to the old Cambodian city of Kratie and eastwards again to Vietnam. It made a rough square about 130 miles on a side, some 17,000 square miles. It seemed impossible to believe, but Derlin claimed Rusty would soon have every rock and tree in it memorized.

"Stay well clear of cities out here, Rusty. They are all infested with NVA or the Red Brigade and there are some pretty heavy weapons right in amongst the buildings. They'll hose you if they can. Now out in the country, you'll find little groups of hootches, and they're usually just native folks. But if there are more than ten hootches or so, the chances go up of them being infiltrated or controlled."

That made sense, too. Rusty sucked up every drop of what this seasoned pilot had to tell him. It was a year's worth of life-saving experience distilled into a few flights together. Other long-time Mike FACS like Kit, Batman and Flip also had pearls of wisdom to share, and Rusty grilled them at every opportunity. It seemed odd that every bit of lore that he'd learned about being a FAC, from Hurlburt field on, had been passed along verbally. Why hadn't someone compiled a written 'tips of the trade' kind of document about this job? Or was the job simply so diverse, so varied, that no such document would have applied in a general sense? Certainly nobody would make a written record of a job as classified as this particular one, but still…

As they flew back to Ban Me Thuot, Derlin gave him one more lesson.

"Rusty, finding a really good infil site is an art as well as a science. We're almost over one I used several months ago. Let me point out to you why I picked it. You see that oval grassy field there?" He dropped the right wing and pointed across Rusty's chest. An egg-shaped patch of yellow-tan grass perhaps two hundred meters by one hundred was surrounded by sparse, single-canopy jungle. "Well, that group of hootches there about two kilometers to the south was the objective for the team to study. Between the hootches and the field, you notice that the jungle is tall but sparse. If we were lower, you'd see that the grassy field is actually a broad flat mound. You'd also see that the terrain to the north and west of the field slopes away down to that small river. Now look real close at the grass. See how it's waving in the wind, like it was water? That tells you that it's tall, standing grass. Okay, now all those things combined are what make that a perfect infil site."

"Tell me more about why."

"It's far enough from the objective that the sound of the helicopters might not be heard if the wind is right, but close enough that the team can get there and back quickly. The tall trees shield the site from direct ground view. The field is just elevated enough that there won't be prying eyes on higher terrain nearby. The tall grass and the nearby jungle will hide the team immediately, and they can move in any direction without being exposed. Plus, the trees are thin enough to allow rapid movement but dense enough to offer both cover and protection. Finally, the nearby river would make it hard for a body of troops on the other bank to get to this side in a hurry if the landing were detected.

Finally, if the team gets in undetected, it makes an excellent place to get them back out again, for all the same reasons. Copy?"

"Yeah, I do. That all makes perfect sense. But how in the hell do you keep helicopters from being seen on the way in?" Rusty asked.

"Ah, that's the clinching factor about the site. That lower terrain to the north and west is the key. I brought the two Kingbees in from the north, plopped them down and then led them off again to the west. We came in right on the trees, just at the altitude of that small rise. They didn't even have to descend to land, just stayed level and the ground almost rose to meet them. Just classic."

"You came in at *what* altitude?" Rusty asked, a bit incredulous, even though he already knew the answer.

"Oh, about twenty feet for the last five miles or so. Here's how it's done: the FAC is in the lead – and you have to hold your speed down to 90 knots so the Kingbees can keep up – then comes the bird with the team, maybe half a click back and directly astern. The empty ship is another half click back and just off to one side so he can keep both of us in sight. The way the actual insert happens is kind of cute. The FAC navigates to the site and gives a short countdown just before he gets there. It goes, 'three…two…one…BINGO! BINGO! BINGO!' When he gets there, team Kingbee plops down, and I mean plops, no slow descent, and no hover, just whomp on the ground. The team bails out and hugs dirt. In the short meantime, the empty Kingbee flies over the team bird. As soon as he's clear, the team bird lifts off and resumes the parade. The team bird is on the ground for only five or six seconds. Somebody on the ground might see three airplanes flying low, but unless he's extremely vigilant, he never catches the fact that the second and third bird change places. If you blink, you miss the team's insert."

"Oh, that is clever," Rusty beamed. "But then what?"

"Oh, you continue leading the parade for a while just to divert attention from what happened back there. After ten minutes or so, you climb to a safer altitude and orbit five or six miles from the infil site. Your little guy listens hard to the radio, and if the team gets hidden and feels safe, they check in with him. At that point, you release the choppers and they fly home. You tool around on orbit until you bingo on fuel, then another FAC with a little guy relieves you. We keep a bird and little guy airborne the whole time a team is on the ground, at least during daylight."

"Tell me again what the little guy does." Rusty knew the answer perfectly well, having flown very similar missions, but with American ground teams, while he was at LZ Emerald. The memory made him wonder whatever happened to 'Joe', his anonymous Special Ops right seater. On their final mission together, Joe and Rusty almost lost their team. They'd flown low and slow over the enemy. He'd been trying to distract their attention from the running team and darned near gotten Joe and himself killed in the process. Their plane was sieved with groundfire – and Joe had one of his toes cut neatly off by a bullet.

While Rusty recalled that terrifying flight, Derlin answered, "Well, the team doesn't speak English, so your robin is there to relay their needs to you. The team speaks in code, and in whispers, by the way. If they start screaming instead of whispering, they're in trouble. All you really need to know is 'whisper good, scream bad'. The rest is just housekeeping." Derlin grinned broadly, his teeth showing through that huge handlebar 'stash of his.

"Of course, when they scream, everything turns into a cluster-fuck. If the Kingbees are still nearby, you pick the team up as best you can. If not, you get the Kingbees to scramble launch and dee-dee mau here as fast as their little rotors can go. In the meantime, your little guy figures out where the team is, where it's going and how to direct them to a good pickup site…if possible. But since it never happens the same way twice, all I can say is that you do what you gotta do."

There that was again. Do what you have to do. Not that Rusty hadn't already learned that – to the cost of many nights tossing and turning while the sight of that other desperate team running frantically through the jungle played perpetually in his mind. The politicians sitting primly in the White House can set all the damn rules of engagement they want, they can make stupid and belated decisions on inadequate information without fear of remorse, Rusty knew. Here, in the field, where the crap hits the fan, the guy who is the actual point of the spear does what he has to do.

"I know. Derlin, just between us chickens, I've already worked with covert teams. With right-seaters, but not little guys. A whole lot of this is on their shoulders – including our own lives. What do we know about them? I mean really know."

"Some of them, like Truong, are so good they could probably do this mission on their own, if they could fly the plane. And Truong dearly loves to hold the controls, by the way. If you ever want to reward him beyond his dreams, let him land sometime. He'd practically kiss you," Derlin chuckled. "But he's exceptional. Some of the others, well, I don't trust them very much. I wouldn't trust any other Chieu Hoy at all, just on principle. Right down there on the deck, all they'd have to do is slam the yoke forward and it's all over. We're pretty sure that's what happened to a guy last year. The impact path of the plane was just a short ditch, and the fuselage rolled end over end into an aluminum ball. The wings came off early, so the fuselage didn't burn until we torched it later. We never got the bodies out," he ended, somberly.

"Why not? Didn't you even try?" Rusty said, shocked.

"Couldn't. The area was swarming with bad guys. The important thing was to destroy the crypto radio and the codes in it. So we used the Green Hornets to torch it. We couldn't use normal assets, as you already know."

"Destroying the crypto radio was more important than getting the guy's body?" Rusty couldn't believe what he'd heard. "What about his family?"

"Rusty, you got the briefing. We're expendable. No, that's not right. It goes beyond 'expendable'...we're deniable. We aren't here. We don't exist. A crashed unmarked plane with burned bodies could be any two-bit Chinese dope smuggler in a commercially available Cessna: completely deniable. But that radio proves otherwise. Besides, a working crypto radio would be invaluable to the Commies. It'd be in Beijing or Moscow within a week. They won't even pick you up alive until you destroy that radio, you know. For a while, the spooks wired a thermite grenade to it so all you had to do was pull the ring. But one of our guys just about shit his flight suit when he found his little guy toying with the damn wire in flight. The pilots refused to fly again until the grenades were taken out. The spooks caved on that, but they also said that if we survived a crash landing, our first duty was to destroy the radio and THEN request rescue. And they weren't kidding."

"Fuck me," was all Rusty could say.

"And no Vaseline, brother," Derlin answered.

The next day, Sanderson scheduled Rusty to go along on an actual insert with Flip. They went to the TOC and sat through the final briefing. Doing the talking was an impressive Vietnamese officer. Rusty had no idea what his ornate rank badge was, but he did have a nametag sewn to his chest: Dinh. A good-looking man if not for the spread of deep smallpox scars on his broad brown face, he treated Flip and Rusty with the same deep deference and courtesy that he showed the Special Forces Captain who also stood at the front of the room. Dinh conducted the briefing, and his English was only slightly accented.

"Operation Silver Tool is a five-day patrol to observe trail traffic and troop movements in this area," Dinh began, tapping a spot on the map with a hard leather swagger stick, the first one Rusty had ever seen except in the movies.

"The ground team consists of three ARVN soldiers and two Montagnard." Rusty thought he saw a brief flash of some emotion – distaste? – flicker on Dinh's face at that last word, but he couldn't be sure. Just the tiniest flare of his nostrils, and that's all. "They are in mixed, non-distinctive uniform and carry the appropriate weaponry and gear. We will use the usual two Kingbees, and the Mike in control will be Dai-wee Five Four." He bowed slightly to Flip, who returned the gesture with a nod of his head. Dinh continued, "The rider will be Van Di." He concluded, gesturing off-handedly with his stick past Flip and Rusty. Rusty turned, surprised to see a small man seated obsequiously mute in the very back of the room. The man sat with bowed head, eyes closed, motionless, and stayed that way.

The Special Forces Captain thanked Captain Dihn (Aha! another captain!) then confirmed the verbal code list of the day and the separate codes to be used by the team and the rider and then a third, completely different set of codes that had been keyed into the plane's crypto radio that morning. The codes were completely confusing to Rusty, but Flip merely nodded in an assured way, so Rusty dismissed his own confusion. The briefing continued with a weather briefing and forecast, a topic that Rusty understood much better. It concluded with the scheduled takeoff time and radio frequencies to talk to the Kingbees. Flip jotted down the last on his kneeboard.

When we were outside again, Rusty asked Flip, "Who were those guys?"

"The Special Forces guy is Captain Brookside. He's the actual chief of the mission, but Captain Dinh is nominally in command. We take orders from Dinh, unless Brookside contradicts them. Brookside won't do that unless something is seriously wrong, out of diplomatic courtesy. But Dinh is pretty good, so in both fact and fiction, he runs the show."

"And the guy in back?"

"Oh, that's our robin. I've flown with him before. He's okay except for the sick sacks." Rusty looked at him quizzically. Flip held up his hand. "Just wait. You'll see. Uh, we have about an hour before takeoff. We'd better go grab an early lunch because it'll be over before we get back. We could even get a box lunch to take along, if it weren't for Van Di."

Again, Rusty looked at him with knitted eyebrows. "Just wait. You'll see," Flip repeated, mischievously. Rusty didn't like the way he said it. Flip was a notorious practical joker.

They ate a pair of sandwiches and a cup of soup each – it seemed to be chicken with rice this time, not monkey noodle. Flip filled a canteen with cold water and they walked to the flight line. From a Conex that served as the equipment locker, they retrieved their helmets and parachutes. They checked their revolvers and the short CAR-15 carbines were loaded, then stowed the carbines behind Flip's seat. Because Rusty would be along, Van Di would ride in the third seat, behind Rusty on the right. He showed up as Flip completed pre-flighting. Van Di wore a set of those odd tiger-stripe cammies and had a parachute slung over one shoulder. He walked up deferentially, bowed and said, "Ready go now, Dai-wee." Flip said "Okay. You strap in now."

Van Di grinned, stuck both arms through the shoulder straps of the parachute and climbed into the plane. Rusty turned to Flip, "Flip, his parachute isn't adjusted to fit him. Hell, it's eight sizes too big for me to wear."

"I know, but there's no way to get any of them to wear it right. Even if he needed it, there's no chance he'd ever make it out of that rear seat, and if he did, I doubt anyone's ever taught him how to open the thing. So the fit is hardly important. The only reason I wear mine is because it makes the seat more comfortable and adds a little bit of protection from ground fire."

It was just one more astonishing thing to add to Rusty's ever-growing list of perplexities. Flip got in and then Rusty did. He noted with some concern that they were only two minutes from scheduled takeoff time. He mentioned that to Flip, who seemed in no hurry at all.

"Oh, that time is for the Kingbees. If you listen, you can hear them idling over on the other side of the compound. But they're so slow that we could takeoff a quarter of an hour after them and still catch up with them before we go across the fence." Rusty nodded.

Flip went through his own checks without ever looking at a checklist. He started both engines when he heard the Kingbees radio the tower for takeoff clearance. Within seconds, he motioned for the crew chief to pull the chocks, and they lumbered out of the parking ramp, through the wire gates of the perimeter fence and down that crooked path of metal planking to the east end of the runway. Flip at least did perform the magneto and propeller checks – again from memory – and then radioed for his own clearance.

"My Fi Fo, you clear takeoff. Ru'way two seben. Wind two fo zeyo at ten." The tower controllers accent was thick, but it was English, and comprehendible if you squinted your ears a little.

Flip added a bit of power and swung the nose towards the runway centerline, shoving the throttles smoothly to the firewall as he completed the turn. Rusty realized that the tower controller hadn't given a barometer setting for the altimeter, but saw that Flip had simply adjusted it to the field altitude of 4,756 feet. Good enough, Rusty realized. As usual, the plane hardly seemed to accelerate at all. It lumbered along, and Rusty checked the engine instruments out of habit. They said that both engines were developing full power. He looked at Flip, who didn't seem concerned at all. One thousand feet, two thousand feet and even three thousand feet of asphalt were behind them when they finally got to 65 knots and Flip gently raised the nose. If this were LZ Emerald, Rusty thought, they'd be smashing into the hootches at the end of the runway now. Just then, he felt that squirrelly little sideways hop that meant the O-2 was ready to take off, and they rose into the air.

"Jesus Christ, Flip! I thought we weren't going to make it."

"Really? Oh, that's about normal performance at this altitude when you have four full tanks, two full rocket pods and three people and combat gear aboard. You should try it when it's hotter. You roll the whole damn runway and have to stick your feet out and shove yourself airborne!" Ever the joker, that Flip.

Eventually, they climbed enough that Flip could retract the gear and flaps. After the inevitable sickening sag, the gear doors closed and they began to climb, almost normally. They continued straight west, and Rusty was able to see the city of Ban Me Thuot from the air for the first time, as Derlin had turned almost due north right after takeoff yesterday. "There's the little Army airstrip they call Ban Me Thuot City," Flip said, gesturing down and to the right. "They still fly a few O-1 missions out of it, and helicopters, of course, but it's phasing itself out pretty rapidly. You can't see it now, but just out my side is the major air traffic control radar facility for the Central Highlands. It's called Pyramid Control."

"Oh yeah. I've worked with them before. Nice to know where they are," Rusty said.

"And there's the city," Flip added. The modern brick buildings, some of three or four stories, surprised Rusty again, the white hotel very obvious among them. In the crowded streets were a few cars and hundreds of little jitney jeeps used as taxis, motorcycles, bicycles and pedestrians, all intermixed helter-skelter. Rusty could even see a busy market square. He wondered where that lovely young woman on the scooter was right now.

"No time to sightsee today, though" Flip said as Rusty craned his neck at the city. "There are the Kingbees right over the Long House. That's where we usually rendezvous."

"What's the Long House?"

"It's a huge meeting hall, I'm told. Maybe a century old and built to house visiting tribal chiefs in regal style. It's almost a hundred yards long, a real monster of a building. They say Teddy Roosevelt stayed there on a hunting trip," Flip added, dramatically.

"Teddy Roosevelt? You gotta be shitting me. I knew he hunted in Africa and South America, but I didn't know he got way out here! What did they hunt here?"

"Well, there's wild buffalo, lots of big red deer, elephant, and even tigers," Flip said matter of factly. "And lots of smaller critters, too. Monkeys and who knows what all."

"I'll be damned. That's news to me," Rusty admitted. But he had no time to marvel at it, as Flip passed the two olive drab Kingbees well to their right. The Kingbees were ancient H-34 helicopters of Korean War vintage. They used huge radial piston engines that would be more at home on the wing of a bomber. That engine was mounted in the nose to a drive shaft that passed on a 45-degree angle between the pilots to the transmission above and behind them. It was a horribly hot, loud and shaky thing to fly. It probably had ten times the moving parts of a modern Huey, and every one of those parts was critical to staying airborne. Rusty marveled at the courage it took just to strap into the things.

Flip keyed his microphone, "Kingbee?"

"Kingbee okay," was the terse reply. Flip clicked the mic switch twice.

"That's the last radio call until the IP," Flip said. "No sense advertising that we're coming."

They got out ahead of the Kingbees, and then Flip throttled back, extended the flaps to takeoff position and slowed down. The airspeed dropped, and dropped some more. Rusty could feel the plane beginning to mush and wallow its way along. He knew they were on the ragged edge of stalling and falling out of the air, and he tensed up. Flip looked over at him and grinned.

"I know," he said. "But this is as fast as the Kingbees can go, balls to the wall. We have to mush along or run away from them. Relax, we have five whole knots between their maximum cruise speed and our stall speed." Flip's permanent grin grew even wider. "Wait until we're trolling along just a few feet off the trees if you want to have white knuckles. No altitude, no airspeed and no ideas. Ahh, it's invigorating!"

Invigorating my ass, Rusty thought. Scary as juggling running chainsaws is more like it. He nearly leapt out of his skin when he felt a tap on his shoulder. He squirmed around and looked back between the seats. Van Di was handing him a white plastic sack – an airsick bag, and it bulged with fluid.

Flip noticed it too. "Oh, he wants you to take that and drop it out of the window," he said, once again as if such a thing were a matter of course. Rusty stared at Flip.

"He has TB. Haven't you heard him coughing? He'll probably fill three or four of those with phlegm during the flight. Normally, he drops them out himself, but he can't reach the window latch from back there. Do him the favor, willya?"

TB? Tuberculosis? Holy living shit! And I'm cooped up in this thing with him? Jesus, Rusty thought to himself as he took the bag as gingerly as he could. He made damn sure it was dry on the outside, then opened the window and held the bag in the slipstream. He glanced down – only trees beneath them now – and let go of it, then squirmed around and looked at Van Di, who smiled and head-bowed his thanks. He already had another bag out and was spitting into it.

To try to put the thought of lethally contagious air out of his mind, Rusty pulled out the map of the area where they were headed and studied it. Flip looked over. "You have the coordinates of the site from the briefing?" Rusty nodded. "Good. This should be a nice, easy insertion. I last checked the site two days ago, and there was no sign of bad guys within several clicks of the place. You never know, of course, but this one seems to be a piece of cake. It's close in for a change, too. We'll cross the fence here in another few miles, then we'll gradually let down and head roughly west. When we pass a big lava chimney, we'll drop down to the treetops for a few miles, and then make a shallow turn to the north. That'll parallel the Tonle Srepok until we get abeam a set of rapids. From there, we turn west again. It's a straight-in shot from there until we reach the infil site."

"What does it look like?" Rusty asked.

"It's at the edge of a big open area. We'll come in parallel to the edge, right next to the jungle tree line, and drop the team within 50 meters of the trees. There's plenty of room for the team bird to climb out straight ahead. There isn't much cover right there, but the team only has to move a few meters to be in the trees. It's not the best site, but it's the only one within five clicks of the objective, and at least it's out of sight and hearing of the village they'll be watching. No waterways to cross, and good cover from there to the objective. The only unknown is what's under those trees."

Twenty miles after they had passed over downtown Ban Me Thuot, Flip said, "Okay, we're over Indian country. Let the show begin!" He started a gradual descent from his current thousand feet or so. "I'll do a little zig here.

≈ 46 ≈

Look back and make sure you can see both Kingbees, okay?" He made a shallow but quick turn to the right. Rusty strained around and looked behind them.

"Yup, two whirlybirds," he said. Flip immediately turned back to the original heading. "Never forget to look back for them once in a while. They won't necessarily call you on the radio if they have a problem and turn back to home. It's embarrassing to get all the way to the infil site before you realize you're alone." That grin again.

In a few minutes, they'd passed the tower of lava that Flip had described. "We call that the nigger toe. It's a great place to get in a little rocket practice." He seemed oblivious to the racial slur. But it did look like a giant's big toe. It even had what looked vaguely like a toenail in the curved shapes that made up its upper parts. And it was a coal-black edifice that stuck up at least a thousand feet above the jungle below. Rusty thought hard, but couldn't come up with a more fitting name – at least without getting pornographic. Flip switched radios and keyed the mic again.

"Mike five oh, Mike five four."

"Go ahead, five four."

"At the toe. Ops normal."

"Five oh copies."

"That tells the TOC that we're still alive and kicking," Flip explained. "We won't call them again until the team is on the ground or everything turns to dog shit."

Flip reached down and picked up his canteen. He took a swig and offered one to Rusty. He shook his head no, and then had the horrifying thought that Flip might offer it to the tubercular lips of Van Di, but he didn't. With the engines throttled back for descent, they could clearly hear the little guy hawking and spitting. Soon, they had descended all the way to the treetops. Just as it seemed they'd settle into them, Flip bumped the throttles up again.

"Okay, this is where it can get tricky," Flip said. "You need to stay low enough that the Kingbees can see you against the dark trees, and low enough that you zip across any small clearings before anybody can draw a bead on you, but high enough to be able to recover from any mild turbulence or bumpy air. Being only a few knots above the stall doesn't help any," he added, delicately working the plane's control yoke like a juggler balancing a broom on his fingertip. Within minutes, a line of sweat began running out of his helmet and down the side of his neck. Flip subconsciously pulled and tugged at his boom mike with his lips.

Down here, all sense of direction and distance seemed to vanish. Rusty was startled to see a broad ribbon of milk chocolate water rush by under them: the Tonle Srepok. A minute later, Flip started a very shallow turn to the right. "Check for the Kingbees again," he said curtly.

Again, Rusty bent his head to look back under the wing flap. Both Kingbees were still there, one immediately behind and a few feet higher, the other off to his left a ways, and a few feet higher still. But even the second Kingbee thumped along no more than 50 feet above the jungle.

"Check your map. We should be coming up on a set of shallow rapids in about two minutes. The river swings back towards us just before that, and you should be able to see the rapids before we get there. I know about where they are, but sing out when you see them as a double-check."

"I will," Rusty promised. He tried to sit taller and peer over the raised nose of the plane. The jungle looked like a flat, featureless carpet of English green from this height, but he soon began to pick out small features; changes in tree height and differences in the light that became clearings when they buzzed past them. Suddenly, he was looking at a long, sinuous depression ahead and to the right.

"River coming up, I think," and even as he said it, he could see that creamed coffee-colored water again. "Roger that, river abeam us now… looking for the rapids. Flip said nothing.

"Okay, I see the rapids coming up," Rusty said moments later. He risked a glimpse at the map. The direction of the river was correct, there was a small island just upstream of the rapids, and up ahead, the river turned to the northeast again. All three points matched the map to the actual geography zipping past. "Stand by…rapids abeam us…now!"

Flip keyed the mic once more, "Kingbee?" They heard two clicks in reply. They were ready.

Flip immediately began a shallow left turn, rolling out due west. As soon as he finished the turn, he reached up and started the plane's stopwatch. "The rapids were our IP – Initial Point," he explained. "We do a mile in about 40 seconds at this speed. Five miles will take three and a half minutes. We should first see the clearing in exactly three minutes, and we'll have the last 30 seconds to maneuver a bit if we need to, and start the countdown to the Kingbees. I want to line up right at the edge of the jungle with the trees on your side. When we enter the clearing, watch that tree line like a hawk. If you see any troops or muzzle flashes, sing out and I'll abort the insertion. If it seems clear, don't say anything. You'll have to look and shout quick, though."

In what seemed like only moments, Flip said, "Okay. Coming up on three minutes. You see a great big clearing up ahead? It should be mostly to our left."

"Tally ho! I see it. We're lined up perfectly, Flip. Right on the northern edge. You might be a hundred meters too far right."

"Nope, we're perfect. I want to drop them damn near under the tree limbs. If there's ten feet rotor clearance, that's five feet too far out. Watch hard, now. Here we go." He keyed the mic, "Kingbee…"

"Three…"

It didn't seem possible, but Flip actually pushed the nose over to go lower!

"Two…"

They dropped over the edge of the clearing, almost clipping the last limbs at the edge, then zoomed along only inches off the ground.

"One…"

Straining to see under the limbs, and suddenly disoriented by them flashing by only feet away, Rusty saw nothing but vegetation. He kept silent. Flip slammed the throttles to full power.

"…BINGO BINGO BINGO!"

He pulled the nose up as they shot over the trees at the far side of the clearing. They popped up to a hundred feet above the trees, then he allowed the plane to settle back down to half that as he pulled back the power again.

Rusty heard nothing on the radio. "Flip, what happened? I don't hear anything. Did the team get in?"

"Rusty, this is truly a time when silence is golden. If the Kingbees couldn't do the insert, they would have squawked. If the team were in trouble already, they'd be screaming. So both events went fine. Now, several things might happen over the next half-hour: either the bad guys detected the insert or they didn't. If they did, they're on their way to shoot up the team. Now that still leaves two possibilities: they find the team or they don't. Either way, the team stays quiet or they scream their heads off. So far, things are quiet and that's very good – quiet good, scream bad."

Rusty tried to calm himself. Combat wasn't supposed to be silent, at least it didn't seem like it should be. This kind was eerily quiet, frighteningly so. He imagined himself as one of the team, jumping out of a helicopter into a place he'd never seen. He'd be disoriented, possibly airsick, surrounded by enemy and have no way to escape. Not to mention being dressed in the enemy's uniform and guaranteed an immediate execution if caught. He'd be petrified.

They trolled around just over the trees for another few minutes before Flip started a slow climb. Behind them the two Kingbees did the same. Finally, Rusty relaxed the white-knuckle grip he hadn't even realized he'd been holding on the seat edges. By now, they were several miles to the southwest of the insertion site, but they could see it as they climbed. Suddenly, Rusty realized that he was hearing something over the radio. It was almost like having his hearing tested: he'd been hearing faint sounds and had no idea how long he'd been hearing them before he realized they were there. Rusty squirmed around and looked at Van Di. He was already busy writing on the window with his grease pencil. The whispers resolved themselves into strange words: "hai... tam...mouiba...mot...sau." Van Di wrote "2...8...13...1...6," then pulled the boom mic of his headset to his lips, pressed his transmit button and whispered back, "chin." Silence again, and Van Di referred to a small booklet of flimsy pink paper. "Team okay," he said over the intercom. "Team go north. No NVA. Numba one job, Dai-wee!" He leaned forward, stuck his skinny arm between the seats and gave Flip a thumbs up sign. Flip looked back and returned the sign, the grim strain of the low altitude flying replaced by his usual grin.

With no further ado, Flip switched radios and said, "Okay. Kingbee go home."

The radio crackled back, "Okay, okay! Kingbee go home!" The exuberance and joy in that pilot's voice was unmistakable, even over the hiss of his radio and thunder of his engine. Rusty wondered if the pilot of that clattering antique was proud of a job well done or if he was simply glad to get out of there and get back on the ground. Maybe both. Probably both.

Flip switched frequencies yet again. "Mike five oh, five four."

"Five four, five oh, go."

"Platinum."

"Copy."

"Now what, Flip?"

"Well, that tells the TOC that all's well. Now we just tool around for three hours and keep our ears open. The team has gotten through the most dangerous first few minutes, but if bad guys are on their way to the infil site, they could arrive at any time. Naturally, the team is already moving away from there, but they could still bump into trouble. If they get through the next three hours undetected, they could be home free. Meanwhile, the Kingbees will go back, refuel and sit on alert, just in case. They'll be on in-seat alert for the rest of the day, and five-minute alert for the rest of the mission."

"In-seat alert?"

"Uh huh. They sit there strapped in, power cart connected and radios on, ready to fire up the engine. They can be airborne in five minutes. And yeah, I see the look on your face. It's miserable duty in this heat and humidity, especially right over an engine that's already smoking hot. I told you these Kingbee pilots were above the cut."

"I'll say. They must be. How do we handle it?"

"You mean do we stand alert? No. But by the time we get down to 'go-home' gas, somebody else will already be airborne and on the way out here to relieve us. We just hand off the job to them as we pass. If things really went to heck in a hand basket, we could get somebody else up in no time, or launch the relief bird early. But we're so much faster than the Kingbees that a true alert status isn't necessary."

"This is all pretty well thought out isn't it? How long has this been going on?"

"Well, I'm not sure, exactly. Special Ops isn't exactly something that gets well documented, you know. I do know, or I'm pretty sure, that the mission we do here is different than the way it's done from other places. The whole thing evolves, too. It's different now than it was just a year ago, even at BMT. For one thing, we don't use GIs as team members anymore."

"Now you're blowing my mind. This isn't the only place this is done? And we used to put Americans on the ground over the fence? Tell me more."

"Uh, maybe that's not a good idea. That need to know thing, you know. But I can tell you what I suspect. okay?"

"Okay, I understand. I never heard a thing."

"Yup, and I never said a thing. But I've heard the radio chatter in the TOC, and I've heard our Special Forces guys talking with a CCC and a CCN. Ban Me Thuot is CCS, so I'm just guessing that the last letters refer to North, Central and South. We're apparently South. There may be others, too. Anyway, I've also heard those other places working airstrikes and extracting teams with non-Asian voices, in English. Draw your own conclusions. I have mine."

"Uh huh, I see. But you said…I mean suspected…that we used to use non-Asian teams out of BMT?"

"Until just a few months ago, in fact," Flip said, nodding. "I think we lost six or seven of them KIA in the past year or so. It got too hard to disguise that, I guess, or some politician found out, or something. But that all stopped very suddenly and we went to all indigenous teams overnight. At least at BMT, that is. Like I said, there are secrets and then there are secrets."

Rusty would have asked more questions, but Van Di tapped him on the shoulder again and handed up another sack of bloody sputum. Rusty had almost forgotten he was back there, and suddenly wished they hadn't been discussing classified stuff with him listening. He opened the window, and carefully dropped the ghastly thing. Flip changed from the main tanks to the auxiliary tanks, first the rear engine, which burned fuel a bit faster than the front, then the other a few minutes later. Staggering the switchover in that order guaranteed that – if you forgot to switch back to the mains in time – both engines wouldn't run dry and quit at the same time.

They gradually settled into cruise mode, and none of them spoke for a long time. Rusty spent much of the time looking at the ground and comparing what he saw to the map. Cambodia was a fascinatingly varied and beautiful place, he decided. Flip tapped Rusty's leg and waggled the yoke a bit. Rusty took over the controls while Flip closed his eyes and rested his helmet against the window. They continued to orbit and before long the constant drone of the engines and the warmth of the sun through the Plexiglas made Rusty a bit sleepy, too. Van Di was snoring. To stay alert, Rusty tried the trick of tuning the ADF navigational radio to the AFVN station in Saigon for some music. The Automatic Direction Finding needle swung dutifully to the south-southeast, toward the Armed Forces Vietnam Network transmitting tower in Saigon. Country music filled Rusty's ear cups. Singing through your nose by ear is what he'd always thought of it, but at least it was livelier than the somnolent drone of the engines.

Time passed, and suddenly the rear engine coughed, sputtered and lost RPMs. Flip jerked upright and quickly turned the right-wing fuel selector back to main. Instantly, the engine roared back to full speed. He switched the left wing selector back to mains, also. The tanks were two-thirds empty and they had been airborne now for three hours. More than two hours had passed since the team went in, and they hadn't heard another peep out of them. Flip shook and stretched, settling himself in the seat, then he turned to Van Di, pointed to his watch, and gave another thumbs up. Van Di came up on intercom, "Very good. Team happy. Van Di happy."

Van Di passed a third sack of mucous forward, this one even bloodier than the first two. Happy now, maybe, but not long for this earth, Rusty thought. Maybe the altitude made his lungs bleed worse. If the O-2 had an oxygen system, he'd probably be sucking on it for some relief. But the plane didn't, and relief would come to Van Di only when they nailed down his lid.

The radio crackled, and both Flip and Rusty stiffened, but relaxed again when the voice came not in a whisper or a scream, but in calm English. "Mike 54, Mike 56." Flip smiled, took the controls back and keyed the mic, "Hey Batman! About time, buddy. Where are ya?"

"I'm crossing the fence now, how about you?"

"Oh, I'd say just about over downtown Orlando at five."

"Uh huh, copy that. I'll be there in twenty or so. You're cleared to head for home. Wave when you go by."

"We'll do that, Batman. Say Hi to Robin for me and we hope you don't hear from the Commissioner."

"Same here. All quiet I suppose?"

"Night before Christmas, bud. Couldn't be better."

That seemed to be all, so Rusty turned to Flip and said, "Okay, explain all that. What the hell were you two saying?"

"First, that's the point. Nobody but us would know what we were saying," Flip said, raising one eyebrow. "Over the fence you already know - he's crossing the border. Orlando is a bit more obscure. There's an abandoned city out here – Chbar - that we use for rocket practice. The bad guys down there use us for target practice, too. It's as much fun as a thrill ride, so we call it Disney World. The real Disney World is about twenty miles south of Orlando, and we're about that distance north of Chbar. See?"

"Now I do. What about the commissioner?"

"Oh, that's because we call Bates Batman, and it's coincidence that our little guys have always been called robins. So it's a natural for him to use code phrases from the comic books. Getting a call from the Commissioner means there's trouble and Batman needs to go fix it. Fun stuff, huh?"

"Yeah, it is. Maybe I should start working on some phrases of my own."

"Hey, yeah! That's good. That'll keep the NVA guessing."

"Flip, do you really think they can hear us? I mean really."

"Oh hell yes. We know they use very capable scanners that sweep all our normal frequencies at high sample rates. They lock on and record any frequency with traffic at that instant. The only way they'd miss something would be if two frequencies were talking at the same instant. They get around that by using multiple scanners. So, yeah - they hear us."

"I'll be dipped. You think we listen to them?"

"I'd bet we do. Electronic intelligence – what the spooks call SigInt for Signal Intelligence – is huge, and growing every day. I'd bet there isn't much that either side misses. The Russians are supposedly very good at it, and they supply the NVA with equipment. Maybe they don't export their best and latest receivers, but these aren't exactly state of the art transmitters, either. Except for that one, of course." He tapped the crypto set at the bottom of the stack between their feet. "That's why we protect that little booger more than our skins."

They headed east, and had flown for only a few minutes when they spotted Batman's O-2 flying outbound. He was just below them and maybe a half-mile off to their left. Flip waggled his wings, and Batman did also. "Well, Silver Tool is his baby now. We're officially relieved," Flip said.

"I meant to ask about that. Silver Tool? What does that mean? I know - all I do is ask questions, but this is all new to me."

"Uh huh. I understand. Go ahead and ask. Better to know the answer than not – for some of this stuff, anyway. Well, somewhere in some deep basement, there's probably some chimp chained to a desk. He has two huge wheels of chance, and each wheel has hundreds or thousands of random words. When they need a name for a new operation, they poke the chimp and he spins the wheels. Whatever two words come up, that's the name of the operation. Some of them make sense, some of them turn out funny, and some are just bizarre. But that's what it gets called, regardless."

"Like what?"

"Oh, we've had missions called Bent Wheel, for example, and another one called Home Street. There was a Clay Book and a Bitter Face. The weirdest pair I remember was one called Weasel Clamp."

Rusty grinned to himself at the mental image of a chimp with wheels of chance. It was probably closer to the truth than not, too. While he mused and concocted odd word pairs, they re-crossed the fence and approached the field. Flip pointed out landmarks and hazards to remember as he maneuvered into the landing pattern. They landed and taxied back into the compound. Waiting for them was BMT's sole crew chief and de-facto maintenance chief, MSgt Mike Cramer. Tall and lanky but with the spring-steel arms and banged-up knuckles that typify all aircraft wrench-turners, he had directed them to their parking spot with arm motions. Their prop wash ruffled Cramer's longish blonde hair as he chocked the wheels.

"Good Mission, sir?" Cramer asked as soon as the props stopped. His eyes automatically scanned the plane's skin for bullet damage. "Any action?"

"Oh, no holes in it today, and no write-ups, Mike," Flip said, jovially. "I guess you'll have to loaf the rest of the day."

"Damn shame, sir. I was looking forward to avoiding chow and happy hour." He said it with a straight face, but it was clear he meant the exact opposite. Rusty could empathize. A cold beer and hot chow sounded awfully good. The three of them climbed stiffly out of their seats.

His appetite wavered a bit as Van Di wriggled from the confines of the third seat. He was carrying yet another sack, this one even fuller than the previous ones. But he smiled and bowed repeatedly to Flip, paying the horrid thing in his hand no mind at all. "You numba one pilot, Dai-Wee. Very good. We fly again some day. Numba one." He bobbed his head some more as he backed away from them deferentially.

"You number one robin, Van Di. We fly again, you bet. Good job," Flip said in half-pidgin, and with his grin at full intensity. He saluted Van Di informally, and then turned away to complete the paperwork for the flight.

"Hey Flip, just one more question, okay? Then I'll quit."

"Okay, shoot, but you owe me a beer if you ask me any more today."

"You get one anyway, brother. But what is this Dai-Wee that Van Di calls you? Even Captain Dihn used it this morning, and it's mystified me ever since."

"Oh," Flip began, as usual, "that's the Vietnamese word for Captain. Van Di probably can't tell one of our ranks from another, but he heard Dihn call me that, so he calls me the same thing. Dihn does know that I'm only a lieutenant —that's a Trung-wee- but he calls me captain as a sort of compliment, as if I should be a captain and would be if our superiors were smart enough to see my true worth. Dihn's saying that we're equals in his eyes."

Rusty looked at him with squinted eyes, not knowing if Flip was pulling his leg or not. It was hard to tell with Flip, who loved a joke more than anything. But it made sense from the Asian viewpoint where precedence and rank meant almost everything. Rusty decided to believe it for now.

"But now let's discuss that beer," Flip said. "There's time to get a quick shower and pop a tab or two before chow. Have you had a chance to get to the canteen yet?"

"No, I haven't, and I need some soap and stuff. Where is it?"

"Just down the street, of course. After all, there is only one street and you can't go far and still be inside the wire," Flip's grin was back. "But I'll walk you there and help you carry the beer back. You are buying, you said?"

"You bet. I might want something non-alcoholic, too. They have soda?"

"Oh yeah, but beer's cheaper. That sure galls Batman."

"Say again? Beer is cheaper than soda? You're shitting me. And why should that bother Batman?"

Flip looked sideways at him as they walked down the ramp to the hootch, "You're doing that question thing again. You now owe me a six-pack, by my count."

"Oh, all right. I'll buy. But let me see if I can put this into a declaratory statement to avoid getting deeper into brew debt. Ahem. I solicit your elucidation as to the seemingly contradictory and obfuscatory commercial conundrum to which you previously alluded, as well as a particular pilot's peculiar potable proclivities."

Flip stopped dead in his tracks. "HUH?"

"Explain the pricing and Batman's choice of drink."

"Jesus, talk about code! Where did you learn words like that?"

It was Rusty's turn to grin. "I'm an English Lit major, my friend, and also a sesquipedalian."

"Well, your religion doesn't matter here."

Still grinning, Rusty said, "No. 'Sesquipedalian' means I'm partial to using big words. I was just showing off. But do explain about the beer and soda. Batman, too."

"Oh, well…" Flip said, still somewhat stunned, "I don't know why, but beer here costs $2.40 a case and soda is $2.65. And Batman is a Mormon, so he doesn't drink beer."

Rusty smacked forehead with palm. "Argh, I forgot that about Batman. Derlin told me that my first day here. Or maybe Kit did. Okay. Lead on, MacDuff. I shall purchase prodigious portions of potables posthaste."

The canteen had a choice of Dial or Zest soap bars, only Colgate toothpaste and very few of any other personal needs. But it had stacks and stacks of canned Budweiser, Pabst, Schlitz and Falstaff beer. There were a dozen cases of Coke and two of Seven-Up. The proclivities of the pilots were apparent. Rusty bought a case each of Pabst and Bud for the fridge in the Big Room. One five-dollar slip of MPC scrip went into the till. With his 20 cents change, Rusty bought a bar of Dial, and the Montagnard clerk behind the counter bobbed his head and grinned at the men in silence. Rusty slipped the bar of soap into his flight suit pocket, and they each toted a case of beer to the hootch.

Glory of glories, Ban Me Thuot not only had a bank of hot water showers, but genuine flush toilets in stalls on the other side of a cement block wall that divided the shower building. A row of basins with hot and cold taps and mirrors stretched along the wall. Even the beer here was better. Falstaff wasn't exactly premium, but it was head and bubbles above the horrible Carling Black Label - and the disgusting four-holer latrine - Rusty had endured at LZ Emerald. All in all, Ban Me Thuot was purest luxury compared to his first FAC assignment. Maybe Special Ops would turn out to be special in other ways.

Rusty changed out of his sweaty flight suit, wrapped himself with a towel and donned rubber flip-flops. Outside his own door, Flip was identically semi-clothed. They walked into the open shower bay, and Rusty stopped dead at the sight of three hootch maids squatting on their haunches. They were busily rubbing laundry on the concrete floor. They gabbled to each other in the high-pitched singsong of Vietnamese between furtive nods and giggles directed at Flip and Rusty. Flip simply ignored them and went to a shower, hung his towel on a hook and began showering. Embarrassed and shy, Rusty hesitated, but did the same. More giggles. Lots more.

Over evening chow the next day, Dave Sanderson addressed Sandy and Rusty. "Guys, you've both done well. Sandy, you've flown with Kit and Batman. Rusty, you've been out with Derlin and Flip. They tell me you're both quick studies and ready to fly solo. Since I'm almost as new here as you two, I'd like to fly with both of you first. Don't think of it as any kind of checkride. I only want to watch how you handle yourselves and maybe learn something myself. It'll almost be like having six instructors for me, since you each had two teachers here. There are two new missions coming up soon. I won't say any more here, but I'm assigning you two as prime FACs for them. I want you to get briefed on them tomorrow in the TOC, and then fly the survey missions solo. When you've found sites you like, I'll go along with you on the inserts. Purely as dead weight, I assure you. But I like to have some feeling about my pilots' flying and thinking styles. Any questions?"

Sandy said, "Nope." Rusty shook his head. It sounded like a perfectly sound idea to him, something Rusty might do if he were in charge. Besides, the last time he'd flown with Dave, Sanderson had been his T-37 IP back in pilot training at Laredo. Rusty hoped to impress Sanderson with how much he'd learned since then. Assuming he had.

"Before I schedule too many days in advance, what are your horse pill days?"

"Tomorrow's mine," Sandy said.

"Say what?" Rusty asked.

"Your day for chloroquine-primaquine."

Rusty still looked back at him blankly.

"Jesus, aren't you on a malaria pill schedule? What the hell were they doing at Cam Rahn, sitting on their thumbs? I hope you don't have malaria already. Well, at least we can plan for your day off a bit easier this way. Let me think. Okay, Sandy, you take your pill tomorrow? Rusty, you take yours on Wednesday. That'll have Sandy off the flying schedule one day and Rusty off the next."

"Why's that, Dave?"

Kit chimed in, "Because the day after you take your horse pill is a crapper day. You'll have the roaring shits. Not a day to be flying, believe me."

"Okay, that's settled," Sanderson said. "Now let's plan for a Welcome Aboard party. Batman, you think you can scrounge up some daiquiri makin's?" The other Dave smiled broadly. "You can count on that, sir. One thing we Utahns understand is getting something for cheap."

"Perfect. Tomorrow night sound good?" Nods all around. "See you all then. Oh, Flip. You have dawn patrol on your team. Keep the uproar to a minimum tonight, okay?"

Flip hung his head in mock disgust and disappointment. He wasn't a heavy drinker, but he enjoyed the club camaraderie. Rusty wished he had Flip for a roommate instead of Richard; who, Rusty had learned, sat alone at the bar every night getting silently but completely drunk. After the bar closed, he'd stagger back to their room, climb into his rack and pass out still dressed. Sanderson showed him no preference and seemed to give him as many early morning missions as anyone else; but Rusty had no idea how Richard flew them while hung over, as he must surely have been every single day.

The next morning, Sandy and Rusty presented themselves at the Tactical Operations Center to be briefed on their first insert missions. Captain Brookside was there again as one briefer, but the other man was new. Brookside made the introductions.

"Gentlemen, I'm honored to serve one of the most prominent intelligence experts we have the fortune to consult. This is Y-Monh, an elder member of the Jarai tribe of Montagnards, and senior officer for the two missions to be discussed. You may treat him as the equivalent of a major." Turning to the man, Brookside held his left hand out toward the two FACs. "May I present our two newest pilots, who seek the honor of performing missions for you. This is Lieutenant Hubert and Lieutenant Naille."

Rusty was amused by the formal, almost diplomatic terms, but managed to keep a serious look on his face. The Montagnard man bowed deeply, and the two pilots rose, then returned the bow with the same degree of stateliness.

When they met his eyes again, he was smiling. Dressed in a mix of tribal and military garb, he wore plain green fatigue pants and shirt, but a colorful, twisted cloth headpiece that resembled a flattened turban. He also wore a black silk bandanna tied snugly around his neck, and had a thick gold ring in one ear. His smile revealed several gold teeth as well. He was short, about five feet three, but powerfully built, and his skin was darker than the other Vietnamese Rusty had seen – more like mahogany than the yellow-pine color of ARVN men. His bone structure was more solid, too; his face and eyes more rounded and his nose more pointed than flat. Clearly, he came from an Asian race or sub-race quite different than the South Vietnamese of the lowlands. All this registered in but a moment, while the man gestured for all to be seated.

"I am happy to meet you both. I have been told many things about you, and I place the lives of my men in your hands."

Rusty hadn't been prepared for his excellent English, nor his way of getting immediately to the root of the issue. The latter impressed Rusty almost as much as his command of language. This man was no lightweight by a long chalk. Almost involuntarily, Rusty bowed again. This Y-Monh had won his allegiance with no more than a score of words. Remarkable. Brookside's diplomacy hadn't been misplaced.

Y-Monh went on, "Two teams of five Jarai each will go to sites far apart. They will appear to be mere laborers separated from their supply teams and lost. They will find and join with the enemy. Each man carries mortar or artillery bombs, but these are special bombs that will explode when fired. They will switch their special bombs with enemy supplies and then become lost again. Then you bring teams home. Maybe many enemy will be killed when they fire our special bombs." He grinned to himself deviously.

Rusty looked at Sandy, and they both grinned back at Y-Monh. This was the kind of practical joke that Sandy loved, and suddenly Rusty did, too. But this was a deadly joke, one that would not only kill or maim the enemy but, as Rusty immediately understood, would strike fear and distrust in others as well. What a masterful stroke!

Brookside and Y-Monh then got down to the specifics of the two missions. They gave the map coordinates where they wanted the teams inserted, based on recently observed trail activity. Sandy's mission was to be called Dusty Wagon and Rusty's was Keel Ship. What great names! The chained chimp had spun well. Both missions were to begin within three or four days, depending on how well the aerial surveys went, and would go in on different days in case the either insert went badly.

When the briefing ended, Y-Monh ceremoniously shook hands with both FACs. His hands were calloused and wiry and his grip like a vise. He caught Rusty unaware, and Y-Monh's grasp only included Rusty's fingers, almost crunching them. Rusty was ashamed of the almost girlish impression the handshake must have given, but there was nothing he could do about it, because Y-Monh immediately turned and left the room. It made Rusty doubly determined to do well on the mission.

He decided to fly out and look for his infil site immediately, and so did Sandy. Dave Sanderson approved, assigning them a plane each for the day. Rusty was a bit nervous because this would be his first solo mission across the fence. He'd made a parts run to Cam Rahn a couple of days before and managed to find his way there and back. But this was different. This time, he'd be on his own over what the other guys called Indian country, out where the Secretary would indeed disavow his existence. Even Mary Beth didn't know what he really did now. He'd written to her several times, and given her only the approved cover story that Dave Sanderson had made them recite to him: they worked with ground teams who patrolled and searched for enemy activity. No other details at all. It was a good cover story because it was true – as far as it went.

In her first letter back, he had been astounded to learn that one of her cousins had been in the Army teaching marksmanship to the ARVN. With cosmic coincidence, John Tarl been assigned to work with the 23rd ARVN in none other than Ban Me Thuot only a year or two earlier. When she mentioned Rusty's assignment to Tarl, he'd raised his eyebrows and whistled, she reported. She didn't say what, if anything, he'd added, but maybe she did know more than Rusty was telling her.

He just hoped that *he* knew what he was doing.

He took off a few minutes after Sandy had gone. Sandy's area was many miles south of his. Rusty's was up to the northwest of BMT, near where Derlin had begun their big counter-clockwise tour of the Mike FAC Cambodian Area of Operation. Crossing the fence and the Tonle Srepok, Rusty flew over a spidery rope bridge across the narrow ravine of an unnamed feeder stream. Discovered by an earlier Mike FAC, the damnable bridge had impertinently survived a fighter airstrike and scores of rockets fired by Mike FACS ever since. The NVA probably still used it to carry supplies along this thread of the Ho Chi Minh Trail. They still called it Dickerson's Bridge: it was Dangling Dick in their radio slang, and Rusty reported his position as such.

Rusty's infil site was more of a region than a point. He was to drop the team within walking distance of Ho's Highway so they could supposedly wander back into contact with NVA. The heavily jungled area was reportedly a maze of trails underneath, so getting the team near one would be easy. Getting them in undetected would be chancier, not to mention getting them out again – especially if the NVA didn't believe their tale of becoming lost. No chance at all if they got caught switching those booby-trapped mortar rounds.

Rusty angled off to the side of the insertion box, tracing it and his path on the map. He knew better than to directly overfly the area more than once. Instead, he set up an orbit several miles wide and a mile or two east of the target box. He searched the area with binoculars every time he flew near it, making two circles before he moved off farther to the north and making two more circles there. There was a small blue line – a stream – running down through the middle of the assigned box, and Rusty assumed that the bad guys had trails that paralleled it. There were several clearings both large and small suitably close to the blue line, but none of them looked especially inviting as an infil site.

All of the smaller clearings were roughly circular except one. It looked like a stretched raindrop, aligned almost parallel with the blue line. About two kilometers west of the center of the box, it might work, Rusty thought. He sketched it on his map, then added the large clearing as a backup. The entire half of the box east of the blue line looked to be impenetrable jungle: useless. If he'd be able to get a team in within the box at all, it'd be the big clearing or the raindrop. For some reason, the raindrop just seemed to look better.

Rusty circled several miles north of the box for a while, as if something there had drawn his attention. He even rolled in and fired a Willy Pete rocket or two into the trees to add to the deception. Besides, he thought, you never knew. There was a story about a FAC up near the DMZ who had been assigned a pair of fighters because they'd been unable to hit their primary target. Told to expend them as he saw fit in the Free Fire Zone he was patrolling, he'd simply launched a marker rocket completely at random and told the fighters to hit it. The first bomb from the fighter had set off a monstrous secondary explosion, and fires and explosions continued for three days. He'd presumably hit a VC ammo dump invisible from the air, by purest luck.

Rusty's two rockets simply puffed their plumes of white smoke with no further results, however. He didn't even see any white sparkles of return ground fire from the spot. Nobody home.

He climbed a bit – just in case – and headed back to the south. This time, he did overfly the little raindrop clearing, but in straight and level flight. He didn't so much as dip a wing as he stared hard at the place through his binoculars: dry grass, reasonably level, plenty large enough for a Kingbee and with no higher terrain nearby. It still looked good, and he made up his mind. That'd be his first insert site.

He hacked the stopwatch and noted his heading: 160 degrees. Out ahead, he noticed one of the many lava upthrusts that dotted the plains. Not a remarkable one, it was a mere heap of black basalt. But it aligned almost directly with his heading. He located it on the map and put a small cross on it. He'd found his Initial Point, too. The next time he saw it, he'd be down in the grass, so he memorized every feature of the landmarks around it as he approached it. When Rusty was directly over it, he stopped the clock and noted the seconds it had taken to fly from the clearing to the lava pile. Later, he'd correct that to account for the slower speed he'd be flying ahead of the Kingbees. He turned and looked back, from the lava to the clearing. He wanted to see it from that direction because the perspective would be different. There was nothing to help orient him on the way in, but no apparent obstacles, either. It'd be a matter of holding heading and speed, watching the clock and making a last-second correction if need be. If he missed the little clearing, the larger one would be just beyond it and to the right. He'd use that rather than circle and try again. It should work, he hoped.

Rusty tooled around a bit longer, getting as familiar as possible with the landmarks. He saw nothing sinister anywhere, but he also knew the bucolic appearance was deceiving: this area was literally infested with enemy troops. He knew they were too smart and too disciplined to shoot at a FAC and reveal their position, so he was relatively immune to danger for now. Go lower, or start circling a small spot, though, and the whole area might light up. Rusty stayed straight and level – and high.

Back at BMT, he landed, taxied in and shut down. Mike Cramer and Mike Lopez helped him button the plane up – how odd that both of the maintenance guys for the Mike FACS were named Mike! – and then he walked back to the hootch. In the big room, Derlin was drawing something, but he put it down when Rusty asked him for help.

"Derlin, look at this with me, would ya? I think I've found a decent infil site for my first mission, but I want to bounce it off of you and see what you think. okay?"

"Sure thing. What you got? Don't talk about any mission details, though. Hootch maids are still around."

As usual, he was right; there were ears within overhearing distance. Rusty could hear sweeping sounds from the next room through the thin plywood wall. He sat on Derlin's cot next to him, and opened the map.

"Here's the box," Rusty pointed, "and there are several clearings in this area, but nothing usable on this side of the blue line. I like the looks of this smaller one, and I could use the large one as backup if I missed the small one." Rusty moved his finger down the page. "This pile of lava should be make a good IP, but there aren't any decent landmarks between it and the clearing. Time and heading, I guess."

"Yeah, I know that area. Not much to navigate by down low. Not many decent clearings, either. You didn't draw an easy one for your first go. Not impossible, though. Let's see…" He took a piece of scrap paper, laid it down between the tentative IP and the small clearing and made two pencil marks. Then he opened the map and laid the paper down against the map's distance scale.

"Uh, about 11 kilometers, maybe six and a half nautical miles. At 90 knots, that's 40 seconds to the mile. Six and a half times forty is, what? Two sixty? That's four and a third minutes. Four plus twenty seconds. Not so long that you'd maybe get lost on the way in. That seems okay. What's the clearing look like?"

"Maybe two hundred meters long, half that wide, shaped like a raindrop with the pointy end on the approach side. Dry grass, but I couldn't tell how high. No big rocks or trees in the middle, no ditches that I could see – at least from two thousand feet," Rusty answered.

"You use the binos, or naked eyes?"

"The binos, of course. But I only made one pass directly over it. From a couple of miles to the side, it seemed like the best bet. The big clearing is a bit bumpy and uneven, with a few scattered trees, but plenty of room for a Kingbee everywhere. Just in case. And it'd be easier to see."

"It's also a bit downwind, if you missed the small one due to crosswind drift," Derlin added, nodding. Rusty hadn't thought of that. "Without looking at it myself, I'm tempted to say it's about as good as you could pick under the circumstances. Now write your call sign on that map, and go file it in the safe in the TOC."

"Huh? Why?"

"Because you marked it up. We don't want to leave it lying around where any set of eyes can see it and pass the info along. Do we?"

"Oh. Oh, right. Of course."

When Rusty got back, Derlin was drawing again. "What's that?" Rusty asked.

"Oh, I'm sketching some plans for a wind sail cart," he said matter-of-factly.

"A who?"

"Wind sailer. Kind of a sail boat with wheels."

"You mean like an ice boat? Those things they sail on frozen lakes?"

Derlin nodded. "Uh huh, but I'm gonna sail it down the runway."

"You gotta be shitting me. Let me see that."

He'd drawn a "T" shaped thing with wheels at each end of the arms and a mast near the front single wheel. A seat where the arms met faced down the long arm of the thing.

"You're actually gonna build this?" Rusty asked, doubtfully.

Derlin grinned. "Mostly done. I'm trying to design some brakes and steering."

"Where is it? I hafta see this!"

"It's over in the motor pool maintenance building. Wanna go take a peek?"

"Hell, yes. Let's mosey."

They walked down the main camp road and turned left at the chow hall. The motor pool maintenance building was a two-story building of sheet iron, blackened by diesel smoke. Inside, two and a half-ton trucks – deuce and a half's – were in various stages of disassembly. In the back, behind one being slowly reduced to nothing through the process of cannibalizing for parts, was a spindly-looking thing just like in Derlin's drawing. Composed of ten-foot lengths of two-inch square steel tubing welded into shape, it was painted cherry red. A jeep seat had been welded to the thing, and the two wheels of an airport fire extinguisher bottle had been welded to either end of the short arm. The wheel-less front arm lay in the oil-saturated dirt of the floor. A third tube comprised the mast; it was bare, but aircraft control cables had been attached to it as stays and stretched tight.

"Geez, you really do have a wind racer. Or most of one. What will you do for a front wheel? And what'll you use for a sail?"

Derlin beamed with pride over the contraption. "The sail's easy. There's parachute cloth by the square mile over at the cargo ramp. The front wheel's got me perplexed, though. I have to figure a way to steer it first, then, uh, liberate the right gear."

"A castering wheel from a chair would be perfect, but it's too small," Rusty mused aloud. "Just stick the post up through a hole in the frame and run two wires back to a crossbar. Steer it like using the rudder bar in a biplane."

"Hey, that's it! I can see it in my mind right now. That's perfect…and easy! Just for that, you get to ride the thing when it's done, Rusty."

"Uh, thanks," Rusty said, uncertain if that would be an honor or not.

"What does that fertile mind of yours tell me about brakes?" Derlin said, turning to Rusty with a gleam in his eyes.

"Probably won't need any. I doubt this thing would hit over 10 knots except in a typhoon. You can always dump the sail or turn into the wind, or just plant your size 11s in the dirt."

"That's true. Okay, no brakes. Only the bold need apply!"

Derlin's enthusiasm was starting to rub off. Rusty could visualize himself zooming along in the thing under wind power. It seemed like it'd be a hoot. He grinned up at Derlin, who grinned back.

That afternoon, Dave Sanderson gave Sandy and Rusty each a bottle of round orange pills. The things were almost a half-inch in diameter and a quarter-inch thick. Horse pills for sure. He instructed Sandy to take one right then, and it took him several long, gasping swigs of water to get the thing down. Rusty should take his first one the next day. Only one pill a week was the dosage, thank goodness.

"You have tomorrow off, Sandy. Have a book picked out, and enjoy the day," Dave quipped. "You take yours while Sandy is indisposed, Rusty."

After evening chow, they all went out to the flightline, where the Mike FAC unofficial party hootch was located. The hootch itself was a CONEX, short for "Container, Expendable" in milspeak. It was a shipping container, about eight feet square and twice that in length, made of corrugated steel and painted the ubiquitous olive drab. Not exactly the Empire Room at the Waldorf, but it was theirs. Inside, Batman had constructed a bar of sorts and by the time the others arrived, his electric blender was already whirring.

The sun was setting, and the oranges, reds and yellows of the sky were mirrored in the concoction that Batman created. He'd scrounged a huge can of peaches and a bottle of maraschino cherries. He'd already mixed a small pitcher using cherries, ice and rum, and as they walked in, he was finishing a larger amount with the peaches. He poured peach and rum slush into a glass, then followed that with a splash of the red mix.

""Mike FAC Sunsetters!" he proudly announced to his astonished 'customers'. "Belly up, boys!"

Derlin said, "Rusty and Sandy, you guys grab yours and sit here." He motioned to a pair of chairs. "We have a little ceremony to perform to welcome you both."

Dave Sanderson was grinning in a silly way, and Rusty suspected something was up, but accepted his drink and sat down. Derlin and Kit stood on either side of him, while Richard and Batman flanked Sandy. Mike Lopez and Mike Cramer looked on, trying to suppress conspiratorial smirks.

Dave raised his glass. "We welcome Rusty and Sandy to the ranks of Mike FACs. In order to forever cement the secret nature of the Mike mission, we hereby perform the secret Mike initiation ceremony, the details of which cannot be revealed to any person, ever. Members of the guard, do your duty!"

Rusty clenched his jaw when Derlin and Kit grabbed his shoulders, trying to be ready for anything. But he hardly would have expected what he got. The next thing he felt was their tongues in his ears. Sandy was getting the same treatment, and he was squirming wildly to evade the sensation. Rusty was laughing too hard to squirm. No wonder nobody would ever talk about this ceremony! After a few seconds, the initiation guards released both and stood back, howling with glee.

"Hey Kit, is it just me, or did Rusty seem to enjoy that?" Derlin hooted.

"I was afraid to say that, but I believe you're right, Derlin. Better watch whom you shower with. Pity Richard. He sleeps in the same room!" Kit said, holding his sides and slumping down into another chair.

"What worries me is that the four of you seemed to enjoy it more then we did," Rusty shot back. "I think I'm going to be the one sleeping with one eye open!"

More howls all round as everyone raised glasses. Rusty sipped the colorful slush.

"Hey Batman, this is great! Sure goes down smooth. You did good," he said, lifting his glass in salute. Batman saluted back with a glass of Coke.

"But they sneak up on ya, Rusty. A two-drinker like you won't be walking back to the hootch tonight, I bet," Richard said with a smile, but also with just a trace of an edge in his voice. It was almost the first time he'd spoken directly to Rusty since that ill-received Hard Dick remark.

Most nights, the Mikes all gathered in the all-ranks bar and either played pool or watched a 16mm movie. Richard would stay on, drinking; Rusty usually left after two drinks and went back to the room to read. By the time

Richard snuck in at midnight, Rusty invariably was asleep. In the day, they somehow never seemed to cross paths, either. It seemed as though Richard was either flying or drinking.

Dave came up and slapped Rusty on the back. "That's true enough. But throttle back a little. This stuff will really sneak up on you."

"I bet it would," Rusty admitted, looking at the colorful, sweet and smooth concoction. "Thanks for the warning," Rusty replied. That suited him just fine, anyway. Rusty knew he was a lousy drinker. If he had too much, he'd puke himself raw and be unable to function the next day. But Batman's daiquiris were damned good, and in his exuberance, Rusty went a bit beyond his usual self-imposed two drink limit by the time the peaches ran out an hour or two later.

He was standing outside the claustrophobic Conex, speechless at the clarity of the stars in a sky untouched by pollution or city lights when a voice inside pierced the buzz of happy pilots.

"Last call!" Batman announced. "Belly up for the final round."

Rusty watched in woozy amazement as Batman added rum and ice to the blender and turned it on, then dropped in a generous handful of Alka-Seltzer tablets. He caught Rusty's eye as the bizarre brew fizzed and foamed. "Another Mike FAC tradition. Keeps the ghouls and goblins away."

"Double, double, toil and trouble. Blender whirl and tablets bubble," Rusty intoned, gravely. "Pour on, Macbeth."

Batman poured a bit of the stuff in each man's glass, and all stood in a circle, some of them swaying and leaning on a neighbor. "To the Mikes." Everyone chugged the evil-looking stuff. It wasn't as bad as Rusty had feared. Not bad at all, in fact. And maybe it'd help in the morning. All of them could still walk, sort of; but none except Batman could manage to do it in a straight line.

For once, Richard and Rusty crawled into their bunks at the same time. Richard was blitzed as usual, but Rusty had managed to keep himself down to a mild buzz. He wasn't to the "swirling room" stage yet, and he dropped off immediately. They hadn't spoken a word to each other.

The next morning brought Rusty a queasy stomach and a mild headache. Not too bad, he thought to himself. Maybe there was something to the Alka-Seltzer daiquiri.

Rusty had just stepped outside when Sandy erupted from his own room down the walk. Sandy hurried down the walk with a peculiar, straight-legged gait, his shoulders pulled up and his back rigid. He stumped along this way, stick-like, straight to the shitter.

Oh, yeah, Rusty remembered, he had to take his horse pill today.

The next day, he more than understood that walk. Rusty was reading a paperback when his guts suddenly seemed to turn to water. Almost involuntarily, all his muscles tensed up in an attempt to control the powerful urgings of his bowels. He hobbled to the toilet. He made it, but just barely. As predicted, whatever effect those huge orange pellets had on malaria, they absolutely prevented constipation. It was too dark in the stall to read, but Rusty wished he had thought to bring that book along. It felt like he'd be there a long time.

CHAPTER FOUR

The pre-mission brief for Keel Ship – Rusty's first team insertion - went smoothly. Dave Sanderson sat next to him, but Captain Brookside and Y-Monh riveted their complete attention on Rusty. In the very back of the small room sat a robin Rusty hadn't met before. He was introduced by Y-Monh as Dak Loi. Rusty turned to meet his eyes, and made a small bow to him. Dak Loi grinned almost eagerly and bowed back.

Rusty copied down all the appropriate frequencies and the daily code keys. The weather would be as good as one could hope: mostly clear with light westerly winds. So far so good. Keel Ship might launch with good luck, he mused.

On the ramp, Dak Loi showed up as expected. He, too, had his ill-fitting parachute dangling over one shoulder. With a crisp bow, but no words, he pointed to the plane's door. It was clearly a question.

"Yes, yes, you get in now," Rusty said. The little 'yard grinned and almost leaped into the plane. Clearly, he'd done this before. Rusty climbed in after him, and then Dave.

"Now remember, I'm just dead weight here unless you ask for help or something," Dave said when the intercom came on.

"I got it. But go ahead and sing out if you need to remind me of something or we're about to die," Rusty said with a smile.

Just as Flip had done, Rusty waited until the Kingbees' takeoff time (listening to make sure they made it) before cranking the engines. He tuned all the radios, checked the IFF in Standby, made sure Dak Loi could hear and jerked his thumbs for Sgt Cramer to pull the chocks. As they wobbled their way through the perimeter wire, Cramer ran up and pulled the rocket arming pins. After the usual engine checks, Rusty turned to Dave.

"I almost feel like I should ask Termite for takeoff clearance."

Dave grinned at the reference to Laredo's runway control tower.

The long, slow takeoff roll didn't catch him by surprise this time, but he was startled by how sluggish the plane was even after they'd lifted off and got the gear up. He'd never taken off this heavy before, and the addition of Dave and Dak Loi plus their parachutes and survival gear made the O-2's already piggish performance noticeably worse. Ahead, Rusty could see the two Kingbees right where they should be over Teddy's Lodge. Again copying what he'd learned from Flip, he dialed to the tactical frequency and keyed the mic.

"Kingbee, check."

"Kingbee okay" was the reply.

Passing the two straining helicopters, Rusty held his breath as he dropped takeoff flaps, then milked the throttles back until the airspeed dropped to 90 knots. The O-2 wallowed and sagged its way drunkenly through the air.

"Dave, you check the Kingbees once in a while to make sure they haven't left the party, and I'll navigate, okay?"

"Will do. What's your plan?"

Rusty had already shown him the planned insertion path before the briefing, and he'd agreed to it. But it never hurt to review things, even to cement them in one's own mind.

"We'll head almost north from here. The IP is this pile of lava right on the border. As we cross it, we'll turn to a heading of 340 for four minutes and twenty seconds. That should put us at the insert site. If we miss it, we should see the backup clearing about 30 seconds later."

"What altitude will you go in at?"

"I plan to start descending as soon as I see the lava pile. A shallow descent will allow me to keep it in view, and I plan to be at 50 feet or so off the terrain when I get there. We'll hold that all the way to the insert and for another five miles or so after that, then climb back up and turn to the west until the team checks in."

"Sounds just like the other guys do it," Dave mused. "That's good – until you create your own ways."

He craned his neck and looked back as Rusty rolled out of the shallow turn that took them to the north. "Two Kingbees in trail. Looking good."

"Thanks. I could probably start down to low level from here, but I think I'll stay up here at three thousand feet for just a bit longer. This thing is mushy and I'm dreading how it'll fly down on the treetops."

"Can't say as I blame you for that."

A minute or so later, they saw the lava pile clearly, and as it disappeared under the engine cowling, Rusty wiggled the throttle levers back a bit. The plane, trimmed to hold 90 knots, obediently nodded its nose and started a shallow descent. The lava reappeared over the cowl, and he set the power to keep it just visible.

"Okay, going down. Fifth floor, ladies apparel."

Dave chuckled silently. Rusty could see him looking out at the lava, then down at the map, and as they got lower, down at the jungle below - checking for the white sparkles of ground fire. Rusty snuck a peek back at Dak Loi, who shot him a thumbs up and smiled widely.

The ten-mile descent went by so quickly that Rusty almost forgot to check in with the TOC. He quickly flipped the radio selector.

"Mike five oh, Mike five eight, fence and normal."

"Mike five oh copies."

That done, he flipped back to the Kingbees frequency, made sure the stopwatch was ready to start, and leveled off at what looked like about 50 feet above the treetops. As the lava pile disappeared under the nose again, he transmitted.

"Kingbee?"

Click, click.

The black mound of lava rushed by under his wing, and Rusty hacked the stopwatch, turned gently left and settled on a heading of 340 degrees. At this slow speed, the nose was high, blocking his view of the horizon. Rusty decided that at two minutes, he'd do a shallow "S" turn to try to see one or both of the clearings.

"Dave, when I make a shallow turn in a minute, try to see if you can see clearings ahead, and also check the choppers, okay?"

"Will do."

The mushy, wallowing quality of the plane's flight made him anxious, made worse by the turbulence of the wind right over the trees. He worked the control yoke rapidly to keep the wings level and the altitude constant. Rusty felt sweat run down out of his helmet on its itchy way down his back. They flashed over a small clearing, and he momentarily panicked that it was the insert site, but the clock showed that only two minutes had elapsed. He started a gentle right turn so he could see better to the front. Only an unbroken stretch of treetops ahead. Dave squirmed around to try to look under the right wing.

"I can't see anything but trees. I'll try another turn in one minute," he told Dave as he edged back to 340 degrees.

"Two Kingbees in trail," Dave confirmed.

Three minutes. Rusty banked left this time to compensate for the earlier right turn. Dave immediately sang out, "Okay, I see a large clearing ahead, just to my side. And a smaller one dead ahead. The smaller one is the insert, right?"

"Yup, that's it. Or should be. The timing is right, but I haven't seen it yet myself to be sure. Let me jink once my way, to be sure." Rusty slewed the plane right again. Yes! He was looking right at the narrow end of the teardrop-shaped opening. Two miles to go.

"Ninety seconds," He announced on the intercom. It occurred to him that the site was so small, and the plane's nose hid so much, that he wouldn't see the clearing until he was almost over it. Rusty found a patch of treetops just a bit higher than the others, just to the left of the clearing, and kept his attention on those trees as they mushed along. Almost there.

"Kingbee…..three…..two……one…………"

Below his wing, the treetops suddenly dropped away to yellowed grass. It had to be the insert site.

"BINGO, BINGO, BINGO!"

He risked a look down at the jungle edge. There were no muzzle flashes, no troops, nothing ominous visible. Just then, the jungle rose again so fast it seemed to be exploding up at them. Rusty snapped his eyes to the front. He was still level, but he'd descended almost into the trees. He tugged cautiously back on the yoke to gain a few feet of altitude. The plane mushed but rose.

Behind them, he knew, five brave Montagnards were leaping out of their helicopter into the unknown. They'd been briefed about the insert site and where it lay in relation to their objective, but placed their lives blindly in Rusty's hands to get there.

"Big clearing on the right, maybe a click away," Dave reported. "No ground fire."

Rusty exhaled in relief. At least he'd found the correct clearing. Now if the team could just avoid a firefight…

They continued on for several miles, as planned, then started a gradual turn to the west and began to climb. Not a sound on the radio yet. Rusty glanced back at Dak Loi. He had pressed his ear cups to the sides of his head, eyes closed in concentration, jaw clenched with the strain. Five minutes since the insert. The Kingbees were still following them faithfully.

Dave had his finger on the map. "Don't get too close to Mondol Kiri here. It's shown as abandoned, but it's right at the junction of two rivers and between two major roads. Gotta be swarming with NVA."

Rusty nodded and turned a bit tighter, rolling out to the south and continuing their laborious, low-speed climb. Ten minutes.

He stared towards the insert site, now a couple of miles off to their left, hoping hard that everything down there was going well, when he again realized he had been hearing whispers. "Moui…nam moui…bay…ban moui nam… tam…"

Dak Loi beamed and keyed his mic, "Sau." He reached up and patted Rusty's shoulder, then shouted over the engine roar, "Numba one, Dai Wee! Numba one!"

Rusty exhaled, not realizing that he'd been holding his breath. He keyed his own mic, "Okay, Kingbee. Go home now."

"Okay, Okay! Kingbee go home!" Again, Rusty heard the joy in his voice.

"So that's how it's done, huh?" Dave said.

"Well, at least that's how Flip showed me and Derlin described. Is there another way?"

"Not really. Variations on a theme, I suppose would be the best way to say it. Maybe you might've taken a more devious course up to the IP, just to throw off any watchers who might report seeing our train. They have learned that an O-2 and two choppers means a team is going in somewhere, you know. They're not stupid; and they've had a long history of observing us taking off with helicopters in tow, followed by discovering a team on the ground. So when their guy in downtown BMT calls them up and says 'Here comes another one' they know to start looking."

"You think that's true? That their intel is that good? And that they have a watcher right in the city?"

"Oh heck, yes. We're not the only ones gathering intelligence, you know. Having observers and agents near an airfield to tally flights and results is an obvious thing to do. We have to assume it, in any case."

"Yeah, I guess that's so. Maybe it'd be smart to vary our routine a bit. Maybe not join up over Teddy's Lodge every time, for instance."

"Hmmm, that's a good observation. I'll bring that up to the Kingbees and the others. In the meantime, you'd best report back to the TOC now."

"Oh yeah, I'd better." He did, using the pre-briefed code word for success, " Mike 50...anchor." Funny how they seemed to choose terms that fit the mission name: "anchor" signaling initial success for Keel Ship. There's somebody with wit in the woodpile, he chuckled to himself.

Rusty pushed the power up, retracted the flaps and allowed the plane to continue its slow climb as they settled in to the radio-monitoring phase of the mission. He made sure the radio was set to receive the team's radios, switched the tanks to auxiliary and took a sip from his canteen. Rusty glanced back at Dak Loi, thankful beyond measure that this robin didn't need to spit into a series of sick sacks. The robin was now slumped down in his seat, enveloped in parachute, seat belt and shoulder harness straps. He reminded Rusty of a fly that he'd watched being trussed by a spider in the toilet stall the day before.

Rusty turned to Sanderson, "So, how did Sandy's insert go yesterday? I was in the crapper all day and didn't get to talk to him at all."

"Pretty well, in fact. For two new guys, you both did a great job first crack out of the box. His objective was a very specific point, and his target box smaller, but he managed to find an insert site that worked. So far, his team is apparently undetected, but having two teams active means we'll have to double bang almost everybody to maintain a cap over both. Two Kingbee alert pairs, too, and that strains them."

"I noticed the schedule. Richard will be relieving me, and Kit relieves Sandy, then Derlin relives Kit, right?"

"Right. Flip is off today, and that's why we set your insert for later in the day — so we'd only need one relief to stretch through dusk. Batman is the standby pilot, just in case. But tomorrow, Batman and Kit are both off, so I'll have to pull one rotation myself. I could work either team, since I know both target areas now, but I don't like to assign a pilot to a mission he hasn't worked. So keeping three of you on each mission is a bitch due to horse pill days."

"Oh, I hadn't thought of that. You're right, it'd be hard for a guy to come out and try to find a team in hot contact if he hadn't worked that area before. I didn't think to brief Richard on this one. How will he know where to go?"

"I took care of that. I showed both Richard and Batman your map, and briefed them on the target box. But if a team goes hot, they're generally running and hard to find no matter what. That's why we lose almost half of them. They just disappear with no contact at all, or they radio for help, but we never find them. So a simple TACAN coordinate for an orbit point is enough to get an experienced pilot to the right general area. Within a mile or so, anyway."

"And if the shit hits the fan, it's just a Chinese fire drill anyway, right?"

"Pretty much. Not much a guy in an airplane can do to find a few guys running for their lives through all that," Dave gestured down at the impenetrable jungle. "They don't exactly have time to stop and leisurely figure out their location on the map."

"How in hell *do* we find them?"

"If you assume they were at or near their objective when they went hot, and that they couldn't have run more than a mile or two from there no matter what, that's a good start. When or if they are ready to be picked up — assuming the Kingbees can get there in time — they'll pop a smoke, flash a signal mirror or set out colored panels. Sometimes, you can spot the smoke and dust from their firefight before that. But, like I said, sometimes they just disappear." He shrugged, but Rusty could tell it was a frustration shrug and not an uncaring one.

"Have you ever lost one?"

"Yes, I did. As I said, it isn't really my job to fly as a primary FAC, but I do have to fill in on orbit missions. On one of them, we suddenly heard excited yells on the radio. It damned near startled my little guy right out of the window – he had been asleep. But anyway, they weren't bothering with code numbers. Just 'Get us out of here, now!' or words to that effect. My little guy listened, talked back to them, and found out they were taking fire and being chased as they ran. I scrambled the Kingbees and the Green Hornets immediately, but they were only on standby alert, and the objective was quite a ways out." He went silent.

"What happened?"

"Well, the team said they were in a decent pickup site and wanted to try to hold out there. That's the last we heard from them. When the Kingbees showed up, I had the little guy call for smoke, and we did see a yellow plume, but when my little guy asked for the authentication code word, a strange voice answered him with the wrong word."

"Bad guy?"

"Had to be. So I cleared the Kingbee gunship and the Hornets to blast the smoke. They strafed and rocketed the whole clearing. We didn't dare try to land a Kingbee and risk losing it."

"Ouch. What if it was just a different team member, maybe the radio guy got hit or something?"

"Like I said, too much risk. Besides, whoever it was gave the wrong code word. No, it's almost certain that the team got overrun and the bad guys wanted to lure a Kingbee in by taking over the radio. Classic VC ambush."

Nonetheless, the notion that they may have attacked and killed their own team was a sobering one. Neither of them spoke again for a long time. Dak Loi snored from the back seat. Rusty wasn't in the mood to listen to music on the ADF radio, and so their only companion was the sonorous murmur of the engines at their loiter power setting. Cambodia slowly turned below them unheeded as they maintained a wide, wide circle at 8,000 feet.

"Mike 50, Mike 59…fence." The UHF radio crackled.

"50 copies."

"Mike 58, 59. On the way." It was Richard, crossing the border to relieve them.

"Mike 59, 58. Got ya loud and clear at 8 K, heading in.

"Copy, at 7. Call tally."

A few minutes later, Dave spotted him on his side, slightly below them.

"Mike 59, 58. Tally ho. At your one o'clock high. You have the ship."

"Uh, roger that."

"Rusty, don't do that," Dave cautioned.

"Don't do what?" he said, quickly scanning the instruments and fuel selectors, thinking he'd forgotten some pilot task.

"Don't get too clever with words on the radio. You said 'ship' and that's way too close to your mission's code name. If the bad guys have any intel about that code name, they might put two and two together."

"But Flip and Batman use cutesy little private codes when they talk. That's what I was doing."

"But I bet they didn't use their mission name as part of the conversation, did they?"

"Well, no, but…"

"No buts. You might have said 'You have the tiller' or even 'the boat' and been okay. But 'ship' is part of the code name. Don't ever use it."

"Yessir. Lesson learned. Anything else I should have done better?"

"Nothing serious…if you don't count almost letting the plane fly into the trees."

"Ah. You caught that, huh?"

"Hard to miss a windscreen full of green. I was one second from taking the yoke when you looked back out front. Remember that the plane usually goes where you're looking. If you look at the ground…"

"Uh huh. You instructor pilots really pick up on stuff don't you?"

"More than you think. I even remember that you tend to leave a bit of nose down dialed in when you trim, so that you always have to hold back on the stick or yoke to hold level flight. Like you're holding the plane up. That's what happened back there. Your nose down trim habit almost took you into the trees."

Rusty turned to look at him in amazement. How in the hell had he noticed and remembered that from way back in T-37s, two years and who knows how many student pilots ago? But he was right, Rusty realized! He self-consciously let go of the yoke, and the nose drifted down. He *did* have a touch of nose down trim dialed in. I'll be damned, he thought to himself. A tiny hint of a smile grew on Dave's lips but he looked straight ahead in silence.

Rusty also kept his mouth shut, but he resolved to deliberately dial in a touch of nose up trim the next time he got down in the weeds.

They landed, debriefed at the TOC and passed along their observations about lack of visible enemy activity to Y-Monh. As they walked out of the TOC, Dave said, "I'd buy you a beer, but we'd best wait until all the flying is done for the day. You never know. So relax but stay in flight gear for the rest of the day."

Rusty went to the big room and found Sandy already landed and there, along with Derlin and Batman. "How'd it go, Rusty?" Derlin asked.

"Real smooth. Not a hitch, in fact. The team is quiet and I apparently passed my checkride."

Sandy said, "Yeah, Dave cleared me yesterday, too. I guess we're officially mission ready Mike FACs now."

"Well, welcome again to the fold," Batman said. "In case you don't remember any of the festivities the other night."

Rusty clapped his hands protectively over his ears. "Oh I remember, all right. Who could forget a wet Willie from two guys with handlebar mustaches!"

Derlin rolled to his side on his cot, roaring in laughter. "Any time you get lonely, Rusty, just whistle!"

"No chance of that, Derlin, especially with you, you two-digit midget. You'd just tell tales about it back in the world."

"Not me, brother! We're all sworn to secrecy here, ya know." He leered lasciviously and winked.

That brought all of them to guffaws. When it died down, Derlin went on, "Speaking of secrets, Rusty, do you think it's time to unveil ours?"

"Oh? Are you two turning Mormon?" Batman asked.

More guffaws.

"No, it's really my little secret, and Rusty just happens to be in on it," Derlin said. "We've built a wind sailer."

"A what?" Sandy squeaked, shrilly.

"Derlin built it, I only made one small suggestion about the design. But it's a land sailboat, like an iceboat. Derlin plans to sail it down the runway."

"Cool! I hafta see that! Where did you build this thing, Derlin?" Batman asked.

"Yeah, and when?" Sandy echoed.

"It's over in the motor pool maintenance area, and I built it out of spare parts and spare time. C'mon, we'll all go look at it."

The four of them walked over to the maintenance building, first leaving word with the radio room guys where they were going.

Since Rusty had seen it last, Derlin had put in a lot of work. He'd constructed a front wheel assembly exactly as suggested, with cables coming back to a cross bar for steering. He'd also added a main boom, a sail and various ropes for controlling the sail.

"Ta Daaa! There she is, the 'Bridge Over Troubled Asphalt!' Ain't she cute?" Derlin beamed.

"Hey, that is cool!" Batman gushed. "The sail might be a bit small, though."

"What does a guy from the Utah desert know about sailboats?" Derlin asked, pretending to be hurt.

"For your information, Utah has lots of sailing. The Great Salt Lake is full of sailboats. Then there's Utah Lake and all the reservoirs, and Bear Lake and Flaming Gorge and Lake Powell, and…"

"Okay, okay, I'm converted," Derlin said, hands out in mock supplication. "Besides, I suspected as much about the sail. I just can't figure out a way to get a bigger one when the length of the scrap tubing here limits me. If there's enough wind, it'll do, I guess."

"I love it," Sandy said. "When can we test it?"

"*We* will be Rusty and I, thank you," Derlin said, changing now to a haughty snootiness. He was obviously loving this and hamming it up. "But to answer your question; as soon as there's enough wind, I guess. That, and enough time. Not much of either for a while, though." He finally became his normal self at that.

"No, I guess not," Batman agreed. "I need to start getting ready for my late go, in fact."

"Huh? You don't take off to relieve Flip for two hours. What's to get ready?" Rusty asked.

"Uh, well, I plan to read a bit before I go. I usually do," Batman equivocated.

"Batman, you go on back to the hootch, and the three of us will hang around here for a while. Maybe we'll push the Bridge over to the ramp and hope for a few gusts," Derlin said.

When he'd gone, Sandy turned to Derlin, "What was that about?"

"Guys, Batman reads his Book of Mormon and prays a while before he flies a mission, if he can. It's kind of his own pre-flight, I guess."

"Really? I'll be darned," Sandy said.

"Me, too. How about that. He's that devout?" Rusty wondered aloud.

"From what I gather, it's not uncommon for Mormons. Like Buddhists, they seem to weave their life into their religion rather than squeezing a religion into their life. The Mormon belief might be a bit quirky, but it produces some upstanding men," Derlin explained.

"If they're all like him, I'd have to agree," Rusty said. "But I don't think I've ever known any others, so I couldn't say."

"What do you mean by quirky?" Sandy asked.

"Well, all that business about avoiding tobacco, caffeine and alcohol, for example: it's almost Hasidic or Islamic in its food proscriptions. And then there's the mandatory missionary service and tithing, the belief in an American Jesus Christ and all that. Not to mention re-baptizing the dead. Just quirky. But I'm not talking it down, and I'm certainly no expert in Mormonism. Ask Batman if you're curious. But watch out, he may convert you!"

Rusty looked at Derlin in admiration. What a deep old file he was!

"Not me. I'm perfectly happy being a Methodist, thank you," Sandy said. "What are you, Derlin?"

"Military Protestant."

They looked at him in confusion.

"Well, I was raised on Air Force bases. There were usually two Sunday services, Catholic and Protestant. But at the Protestant one, there might be Methodists, Baptists, Presbyterians, Unitarians, Episcopals, Lutherans...you name it. So they held sort of mixed-bag services that hit everybody's main beliefs without trodding on any doctrinal toes. Military Protestant. How about you, Rusty?"

"Oh, born and bred Catholic. Sixteen years of Catholic education, in fact. But I'd have to say that it may have been too much. Like too much propaganda, maybe. Anyway, I'd have to say that I'm firmly agnostic."

"You don't believe in God?" Sandy asked in surprise.

"No, no. That's not what agnostic means. Atheists say there is no god. An agnostic says there's no way to know."

"That's the same thing, isn't it?"

"Nope, it isn't at all. Look, it's a matter of faith. Believers must have faith that their belief is correct, right? Because they can't reach out and touch God."

Sandy nodded.

"But so do atheists. But theirs is faith in what they don't believe. Just because they can't touch a god, they say God doesn't exist. But it also doesn't prove that God *can't* exist, so theirs is a faith-based statement, too. Agnostics say that there might be a god, or there might not. No faith required – or allowed, for that matter."

"The universal cynic?" Derlin quipped.

"Actually, that's almost a brilliant description. I'm dubious about both versions of how the universe runs, and none of us will ever know for sure which is right."

"You are weird, Rusty," Sandy shook his head.

"No argument, brother," he said, putting his arm around Sandy's shoulders. "No argument."

Sandy and Rusty took off at dawn each day, went to their mission areas, and orbited on radio alert. After about four hours, they'd each be relieved by another Mike and his robin. Three FACs flew each mission every day, with Dave Sanderson filling in for anybody who happened to be on his horse pill-induced crapper day. Neither team went hot the entire time, checking in each morning and evening with lists of whispered numbers to report their findings.

Sandy's mission ended first, his team having a much more specific target to watch. On the final morning, Flip flew the dawn patrol so Sandy could run the extraction later on. The team didn't perform their morning check-in. Flip called back to the TOC and reported the non-contact via his crypto radio link. It wasn't unusual for the team to stay silent until just before the pickup, as they'd have time to debrief their intelligence in person instead of via code.

When Sandy got there and took the handover, his little guy tried to call the team. No reply. They tried for almost four hours, three hours past the scheduled pickup time. Nothing. Short of gas, Sandy came back, refueled and went back out again. At dusk, he gave up and landed.

In the big room that evening, they all gathered together, including Dave Sanderson and Major Esterhouse.

Over cold beers, Major Esterhouse explained. "Guys, I'm afraid we've lost a team. For most of you, it's happened before, but as it was Sandy's first insert, and his first loss, I thought I'd come and tell you everything we know."

Somber nods all round. Even Derlin and the irrepressible Flip looked subdued.

"The team was sent to watch a particular pair of hootches we suspected the NVA were using as a staging point for ammunition."

"Sorry, but what does that mean?" Rusty interrupted.

"Oh. Well, what we call the Ho Chi Minh Trail is about 250 miles long. Materiel moves down the whole length, or to where it's needed, but it isn't moved non-stop. In other words, one guy doesn't carry his rocket all the way from the Mu Gia pass in Laos all the way to its launcher in the Mekong delta. He may carry it for ten miles or 50, but then somebody else takes it, and the first guy goes back for another load."

"Like a relay race with explosive batons?" Rusty asked.

"You got it. Anyway, we suspected that these hootches were one of those handoff points. The team was to monitor the place, and if the occasion arose, sneak in and switch some of the mortar rounds in there with their booby-trapped ones. They gathered a lot of information, watched a lot of traffic and gave us beaucoup poop about the amount and type of stuff being moved. But there was never a time when they felt they could sneak into the hootches undetected. Last evening, they expressed a strong desire to achieve that. You probably saw how much Major Y-Monh loved that scheme, and the team was highly motivated to do it."

Sandy and Rusty nodded. They'd loved that idea, too – and Y-Mohn would motivate anybody to succeed.

"Well, we surmise that they tried to make the switch either under cover of night or as their last act this morning. Odds are, they got caught at it. The bad guys didn't try for an ambush, so we're fairly sure the team hid their radio before making their attempt. Let's hope that it remains hidden forever."

"So the ammo switching scheme is now scrapped, huh?" Sandy asked.

"No, not at all. Even if the NVA confirms that we're booby-trapping some of their ammo, it doesn't decrease the ruinous effect it has on their morale. It makes it worse, in fact. Now they know the explosions they've experienced weren't just shoddy material from the Russians or Chinese, but deliberate sabotage. None of them will ever drop a round into a mortar tube again without having doubts. It's just a shame that we lost five damned good men in the effort. A real shame. Besides, they may have actually completed the swap before they got caught. It'll be interesting to find out."

"How could we learn that?" Kit asked.

"Oh. The spooks higher up will monitor NVA radio traffic and such for any warnings about bogus ammo. If they hear that, we'll know the team got caught trying to make the switch. If we only hear reports of firing crews getting blown away, we know they got the job done first and then got caught. If we hear no reports either way, then something else happened to them."

"Like what?" Sandy beat us all.

"Who knows? Maybe they were discovered by a patrol that missed finding the hidden rounds or the radio. Maybe some locals turned them in to the NVA for a reward. Maybe they all came down with food poisoning or dysentery and are still out there too sick to use the radio. Or maybe a tiger ate them."

"Jesus, what if they are still alive out there," Sandy blanched.

"We'll make an over flight of the area every day and transmit on their frequency, just to be sure. But if we don't hear anything for three more days, or if the signals guys pick up some of that other intel, we'll call it off. That's all we can do, really," Dave Sanderson suggested. Esterhouse nodded in confirmation.

They were right. There was nothing else that could be done.

The next morning, to his immense relief, Rusty's team checked in as usual, whispering a long list of numbers that his robin copied on the plane's window with his grease pencil. He then read back a much shorter list of numbers, presumably to remind the team that tomorrow would be pickup day. As if they could have forgotten, Rusty thought.

Richard relieved Rusty on schedule, and heard nothing at all, as expected. Batman had the evening flight, and the team once again read up a numbered report. After Batman landed at dusk, the report got de-coded in the TOC, as every report did right after landing. Dave came to see Rusty shortly afterwards.

"Rusty, we normally wouldn't reveal things like this, but in light of what happened to Sandy, well... Anyway, your team says that they successfully made an ammo swap. They've already moved back to the infil site, and want to be picked up as soon as possible in the morning. So we'll have you do the dawn patrol as usual, and if they check in alright, we'll launch the Kingbees immediately. Do you know how to run a pickup?"

"Actually, no. I've never seen one, and I've never asked in detail."

"I thought so. Okay. It's very much like an infil in reverse, but doesn't have to be quite as covert. You rendezvous with the Kingbees a few miles from the team, then lead them in. There's no need for low-level work inbound. You dive down and do a bingo call over the site, or have the team pop smoke. Do both if the Kingbees have trouble finding the right spot. The slick will land while the gun ship orbits. As soon as the team gets aboard, everybody heads home deedeemau. Got it?"

"Yes, that sounds plain enough."

"There's only one really, really mandatory thing to do, and that's to absolutely, positively verify that the team is in fact *our* team," Dave said, raising one finger in emphasis.

"Ah ha. Yeah, that would be a major point. How do we do that?"

"Your little guy is the key. He knows the guys on the team, both by voice and by a secret password. He'll make sure the voice is right, and he'll also ask for the official authentication word. If he's at all suspicious, even after that, he may ask for some other detail, like the name of the meanest dog in their village or something. Unless the robin is happy, and I mean totally convinced happy, you do not pick up anybody. Got that?"

"I copy that in indelible ink, Dave." Then, as counterpoint to that heavy thought, "Hey Dave, what happens if the guy on the ground has been screwing my robin's wife or vice versa, and the robin wants to do him in? What if the robin lies and tells me they're enemy?"

"Then the team is fucked."

"Yeah, they would be," Rusty reflected, his half-grin collapsing instantly. "Completely."

"Rusty, you don't know Montagnards. They are beyond tough. That team would probably walk home, and then your robin would be worse than fucked. He'd be fucked five ways."

Rusty's grin bounced back with a vengeance. It wasn't beyond believability. 'Yards *are* tough bastards, he mused.

When Rusty took off the next morning, he couldn't help casting a curious look at Dak Loi. How did he feel about the team members? Oh, hell, some of them might be his relatives, Rusty realized. He settled himself to make the extraction successful. It was his day to take another horse pill, and he wouldn't be able to fly tomorrow.

Every morning of the mission so far, Rusty had taken a different flight route to the area, but had maneuvered within radio range by full daylight. Today, he simply flew directly there. He was still a few miles from the site when he heard those familiar whispers in his ear cups. They must have heard the plane coming. Dak Loi scribbled numbers on the window, then thumbed through his little pink codebook.

He turned to Rusty, "Team okay. Ready go home now."

"You sure this right team? All numba one? No NVA?"

"No, no, no. No NVA. All good team. Him friend me."

Rusty gave him a smile. "Okay, good. We call Kingbee now."

Dak Loi grinned and keyed his mic, but instead of numbers, spoke in clear words.

"What did you say?" Rusty demanded. Dak Loi had clearly broken radio protocol.

"Say him monkey...uh…" Dak Loi pointed to his butt, his whole skinny body shaking with glee.

Rusty laughed as well as he switched the radio selector. "Mike 50, 58."

"58 go ahead."

"Ops normal. Launch."

"Copy all normal and launch, 58. Advise any changes."

"Will do, 50. 58 standing by."

The Kingbees, briefed and sitting with their engines running, were airborne within minutes. Their flight time directly from Ban Me Thuot to the team site was a bit over twenty minutes. To keep from attracting any unwanted last-minute attention, Rusty flew straight past the pickup site and continued on for ten minutes. By the time he turned and flew back, he figured, the Kingbees should be nearby. While the minutes expired, Rusty began a slow letdown, planning to lose half his altitude while outbound, and then most of the rest while coming back. It worked perfectly. Just as he passed abeam of the teardrop clearing, he saw the two Kingbees just a few miles away.

Rusty turned to Dak Loi. "Team have smoke?"

"Yes, yes. Have smoke."

"Tell them pop smoke now." Rusty switched him to the FM radio. Dak Loi spoke.

Rusty was watching the small clearing intently, and was surprised to see a plume of purple smoke spurt up from the larger clearing a half-mile away. He was about to ask Dak Loi what was up when a plume of green smoke rose from the smaller clearing.

"Quick, ask what smoke." Dak Loi turned white, then babbled a quick string of words. Rusty heard the answer, repeated twice, but Dak Loi just stared at him.

"Uh, uh…."

Oh shit. Dak Loi had forgotten the English words for colors, Rusty realized.

"That one? Rusty pointed. "Or that one?" Rusty jabbed his hand towards the larger clearing.

"That one! That one!" Dak Loi stitched his brown finger needle-like at the smaller clearing.

Christ, he'd better be right, Rusty thought. And this had better go right the first time or everything is gonna turn to dog shit. Rusty keyed his own mic.

"Kingbee, team maybe go hot. You ready for bingo now?"

"Kingbee see you. Kingbee ready."

Rusty jammed the prop and throttle levers to the firewall and peeled off left into a dive, aimed right for the center of the small clearing. Just as he leveled barely above the trees, he saw small figures running toward the center of the clearing. No telling who they were, and there was no time to get further authentication. Rusty would have to trust Dak Loi.

"BINGO, BINGO, BINGO!"

"Kingbee go down now!"

Rusty zoomed up out of his dive, rolling left and searching for the Kingbee. The lead chopper made a beeline for the clearing Rusty had just buzzed, while the second angled off to the west, where he could keep the machine guns in his right-side door trained on the clearing. He passed under Rusty just as the first Kingbee touched down. Moments later, the team Kingbee lurched up and then seemed to stagger a bit to his left, but managed to clear the trees at the edge of the clearing. Instantly, the gun Kingbee opened up, and Rusty saw tracers arc down into the clearing. He heard a few high-pitched words in Vietnamese, then some more from a different voice. Alarmingly, the lead Kingbee now trailed a thin stream of blue smoke. He had also turned to the west, but hardly climbed at all.

After a few seconds, the radio crackled a bit, and Rusty heard the thunder of a Kingbee engine for a moment, then a voice, "Kingbee hit. Maybe no good."

"Okay, Kingbee. I see you. Go home, and I'll watch. Kingbee gun, you okay?"

"Kingbee gun okay," said a second, calmer voice.

"Kingbee, team okay?" Rusty asked, hoping.

A long pause. "Team hit. One dead. All hit. All on Kingbee. Kingbee maybe go home. Maybe."

Rusty could feel his face blanch. "Okay Kingbee, copy."

Rusty snapped the selector. "Mike 50, Mike 58. We have one Kingbee hit and damaged, possibly bad. The team is extracted with casualties. I'm escorting the choppers. Launch the alert just in case of another pickup. Alert the medics. Copy?"

"Mike 58, copy all. Go black."

Rusty switched the crypto radio out of standby, and keyed the mic. There was the usual sound of the thing spinning up, then a click. "Mike 50, 58 on crypto. Over."

"58, this is 51. What happened? Over."

Again Rusty had to wait for the spin up and click. "Sir, the team was bait. The NVA popped a smoke when we asked the team to, and tried to trick us. They opened up on the Kingbee when he landed. Kingbee Lead reported that one team member is dead, the rest wounded, and he's trailing smoke from his chopper. He may not make it all the way back. Over."

"You did authenticate, correct? You do have the correct team? Confirm, over."

"Affirmative, sir. Dak Loi was perfectly sure he was talking to his friend. I asked him twice. Over." Rusty sure hoped so. He looked at Dak Loi, whose coppery face now appeared a bit green. Whether from air sickness or aware of his possible major screw-up, Rusty couldn't tell.

"Alright, Rusty. Can you get an idea of how badly the team members are wounded? Over."

"Uh, I doubt it right now, sir. Kingbee has his hands full just flying. Just assume bad and you'll probably be right. Over."

"Yeah. One last question. What's your arrival time if Kingbee makes it? Over."

"Twenty minutes from the site, maybe fifteen from now. If he makes it. You launching the alert Kingbees? Over."

"And the green Hornets. Just in case. They'll rendezvous with you on this frequency. Go back green now. Over."

Rusty switched the crypto radio back to standby. "50, 58."

"Got you loud and clear again, 58. Stand by." It was Sgt Hannah's voice again.

"Standing by, 50."

Rusty stared at the thin trail of blue smoke coming from the humped back of the lead Kingbee. It had to be an oil leak from the transmission. If it ran dry, Rusty knew, the helicopter's transmission would seize and the rotors would instantly snap off from their own inertia. The Kingbee would plummet to the ground like a stone. Keep on truckin' baby, he murmured to himself.

Somehow, it did. Halfway home, they'd been met by a veritable cloud of helicopters. Rusty gaped at the pair of backup Kingbees, two of the Green Hornets' fast twin-engine N-model Hueys, and even two wickedly powerful Cobras. Esterhouse had sent the whole friggin' package, everything on the base with rotors.

Somehow, the stricken Kingbee, still trailing that ominous blue string of smoke, crossed the border, then skirted around the city and finally plumped down – no formal approach pattern, just straight in – on their home ramp.

Rusty saw the flashing red lights of fire trucks, ambulances and more waiting for them. With plenty of fuel aboard, he orbited high until all of the helicopters landed, then landed himself and taxied in. Mike Cramer met them, his face beaming.

"You sure know how to stir up the Hornets, sir," he laughed. But his eyes swept Rusty's plane for new holes as he did so. "Any trouble?"

"Not with this bird, Mike. But I'm burning to know what happened to them." Rusty gestured to the other side of the tiny base, where the Kingbees were based.

As they talked, Dak Loi bowed jerkily in Rusty's general direction and ran off, dropping his parachute on the ground.

"What has his pants on fire, sir?"

"I'm pretty sure he has a friend on that chopper, Mike. Or he doesn't, and that would be a whole lot worse."

Cramer looked at him, puzzled. Rusty didn't elaborate.

CHAPTER FIVE

Rusty woke to a pair of different but oddly complementary sounds. Richard was snoring in his usual rhythmic buzz, and the wind soughed outside in a slower but more powerful cycle. Rusty lay there amused by the way the sounds rhythmically interacted, when Derlin tapped on the door.

"Rusty. Hey Rusty! Surf's up! Time to fly the Bridge!"

Rusty got dressed and hurried out to the ramp. Ban Me Thuot's parking ramp was a rectangle of solid aluminum matting stretching almost 600 by 200 feet. It almost filled the northeast corner of the entire compound, and it had revetments around three sides to protect parked aircraft and helicopters. Made of interlocking plates about five by ten feet, it was amazingly level. A lot of preparation had gone into the ground underneath before it was laid, Rusty was sure. But for now, it made a perfect test area for Derlin's wind sailer.

A small crown of curious 'yards had gathered along the south side of the ramp as Derlin pushed the sailer onto the matting. The wind was from the west, right down the long axis of the ramp, and the craft almost leapt from his hands as he pushed it up onto the smooth surface.

"Rusty, you hold onto the mast while I get on, and when I'm ready, I'll let the boom out to catch the wind, okay?"

"Okey doke. If you let the boom go to the right, I'll brace the mast from the left. That way, I won't get clobbered with the boom."

"Good idea…Okay, I'm ready, step back!"

Rusty quickly backed up three steps, and Derlin let the boom swing to his right. Immediately, the sail popped full, and the sailer jumped forward. He steered toward the opposite corner of the ramp, and then did a few crisp "S" turns by pushing the steering bar with his feet. Derlin whooped with joy, and the 'yards echoed him with shrieks and laughter. At the far end, he made a big swooping turn and tried to angle back up the ramp, quartering into the wind, but the sailer crept to a stop.

"Yee-haw!" Rusty yelled, running down the ramp. "That was shit hot!"

"I'll say! That was fun! I wonder how to make it go across the wind, though. Do you know?"

"Nope. I know it's called tacking, but that's it. I've never been on a sailboat in my life. Let's just push it back to the other end."

"Okay. Then it's your turn, like I promised," Derlin said, beaming from behind his mustache.

"Really? Hot damn!"

Derlin clambered out of the seat, they pushed the sailer back, and they traded riding and holding roles. Rusty had to slouch down, his butt on the very edge of the old jeep seat to reach the steering bar - Derlin had obviously positioned it for his own six-foot-six frame. Derlin stepped back, and Rusty let out rope to hold the boom perpendicular to the sailer's long axis. Pop, went the parachute cloth, and the sailer again leapt forward.

Rusty steered left across the ramp, then turned across the wind. As he did, he had to quickly pull in the boom and flip it to the other side to catch the most wind. The sailer slowed while he did so, then leapt forward again. At the bottom end of the ramp, he made a swooping turn the opposite direction Derlin had, and pulled the boom in tight, right ahead of his face. The sailer slowed, but didn't stop, and tacked across to the other side. It hadn't gone into the wind by much, but it did go back west a few yards.

The 'yards giggled, shrieked and pointed again. Rusty was grinning broadly when Derlin jogged up.

"I saw how you did that. Pretty slick, bro."

They took turns riding the thing, and it soon became an undeclared contest to see who could sail back up the ramp the farthest. Derlin eventually won, but he started his swooping turn a few feet before Rusty had, which gave him an automatic advantage. With a little experimenting, they were able to sail across the wind, tacking up a few yards, then making the tightest possible turn downwind while swapping the boom over. By repeating this over and over, they could cut a kind of figure eight. Before they had the maneuver perfected, the 'yards had long since lost interest and wandered off.

"That's a trip, Derlin," Rusty said after they'd secured the Bridge inside one of the unused revetments. "But I think it needs more sail or something. It just doesn't have enough thrust to tack the way it should. Unless I'm overestimating what 'should' means for these things."

"Yup, I agree. I can't figure out how to make the boom longer, or the mast higher, though. I can't find any more tubing, and even if I did, a longer boom would hit the guy wires holding the mast up. I'm out of ideas."

"Yeah, I see what you mean. I'll think on it, but I'm stumped, too."

As they rounded the corner of the hootch, the others were just coming back from the chow hall. "Hey, where you two get off to? We missed you at breakfast," Kit yelled when they were still fifty yards away.

"We went sailing," Derlin boomed back. "The wind sailer."

"No shit?" Kit answered. "I gotta see that." "Yeah!" and "Me, too," the others echoed. So they all turned around and went right back to the ramp. Naturally, they all had to have several turns, but none of them were ever as adept a tacking into the wind as either Derlin or Rusty. By the time everybody had his fill of riding it down and pushing it back for the next guy, breakfast hours at the chow hall were long over.

Oh well, a little exercise and fresh air was probably better for him than another plate of those godawful powdered eggs and even worse powdered milk, Rusty consoled himself.

Try as they might, they never found a way to add extra sail area, and Derlin never did get to sail it down the Ban Me Thuot runway.

A few days later, Derlin flew his last mission at Ban Me Thuot. As he taxied in and shut down, Kit and Batman pulled out one of the fire-fighting hoses. When Derlin emerged from the plane, they turned it on him, soaking him to the skin. Yelling like a banshee, Derlin charged against the stream of water, wrestled the hose away from the two, and turned it on them. He quickly sprayed everyone anywhere near, including the crew chiefs, a few Montagnards, and even Major Esterhouse.

That evening, Derlin was the natural center of attention in the big room. He sat on his bunk with his guitar in his hands and a peculiar chromed wire frame around his neck that allowed him to play a harmonica while he strummed. Long into the night, and deeply into the beer, they all sang FAC songs, satires and popular ballads.

The music ran out. The beer ran out. Finally, their emotions ran out. As the senior FAC, and quintessential Mike FAC, Derlin meant a lot to all of them. In the end, nobody wanted to say anything maudlin, and they all spontaneously wandered to their beds. In the morning, they shared solemn handshakes all around, and then Esterhouse flew Derlin and his bags to Cam Rahn Bay.

That afternoon, Kit ran a successful and uneventful extraction of a team he'd put in. Suddenly and uncharacteristically, the Mike FACs were temporarily without any activity across the fence. To fill in the time, Flip decided to make some lounge chairs. Gathering a half dozen rocket boxes, he somehow got his hands on a handsaw, hammer and some nails. He knocked down the boxes and then, with no plans, proceeded to saw out and assemble two Adirondack-style lawn chairs. As Rusty watched him work, he marveled at the talents some people are blessed with. When Flip finished, he positioned the chairs, then with a flourish plumped down and invited the rest of them to compete in a horseshoe game while he lounged in the sparse shade of the two scraggly trees in the courtyard.

Rusty lost his game almost immediately, and sat down next to Flip. "You're quite the man with a hand saw, Flip."

Flip waved his right had in a self-deprecating way, but his even white smile showed that he appreciated the compliment. They watched Kit play Richard for a while, both of them evenly matched at the game and doggedly trying to knock the other's horseshoe away from the peg while leaving his own shoe closer to it. Back in Chicago, Rusty had watched Mary Beth's family play the Italian game of bocce ball with the same silent but fierce determination.

"Quite a sport, isn't it?" Flip finally said, idly.

"Actually, no, I don't think so, Flip."

"Huh?" He looked at Rusty quizzically. "What have you got against horseshoes?"

"Nothing. Nothing at all. But I wouldn't call it a sport. It's only a game. Sport is a higher calling, like hunting or fishing or golf."

Flip's eyebrows knotted even deeper as he stared back, but he said nothing. Rusty took the invitation.

"Well, it's like this. I think that true sports are those where there is no real score, no referees and no winners or losers. In a true sport, you are your own judge. You follow the rules, and sometimes even formulate rules for yourself. You might be the only one who knows if you followed those rules – if you played fair. Sport improves your character. All the rest of what the newspapers call sports are merely games. Things like baseball and football destroy character, because the players look for every opportunity to bend the rules or even break them without being caught at it. That's why games need referees and penalties and such. The only good thing about them is the pure physical exercise. Games might build physical skills, but they destroy character because the winners are those who cheat the best."

"Hmmm. I can see how you might call golf a sport under that kind of reasoning, but hunting and fishing?"

"Those may be the purest form of sport of all, Flip. From the ancient Greeks to our own founding fathers, all the sages and educators counseled young men to adopt the bow or the gun as the best sport. Because you hold life and death in your hands, they force you to make some very tough decisions – and nobody is there to enforce any artificial rules. Some of the brightest minds in history extolled it: Cicero, Ortega, Jefferson, Teddy Roosevelt…heck, even Shakespeare."

"I just can't see how walking around killing animals can build character. Besides, there are lots of hunting laws. You don't get to make up your own. And there are game wardens, too."

"Well, yeah, that's true. But think of it this way: most game laws are there to preserve adequate numbers of animals. They might set the 'when' of seasons and the 'how many' of the bag limit, but they don't often address the 'how' that game is taken. Take quail or duck hunting as an example. The law says you can take so many each day and that you have to use a shotgun. But there is no law that says you can't shoot them while they're on the ground or the water. Hunters themselves decide to take shots only at flying birds. Shooting them on the ground would surely be easier, but virtually nobody does it. And as far as they know, nobody is watching them, either. The game warden doesn't follow along like a football referee, watching for infractions. It's just more 'sporting' to restrict yourself to shooting at flying birds only. Some big game hunters use only primitive kinds of equipment, like bows or muzzle loading rifles. It's much harder to get an animal with equipment like that, and the law would allow them to use modern arms. But they choose to make it harder, more sporting, to hunt with a self-imposed handicap. See?"

"You know, I'm beginning to. I'm not a hunter or a fisherman, so I never thought about it. In the city, guns are what criminals use. We called baseball and football sports and thought they built character. But you throw a new light on things." Flip turned and raised his voice. "Hey Kit, Richard. Are you guys hunters?"

"Oh yeah. Big time. Been hunting since I was knee high to a grasshopper. Love it," Kit responded immediately.

"Nah. Not me," Richard said, laconically. "Spent most of my weekends partying."

"What about this shooting flying birds only thing, Kit? Is that true? And there's no law against it?"

Kit looked at Flip a second, thinking. "Well now, it's true that nobody ever shoots at a bird on the ground, unless it's wounded. But now that I think about it, I don't think it is a law. Just how it's done. Wouldn't be giving the birds a fair chance to shoot 'em on the ground, would it? Why do you ask?"

"Well, Rusty here was saying he thinks hunting and fishing are the purest form of sport because they build character with unenforced laws like that bird shooting thing. He says so-called sports like football are mere games that encourage cheating to win. That make any sense to you?"

"Just a sec," Kit said as he tossed his last shoe neatly around the peg. "Ringer. I win, and you lose," he said, pointing at Richard derisively.

Kit walked over and stood between the chairs for a bit, thinking. "Yeah... yeah, it sure does. When my daddy taught me to hunt, he always said to give the animals a fair chance. To kill humanely, use what I kill, and respect both what I caught and what got away. But when he taught me to play football, he coached me how to get away with holding a lineman and how to keep a receiver from catching a pass by 'accidentally' tripping him or running into him. It never occurred to me to see the discrepancy between the two until now. But now that I do, I have to agree with Rusty."

"I'll be damned," Flip admitted, leaning back. "Now I'm starting to see it, too." He turned to Rusty again. "You know, Rusty, you have the damnedest way of making a guy think about things."

"Or just being a fucking know-it-all," mumbled Richard over his shoulder - just loud enough for all to hear - as he walked away.

"Sarcastic SOB, isn't he?" Kit said after Richard had gone into his room and closed the door.

"I'd correct you and say he's actually sardonic rather than sarcastic," Rusty said, "But that would just prove that he's right."

Flip's broad white grin erupted in a hoot of laughter, and he reached over to slap Rusty on the thigh.

"Christ, that does it," Kit said, also grinning. "Time for a beer. If anybody has to scramble aloft for the rest of the day, let ol' Richard do it."

"It'll probably have to be Batman. The club opens in half an hour, and the minute it does, I bet Richard is there at the door," Flip came back. "Nothing increases his thirst like a foul mood, and I bet he's plumb dehydrated now!"

"Drier than a popcorn fart," Kit chuckled as they all started towards the big room.

They had a couple of brews each, then collected Batman from behind a book and went to evening chow. Rusty didn't see Richard again until he staggered in after the club closed. He'd apparently drunk his supper. Rusty pretended to be asleep when Richard came in the room. He lost his balance while taking his pants off, and lurched sideways into the chair. When Richard finally crawled up into his bunk, he immediately began to snore heavily. He kept up his raucous snorting until the heavy mortars fired their inevitable four rounds of midnight harassing fire, at which he jerked up with a startled grunt, then tossed onto his side and passed out again in silence.

The next morning, Rusty slipped out of his rack, went for a shower and dressed as silently as possible. Richard was still out cold when he left for breakfast. Rusty dallied over his powdered eggs, canned bacon and bitter coffee as long as he could. When he peeked back into the room Richard was gone. Rusty sighed with relief at avoiding another confrontation. Sooner or later, though, he knew the enmity between them would come to a boil – or an explosion.

With the lack of working teams, Rusty wasn't scheduled to fly, and with nothing better to do, he wandered over to the radio room to shoot the breeze. Staff Sergeant Hannah and Sergeant Young were the two radio guys, and they alternated shifts while anyone was in the air during the day. The SOG team maintained a 24-hour radio watch on their own net from within their bunker, so Hannah and Young worked only the Air Force side of things. The two were both enamored of the rock band Crosby, Stills and Nash, which they played incessantly on a tiny cassette player. So incessantly that the FACs joked that what went out over the "Mike 50" airwaves was Crosby, Stills, Nash, Hannah and Young. This morning, Young sat crouching over the microphone, squinting over his horn-rimmed glasses at a crossword puzzle.

Leaning into the back corner of the room was one of the Special Forces guys, Master Sergeant McGuire. McGuire might have served as the dictionary illustration of "grizzled." He was over forty years old, but his five feet eight frame was as solid as a safe. His face was sun-blasted a deep mahogany, reddened even further by a masochistically fierce morning shave.

Sgt McGuire's left hand was seemingly grafted to a battered, chipped beer stein from which he continually sipped coffee. The inner surface of that mug was coal black from lip to its stygian depths.

"Sergeant, I'm just curious. When's the last time you washed that mug?" Rusty asked.

"Lieutenant, the secret of this mug is that it has never been washed," McGuire growled, taking yet another sip. "Not since I got it. That was before Korea almost twenty years ago."

"Never been washed? How is that a secret?" Rusty replied.

"Well, sir, I'll just have to show you." With that, he ambled to the door. Opening it briefly, he tossed the contents of his mug onto the parched red clay. Recrossing the room to where Rusty stood, he tilted the mug's rim. "Look in there, sir."

The inside of the mug tapered cone-like from the rim down. The coating must have been more than in inch thick at the spoon-sized space at the bottom. Rusty screwed up his face in disgust. "Yeeeuck! That's ugly."

"Ah, sir, ugly it may be, but that's also the secret. Step this way and watch…" He crossed over to the coffee urn with Rusty close behind. Pulling the toggle, he ran plain hot water into the mug. He pulled a spoon from his breast pocket and began stirring the water vigorously, scraping the spoon against the coating. After a few seconds of determined stirring, he flicked the spoon twice and returned it to his pocket; then reached for a clean coffee cup and poured out some of the mug's contents. In the cup was a light brown wash with a foreboding oily sheen floating on the surface.

"Lieutenant, with this mug, as long as I can get hot water, I'm never without my coffee," he grinned triumphantly.

If you can call it that, Rusty thought wryly, but then he imagined waking up in a frozen foxhole in Korea. No question that it'd be the best coffee around, if only by default.

"Sergeant, how does this war compare with Korea?" Rusty asked.

"Same shit, different day, sir." McGuire gave a quick half-smile but his face immediately hardened. "We'll pull out of this without winning too," he shrugged, and then sipped the weak brew with a grimace.

"You think we'll lose this war?" Rusty asked, taken aback at his nonchalance.

"Not 'lose' in the sense of us surrendering, sir. But in Korea we just stopped fighting and called it a draw. We're still there, there are still two Koreas, and the only change is that neither side shoots at each other quite as much. I don't know how this war will end, but it wouldn't surprise me to see things much the same some time down the road." He shrugged. "And the end of the road isn't far off, either. This 'Vietnamization' crap is just a copout for us getting ready to abandon these people. Politicians…" he said with sudden disgust, and spat on the floor.

"I think that's a pretty ugly accusation, sergeant," Rusty said sternly.

"All due respect, sir, but college pukes don't know shit about the real world," he replied, meeting Rusty's eyes fearlessly.

Rusty paused a few seconds, noting that there was determination but no anger in those black eyes. "Whereas grizzled old non-com farts are savvy enough to couch an insult behind an 'all due respect' so they can't be accused of making the insult?"

Just as Rusty saw a hint of a smile begin, McGuire raised the mug in front of his mouth, hiding it. "There may be hope for some of you...sir," he ended, nodding imperceptibly as he turned on his heel and marched out of the radio room.

Pretending not to have overheard the exchange, Young turned around and said, "Good morning, sir! Glad to have you here. Anything I can do for you, sir?"

"No thanks, Young. Just came by to kill time and see how the other half lives."

He chuckled. "Slumming with the enlisted swine, huh, sir? Or just checking up on me?"

"Gotta make sure the galley slaves are still chained to their benches, don't we?" Rusty echoed the joke with one of his own. "No, seriously, I just popped in to see how this works. I've never had the chance to do it until now. What does all this gear do?" Rusty waved a hand to encompass the banks of olive drab radios that filled three sides of the cave-like room with bright red, orange and green lights and dimly glowing white dials.

"Well, sir, we monitor all the airborne frequencies you pilots use, plus the ground FM frequencies, plus links to Pyramid Control, SOG headquarters and more. Oh, and the high-frequency set that links us stateside. We can talk to pretty much anyplace on the globe if we have to – allowing for atmospherics, of course."

There was an undeniable pride in his voice, and he stroked the microphone almost sensually as he spoke. Clearly, the man loved his job and his tools.

"Very impressive, sergeant. I'm very glad you understand it all. Electronics have always baffled me a bit." Rusty allowed the implied compliment to sink in, then asked, "So what's going on this lovely morning?"

"Not much, sir. Lt Fillipini is on the weekly parts run to Cam Rahn, and Lt Hrducik is up with a robin doing some visual recce. For a mission that's coming up, I guess. But that's all. Pretty quiet today, thank goodness."

"Uh huh," Rusty answered automatically, his mind marveling that Richard could even walk this morning, much less fly. If he had drunk as heavily as Richard had last night, he'd be in intensive care this morning, Rusty thought. Or worse. He bantered with Young a few more minutes, then wandered back to his room. The place still carried a stale fog of alcohol from Richard's sleeping breath. He took a book and went out to one of Flip's chairs to read.

Rusty was deeply engrossed in the book and had lost track of time when he became aware of Dave Sanderson shouting. "Rushing! I need you to launch ASAP! Grab your gear and I'll brief you on the way to your plane."

Kit and Batman both peered out of their rooms, then Kit ducked back inside to grab his gear. Batman and Rusty hurried over to where Sanderson stood.

"What's up, Dave?"

"I'll fill you in when Rushing gets out here. Where's Hubert, in the shitter?" They nodded. He looked worried, and it was clear that whatever was going on was serious.

In moments, Kit appeared, carbine in hand. As soon as he got near, Dave looked all three of them in the eye, then began. "Hrducik is overdue. He hasn't made a position report in two hours, and we can't raise him on the radio. Rushing, I want you to take off and see if you can spot him or reach him on the radio. He might just be flying at low altitude and below the radio horizon. Or not," he added ominously, then went on.

"Naille and Bates, you two suit up and stand by. I may need you to launch later if this turns into a search."

Search. The thought of what that meant – and the fact that Sanderson was using their last names - brought a cold chill to Rusty's spine. Images of Crazy Eddie flashed through his mind, and the similarities of his disappearance back at LZ Emerald stunned Rusty. As quickly as the pulse of alternating current, another emotion flooded in and he gloated 'Serves the sonofabitch right.' The ricocheting pulses buzzed in his head until he quashed them both. Nobody deserved...whatever had happened to Crazy Eddie, not even Richard. Still... Unable to decide what he really wished for, he just stared dumbly at Dave.

"Okay, Rushing. You get airborne. You two suit up and meet me in the radio room," Dave ordered. Sanderson and Kit spun around and jogged off around the end of the hootch as they headed for the ramp.

As Rusty stared at their departing backs, Batman said quietly, "Oh Heavenly Father, help us now."

A short time later, almost everyone who could squeeze in on some pretext had huddled together in the tiny radio room. Dave Sanderson, Batman and Rusty pressed in close behind Sgt Young on the radio. Sandy Hubert stood near the door, rushing out at intervals in response to the urges of his bowels. Hannah stood beside Young's chair. Outside, crew chiefs Mike Cramer and

Mike Lopez hovered, straining to hear any clue of what was happening. The only Air Force people missing were Major Esterhouse, who was once again off base doing air liaison work at SOG headquarters, Flip on his parts run, Kit... and Richard.

"Mike 59, this is Mike 55, over." It was Kit transmitting, trying to reach Richard. If Richard answered, his signal might not be heard at BMT, but Kit's reply to Richard would. Everyone inside and out held their breaths. A long pause.

"Mike 59, 55. Come in please," Kit called again. Another pause. Again. Another long pause.

"Mike 59, this is Mike 55 on Guard channel. Come in." Kit had switched to the universal emergency frequency that all pilots monitor. Nothing.

"Mike 59, Mike 55 on Guard. Come in please."

Then, loudly, "Mike 55, this is Hillsborough on Guard, do you need assistance?" Hillsborough was a high-altitude aerial command post dedicated to monitoring and managing emergencies such as bailouts and searches for pilots.

"Uh, Hillsborough, Mike 55. Standby."

"Mike 50, Mike 55, did you copy Hillsborough?"

Dave Sanderson stepped forward and took the microphone from Sgt Young. "We on our own push?" Young nodded.

"Mike 55, Mike 52 here. We did copy. You cannot use Hillsborough. Tell them to disregard and then go back to this push for your mission. Do you copy?"

"Mike 52, Mike 55. I copy. Sorry, I forgot."

"That's okay. Just go back and tell them. Mike 52." A moment passed.

"Hillsborough, Mike 55 on Guard. Disregard previous transmission."

"Mike 55, Hillsborough, are you sure? Do you need assistance?"

"Negative, Hillsborough. Disregard. Out."

Rusty turned to Dave. "What did Kit forget?"

"That we cannot use regular SAR assets. Period. We aren't there, Rusty, remember?"

The reality of that briefing a few weeks ago suddenly came back in full force. Rusty had forgotten, too.

Kit tried to raise Richard on several different frequencies for about ten more minutes. No reply.

Dave took the mic again. "Mike 55, 50."

"Go ahead 50."

"Mike 55, begin a pattern search as briefed. We'll send up a relief in one hour."

"Mike 55, I copy." The disappointment and despair were heavy in Kit's voice.

Dave turned to Batman and Rusty. "You two get ready to relieve Rushing. Takeoff in one hour. I'll have search grid boxes drawn up by then. I'll have the Kingbees and Green Hornets standing by."

They all stood there staring at the radio, as if they could make something happen by sheer will power. Half an hour dragged by like one of those nightmares where you cannot move despite an approaching horror.

"Mike 50, Mike 55." They all jumped as if a shot had been fired.

"Mike 55, 50 go ahead," Young replied instantly.

"Go crypto." Rusty's heart sank. It had to be bad news. Young reached down and flipped the switch that linked the UHF radio to the coded scrambler. When the green light came on, he keyed his mic. The familiar rising whine peaked and there was a click.

"55 this is 50 on crypto. How copy? Over." A two-second pause came as Kit's radio also whined up.

"Have you five by five, 50. I found him. He's down about ten miles east of Disneyland. The plane is mostly intact, and he appears to have hit in more or less level flight. Steep angle of impact, though. Not much of a skid line. I can't see any evidence of survivors. Repeat. No survivors sighted. Will keep looking. Over."

"55, we copy. Pass map coordinates in crypto when able. We'll launch helos ASAP," Young looked up to Dave, who nodded. "And be advised, 52 also copies. Repeat, launching helos from alert. Can you orbit the site? Over."

"Affirm." A few minutes later, Kit read them the six-digit map coordinates of the crash site, then confirmed he could continue orbiting for at least two hours. He and Young switched back to non-coded transmissions.

"Batman, I still want you to launch. I guess you're senior FAC now that Derlin's gone. Go out there and orbit high, in case Kit needs to go low. You can relay between him and us if need be. You'll be the on-scene airborne commander."

"Yessir. I understand. I'll get airborne as soon as I can. You want me to escort the helos, or just burn out there?"

"It's probably better to get there ahead of the helos, so you can get the situation clear in your mind. I'm going to assign this to the Green Hornets.

They're faster than the Kingbees and carry more firepower in case this turns into a hot rescue." Dave said. "I just hope it is a rescue."

Batman left immediately, and most of the rest of the non-essentials drifted back to their jobs as well. There was nothing anyone could do now but wait. In the background, Rusty heard the Green Hornets firing up their powerful twin-engine Hueys. Each carried two door-mounted General Electric mini-guns capable of firing up to 6,000 rounds of 30-caliber ammunition a second. Each chopper also carried two nineteen-round pods of high explosive rockets. Even with all the ammunition for the guns, the two engines gave them the power to carry as many as six men in full combat gear. They were awesome machines, and if anyone could get survivors out alive, it'd be the Green Hornets.

But the time dragged on mercilessly. The helo team maintained radio silence as usual, and it would be at least a half hour until they got to the crash site. Rusty stayed in the radio shack, waiting for Dave's order to launch, but wanting to hear, too.

"Mike 55, 56."

"56, go"

"I'm overhead. I see you, and I see the object. Anything new?"

"Negative 56. Still no show from either player." It meant he hadn't seen any movement at the crash yet. Not good.

"Copy 55. Golf Hotel on the way." Golf Hotel, the military way of saying G and H: the Green Hornets.

"Copy."

"I'm the on scene commander, 55. I'll stay high for contact."

"Copy, going for the weeds." Kit knew he could now go below radio reception altitude for a real close look. With the choppers on the way, there was little risk in making multiple low passes. The bad guys wouldn't get there before the Green Hornets – if they weren't there already. But it also meant those in the radio room would hear only one half of the deliberately ambiguous conversation. More minutes dragged by.

"55, 56.........Golf Hotel in sight."

"Hornet, this is Mike 56. Have you in sight. I'm at seven, Mike 55 is in the weeds at the object."

"56, Hornet lead has the low bird in sight...and tally on the object. Who runs the show?"

"Hornet, I'll be the on-scene, but 55 will task you directly. I'm also relay."

"Hornet copies. 55 you read me?" Kit's reply takes several minutes – unheard in the radio room.

"Hornet copies. Going in."

"What's happening?" Rusty asked nobody in particular. "Why doesn't Batman tell us what's happening?"

"Because he'd just tie up the frequency. There's nothing we can do, anyway. Just let them work, Rusty," Dave said, in an avuncular voice.

The clock's hand moved like a glacier. Not a sound from the radio for twenty more minutes.

Then, "Mike 50, Mike 56. Go crypto." Here it comes, Rusty thought.

"Captain Sanderson, you there?" Batman's voice sounded metallic and emotionless through the weird encryption circuits.

"Go ahead, Batman."

"The Green Hornets say they have recovered two bodies and burned the plane. They ripped out the crypto set first. There was no enemy contact on the ground and no ground fire during the recovery. All of us are now inbound. Sorry, sir."

"Understand plane destroyed, crypto removed, two KIA recovered. Good job, Dave. Go back to company push and maintain radio silence until you contact the tower. I'll debrief you all on landing. Over."

"Copy. Crypto out." Dave handed the mic back to Young. He turned and started for the door, head down and walking like an old man. "Fuck," he mumbled as he pushed at the door. Rusty had never heard the word cross his lips before.

That afternoon, Dave called Rusty into his room.

"Yes, Dave? What happened?"

"I'll tell you in a second. I'm going to brief all of you guys in the big room in an hour anyway. You all deserve to know as much as I can tell you. But first I need you to take charge of Hrducik's things."

"Yeah, I know. I've done this before. Back at Emerald."

"You have? Not for a roommate, I hope."

"Unfortunately, yes. We all bunked together, but yeah."

"Oh, I'm so sorry." He paused, then went on, "We don't have a mortuary affairs officer here, Rusty. I guess I'm naming you to be one as an auxiliary duty. Here's a footlocker. Find everything that conceivably is his and put it in here. Use a little discretion if there's anything that might embarrass his family, though, huh? It wouldn't do for his mother to open the thing and find a carton of condoms or something. Use common sense, but remember that you are personally on the hook if anybody claims he owned a diamond-studded Rolex. When you're done, I'll come and inspect the room."

"Okay. I'll make a list of it all, too. I think that's required. But Dave, I have to know. What happened? Did his robin crash the plane on purpose? Or was Richard…impaired?"

"No. It was a Golden BB. One hole was all they found in the plane, but it was in Richard's side window. He must've been looking right at the shooter. Hit him right in the face. Never knew what hit him, as they say." Dave stopped and stared at the floor for a second, then turned back to me. "His robin wasn't a Chieu Hoy, by the way. New guy, but no suspicion attached to him. He died at impact, they said." Dave shrugged and looked at Rusty with disbelieving, almost plaintive eyes. "The Golden BB."

Rusty was glad Dave hadn't addressed Richard being impaired. Maybe he hadn't heard the question. Or maybe he had, but chose not to discuss it. Either way, Rusty realized, Dave never would bring it up.

Rusty took the empty footlocker back to their – his – room. Folding Richard's uniforms and shirts wasn't too bad, but handling his underwear and personal stuff was creepy. Rusty felt revulsion, anger and loathing just touching Richard's things. There were tiny hairs encrusted on his razor, and brown stains in his boxers. Curling his lips in disgust, he wished he had tongs or even pliers. He lifted the repulsive things using two fingers and dropped them into the box. Fortunately, there were no cartons of condoms. Not even a Playboy magazine or a photo of a wife or girlfriend. Rusty had seen a wedding band on Richard's finger, but had never seen him read a letter from home, or write one. His belongings were as emotionally sterile as if they'd been washed in alcohol. Which, Rusty suddenly realized, they had. He regretted that he knew virtually nothing about the man. But he was glad, too. Rusty hated himself for feeling it, but was happy Richard was gone. Staring at the half-filled footlocker, Rusty explored those feelings. He wasn't exactly glad Richard was dead, but was glad to be rid of the drunken sot. Not that he'd ever admit that to anyone else, he told himself. No one speaks ill of the dead.

Christ, roommates shouldn't have to do this, he thought, suddenly feeling an unexpected red-hot anger. It's too personal, too…intimate. He hadn't liked the sonofabitch, and now he hated Richard for making him touch his things, Rusty grumbled under his breath. He set the locker's upper tray in place, filled it with the man's small items, and then slammed the lid. Closing that footlocker was like closing his heart on the man, and Rusty miraculously felt better the moment the lock snapped. He went to fetch Dave.

Sanderson came in, examined Richard's end of the room, checked the desk and asked if a few items he found in its drawer were Rusty's or Richard's. Only

Richard's steel helmet and flak vest remained, still hung on the end post of his bunk. Dave agreed that they weren't personal items.

Dave opened the locker and wordlessly compared the items against the list Rusty had made. When it was done, each of them signed and dated the sheet, then Sanderson locked the box.

"I'll have one of the enlisted guys come get it later. Let's get to the big room so I can brief you all."

He told them all what he had told Rusty: the Golden BB and all. Kit asked about the robin, and Flip asked about the fuel selector switches. Dave replied the Green Hornets didn't know enough about the O-2 to check that before they burned the plane. Now nobody would ever know. Then Dave emphasized that they shouldn't talk about it to anyone, especially their families. He said there had been terrible instances of families finding out about a loved one's death through the grapevine before a chaplain could officially notify them.

Finally, Dave added, "Major Esterhouse is on his way back from An Loc. I'm sure he'll say the same thing I'm about to, but I want to say it first. Losing one of you is my worst nightmare. This is combat, and losses do happen. But I don't want it to happen again on my tour. I want all of you to do your jobs the best way you know how, but I will not allow you to risk yourselves needlessly. No hot dog stunts, no stupid mistakes, and no lapses of judgment. That's an order." He looked each of them right in the eyes, going slowly around the room. "You hear?"

Dutifully, they all said "Yessir!" They said it with authority and maybe even with good intentions. But they all knew that nothing, not anything, can stop a Golden BB.

Dave wasn't the only one with nightmares. That night, Rusty lay there staring up at the bottom of Richard's bunk. His heart thudded and he felt cold sweat running through his scalp. Another rivulet pooled in the hollow over his heart. Mixed streams of fear, dislike, worry and relief fought with each other as he lay there in the silence. As much as he had hated the guy and his drinking problem, Rusty wished that he could hear Richard shuffling unsteadily back to this room right now. Suddenly, he realized he didn't even know what had become of Richard's body. What had they done with him after they recovered him? Where was he right now? Still here at Ban Me Thuot? What about the robin's body?

"Boom! Boom!" The nightly outgoing mortar rounds woke him with a start, and he found himself twisted up in the sheets. Rusty unknotted himself from the soaking wet bedclothes and got up. He was shaking, heart hammering, and he felt the creeping edge of panic not far off. He stood there dripping in the dead silence and pitch-blackness until his nerves calmed and he felt chilled. Rusty walked to the showers and stood under hot water until calm and warmth returned, then shuffled back to the room.

Rusty wadded up his clammy sheets, then discovered that his mattress was soaked as well. He wondered groggily where he could finish the night. Richard's bunk was still made with his sheets, but Rusty shuddered at the thought of climbing between them. Finally, he knocked on the door to the big room. Flip mumbled, but woke and came to the door.

"Jesus, Rusty, you look like hell. What's wrong?"

"Nightmares. About Richard…and stuff."

"Ah. Want to talk about it or something?"

"No. Not now. But my bed is too sweaty to sleep in, and I can't bring myself to sleep in his bunk. Mind if I take Derlin's bed for the rest of the night?"

"You wet your bed, huh?" Flip grinned in his irrepressible way.

"Yeah, I guess you could say that, you cold-hearted bastard," Rusty couldn't help but laugh.

"Well, I guess it's okay. But I'm not sure you don't have another reason for coming into my room in your underwear. I'd better stay awake and watch you!"

This broke Rusty's black mood. He shook his head and laughed manically. But before long, the laughter evaporated and he stared at Flip blankly. Rusty sat down on Derlin's bed and put his face in his hands.

"Okay, Rusty, now talk. Let it out."

"Christ, Flip, that's twice for me." For almost ten minutes Rusty went on about Crazy Eddie while Flip just sat and listened. Finally, he wound down. There was silence for a few seconds.

"Rusty, forgive me for saying this, but ten times that many guys died in the first five seconds on Omaha Beach."

"So what?"

"Well, it's war. People die every day, with you or without you. I mean, you did nothing whatever to cause either of their deaths. Aside from living with them, it has nothing to do with you." He spread his palms in a helpless gesture.

"You mean Richard's death doesn't affect you?

"Uh, no, I can't say that. I was shocked, and I confess, I had a hard time trying to get to sleep tonight myself. Kept visualizing a Golden BB coming right for my head. But that's a one in a million thing. I know it's not going to happen to me. One guy getting killed is tragic, and things won't be the same around here for a while. But everything will go on." Rusty could see him shrug in the dark. Silence again.

"We're not going to pack up and leave Vietnam in defeat, and the VC aren't going to celebrate a holiday because one guy died," Flip resumed. "It's not even going to make the papers."

"So he died for nothing? It doesn't count?"

"I didn't say that. I said even one guy getting killed is tragic. It is. But it's one raindrop in a storm. Hell, everybody dies sooner or later. We can't stop fighting because it happened. If anything, it's cause to fight even harder."

"You mean like in the movies where William Bendix charges the Japs single handed when the underage soldier in his squad gets killed?"

"Well, sorta. But I don't mean you should go berserk. That's what Sanderson meant: fly hard but fly smart. What made you think of William Bendix for Pete's sake?"

"I dunno. I just suddenly saw myself as a bit like that lovable goof."

"Uh, I'm not going to sit here in the dark and in my underwear and call you lovable…"

Rusty could see his grin glowing across the room.

"…but a goof you're not. You're a good pilot and a good FAC. We've heard a few things about your first time in 'Nam, ya know. You're good enough to survive this and go home in one piece. Provided you don't go nuts and charge any Japs."

Flip turned and slumped onto his pillow: counseling session over. Rusty lay back, too. He thought about what Flip had said and about what Dave Sanderson had said. He was still thinking when he awoke and realized it was light outside.

"Mornin' sleepyhead. Time to get dressed or you'll miss chow."

Rusty looked over at Flip, who was sitting on his bunk again, but now fully dressed. Rusty rubbed his eyes and staggered out to his own room. As he entered, he looked at Richard's bunk, and there wasn't a trace of emotion left in him. The ghost was exorcised.

At breakfast, Richard was the sole topic of conversation, of course. They learned from Hannah that his body had been taken to the clinic. It now awaited air shipment back to the world. Hannah didn't know what had become of the robin, but suspected that it had been turned over to the locals.

Batman said, "I'll pray for his soul and ask that it be baptized."

"Say again?" Kit asked.

"Baptize his soul," Batman repeated. The rest of them stared back blankly.

"Well, we Mormons believe that no one can enter God's celestial kingdom unless he's baptized a Mormon. So we spiritually baptize the souls of the dead."

"You gotta be shitting me," Kit spluttered. "You're telling me that no matter what religion I am now, that if I get killed, you intend to make me an ex post facto Mormon? Without so much as my approval or even knowledge?"

"Actually, no, I wouldn't if I knew you didn't want that. But if your wishes aren't known, then yes, I would. I wouldn't want to keep you out of heaven."

"Hey, I'm a good Southern Baptist," Kit said. "I think I can find my own way to heaven, thank you very much." He said it with a smile, but there was a hard edge underneath it.

Batman raised his hands, palms out. "No problem. You're hereby on your own – at least on my account. We all have free choice, even Gentiles."

"Gentiles? What do you mean?" this time Flip chimed in.

"Well, again, that's a Mormon belief. Everybody is either a Saint – a member of the Church of Jesus Christ of Latter Day Saints – or not. The 'nots' are what we call Gentiles."

"So all non-Mormons are Gentiles?" Rusty asked, and Batman nodded. "I think that would be a source of merriment to one of my pilot training classmen: Ike Silverman."

"Yeah, that's for sure," Flip grinned. "But, Batman, if you baptize Richard's soul and make him Mormon, his heaven will be purest hell."

"How so?" Batman asked.

"You Mormons don't drink," Flip deadpanned.

For one full second, there was silence, then Rusty roared, and Kit hooted in glee. Even Batman smiled and hung his head. Sandy Hubert remained silent, but his chest heaved and his face reddened until a tear rolled down his cheek.

CHAPTER SIX

A week later, Rusty was in the combined shower and shitter, shaving. He peered at the oddly reddish mustache he was growing, wondering why black-haired guys like Dave Sanderson could have a recognizable 'stash in only a few days while it seemed to take weeks for his to be even visible. He wondered how long it'd be before he could twirl the ends into a handlebar. He was still peering intently at his reflection when Batman walked in.

"Who was that guy in Greek mythology that spent all his time staring at himself in a pool of water?" Batman asked, smirking.

"Uh, Narcissus, why? Oh, I see. Very funny, Batman. It's just that there isn't much to do between horse pill shits. No sense leaving here, but even sillier to stay in a stall the whole day."

"Yeah, I know. I usually bring a book and just sit right outside the door there. How's the 'stash coming?"

"Slowly. My hair just doesn't grow fast. I can go a month between haircuts. Why aren't you growing one? You're the only Mike FAC now without one."

"Not for long."

"What d'ya mean?"

"We're getting three replacements in today. Two new FACs and a new ALO."

"New ALO? What happened to Major Esterhouse?"

"Dave said that he had a family emergency back home and got an emergency DEROS. He already left."

"No party, no goodbyes, nothing? Just left?" Rusty was incredulous.

"Yeah, I know. But it was one of those 'deedeemau now or never' things. You hear that C-130 take off a while ago?"

Rusty nodded.

"He was on it. Cleared direct Saigon, direct world. Only took one duffel, and we're to ship the rest of his stuff whenever we can. He shook hands with a few of us, but he was already in the jeep when he did. Hannah took him to the 130, which didn't even shut down engines. Just popped the ramp and Esterhouse sprinted in."

"Damn. Bad problem back home?"

"Don't know exactly. Some medical thing, I'd guess. That's about the only reason they give those emergency DEROS orders."

"Well, at least he got news from home. I haven't had a letter from my wife in five weeks," Rusty said, morosely.

"Five weeks? You're kidding. What's wrong?"

"Beats me. The letters just suddenly stopped. I'm worried because I go on R&R in two weeks, and I don't even know if my wife knows it. I'm booked to Hawaii, and I just hope she is, too."

"That's awful. Have you tried to call her?

"Once, but I never got a time slot on the MARS radio net. I'll try again tomorrow."

"I got through once, but I screwed up the time change and it was something like 3 a.m. there," Batman said. "But I have it straight now."

"What is it?"

"Well, let's see," he looked at his watch. "It's 9 a.m. here, so it's 7 p.m. yesterday evening in Salt Lake City. Your wife is in Chicago?"

"Uh huh. So it'd be 8 p.m. Central time, right?"

"That's how I figure it. For you, subtract an hour and a day and flip morning to afternoon."

"I'd try now, but my gut is rumbling again. See ya, Batman."

Rusty hurried into the first stall and let his bowels flood out. Between watery gushes, he read some of the half-literate, raunchy sayings and doggerel scribbled on the walls, some of it so universal that it seemed to be inscribed in almost every toilet stall he'd ever visited. Rusty wondered if Shakespeare had read that same abominable drivel in the outhouse behind the Globe Theatre.

> He who writes on shithouse walls
> Rolls his shit in little balls
> He who reads those words of wit
> Eats those little balls of shit

Beneath that one ran the other inevitable ditty:

> Here I sit all broken hearted
> Came to shit, but only farted

That certainly wasn't Rusty's problem at the moment. He turned to the other wall, where a list described various people as fuckoffs, queer or worse. He was glad not to see his own name there. Determined to rise above that level of dubious humor, he took a pencil out of his pocket and wrote, "Margaret Mead is a pedophile." Maybe somebody would get it.

That afternoon, drained of every vestige of whatever he'd eaten the past few days, he went back to his room and lay down, exhausted. Before long, he heard strange voices walking past.

Dave Sanderson tapped on the door. "Hey Rusty, come meet the new guys." He got up and went around to the big room, where he himself had stood for introductions not so many weeks ago.

"Okay, now that everybody's here…Guys, meet your new ALO. This is Major Allen Bridgewater. He's fully mission briefed and despite that has foolishly agreed to act as your Mother away from home." Bridgewater was a slender, shortish man with thinning brown hair, and an impish glint in his deep blue eyes. Before anyone could shake his hand, Dave turned to the two First Lieutenants.

"Next is Danny Craig, new in country, but highly thought of. He'll be the new Mike 59. And this is Jack Buchenhardt, up from Four Corps, who'll be Mike 53."

Craig was built like a fireplug, much as Richard had been. Maybe that's why he got Richard's call sign. But Craig was not the dark brooding lump that Richard had been. Round-faced, with short, curly, caramel-colored hair, he looked almost like a bust of Julius Caesar. Buchenhardt, on the other hand, was tall and athletically thin, with an aloof, haughty look on his thrown-back face. A severely short crew cut made it hard to tell what color his darkish hair might be. Hand him a quirt, and he'd pass for a Prussian cavalry officer, Rusty thought.

"Call me Dan," Craig said instantly. He smiled at everyone, and offered his hand to Flip, nearest him.

"Hello," said Buchenhardt, tersely. He nodded jerkily to nobody in particular.

Sanderson repeated everyone's names to the new folks while Craig and Bridgewater looked at each man and shook hands. Buchenhardt stood rigid, hands clasped deliberately behind him. He surveyed them all with an unfocussed, disinterested glance about the room. Rusty made an effort not to think of him as a complete prick, but he'd have to go some to break down the first impression he'd made.

Major Bridgewater, however, won them over instantly with his humor and soft Texas accent. "This is quite the dump y'all live in, ain't it? What do we call this décor? Early hippie?"

"More like Baux Rokette," Flip quipped right back.

Bridgewater laughed hard and shook his head. "Well, maybe we can come up with something that makes up for all that. Soon's I get up to speed on this here spooky stuff, I'll look into it. But right now …(he pronounced it rat naow)…ah'm gonna be busier than a green fly on cow flop."

With that, he and Sanderson excused themselves and left.

Craig immediately asked about the briefing they'd had from No Name. "Is all that stuff true?" he asked.

"And then some," Flip came back. "Did he mention the cyanide pills?"

"Cyanide pills? No!" Craig went ashen.

"Oh, don't do that, Flip," Batman interjected. "He's new in country, after all."

"A virgin FAC?" Kit asked with mock astonishment. "Is there such a pitiful thing?"

"Just as a FAC, maybe," Craig smiled. "I've got three kids already."

"Three kids! How'd you manage that?" Kit said, with genuine astonishment this time.

"Got married when we were both sophomores. Had to," he actually blushed. "Then they just kept coming. One in senior year and another while I was in UPT."

"You didn't go to BYU, did you, Dan?" Sandy said.

"Huh?" Danny Craig said, now confused.

"Let Batman here explain it to ya sometime." He snuck a sideways glance at Batman, who stuck out his tongue at Sandy.

Rushing preened his coal-black mustache and pointed his other hand at Buchenhardt. "How about you, Jack? What'd you think of the Mike FAC briefing?"

The tall man shrugged. "Sounded like a bunch of crap to me. Is that all there is to this pussy mission? No air strikes? Just fly around until you run out of gas? I think it's a job for weak dicks."

Rushing's nut-brown face went instantly red and hard, and he started to come up from Derlin's old bunk. Rusty put a hand down on his shoulder to hold him there. "Hold on, Kit."

"I think you shouldn't judge the mission until you've flown it, Jack. We might not run air strikes, but what we do out there is just as dangerous as any other FAC job. We just sent two guys home in body bags and neither of them was a weak dick. One was literally a hard dick, in fact." Across the room, Flip snickered while Rusty went on, "Neither of them took the job lightly, and you shouldn't either."

"Fuck you," Buchenhardt said. This time Rusty felt himself coloring. Rushing surged against his hand again; but Rusty pressed down against his shoulder without looking down.

"Look," Rusty said, "You're here now. You can't back out and you can't go back to wherever you came from. Maybe it'd be best if you made the best of things. Batman, are you ready for an initiation bash?"

"I can be," Batman said, eager to change the topic. "I'll raid the kitchen for whatever they have. Tomorrow night good for everyone?"

There was no reply, and he went on, "Okay, tomorrow it is. Two new Mike FACs to be initiated into the Hole of Flame."

Neither of the two new recruits was assigned to Rusty's room. Craig was nice enough, and Rusty would have welcomed him as a roommate; but the thought of rooming with Buchenhardt turned Rusty's stomach. Maybe it was better if he lived alone for a while.

The next day, Rusty took Dan Craig up for a tour of the area. Batman had been saddled with Buchenhardt for his "dollar ride." Dan - because he'd come to them directly from Cam Rahn's FAC U - had no clue about real-world enemy tactics or ground fire or anything else. Rusty tried to get them shot at by way of a quick introduction, but the bad guys stayed hidden.

"Dan, I'm sorry that I can't seem to buy any ground fire today," he said as they orbited over a normally hot area. "You really need to know what small arms fire looks like."

"You mean you're TRYING to get shot at?" Craig squeaked, "on purpose?"

"Yup. If I could, I'd not only show you what muzzle flashes really look like, but how they sound, too."

"SOUND? You can HEAR them?" He turned , his face paling rapidly.

"Uh huh. Two ways, in fact. If you get low enough and they miss you close enough, you can hear the little sonic booms – more like sonic pops - that each bullet makes in your microphone. Or if your team is in real trouble, you can hear the enemy muzzle blasts over the radio when they transmit. Neither one is good, but you need to know what you're hearing when it happens."

"For God's sake, why?"

"Well, like I said: neither is a good thing. If you hear bullets popping over the intercom, it means they're passing within a few feet of your mic – and your head. If you hear them over the team's radio, it means you're likely to lose the team. At best, it means a hairy exfil for the Kingbees."

Craig turned even whiter, until he really did resemble a marble bust of Caesar – a terrified Caesar.

"Oh well, maybe next time," Rusty shrugged. "Did you ever get exposed to any ground fire while you were at Cam Rahn?"

"No, none at all."

"You gotta be shitting me. None? Not even when you did rocket practice out west of the bay?"

"No, none. We only fired rockets on one mission. We did do some map reading and stuff, but most of my flights were in the traffic pattern."

"Oh, my bleeding asshole. What has become of FAC U?" Rusty wondered aloud. "Well, I guess we'll have to finish up your grad work as OJT. Danny my boy, I'll have Dave schedule you and me for a few more flights together, and we can amalgamate your distinctly amorphous training."

"My who?"

"Never mind. Let's just say we'll get you ahead of the power curve. That better?"

"Yeah," he said, brightening. "That I can understand."

"When I get done with you, the little guys will say, 'You bic FAC numba one'"

"That's good?"

"That's very good. It means you understand the job and are first rate with them."

"What's it like working with…them?"

For a few seconds, Rusty's mind reeled. Could it be possible that at one time he had never met a Vietnamese or had a clue about their pidgin English? That he had never seen ground fire? Or that he had asked the very same things of Derlin that Craig was now asking him. Had he learned so much so fast that he now seemed the expert? Hell, Rusty still felt like a novice in his own mind. Is the learning curve that fast in combat? Did Derlin feel this way when he was teaching *me*? Rusty shook his head and told Dan all he knew about little guys, Chieu Hoys and such. While he spoke, he gave Craig the controls and let him fly them home. Rusty was still talking when they landed. In the back channel of his mind, he told himself, yes, Rusty, you have learned a lot. Seen a lot, too.

After they hung up their gear and had a cold drink, Rusty excused himself and knocked on Dave Sanderson's door. "Got a second, sir?"

"Sure thing, Rusty. What you need?" He turned away from a pile of papers and motioned Rusty to an empty chair.

"I just flew with Craig, and he's very green. He's never even seen ground fire, and they gave him almost nothing but pattern work at Cam Rahn."

"Yeah, I know. If we weren't so short of pilots we'd never have taken a guy straight out of FAC U." Sanderson paused. "What are you saying?"

"That I think I'd like to have a few more flights with him to teach him a few things. I know I'm not the senior FAC, but we seemed to hit it off, and I just thought…"

"I know you're not senior FAC. But, Rusty, I assigned him to you for a reason. Remember, I've flown with you; way back when you were a student pilot, and when you first got here. I already knew you have great hands, and I actually learned a few things from you when we flew here. I think you're a natural teacher, Rusty. You can have as many flights with Craig as you think he needs. I'll fly with him, too, but I want you to be his IP of sorts. That's unofficial, and don't mention it outside this room. I have other egos to contend with. Copy?"

Rusty could himself reddening with self-conscious pride, but managed to blurt, "I copy. I'll start with him tomorrow."

"Good. Oh…try to stay at least half sober tonight. I have you on an early scouting flight for the next team insert. Brief is at 0800. You can take Craig along with you if you want. You won't need a little guy for the first scouting trip."

"Roger that." Rusty stood up to leave, but turned around at the door. "Dave? Thanks. I needed that."

"I knew that, too, Rusty."

That evening, Batman once again reveled in his bartender skills as he churned out blender after blender of daiquiris; pineapple this time. The air in the flightline Conex seemed somehow thicker, and the sweaty fug of nine pilots and three sergeants was almost palpable. Rusty managed to stay convivially sober by nursing one large tumbler for most of the night, but the heavy air made it hard not to drink more.

Finally, it was time for the Mike FAC initiation. They put Craig and Buchenhardt in chairs back to back, so neither could see what was happening to the other. Rusty made it a point to stand next to Craig, along with Sandy. Kit and Flip stood beside Buchenhardt. Batman made the speech, and at the right moment, the four of them grabbed the two victims and stuck tongues in their ears. Craig hunched his shoulders and giggled in surprise.

But Buchenhardt leapt up, elbowing Kit and Flip hard as he did. He bellowed at them, and everyone else, "Get off me you stupid fuckers!

Goddamn queer motherfuckers!" He swung a fist through the air as if to ward anyone off.

"Jesus, Jack! Calm down! It's just an initiation. What the hell's wrong with you?" Kit bellowed back. He raised his fists in self-defense.

Batman jumped between them, "Whoa. Whoa! Everybody throttle back! We don't want any fistfights tonight. It's over. okay?"

"I'm not having any queer motherfuck French kiss my ear," Buchenhardt said, ignoring Batman and staring hard at Kit.

"Hey, listen you prick, you called me a weak dick the other night, and now a queer. I'm not taking that a third time. You copy that, asshole?" Kit was coloring now, his temper rising by the millisecond.

Before anyone else could say anything, Dave Sanderson stepped up next to Batman. "Ok, that's it. Bar's closed. Everybody out. And that means straight to your rooms. Anybody so much as looks hard at anybody else tonight, and there'll be an Article 15 in it for all of you." He looked at all of them in turn, then went back to Kit and Jack to meet their eyes. "Copy that, you two?"

Kit said, "Yessir." Buchenhardt snorted.

Batman busied himself packing up the blender. As Rusty tied the official Mike FAC red bandanna around Craig's neck, he noticed Flip stuffing what would have been Jack's back into his pocket. Rusty met Flip's eyes, and read in them exactly what he himself was thinking: Buchenhardt might be assigned here, but he'd never be a true Mike FAC.

Rusty walked back to the hootch with Major Bridgewater, who hadn't said a word either during the fracas or afterward. Rusty suddenly realized that they should have initiated him, too. "Uh, sir, sorry we didn't get to initiate you. I mean, the ear thing…well, you outrank us, and…" he let it trail off, feeling embarrassed and awkward.

Rusty turned and saw the man smiling in the light of the half-moon, just risen. "Oh, that's alright, son. I 'spect it's a perk that a field officer has to forego. Even if you are the only roundeyes I've laid eyes on since Hitler was a corporal."

Rusty groped for a risqué comment, but at that moment a flash lit the cloud bottoms and a split second later came the Boom BaBoom Boom of the midnight mortars. Both of them jumped involuntarily. "Christ! Those things startle me! I do that every night. Damn near levitates me out of the bed," Rusty said.

"No s'prise at that, son. But hush up, listen close now…" He stopped and held Rusty's arm for what seemed a long time, but was probably about thirty seconds. Far off in the distance, they heard Whup whump…whump…whup. "Ah, there. Let's hope some VC just had his sleep prolonged permanently." An entirely new glint glowed in the major's eyes, this one predatory, almost feral. His grip tightened even more, and then his eyes focused on Rusty again. He relaxed his grip and turned to the hootch again. Speechless and amazed, Rusty followed a step behind him.

In bed, Rusty mulled over everything that had happened that day. The almost cosmic shift that had transformed him seemingly overnight from rookie to wise old head. Then he marveled at what Dave had said about being a born teacher. He wondered what might happen between Kit and Buchenhardt, and finally he marveled at the sheer predatory hunger he'd seen in Bridgewater's eyes.

In the morning, Rusty knocked on Dan and Kit's door – Dave had fortunately bunked Dan in with Rushing and put Buchenhardt in the big room with Flip. "Hey, Dan. Suit up. We brief in an hour. Skweet! Kit, yungry?"

"Yeah, mungry. Skweet," Kit came back instantly.

Rusty grinned to himself at the confusion on Dan's face. It felt good to pass those same odd verbal contractions on to an initiate. "Breakfast, Dan," he finally said. "Powdered yellow shit, burned black shit and greasy brown shit. Yum!"

Rusty saw his shoulders slump. His smoothly rounded torso proved that he liked food. Rusty did, too. In fact, he found himself actually gaining weight on Ban Me Thuot's unorthodox fare. But this wasn't the time to tell Dan about monkey noodle soup, water buffalo steaks or dog stew. Not to mention nuoc mam and fecally fertilized lettuce. Better to save that for Buchenhardt - preferably in mid-chew. He smiled evilly at the thought.

They walked into the chow hall to find Batman, Bridgewater and Sanderson already there. Heads together, they were in the midst of a hushed, intense conversation

"Morning all," Kit said, cheerily. The three half-turned and waved back cordially, but they were clearly preoccupied. Rusty raised his eyebrows involuntarily as they turned through the small door that led to the chow line itself.

Once out of sight of the others, Kit leaned close to Rusty, "What was that all about?"

"Beats me. But those were the only three sober guys last night. Maybe they're figuring out how to have the rest of us shot at sunrise," Rusty said, trying to be funny. It failed.

"Jesus, I hope Sanderson isn't serious about that Article 15. A disciplinary letter in my file would kill my chance of promotion."

"Nah, I was just kidding, Kit. I don't have any idea what they're discussing. It might just be an ops thing. Batman's senior FAC now, after all. There were some 'yards in there, and they're being discrete is all."

"Still, if anything bad happens to my records, I swear I'll frag that Buchenhardt bastard. What a dildo he is."

Craig added, "I'll say. All the way over here from Cam Rahn, all he did was bitch about this assignment. Said he was too good a FAC to go to some pissant unit nobody ever heard of. Stuck me in the back seat without even asking, too. Like he owned the fripping plane."

Rusty saw Kit's brow furrow as he homed in on something. "Assignment? You mean he was sent here? He wasn't asked to volunteer?"

"I don't know, but he used the word 'assignment' himself. Now that you mention it, when we got our secret briefing that first day, the briefer asked me if I chose to volunteer, but he didn't ask Jack. He talked to me during the brief, but he hardly looked at Buchenhardt. It was almost like I was the only guy in the room. I didn't even realize it until you just mentioned it. What the heck!"

Kit nodded. "Just what I suspected. The sonofabitch is a pariah. I bet he got booted out of his last assignment in Four Corps, and they sent him to us because you can't go anywhere else once you're here. We're fucked permanently with this toad. I just fucking knew it!" Kit exclaimed, pounding his fist on the bars of the serving line in emphasis. The startled Vietnamese cook behind the line looked up in shock and fear.

"I believe it," Rusty said. "That makes perfect sense from what I see. He wasn't here ten minutes before he pissed us all off. Well, me, anyway. And then last night, well…"

"Absofuckinglutely," Kit said. "Posifuckingtively, too."

"Well, for what it's worth, I don't like the…jerk," Craig said.

Rusty turned to him, amazed at his avoidance of any cuss words. "Dan, tell me. I haven't heard you use any curse words. Any reason for that?"

"I just don't like them. No religious reason or anything. I just imagine myself in front of my mother or my kids. I can't bring myself to say any."

"I know just what you mean," Rusty said. "I love spoonerisms, like flutterby or pewsnaper. But one time I was reading Mark Twain. My Mom was in the room and without thinking I blurted out, 'I love this Fuckleberry Hinn.' She just stared at me. Embarrassed the hell out of me."

"You didn't," Dan said, aghast.

"Yup, I did; without even thinking. I think I was as stunned as she was. I still tone down my language a lot."

"You're both fucking nuts," Kit said, with a grin.

"Amen to that," Rusty came back, grinning too.

By the time they went through the line and got out to the tables, the others had gone. They ate the gross eggs, slippery bacon and bitter coffee in near silence. After they finished, Kit went back to the hootch alone while and Dan and Rusty walked to the briefing room. There, they settled into chairs in the front row, the first two to arrive.

"Not much like pilot training, is it?" Dan asked.

"Nope. Not even like fighter lead-in school in New Mexico. No time hack, no safety brief and no pop quiz of procedures. There will only be four of us, probably. The man nominally in charge will be the Vietnamese Intel guy, and the other guy will be Special Forces. Sometimes it's hard to tell who's really in charge, but it's best to assume it's the Vietnamese officer. A guy named Y-Monh is the best. He's actually Montagnard and he's...well, I'll let you form your own opinion. The Special Forces guy is Capt Brookside. Just as good, and technically in our chain of command. Kind of, anyway. It's confusing. But it really doesn't matter. They give us the target box and the goals of the mission, and we fly it. Simple."

"That's it? No detailed instructions or anything?"

"Nope. We're on our own. Or, more precisely, they set the broad parameters and let us work out the details. Mike FACs are adults, as it were."

"I'll be...darned," Dan said.

"That's possible. Or damned, if you...*mess*...up," Rusty chuckled. At that moment, Brookside and Y-Monh entered. Y-Monh smiled at Rusty, then glanced quizzically at Craig.

Rusty stood, and Craig followed suit. "Sir," Rusty said, addressing Y-Monh directly, "This is Lieutenant Craig. He's new, and it is my honor to teach him the Mike FAC way."

"Then he is honored as well," Y-Monh graciously said. He looked at Dan, "The Dai-wee Naille is one of our bright stars. Follow his way and you will shine also."

Rusty almost blushed. Y-Monh motioned them to their seats, and he went straight into his briefing. He revealed the name of the mission – Cedar Ship – and told them it was a routine trail watch. No mingling with the enemy, no sneaking through the jungle, just a fixed objective to watch. That objective was a trail junction where two ribbons of the Ho Chi Minh Trail from the north merged into one broader track to the south. The team would count traffic and take notes for five days and nights, then be recovered. Very straightforward and safe – unless they were detected, of course.

The weather forecast, from Brookside, surprised Rusty a bit. He said the monsoon was imminent, and that the NVA were thought to be doubling or tripling their movements to beat the rains. The downpours might start within days, perhaps while the team was still in place. If possible, they might even advance the insertion to tomorrow, he said.

Rusty knew a hint when he heard one: find an infil site today.

With that, Y-Monh ended the brief and strolled out.

"What'd you think, Dan?"

"Jiminy, that Y-Monh guy is amazing. I never would've thought he spoke English like that."

"He speaks four languages fluently. His own tribal Montagnard, of course. He's a Jarai, by the way. Then Vietnamese and French besides English. What else did you think about him?"

"That I'm glad he's on our side. I can't put my finger on it, but he's the most frighteningly powerful man I've ever seen," Dan said, in awe.

"Uh huh. That's the same first impression I got. It's not a false impression, either. That man just exudes power."

"No foolin'," Dan said. "But tell me about the monsoon."

"That surprised me, too. I've noticed that it's gotten a lot more humid over the past few days, and the sky has gone from a clear, deep blue to a sort of depthless white, but beyond that, I guess I lost track of time. I didn't realize it was monsoon time again. I saw it the first time I was in 'Nam, but it cannot be described. Trust me, you'll agree when you've seen it."

Craig shrugged, "Well, it's beyond our control, anyway. What time do we take off?"

"Anytime we want, but that hint to hustle was plain. So let's go right away."

They pre-flighted and Rusty let Dan take the left seat. He wanted to check Craig's rocket firing technique, and Rusty could read the map while Dan flew. After they crossed the fence, Rusty told Craig to stay high while they transited almost directly to the target box. They had brought binoculars so they could examine the target box without drawing too much attention to their flight path.

True to his training, Dan turned on the TACAN navigation radio and tuned it to Channel 117, the station near BMT. "What's the radial and DME of the target?" he asked when they were airborne.

"Beats me. We never navigate that way. Or at least, not outbound. Everything is by map and eyeball. We only use the map for confirmation of coordinates, in fact. Everything else, we memorize."

"What do you mean by memorize?"

"Just that. We navigate by the terrain itself, which we memorize. Before long, you could be flown around blindfolded for hours, and with one quick peek, know exactly where you are and which way is home."

"Over how much area?" He was incredulous.

"Roughly 130 miles on a side. From the fishhook to the Laotian border and from the Vietnam border to the Mekong."

"And you have..." he paused to grease pencil numbers on the cockpit window..." 17,000 square miles of land *memorized*?"

"Not perfectly, but I'm working on it. The parts I know well, I know down to the last creek, hootch and burned out truck. So will you before long."

"It's not possible."

"Oh yes, it is. You'd be amazed. I didn't think it was, either, but if you keep your eyes open, it just kinda accumulates with no special effort. Look... back home, did you drive a regular route to school or work or anything?"

"Yeah, why?"

"Do you think you'd notice if a sign got put up or a tree cut down on that route?"

"Sure. But that's not the same thing."

"Yes, it is," Rusty said. "Suppose I made you close your eyes and let you peek for a second while I drove that route. Would you know where you were with that one itty bitty peek?"

"I see what you mean. Yeah, I would. So you're saying that it's the same out here, even in an area that big?"

"It is, Dan. It's just the same. I can tell you if a stream's been crossed, by about how many people, or animals, or trucks, and which way they went, and almost to the hour when. I can tell you when a village has VC in it and when it doesn't. I can even tell you if an elephant is wild or a VC pack animal."

"Oh, bull. Now you're pulling my leg."

"No, I'm not. That one's the easiest, in fact. Just fly low over the elephant. Not buzz him, just cruise over him at 500 feet or so. If he bolts and runs, he's wild. But if he stands still, he's used to motor noises. Pack animal; bet on it."

"I'll be flipped. I'd never have thought of that. How do you learn that kind of stuff?"

"You learned it just now, right? That's how. We teach each other. Long bull sessions at night, war stories; call it what you will. It's life insurance. You pick people's brains, ask questions, and pose problems. One of these guys has seen it, done it and figured it out. I learned from a master, and if he were still here, I'd still be learning from him."

He just shook his head in wonderment. "Prove to me that you know the terrain."

"Ok, it happens that I do know the area where we're going. Look at your map. You see that small hill almost in the center of the box?"

"Uh huh."

"Well, just beyond it, there's a long oval clearing. It's thick jungle all around except for that one clearing. The clearing is dry grass, no trees at all and no ravines cross it. The team is supposed to sneak to this spot right here," Rusty touched the map with a pencil, "and that's about two clicks northwest of the hill. What I plan to do is to come in around that hill real low and from the south, drop the team into that clearing and then curl right back to the east around the hill. I'm hoping there won't be any bad guys on that hill, but that's the biggest risk. If not, nobody will see us coming, and even the sound of the chopper rotors will be masked. We'll duck in, duck out and nobody will be the wiser."

Rusty explained to him the trick of the lead helicopter dropping to the deck only long enough to drop the team, then popping up in trail of the empty gunship.

He stared back open-mouthed. "That's magic."

"Nope, just applying what I was taught. You approach right on the deck, avoid the target area itself, drop the team where they can either disappear in a hurry or you can make an immediate pickup if things go to hell, then get the helos out so they have the least chance of being spotted. From there on, it's up to the team and your little guy."

A few minutes later, they'd flown almost to the hill.

"Now angle off a bit to your side. I want to take a close look at the clearing and that hill with the glasses. Just hold a straight heading and altitude. I don't want to betray any interest in this spot at all."

"Got it. This is almost like chess, isn't it?"

"Yeah, that's what I like. I get to outwit the little bastards. And they're no dummies, by the way. Few tactics work more than twice. The bad guys spread the word about our tactics much better and faster than we do. How, I haven't a clue, but they do."

As they flew slowly past, Rusty spent the next two minutes staring intently at the clearing, and even harder at the hilltop. He saw no evidence of anyone having been up there or in the clearing recently: no paths in the grass, no cut trees, no smoke. He stared down, first forwards and then gradually back until he couldn't turn around any further in the seat, then turned to Dan. Rusty told him everything he had looked for, and why.

"Okay, now just fly on for a few miles and we'll do some sightseeing. On the way back, we'll fly past the hill again on the same path. That'll put it on your side. Then I'll point out all the things I saw. I just hope that red crested sap sucker is still there." Rusty looked at Dan out of the corner of his eye to see if he was buying that. He wasn't.

On the way back, Rusty flew while Dan looked from the map to the ground, then through the field glasses. "I'll be darned," he finally said. "It is just the way you said: the low hill, the clearing, the grass, the jungle all around and all the rest. You did have it memorized!" Then he turned to Rusty, "But the sap sucker is gone...unless you meant the female."

Rusty guffawed, "See, you *are* learning!"

They went south, where they fired some rockets at the ruined hootches at Disneyworld. Rusty taught him the turning, pull-through rocket pass he'd learned from good old Chuck McKenzie at Cam Rahn.

As they pulled out after the fourth pass, Rusty calmly said, "Hey Dan, look down there at about the fifth hootch from the south end. See those cute little white sparkles?"

He looked, then did a double take, "You mean, that's ground fire?"

"Uh huh. Just one guy, with an AK-47, judging from the number of rounds per clip."

"What's he shooting at?"

"Well, that's another thing you can learn. If you see the sparkle, you're looking down his barrel."

"He's shooting at *US*?"

"Yup, but we're way out of range. He may or may not know that, but he's trying to kill us, regardless. Wanna shoot back?"

"You bet your ass I do!" He whipped the plane around, armed up and sent a smoke rocket down very near to where the sparkles still blinked. It was a good shot. The sparkling stopped. "Take that, you piece of shit!"

"Why Danny Craig, what would your mother say?" Rusty quipped. Then to put things into perspective, Rusty tapped the map and said, "Dan, fly me to this spot and tell me what you see." Craig turned the plane east and flew for a minute or two.

"There's a black spot on the ground. It looks like...hey, is that a plane? It looks like an O-2!"

"It is, Dan. And you should know one more thing. That wreck down there was the previous Mike 53 - the guy you are replacing. He took a bullet right in the face, very near here, and maybe from that same guy that just shot at you. So keep that in mind any time all this starts to seem like only a chess game or a thrill ride."

Craig gulped and swallowed. "I sure will."

Back on the ground, they debriefed with Brookside, passed along the insert site coordinates and a small drawing of the path Rusty planned to take both in and out – which would be given to the lead Kingbee pilot in a separate briefing – and confirmed that the mission could be moved up to tomorrow.

Barring an emergency, they were done for the day, so they wandered into the big room for a cold one. Flip was there, but Buchenhardt was gone.

"Where's Jack?" Rusty asked, hoping he'd be gone for a while.

"Moved out," Flip said, with a sly smile.

"Moved where? Da Nang, I hope." Rusty opened the mini-fridge and popped a Coke.

"No, just to the empty room on the end. Said he'd prefer being by himself. But I think the truth is that he didn't want to be here in the big room where people drop in all the time," Flip said in a stage whisper, cupping one hand next to his mouth.

"You mean cooped up with inferior beings? That sounds about right for him. Did he need the door widened for his head to pass through?"

"Ha! Probably! He made it out of this one easy enough. Quick, too. He never even unpacked. First thing this morning, he talked with Major Bridgewater and while I was at breakfast, his stuff just disappeared. I wonder what shape that last room is in? Nobody's lived there since I came here eight months ago."

"Man, that's good," Rusty said after a big sip of the soda. Then, "Gotta be filthy in there. You think we should tell Mama-San to have one of the hootch maids clean it out?"

"Hell, let him make cleaning arrangements. His room, his problem is the way I see it."

"You got that right," Rusty nodded, convinced. "What's on the agenda this afternoon? Anything?"

"Well, let's see." Flip ticked items off on his fingers. "I'm going to jog a while before lunch, Batman is up on some mission or other, Kit's in the shitter today, Sandy is going to take one of the planes down to Cam Rahn for maintenance and an overnight, Dave is going to take the Bucher up for an orientation flight, and...I think that's about it."

"You not flying today, then?"

"Nope. No teams across the fence right now, so no cap mission needed. A good day to get laundry and stuff sorted out. You?"

"Thought I'd write another letter to my wife with my flight details for R&R. I have no idea if she's getting any of them. So I'm writing the same thing every day in hopes she gets at least one of them."

"You mean you don't know if she knows about your R&R? You're kidding!"

"No, I'm not. I haven't a clue if she'll be there when I land or not. I might end up on Waikiki Beach alone for all I know. I've tried to get through on the MARS circuit several times, but never did. I'll try again tomorrow morning before my insert."

"Man, that's awful. How long has it been since you got a letter?"

"Over five weeks now. I got some the first few weeks here, but nothing since then. The exact same thing happened to me back at Emerald. I'm beginning to think I'm jinxed or something. And the stupid Army mail service is no help. When I ask them to check on it, they want to know how her letters were addressed. How the hell am I supposed to know that if I haven't gotten the goddamn letters?"

Flip just shook his head in amazement and empathy.

Rusty changed the subject. "You say you're going to jog?" Flip nodded. "Beats me how you can with this new weather. It's got to be close to ninety out there, and the humidity is enough to curl my writing paper in the damn drawer. How do you stand to run in it?"

"I feels worse if I don't, somehow. You oughta start, you know. You're getting a little pudgy. You don't want you wife mistaking you for a beached whale on Waikiki, do ya?" He grinned.

"I'm hoping she'll be interested in parts other than my waist, Flip." Rusty leered at him. "Concupiscence obviates finicality, after all."

"There you go with that six-dollar word stuff again. What's that in fifty-cent talk?"

"Horny ain't picky. How's that?"

"Now you're talkin'! I bic that. Much longer here, and I'm gonna think Mama-San is worth a tumble, ha ha ha!"

Rusty flashed a mental picture of Mama-San naked, with her pocked face, black teeth and saggy, flat boobs. "The war ain't gonna last long enough to make her look good, brother. But I confess, that little Mai Lin is looking better every day."

"Ah ah aaah!" Flip waggled his finger, "That's what Derlin warned you about! Remember?"

"Yeah, my first day here. She's no real temptation yet, but if I come back from R&R without getting my rocks off, I'm not promising anything."

"Time for a trip to the Bakery, huh?" That sly, conspiratorial grin of his again.

"No, not really. I'd still be scared of catching the clap. It wouldn't do to bring that home."

"They can cure that, you know. Six sticks for the drip." He mimicked a needle being injected in his arm.

"Uh huh, but it goes in your records. And if I'm ever asked 'Have you ever had...' I want to be able to say 'No' with a straight face and a clear conscience."

"Yeah, that's probably the best. Besides, the rumor is that there's a strain of the clap that they can't cure...ever."

"And it'd be just my luck, too," Rusty said, shaking his head ruefully. "Nah. I can stand not dipping my wick for the duration. At least, I hope I can."

"Better stay away from nam pei parties, then."

"What's that?" Rusty realized there were some things he hadn't learned yet.

"Nam pei parties? You've seen those brass wire bracelets some guys wear?' Rusty nodded.

"You get one if you're the guest of honor at a nam pei party. The chief invites you to a 'yard village, and they feast and toast you. It starts with a big clay pot in the center of the village. That's where they make the nam pei. It's rice wine, sorta. The village women chew up half-cooked rice and spit the stuff into the pot. When it's half full, they add water and tie a leather cover over it. It ferments in the sun for a week before the party. Then, they lead you – the guest of honor – to the pot, slit it open and hand you a straw."

"You're kidding," Rusty said, incredulous.

"Oh no, I'm not. And that's not all. You have to drink until they think their honor is satisfied. All in one long swallow. It might be a gallon before they cheer and you can come up for air."

Rusty stared at him. A gallon of fermented rice spit – in one long swallow!

"Then the feasting starts. Pig, dog, dried fish, rat and the piece de resistance, live monkey brains."

"*Live* monkey brains? Did you say that right?"

"Yup. They have a round table with a hole in the middle. They shove a live, kicking monkey headfirst up into the hole, and slice off the top of his skull with one blow of a machete. Then everybody digs in with spoons. Honest."

"Jesus Christ," Rusty muttered, "That even trumps a naked Mama-San for gross."

"But here's what I meant before. When that's all done, they lead you to one of their raised houses for the night. You crawl up the entry log, and a pubescent little virgin crawls up right with you. You're expected to uphold the village honor again. Do I have to explain?"

"You don't. If it takes a gallon of nam pei to satisfy their honor, then…"

"Uh huh. You get the picture."

"How exactly does one avoid this…um, honor?" Rusty asked, very eager to know.

"You're in serious danger of it already, brother. Y-Monh is the chief of chiefs in these parts, and he thinks you're numba one Mike FAC."

"Oh shit. Really?"

Flip just nodded, glee in his eyes at Rusty's distress. Then he glanced at his watch and said, "Well, I gotta get going if I'm gonna get a run in before lunch. Wanna join me?"

"Uh, no thanks. I'll just see you later." Rusty left, wondering yet again how much of that was true. Coming from Flip, it was hard to say.

After lunch – during which Buchenhardt sat by himself, his back to the rest of them – the sky rapidly went from an opaque sheet of white glare to gray, then black. Lightning cracked and thunder boomed, then came a sheet of heavy rain amid strong gusts. The drenching continued for a half-hour and then ended. In the storm's wake, the ground steamed with ghostly white fingers and sheets of water vapor.

Rusty turned to Craig. "You are about to experience the monsoon, Dan. The passing of which may extract an explicative even from your lips."

They were sitting out in the courtyard just after sunset, enjoying the cooling, wet air, when a tobacco-brown insect fluttered down from the sky and landed on Kit's foot. The bug, a solid inch long and almost as fat as a cigarette, had four wings, but as they watched, all four wings suddenly detached from the bug's body as it crawled off. Rusty was about to comment on it, when two more identical things landed, shed their wings and crawled off. Then came a dozen, a hundred. Suddenly, the air was filled with thousands of the things, whirring down on four wings, which immediately fell off. The bugs quickly blanketed the ground, the trees, the blast barrels and the sides of the hootch – even the men themselves. All of them leapt up and began slapping at the things, even though the creatures didn't seem to bite or sting. It was the suddenness of the attack that caused a spontaneous, instinctive defense reaction, and they ran for their rooms. Rusty slammed his door, but discovered that a dozen or more had already gotten in. More were crawling under the door, and he wadded a towel into the gap at the bottom. That stopped them, and he was free to watch as the screen filled with their bodies, scurrying madly in every direction. Rusty yelled through the window screen, "Hey Flip, what the hell are those things?"

"Beats me, but whatever they are, I think this is called a swarm. It's when a whole colony abandons its home and flies off to find another."

"Yeah, I've heard of that," Rusty yelled back. "Bees do it when they establish a new queen. The soldier bees escort the queen to a new home site. You think that's what this is?"

"Well, these aren't bees, that's for sure. They look like giant ants or something."

Then the truth dawned. "Nope, not ants. These are termites; giant, flying swarming termites. I saw something like it on TV once, but those were in Africa. They come out at the first rain of the wet season, when the ground gets soft enough to tunnel into. I bet that storm is what triggered this."

"I bet that's right. Man, I hope they don't eat the hootch!"

From down the way, Rusty heard Kit's voice as he joined in. "Hootch? Who cares about the hootch, I hope I don't wake up with a woody myself, only to have them gnaw it off!"

Rusty collapsed into gales of laughter until his sides hurt. He wasn't the only one. When the guffaws ended, the bugs were still swarming against the window, and so Rusty turned out the light in case it was attracting them. Standing there in the dark seemed silly, so he undressed and went to bed. He lay there a long time, thinking, but every time he remembered Kit's joke, he laughed to himself again.

In the morning, the skies were blue again. It was not the deep sapphire of spring, but a pale hazy blue that looked as though it wanted to coalesce into more storms. Rusty went outside, and immediately noticed the ground, which was covered with millions of shed wings. They covered every surface, and in some places the wind had blown them into drifts four or five inches deep. He picked up several from the top of a blast barrel.

The cellophane-like discards were a transparent, light tan color, each one an inch long and shaped exactly like half a propeller. He held one up and was enthralled by the network of veins traced between the thick black leading edge and the gently curved, transparent trailing edge. What a miracle of pure design for something that apparently was only to be used once, Rusty marveled.

But where had the insects all gone? There wasn't a single one visible anywhere, except a few that had been squashed underfoot the evening before. Were they even now inside the walls of the hootch, preparing to devour it? Where could they have gone?

But his reverie couldn't last. There was breakfast, a briefing and an insert to be flown today. He knocked on Dan's door and found him dressed and waiting. They ate and went to the command post for the mission brief. Once again, Y-Monh and Brookside presided, and Rusty was delighted to see Truong in the last row of the room as their robin.

After he'd briefed the frequencies, codes and other essentials, Brookside said that the storm last night might be the first of the monsoons. If the weather got really bad, they'd pull the team early. Rusty nodded curtly, knowing it would be up to him to devise a way to do that, making decisions on the spot as the situation dictated.

Rusty noticed Y-Monh smiling at them, and had a sudden fear that he'd invite him to a nam-pei party. Rusty desperately tried to put the Flip's vivid images out of mind, but he still missed something Brookside said and had to have it repeated. Instantly, Y-Monh's smile disappeared, clearly upset by Rusty's obvious daydreaming. Oh well, maybe that was the answer to Rusty's fears about a nam pei invitation.

Truong, as usual, said nothing during the briefing, nor was he asked anything. When the briefing ended, he left silently, while Dan and Rusty walked to the ramp. There, they retrieved helmets and chutes and started the preflight. Truong came ambling up right on time, and got into the back seat.

As pilot in command, Rusty climbed into the left, and Dan strapped in to the right seat.

Rusty felt a wave of deja vu as he explained to Dan about the Kingbees' versus their own takeoff time. His words sounded so much like Flip's had that Rusty half imagined he'd be able to do carpentry after the mission. Could it have been only two months ago that he'd been sitting in that seat on his first insertion?

Rusty talked almost constantly on the way out to the fence, weaving the plane regularly so that he or Dan could check on the Kingbees trailing behind. They made the usual sparse radio calls checking them in and reporting crossing the border to the command post. Soon, it was show time, and Rusty slowly eased back the power and lowered the nose. He'd told Dan that they'd be going in low, but he hadn't said how low, and he watched amused as Dan squirmed in his seat when they finally leveled off only a few feet above the treetops. They skirted a village that was supposed to be abandoned, and Rusty explained that they never assumed anything about bad guys.

In the distance now, they could see the rounded top of the hill they were aiming for, and Rusty made a final little jinking turn to eyeball the Kingbees. They lagged behind a bit farther than usual; but so far, so good. At the last minute, he had a thought.

"Dan, I'm going to fly closer to that hill than I originally planned. It's still early in the day, and if there are any bad guys up there, they just might have a fire going to dry out from the storm. Look close as we go by, and if you see any smoke or troops in the open or ground fire, yell out and we'll abort the insert. okay?"

"I copy," Dan said, his voice tight with discomfort at the low altitude and slow speed.

"Don't worry, I'll push up the power soon, so I can maneuver easier."

"Good," Dan said, relieved.

Rusty checked the radio selector, then thumbed the transmit switch. "Kingbee okay?"

They heard two rapid clicks in reply. Good to go. They were still a mile from the hill, but Rusty shoved the throttle up and aimed for the edge of the hill itself. "Watch that hill close now, Dan."

"All clear so far. No smoke that I can see."

"Okay! Here goes," Rusty said moments later as he rolled the plane sharply, right around the contour of the hill. The trees whizzed past only feet from the right wing as he dropped the nose in the turn. Aiming right for the center of the clearing now, Rusty let the airspeed build.

"Kingbee, three…two…one…Bingo, Bingo, Bingo!"

Rusty eased the yoke back, leveling off as they dropped below tree level in the clearing.

Just as he did, over the radio came, "Kingbee no see bingo! No see bingo!"

Oh shit. Rusty realized instantly what had happened. He'd pulled away from the slow choppers, and when he whipped around the very edge of the hill, he'd disappeared. Before they could catch up, he'd already called the bingo. Shit, shit, shit!

He only had a few seconds before the Kingbees would come around the hill, and if he wasn't in place for another bingo, they'd overshoot the clearing. It'd be impossible for them to turn around, and if they went around the hill again, they might as well drop engraved invitations to the bad guys to come greet the team. Rusty decided in a heartbeat what to do.

He pulled the nose up sharply, went to full power as they popped up a thousand feet, then he relaxed backpressure on the yoke, rolled and shoved in full left rudder. The O-2 slewed left, pivoting 180 degrees around the left wingtip, and then plunged again for the ground. From the corner of his eye, he saw Dan's hands come up, reflexively reaching for the yoke, as both he and Truong sucked in their breaths in fear. "I got it!" Rusty yelled, "I got it!"

He was shoving the throttles hard enough to bend them as he milked the nose back up, and they leveled off just above the grass and shot across the clearing back the way they'd come. Rusty stared at the edge of the hill, and just as he saw the lead Kingbee appear, hit the radio button again. "Bingo, bingo, bingo!"

"Okay, okay!" he heard. He looked straight ahead, and his heart stopped. Trees!

The trees at the south end, the ones they'd dived over mere seconds before, now loomed high above them, and the plane hurtled right at them. Rusty pulled the yoke, then pulled harder. The windscreen was still filled with solid green. He heaved back hard on the yoke, slamming them down in their seats. The nose shot up, but just as some blue appeared at the top of the windscreen, they hit. Bang! Leaves and twigs pelted the windscreen. Rusty heard broken branches screeching against aluminum, and he thought it was the end. Then, suddenly, they were free. The O-2 mushed along, the impact stealing much of his airspeed, and he unloaded the backpressure to let the nose fall on its own. As it neared the horizon again, he slowly milked in a tiny bit of backpressure with his left hand, the right still leaning on the throttles for full power.

They held their altitude only feet above the jungle, levitating by pure will power. Slowly, the airspeed built back up. They were flying again. Rusty very cautiously turned back to the north, and caught sight of the two Kingbees just above the jungle, headed east. Had they actually done the insertion, or were they headed home to report that the FAC had crashed?

There was only one thing he could do. Rusty managed to take two deep breaths — and realized he'd been holding it - clicked the mike button and said, "Kingbee?"

"Kingbee okay," was the calm reply. "Go home now?"

Christ, they had done the insertion! There was no other way to interpret that reply.

"Negative Kingbee, stand by."

"Okay," the Vietnamese pilot said, and there was a questioning note in his voice, as if to say, why are you talking to me now?

Then Rusty realized that the helos hadn't seen them hit the trees. They'd flown right over the O-2 as they went for the clearing. He'd pulled up under and just behind them. As far as they knew, the FAC had merely turned around and flown under them.

Rusty gained altitude and turned east. Craning his neck, he could see green stains the length of the left wing, on the rocket pod, the wing strut and across the windscreen. At least nothing seemed bent or broken. As he looked to the right, he came face to face with Dan, whose eyes bulged like cue balls.

As normally as he could pitch his voice, Rusty said, "And that's how it's done."

"Jesus Fucking Christ," said Danny Craig. Truong cackled in mirth.

Rusty let the next fifteen minutes go by in utter silence, mostly to let his heart rate drop under a gazillion gigahertz. As always, Truong hunched his head, eyes shut to better concentrate on the radio. When the expected whispers came, he scribbled his columns of numbers on the side window, and gave a thumbs up. "Team okay, Daiwee. Numba one job, you bet!" He mimicked the tree limbs exploding over us with his hands, shouting "POW!" into his mike. Then he convulsed with laughter again, sliding down into his harness. He had loved it!

Finally, Dan cleared his throat and said, "Is that really how you do an insert?"

"Well, all but the tree trimming part," Rusty said, casually. "That's optional. But I thought I'd show you the whole shooting match. You needn't try it on your own if you don't want to."

"Thanks, I think I might not." Dan sat there for a second. "Um, just how many G's did we pull back there?"

"Two," Rusty said flippantly. "Too many. I think we may have stressed something a bit, actually."

"Uh huh, I thought I heard something bend in a creaky kind of way."

"Yeah, me too. Time to fess up, Dan. I didn't do that on purpose. I screwed up. Big time. Scared the shit outta myself, to be honest. I don't think I'll be able to get the seat cushion out of my asshole with a chain and a John Deere. You?"

"I sucked mine up all the way to my Adam's apple, feels like."

"Truong loved it, though. If we asked him, he'd be ready to do it again."

"Don't ask him," Dan said. "Please."

"I don't think we actually broke anything. It flies okay and I don't even see any dents."

"Whattaya you mean 'we' didn't break anything? I was sitting on my hands the whole time, mister pilot in command."

"Uh, yeah. I know. I'll swear to that, if it comes up. It was my screw up all the way. You have my word."

"Thanks. You think we should do a controllability check or anything?"

"No. We'll know if it's bent when we try to land. That's soon enough. No sense reporting it till we get back, either."

"You just want to delay the inevitable, don't you?"

"Oh yeah. Sanderson is gonna kill me. My first insert after his big 'Fly safe' harangue, and this happens. Oh, brother."

Dan looked at Rusty with pity in his eyes. "It was nice knowing you."

"Thanks a bunch."

Rusty released the Kingbees, climbed to 5,000 feet and set up a long racetrack orbit ten miles southeast of the team. He explained to Dan what he'd done wrong, and what had gone right. They talked softly while Truong listened for any emergency calls from the team. None came.

Three hours later, they heard Kit check in with Ops and then cross the fence. He checked in with Rusty, and asked if everything was normal.

"Uh, the mission is fine. Go nickel."

Going nickel was a private code between Mike FACs. It meant to drop five megahertz or kilohertz on the radio in use so Ops couldn't listen in.

"What's up?" Kit said immediately on the new frequency.

"Um, well, I may have bent the bird a bit. Trimmed a tree in the bingo."

"Uh oh. Graze a branch?"

"I wish. Flew through a whole damn tree. A big mother. From underneath. Plane's green all over but I don't think it's dented. But I yanked a few extra Gs trying to miss it."

"What's a few?"

"If this thing had a meter, it'd be pegged."

"Ouch. How's it flying?"

"Just fine, actually. Can't feel any tendency to roll or anything, and the airspeed is normal for the power setting. Can't detect any fuel leaks, either. If I bent the wings, they're bent equally."

"You want me to join up and give you a look see?"

"Maybe you'd better." Rusty gave him their position and altitude. "Make it quick, a handoff isn't supposed to take long."

"I know."

A few minutes later, Kit said, "Okay. Have you in sight. Start a shallow right turn for a rejoin."

Rusty did. Within seconds, Kit was sliding up from inside the turn. He slid into position, stabilized, and Rusty rolled level. Kit dropped back and slowly passed under them, then slid forward again on the left side until he and Rusty could make eye contact.

"Boy, you ARE green. Even my little guy is impressed. You really go through a whole tree?"

"Uh huh, from below. Had to snatch it up and almost made it. Not quite, though."

"Looks like you may have missed all the big branches and stuff. I don't see any dents anywhere, and everything is still attached, even your antennas. Beats me how, though." Kit paused and looked closer, then said, "Maybe it's nothing, but your main gear doors look like they're loose. Not hanging, but there might be extra gap at the leading edge. Or not. I've never seen anybody else's doors in flight before. There's no green there, so maybe it's normal."

"Yeah, I understand. Well thanks. We'd better get back on Ops freq."

"Going."

After he retuned, Rusty hit the switch. "Mike 55, 58 has you in sight. You have it."

Kit answered, as if nothing abnormal had happened, "Roger, you're relieved."

Rusty turned and headed for home, waving to Kit as he turned away.

When they crossed the fence, he said to Dan, "Well, time to bite the bullet." Then Rusty transmitted, "Mike 50, 58.

"Go ahead 58."

"50, 58 may have contacted a tree during the mission. Will you alert the Ops officer?"

"Copy 58, do you have structural damage?"

"Uh, we don't think so, 50. Just some…stains. Will advise."

"Stand by 58."

"Well, here it comes," Rusty said to Dan. "He's fetching Sanderson right now."

But a few seconds later, they heard Major Bridgewater's voice instead. "Mike 58, this is 51. Understand y'all may have pureed some spinach, is that raht?"

"That's affirmative. We passed through some, actually."

"Any damage y'all can eyeball?"

"None as far as I can tell, but I'm still in cruise configuration."

"Ah see. Well, the active runway is currently 09. So I want y'all to set up for a long easy straight in, y'hear? Drop the flaps to takeoff, no more. Then if that works out all raht, drop the gear. If that works fine – and you be damn sure now, y'hear? Then you come in raht easy like. Grease this'n for me and I'll be out there awaitin' fer ya."

Bridgewater's Texas drawl had gotten about thirty times thicker, and Rusty knew it was because he was trying to keep things calm.

"I'll reconfigure now so you'll know how it went."

"That's good thinkin', 58. Go on now."

Rusty lowered the flaps. Normal. Then, with some trepidation, he moved the gear handle to DOWN. He heard the huge aft doors come open, felt the drag, and felt the gear drop into place. The gear handle popped back into Neutral, the hydraulic pressure dropped back to normal, and all three green lights came on solid. Down and locked.

"Mike 51, we have three green, good flaps and nothing squirrelly. I think it's fine."

"Raht fine, 58. All raht, you go on to tower now, and bring that thing on home."

"58 copies. Going to tower now."

"See y'all on the ramp."

Rusty called the tower, asked for a straight in approach to runway zero nine, which they granted and cleared the O-2 to land. Rusty set the power and trimmed the plane, and it flew itself down to the numbers just like sliding down a banister rail. He squeaked the tires and taxied down to the far end. But when he got to the winding, rickety taxiway into the Mike compound, two jeeps were there. Major Bridgewater was in one, and Dave Sanderson was in the other. Both stared hard at Rusty and the plane. Rusty saw Dave's eyes go wide, but when he looked at Bridgewater, the man was actually chuckling!

Rusty trundled in, parked and shut down. Sgt Cramer set the chocks, then stood there with his face a solidly stoic mask. While Rusty took his time turning off the radios and going through the checklist, Bridgewater and Sanderson walked around the plane, pointing at various things. Rusty's heart sank. He was dead meat and he knew it.

When they popped the door open, Sanderson charged at it, his face red and hard. But Major Bridgewater stuck his arm across Dave's chest and stopped him. Then the major sauntered over, still looking up at the wings. When he got to the door, he looked in at Truong, who was grinning and giggling like a lunatic, then at Dan, then Rusty.

"Rusty, ah know you like working this mission, and ah know you are honored to be associated with the Special Forces. But ya needn't go a-paintin' your plane Army style." Then he turned and walked off, grabbing Sanderson by the arm and dragging him along.

"I do not believe it," Dan said. "I simply do not believe that. In any other unit, anywhere in this man's Air Force, you'd be in chains now on your way to a court martial via the Flight Eval Board to yank your wings.

"Don't I know it. I was positive that was my last landing. I was saying goodbye to my wings as I sat here. What do you think just happened, Dan?"

"I don't know. All I do know is I'm going to love working for that man."

CHAPTER SEVEN

I n the Special Forces all-ranks club, Sgt Young started the 16mm projector and the crowd settled in to watch "McClintock" for what must have been the eleventeenth time. The barmaid slithered between the rows of folding chairs, futilely trying to avoid getting her butt pinched. Sitting next to Rusty, Kit asked her for a scotch and water.

"Scot wat!" She yelled to the bar, then turned back to Kit, "Ba-muoi nam." He handed her what passed for money: a quarter and a dime in MPC paper scrip. Then she turned to Rusty. He ordered a Canadian Club and Seven-up, mostly to see how she'd pronounce it. "See-see seben!" He should've known. At thirty-five cents a drink, he'd be plastered before he got to the bottom of his wallet – or her entertaining vocabulary.

She was so close that Rusty could see the stitches in her bra right through the tight white silken sheath of her ao dai. The tiny but seductive mounds were only inches from his eyes, and he stared. She playfully slapped his cheek but smirked slyly. "You dinky dau GI," she pretended to scold, "Look me too much!" Rusty flicked his eyebrows at her in a silent flirt. She giggled but moved on to Danny.

Two rows of chairs were set up, room for a dozen movie watchers. But seldom were that many filled except on the rare occasion that a new movie had been flown in. Most of their supplies were flown in, as the roads across the central highlands were very dangerous for truck convoys. Oddly, the only things that the Army trucked in were heavy supplies like aviation gas, ammunition and booze. With prizes like that, no wonder those serpentine mountain roads were dangerous.

On the screen, John Wayne once again came home to Maureen O'Hara, only to be accused of infidelity. Given his thoughts of only minutes ago while he stared at the barmaid's pubescent bosom, Rusty squirmed a bit in his seat. Kit roared with laughter as G W McClintock, powerful cattle baron, tried to match wits with his wife. Rusty concentrated on O'Hara.

"Kit, I just can't decide," he finally said.

"Decide what?" he said, wiping a laugh tear from one eye.

"Well, some actress or other came to LZ Emerald on a USO tour while I was there, and I didn't catch her name. I thought it might have been her," Rusty said, pointing at the portable screen.

"You're shitting me. Maureen O'Hara? At LZ Emerald? I'm calling bullshit."

"No, I'm half sure it was her. Hard to tell, though. The woman I met wasn't in full movie makeup, and that's the only way I've ever seen Maureen O'Hara."

"How'd she look?" Kit asked.

"Half plowed, a little wrinkly and exhausted." Rusty shrugged. "Guess I'll never know."

"Was she alone?"

"No, Doug McClure was with her – whoever she was."

"No shit? Doug McClure? Did you get to talk to him or anything?"

"Nah. Kit, the only guy he talked to was the bartender, and all he said to him was 'Another double.' He pretty much ignored the rest of us, actually."

"He shoulda met Buchenhardt. I'd have paid to see that battle of egos!"

Rusty almost choked on his drink. "No kidding. I wonder if Hollywood trumps the Citadel?"

"Didn't McClure play a military cadet in some movie? All duded up in some Citadel-style grey wool uniform? I bet Buchenhardt would've looked just like that."

"Yeah, me too. I can almost picture him in one of those tall plumed hats with a saber at his side. You know, that first night he was here, I thought he resembled a Prussian cavalry officer – even before he bragged about going to the Citadel."

"Now that you mention it, that's about how I saw him, too. But I saw him as the horse. Not the head end."

Rusty laughed, and they both turned back to the movie. Before they could enjoy the first of the two hilarious spanking scenes, there was a colossal boom of thunder and the lights flickered.

"Uh oh, here we go again," Danny said. "I don't know about you, but I'm going to make a run for it before it starts pouring again."

"That's a helluva good idea, Dan," Kit said. "I'm outta here, too. Hey, sweetie, one to go!" He waited long enough to get a fresh drink while the rest of them ran for the hootch. Kit slid to a stop outside his door just as huge drops began to pelt down. Dan held the door for him and slammed it shut as Kit ducked inside. Rusty stood at his window and watched, wondering if there'd be another swarm of termites. Sure enough, a short while after the deluge gradually wound down to a drizzle and then stopped, another cloud of dark brown termites rained down. They shed their wings and began frantically searching for whatever it was they sought.

Rusty wondered if his team members were scurrying for shelter as well. He was glad for the rain, because with everyone huddled in their own rooms, nobody had as yet asked him about the tree strike. Whether they hadn't heard yet – which was extremely unlikely – or somebody had told them to lay off, he didn't know. If it was the latter, who'd give that order? Not Sanderson, he had looked mad enough to fire Rusty on the spot. It had to be Bridgewater.

It had been Bridgewater who debriefed Rusty about it. He'd called Dan and him into the Command Post right after they'd secured the plane. Amazingly, there wasn't any damage to it other than green stains. MSgt Cramer had assured them that a good scrub down would fix everything, and Rusty was still standing there shaking his head when word came for both of them to report to Bridgewater. They left Truong pointing and giggling to Cramer, repeating his "POW!" sound and throwing his hands up past his head to imitate the hit.

Bridgewater asked what had happened, and Rusty told the story, emphasizing that it was entirely his own fault. "The big mistake was in getting out too far ahead of the Kingbees, and then cutting the corner too close to that hill," he said. "That's why they lost sight of me. I was flying, and Craig had nothing to do with my decision."

"Does that accurately sum it up?" Bridgewater asked, turning to Dan.

"Well, that's what happened, sir. I'm not sure if there was a mistake made. It was my first insertion, and I have no basis to judge anything."

"That's true enough. By the way, I've already spoken to the Kingbee pilot, and what he says substantiates your story, Naille. So I guess that ties it up." His drawl was completely and mysteriously absent.

Rusty looked at him dumbfounded. Was that all there would be to it? He had to ask. "Is that all, sir? No court martial?"

"Court Martial? Hell, no." Then the drawl came back, "Hell son, we don't shoot a pup for whizzin' on a truck tahr. We jist hose off the damn tahr. That's all we need heah – a hose."

Rusty couldn't help laughing.

Now, standing in his room, he exhaled again in relief. He'd been sure he'd lose his wings for that incident, and his wings meant everything to him. Maybe even more than Mary Beth meant, although that might only be because he'd been away from her for so long.

That thought abruptly reminded him that he still hadn't gotten a letter from her, nor had he been able to get through via a MARS call. He had to remember to try again first thing tomorrow. Rusty vowed to get up as soon as it was light, or even before, to try to get through. His flight to Hawaii was just a few days away.

At six the next morning, he went to the radio room and Sgt Hannah helped get an outside phone line through the Army base at Qui Nhon. Rusty finally got to a MARS radio operator, who told him the airwaves were awful and that getting through to another MARS HAM in the US would be unlikely. Sunspots, he thought. Rusty's shoulders slumped.

The sky matched his mood as Rusty walked back to the hootch. There were thick swaths of fog swirling around, and an impenetrable gray overcast looked like it was hardly more than a hundred feet above his head. He was crossing the center of the red dirt road when he heard his name being called.

"Naille! Hey Rusty!" It was Bridgewater, and as he turned to look for him, Rusty saw him striding rapidly his way from the Special Forces bunker. "You need to scramble. Your team's in trouble. They need to deedeemau outta there soonest – ricky tick."

"You mean take off? In this? You're kidding! It's below IFR minimums, for sure!"

"Yeah, it is. So go VFR. However you do it, you have to go. It's an emergency."

Rusty looked at him, stunned. Take off under Visual Flight Rules when it was below Instrument minimums? Was he nuts?

Bridgewater got closer, and he caught Rusty's expression. "Hey, ya do what ya gotta do, ya know. Now don't just stand there, get your vest and hustle. Truong is on his way. If you get him there, he'll get the team out. He's the best. Kingbees will launch in ten minutes, so hustle."

He wasn't kidding. Rusty started to turn, but then looked back at him. "Wait. If nobody's out there flying, how do you know the team's in trouble?"

Bridgewater slid in the red goo of the road, catching Rusty's arm for balance. "Never you mind, son. We know, is all. Now you just saddle up and get to ridin' ya hear?" Funny how that drawl came and went, but when it came, he was being avuncular – and serious.

Rusty grabbed his vest and carbine, then sprinted around the end of the hootches to get to the ramp. As he passed Kit and Craig's room, they were just coming out to go to breakfast. "Hey, what's up Paul Bunyan? Remember a tree that's still standing?" Kit slapped his thigh.

"Not now, Kit. My team's gone hot. It's boogie time."

"Oh shit. In this weather? Man oh man, good luck!"

Rusty got to the ramp, and realized he had no idea which plane to take. But Mike Lopez was hustling around the third one down the line, so he ran there. "This the one, Mike?"

"Yessir! It's got the best radios. You're gonna need 'em. Jesus, what shitty weather."

"Yeah, I know. Beats me where I'll land. You got a full load of IFR pubs aboard?"

"Uh huh. Enroute charts, letdown plates, approach book, the whole works. You taking an RON bag?"

"Didn't have time to pack. Besides, I think I'll have to come back here. How would I explain Truong?" Rusty said as he glanced at the plane - it could never be called a real pre-flight. But he trusted Lopez. If he said this plane was good to go, it was.

"Jesus, I never thought of that," Lopez said. "Where is he, anyway?"

As Rusty shrugged into his parachute, he saw Truong appear out of a fog patch that obscured the other side of the ramp. What could the visibility be, he wondered, fifty yards? It'd be dangerous to drive in this, and he was about to fly?

Truong slid to a stop on the wet aluminum ramp, shrugged more or less into his parachute, and grinned at me, "We go, Dai-wee? Shit hot!"

Rusty had never heard him use that phrase before, and he had to laugh at it despite his forebodings. "You bet, Truong. We go now. You have code book?"

"No code now, Dai-wee. Team talk big."

Rusty guessed that he meant not only in the clear, but out loud. No whispers or number codes today. "Okay, we go."

Rusty slid across into his seat, and Truong jumped up into the right-hand one. Lopez closed the door and stood there under the wing waiting for Rusty to start the engines. Instead of the usual hand signals, Rusty yelled to Lopez, "Cranking one!" He nodded and Rusty hit the starter for the front engine. It fired, and he immediately hit the rear starter. His hands flew across the various switches, knobs and circuit breakers out of muscle memory.

When the radios whined into life, he called the TOC. Bridgewater answered and confirmed the mission was still on. Rusty motioned to Lopez and he pulled the wheel chock, then scooted out to the front to help guide them out of the revetment. When Rusty was clear, Lopez snapped a very sharp salute. Then he jumped into a jeep and raced off to open the compound's barbed wire gate so Rusty could taxi out. There, he pulled the rocket safety pins and handed them in through the plane's little side window. He stuck his face close and shouted, "Bring these pins back, sir. We're running short of 'em."

Rusty smiled at his off-handed way of wishing them luck

As he wound his way down the twisting perforated plank taxiway, he changed to tower frequency. It took two calls to rouse them, and they replied to the takeoff request with astonishment. "My Fi Ay, Ban Me Too field close. Below IFR minimum."

"I copy, Ban Me Thuot Tower. Repeat, Mike 58 requests immediate takeoff."

"Uh, roger, My Fi Ay. You are clear takeoff runway two seben. Pilot discretion. Wind calm, altimeter two nine ay seben." Utter amazement and disbelief permeated the Vietnamese controller's voice. Rusty knew just what he was thinking: what kind of absolute idiot would take off when it was impossible to land again even if he experienced an emergency right after takeoff?

This kind, Rusty thought, as he shoved the throttles to the wall.

Rusty could see only the painted centerline of the runway. It disappeared in the fog, alarmingly nearby. Between fog patches, he got one glimpse of that titty-pink tower as he sped past, but only the lower half of it. The clouds hid the top half. He rotated, broke ground, and immediately was in complete grayness. Watching the rate of climb, airspeed and heading with his breath held, Rusty waited until he'd climbed well clear of the ground, then shot a hopeful glance at the engines gauges before he slapped the gear handle up. The plane gave its customary sag as the gear doors opened, and the rate of climb needle sagged towards zero climb. Then, the gear was up, and the airspeed crept up. They were climbing again. Rusty didn't breathe until they rose above the height of the several radio towers that jutted up near the outskirts of the city, but then he started to relax a bit. So far, so good, he thought.

Rusty looked over at Truong. As usual, he was grinning, and he nodded in pleasure. If only he knew, Rusty thought to himself. Or maybe he did, but his cultural views of fate reassured him. Either you die today or you don't.

With absolutely no visual cues at all, Rusty droned west and dialed up the TACAN. He unfolded his maps and made a rough guess of the radial and DME of the target area. He planned to drive out to where he knew the ground was relatively flat, then let down until he either broke out of the clouds or he got down to 200 feet above the ground. It seemed like a safe plan. Then Rusty remembered that damned hill. It'd be just his luck to let down and smack right into it.

The one thing he had going for himself was the fact that Ban Me Thuot was almost a thousand feet higher than the target box. Near the border, the land began a long slope down towards the west. In reality, it sloped down from Vietnam's craggy mountain spine all the way to the Mekong River. But right near the border, the broad plateau on which Ban Me Thuot sat dropped off to the plains of Cambodia.

In effect, if the clouds were on the ground at BMT, he might have almost a thousand feet of airspace underneath them by the time he got to the box. At least, he hoped he would.

When the TACAN told him he'd crossed the fence, he keyed the mic, "Mike 50, Mike 58."

Rusty heard a click, and then, "Mike 58, Mike 50, stand by…" Hannah was holding down the transmit key, maybe on purpose, maybe not. But what Rusty heard in the background was Hannah's favorite Crosby, Stills and Nash song. It was "Wooden Ships" and by chance, the lyrics of this blatantly anti-war, post-nuclear exchange protest song were:

> I can see by your coat my friend that
> You're from the other side.
> There's just one thing I gotta know,
> Can you please tell me who won?

Rusty heard the cassette player click off, and then, "Mike 58, go ahead."

For a microsecond, Rusty wondered if Hannah had been playing that song because this team was code-named Cedar Ship, and then he realized that Hannah shouldn't be privy to such information. Still, he wondered of the lyrics were in any way prophetic: who HAD won out there in the Cambodian jungle? Rusty keyed his own mic, "58 at the fence."

"Roger, copy the fence. Kingbees up"

And then Rusty had no time to wonder about the aftermath of a fictional nuclear exchange, or of almost anything else. The Kingbees had somehow managed to get airborne. It was up to their flying skills and his, now. Rusty started his descent.

According to the map, the ground below was already lower than the field at BMT. He was cruising at 6,500 feet, and the runway at Ban Me Thuot East was at 4,750 above sea level. Rusty pulled back the throttles and held his heading as the altitude slowly unwound. At 4,500 indicated, they were still solidly in clouds. He could hardly see his own wingtips, the clouds were so thick. Rain pelted off the windscreen as he passed from shower to shower, the drops exploding into a powder-like puff as they hit the Plexiglas.

The ground beneath them should be about 3,500 feet above sea level, or ASL. He was therefore about a thousand feet above it. Rusty continued to let down, stealing glances out over the nose or out the side window in addition to his constant scan of the instruments. He decided that he'd let down another 500 feet and level off if he hadn't broken out yet. As he expected, the TACAN began to break lock – lose its contact with the ground station. Rusty leveled off and got a final electronic fix of his location. He was still some ten miles from where the team might be when the small red warning flag in the TACAN indicator dial popped up – "OFF" and then he was truly flying blind.

He set the VHF-FM communications radio to the team's frequency, and told Truong to try to contact them. The robin nodded, and pressed his transmit key, whispering a few words. Immediately, he got a reply, not in whispers, but in full high-speed Vietnamese babble. It wasn't a good sign.

Truong listened and then scribbled numbers on his window with his grease pencil. What he wrote looked like map coordinates, and Rusty looked from the scrawled numbers to his map several times to plot the spot. If they were correct, the team was now well north of the hill and their insertion clearing, next to a stream. He asked Truong to relay that guess to the team for confirmation. Yes, they were near a stream, but were moving as fast as they could along it to the east, Truong reported back.

Again, Rusty darted his eyes between his instruments and the map, meanwhile racking his brain to remember the terrain in that area. Then, he pictured it clearly. The team was headed towards an area where the jungle thinned a bit. If they could get there, and if the trees were thin enough, perhaps a Kingbee could extract them with a rope ladder. But it would be chancy.

Rusty turned right, hoping to avoid the granite surprise that lurked next to the original clearing. Hoping for the best, he started to let down again. He hadn't dropped more than a hundred feet when the light from below began to brighten. Suddenly, he saw scattered bits of sopping wet jungle, then things abruptly cleared. Rusty made a sharp, full-circle turn to get his bearings. The dreaded hill was a couple of miles to the west, and it did indeed stick up into the base of the clouds. More luck than skill had kept him clear of it.

But now the real battle began. Suddenly, Rusty realized he didn't know if the Kingbees had a TACAN or not. If not, how could they ever find their way to this vicinity safely? It was no use asking Truong. He wasn't a pilot.

He did the only thing possible: he called base and asked. Hannah hurriedly found Sanderson. Yes, Hannah reported back within moments, the H-34s did have TACAN. What a miracle.

Changing to their frequency, Rusty called, and the lead Kingbee answered immediately. "Kingbee, come to TACAN 290 for 65. Copy?" Rusty dared not give him the TACAN station identifier for BMT, or anyone listening would know that they were flying over Cambodia. But the Kingbee pilot was good. "Copy 290 and 65, Mike 58. We come now."

"Okay, Kingbee, good job." Rusty briefed them to come out to the 50-mile point and then let down .

Truong called the team again. He learned that they'd been discovered and had been evading the enemy all night, moving when the rain covered the sound of their movements. They were soaked, cold and had had neither sleep nor food, but all of them were alive. They had discarded all their gear except for their guns, ammo, canteens and the radio. Even Rusty could hear the fear in the radioman's voice.

Truong talked to them calmly – or what passed for calm in an Asian – and told them help was on the way. Or so he reported to Rusty. "Team okay now. Happy see you, Dai-wee," he summarized.

Within minutes, they arrived in the general area, and Truong reported that the team could hear their engines. Rusty flew to the spot on the map they had given and turned to parallel that stream the team thought they were following.

A sudden excited gabble on the radio told him the news even before Truong could translate: the team had seen them fly over. Rusty deliberately flew past them almost a mile before setting up a wide circle orbit. Best to not circle the team and lead the bad guys right there. Truong told them to stay put and be quiet until the Kingbees arrived.

Five minutes went by, and finally, the Kingbee lead pilot reported that he was now below the clouds and headed their way. Rusty turned toward the spot he thought they'd appear and flicked on his landing lights for a few seconds. Almost immediately, he saw an answering pair of lights almost where he was looking and turned his own back off. The others went off, too.

"Tally ho, Kingbee!" Rusty said into his mic. "Kingbee see you," was the reply.

Quickly, Rusty turned back up the stream, racing to where he thought the team might be. Halfway there, he spotted a series of muzzle flashes and green tracers coming up from the jungle. The bad guys were less than a mile from where the team was, and they now knew what was afoot. "Kingbee, VC shoot at Mike FAC now. Maybe one click from team."

"Okay" was his reply.

"Truong, tell the team the bad guys are maybe a click away. Find a small clearing if they can and be ready to pop smoke." That was a lot of English in one bite. "You bic?"

"Sure, sure, I bic. Okay." He babbled excitedly into his mic. More babbling in reply.

"Team say they hear VC shoot. Close. They find clear place now. Wait."

"Okay, Truong. Let's see if we can warm things up." Rusty armed up his rockets and rolled in on where the muzzle flashes had been. He fired two rockets from each pod, and moments later the four warheads slammed into the jungle at supersonic speed. Huge clouds of white phosphorous smoke billowed upwards. Marking rocket warheads weren't fatal unless they happened to hit someone directly, but chunks of burning phosphorous would get the bad guys attention, as would the bang of the explosions. It worked. More muzzle flashes twinkled from the trees now. Good. Rusty hoped that they were paying attention to him and not the team.

"Kingbee, white smoke on VC, you copy?"

"Kingbee copy. Where team?"

"Stand by, Kingbee, team running. Maybe pop smoke soon."

"Okay"

Rusty turned and rolled in again, this time firing a single rocket from each pod. No telling how long he'd have to keep this up, and he had started out with only fourteen rockets total. He'd already fired almost half.

He heard the team radioman talk again, this time gasping for breath. Before Truong could translate, Rusty saw a thin stream of purple smoke coming from a tiny clearing.

Rusty asked Truong to confirm the team smoke was purple, but he didn't seem to understand the word. No time to worry about it, Rusty thought to himself. Purple was the only smoke he saw. He could only hope it was the team.

"Kingbee, you see smoke?"

"Kingbee see. Team?"

"I hope so, Kingbee. Kingbee cleared down."

"Kingbee go down now."

Rusty rolled into another rocket pass and missed seeing how the helo pilot had done it, but when he looked, the lead Kingbee was sitting on the ground in a clearing that Rusty could swear was smaller than his rotor diameter. As he watched, the helo lifted off, and Rusty distinctly saw leaves and small branches whirling in his rotorwash. Rusty rolled back and fired one more pair of rockets, and as he pulled out of the dive, he heard "Kingbee come up now. Team on Kingbee."

Once again, Rusty turned until he could see. The lead Kingbee was just above the trees and picking up speed. The second helicopter was weaving behind, and Rusty saw a long series of muzzle flashes pour down out of its right-side door. The ground below and behind them – almost exactly where the team had been – was now alight with muzzle flashes and tracers. Rusty jinked and fired his last four rockets into the spot.

Truong turned in his seat and said, "Numba one, Dai-wee! Team all okay. Numba one! Shit hot!" He was literally jumping in his seat with excitement and glee, but Rusty knew the job wasn't over yet. The two Kingbees still had to somehow get back home and land. So did he, for that matter.

Rusty slowed down and followed the two choppers for a few miles. Suddenly, Rusty's stomach knotted. He clicked his mic, "Kingbee okay?"

"Kingbee numba one, Mike. Team all okay."

"How Kingbee go home?"

Silence. Either he didn't fully understand the word 'how' or the helo pilot had just realized he had no way to let down through the clouds and land at Ban Me Thuot. That's what Rusty had realized.

"Stand by Kingbee."

Rusty changed channels and reported home. "Mike 50, Mike 58 inbound with the package. All safe. Say current weather."

"Mike 58, copy package okay. Stand by for weather. Good job."

A minute or so later the radio crackled, "Mike 58, weather sucks. Ceiling 100, visibility one eighth in fog, winds calm. Field reports closed."

"Copy sucks, 50."

For a brief moment, Rusty considered having the two Kingbees fly formation on him while he led them back through the clouds. Even though the field was closed and had no published instrument approach, he might be able to grope his down below official minimum altitude and somehow find the runway. Then he imagined what would happen if the least burble of turbulence tossed one of the Kingbee rotors into his plane. Nor did he know if either

Kingbee pilot could even fly close formation. He dismissed the whole idea. They had both somehow gotten airborne and found their way to the team; Rusty could only hope they were skilled enough to make it home.

No matter what, each of them was on their own. Come what may, it was every pilot for himself.

"Kingbee, you go home. Mike will follow. Good luck."

"Okay, Kingbee go home. Copy."

Rusty switched frequencies again. This time, Major Bridgewater was on the mic. Rusty explained that he had no choice but to release the two Kingbees and hope for the best. Bridgewater agreed. "Why don't ya'll just toodle around a spell and give those two whirlybirds a chance to find their nest. Mebbe the weather'll improve in the meantime. I have an idea to help the Kingbees."

That sounded as good as anything. Rusty still had two and a half hours of fuel. He could loiter at maximum endurance airspeed for a half hour, try one approach to Ban Me Thuot and still have enough gas to get north to Pleiku or even the coast if he had to. He took one last look at the two choppers, still flying along just barely above the trees but headed straight for home, and then climbed up into the clouds. He wondered what Bridgewater's idea for the Kingbees was, but didn't ask. None of his beeswax now, he mused.

He'd been orbiting at 6,000 feet for only about twenty minutes when the radio crackled again, "Mike 58, Mike 51." It was Bridgewater.

"Go ahead 51."

"58, we have two birds in the nest. Y'all can try to find your own perch whenever you're ready." The Kingbees had landed already! How in hell did they do that? "58 go to Pyramid and call for an approach."

"Copy, 51. 58 going."

Rusty dialed in the frequency for the radar control station located in Ban Me Thuot city, then hesitated. It was probably illegal to even be airborne in this weather. He had no clearance, and no flight plan. Oh well, Bridgewater said to do this, so...

"Pyramid Control, Mike 58 at six thousand. Request approach to BMT East for landing."

"Mike 58, roger squawk 1220 and ident."

Rusty turned on his radar transponder, set the code and hit the IDENT switch that would send a signal back to the ground radar.

"Mike 58, radar contact one zero miles west. Be advised BMT East reports field is below IFR minimums at 100 overcast, one-eighth mile viz. Winds calm and altimeter two niner eight niner. Say intentions."

"Two nine eight nine. Mike 58 requests radar vectors to runway zero nine for a circling approach." He was asking to be directed to the vicinity of the field using ground radar. He'd descend to the legal minimum of 200 feet above the ground on a path that would roughly align with the runway. Legally, if he didn't see the runway at that point, he would have to abort the approach and climb back to safety. But he didn't plan to do that. He couldn't legally go below 200 feet unless he had the field in sight. But "field" could be loosely defined, right? Rusty was now accustomed to flying as low as ten feet from the ground, and the area around the field was now as familiar to him as his childhood neighborhood.

"Mike 58, roger. Turn left, heading one zero zero. Maintain six thousand until directed. Be advised, tower is closed. Land at pilot's discretion."

That was even better! Well, in a warped kind of way it was. With the tower closed, he didn't need a landing clearance. Nor could he be reported for violating any flight technicalities. And he fully intended to violate some.

Truong had no clue about all this, and he had been slouched down in his seat since they had re-entered the clouds back in Cambodia. But when Rusty dropped the landing gear and flaps and set the propellers for landing, Truong sat up and looked around. The clouds were still thick and heavy all around them, and nothing beyond the wingtips was visible. Still, he grinned. "We go home now?"

"You bet, Truong. We go home." At least, he hoped so.

"Mike 58, turn left heading zero nine zero. Descend and maintain five thousand."

Rusty made the slight turn as he let the plane sink slowly down to 5,000 feet, where he leveled off. All kosher so far. But he was still in clouds. He could glimpse a few hootches below through occasional thin spots in the clouds. Then there were buildings and streets. The city! He was doing perfectly. Glancing straight down while he also watched his instruments, he saw the manicured rows of low trees that were the tea plantation due west of the field. He was splitting his attention from the instruments to the ground rapidly, and almost missed seeing what he was straining for: a sprawling L-shaped building with a shiny tin roof that he'd flown right over dozens of times in the landing pattern. He knew the runway was only about a half mile ahead. He still couldn't actually see the runway, but he knew exactly where he was. As far as he was concerned, that odd building said "field" loud and clear.

"Field in sight, Pyramid. Thanks!"

Rusty milked the power back a bit and let the plane settle. More. A bit more. The clouds bottoms got ragged and thin. Ten more feet down. He was only about 50 feet off the ground when he actually did see the runway itself, and he was almost over the end of it when he did. Rusty kicked a little bit of rudder and sideslipped to the left, touched the right rudder to straighten out, and pulled the throttles to idle. Squeak! They were home.

Taxiing in through patches of zero visibility was an anticlimax. Truong trotted off in the rain, grinning as broadly as always. Rusty went straight to the TOC to debrief. Major Bridgewater was there waiting, a bemused smile on his face.

"Lordy, Rusty, that was slicker'n a greased blacksnake. Ya done real good. I'da bet we'd lost that team for sure."

"I wasn't sure how I was going to manage it myself. But I lucked out with the weather, I guess. We had just enough room underneath it to work. Getting out there and back were the only rough spots. Which reminds me; how the hell did the Kingbees manage it? I didn't think that bird was IFR rated."

"Well, it ain't, actually. But that pilot is one gutsy mother. His name's Chau Le Quang, and I don't think anybody on God's green earth could fly a Kingbee better'n him."

"Don't short that wingman, either. There were times when I couldn't see my own wingtips. How they kept formation, I'll never know," Rusty said. "But I have to know, what was your little secret for getting them back on the ground here?"

"Oh, that's easy. I called down to Pyramid Control, and they gave vectors to them. When they painted the Kingbees almost over the compound, they gave them the word and the Kingbees just let down real slow until they could see. They broke out about 50 feet above the wire, and only had to move a few yards to land." The drawl was gone again, but the grin stayed.

"I didn't hear any of that on the radio!"

"No, they switched to VHF. Pyramid was able to skin paint them – they don't carry IFF transponders but those rotors make a huge radar target. Besides, you three were the only planes airborne in this whole sector. Pyramid wasn't exactly overwhelmed with traffic."

"How's the team?"

"'Bout like you'd 'spect," he drawled. "Colder'n wetter'n a well digger's ass. Happier, though. The team leader says he didn't think they had a chance. Been chased all night, and what with the weather, well…"

"But how did you know to scramble me? I still don't get that."

"Let's just say that Mike FACs aren't the only folks who 'aren't out there', shall we?" He put a forefinger to his lips.

"Ah," Rusty answered, raising his own finger likewise.

"By the way, don't go getting' all big-headed, but the Mike Force Commander has already put you in for a medal."

"Who, me? A medal? For what?"

"For getting that team back at all, much less uninjured. And the Mike Force Commander is the ARVN commander of this operation. My SOG boss's counterpart, sorta, except that he commands a couple hundred Vietnamese, 'yard and mercenary troops, whereas I only command a few dozen yahoos and misfits like you." He grinned again. "And you'll probably never see that medal. Those things hardly ever make it up one chain of command and down the other intact. Most get disapproved, or just plain lost in the paper shuffle. So instead of that, what say I buy you lunch at the country club?' Bridgewater joked.

Lunch. The very word made Rusty's stomach growl. He'd completely missed breakfast, and was starving. He hadn't even managed to grab any coffee before he launched. Rusty looked at the clock: 10:30. Then he remembered another unfinished chore. "Sgt Young, do you think I could try to get a land line out now? I still need to reach my wife."

"Stand by, sir. It'd be my pleasure. He turned and picked up an ancient black handset that didn't even have a dial. But it must've rung somewhere because Rusty heard him ask for Nha Trang. A few seconds later, he asked for yet another connection. More seconds, and then he talked back and forth with someone. But then he hung up. Rusty's shoulders slumped.

Young spun around. "Sorry, sir. Nothing going out yet. It's all official traffic this time of day. And the atmospherics are still shitty. You might try again this evening or tomorrow morning.

Rusty calculated. Late evening here would be early morning in Chicago. Maybe he could catch Mary Beth before she left for work. "Okay. Yeah, that might work out."

There was still an hour before the chow hall opened, so Rusty walked over to the hootch. He changed into a fresh set of fatigues and poked his head into the big room. Everybody was there, lounging on the two bunks or in chairs. Everyone asked at once how it went, and he filled them in on the whole story. He told them everything except the part about the medal recommendation.

"Shit hot!" Kit, Danny and Sandy said simultaneously when he'd finished. Flip gave a big thumbs up, and Batman stood to shake hands. Buchenhardt, in the corner, mumbled something inaudible.

"Thanks, guys. The weather had me scared shitless, but the team pickup actually went pretty smooth, I thought. Not that big a deal on my side. The Kingbees were the ones with brass balls, believe me."

"Ah, bull," Buchenhardt said. "Those zips can't fly for shit. And they have no balls at all. Run away at the first hint of ground fire."

"Now wait," Flip said. "How can you make that judgment? You haven't flown with Kingbees at all yet."

"Hell, they're all the same. Every ARVN force I've ever worked with has been all blow and no go. They strut around like banty roosters until the first shot gets fired, then they throw down their guns and scream for air support and evacuation." Buchenhardt said, covering his head with both arms in derisive mimicry. "Complete cowards, every one of them."

"Then you've never worked with the Vietnamese Marines, or Rangers, or even our 23rd ARVN here. Who'd you have, Ruff Puffs?" Flip came back.

"Ruff Puffs? What are they?" Danny managed to interject.

Kit turned to him, and half whispered, "Regional Forces Popular Forces. They're sort of a half-trained half-equipped militia. The same idea as our National Guard, but at idle power.. Pretty sad as soldiers but still better than the CIDG or Civilian Irregular Defense Group. Those guys are really sad."

Over Kit's explanation, Buchenhardt loudly answered Flip, "Hell no, they were regular ARVN. I don't think there is such a thing as a good zip soldier anywhere in this country."

"So the NVA who are kicking our butts are poor soldiers? What does that make us?" Batman asked, calmly.

"It might prove what some of us have always known about ROTC pukes," Buchenhardt said, glancing at the rest of them.

"Okay, that does it," Kit said, standing up. "I'm leaving before I break something – like a nose." He spun and left. When the door closed behind him, Buchenhardt snorted, his lip curled into a sneer.

"I wouldn't push things with Kit," Batman said. "You've gone about as far as you can go with him already."

"What's that supposed to mean? Are you threatening me?"

Batman held both palms out, "Not me. I'm too short for that. But Kit's fuse gets shorter every time you light it. Both of you are already in Sanderson's gun sight. You light that fuse again, and the explosion will blow holes in both your records. That's all I meant."

"Then you're as yellow as any zip," Buchenhardt spat.

Sandy now came to his roomie's defense, "If you think Batman and Asians are creampuffs, then I cordially invite you to call any South Korean a coward. Because before you finished the word, he'd cut your balls off and stuff them down your throat. Not that it'd shut you up, apparently."

"Yeah," was Rusty's uninspired addition, as the image of a ROK troop doing just that flashed through his mind.

Lame or not, that was the final word of the interchange. Buchenhardt snorted again and swaggered out.

"Well, that's three enemies Buck'n'fart's made for himself," Craig said.

"Three and a half. I can't stand the sonofabitch, but I couldn't fight him," Rusty said. Then he smiled at Dan, "Buck'n'fart? That's good."

Even Batman grinned, but then said, "He's not my enemy. I don't like him, but I don't feel hate for him. I'll put him in my prayers."

The mention of prayer seemed to dampen the conversation a bit. After a bit, Flip started a line of small talk to clear the air. After a while, they rose and walked down to the chow hall. Bridgewater, Sanderson and Buchenhardt were already there and eating together. Bridgewater saw them come in and raised his voice, "Remember, Rusty, lunch is on me!"

"Oh, thanks a heap…sir," Rusty said, smiling. "You're too generous." They all laughed. The "country club" lunch that day was the usual monkey noodle soup plus fried Spam and cheese sandwiches. Rusty was surprised to find any of the Spam left. The 'yards wouldn't touch cheese, but they simply adored Spam in any guise.

"Well, I guess none of us can ever die now," Rusty mused. "What with all the preservatives in this Spam and the chlorine in the water they use to make the bug juice, we should be germ-free and immortal."

"But is it worth it?" Dan said, making a face at the bleachy fruit drink.

"At least the bread here is good," Sandy said. "You guys are lucky you don't have to eat that awful Army stuff. Canned bread. Yuck!"

"Living off of the local economy does have mixed blessings," Batman said. "This bread and the soup on the one hand, but the dirty lettuce and those horrible peppers on the other."

"What peppers?" Rusty perked up. "I love peppers."

"Oh, not these! These are so hot they peel paint," Batman said. "Turn around and look at the 'yard tables. See those glass jars with the little yellow things in them? Those are the ones. Inedible."

Rusty had scrunched around and now noticed, for the first time, what resembled regular Mason jars on most of the tables on the far west side of the hall. As he watched, one of the 'yards reached in and plucked out a small yellow pepper from the clear liquid. Holding the inch-long conical pepper by the stem, he popped it behind his teeth and tugged the stem free.

"I want one of those," Rusty said "It'll wash away the chemical taste in this bug juice."

"It'll burn your lips off, you mean," Batman said.

Ignoring him, Rusty got up and walked back a few rows of tables to where one of the regular robins sat. He rose and smiled broadly at Rusty, who bowed back politely, pointed at the jar and said, "Nguyen? Okay I have pepper?"

Abruptly, Nguyen's face turned to one of fear and horror. "No no no, Dai-wee! No for GI. No good. No GI!"

Rusty bowed again and insisted. "Yes, yes. Ok for me. Mot?" He only wanted one.

Nguyen visibly squirmed, torn by a cultural inability to refuse a direct request, but plainly unwilling to meet this one. Finally, he bowed slightly and nodded. He raised one finger as if in caution, then pantomimed the practice of holding the stem and popping the pepper off behind his teeth. He did it again until Rusty nodded, and only then did Nguyen fish one very small pepper out of the jar. Rusty took it back to his own table, where he sat down in triumph.

"Ah, now let's see just what these are," he said. He dutifully held the stub of stem and opened his mouth. At the last second, wary of eating the whole thing, he decided to take a small bite of it. Despite Nguyen's careful pantomime, Rusty bit it in half.

For one brief microsecond, Rusty tasted a delightful vinegary sharpness – and then his lips caught fire. It was as if someone had turned a propane torch onto his lips. Rusty's eyes slammed shut as they brimmed with tears. He gasped – or tried to - but even his breath had stopped.

Recalling his first taste of jalapeno peppers back in Texas, Rusty lurched for a slice of bread and crammed it between his lips. Back then, he had still thought of jalapenos as hot. After a year, he could eat jalapenos like popcorn, which was why he thought these 'yard peppers would be merely a tasty condiment.

He was wrong. The little nuclear inferno he had just stuck between his lips made a jalapeno seem like cotton candy. Rusty held his hand over his mouth until the bread took effect, then gasped in air. "Ack!" he rasped. "Holy shit!"

Rusty finally took his hand down, and Sandy's eyes went wide. "Jesus, Rusty, you have blisters on your lips!"

Dan nodded to confirm the assessment. Batman said, kindly but with resignation, "I tried to warn you, didn't I?"

Rusty managed to chew up the tip of the thing and swallow. He was startled to realize that behind the white-hot pain in his lips, the pepper itself had been tasty! He instantly understood the importance of the stem-popping act: you had to keep the pepper's volatile juices off your tender lips, but if you did, the things were good. Not for the faint of heart, certainly, and not for anyone who thinks Tabasco sauce is hot, but for a true pepper lover, darn good. To the utter astonishment of all, he popped the remaining half of the thing behind his teeth and tugged out the stem.

Nguyen rushed over, having watched the commotion in horror. He looked at Rusty's blistered lips and went white. If he had had a sharp knife, he might have committed suicide on the spot, but he simply wrung his hands and muttered to himself in anguish.

Rusty turned to him, and between gasps for cool air, said, "No sweat, Nguyen. No sweat. Numba one!"

But Nguyen was so flushed with guilt that Rusty knew there was only one way to mitigate the poor man's loss of face. Rusty got up and walked to the 'yard table, plucked another pepper from the jar and ate it – this time following the stem-plucking routine carefully. Two of the little bomblets pressed right at the limit of his abilities, but it was the only way to relieve Nguyen's distress. "See, Numba one!" was all Rusty could manage to gasp.

Back at the pilots' table, everyone stared at him in silence. Finally, Dan said, "I cannot believe you did that. Twice!"

Before Rusty could answer, he had to get something down on top of the growing ball of lava in his stomach. He wolfed his own Spam sandwich, then reached over and grabbed what was left of Batman's. When the bread and grease had at last taken the edge off the pain, Rusty wheezed, "See, I was right. No chlorine taste now."

"Son, yore gonna regret eatin' them ice cream peppers, Bridgewater chuckled across at Rusty.

"Ice cream peppers? They were nothing like ice cream, sir."

"No, it didn't look lahk it. But if what I hear is true, tomorrow when yore on the shitter, you're gonna wish you'd had ice cream for dessert, 'cause yore gonna be a-thinkin' 'Hurry up ice cream!'"

Later that day, Sgt Hannah excitedly found Rusty and said, "Lieutenant Naille, you may be in luck, I think I can get you a MARS line right now! Come over to the radio room while I try."

As Rusty watched, Hannah seemed to go through the same series of connections that Young had tried earlier. But this time, Hannah finally beamed a smile, and held the handset out. "When you get through, remember that you're talking through two HAM operators between you and your wife. You have to say 'Over' between sentences, so they know to switch from transmit to receive. Tell your wife to do that, too."

Rusty nodded and took the handset. "Hello? Mary Beth?"

"Stand by one second, sir, they're still trying to connect at the other end," said a male voice. Distantly, Rusty heard a ring tone then his mother-in-law's voice. Before he could say anything, a second male voice said, "This is a radio relay call from Southeast Asia. Will you accept the call?"

Rusty heard the socially proper woman say, "I beg your pardon, do I know you?"

He had the awful feeling that she was about to hang up out of suspicion, but she said, "Oh, I see. Yes. Just a moment…"

A few moments later, he heard Mary Beth say, breathlessly, "Rusty? Rusty? Is that you?"

"Just one moment, m'am. Have you made a MARS call before?"

"Yes, yes I have. Um, over."

The second male voice then said, "Go ahead, Lieutenant. He heard two clicks, and said, "Mary Beth, it's me. I love you, but I have to know first: have you gotten my letters? Do you know about Hawaii? Uh, Over." Two more clicks.

"Yes, of course, why? She said, and then after a short pause, "Over."

"I haven't gotten any letters from you in almost two months. I was afraid I'd show up and you wouldn't know I was even coming. Over"

"No mail? Again? Oh no! Um, no, everything is fine. I'm getting all your letters. I arrive about an hour after you. I can't wait to see you. I miss you so much. Uh, over."

"Me too, honey, me too. I want to kiss you all…over," Rusty said, feeling clever and hoping not to get cut off for vulgarity. But they talked for another minute or so before one of the male voices cut in.

"Sorry, Lieutenant, your time is up. More GIs waiting. Five more seconds."

Mary Beth said, crying, "I love you!" and Rusty managed to say, "See you in a few days!" before there was a click and a hiss and the line went dead. But he didn't think she heard it because she hadn't said 'over' and the connection hadn't been switched her way again.

Rusty stared at the handset as if Mary Beth had just been right there inside it. It was a wrenching feeling somehow to suddenly hear her voice again after all these months, and then have it click out of existence again. He abruptly felt a bit disoriented and light-headed. Hannah reached out and took the phone from his fingers, "Finished, sir? Did you get through?" As if he hadn't been sitting right there hearing this half of the conversation. It was a very gentlemanly and kind pretence, and Rusty felt immediate warmth towards him for it.

Rusty continued the fiction, "Yes, yes I did. The guys in between were super. Explain that MARS thing again, will you?"

Clearly delighted to expound on his area of expertise, Hannah swiveled in his chair and leaned forward, elbows on knees as his face brightened. "Well, sir, it works like this: Starting from a land line connection at this end, you get connected to a volunteer HAM radio operator somewhere on this side of the world. Maybe that's some off-duty GI in Saigon or a civilian. It could even be some Aussie or somebody in Japan via an oceanic cable. Anyway, that Ham operator fires up his set and tries to reach another HAM stateside. If everything lucks out, that second HAM will be near where you're calling. So then that guy patches his radio to a phone line and dials your party. When everything's connected, you're speaking to your party, but relayed by radio between those two HAMs. You see?"

"You mean, those HAM guys volunteer to do these relays? They don't get paid for it?"

"No, sir, not even the guy at the other end; he might have to make a long-distance call to reach your party, too." He shrugged, "They just love doing it to help, sir. Radio people are good folks."

"They are, Hannah; they sure as heck are." Rusty stood up and patted him on the shoulder as he turned to leave. "All of 'em."

In the big room, Flip was stretched out on his bunk reading, and Kit was strumming his guitar. Batman perused the library of paperback books, hoping to find something different. There were almost 500 of them on handmade shelves all around the room. Rusty was still pumped up from his call.

"Hey guys, I finally got through to my wife on a MARS call! She does know about R&R after all. Man, what a relief!"

Flip lowered his book, "Hey, that is good news. Shit hot!"

"The MARS connection worked, huh? Remarkable," said Batman. "I've never been able to get a whole call through myself. Usually, it gets cut off in the middle or the connection just dies."

"Me too," Kit said. Those HF radio connections depend so much on the condition of the ionosphere that you never know when your skip path will fade."

"Your who?" Rusty said, still fascinated by how the system worked.

"Well, you know that all our regular radios are line of sight, right?"

Rusty nodded.

"Okay, unlike Ultra High frequency – UHF; or Very High Frequency – VHF; plain old High Frequency is at a much lower frequency. That means longer wavelengths. Well, those long HF waves bounce off the electrified layer of the upper atmosphere. They can come back down hundreds or thousands of miles away. Sometimes, they can bounce more than once. That's how HAMs all over the world can talk to each other. Because of the bounce."

"I get it," Rusty said, envisioning a kind of global billiards, with radio signals bouncing around the world. "Go on."

"Well, the problem is that you never know when the ionosphere is going to pulse or buckle or wobble, and that changes the bounce. And you lose your connection. It's worse when there's a lot of sunspots, because they make the ionosphere squirm like a worm on a hotplate," Kit said.

"How come you know all this stuff Kit?" Flip said.

"Oh, I dabbled in it when I was a kid. I was studying for a HAM license and all. I learned Morse code and radio theory. Even made a couple of Heathkit radios. But then I discovered girls," he grinned through his mustache. "Much nicer waveforms on girls."

"Yeah, but breaking their code is a lot harder," Batman said.

"I can't wait to get a little waveform bounce," Rusty grinned lasciviously.

"You have to get to Saigon first," Flip said. "You think any MAC birds will be able to get in here before your flight to Hawaii?"

Rusty hadn't even thought of that. He had orders and a ticket from Ton San Nhut airbase to Hawaii. But how would he get to Ton San Nhut? Rusty blanched.

"Oh shit! I don't know." Rusty automatically looked out the window at the heavy gray overcast. Military Airlift Command flew cargo missions into BMT three times a week, but none would be able to land unless the weather lifted. He could be stranded here and miss his flight altogether. Mary Beth might be the one to be alone in Hawaii. What a cruel twist of fate!

Rusty left and hurried to Sanderson's room. "Dave, you there?"

He invited Rusty in. "If you're coming to finally explain your tree strike to me, don't bother. You've managed to wipe out your 'oh shit' with a giant 'attaboy.'" He looked at Rusty poker-faced.

"Uh, no. That wasn't it at all." Rusty had forgotten that he still might be on Dave's shit list. Would Sanderson punish him by somehow preventing Rusty from making his R&R connection? Was there a vindictive side to the man? If so, this was a perfect chance for him to indulge it. "I just realized that I might have a problem getting to Ton San Nhut to catch my flight out." Rusty blurted, shrugging lamely.

Sanderson looked up, and the look on his face said, "Why is he bothering me with such a pissant problem?" But his mouth said, "Hmmm. When is your flight out?"

"Uh, in four days. Early morning, so I need to be there the night before just to be safe," Rusty said, starting to feel relieved.

"Let me work it. Check with me later today."

"Yessir! Thanks, Dave," Rusty said, exhaling in profound gratitude. He turned to leave before the ops officer could bring up that other topic, but he wasn't quick enough.

"Just a second."

Rusty turned back, knowing what was coming.

"Do you know how much you disappointed me the other day?"

"Yessir," Rusty said, looking sheepishly at the floor.

"I put my trust in you to be a teacher, and the very next trick out of the hat, you came within an ace of killing yourself and two others. Not to mention losing an airplane and completely ruining a whole intel mission. Is there anything you can say for yourself?"

"No, sir. I just flat screwed up. I can see in hindsight just how and when, but at the time, nothing seemed to be going downhill until I was in a box with no way out."

He nodded. "That's the lesson I hoped you would have learned: the primrose path ends in thorns. Is that clear?"

"Oh, yes," Rusty said, looking up again. "That is a very clear image. So is that wall of green I hit. I won't forget it."

"Good. Okay, get out of here."

Rusty wasted no time in doing that. He went back to the big room.

"Flip, have you been on R&R?"

"Yeah, I got back just before you arrived here. Why?"

"What did you take with you? I mean, clothes and stuff."

"Oh. Well, you won't need more than two uniforms. Fatigues and a Class C set for travel to and from. Just civvies for your time there. Take your camera for sure. That's about it."

"That'll be a light bag. I don't have many civvies. Just a pair of jeans and a polo shirt. Come to think of it, I don't have a bag except for my duffle."

"That's no sweat." Flip reached under his bed. "Here's a B-4 bag you can borrow. I have a few shirts you can use, too. Or just buy some. Anything you have will look out of place in Hawaii, anyway. Just get some shorts and Hawaiian shirts there. It's like wearing a different kind of camo," he grinned.

"Yeah, I guess it is," Rusty said grinning back. "Thanks."

Rusty was pushing open the door to his own room with Flip's B-4 bag in hand when Dave Sanderson came out of his room. "What are you, psychic?"

"What do you mean?"

"Get packed. There's a C-130 scheduled to land here in a few hours, and if it does you're going to be on it when it leaves. No sense you sitting here if we're grounded for weather, and this might your only chance of getting to Saigon. So hustle."

"You bet! I'll be ready to go in half an hour!"

"No need to get in that much of a hurry, but be ready to go if I call you. Make sure you wear a uniform with name and rank. And don't forget to put copies of your orders in your bag, too. I'll cut you some general in-country travel orders so you can catch a ride anywhere on anything moving. That'll get you back here afterwards, too," Dave said.

"I copy all that. Thanks again, Dave. I owe you."

He rolled his eyes. "Of course you owe me, dipstick. I still haven't told these guys about your student pilot days at Laredo. I'll just add this to the growing list."

Rusty dropped his head in mock shame as Sanderson went on in a mellower tone, "Say hello to Mary Beth for me, will you? She's better than you deserve."

"Thanks, I will. She knows that already. Me, too. How's, uh…Judy, by the way?"

"Just fine. I'll be seeing her soon myself. In fact, I'll be leaving for my R&R while you're gone."

"Where are you going?" Rusty had visions of bumping into him yet again in Hawaii, just like he had at almost every post he'd been to since Laredo.

"Sydney. We've both been to Hawaii already, but we want to see Australia."

"Oh, well, give Judy my best then." It felt a bit awkward for Rusty to be social with Dave. Despite their being rough equals at aerial gunnery school at Cannon AFB in New Mexico, he'd also been Rusty's T-37 instructor before that at Laredo and was now Rusty's direct boss, after all.

Dave nodded and went back to his room. Rusty got out a clean Class C uniform and low-quarter shoes, packed his own few civilian clothes and the two shirts Flip had loaned him. As he packed, it suddenly struck him that all his underwear and T-shirts were now a pinkish orange color instead of white. Then he held up his original fatigues with name and rank patches on them. Compared to the clothes he'd been wearing every day, they were still green. He hadn't noticed how red everything else had become. Vietnam was apparently a permanent part of his clothes, he mused. Maybe it was part of more than just the clothes.

As he packed, Rusty thought of all the bizarre things he had seen and done since his first partial tour in Vietnam, how much death and destruction he'd seen and even caused. He marveled at how he'd almost wet his pants that first time he'd been shot at, and how he'd almost done it again when he'd been nearly shot down flying with the Special Forces agent "Joe" back at Emerald.

What a change between then and just yesterday when hundreds or even thousands of shots had been fired at him – and he'd thought nothing of it. It was routine now to have someone trying to kill him. How can a man get to the point where such a thing is routine? What does it mean when killing *them* is just as routine?

And yet, I am still me, he thought: I can follow myself through every moment of the path between being a hotshot student pilot up to this moment. Somehow, somewhere I cannot pin down, I changed. I'm a very different person now. It's all gone just like that last insert had: everything I've done seemed right at the time, but I still found myself smacking into a tree. If my life has been a primrose path, just how close am I to those clutching thorns? Will I someday look back and know that everything I've done was a colossal screw up – and I never even saw it coming?

Rusty shook himself. Snap out of this, Rusty. You're on your way to Mary Beth. This is no time to be morose, he told himself.

Through the wall, he could hear Kit belting out a song: The House of the Rising Sun. Ah, yes, he half-smiled to himself. "It's been the ruin of many a poor man, and Lord, I know I'm one." Well, if a little "it" will ruin one, let this one be ruined!

Before long, Rusty was sitting in a jeep in front of the tiny MAC aerial port under the pink tower. Mike Lopez was in the driver's seat, and he heard it before Rusty did. "One thirty on final," he said, his head cocked a bit to the side. "On 27."

Rusty turned to look over his right shoulder, and as he did, a dark patch in the clouds got darker, then abruptly brighter. Landing lights popped out of the bottom of the overcast, materialized into a hulking C-130, and settled directly to the runway. The roar of four turboprop engines rose to a scream as the pilot reversed thrust, and then settled into a pervasive hissing roar. The dripping green plane taxied in to the ramp like an amphibious dinosaur coming ashore. It did not shut down its engines.

They watched as the rear ramp opened and a crewmember jumped down. In short order, two pallets of plastic-wrapped boxes and odd shapes slid down and were carted off by ground workers with a huge olive-drab forklift. The plane's crewmember pointed at them questioningly. Rusty waved, and the man motioned back to hurry. As Rusty got close the crew chief yelled, "You our pax, sir?" Rusty nodded as he wrestled with the awkward B-4 bag. The other man reached for it. "Okay, climb aboard. Sling seats are along the port side, sir. Strap in while I get this stowed."

By the time Rusty had strapped into an empty sling seat alongside three other passengers, the ramp had closed with an electric whine. The seats were forward of the main landing gear wells, and their backs were only inches from the rotation arcs of the massive propellers. The scream at idle power was deafening. As he scurried by, dragging an intercom wire from his headset, the loadmaster dropped a little cardboard pack of earplugs into Rusty's lap. He eagerly compressed the yellow foam plugs and stuffed them deeply into his ears.

In moments, he could feel the plane moving. He could see only through a narrow slit between two pallets in front of his knees, but that view included the tiny porthole of a window on the opposite side of the fuselage. Through this keyhole-like view, Rusty saw the tree line that marked the northern edge of the airfield. The view swung wildly as they turned first onto the taxiway, and then again as they entered the midpoint of the runway for the short trip to the takeoff end. He saw his tiny compound slide by, or rather the wire-topped earthen berm that formed its safety perimeter. Just as he noticed the serpentine path they used to taxi into and out of the compound, the view careened wildly again as the plane's pilot spun the plane around. They sat still while he completed his pre-takeoff checks; but before long, Rusty felt a lurch when the pilot released the brakes. Immediately, the engine roar wound up through several octaves and dozens of decibels. They slid sideways in their flimsy seats as the massive plane accelerated. Rusty felt the rotation for liftoff, and the porthole view abruptly changed to dark grey. He uncrossed his fingers. He really was on his way to Hawaii.

They made one more landing stop somewhere - Rusty hadn't a clue where - and unloaded the last two pallets. Again, the engines never stopped, and they were soon airborne again. Only a few minutes later, it was obvious they were landing yet again. Rusty wondered if something was wrong, but the busy loadmaster never got close enough as he checked things in the cargo compartment for Rusty to shout a question. Moments later, they thumped down and taxied. Eventually they stopped, and then with a grateful whoosh almost like a swimmer blowing air after a long dive, the engines wound down to a stop. Oddly, the roar in Rusty's ears and the hammering vibration in his spine did not stop, but they were merely the "afterimage" of the din that had pounded him for the last hour or so. He struggled up out of the painful strap seats and rubbed his legs where the metal support bar behind his knees had cut off almost all blood circulation.

"Scenic downtown Ton San Nhut, gateway to Tu Do Street and points south," said the loadmaster jovially. "End of the line. In more ways than one," he added, only half in jest. The others – two Army grunts carrying their M-16s and an Army helicopter pilot in his two-piece flight suit – merely filed out without a response. Rusty smiled at the loadmaster. They were fellow Air Force types, after all. The loadmaster unstrapped the B-4 bag and handed it to Rusty. "Passenger Assistance is right inside the terminal, sir. In case you need a ride or something."

Rusty thanked him and waddled down the ramp, the damn B-4 bag banging into the back of his calves at every step. He hoisted it up onto his shoulder to cross the wet ramp. Fortunately, it wasn't raining at the moment and the cloud ceiling looked much higher here than it had been at Ban Me Thuot. Rusty slogged inside and found the counter. The clerk checked his orders, noted that the lieutenant appeared to be two days early for his contract flight to Hawaii and suggested he check in at the Visiting Officers' Quarters. A regular bus ran by there, leaving from out front every ten minutes. It was almost like civilization, Rusty thought, if you could ignore the overwhelming and pervasive odor of diesel and jet exhaust, decaying fish, sewage and something else unrecognizable but nauseating.

He went outside and waited. Shortly, a dark blue bread truck pulled up and an airman two-stripe in the driver's seat slid open the door. "VOQ," Rusty told him. "And tell me when we get there. It's my first time here."

"Yessir, happy to. Where you from?"

"Here in country, you mean?"

The airman nodded.

"Ban Me Thuot."

His eyebrows knitted. "Never heard of it. What you fly?" He had glanced down and seen Rusty's wings.

"O-2. A FAC."

"Jeez Louise, you mean those little puddle jumpers? You run airstrikes and stuff, right?"

"Uh, yup, that's it." He didn't dare tell the man what they really did – or where.

"Holy cow, I've never met a FAC before. You ever been shot at?"

"Oh, not above seven or eight thousand times," Rusty smiled to himself. The driver was already pulling away and was watching the millions of pedi-cabs and jitney taxis that swarmed everywhere. "This month," Rusty added, for effect.

The driver slammed on the brakes, right there in traffic, and spun around to look at Rusty. "You're pulling my leg, aren't you sir?"

Rusty reflected a bit, and then answered, "No, not at all now that I think back. If anything, it's way low. I'm certain I've had lots more than a thousand rounds fired at me during just one mission, and I've already flown more than a hundred missions."

The airman's jaw dropped wide open. "Jeez Louise," the man murmured over and over again all rest of the way to Rusty's temporary quarters. When he pulled up there and stopped, Rusty grabbed his bag and stepped off. As the door slid shut, Rusty heard him say "Jeez *fucking* Louise!"

Rusty checked in and got a room. The clerk looked at him a bit funny, but didn't say anything, and gave directions to the barbershop, laundry and O'Club. The O'Club made sense, but why in the world did he mention those other two, Rusty wondered. He flung the bag onto the bed in his room – which had an air conditioner roaring away in the window! It felt freezing cold to him, and he turned the thing off. An honest to God air conditioner, he marveled. And the bed had ironed sheets! Jeez Louise!

Without further ado, Rusty pronounced it happy hour and walked straight to the O'Club bar. He already knew what he wanted: a good martini. The hired 'yard they had for a bartender at BMT could mix any liquor with any mixer, but he was totally clueless about more sophisticated cocktails like martinis.

Before Rusty could get this bartender's attention (Rusty all but stared at his heavily starched white shirt and black bow tie) a full colonel on the next barstool spun towards Rusty and wrinkled his nose.

"Lieutenant, it is customary to bathe before you enter the Officers' Club."

Rusty turned to him in amazement, but before he could answer, the colonel looked him up and down with disgust.

"Your uniform is filthy, you are grossly in violation of both haircut and facial hair limits. And that," he pointed at Rusty's red neck bandanna, "is completely unauthorized. How do you explain yourself?"

Rusty stared at him. He'd never met one, but the man before now had to be a certified REMF, a Rear Echelon Mother Fucker: the kind of high-ranking clueless prig who thought a regulation haircut and shiny shoes would win the war.

"Sir," Rusty said, just to get it out of the way up front, because he never intended to honor the man's rank again, "this is as clean as our uniforms get in the field. This is as clean as *we* can get in the field. I'm a FAC, and no fighter pilot I've ever controlled and no ground pounder I've ever saved has complained about my haircut or mustache. Furthermore, *this* is not only authorized, but is an assigned part of my unit's gear." Rusty lied about the bandanna, but this pretentious, fatuous weasel had gotten his dander up.

"And in precisely what misbegotten unit would this be?" he said, challenging right back.

"MAC...V...SOG," Rusty said, very slowly, and turned away. Let him chew on that.

The REMF didn't respond. He harrumphed but made it a point to stare at Rusty's nametag before he spun off his stool and stomped away. Rusty had the feeling he'd go straight to a phone and try to track him down. Let him try, Rusty snorted to himself.

Alerted by the commotion, the bartender hovered expectantly across the bar from Rusty, eyebrows arched in bemused anticipation. Rusty ordered, and watched the bartender perform a miracle. He took a chilled martini glass and swirled a spoonful of dry vermouth in it before dumping it out. Then he reached into a small freezer and took out an ice-rimed bottle of Tanqueray gin and quickly filled the glass. He slid it across and smiled, "On me, fly boy."

It was the distillation of alcoholic nectar. Rusty quaffed it with almost religious awe while the bartender watched Rusty's face - his own enjoyment plainly visible. Before Rusty had even finished, the barman took a fresh glass and made another. "Your drink, sir. That'll be fifty cents."

Rusty laid limp MPC notes on the bar, and added a dollar to the tip jar. After a while, after he had reverently sipped away the second glorious martini, Rusty waved for the bartender again. He came over, but instead of mixing another of those bits of Nirvana, leaned across and said, "You know Lieutenant, perfect martinis are like perfect breasts: one is obviously insufficient, but three are entirely too many." Rusty laughed, tipped him again, and left. The REMF colonel had never returned.

Rusty ate in the dining room and then went back to his room. He took off his fatigues and sniffed them – they weren't nearly as smelly as the damned air here - and slid between those crisp cool sheets. The next thing he knew, it was mid-morning.

A long hot shower in a private stall continued the unworldly feeling. Rusty shaved and put on the khaki pants and shirt of his Class C uniform. The laundry said they couldn't guarantee getting the fatigues back to him overnight, so Rusty took them back to the room uncleaned and tried the barbershop. The barber put him in his chair and cut Rusty's hair to regulation standards without even a word of instruction, but did ask about the mustache. Rusty debated it. He had just barely gotten it long enough at the corners to get a crisp full turn handlebar, and he was proud of it. But it was also was far beyond Air Force limits. Hell, Hitler would've just barely passed Air Force mustache limits, Rusty groused to himself. But he reconsidered, and let the barber trim it until it no longer extended beyond the corners of his mouth. Two snips and two smoothly waxed curls lay on the cloth tied under his chin. Oh well, they'd grow back – eventually.

And it might keep the REMFs off his back.

He bought two more civilian shirts and a pair of nice slacks in the BX, plus two six-packs of new underwear. He threw all the old ones into the trash basket in his room, but took one back out to show to Mary Beth. She'd get a laugh out of him wearing pink underwear, he mused.

It rained the rest of the day, and Rusty sat in the VOQ day room watching Armed Forces television and thumbing through several weeks' worth of Stars and Stripes. The TV was wall-to-wall officially massaged "no news is bad news" pap, but it was the first television he'd seen in months. It was awful. The "teaser" came on for tonight's movie…John Wayne in "McClintock." Naturally.

That night, he was so keyed up to see Mary Beth that he hardly slept at all. He tossed and turned and finally drifted off, but woke again hours early. He got up. A hot shower and shave followed by a huge breakfast (real eggs!) got him going. It was still raining, and Rusty spent the day reading a dog-eared paperback in the day room, but his mind was so taken up with excitement that he had no idea what he had read. Finally, he got his bag, checked out and waited for the blue shuttle bus. It was a different driver, and this one never spoke a word. At the terminal, Rusty sniffed. Either the rain had washed the air a little cleaner or he was getting used to the stench.

At the airline counter, the civilian clerk was too bored to make eye contact, much less smile. He riffled through Rusty's ticket and travel orders perfunctorily and stuck a claim tag on the B-4 bag. He wrote a few numbers on the ticket, handed them back and said, "Next." On the way to the gate, Rusty checked what he'd written. He'd been assigned an aisle seat back near the smoking section. Rusty asked the gate clerk to re-assign him farther away from the smokers, but was told it'd be easier to swap seats after takeoff. Too much trouble for the clerk, Rusty guessed. More REMFs of a different flavor, he thought to himself. Finance clerks changed the passengers' MPC scrip for real US greenbacks and then locked all of them into a room made of chain-link fence from floor to ceiling. Armed guards outside the wire made sure nobody could pass the hard currency to anyone. The sight of real dollar bills hit Rusty strangely. He hadn't realized until then how completely alien it was to be here, how far removed from every single aspect of his previous life. It might as well be another planet. And he instantly knew why all the Army grunts referred to the US as "the world."

When he saw TWA printed on the ticket, he had hoped this would be a regular commercial flight. Rusty held to that hope until the last moment. When they finally boarded, it was apparent this was yet another government contract flight: the seats were crammed as close together as could accommodate the human frame. Provided those frames were midgets – and anorexic.

After the usual silly emergency briefing, they took off into the sunset. The cabin crew announced that they'd be served dinner in about two hours, and that flight time to Guam would be about seven hours. Rusty was already tired from his excited and sleepless night, but decided to stay awake until after dinner. He'd stupidly forgotten to bring anything to read, and the time passed as slowly as if it were a cosmic-sized hourglass, the individual grains of sand falling across the light-years.

One refueling and fourteen hours later, Rusty's plane taxied in to the terminal in Honolulu. By now, unable to sleep, dehydrated and painfully cramped, he looked like a hobo. Two salt-crusted stains spread from under his arms, and a long oblong stain stretched down from his neck. The wrinkles in his uniform pants had set into accordion folds all across his lower stomach.

Nonetheless, as he left the plane, he was startled to have a beautiful young Hawaiian woman come up to and place a loop of flowers around his neck. Smiling as if Rusty was the only one she were there to meet, she kissed him on the cheek before moving with equal eagerness to the next GI.

Rusty retrieved his luggage, wandered to the concourse where Mary Beth's plane was scheduled to arrive, and collapsed onto a bench. From deep inside a fog, he dreamt he heard Mary Beth's voice excitedly calling his name. It was a wonderful dream until his shoulder shook. He jerked awake, and there she was. The moment he lifted his head, she pulled back as though he'd been a snake.

Then, amazement plain on her face, she looked closer and said, "No, it is you, but what is that thing?"

"Huh?" Was his groggy, disoriented reply.

"That thing on your lip. Oh who cares? It's you, and that's enough." They hugged and kissed for several minutes while Rusty gradually came to life and the present. He revived enough to help collect her bag and they got a cab to Fort DeRussy, where he had to report in order to sustain the fictional military purpose of his orders.

At the Fort, the Army clerk in the Orderly Room took one glance at the orders and said, "Welcome to Hawaii, Lieutenant. I imagine you need transport to your room first thing?" He'd certainly seen thousands of sex-starved couples like them, and knew full well what R&R was really for. The clerk called the hotel where Mary Beth had made a reservation, but they claimed to have no record of any such reservation. It was mid-afternoon now, in one of the most crowded vacation spots on earth, and the clerk said there probably were no rooms anywhere. Rusty let out a weird, whining growl from frustration, exhaustion and sudden overwhelming anger. May Beth again looked at him as though his body had been taken over by a space alien.

The clerk said, "Just wait a moment, sir. Let me call somewhere." He dialed a number, and spoke in hushed words for a second. There was a pause, and then he said, "I understand, but this is an R&R. From Vietnam." Another pause, and he hung up. Rusty braced himself for the bad news, but the clerk smiled and said, "You have a room for four nights at the Holiday Inn Waikiki. It's just down the street. I'll have someone drive you and your bags there right now."

Rusty was too groggy to be coherent, but Mary Beth gushed her thanks and even bent down to kiss the clerk. There were tears of gratitude in her eyes. The clerk blushed.

They got to the hotel, registered, and the bellman put their bags on a trolley before he led them to the elevator. He had also apparently dealt with many R&R couples before, because he opened the room, placed the bags by the wall, and immediately left, smiling broadly. He didn't even hang around for a tip.

They woke each other some time later. It was dark outside, but only mid-evening by the clock. Rusty went in to shower and was shocked at his own image in the mirror. He was red-eyed, haggard, and his skin had a sickly yellow cast. His hair was matted and stringy. Staring, he couldn't understand how Mary Beth had even recognized him in the airport. He hardly recognized himself. But a hot shower, shampoo and shave improved things. While Mary Beth showered, he got out his civvies. When he picked up his hastily discarded uniform, he reeled back. It reeked, and so did the set of fatigues that he next pulled out of the B-4 bag. Had his nose gotten so inured to Vietnam that he hadn't even noticed? Rusty wadded the mess up and dressed.

Mary Beth came out of the bathroom, sniffed and said. "Whew! What IS that?"

Rusty pointed to the ball of clothes, and she bent to it. "Wow. Is that what Vietnam smells like?"

"You mean that's not all from me?"

"No, I know what you smell like. There's some of that in there, as I'd expect, but there's a lot more in that smell than just a sweaty man. Lots more."

"I guess so. I must be used to it. But yeah, that's what Vietnam smells like. Except that this is but the faintest, dimmest, fragmentary whiff of the real thing."

"Yuck."

"I think that pretty much describes everything about Vietnam in one word, yes."

"Let's get that mess to the concierge for cleaning. I want it out of this room."

"I do, too. Give to it to the what?"

"The concierge," she said. He looked blank. She went on, "He's the hotel's do-everything guy. Reservations, tickets, helpful info, whatever. He arranges things. Haven't you ever heard of a concierge?"

"Nope. Must be a city mouse thing. Us country mice just does things ourselves."

"Okay, hayseed. You want to wash those things yourself?"

"Uh, no. Let's find that guy. And something to eat, too. I'm starving."

"Good plan, country mouse. You look a wreck. Maybe a decent meal will help."

They dropped off the foul uniforms with the concierge. To his credit, he managed to accept them without cringing or turning his head away. Then they headed to the hotel dining room. They'd hardly been seated and given menus when a waitress walked briskly up and set a huge, frosted glass of frothy milk in front of Rusty. He looked at it and at her in amazement – for about a half second – then wolfed down the entire glass in one swallow. Mary Beth stared at him, then looked to the beaming waitress for an explanation.

"The house wishes to welcome you for your R&R, with our thanks."

With milk in his mustache, Rusty said, "Thanks for what?"

"Why, for going to Vietnam. Or for coming to Hawaii for your R&R, or just for eating in this restaurant. Take your pick, but we mean it. Thanks."

He looked at Mary Beth. It was the first time anyone anywhere had thanked him for going to Vietnam. He'd been reviled, insulted, shunned and even spat on – but never thanked until that moment. He couldn't help it, his eyes brimmed over and spilled down his cheeks.

He spent $20 on the meal and left a $20 tip. It was worth it.

Afterwards, Mary Beth asked about the milk. Rusty explained the godawful dry milk mix that they got, and how he'd heard so many guys fantasize about getting a cold glass of real milk the first minute they got back in the world. "I bet they've heard that more than once in this hotel," he mused.

"Apparently it was one of your wishes, too."

"Yeah, but it wasn't the very first thing I wanted, was it?" he leered at her.

"You ready for seconds?"

"You mean milk?"

"No," she said coyly.

In the morning, they rented a car and drove up the coast, stopping to marvel at several of the "blow holes" where the surf shoots up inside lava tunnels and bursts out in a spectacular, explosive fountain. They ate lunch under a spreading banyan tree the diameter of a tennis court, and then simply walked in silence, hand in hand.

When they got back to the room, there was a fruit basket complete with dewy fresh pineapple, papaya, guavas and more, compliments of the hotel. Rusty ate most of it greedily. That evening, they went to the regular weekly luau at Fort DeRussy.

Rested, full and cuddling together in bed that evening, Mary Beth wanted to talk about the war. "Ok, I've gotten your letters, and I've talked to my cousin John who was in Ban Me Thuot. He was Army and assigned to something else, but there's a lot that doesn't jive between what he tells me and what you tell me. We're all alone now. Tell me what you really do."

"No."

She rose to one elbow and glared down at him. "What do you mean 'no'? Don't you trust me?"

"I trust you completely, but I cannot tell you what I do. It's classified."

"Oh, screw that. I'm your wife, and I have a right to know."

Rusty sat up, too. "Yes, you are my wife. And you have a right to know almost anything about me. Almost; but not this. I just can't."

"But you already told me in a letter that you work with small reconnaissance teams. Was that a lie?"

"Yes, I did say that, and it's not a lie. But it is also just my cover story."

She reddened, visibly angry. "Is a stupid government secret more important to you than I am?"

"No, never." He reached up and stroked her cheek. "But it's not the secret that's the problem. The secret itself is pretty lame, if you want to know. The problem is that I took an oath not to reveal it…to anyone."

"That makes no sense. If the secret is lame, what difference does it make?"

He looked at her for a long moment. "Let me explain it this way. When we were married, I took a vow to be faithful to you and only you. One could argue that where I put my dick when you're not around doesn't matter much as long as I love you."

She reddened even deeper.

"I didn't say I agree with that," he hurried to say, "But even if it were true, it's not the important thing. It's the vow. If I did screw around, would you feel more betrayed by the act, or the fact that I broke my vow?"

"Both, but maybe I see what you mean. It's not the secret that matters, it's your oath to keep it?" she said, calming.

≈ 169 ≈

"Bingo. My oath, my vow, my word, my promise...they're my honor. That's all I truly own. Honor. If I broke that oath, you'd be disappointed; soon you'd begin to wonder if I might violate some other promise. You'd lose your trust in me. If I lose my honor, I'd eventually lose you. It's not gonna happen."

There was a long pause, then she said, "Have I ever told you that I love you?"

"Uh huh." He was about to suggest something in the way of a demonstration when his gut rumbled. The fruit had hit bottom like a malaria pill. Rusty leapt out of bed and hurried into the bathroom.

In the morning, they drove down to Pearl Harbor and took the motor launch out to the Arizona Memorial. They were asked to speak quietly, as the entire sweeping structure is considered holy ground. But the guards needn't have bothered with that superfluous request. Everyone could feel the spirit of the place. It was awful in the original sense of the word: full of awe. They were looking down at the remains of the number three gun turret when a black drop of fuel oil rose, burst and spread across the surface in a rainbow. The docent noted it too. "For thirty years, the Arizona has continued to leak its fuel a drop at a time. We say that she's bleeding on behalf of her crew." Mary Beth squeezed Rusty's hand convulsively. He continued to look at the spreading rainbow, and managed to choke out, "Those are my brothers down there."

On the trip back ashore, they saw more than a few bright eyes among the other tourists. No one spoke at all. In the parking lot, Mary Beth said, "I knew intellectually what happened at Pearl Harbor, but the dry facts never made a deep impression on me. Until now, that is. I think I'd like to go to the cemetery."

They drove to the top of Puowaina Crater and the National Cemetery of the Pacific. They gazed across the thousands and thousands of small white stones that filled all 120 acres of smoothly curving crater floor. The guidebook explained that the site contained the remains of more than 13,000 soldiers and sailors who had been killed across the Pacific – and one civilian: Ernie Pyle.

Finally, still without saying a word, they drove back down into Honolulu.

They walked out onto Waikiki Beach and strolled around. Rusty tried his best not to stare at the flocks of unbelievable beauties in the tiniest possible bikinis. Mary Beth caught him at it and dug her elbow into his ribs. "Some faithful hero you turned out to be," but she was laughing when she said it. "They really are something, aren't they?"

"That, my city mouse, is a distinctly loaded question. I will excuse my looking with the fact that they – and you – are almost the first roundeyes I've seen since Cam Rahn Bay."

"Roundeyes?"

"Yeah. You know, anything but an Asian. You cannot imagine how much we all miss seeing roundeyes."

"I suspect that it's more than eyes that you miss. How about having lunch at this restaurant? We can sit right out here on the boardwalk and you can ogle to your heart's content."

Rusty grinned at her, but made it a point to sit with his back to the beach. He had barely congratulated himself for being a martyr to voyeurism when a tall strawberry milkshake materialized in front of him. The waitress smiled and said, "R&R, right? With our compliments!"

This time, he had to ask, "How the hell do you know?"

She laughed in a fluid trill. "Your clothes. Dead giveaway. They may as well sport a big neon sign that says BX." She shook her head in mock pity. Her long blue-black hair shimmered in the sun like an ebony waterfall. She touched his shoulder with two fingertips. "Your clothes say Vietnam. We say thanks."

Rusty tipped her 100% of the tab.

They walked along the boardwalk, popping into the shops. Mary Beth picked out a Hawaiian shirt, shorts and sandals for Rusty, and he asked that they be delivered to the hotel.

"No, he'll put them on here. You may send his old ones to the hotel – or burn them," Mary Beth told the clerk. Then to Rusty, "We can't have you looking like a turd in the punchbowl any longer."

"But it doesn't bother me what I look like. Besides, these duds are new, and they get me free milkshakes," he protested.

"I'll buy you milkshakes if you want them. I do care what you look like. 'Duds' describes those perfectly."

"Ok, Ok. I'll wear a Hawaiian shirt, but only if you wear one of these muumuus."

"Are you implying some bovine comparison?"

"No way. Don't blame me for their language. You had no objections to getting a lei, did you?" He smirked lasciviously.

"Just can that talk in public, you lecher."

"Yes, dear," Rusty sighed, hanging his head and pulling a theatrically submissive face.

She laughed. "Just you get that learned pat, buster."

"Can I wear black socks with those sandals?" he teased.

"Arrrrgh! Hayseed! Hick! Maroon! What must I do to civilize you?"

Rusty leaned close and whispered in her ear, grinning.

"I've changed my mind," she said to the clerk. "We'll carry our purchases back to the hotel ourselves."

Back in the room, there was another fresh pineapple, and Rusty's uniforms had been returned. There was a note on the bag that covered them. It said, "We regret that we were unable to remove the stains from these garments. The stains may have set permanently before we were asked to launder them." Compared to the white paper hang bag, they had a distinctly orange-red tint.

"Are all your clothes like that?" Mary Beth was looking over his shoulder.

"No, most of them are much worse. Look," he said, and dug around until he found the set of formerly white underwear that he'd brought to show her.

"Oh, my. That's terrible…that's beyond ugly. How do they get like that?"

He shrugged. "That's how they come back from the laundry. The ground is that color, and the clothes get dusty or muddy. The dirt stains the wash water, I guess. Before long, everything turns red like that. Even our gray airplanes are kinda pink. So are the elephants," he joked.

"What?!? Elephants? Pink elephants? Now you're pulling my leg for sure."

"No I'm not. Not at all. There are elephants in Cambodia. Some are wild and some are tame, but they all like to roll in mud. The mud dries to this color, and the elephants look pink. Even when you're stone cold sober," he added, laughing.

"You've seen elephants?" She was delighted.

"Um, yeah, lots of 'em." he shrugged, suddenly wanting to change the subject as he recalled the scenes. When they spotted what seemed to be tame elephants, they attacked and killed them with rockets. Rusty hated doing it. The rockets they used for that job carried thousands of flechettes, which were little more than inch and a half-long nails with fins where the head would be on a regular nail. Flechettes zipped through almost anything at supersonic impact speeds, but they were too tiny to kill elephants outright. The animals writhed and rolled in agony until they bled to death internally from hundreds of puncture wounds. It was a gruesome and pitiable sight but a necessity. Tame elephants were inevitably NVA pack animals, and killing one might save a soldier's life.

Mary Beth saw his mood change. "Something's not pleasant there. Right?"

"Uh huh. Can we move to something else?"

She lay back on the bed. "How's this?

≈ 172 ≈

In the evening, they strolled back down the boardwalk again, poking into souvenir shops and getting sweet mai-tais from a bar with a take-out window.

"This drink tastes just like a New Orleans hurricane, but from a parallel dimension," he said. He stopped abruptly and stared off at the purpling horizon, "That's what Viet Nam is like, in a way. It's like a world where you recognize some things except they're from another dimension or on another planet. You want to hear something silly?"

"Sure, what?"

"When I was at LZ Emerald, I went out one night when there was a full moon. I was looking at it, and I wondered what phase of the moon it was in Chicago."

Her eyebrows wrinkled, and then it hit her. She looked at him with eyes narrowed and her face slightly cocked away in disbelief.

"You see? It made sense to me that the real world, the one where you were, would have a different moon than Viet Nam. It still does. I can't ever seem to shake the feeling that I'm in some completely bizarre, nightmare place. A place that's so horrible, so ugly, that it can't be real."

She squeezed his hand, and her eyes brightened wetly.

The dam had burst, and Rusty couldn't stop. "Things happen there that seem to be consistent and sensible, but if I told them to you now, they'd cause you to shrink from me like I was a leper or a lunatic. It's like *Alice Through the Looking Glass*. In Nam, the Mad Hatter makes sense, and you have to *let* him make sense or nothing else does. Time might run backwards there and water might run uphill; but to survive, you learn to dry yourself off before you stand over the showerhead. Can you understand?"

She shook her head. "No, but I haven't been there. You have." She thought for a second, then, "Just remember that Alice found her way back home. You can, too."

He walked on for a few feet before he tossed his drink into a trash basket. "Remind me to stay away from these things, willya? I think maybe there's LSD in them."

"No...it's truth serum," she murmured. "But I think I have something that will take your mind off it all. I saved it as a surprise."

"Huh? What do you mean?"

"Do you remember that old TV series *Adventures in Paradise* about ten years ago?"

"I sure do. That's what got me hooked on reading Michener. Why?"

"Well, the schooner that was in that show...the Tiki, remember? Well, that actual boat is here in Honolulu. They offer dinner cruises on that very boat right here. And I booked us on it for tomorrow night!"

Rusty turned to her in utter delight. "How in the heck did you manage that? It's wonderful!"

"Hey, country mouse. Remember what I told you about the powers of a good concierge? Well, I saw a brochure about the boat in the hotel, and had the concierge get us tickets. I called down while you were in the shower. Anyway, surprise!"

On the morning of their last day in Hawaii, they called their parents, had breakfast – where Rusty was presented with another gratis tumbler of cold milk – and then went down to the hotel's beach for the day.

Finally, they put on their Hawaiian outfits and took the hotel's courtesy car to the boat harbor for the dinner cruise. Rusty had never been on a sailboat of any kind, and the experience captivated him. The schooner 'Tiki' putted smoothly out of the harbor under engine power, then its small crew ran up the crisp white sails. As it leaned over slightly to the pressure of the ever-present trade winds, Rusty marveled at the utter silence of it all. The susurrant hiss of the water sliding down the hull was the only sound, and it was mesmerizing.

"I don't want this to ever end," Mary Beth said, wistfully.

"Shhh. There is no time but now," Rusty said. Then, trying to recover from such a lame comment, he added, "Besides, when you say that, you don't mean this boat ride – as nice as it is. What you mean is that we never end. I don't need to tap on teak to wish for that. It just will be. We won't end, and that's just the truth. I promised you that I'd come home safe. I have so far, and I'm past the learning curve now."

"What do you mean?"

"I mean that I know how to do this thing, this job. I'm well past the most dangerous time – when I didn't know the things that can hurt me. I've made it through the rough spots and over the hump."

"You know, you never write and tell me anything about your flights. You've told me that your superiors have been pleased, but you've never said why. Even before you started this new mission, all you've really talked about in your letters are the weather and the funny things the other guys have done. So I don't know what those rough spots were. Were they so bad that you couldn't talk about them?"

He pondered how to answer her question. If he said being a FAC wasn't dangerous, she'd know he was lying. But if he said they were as bad as they could be – had been – she'd go crazy with fear and worry for the next six months.

"I don't know how to answer that. Yes, there have been some times that I may never talk about. But a lot of my missions aren't much more than sightseeing. I fly around and look for things. If I see something, I report it. That's truly all that a lot of it is."

"But not all."

"No. Have you ever had a near miss while you were driving?"

She nodded. "Of course."

"Well, it's a lot like that. They say flying is hours and hours of boredom punctuated by moments of sheer terror. That's true of any kind of flying, mine included. It's true of driving, too. I worry about you as much as you worry about me, when it comes down to it."

"Nobody's shooting at me."

"No, that's true. But nobody's hit me yet, either. That's what I mean: I'm a pro now, and most of them are amateurs."

"It's that little word 'yet' that worries me. And you did write me about your roommate. What did you call it? The Golden BB? It's this secrecy thing that gets me. Not knowing what you do is the worst."

They were back to that again. "I understand. I do. But I cannot and will not violate my oath. Nor should we be talking about it here in public. Let's try to put it aside for the evening, please?"

The sun plummeted down in a huge red ball that splashed gold back into the sky. The graceful boat glided sibilantly on. It all ended too quickly. More drinks, dinner and before they knew it, the boat was tied up at the dock.

The drinks and the unvoiced knowledge that it was their last evening together spurred them to desperate lovemaking. Afterwards Mary Beth cried softly, her head buried against him. He could feel her tears running down his chest, one at a time. He could do nothing except hold her tightly and kept silent. Nothing he could say would help or even matter. She simply needed to cry.

Mary Beth's plane left first the next morning. They hugged and kissed until her flight was called. When they pulled apart she walked quickly aboard, sniffling back tears as she went. To help settle his mind, Rusty bought and savored one last giant milkshake. Chocolate.

He landed in Saigon late at night, and when they opened the cabin door, there was a collective groan as the nauseating stench hit them all. Mary Beth, the flower-perfumed atmosphere of Hawaii, real milk, sex, and perpetual tropical beauty receded once again to a world a million light-years away. Rusty stood in the plane's door, retched once at the smell and stepped back into the realm of the Mad Hatter.

In the morning, he caught a C-123 that ultimately would stop at BMT. The squat, obsolete cargo plane had two piston engines augmented by two auxiliary jet engines used only for takeoff. The thing was so noisy – especially on takeoff - that earplugs were mandatory in the cabin. The flight left him with a splitting headache because they lumbered through five takeoffs as the crew dropped off and picked up various kinds of cargo. At one field, they landed under fire, and Rusty watched as small spots of sunlight magically and soundlessly appeared in the cabin walls: bullet holes. The loadmaster eyeballed them, shrugged, and went about his chores.

They landed again, and this time the loadmaster motioned to Rusty that this was BMT. He unstrapped, grabbed his bag and hustled down the open tail ramp. Rusty waved his free hand to wish the crew luck, but could not raise his eyes into the propeller-whipped rain.

There was nobody there to meet him. He found a phone, and a few minutes later, Major Bridgewater slid to a muddy stop just outside. He was dressed in a dripping poncho, the hood tied snugly around his face. Rusty swung the B-4 bag into the back and plopped into the soggy passenger seat.

Bridgewater asked him something, but Rusty failed to hear what over the ringing C-123 scream still echoing in his ears. He pointed to them, "I can't hear you. That sonofabitch trash hauler made me deaf!"

"How was R&R?" Bridgewater shouted into Rusty's left ear. "Ya get enough nookie?"

Rusty grinned ruefully, shocked at his superior's crude remark. "Yeah, I guess."

"No ya didn't. Ya can never get enough nookie," the major shouted, grinning, as he popped the clutch and spun all four tires through the greasy red mud.

They slipped and slid their tractionless way through the main gates a few minutes later. Rusty was already soaked through, both from rain and sweating in the sauna-like heat. Blood-red water ran down the central camp street, water ran in sheets from the sandbag-weighted tin roofs of the hootches, and the clouds hung leadenly just above the single tree outside the Special Forces club.

Home sweet hell.

CHAPTER EIGHT

For a few days, Rusty was subject to the usual locker room humor of sex-starved men. He grinned and played his part in it, comparing experiences with others who'd gone to Hawaii and those who had gone to Australia. The latter guys – all single – bragged about the lusty Aussie women who seemingly couldn't wait to bed any GI they found. Rusty grinned appreciatively at their lurid stories, but secretly felt sorry for anyone without a wife. He could almost still feel that convulsive squeeze of Mary Beth's hand as they stood on the Arizona Memorial. No Sheila, no matter how sultry, could ever share feelings like that.

The monsoon was still in full force, and there'd been hardly any flying while he'd been gone. The leaden skies would pour for hours or days straight, then there'd be three or four days of patchy sun punctuated with thunderstorms. Whenever possible, they flew out over Cambodia looking for signs of enemy travel: new truck ruts, rope bridges, log-filled low spots in roads or hidden ferry boats.

Buchenhardt hit the jackpot one morning when he spotted thirty or forty enemy troops desperately trying to free a mud-bogged truck. The Green Hornets had a field day rocketing and strafing the truck and the few troops stupid enough to try to defend it with small arms. The truck itself exploded in a massive gray-black fireball.

Buchenhardt became an even worse insufferable rodomontade in the O'Club that evening. Worse, the Green Hornets backed up his bragging.

"Hey, Buckandfart! If you're such a hero, why not buy the house a round?" Rushing yelled to him.

"Why don't you buy one for me, Rushing?" Buchenhardt turned to Kit, his face darkening at the nickname he hated.

"Because I only buy for my friends," Kit said, levelly. "And you don't fall in that category."

Buchenhardt stared hard at him but didn't respond.

Rusty was sure the two would finally come to blows, and he didn't want to be in the middle of it. He got up from his chair and casually walked into the small adjacent room that held a pool table. Just going in there was an exercise in masochism. At some point in the past, one of the Special Forces grunts had gotten soused and decided it would be great fun to gas the place. He'd tossed a CS tear gas grenade into the Club, and the damn thing had rolled right into the billiard room. The eye-watering remnants of its microscopic crystals were imbedded in the felt of the table, and every rolling ball released a whiff of it.

There was a game in progress, and the two-stripe airman doing the shooting had his back to Rusty. He was stretched out across the table as he played an awkward lie. He stroked his shot, and quickly leaned back away from the plume of irritating gas. He spun around and Rusty stared straight into the unmistakable face of Eddie Haskell.

"Hey, you're…you're…" Rusty stammered.

"Ken Osmond, sir." The airman grinned that same sly, crafty smile for which he'd become famous, and added, "But, yeah, I did play Eddie Haskell."

Rusty was thunderstruck. Suddenly, it really did feel as though he'd fallen through the looking glass with Alice. "What in the hell are you doing here?" he finally asked.

Osmond/Haskell smiled again. "Long story, sir. After *Leave it to Beaver* I couldn't get any other parts. I guess no matter who else I ever played, I'd always be Eddie. So after a while I enlisted in the Air Force. I'm a sky cop and love it."

"But how in the world did you wind up in Ban Me Thuot?"

"Oh, I'm only here overnight. Came in on a truck convoy and we'll head back out again tomorrow. I'm detailed to these Green Beanie guys as Security."

"But, you enlisted?" Still off balance mentally, Rusty couldn't believe a TV star would ever volunteer for this unpopular war, or even for the military at all.

"Oh, yeah. I know, I could've pulled a few strings and gone to Officer Candidate School, but I didn't plan to make this a career. I thought I wanted to be a cop, and this was an easy way to try it out for a while. Turns out I was right. I like it. I think I'll join the police force in L.A. when this is over."

"I'll be damned."

Osmond grinned that famous smile again, then turned back to the tear gas-infused pool table.

Rusty went back out to the bar, where he noticed that Kit had left, but Buchenhardt was still basking in the light of his own lamp. Rusty sat down next to Sandy, wiping his eyes with a handkerchief. "Do you know who's in there?" he said, jerking one thumb over his shoulder.

"Eddie Haskell? Yeah. I talked with him a while. Nice guy, isn't he?"

"Too weird for words is what it is. Of all the faces I'd expect to see in a uniform and in this dump, the last one I would ever have bet on is Eddie Haskell. I mean, in my wildest dreams…" Rusty shook his head.

"Uh huh. I know what you mean. Blows my mind, too."

"He said he wants to be a cop in Los Angeles. Can you imagine the look on some guy he's trying to arrest? Man, what a story: punk turns cop, burns punk."

Sandy laughed so hard he sprayed some of his drink into a cloud. "Hoo Hoo! Boy, that says it all! Sorry about that!"

"No sa-vet, GI." Rusty mimicked the bar girl's pigeon English.

His eyes still smarted a bit from the potent crystals of CS, and Rusty soon excused himself. He went back and wrote Mary Beth about Airman Osmond, the lousy weather and how much he missed her already. Just thinking about her made his eyes brim even more than he could blame on tear gas. Before long, the nightly blasts of mortar fire boomed into the dark: midnight. He turned in.

The next few days brought yet another of the broad, sweeping bands of low clouds and rain across Southeast Asia. Between downpours, some of them drove out to the old artillery base just east of the fenced compound, and did a little target practice. Ammunition for their compact CAR-15 carbines was easy to come by, naturally, and so they burned magazine after magazine of it. Rusty loved to watch the way tracer rounds would embed themselves in the dirt and smoke. Sometimes, if they hit something harder, they'd only penetrate a short way and you could see them sitting there half-buried and spitting a tiny ball of red flame.

They also had some unusual guns to shoot. The Special Forces guys somehow had gotten hold of an ancient M-2 "grease gun" that fired .45-caliber pistol ammunition. The crudely made gun nonetheless was unstoppable, shooting in a measured "pom..pom..pom..pom..pom" as long as the trigger was held down and ammunition remained in the magazine. It contrasted so much with the ripping fire of the CAR-15 and its individually indistinguishable shots that they laughed and whooped. There were also a few captured enemy AK-47s, and the pilots quickly developed a true respect for this weapon. Like the grease gun, it was cheaply made but completely reliable, simple where it could be but sophisticated where it needed to be. Its effect on inanimate bits of trash was sobering. This is what the bad guys shot at them, and the terrible damage it caused made them secretly squeamish.

Even more sobering was the pathetic performance of their issued .38-caliber revolvers. Mere popguns. Rusty realized there'd be no way to defend himself against soldiers armed with those awesome AK-47s. He decided he'd use his solely as a signal device if he were ever forced down. He'd reload with six rounds of tracer ammo and carry it that way from then on. If he needed to signal to rescuers, they'd work. And if he were about to be captured…well, it wouldn't matter what ammo he had. One would do.

He earnestly tried to put that scenario out of mind when he flew a visual reconnaissance mission the next day. The backside of the broad rain band brought its usual towering but scattered thunderstorms, and several pilots eagerly got airborne to look for new signs of movement on the Ho Chi Minh trail. Rusty marveled at the changes that the monsoon had brought. The sinuous black snake of the Tonle Srepok river he remembered had become a roaring anaconda, a quarter-mile wide swath of caramel-colored roaring runoff. What he knew had been house-sized black lava boulders sticking several feet out of the river were now merely boiling spots of turbulence, the rocks completely submerged but defiant against the surge. Whole trees, logs and debris of all kinds tumbled and spun along, disappearing, reappearing and slamming into crumbling banks. It was as if God were flushing the toilet that was Vietnam.

In contrast, the jungle itself seemed to glow with a new inner light. The treetops glistened in darkest green, and where patches of sun raced across them, they sparkled in prismatic glory. Rusty didn't see any sign of the enemy – no helpless trucks to decimate. But he did spot new activity around a small group of thatched hootches.

He'd flown over these hootches many times, noting occasional wisps of smoke, so he knew they were occupied. There'd always been evidence of gardening, and because the activity was nearly constant and overt, he presumed the people were indigenous and not NVA. Today, he spotted someone actually out working in the garden area. Curious, he cut his engines to idle and made a swooping dive down low to get a better look.

Rusty glided down, the plane as quiet as the Oscar Duck can get, and he got quite close before the gardener – perhaps preoccupied with a daydream – suddenly became aware of him and spun around to gape. Rusty pulled up not over a hundred feet from her, grinning appreciatively to himself. It was definitely a she, because she had adopted the simplest possible way of keeping her clothes dry – she wasn't wearing any.

Rusty blew a kiss to this delightfully au naturel gardener, shoved the engines to full power and performed a graceful chandelle climbing turn in her honor. One pretty curve as a poor mirror to hers, he thought. Over his shoulder, he saw her slip-sliding her panicky way through red clay gumbo towards the hootches, her hoe lying abandoned where she'd dropped it. Suddenly, he felt ashamed of himself for scaring her. Perhaps she thought the swooping plane would shoot rockets at her at any second. Rusty rocked his wings, hoping she'd recognize it as a wave and not a threat, but also knowing she wouldn't have any concept of that. She'd been frightened for her life, and he envisioned her shaking in fear. For the rest of the flight, he wondered how he could possibly make it up to her.

But that wasn't his only preoccupation. Throughout the flight, and even more so now that he prepared to navigate his way home, Rusty had noted that the thunderheads had constantly multiplied and grown. Only narrow alleyways of clear air now separated them. Flying in clouds is no difficulty to a trained pilot, of course, but only an idiot tries to penetrate the violence of a thunderstorm. Intense turbulence can slam a plane out of control or even rip it apart. Hail could blast through the windscreen like ice bullets, and thick coats of condensing ice could make a plane too heavy to stay airborne at all. No, thunderstorms are best flown around.

Except that now there was little "around" left.

Rusty radioed in to give his position and intent. Sgt Hannah's voice was calm as he advised Rusty he was the last one airborne, but Hannah sat in a snug radio room, not staring into menacing anvil heads of violent weather. Rusty had plenty of gas to make it home, but not enough to get anywhere else, he realized. There'd be no weather divert for him today. He worked his way between storms, always trying to angle to the east. But he found himself forced to deviate far off course to get around the rapidly swelling columns of evil black storms. Lightning stabbed down to the jungle below, and solid columns of dark gray rain looked like massive concrete pillars supporting the heavy storms.

Finally, he glimpsed the Tonle Srepok again just ahead, and knew he was nearing the border. Another half-hour and he could be landing. But the direct path home led between two of the biggest storms. The space between them looked to be less than a few hundred feet, and that gap was closing like two giant hands about to slap a fly from the air. Rusty was that fly.

He charged for the opening, hoping to get through before it closed. Just as he reached almost to the narrowest portion of the gap, a panicky thought sparked through his mind: his pods still held all fourteen rockets with warheads. Worse, his gas tanks were nearly empty – the time when they were most susceptible to flash ignition. Rusty was about to bridge the gap of those two huge lightning generators with his aluminum plane.

Just the thought of it made him scrunch his eyes tight and hunch his head down between his shoulders in anticipation of the strike. As though his actions were a trigger, it happened.

KABOOM! A blue-white flash that filled his whole world lit up the cockpit. Even through Rusty's closed eyelids, it was blinding. The crack of the thunderclap was like a rifle blast right next to his ears. He squeezed the yoke convulsively, waiting for the explosion of the rockets, the gas tanks or both. He braced for the sickening drop that would follow as his wings collapsed, the fiery final plunge, the crunch of impact...

...and was amazed that all he heard was the steady drone of the engines. He opened his eyes and discovered he was in level flight. An intensely orange afterimage danced in his eyes, and his ears rang, but he was still flying. He looked anxiously at every instrument and every radio. All working! He looked out at both wings. All 14 rockets were still there in their pods. Nothing looked bent or burned.

Rusty flew on, just holding level flight until his fluttering heart rate slowed. He felt tingly twitches in his muscles, a hollow ball of semi-nausea in his gut, and cold drips of sweat under his arms and in his groin. But all that was familiar, the adrenalin hangover that always followed extreme danger.

"Mike 50, 58."

"58, go."

"Uh, 50, I've just had a lightning strike. Big mother. I don't think anything is damaged, but it was a direct strike. Anyway, I guess I'd better declare a precautionary emergency. I'm ...uh...one five minutes out, at the fence, northwest."

"Copy lightning strike and precautionary, 58. Copy one five ETA and negative damage. I'll alert the tower and crash crew."

"Thanks, 50."

"How was it, 58?"

"Jesus Christ O mighty, 50. Like being inside a flashbulb. But lots louder."

"Copy that, too, 58. Stay on freq for flight following until you go tower. Report if the wings fall off."

"58 wilco." Droll, that Hannah.

But nothing happened. Rusty droned on the last few miles, noting over his shoulder that the storms were mysteriously lined up shoulder to shoulder right over the border as if they had no passport to enter Viet Nam. Over the city, he told Hannah he was going off frequency to contact the tower. He made an uneventful landing pattern and landed back to the west, the only thing out of the ordinary being the crash fire truck parked next to the runway with its red lights twirling. He turned around on the runway and taxied back to the decrepit taxiway, the fire truck escorting him the whole way. At runway end, Sgt Cramer pinned his rocket pods, and Rusty saw him do a double take look at the right wingtip. As Rusty entered the parking ramp through the gate, the crash truck shut down its lights and peeled off.

In the chocks, the whole maintenance crew waited for him, along with Dave Sanderson. As he unstrapped, he noticed Sanderson and Sgt Cramer pointing to the right wingtip. When Rusty clambered out, he saw what had drawn their attention. The fiberglass wingtip had been blown away, leaving the wires to the position lights hanging. On the other wing was a small black hole burned into the trailing edge of the aileron. The stroke had apparently entered at one, and exited at the other, the plane serving as the conductor between those two storms.

"Well, sir, this one will be grounded for a while," Cramer said, shaking his head. "We'll have to go through the whole thing looking for internal damage."

"Did you have anywhere else to go?" Sanderson joked.

"Guess not, sir," Cramer answered, shaking his head and half-grinning.

Sanderson turned to Rusty. "How about you? Any injuries or anything?"

"Well, I gueth you could thay I'm a little Thor," Rusty said, lisping outrageously.

"Oh, god," Sanderson said, dropping his head to his chest and shaking it ruefully. "I hope that's not a permanent affliction. You were bad enough before."

"Maybe that's because I've been hit by lightning before."

His eyebrows went up and even Cramer's head snapped around to gape at Rusty.

"Hit by lightning before? You mean in a plane? Because I've been with you since you were a student, and I don't recall anything like this before," Sanderson probed.

"No, I mean hit as in struck. Not in a plane. On the ground."

They both stared. "You gotta be shitting me," Sanderson said after a long pause.

"Nope. I was in the Civil Air Patrol, and we were in our summer encampment at Chanute Air Force Base in Illinois. There was going to be an inspection the next morning, and I was adjusting the spacing of uniforms in our barracks. They had a long pipe along the wall as a clothes rod, and I was touching it when lightning hit the barracks. I remember a big blue basketball of fire around my hand, and my whole body twitched uncontrollably for an hour. Burned all the hair off my arm, and all the uniforms had burn marks where the metal hangars touched them. Real fun. But no permanent affects," Rusty smirked, bobbing his head and batting his eyes while he jerked his arms spasmodically.

"Jesus," Sanderson said. "Twenty thousand comedians out of work, and you're working for free. You are kidding us, right?"

"Nope. I'm not. It happened just that way. Honest. I thought I was immune from lightning. That 'never strikes twice' thing, you know? Until now," Rusty said, looking suspiciously at the sky.

Cramer edged away from them as he looked up, too.

"Jesus," Sanderson said again to Rusty's back as he turned and walked to the parachute Conex.

That evening, it was Rusty's turn to be the center of attention in the O'Club. The Special Forces guys asked a million questions about the storms, the lightning strike and all. But all Rusty could really say was that it hadn't hurt anything except the wingtip damage - as far as he knew. The story about the time he'd been struck in his youth made a few eyes go wide, but he downplayed it again.

It wasn't until later when he was alone in bed that he remembered that tawny young Cambodian woman in all her natural beauty. He wondered how he could possibly help those people, the innocent survivors of this damn war. It wasn't until he'd dropped down through the misty veil of half-sleep that the germ of an idea came.

The next day, Rusty was assigned to fly two Special Forces soldiers to Qui Nhon. He'd never seen them before, and they said nothing about themselves or how they came to be at BMT. But by now Rusty was well used to not asking questions about strange things. As he briefed them about the plane and the few emergency procedures they needed to know, one of the guys said he had never flown before.

"How did you get to Viet Nam?" Rusty asked, incredulous.

"A ship," he said, "It took us almost a month and I was sea sick the whole time. I hope I don't get sick up there." He pointed to the leaden sky.

"Me too, brother," Rusty answered. "But if you do, you clean it up. I have to live in that thing." Rusty smiled to him, but the soldier immediately understood that Rusty wasn't altogether kidding. Rusty made sure to grab a few extra sick sacks, even though he knew there were several in the pocket behind the seat.

After they got the other soldier strapped into the rear seat, Rusty climbed in. Sgt Lopez helped the virgin flier get strapped in last of all, and Rusty made sure he explained as much as he could to him. He surely didn't want anything to be a surprise, and he knew that being in the co-pilot seat would lessen the chance the man would get queasy.

The only sign of anxiety Rusty noticed was when he firewalled the engines for the takeoff roll, and he saw the soldier's hands reflexively tighten on his thighs. As expected, the hands clutched even tighter when the plane broke ground and lurched into the sky. In the back of his mind, Rusty remembered the way his own stomach seemed to flip-flop the first time he flew, and he smiled to himself.

They immediately entered the thick, dark grey clouds, and Rusty headed northeast for the half-hour flight. The clouds were solid all the way to their cruise altitude, but once there, they broke out between two cloud layers. Now that he could see outside, my new flier seemed to be enjoying himself, but he'd been nervous the whole time they could see nothing.

"Excuse me, sir, but how the hell do you know where we are when you can't see the ground?"

"Well, the only way is by these navigational radios," Rusty said, tapping the dials. "We actually have two of them. This one is the primary one. It gives us our bearing and distance to a ground station. There are lots of those stations, and by dialing in the right one, we always know where we are."

Rusty opened out the instrument flight navigational chart he was using. It was a white sheet with blue circles and lines on it, but no ground features: no cities, no roads, no highways.

"So if I dial in this station here, Channel 74," Rusty pointed to the radio and the little window with the channel number showing, "then read this dial here, you see that we are on the 300-degree radial – that's the same as being 300 degrees on the compass – and 64 nautical miles out." He pointed to the map. "Here's that station, and so we should be about…here." He tapped the chart.

"Now, if Qui Nhon had its own radio station like this, we could just tune it in and home directly there. But since it doesn't, we just navigate to the bearing and distance where it lies from this station we're using. These lines between stations are like highways, and where they cross are like intersections. So we can just drive from one place to another."

"Oh, that's not so hard," the soldier said, brightening.

"Well, there's a lot I left out, like Instrument Flight Rules and such, but the actual getting from point A to B isn't hard, no. Of course, there's the problem of what to do when we get there," Rusty grinned. "Getting down to the runway without hitting a mountain, for example."

The right-seater blanched a little, and said, "You do know how to do that, don't you, sir?"

"Yup, but if I have trouble, can I ask you for help?"

"Don't joke with me, sir. I've never flown before, and there's no way I could fly this thing."

"Wanna bet? I think you could fly it just fine – at least here at altitude. You want to try?"

"Huh? You mean actually fly? Really?"

"Sure. Look, just put your right hand on the yoke and your feet on those two pedals." He did, and Rusty went on, "Now it doesn't take any actual movement. Just very gently apply pressure either forward or back, or turning. Now look straight ahead. See where the front of the plane lies just below the cloud line there?" The man nodded.

"Ok, just hold the nose there. If it drops, just hold a little back pressure. If it goes up, just press a little bit forward." While Rusty talked, and the soldier stared at the horizon, Rusty relaxed his own grip and let go of the yoke. "And if we roll a little bit, just pull down or push up a little bit to correct it. You got that?"

"Uh huh, I guess so, sir. That sounds easy. Okay, I'm ready to try when you are."

"You're already doing it. Look." Rusty showed him both hands.

His eyes went big for a second, then he snapped his attention back to the gray line of the horizon. "Holy smoke!" The movement caused the nose to dip slightly, and he pulled back on the yoke. The nose shot back up and he gasped a little.

"Ride 'em cowboy," quipped the backseater. "You got those reins tight, Steve?"

"That reminds me," Rusty said, "Don't choke the yoke, just hold it lightly. Remember, it only takes pressure. Don't chase the nose, just hold gently one way or the other until it goes where you want it to, and then relax. See, that's better," he said as the nose settled down again. "Hey, you're a natural. Give me a few flights and I could make a pilot outta you."

"I doubt it, sir. I could never figure out all those funny clocks and stuff."

"Oh, they only look complicated. Each one just tells you one thing: your heading on one, your altitude on another, your speed on another, and so forth. Heck, your grandmother could learn it."

"Well, maybe, sir, but my Gram is a whale of a lot smarter than I am," he grinned. "But I'm honored. I've never had an officer treat me like this before. You're alright, sir, really alright."

"We're all in this together, corporal. We all have different jobs to do, but it takes all of us doing it. I don't think I could do what you do, either. Whatever it is."

He grinned back. "You wanna try?"

"No thanks. I think I'd be more afraid than you are of flying. And not as good at it."

Rusty let him fly until the cloud layers closed in and he had to take the controls and go back on instruments. He got out all the charts and approach plates he might need, deliberately arranging a few more than absolutely necessary. His passenger watched, squinted at the instruments and peered out into the thick wool that surrounded them. Rusty made the usual radio calls and switched from enroute control to approach control at Qui Nhon, dialed in the altimeter and radio settings and followed the controllers instructions for an instrument approach. The radio chatter was pretty constant between the controllers, other planes and them, and Rusty could see the questioning looks his passenger was shooting at him, as well the man's increasing anxiety.

Rusty said nothing to him for a while, having to concentrate pretty hard on things himself. When they broke out of the clouds only a half mile from the runway, the passenger exhaled a big breath and said, "Sir, you told me a big 'un back there. Either that or my Gram is one HELL of a lot smarter then even I thought!"

As they taxied to the ramp, Rusty asked him, "Well, what did you think of your first plane ride? Was it better than an ocean cruise?"

"To tell you the truth, sir, I was starting to feel a little green there at the end when I couldn't see anything outside and my stomach felt like it was moving around on its own inside me. But I sure did like it when you let me drive this thing."

"That's perfectly natural when your eyes and senses don't agree. Did you get queasy back there, too?" Rusty turned to peer at the backseater.

"Sure did, sir," he said. "I was starting to look for one of those bags. But I'm fine now. May I say, sir, that Steve was right? You're an alright officer. I'd fly with you any time."

"Teeny Weeny Airlines at your service, guys. It's been my pleasure."

They pulled up in front of a waiting jeep and shut down. After his two passengers got out, Rusty made sure the headsets, seatbelts and straps were stowed correctly, then started up and flew back to BMT. On the way, he reflected. Just a little over a year and a half ago, he'd been a student pilot. Students weren't permitted to fly solo in the weather, and in fact he'd done very little actual weather flying at all in deep south Texas. And now here he was, not only entrusted but rather casually assigned to fly in serious weather, alone, over a combat zone. Even more astounding, he seemed to have achieved all this effortlessly. What incredible changes flying had brought to his life. His thoughts turned philosophical.

Life, he mused, is like flying. We struggle to get off the ground and achieve independent flight burdened with all the fuel we will ever have, unable to change the craft we're in or even repair it. Sometimes, that craft breaks through no fault of our own. Once in flight, we can never stop, but must keep hurtling forward for every moment of our time. Completely isolated from all others in the uncharted sky, we must navigate our own way, maintain control of ourselves, stay alert and avoid storms. Some of us spin in, out of control. Others fly on in perfect confidence. Some of us lose our way, but some keep their bearings. Some of us crash, unknowing and unaware, into an invisible, fog-shrouded mountain. Sometimes the route is a straight one, and sometimes we are forced to change destinations unexpectedly. Almost always, the view is glorious; but sometimes there is unforeseen turbulence. And when we finally exhaust the fuel that keeps us going, we inevitably return to the earth. Every flight and every life ends the same way: full stop.

Gotta write that all down someday, he concluded. Nah, too corny.

He was roused from these musings by a call on the radio. Time to start his descent into BMT. The weather had improved a bit, and he caught sight of the field several miles out. Another uneventful landing for Teeny Weeny Air.

Rusty checked on his little group of Cambodian hootches from a distance several times over the next week. He never saw anyone else outdoors, but the garden was well tended, and he could detect changes from day to day. They hadn't abandoned the place.

Meanwhile, he scrounged the items he needed for his plan. Wandering outside the compound, he located parachutes from a couple of spent mortar illumination rounds. The mortar crews gave him some cardboard tubes in which mortar rounds had been shipped, and he scrounged some heavy wire and some sheet metal. Rusty borrowed tin snips from Cramer. In his room,

Rusty made paper forms, cut sheet metal to match and tested the idea. It might work!

Finally, he asked the other FACs for the rest of what he needed, without revealing why. From the uneaten portions of ration packs, he collected chewing gum, cigarettes, packs of fruit drink mix, hard candy, matches and packets of salt and pepper. He bought packages of single-edge razor blades, bars of soap and toothbrushes. All these he carefully test-fit into a mortar tube and taped on one end cap. At the other end he assembled the other items he'd collected.

Before his flight the next day, Rusty surreptitiously carried the device out to the plane. He'd already conspired with Sgt Cramer to be his crew chief for the day, and Cramer knew what he'd planned. Cramer latched the tube under the right wing outboard pylon, grinning conspiratorially as he did. Without further ado, Rusty took off and headed west. So far, he'd gotten away with it!

Over his friendly hootches, Rusty cut the throttles and glided down. As before, the people must have heard his approach, for no one was visible. He flew straight towards the hootches, leveling at 300 feet. As he neared the tiny village he set the outboard pylon switch for DROP, flipped on the Master Arm and when he was directly over the hootches, touched the trigger.

The tube fell free until it hit the end of its trip wire. The stiff wire pin looped to the end pulled free of the sheet metal flap Rusty had fashioned. Out popped the six-foot diameter parachute, inflating perfectly.

Circling, Rusty saw the chute descend, finally plopping down lightly in the center of the village. Nobody came out. Nothing happened at all. Rusty flew off to complete the rest of his assigned mission uneventfully, but with a broad smile and a twinkling eye. He'd just candy-bombed Cambodia.

A few days later, Rusty flew back over the spot. The parachute and tube were gone. But he saw two faces peeking out of one hootch. Laughing to himself, Rusty dropped a second candy bomb. It had hardly touched the ground before he saw two figures run out and grab it up, then scurry back into the hootch. Rusty made a final pass, waggling his wings wildly as he passed over. From the door of the largest hootch, he glimpsed a hand waving back.

They'd resumed working a few teams by then, and Rusty flew a few days of cap missions orbiting high over Cambodia a few miles from the target box. He had one parachute left, but he'd stripped the camp of candy and other goodies. To fill the last tube, he'd had to confide in the guys. When he told them what he was doing with the stuff, they'd all been delighted. Batman was especially enthralled, and promised to find some other things that the villagers might find useful. Rusty reminded him that whatever he found had to fit inside a three-inch diameter tube.

When Batmen knocked on Rusty's door that evening, he came in with a laundry bag almost bulging full. He dumped it out on Rusty's bunk, and out flooded packs of new cigarettes, candy bars, razors, bags of candy, bars of soap, canned fruit and GI can openers, even two brand new pocketknives.

"Batman, how and where did you get this stuff? Some of this stuff I can't even get for myself!" Rusty looked at the Snickers bars with real yearning.

"Not your problem, brother. Your job is to drop it, mine is to gather it. Now let's see that mystery bomb."

Rusty opened the spare locker – it had been Richard's – and dug out the mortar tube, parachute and end pieces he'd already fashioned.

"These are the last ones. I can't find another spent flare parachute anywhere, and I'm afraid to walk too far outside the compound to go looking."

"Hmmm. Can't blame you for that, I guess. So this will be your last drop?"

"Unless I find another chute, yes. The tubes are easy, and everything else I can make, as you see."

"Uh huh. You clip these wire rings into the pylon shackles?" he asked, and Rusty nodded. "Then you fasten the end of this wire to the pylon so that when you drop the tube, the pin pulls the cover loose and the parachute pops out. Clever. What happens to the wire?"

"It just trails behind the pylon until I land, then Cramer removes it when he safes the rocket pods. No evidence of anything when I taxi back inside the compound."

"Very cute, indeed. Where do you drop them?"

"You know that little group of hootches about twenty clicks west of the Toe, the one where the jungle ends and the grass plain begins?"

He nodded. "Yeah, I think so. Four hootches and a few gardens?"

"That's it. Well, a few weeks ago, I spotted a girl hoeing there, and I scared her silly by making a low pass. I wanted to make up for that, so…" Rusty shrugged, and decided not to tell Batman that he'd first seen her gloriously naked, shining wet and tawny brown.

"I think that's great. How many have you dropped?"

"Two. The first one must have scared them at first, but apparently they got over it and opened it because they ran out and scarfed up the second one before it even landed. Must've been a success!"

"I'll say. But if there's only one chute left, we have a problem. All this stuff isn't gonna fit into that little mortar shell tube."

"That what I was thinking, too. Maybe I can find a bigger tube of some kind."

"Again, you leave the gathering to me. I'll be back when I've located what we need."

Batman left, taking the bag of goodies with him. Damn. Rusty thought he deserved one of those oh-so-rare Snickers bars.

Batman was as good as his word. The next evening, he knocked again. He had a silly grin on his face, and he hid his right arm behind the doorframe out of Rusty's sight. "Ta-Daaa!" Batman announced, displaying a bright aluminum tube, six inches in diameter and four feet long.

"Holy crap, Batman, where did you get that!" Rusty exclaimed, an octave above his normal voice.

Batman waggled his left forefinger. "Ah ah ahhh! No fair asking questions, remember? I merely provide. You utilize."

Rusty stared at the beautiful, pristine tube. "Uh, okay. It's better if I don't know, huh?"

Batman nodded, a sly smile spreading across his face.

Rusty returned his conspiratorial look with a wink. "Very well. I copy. But boy oh boy, this is a whole different kettle of sardines. This is gonna need some extra engineering and labor. It's gonna be at least five or six times heavier, for one thing. So it'll hit the ground like a ton of bricks. Well, half a ton, anyway. With this small parachute, I mean."

Batman nodded, still grinning.

"But I doubt we can find a bigger 'chute, so maybe we can just pack the goodies better or something. And there's no pre-made end cap for the bottom end, so we'll have to make something that will hold shut against the shock of the parachute, but can still be opened with no tools. Let me think."

"I'd bet on their ingenuity if I were you. You get it there, and they'll get it open."

"Batman, you're spot on, as usual. I'm sure they trust me now. They won't scruple to bash it with a rock if they have to. Silly me."

"You just underestimated them for a minute. They survive against incredible odds out there. Subject to all the vagaries of nature, and regularly robbed by the NVA to boot. But they're still there kicking," Batman said.

And one of them is quite fetching as well, Rusty thought to himself.

By the next day, he had it figured out. He asked Flip if he could saw out a six-inch circle of wood.

"No sweat. I'll just start with a square of rocket box and keep gnawing off the edges. How perfect does it have to be?"

"Not very. Here's a paper tracing and you just make it that size. We can refine it if we need to. I'll need two of them."

"Okay. Two it is." And a few hours later, he presented them. They were an easy slip fit inside the tube. Perfect.

Sgt Cramer used his sheet metal skills to punch six evenly spaced holes an inch from the bottom end of the tube and another set six inches from the top end. They nailed one of the wooden disks firmly in place at the top end, forming the parachute chamber. Cramer also made a sheet metal lid for that end with his tin snips. They packed the parachute into its chamber, then closed and pinned the lid in place. For the loops that would hold the tube to the pylon until release, Cramer wrapped thick wire around the tube, leaving an exposed twisted loop at the top. Heavy strapping tape secured and smoothed the wrapped wire.

Back in Rusty's room, he and Batman carefully packed all the goodies inside, lighter items went in first to be near the parachute end, the cans and heavy items near the bottom. They wrapped every item in towels and clean shop rags, until Batman said, "It'll be like a Christmas present."

Rusty secretly hoped that all the Snickers bars wouldn't fit, but everything did, with a bit of room to spare. Flip contributed two pairs of heavy socks to fill the space, serve as cushioning, and maybe even be something the Cambodes could use. Who knows?

Finally, they slid in the bottom round of wood and pinned it in place with three pieces of heavy stiff wire stuck through the six opposing holes at the bottom. Rusty bent the ends of the wire back and taped over them. It should hold the contents in place but be simple and intuitive to open. At least he hoped so. Then they hid the thing in the spare locker.

They were all grounded by rain the next day, but Rusty was scheduled for a radio cap flight the day after. He and Cramer carried the tube to the ramp, sneaking around the far end of the FAC hootch in hopes that neither Sanderson nor Bridgewater would see them. Cramer locked it to the right outboard pylon as usual, and Rusty waited anxiously for his robin to show up, sweating in fear of discovery before he arrived.

Rusty breathed a sigh of relief when he got airborne undetected. His orbit zone was many miles from the village, but he made a detour to go past it first. Truong cast wary glances at the unfamiliar shiny tube hanging from the right wing, but said nothing. With little time to spare before he had to fly to his real mission, Rusty made no preliminary scouting circles around the village, but just bored straight in, diving to the usual 300 feet. He hoped that the village hadn't been abandoned or worse yet taken over by the enemy, but there was no time to scout the place to be sure. He felt like an F-4 pilot, making that fuel hog's typical "one pass haul ass" delivery. He armed up, and pickled the tube right over the village, as before, then made his usual climbing left turn to watch what happened. As he'd feared, the much heavier load plummeted down at several times the gentle pace of the previous drops, even though the parachute again opened perfectly. He saw the shiny tube thump down, bounce and tumble to a stop just outside the edge of the gardens, hopefully intact. It had landed long due to its greater forward momentum and Rusty's higher airspeed this time, but he was sure they'd find it. He couldn't hang around to be sure, though.

Rusty checked in with Danny Craig and relieved him from dawn patrol. The rest of the cap mission was as boring as ever, and Truong unbuckled his seat belt, slid down and fell asleep the moment Rusty had completed the handoff. In mid-afternoon, Kit relieved Rusty in turn, and he considered flying down to check out the village. The fuel gauges ruled that out though, and Rusty decided against it. Oh well, the villagers had either found it or they hadn't.

Nature and events conspired against going to the village again for many days. Heavy weather socked in again, forcing Danny to pull his team and grounding everyone. Two planes had to be flown down to Cam Rahn for routine inspections and service. With Rusty's lightning-blasted plane still being inspected for lightning damage, there weren't any to spare for visual flights.

While Rusty chomped at the bit to go see if the villagers had found the tube, he toiled away at his new additional duty. Major Bridgewater had learned that Rusty was literate. So he became Awards and Decorations Officer. That meant that Rusty spent many hours writing up recommendations for people to get medals. Everyone but himself, of course, as that would be most unseemly. He was tearing out his hair over one such recommendation. One of the enlisted guys had gone downtown to the Bakery and gotten oral sex from one of the local girls. Somehow, he'd angered her and she bit him hard enough to draw blood. Weeks later, she'd been arrested by the 23rd ARVN as a VC agent. The intrepid airman, reading the regulations very carefully, had applied for a Purple Heart: he'd been wounded in action by the enemy. Rusty was dutifully trying to compose the award recommendation without mentioning oral sex when Major Bridgewater called to see him.

Rusty reported to the TOC, thinking it was about this ridiculous Purple Heart. Bridgewater motioned him to a chair.

"I hear you're pretty good at dropping things from the O-2." He said, blank-faced.

Oh shit. I'm screwed to the wall, Rusty thought. "Uh, what do you mean, sir?"

The major grinned. "Sheeyit, boy, this little 'ol camp is tighter'n a tick's asshole. Ever' body hereabouts knows you been dropping candy to some teensy village out there across the fence. Ya don't think ah wouldn't a heert of it, do ya?"

Rusty couldn't help smiling at that cornpone accent again. "Uh, I guess so. Or not...sir. Whichever."

"Wheyall, here's the deal. Since you're the nearest thang to a bombardier we got, you're just the guy for a little job we have comin' up."

"Sir?"

"In a day or so, you're gonna take off with a few...parcels. And you're gonna deposit those parcels smack dab on a map coordinate."

Rusty's half smile evaporated. He waited.

"Is there somethang else you need to know, Lieutenant?"

"Uh, um...no. Sir. I guess not. When was this, did you say?"

"Raht soon. Don't matter. I'll make damn sure you're available." He looked at Rusty for a few seconds wearing a mischievous grin. "That's awl."

Rusty jerked as if he'd been stuck with a pin. "Uh, Yessir. Yessir. I copy. Thank you, sir. Good day, sir." He backed out of the tiny office and closed the door.

Now what? Two days later, He found out.

Rusty was sitting in the usual briefing room in the TOC just after breakfast. At the podium were Major Bridgewater and a man Rusty had never seen before. He was dressed in brand new sterile jungle fatigues: no name or rank. The anonymous dress by now was perfectly routine to Rusty, but this man didn't look like he belonged in them. His shaggy, unkempt hair and loose posture said it all: "Company" man.

"Lieutenant, here is a set of map coordinates." He handed over a slip of paper with two letters and six digits penciled on it. "Can you please locate them on the map on this easel?"

Rusty looked at him with disbelief. What the hell was this, some kind of pissant test? Major Bridgewater caught Rusty's eye and made a "humor him" facial expression. Rusty shrugged and walked up to the easel, read the coordinates from the paper and traced them very deliberately on the map. "About here, I'd say. Within a furlong. Perhaps a chain or two. You need it down to a few cubits?"

Bridgewater rolled his eyes. "Lieutenant Naille is quite good at map reading, I promise you. But perhaps a tad whimsical at times. He can find it."

The Company man cleared his throat. "Harrumph. Well, he'd better." He glared at Rusty. "You are to deliver the objects to that location within ten minutes of 1430 hours today. No exceptions, no excuses. Do you understand?"

"The time and place, yes. Sir." Rusty added, just in case. "But the what and the why are unclear. What objects? And delivered to whom? For what reason?"

The spook harrumphed again. "That does not concern you. At all."

Bridgewater butted in. "Rusty, there are four…um, containers. You will drop them from an altitude of exactly three hundred feet and a speed of under one hundred knots. Drop them all at once, on one pass. You'll have to find the exact spot from a distance and make one pass. No circling the drop zone. Understand?"

"That part's no sweat. What am I carrying?"

"Just 'containers' is all I can say. You'll see them when you preflight, not before. You won't be carrying rocket pods, and you'll have main tanks only to hold down your takeoff weight. Just fly out, drop and come straight back. No radio traffic at all except to the tower, not even position reports. Copy?"

"I guess so, Major. More sneaky Pete stuff, obviously. No clue as to who's on the receiving end of this?"

"No." said both Bridgewater and the Company guy simultaneously.

"Ah ha. I get it."

"And no discussing this with your fellow FACs," Bridgewater said. "Not beforehand, at least."

"I copy, sir. A monosyllabic chrysanthemum is a singularity of verbiage."

Rusty watched the Company guy out of the corner of his eye. He was shaking his head in silent disbelief – or possibly despair.

An hour before his scheduled drop time, Rusty walked out to the ramp. Parked between the revetments was his favorite plane, tail number 012, but what was bolted to it stopped him dead in his tracks. Attached to each of the four pylons was a length of what appeared to be drainage pipe, each one about a foot in diameter and seven or eight feet long. Except for being blunt-nosed and lacking fins, they looked like 1,000-pound bombs!

Bridgewater was there, but the Company guy wasn't. "Well, I told you. There are your four containers. You have that slip of paper with you?"

"Uh yeah, of course. Sir, what do those damn things weigh? I swear the tires on that plane look like they're half flat."

"Never mind that. You'll make it off. It's been tested. You just put them where and when you've been briefed. Is that clear?"

There'd been no fake Texas drawl. This must be serious.

"Yessir. I copy. And radio silence. I remember. See you in three hours or so."

"Less. Y'all don't have gas for three ahrs". He avoided Rusty's sidelong look.

Oh shit. They had to offload gas to get within extreme maximum takeoff weight. "Uh, if it's all the same to you sir, I think I'll leave my parachute behind this time. And my helmet." Rusty wished he had time to take a massive shit as well, he thought to himself. Every ounce was gonna count.

"Fahn by me," Bridgewater drawled. "Raht fahn."

Rusty found out just how heavy the load was when he tried to taxi: it took almost half throttle just to get rolling. And here he was, attempting a takeoff in the hottest part of the day, when engine performance was at its lowest. Rusty could already envision himself in a smoking hole just off the end of runway. Or plunging into the Bakery and its prostitutes, he thought, irrationally. Well, if they beat him to death in anger, he'd at least get a legitimate Purple Heart.

Rusty did a very careful engine check at the end of the runway, squinting closely at each magneto for the slightest indication of ignition weakness. But all four looked good, so he shrugged and committed himself. The tower cleared him for takeoff, and he rolled out, not pausing at all, but firewalling both engines before he'd even gotten off the taxiway. Still, the plane hardly accelerated. It rolled, and it rolled. It hadn't even reached 65 knots by midfield, half a mile down the asphalt. Twenty knots to go before Rusty could even think about rotating the nose upwards. It was as if he'd left the brakes on.

Finally, less than two hundred yards from the end of the asphalt, he lifted off and wallowed clear of ground effect. Rusty's heart hammered, and he decided to leave the gear down until he'd climbed to at least a hundred feet of altitude. He knew he'd never stay airborne with the added drag of those cursed gear doors. Wallowing along, Rusty pushed stiff armed on the prop and throttle handles for all he was worth, trying to force them an extra fraction of an inch forward. It wasn't until he had skimmed across the tea plantation between the field and downtown Ban Me Thuot before he felt he could retract the gear. When he did, the plane sagged and slowed frighteningly until the doors closed. Slowly but encouragingly, good old 012 accelerated. He felt the speed build even before he could actually see the airspeed needle creeping upwards. It built still more when he milked up the flaps, and Rusty started breathing once more.

My God, what kind of weight was he carrying in those tubes, he wondered. If either engine were to suck up a drop of water from the wing tanks now, he'd be in the trees in moments. Rusty tipped the left wing down a few degrees to slide south of Ban Me Thuot city. He'd arc back around to the northwest when he was well clear. It was a good thing the terrain sloped downwards to the west. He'd be lucky to climb up to within a few hundred feet of the cloud base.

Crossing the border, he looked again at the small section of map where he was to drop the tubes. He already knew almost exactly where the place was, of course. That part of Cambodia was one of his best-memorized areas. Rusty could fly to within a quarter mile of it even without looking at the map. After that, he'd map read until he had the spot pinpointed.

As the engines labored on, Rusty wondered who could be down there waiting for whatever he carried. He knew that the Mike FACs had no teams operating near the abandoned city of Lumphat, but as he'd learned before, they weren't the only people 'not out there' doing intelligence gathering in Cambodia. Oh well, it wasn't absolutely necessary to know what he was dropping, or to whom, he surmised. His job was to put the damn things where and when ordered to. He could certainly do that.

On the topographic map, the drop zone was shown as a fairly level, unobtrusive, almost anonymous place. Nothing distinguished it from thousands of square miles of other terrain out here. That was probably its main attraction to…somebody.

Once he spotted a particular sharp bend in the Tonle Kong river, a broad blue line that fed the Tonle Srepok, he'd be able to identify the drop zone to within a few meters. He'd like to circle until he had it positively identified, but he couldn't. This had to be a one-pass drop. Bridgewater and the spook had emphasized that. But Rusty hoped that maybe he could pass the place a few miles offset to the side, then fly on a few miles before making a U-turn for the drop run. At least, that's what he planned to do. But that plan would take him right up to the Laotian border, which he was forbidden to cross. Lord knows why not; it was a poorly kept fiction that the US was running massive covert operations in and over Laos under the banner of civic assistance.

Even in the hazy, bluish air, Rusty could see at least fifteen miles, as long as he wasn't trying to see through one of the gray columns of rain that slanted down in scores of places like elephant legs. As he neared the sharp angle in a river that they called the "Elbow" he reflexively thumbed the microphone switch to make a position report; but even as his lips met to say "Mike…" he remembered that this was supposed to be a radio silence mission. Rusty released the switch.

Now he was past the Elbow. Down to his left front should be the pronounced U in the Tonle Kong where the Prek Noi entered it. Tonle meant river, and he'd assumed that prek meant creek. On the map, it was drawn as a tiny waterway, but in reality the rains had swollen every trickle into a torrent. The Tonle Kong flowed high, wide and muddy through the jungle. Nothing much resembled the 30-year-old map. Nearer to him should be the drop site, but all he could see was thick jungle. Hurriedly, he compared the topographic contour lines on his map with the ground, hoping to match the real ground to the largely inaccurate data that had produced this map.

Almost where he'd been looking, Rusty noticed a thin spot in the jungle. Even from this distance, he could see bare ground through the trees. That had to be the spot. Anywhere else nearby and he'd be dropping into thick jungle where nobody would ever find the damn canisters. He checked the clock. All he had to do now was fly on for half the time remaining before the drop, turn and come back. Sixteen minutes to go. Perfect.

Rusty flew straight on, but he craned his neck and twisted in the seat to keep the drop spot in sight as long as possible, and then kept track of other landmarks that he could recognize on the drop run. When seven minutes had elapsed, he started a wide left turn. He wanted to make the approach run with the spot just off his left side so he could see it better, then he'd make a last-second jog to put himself right over it. He'd just rolled out on his drop heading when he saw a chilling sight: a rain column had moved in right where the drop zone should be. Would he be able to see at all in that rain? If not, should he drop blind and hope whoever was down there could somehow find it? Would it be better to turn away and come back later, even if he missed the drop time? Or should he abort the drop altogether?

Rusty ruled that option out immediately. Whoever needed this stuff might really need it. Worse, there might not be another chance for them to set up a new drop. He made up his mind to drop as planned: one pass, on time. He'd try to get as close as he could. If he missed…well, he'd have done his best.

Before he got into the rain, Rusty pulled back the power and started a smooth descent down to 300 feet above the ground. As heavy as the plane was, losing altitude was the easy part. He dropped a touch of flaps for insurance, and added power until the airspeed held at 100 knots. Heavy and slow, the plane wallowed again, rocked by low-level wind eddies and gusts. Rusty juggled the controls, desperately looking outside while keeping close watch on his airspeed and altitude instruments. He strained to see through the gray veil of rain and mist, dismayed that visibility had dropped to less than a half mile. He could see clearly only straight down. Suddenly, water flashed below and he saw a sharp curve. It had to be the Prek Noi, he said to himself. He quickly flipped all four pylon switches to Drop and raised the safety cover on the Master Arm switch. The drop spot should be coming up now, any second. Rusty squinted ahead and left, unable to see anything but gray rain and deep green jungle. Where was it? Then, with no warning, a thin spot flashed below, red mud showing between sparse trees. Rusty stabbed at the Master Arm switch and pulled the firing trigger at the same time.

He never saw them drop, but he felt it. The plane suddenly shot up more than a hundred feet, the ground simply vanishing in grayness. He snapped his eyes to the instruments, slammed in full throttle and climbed straight ahead. In moments, he shot out of the edge of the rain column and was in clear air again. Rusty twisted to look back, but could see nothing except the column of rain, the jungle and clouds.

Well, at least they'd all come off cleanly, he thought. Suddenly, the thought of what would have happened if one of the heavy cylinders hadn't dropped made him feel a little queasy. With all that weight far out under one wing, the plane would have rolled uncontrollably. By now, he'd be dead. Rusted pylon latches were common, he knew, because the maintenance crews hardly ever removed rocket pods once they'd been installed.

Rusty resolved to buy drinks that evening for Lopez and Cramer. Whichever of them had loaded those awful tubes onto his plane had made sure those latches worked perfectly. He owed them. In fact, maybe he should spend a little more time out there on the ramp with them. His appreciation for wrench benders had once again come into sharp focus.

Good old 012, now shorn of her heavy cargo, climbed even more smartly and nimbly than usual. If it weren't for the low clouds, he'd have been tempted to fly a few aerobatics, just for the hell of it. Sadly, he had neither the altitude nor the fuel to lark around. As Bridgewater had said, he wouldn't be up long. Rusty was already down to less fuel than he'd usually have at the end of a four-hour flight, and he'd only been airborne for one hour. He headed straight home.

Taxiing in, he noticed wires trailing from each pylon. Chuckling to himself, he realized he wasn't the first one to rig a parachute to open that way! Bridgewater was there at the revetment to meet Rusty when he taxied in, and they walked immediately to the TOC for debriefing.

The CIA spook scowled when Rusty insisted the tubes were far too heavy to be carried on the O-2. The scowl turned to a glower when Rusty said he couldn't be positive he'd dropped at the assigned coordinates. Bridgewater asked why not, and Rusty explained about the rains. Bridgewater nodded and dismissed Rusty.

Later, Bridgewater called Rusty to his room again.

"You were right about the weight," he said before Rusty even sat down. "Good thing we only partially filled your main tanks, or you'd have never made it off the ground at all."

"No shit. What did I weigh?"

"Way over gross. Probably near 5,500 pounds."

Rusty stared at him. The usual combat takeoff weight was already over 'book' maximum: 4,850 pounds versus the 4,400 that Cessna recommended. Rusty had been as much as 1,100 pounds – 25% - over the maximum allowed takeoff weight. Worse, that allowed weight had been established for sea-level takeoff on a cool day. Ban Me Thuot was both much higher and hotter.

"No fucking wonder I almost lost it. Tell me, did you know this before you ordered me to go?" Rusty suddenly felt an intense flash of paranoia. Was Bridgewater out to kill him?

"No, I didn't, Rusty. Honest. The..uh, agent told me to fuel only your main tanks, but that's the only instruction he gave me. When I finally wormed the real information out of him, I damn near slugged him. You can believe me, I'll never let that happen again."

Well, Rusty noticed - no drawl. Bridgewater was being serious.

Rusty nodded, "Ok. No problem. But if we ever have another drop like that, you should insist on only two tubes. That should be manageable. And it'd be damn smart to have the firing switches set up to jettison 'em on takeoff, too. Just in case."

"Sounds like a smart idea. I shoulda thought of it. We will, next time."

"So there will be a next time?"

"Yup, in about two weeks, probably. That's all I know for now. Nothing's certain, though."

"Yeah. Hey, tell me. How long have you known about those candy bombs?"

"Jist about from the start, I reckon. Yore strolls outside the wahr to collect parachutes was reported. Didn't take long to figger why."

"I'll be damned," Rusty admitted. He leaned forward and added, "But you couldn't have known why I was doing it. I surprised a young honey out there tending her garden in the rain. Naked. Nice, too."

Bridgewater leaned back and that familiar grin spread across his face. "Knew there had to be something to it. Happy to help out."

"Huh?"

"Sheeyit, boy. Whar'd ya think all them goodies came from, huh? Ah hauled summa that shit all the way from Dalat, jist so's y'all could shine yore ass for some Yard snatch. Pity ya ain't never gonna get any o' that nookie fer yore troubles."

CHAPTER NINE

Gradually, the monsoons abated as autumn deepened. The days between rain bands increased and the thunderstorms weakened. Rivers slowly lowered from roaring red torrents to snaking black normalcy. Everywhere, peasants planted rice in flooded paddies, toiling from dawn to dusk hunched over as they shoved rice slips into the stinking ooze.

Out along the Ho Chi Minh Trail, the enemy was also toiling with renewed vigor. New missions came down to the Mikes with almost frenetic speed. Hardly a day passed that they didn't put in a team, or pull one out. They also began to lose teams completely. Someone would insert a team, and they'd either go hot within hours or simply vanish soon after insertion. Whoever flew the dawn cap mission would try to contact the team, and there'd be no response.

They'd lost four of seven teams over two weeks when Major Bridgewater gathered them together for a strategy session.

"Boys, y'all know it ain't goin' too good out thar. We're flat runnin' outta volunteers." He grinned. Many team members were either fiercely ferocious Montagnards or well-paid Chinese Nung mercenaries. Few served on capricious whims.

"So we're gonna start providin' 'em with some cover and support round the clock." Bridgewater paused to let that sink in.

Flip was the first to react. He sat up straight and asked, "You mean overnight? We're gonna fly night caps?"

"Ah'd hope that you'd be a-flyin' sober," Bridgewater jibed. "But yeah, we're gonna fly cap missions at night. For a while, anyhow."

They stared at him, dumbfounded.

"Ah know it's not been done before. Here, anyways. And Ah ain't exactly been ordered to do it. But Ah want y'all to give it a shake. Sanderson has worked up a schedule. We'll start it tonight. No sense puttin' it off none, I reckon."

He briefed them on how he wanted the flights conducted. There'd be two pilots plus a robin on all night flights, for safety. They'd carry one pod of rockets, two racks of parachute flares plus a rack of log flares. Yes, that'd put them seriously over gross weight, but night air would be cool enough to make up for it with better engine performance. He hoped.

Rusty looked at him with eyebrows tightly arched. Bridgewater shrugged.

Because the civilian tower controllers left at sunset, one pilot would have to be up there at night, if only to turn on the runway lights and man the tower radios. Three flights per night should just cover the ten hours of late-summer darkness, Bridgewater said, and that would allow them all to work on a four-hour on and four-hour off schedule.

Rusty realized the fallacy of that plan immediately. Pre-mission brief, post-mission debrief, eating and showering would consume a lot of that "off" time. It took closer to six hours to perform a four-hour mission. Nobody would be getting much rest while this went on. He mentioned it.

"Ah know," Bridgewater said. "Sanderson and Ah will be flying missions raht alongside ya'll. That'll help out enough to get ya a leetle bit 'a time off. Mebbe a half day or so. We'll plan it around yore horse pill days fer a start."

A whopping half-day off, but not to sleep - to shit. Just great. Each of them would be flying two or even three maximum-duration flights every day – plus tower duty. No booze, either, Rusty realized. The "eight hours from bottle to throttle" rule pretty much ruled out any of the "bottle" when there were only four hours between every landing and the next takeoff.

True to his word, Bridgewater scheduled himself for the first night's toughest go, the midnight to four a.m. mission. Not to appear a slacker, Sanderson penciled himself in for the very first night sortie. Bridgewater would relieve him.

Before the day was out, Sanderson had a schedule worked out and typed up. It even looked brutal. The next day was Rusty's usual day off, due to his malaria pill schedule. Sanderson had scheduled him for tonight's second tower stint: midnight to 0400. Then Rusty would have twelve hours off and take the 1600 until 2000 flight.

Rusty looked over the list and realized that Sanderson had somehow arranged it so that Rushing and Buchenhardt never flew together. Good thing; they'd probably kill one another. Rushing, in fact, would be the first to pull tower duty, to be relieved by Rusty. Buchenhardt, Craig and Flip would fly the first night's right-seat missions. Thank goodness they only needed one pilot aboard for daytime missions.

Kit and Rusty took a jeep and drove to the civilian terminal. Parking next to the titty-pink control tower, they went inside and climbed the stairs to the top. There, the Vietnamese controllers showed them the controls for the lights and radios – all labeled in English, thank goodness. Fortunately or unfortunately, there'd be absolutely nothing for them to do except for the single takeoff and landing at each end of their shifts. The tower was normally closed from dusk until dawn and there'd be no other traffic but the Mikes. Rusty resolved to turn the radio volume up and perhaps nap on the floor for his four hours. The radio would wake him, he rationalized, and all he'd have to do would be to turn on the runway lights for a few minutes, then off again. Maybe it wouldn't be so bad after all.

That evening, they all went to the chow hall together to talk it through. Immediately afterwards, Rusty went back to his room and tried to get some sleep. Naturally, he couldn't. Batman had inserted a second ground team that afternoon – Flip had inserted one two days before that had managed to stay undetected. When Batman landed just before sunset, it would be the last capless gap over the teams. One of the enlisted guys had taken Kit to the tower, and shortly before twenty-hundred hours Rusty clearly heard Sanderson and Buchenhardt take off for the first ever Mike FAC night cap mission.

Rusty's alarm clock clanged cruelly at 2300, and he jerked bolt upright. Shaking his head in a futile attempt to rid it of cobwebs, he slipped into fatigues and boots. He had planned to shower, but blew it off. Who the hell would he offend up there in the tower? On the way to the TOC, he saw Flip come out of his room and meet Bridgewater. The pair walked to the ramp to preflight as Rusty went the other way to the radio room. He opened the door and found Young on the radios.

"How's it going?"

"Oh, pretty calm, sir. Both teams checked in fine and everything's quiet. Coffee's on if you want some before you relieve Lt Rushing, and the jeep's right outside."

"Bless you for the coffee, my son," Rusty said, with wholehearted gratitude. "I'd take a gallon of it with me if I could."

"There's a Thermos right there, sir. Fill 'er up. Lt Rushing took one, too. You know, avgas keeps pilots up, but coffee is what keeps us enlisted guys running."

"It oughta," Rusty said, taking a sip of the steaming brew. "This stuff has more octane than avgas. Wow!"

Young grinned from ear to ear. "Yessir, it does. We do brew it a bit stouter for night duty. Even Sergeant McGuire approves."

"Now I know how that mug of his got that way," Rusty nodded. "This stuff has more solid stuff in it than the Tonle Srepok. And that is saying something."

Young turned rueful. "You know, sir, I sure wish I could see some of the sights you pilots do. I can only imagine what it looks like out there." He jerked his head westwards. "It must be beautiful."

"It is. Or at least it is sometimes and in some places. It's a bit scary at times, too, you know. You might not like it so much then. But, in general, I'd have to agree: it's gorgeous to fly over." To himself, Rusty wondered if Bridgewater might let them take the enlisted guys up once in a while, especially the radio guys. It might be invaluable for them to actually see the ops area and put the landmarks in perspective. It would be completely unauthorized of course; but then so was everything else they did here.

For that matter, Rusty had long wished to go along with the Green Hornets on one of their flights sometime. He used the same reasoning: he'd have a better idea of what they did and what they could and couldn't do. He'd draw the line at flying aboard a Kingbee, though. Those guys might be good, but they were nuts, too. Rusty would probably be petrified.

As he mused, he finished filling the Thermos. Turning to the door, he bid goodnight to Young. At the main gate, the guard unlocked the gate and swung it open. Rusty drove slowly down the dirt road to the air terminal. The only light showing anywhere was that which gleamed from the green-tinted windows of the control tower, and Rusty clearly saw Kit walking around up there. Rusty parked and went in, his steps pinging on the steel stair treads as he climbed. He found Kit smiling down as Rusty emerged from the stairwell and rose above the floor level.

"You're a welcome relief, bud. It's quieter than a tomb up here and twice as boring. I wish to hell I'd thought to bring a book or something," he said. "Or maybe a hootch maid."

"Uh huh. Now that you mention it, I wish I'd have thought of a book, too. Nix on the hootch maid. With my luck, the only one willing to come with me would be Mama-San."

Kit laughed aloud. "Well, maybe the fuckyou lizard will oblige you. It's sure big enough."

"The what?" Rusty said.

"The fuckyou lizard. Look." He pointed to the ceiling. In the center was a square steel plate that supported the signal lantern used to flash instructions to radio-less airplanes. The support plate hung on its bolts free of the water-stained acoustic tile ceiling by an inch or so, and through that gap protruded a large, green-scaled foot.

"Holy shit! What is that thing?" Rusty stammered.

"Just what I said: a fuckyou lizard. I think it sits up there and ambushes insects that fly past the gap. All I've seen is that one foot, but based on that, the whole lizard has to be a couple of feet long. And every few minutes, it cusses at me. 'Fuck you!' it says."

"You're shitting me."

"No I'm not. Just let things quiet down and he'll start in again. Make a noise and he goes quiet for a while. You'll see."

Before they could talk more, the radio crackled. "Bang My Twat tower, Mike 51 for takeoff."

Kit picked up the silver, bullet-shaped microphone stand and squeezed the switch on its side. He glanced at the dials glowing softly in the slanted panel and replied in a horribly mangled accent, "Uh copy, My fi won. You queer for tay-awp. Wins com. Ahtimmer tree zeoh won tree. okay?"

As he spoke, he turned a saucer-sized black rheostat. In response, the runway lights came on, growing brighter as Kit twisted the knob. Rusty looked to the east end of the runway, and saw the lights of an O-2 as it swung onto the asphalt runway.

"My fi won rowing." Bridgewater replied, with an equally outrageous accent. Kit's teeth gleamed from behind his coal-black stash. In seconds, the plane was gone to the west and Kit spun the rheostat back to off. With the runway lights out, Rusty could see nothing but his own reflection in the control tower windows.

"Well, that's about it, I guess," Kit said. Sanderson should be back in 30 minutes or so. Just turn the lights on and clear him to land. Unless the boss has a plane malfunction, he'll be gone until four a.m. Batman and Craig will takeoff, Bridgewater and Flip will land, and you can just call the TOC on land line for a ride home. Nothing to do here but turn out the lights, I guess. The regular control crew should come in about eight, but it'll be light by then and Batman won't need runway lights.

"What if Batman has an emergency while it's still dark?"

"Hmm. I guess somebody'd wake you up and you'd hurry back here. I'll tell them that at the TOC."

"Gee, thanks."

The nightly harassment mortar fire went off just then, rattling the windows.

"There's my end of shift whistle," Kit said. "See ya at the bar." He stepped to the opening in the floor and disappeared down the stairs. Rusty heard his steps go down, then the screech and clang of the door. He didn't hear the jeep start, but saw its headlights pull away.

Alone, there was nothing for Rusty to do but explore the tower. He checked out the meager assortment of communications radios, the displays that showed the barometer setting, wind speed and direction, and the small boards that held flight strips for aircraft traffic, all blank now. Suddenly, he heard a scratching sound from above him, and looked up. The lizard had shifted its foot. Maybe it had caught a roach or something.

Standing there, Rusty suddenly got the feeling of being watched. He remembered how clearly Kit had appeared from below, and realized how plainly visible he also must be at this moment. Hell, he made a pretty easy target! He didn't exactly fall to the floor, but he did step smartly over to a chair and sat down. Rusty gauged the height of the windowsill, and calculated that he must be out of sight from the ground when seated. He sure hoped so; he was alone up there. Alone, visible – and completely unarmed! Worse, the civilian tower stood outside the secured compound. Suddenly, he realized that the entrance door was unlocked. All an enemy had to do was walk to the door, climb the stairs and kill him. Cripes! That sure wiped out any ideas of a catnap. He wished they'd thought this through a little better!

Rusty rolled the chair over to the lighting panel and dimmed the tower's inside lights. As they dimmed, he felt less and less vulnerable. But he stayed seated, nonetheless. Rusty leaned back, straining his ears for the smallest sound of his impending demise. Long minutes went by. He heard nothing but the faint, lulling hum of the radios. Eventually, he nodded and his eyelids crept down.

"Fuck You!"

Rusty leapt out of his chair, but not faster than his heart had leapt out of his chest. His eyes flitted to the stairwell, expecting his last vision to be a black-clad VC with an AK-47 aimed at him. Nothing.

Above the hammering of his own blood in his ears, Rusty detected a faint scrabbling sound. He looked up. The foot had vanished. Jesus! That damned lizard *did* say "Fuck You" as plain as day.

Rusty gradually calmed down, the familiar twitchy muscles and nausea of a severe adrenaline dump slowly ebbing away. He poured a cup of Young's potent brew and tried to think about something besides VC assassins creeping toward him in the dark; not with complete success. He forced himself to think about what Bridgewater and Flip were doing now, what they would talk about

out there in the dark over Cambodia. He wondered if the insert teams slept at night – or could.

Funny that he'd never thought of that before. Somehow, it just seemed that the war ended for everyone at sunset, like it did for Mike FAC pilots; a gentleman's agreement, sort of. But it didn't, he knew. Men fought and died no matter what the hour of day or night. He'd experienced rocket and mortar attacks during the night, and certainly knew that his own side fired rounds at the enemy at night. There were even FACs who specialized in night work against trucks along the Ho Chi Minh Trail in Laos. If those VC trucks rolled throughout the night in Laos, they certainly did the same in Cambodia. Maybe the intel teams were actually busiest at night. It came as a revelation.

Those teams weren't on a lazy camping trip, with a pleasant fire, ghost stories and hot chocolate at night. Did they even get hot food at all? Was their day divided into four-hour watches? Did they strain their ears and eyes at the darkness around them? Were they as perpetually afraid as Rusty knew he would be in their place?

That thought brought him back to his own situation. He'd hate to admit it to anyone else, but he was afraid, right now. The cold wet patches under his arms and his shallow breathing betrayed him to himself. It was funny, he mused: I'm petrified here on the ground, and ground troops get scared in the air.

Rusty remembered an Army Ranger he'd taken up on a routine visual recce flight at LZ Emerald. He was a member of a Long Range Reconnaissance Patrol, a member of a team much like the 'yard guys. He'd walked into bad guy country dozens of times to gather intelligence, capture people who could be interrogated and done even more dangerous things. One of the meanest, toughest, ice water-veined men to walk the planet. Yet, when he flew in Rusty's plane, he literally squirmed in fear. He kept muttering, "Jesus, they can see us up here! All of them can see us! There's nowhere to hide, no cover, no nothing!" And when they landed, he'd turned to Rusty white-faced and swore he'd never leave the ground on a combat flight again.

In the bar at Cam Rahn once, an F-4 driver had shivered when Rusty told him he was a FAC. "Goddamn! I worry about getting blown out of the sky, and I fly at 30,000 feet and 500 knots. You crazy bastards work down on the treetops at one hundred knots! No fucking way you'd get me in one of those kites." So, Rusty thought, maybe we all felt comfortable in our own environment, while somebody else's – anybody else's – might scare the bejeezus out of us. How would he feel in a helicopter, he wondered?

The radio suddenly hissed a stream of static. Rusty jumped a little and stared at the speaker. No voice came out, and the white noise stopped in a few seconds. Silence again. He looked at the clock: 0135. Time sure crawls when you're scared shitless. He poured more coffee. The lizard had disappeared. Maybe his duty watch had ended, too. A shame: Rusty missed his company. His vocabulary might be limited, but he used it well.

"Tower, Mike 56 for takeoff."

Rusty started violently and stared at the speaker, then at the clock. It was 0340. Christ, he'd fallen asleep. He grappled for the mike, "Go ahead, 56." It came out as a croak.

"Ready for takeoff. What I do, wake you up? Sounds like it." He could hear the glee in Batman's voice.

"Uh, no, no. I was just, um…oh all right; you got me. You're cleared to go. Winds are 240 at five, altimeter 3009." Rusty reached for the rheostat and twirled it up to the maximum. In response to the blaze of runway lights, Batman flicked on his landing lights and trundled onto the asphalt. Rusty absently watched as Batman started his roll, then snapped to full attention.

"Mike 56, you're taking ground fire from your three o'clock side!"

A string of tracers wavered and snaked their way towards and around the accelerating plane. Some arced over it and seemed to plunge into the compound beyond. Some ricocheted off the runway and bounced sharply upwards.

"Douse your lights, 56! He's tracking your lights," Rusty shouted into the mic. Instantly, all Batman's external lights went out. Rusty saw the runway lights eclipsed in sequence by the plane as it rolled by. The path of the tracers was behind him now, and the gap was growing by the second.

The shooter now had other worries besides missing Batman. Rusty could see other tracers in the air, and these came from the compound's watchtowers. The mercenary guards on duty there loved to shoot their machine guns, and wasted no excuse to do so. Now, they must be cackling in glee as they poured long streams of red-dashed light towards the source of the ground fire. Seconds later, two parachute flares popped open to bathe the scene in surreal orange light. The shooter had stopped, either because he'd run his magazine dry or because the tower shots were coming close.

The whole compound would be awake now, Rusty thought. The steady roar of the tower guns, the thump of mortars launching new flares as well as explosive rounds and the *crump crump* of the HE rounds going off just a few hundred yards away would wake them all. Rusty laughed when he thought of them all tumbling out of their bunks and scrambling for helmets, flak vests and guns. Then he remembered where he was: alone and defenseless in this lighthouse. That didn't seem funny.

Rusty keyed the mic. "56, you get off okay?"

"Affirmative, tower. Thanks for the heads up. We didn't see the groundfire until one bounced off the runway ahead of us. That was after your call. No hits, and we're proceeding as planned."

"Ok, 56. Be sure you report in to Mama so the big guy hears about this. Might make his night interesting."

"Yeah, it just might. Will do. 56 going off the push."

"Bye."

Batman would report his status to the TOC. Bridgewater was sure to overhear, as he'd be on the same frequency. He'd be landing in just a few minutes, and knowing that he might take ground fire in the landing pattern would get his attention. Sure enough, ten minutes later, the tower radio crackled to life again.

"Tower, Mike 51 ten west. Say conditions."

"51, winds are 240 at six, altimeter 3009. Tracers seen northeast end of the field. Land at your discretion." Rusty knew that the bad guys could monitor any frequency in use, and they certainly knew this one. Rusty didn't want to give any nearby VC the news of which way Bridgewater would be landing. Luckily, he'd forgotten to turn the runway lights off in all the excitement, so turning them back on now wouldn't serve as an arrival warning. He might even claim later that he'd planned it that way.

Still, even Rusty was surprised a few seconds later when he again saw the runway lights being eclipsed. Bridgewater had landed already! He'd landed downwind, as Rusty suspected he might. Landing to the east, he didn't have to stop, turn around and taxi back to the only taxiway exit at the east end of the field. He'd somehow come in silently, too. Rusty made a mental note to ask how he did that!

When Rusty thought he'd had enough time to clear the runway, he turned the rheostat down to off. Then, crouched down out of sight, he dialed the TOC on the land line and asked them to come get him in a jeep. "Make sure you bring a rifle. No, two rifles! And extra ammo."

It was Sgt Lopez, and he had indeed brought a rifle for himself and another one for Rusty. He was smiling, but nervously: they both knew they were essentially alone out there. Lopez spared none of the four-cylinder horses on the half-mile drive back to the main gate, but he did slow down well short of it. When he almost stopped, he gave three short and one long blast on the jeep's mule-like horn. Rusty looked at him in the pitch darkness, and Lopez said, "We arranged that as I left. Now the guard knows it's us. I wouldn't want to get a fifty-caliber surprise by roaring up to the gate in the dark. Not tonight, especially."

Neither would Rusty. Bullets from the heavy Browning machine gun that guarded the gate would zip through jeep and flesh like x-rays through a hummingbird. But messier...lots messier.

By the time they got to the TOC, Bridgewater and Flip were already there.

"Where exactly did the ground fire come from and how much of it did you see? One source or more?" Bridgewater prompted Rusty the instant he came through the door.

"It looked like one source, one guy. He emptied one magazine at Batman before he went cold and then deedeemaued out of there. Or I guess he did. That's all the fire there was, and I didn't see any directed at you when you landed. How'd you do that anyway? Silently, I mean."

"Later. Batman said you directed him to roll lights out. Is that right?"

Rusty nodded.

"That was quick thinking. Smart, too."

"It seemed obvious at the time. The bad guy was obviously aiming at the plane's lights. Hell, with his rotating beacon, nav lights and landing lights on, Batman looked like a rolling carnival. As soon as he went dark, he became the Invisible Man. I left the runway lights on so he still had visual references for takeoff. No sweat. Same for your landing," Rusty tossed in.

"Good thing you did. I needed all the visual reference I could get. I flew a flameout approach. That's why you didn't hear us. I stayed at altitude when I heard about the ground fire, and when I was directly over the field, I pulled both engines to idle and flew a steep spiral right down to touchdown. Lights out, of course."

Rusty's eyebrows went up. That type of landing pattern was extremely hard to judge in daylight. In a blacked-out plane to a nearly blacked-out runway, it would have required nearly miraculous eyesight and depth perception. The old man was a stick!

Flip must've noticed Rusty's eyebrows, because he nodded silently and raised his own. He'd been impressed, too...and he'd been in the plane with Bridgewater.

Before long, they received a situation report from the Army guys, but it was only what they suspected: probably a single bad guy. They'd send out a

≈ 211 ≈

patrol in the morning to try to find where he'd fired from and maybe find some evidence that the tower guards or the mortars had hit him. But they'd likely not find anything. It was all over now.

Bridgewater asked that they all sit down later in the day and go over lessons learned. Rusty certainly had a few things to say, but they'd keep. Besides, it was almost daylight by now, and he had already felt the first rumblings in his gut that presaged a day of the runny shits from yesterday's horse pill. He'd certainly be sitting down.

By the time they all got together at lunchtime, Rusty was empty from stem to stern. The others contributed a few observations while he wolfed down his soup and sandwich. Then Bridgewater turned to him and asked for his input.

Rusty first told them how naked and defenseless he felt in the tower, and how nervous he'd been due to the unlocked access and no transport. He also opined how pointless the tower exercise was. There was no other air traffic into or out of BMT at night, so what was the point of takeoff and landing clearance? Couldn't they simply arrange for the Vietnamese controllers to leave the runway lights on all night?

Both Sanderson and Bridgewater nodded in agreement as Rusty spoke, and when Kit admitted that he'd also felt like a prime target in that lighted tower, that clinched it. Tower duty was out. Sanderson said the decision would greatly simplify the scheduling, and make our rotations better, too. He'd rework the schedule right away.

Rusty was still scheduled to fly the 4 to 8 pm cap, and he was logy from last night's work plus the debilitating effects of the horse pill, so he went back to his room for a nap. When he opened the door, there squatted Mai Lin. She had a tiny electric rice cooker going in the center of the floor; the pungent odor of nuoc mam and rice filled the place. But what drew Rusty's instant attention was what the hootch maid had chosen to use as a lid for the rice steamer: his brand-new copy of Outdoor Life magazine. Rusty exploded.

"Hey, you no cook here! Out! Out now! Goddamn!" He reached down and jerked the magazine – now curled and congealed into a solid mass – off the cooker. "Goddamn it!"

Her baby girl smile vanished, and she went stony. She instantly looked down at the floor and scrabbled first to the wall plug and then to the cooker. She wrapped the scalding hot thing in a cleaning rag and scuttled backwards out the door, bowing obsequiously and silently as she did.

Rusty immediately regretted the outburst, but a glance at the ruined magazine rekindled his fury. He threw the useless thing into the trashcan and flung himself down on the bunk. But he knew he'd stew the event over in his mind for hours, making a nap unlikely at best, so he got up again and went to retrieve a book from Flip's room.

He had no sooner gotten back than Mama-San burst in. She railed at Rusty in her steam-whistle screeching Vietnamese, black eyes and the disturbingly black teeth of a habitual betel-nut chewer flashing in accompaniment. All the while she waved her hands and arms like a scarecrow in a Kansas twister. When she finally wound down, she stopped abruptly, shot a look at him and said, "You numba ten GI. No clean room. No more." She whirled and stormed out.

Big whoopee, Rusty thought to himself. All Mai Lin had ever done was carelessly fling up his poncho liner blanket, and sometimes sweep the floor. Unlike some other of the men, Rusty had never had anything "disappear" from his room, but what little Mai Lin had done for him as a maid wasn't even worth the paltry three dollars a month he'd been asked to contribute. Good riddance, he fumed.

Knowing that sleep would now be completely impossible, Rusty decided to fulfill a promise he'd made to himself. He walked out to the ramp to visit with the maintenance guys. Sgt Cramer and a two-stripe airman had the engine panels and access plates removed from tail number 068. Both of them had their arms deep inside the rear engine compartment when Rusty walked up. He overheard Cramer ask the other man to fetch a particular wrench for him.

"Never mind, airman. I'll get it. Where's that wrench, Cramer?" Rusty said, interrupting.

"Oh, hello sir, I didn't see you," Cramer began extricating himself.

"No, no, don't stop. Either of you. I'll help." Rusty stooped to the tool chest and selected what seemed to be the right wrench. "Is this the one you need?"

"Almost. It's the one in the next drawer, the half-inch box with the offset. I can't reach this nut with a straight-handled one. Thank you, sir."

"No thanks needed. Here ya go." Rusty passed a wrench with a double bend in the handle, worming it deep inside the cowling where Cramer could grip it. Cramer manipulated it as best he could, but slipped and barked his knuckles twice. He eventually backed his arm out, and Rusty saw his oil-blackened hand also coated with blood. Cramer wiped his knuckles with a rag with complete unconcern, still staring into the dark engine cavity.

"You gonna get that treated, sergeant?" Rusty asked.

"Huh? I mean, what, sir?" Then he looked down at his hand. "Oh, this? Oh heck no, sir. Geez, if I walked to the clinic every time I busted a knuckle open, none of these things would ever get fixed." He shook his head in amazement at the question. He turned to the airman. "Imagine that, Andy! Go get a busted knuckle treated! Oh Lord." They both laughed.

The airman came around to see what kind of idiot would suggest such a thing, and Rusty read his nametag: Corso.

"Corso? Andy Corso?" Rusty asked.

"Yessir, why?"

"Hell, I had a good buddy named Andy Corso back in ROTC at St Louis University. He was in my class. Any relation, maybe?"

"Uh, not that I know of, sir. I have lots of cousins, but I don't know of any others named Andy. And none that went through ROTC. College either, for that matter."

"Well, nonetheless, he was a helluva fine guy, and I'm sure you are, too. Glad to meet you." Rusty stuck out his hand. Corso stiffened a bit, but offered his own, a bit hesitantly. It was as black as Cramer's with oil, but Rusty took it and shook it firmly.

Corso immediately beamed and looked to Cramer.

"That's right, Andy. He's one of the good pile its," Cramer said. Then to Rusty, "No offense, sir, but not all officers fit that description. No names, but…"

Rusty held up his left hand, still shaking Corso's with the right. "No need to finish, Cramer, I'm pretty sure I know at least one example."

"Yessir, I think you do." They both chuckled.

"What's left to do in there?" Rusty motioned to the plane, changing to a more neutral topic.

"Oh, just safety wire and button it up. That was the last nut. We had to change out the generator. It takes four hands to set the belt tension and tighten down the adjustment. You might not believe it, sir, but handing me that wrench saved us a lot of time. If Andy here had had to let go to reach for the wrench, we'd have lost the adjustment. Your fifth hand really made a difference."

Rusty shrugged. "More than happy to help. Show me how you safety wire, will you? That's always interested me."

"Safety wire interests you, sir? You're pulling my leg."

"No, really. I know that it's designed to keep nuts and fastenings from getting loose, but it always looks so neat and cleanly done. I can't twist wire and get it to look like that. What's the secret?"

Cramer absolutely lit up. With childlike delight, he whisked a strange-looking pair of pliers from his back pocket. "Safety wire pliers, sir. Watch." He pulled a length of thin stainless steel wire from a spool and cut it. Then he threaded it around the handle of his toolbox and clamped the jaws of the pliers where the two ends of wire crossed. Then he gripped a third leg of the pliers that extended back between the two regular ones. "Now I just pull." The pliers spun as the center leg extended, and the wire coiled sinuously and smoothly around itself. "Nothing to it."

But despite that denouement, Rusty saw a glint flash in his eyes. Clearly, this simple act was one in which Cramer took great pride. There was art in this artisan.

Corso shook his head ruefully. "Yeah, nothing to it for you. I can't get it to look like that either, sir. He makes it look easy. It isn't, or I'm the clumsiest dago there ever was."

"I doubt that, Corso. I never met an Italian who didn't delight in smooth flowing lines, symmetry and beautiful things. Isn't that why the greatest artists are Italian? You just wouldn't be happy with less than perfection is all. There's as much beauty in your blood as there is carbonara sauce and Chianti."

It was Corso's turn to beam. "Carbonara, sir? Most non-Italians just say spaghetti sauce. As if there were only one kind." He rolled his eyes. "How do you come to know carbonara?"

"My wife is a Schiavone, Andy. I had to learn, but now I speak carbonara. Also marinara, bolognaise, Florentine, primavera and even pesto."

He stuck out his hand. "Put it there again, sir. This time it's my pleasure."

Cramer interrupted. "I hate to put a damper on this, but we have to get this plane finished. With this added flying, it's elbows and assholes to keep them all in service. Sir," he added, not without due respect.

Rusty pitched in again, handing them tools, carrying removed panels and otherwise serving as unskilled labor. He was soon soaked with sweat in the muggy air, hands black with oil, and he'd even managed to bleed a little due to a rough edge of metal. But he was thoroughly and joyfully absorbed in the labor when he heard a plaintive Vietnamese voice close behind.

"Daiwee! Daiwee, we fly now? Go now!"

Rusty looked at him, then at his watch. Cripes, it was almost four o'clock!

"Shit! Cramer, I'm late for my mission! Christ, I forgot my flight." Rusty thought rapidly. He'd have missed the pre-flight TOC brief, and they must've already gone to look for him. "Where's the flightline phone?"

"Right there in the Conex, sir," Corso shot back. "Here, I'll show you."

Cramer yelled to Rusty's retreating back, "The sixteen hundred go, sir? That'll be 014. I'll get started on your pre-flight. Just grab your chute and stuff. I'll get the robin ready."

Inside the oven-like steel Conex, Rusty grabbed up the phone and cranked the handle. The TOC answered: Sanderson. "Naille, where the hell have you been? We've searched the whole damn compound."

"I'm sorry, sir. I'm right here on the ramp. Um, doing my pre-flight. Nguyen's here, too. I'll be off in a minute or so."

"Why weren't you at the brief?"

"Uh, well, it's just a cap mission, and I already knew the freqs and stuff. So I came right to the ramp." Rusty lied. He did know almost all he needed to know, but there may have been last-minute intel or weather data presented at the briefing. Missing the pre-brief was unforgivable, almost gross dereliction.

"Report to me when you land, Naille." Sanderson said in a forced calm. That meant he was really, really mad.

Rusty acknowledged him and hung up. He grabbed his chute, helmet and vest from the gear Conex, and ran to 014. He wished there were time to go back to the hootch for his CAR-15, but he'd never make takeoff time if he did. Now sweat was really running; down his arms and legs, from his chest and back, and especially from his scalp. As he ran to the plane, he felt suddenly woozy. The edges of Rusty's vision went black.

Cramer saw him approach. "Sir, you feel okay? You've gone really pale. The plane's ready to go, but you don't look so good."

Rusty realized what was wrong. "I think I'm really dehydrated. I had the horse pill shits this morning, and now…"

"Ah, yeah, that would explain it. Corso! Get a full canteen here right now. The lieutenant needs a drink." Then back to Rusty, "You strap in, sir. Crank up and get ready to taxi. I'll catch up with you in the arming area."

Rusty climbed in, head aswim, but managed to go through the pre-start items from memory as Cramer strapped in Nguyen. The cool air that rushed in through the cockpit window after the engines were running helped. Cramer pulled the chocks and raced off to his jeep.

Rusty taxied out through the gate, then meandered down the bumpy taxiway. At the hammerhead area where they armed their rockets and checked the engines, he stopped. Cramer slid his jeep to a dusty stop ten yards off the right wing and leapt out. He pulled the rocket pod safety pins and handed them in to Rusty, along with two full canteens. "There you go, sir. Get some of that down you right now, and finish the rest of it after you get airborne. Take this salt pill, too." He fished inside his shirt pocket and pulled out what had once been a white pill. When he dropped it into Rusty's palm, it was coated with oil and pocket lint. Without a second thought, Rusty popped it into his mouth and swallowed it with a long pull at the canteen.

Cramer smiled and nodded his approval. "Good to go now, sir. See you later this evening." He turned and strode confidently and purposefully back to the jeep. He raised his right fist with the thumb up, then smoothly swept it into a crisp salute.

By the time they crossed the border, Rusty had finished the first canteen and was feeling much better. His soaked fatigues were drying rapidly now in the cooler, drier air, and Rusty gave one large involuntary shiver from the resulting chill. Nguyen looked at him with concern, but Rusty shook his head. "No problem, Nguyen." Rusty attempted it in Vietnamese: "Khong Xao." Nguyen grinned at what was probably reverse pidgin.

The cap was uneventful. Rusty set up a large circular orbit about midway between where the two teams were supposedly working. At ten thousand feet they droned along. The sun poured in through the Plexiglas, the engines droned monotonously and Rusty grew irresistibly sleepy. He turned to Nguyen. "You want fly?"

The robin nodded excitedly and pushed himself up from his habitual slouch. Grinning wildly, he put his hands on the yoke and stared fixedly out over the nose. Rusty watched him for a few minutes, and when it was obvious he could hold altitude and heading pretty well, Rusty leaned his head against the side window. I'll just rest my eyes a bit, he thought.

Rusty awoke with a start and automatically glanced down. Not surprisingly, they were over jungle. Then he glanced over at Nguyen and his heart nearly stopped. Nguyen was curled up in his seat...asleep!

Rusty looked at the clock. Christ, he'd been asleep for half an hour! How long had they droned along with nobody at the controls? And where the hell were they? In a glance, he saw that they'd climbed to twelve thousand feet. He turned on the TACAN display and cringed. They were far, far out over Cambodia. Before he figured out just where, he made a quick turn and headed back east. The motion awakened Nguyen. Rusty wanted to hit him, but it wouldn't have helped. Nguyen smiled in pure innocence and blissful unawareness.

Rusty switched the fuel tanks to auxiliary, started a slow descent and got out his maps. He'd been trying to find something recognizable on them for a few minutes without success when a broad band of brown appeared ahead. Jesus Christ, they were miles west of the Mekong, about a hundred miles from where they should be orbiting. And, it stabbed through his awareness, far out of either team's radio range. If they'd come under attack while he slept, they'd be dead now. Rusty imagined them screaming into their microphones, getting no answer. He shivered again, but not from cold. God damn, he'd really screwed up this time.

To make things worse, his head pounded and throbbed. Hypoxia, probably. Flying above ten thousand feet gradually deprived the brain of oxygen. The first effect was a massive hangover-like headache. Eventually, you'd pass out and die. Well, Rusty had sure passed out. He just hoped that nobody had died as a result.

Back east of the Mekong, they were also back on Rusty's maps. He knew the area now below them by heart, and flew back to where he should be. By now, Nguyen was again slouched down and nodding off, the radios still silent. Rusty set up another long racetrack and settled in. But his mind was far from settled. He fretted in fear that one or both teams had been lost while he slept.

Just before it was time to head back to BMT, Rusty heard a faint whisper in his headset. He shook Nguyen, who scrunched up his face in concentration, then pulled out a pink-paged codebook. He whispered back once, then scribbled numbers on his window. Before he finished, Rusty heard a different voice also whispering. Nguyen wrote again, in a different column of numbers. Finally, he turned in his seat and said with complete indifference, "Teams okay. Night soon."

Rusty released a big breath he didn't realize he'd been holding. He held up fingers. "Two teams? Two okay?"

Nguyen nodded and shrugged as if to say, "Of course."

It was the best news Rusty could have heard.

Shortly thereafter, he heard a more familiar voice from a different radio. "Mike 58, 52." It was Sanderson on UHF.

Click. "Go ahead 52."

"52 is at the fence for handoff."

Again, Sanderson had taken the first night flight. If Sanderson was Rusty's relief, he'd been reprieved from an ass-chewing at least until tomorrow morning. But no amount of trouble for missing a briefing would compare to the self-punishment Rusty would surely give himself for falling asleep in the air.

"Roger, 52. 58's inbound. All quiet on the western front. Break. Mike 50, you copy?"

"50 copies all."

By the time Rusty got back, it was deep twilight. Only the distant tops of mountains to the east had a sliver of golden light left on them, and that winked out as Rusty watched, spellbound at the beauty. He'd set up for a long straight-in approach, thinking that he'd make it steeper than usual with the power at idle - just in case there was another shooter lurking near the runway. But as he got closer, Rusty noticed that there were no runway lights.

"Ban Me Thuot tower, Mike 58."

No reply. He tried again. Still nothing.

"Mike 58, this is Pyramid Control on your push. East field has closed for the night. Altimeter 2999, winds calm. Land at your discretion, no traffic reported in the area."

"Uh, copy, Pyramid. Any way to get the runway lights turned on?"

"Stand by one, 58." A short pause.

"Uh, 58, we show a request to have them on. Do you have them in sight?"

"Negative, Pyramid. I can see the tower beacon, but negative on the runway lights. It's black out there."

"Copy, Mike 58. Uh, all I can say is land at your discretion. Would you like vectors to an alternate field?"

"Negative, Pyramid. Thanks. I'll report if I can't make it."

"Copy, Mike 58. And do call on lima-lima if you do land at BMT. Wouldn't want to sit here all night in suspense." He said, lightheartedly.

"Wilco, Pyramid. Thanks for the thought."

Rusty smiled to himself, but quickly settled down to focus his concentration. He'd already decided to land lights out. But with no landing lights, and no lights on the ground to outline the runway, he'd be landing totally blind. Thinking rapidly, Rusty scuttled the idea of landing straight in from the west. There were very few visual cues from that direction. Instead, he'd circle over the compound, where some lights always burned, and land to the west and towards the faint sky glow still visible. He'd have a better chance gauging where the runway was by his distance from the compound than otherwise.

Rusty flew directly over the center of the compound, then started a left turn back to the west. Halfway around, he was happy to see that the runway glinted eerily from the reddish sky's faint light; and he touched down without incident. Rusty braked to a quick stop, spun around and taxied back towards the tiny taxiway, keeping an eye on the spot where last night's tracers had originated. But no green arcs came out of the tree line. Sgt Lopez met them at the gate and took the rocket safety pins. While he inserted them, Rusty glanced up and saw a shadowy figure staring out from behind that gate's .50-caliber Browning. He hadn't been the only one looking anxiously for ground fire. After Rusty passed through the gate, Lopez closed it and secured the wire to the grapefruit-sized grenade that hung there to ruin the day of anyone fooling with the gate latch.

After Rusty unstrapped, he went straight to the TOC for debrief. He confirmed that both teams were fine, but didn't mention his aerial nap or his sojourn far out beyond the Mekong. Finally, he called Pyramid Control by landline and thanked them for their help. Knowing there was little choice, Major Bridgewater asked Rusty to drive to the tower and turn on the runway lights, but when he got there, the entrance door was padlocked. Bristling as he stood there, he briefly wondered if a clip of CAR-15 ammo might open the lock, but decided not to try.

"What do you think?" Major Bridgewater asked when he got back to the TOC.

"I think Dave Sanderson had better have the eyes of an owl, because there's no way we're gonna get runway lights on for him."

"Uh huh. Takeoff wouldn't be bad. Barring another shooter out there, we could takeoff with the landing lights on but otherwise blacked out. That'd give centerline cues at least. But landing…Maybe we should cancel cover flights for the rest of the night. I hate doing it, but teams have survived out there at night for years without cover," Bridgewater said, obviously thinking out loud.

Sgt Lopez spoke up. "Sir, we could take two jeeps out there and set up facing each other at the end of the runway. If we left our headlights on, would that give enough light to land?"

Bridgewater looked at him and his eyebrows knitted. "Hmmm. You know, that's a thought. Damn clever, Lopez. But whoever went would be exposed to enemy fire the whole time. Pretty risky. How about this: we take the jeeps out but with no lights on. We carry a portable FM radio just like the teams carry. When whoever is landing thinks they are close, he calls for the lights. That's when the jeeps switch their lights on. The plane lands between them, the jeeps douse their lights and everybody hauls ass for the gate. Thoughts, anyone?"

Rusty mulled it over for a second. "Yeah. That might work. But instead of parking at the end of the runway, have them park a thousand feet down it. That'd give some leeway in case of a short landing. Actually, it might be better to land short of the jeeps on purpose. That way, you'd still have light cues until touchdown."

Bridgewater stared at the ceiling, head cocked slightly aside.

"Yeah. That's good, too. Anybody else?" He looked around the room. "Ok, that's how we'll do it. Now the hard part…any volunteers for the jeeps?" It was a facetious question: there were only four of them there.

Lopez piped up first. "Yessir. I'll go."

"Me, too," said Young.

"Count me in, too," Rusty echoed. "You need one pilot out there to gauge the right spot to park. Two drivers and a pilot ought to be plenty."

"Agreed. But ya'll wear a hard hat and vest. And don't fergit yore shootin' ahrns, ya hear?"

The drawl had crept back into his voice. He was comfortable.

Suddenly, Rusty wasn't. Me and my big mouth, he thought to himself. He'd volunteered to go out beyond the wire at night, right where Charley ruled. "Uh, Major, none of us are exactly combat trained. Do you think we might get one of the Special Forces guys to tag along?"

"Skeert of the boogie man, are y'all?" Bridgewater chuckled, then turned serious. "I'll do that. I'd be nervous out there myself. Stay here and I'll be right back."

A few minutes later he came back, "Wayal, Ah cain't blame 'em. Them green beanie fellers say they'd be as jumpy as a long-tailed cat in a room full of rockin' chairs – what with all' a you blue-suit idjits havin' guns - AND itchy trigger fangers. But they'll ride shotgun. Fact is, they'll send two, so you can rest easy, Young. Lopez and Naille here will go."

The two went to fetch helmets, vests and rifles, then came back to the TOC. On the way, Rusty passed Flip and Buchenhardt and told them what was afoot. Flip wished him well, but Buchenhardt pulled himself to his haughtiest height and said his Citadel training would make him a better choice if enemy ground action might ensue.

"Nothing's stopping you from volunteering in my place," Rusty said calmly, but inwardly seething at the implied insult.

"I suppose the two Special Ops guys are enough this time," Buchenhardt weaseled.

Back at the TOC, Bridgewater said that he'd already radioed Sanderson about the runway lights and our proposed solution. He'd also offered to let Sanderson break off his mission and divert to Pleiku if he thought that would be best. But Sanderson said he'd just as soon try to land at BMT first. Bridgewater then told him to start back immediately, so he'd have enough fuel to divert if the jeep trick didn't work out. Sanderson would be here in a half-hour to try.

"Ah told Capt Dinh, too. He shore didn't like leavin' the teams uncovered without tellin' 'em about it. Cain't blame him, but it cain't be helped, neither. We'll launch the regular dawn bird, and jist hope fer the best."

As he talked, MSgt McGuire and a Special Forces guy Rusty didn't know walked in. They were loaded for bear with rifles, ammunition and grenades hung from web harnesses. McGuire immediately took charge.

"Sir," he said, addressing Major Bridgewater, "I'm told we'll be providing security for a little detail outside the wire tonight?"

"That's right, sergeant, and thanks," Bridgewater said. "If you agree, I'd like you to escort these two out onto the runway so they can provide a bit of lighting for a bird we have up." He went briefly over the plan and asked them for their input.

"Sounds basically sound to me, sir," McGuire said. "I think it'd be best for your two men to do the driving, and we'll provide the eyeballs and muscle. I'll ride in one jeep, and Spec One Redmond here will ride in the other." He glanced at the guns Lopez and Rusty were carrying, then added, "Major, if there's any shooting to be done tonight, may I tactfully request that your Lieutenant and Sergeant take instructions from me?"

Rusty grasped what he meant and replied before Bridgewater could, "Sergeant, if any shooting happens, I gladly put myself under your orders. I assure you there will be no pulling of rank."

McGuire nodded and gave a sly smile. "Thank you, sir. I may have been right when I said there was hope for some officers."

Rusty returned the smile, openly. "Thank *you*, sergeant." And meant it. If this Korean combat veteran saw hope for him, it might wipe out a fraction of the shame Rusty felt for his colossal but secret screw up.

Bridgewater knitted his eyebrows at the exchange, but shrugged his shoulders and nodded his head once in satisfaction. "You boys oughta saddle up. Sanderson'll be comin' quicker'n two rabbits." He passed Rusty a handheld radio. "That's already tuned to the raht push. He'll give a shout when he's close."

"I understand. Okay, troops, let's go."

They went outside and climbed into the two jeeps. Lopez and the SF guy Redmond took one, and McGuire and Rusty climbed into the other. "You blue suit types drive," McGuire repeated. "And we'll do the rest." They drove across the aircraft ramp to the gate, where Cramer waited. They briefed him how they planned to operate, and he agreed to stay there until everyone got back. He warned them that he'd re-lock the gate until he heard Sanderson or the jeeps coming up the taxiway, and then open it again. McGuire agreed, motioning them out into the night, all lights doused.

Heavy clouds were scudding across a sliver of moon, just risen. In the intervals of dim silver light, they could make out the taxiway, and then the slight sheen of the runway asphalt. Once on the runway, they drove next to each other. Nerves had their effect, and they continued to accelerate gradually as they got farther and farther from the safety of the gate. It was almost a surprise when Rusty suddenly perceived the lighter look of vegetation at the far west end of the runway. He braked to a stop.

"We need to go back down the runway a ways," Rusty whispered hoarsely to McGuire and the other jeep. I want to leave some room in case he touches down early."

"That's your part of the job, sir. You call the shots unless the gooks want to party." McGuire kept his head swiveling, eyes scanning the nearby and distant terrain ceaselessly.

"Okay then. Sgt Lopez, we'll go back east a bit. I'll take the south side and you the north. Park just off the asphalt pointed at a small angle towards the east. That way your lights won't be shining on us, and vice versa. They won't blind Sanderson, either."

"I understand, sir. I'll turn mine on when I see yours. You want high beams?"

"Um, no. Low beams will show the runway surface a little better, maybe. Let's go." Rusty started back eastward, slowly. He tried to figure how many seconds a fifth of a mile would be at ten miles an hour, but gave that up and just drove for what seemed about a thousand feet. When it felt right, he swung his jeep to the right and heard Lopez go left. He drove right to the edge of the runway and off, then made a tight little turn until he faced a few degrees more than perpendicular to the runway. Rusty could barely see Lopez 150 feet away when the moon was behind the clouds, but when it came out, the light glimmered faintly on the jeep's windshield. Good enough.

Rusty left the engine idling. He would have liked to shut it down to hear better, but he was afraid it might not start when he needed it again. He mentioned it to McGuire.

"What little noise it makes idling won't matter, Lieutenant. If they didn't hear us drive out, they won't hear this. And if they did, it'll soon be a whole lot noisier out here than that dinky engine." He didn't bother to whisper.

His matter of fact words made Rusty's skin crawl.

The minutes crawled by. Rusty was beginning to wonder if he should call the TOC on the radio when it emitted a tiny squawk and then Sanderson's voice blasted out. "Mike 58?"

Rusty fumbled for the volume knob and frantically turned it down. Then, "Go ahead 52."

"About five miles out. Say status."

"We're ready here. Just line up as best you can and when you're on final, say when. We'll give you what we can and then we'll follow you in if you make it down."

"Copy. Stand by."

Rusty strained his ears. Suddenly, in addition to the jeep's exhaust, he heard the distinctive muttering whisper of an O-2 in a glide. Close by...really close. He found the jeep's headlight switch with his left hand and waited.

"58...NOW!"

Rusty twisted the switch. Across the runway, Lopez' lights came on at almost the same instant. He must have heard Sanderson's engines, too. The yellow stab of light was temporarily blinding, weak though it was, instantly erasing Rusty's night sight adaptation. Too late, he wished he had remembered to close one eye to preserve at least some of his night vision.

Seconds later, he heard tires screech and Sanderson's O-2 whooshed past. As soon as he'd gotten well clear, Rusty again twisted the headlight switch to off and hit the gas. Lopez was only a moment behind as they roared down the runway. Rusty at first headed for the center of the asphalt, then realized that he might run into Sanderson, so he quickly angled off to the runway edge. He looked around to see if Lopez had noticed, and was relieved to see that he had. In seconds, the grayish blur of the plane loomed up ahead, and Rusty braked to stay behind it. Sanderson taxied at jogging speed down the center of the runway. He slowed near the end, probably trying to make out the narrow taxiway. Rusty flashed his headlights on for another second or two, and

Sanderson immediately swerved towards it. With the gate and relative safety only a few hundred yards away, Sanderson turned on his landing light to negotiate the narrow aluminum path.

In the glare of those powerful lamps, Rusty saw the gate slide open. As they all neared, Rusty could see Cramer and another man standing on opposite sides of the taxiway, ready to pin Sanderson's flares and rockets. It took them only seconds, and as they did so, Rusty glanced up at McGuire. He was standing up, turned to the rear, still scanning for any sign of the enemy, a pose he held until all had dashed through the gate in turn. Cramer slid it closed, the gate squealing on its rusty wheels until it clanged shut.

"How did that work?" Rusty asked a few minutes later as Sanderson shrugged out of his gear.

"Passably well. Four jeeps would be better. The gap between the two on each side would give some sense of sink rate. As it is, it's like dropping into a black hole – no sense of your descent rate. But it's doable. Just."

True to his word, Bridgewater cancelled flights for the rest of the night. "We'll see if we can get the lights on for tomorrow, boys. But Ah'm not sending any more of ya out there until then. Might not git away with it twice."

Sandy and Flip were relieved to hear it. They'd been getting ready to take off when Sanderson came back early. "Good enough for me," Flip said, "I'm off to bed."

"Good ideer," Bridgewater said, "Ah'm tarder'n the only rooster on an egg farm."

In the morning, Kit got airborne just as dull gray light began to tinge the eastern sky. Both teams checked in safe, and everyone in the TOC breathed a sigh of relief. Kit's mission was uneventful, but Batman had to extract one team under fire in the afternoon. He managed to get them all out uninjured, although the low Kingbee took a dozen non-critical hits from small arms as they lifted out of the jungle.

Jack Buchenhardt had the evening go, which again was uneventful for the single team left out. While he was up, Bridgewater called Rusty, Craig, Flip and Sandy in for a confab. "Boys, I hate to break it to ya, but the tower guys say they haven't gotten permission to leave the runway lights on all night."

They responded with a babble of incoherent complaints and questions, which Bridgewater silenced with upraised palms. "Naow boys, Ah don't know any more than that. I jist cain't say what the problem is. I 'spect it's some damn fool official who wants his palm greased and there ain't so much as a biscuit crumb's worth of pan drippings in sight. But there ain't gonna be no lights t'night."

"Do we have to pull tower duty again to turn 'em on?" Flip asked.

"Cain't do that, neither. Somebody got a hair up and decided that we don't qualify as air traffic controllers. Not even in this shit hole country. So they're gonna lock 'er up."

"So we jeep it?" Sandy got in his usual succinct summary.

"Yup, we jeep it," Bridgewater confirmed. Then he got a devilish look in his eye that Rusty had seen before. "Flip, you and Sandy will be up first, and Rushing will be your jeep controller. Naille, you git the honor of flying the last night cap. And jist to show that turn about's fair play, we're gonna have Captain Sanderson providin' the lights for Rusty here. Tomorrow, we'll pull that last team and that'll be the end of this here owl experiment."

"Thank God for that," Craig said. "I'm afraid of the dark."

"If I'm the last, what about the 0400 till dawn go?" Rusty asked.

"Why, Ah'm gonna fly that'un mahself. By the time Ah'm down, it'll be light."

They all hustled to the chow hall for supper. Craig and Rusty went to their rooms to try for some sleep before their midnight takeoff. The others gathered in the big room and hung out until it was time for Flip and Sandy to preflight.

Far too early for bed, Rusty flailed about on his damp sheets until well after dark. He awoke groggy and crusty-eyed when Craig tapped on his door just before eleven. Coffee from the TOC helped, but Rusty was still yawning and shaking the cobwebs out of his skull when they taxied out a few minutes before midnight. As they crossed the border westbound, they checked in with Flip and Sandy to relieve them. When he and Craig saw their position lights pass by in the distance, Rusty reached over and turned off his own outside lights. "No sense advertising ourselves as a target," he said.

"Amen to that," Danny said, then, "Are you as sleepy as you look? You've been yawning non-stop since we started pre-flighting."

"Yeah, I sure am. You think you can take it for an hour or so? We can take turns flying and napping. Our little guy is already out," Rusty jerked his thumb at the interpreter in the rear seat. He was slouched down as far as his seatbelt would allow, his head already lolling side to side.

"Yeah, sure. No sweat. I'm fine."

"Are you sure? Just don't nod off while I'm asleep. It's scary when nobody flies."

"Yeah, I bet," Craig laughed as he took the yoke.

If he only knew, Rusty thought to himself. He slid his seat back a few notches and squirmed around until he could wedge his helmet between the edge of the backrest and the side window. In seconds, he was out.

Music roused him to half-consciousness, but Rusty didn't stir. Craig had tuned in AFVN radio on the directional finder set. Rusty drowsily considered unplugging his headset, but drifted back to nothingness before he could decide if it was worth the effort.

Pain from his cramped neck woke him. Twisting upright, Rusty groaned as it shot up and through his brain until it speared into the back of his eyes. Craig had the instrument lights turned as low as they would go, but they were still the only things visible anywhere. The entire world outside the cockpit was an utter black void. Not a single speck of light appeared anywhere at all.

"Jesus, it's dark out there," Rusty mumbled.

"Sure is. I've been on the gauges for an hour. No horizon at all. No moon visible tonight either. I think we're completely cloud bound. There was some rain a while ago. Did it wake you?"

"Not even Gabriel's trumpet could have woken me up, brother." Rusty squinted at the clock: 02:10. "Holy smoke, why didn't you wake me? The mission's more than half over."

"I'm fine. Well, mostly. I was about to poke you, actually. Tooling around in this ink pot is pretty boring. I even got a case of vertigo a while ago. Not bad, but I sure had the leans. Coulda sworn we were flying sideways. Must be because I'm looking at the gauges cross-cockpit. I never believed you could get so whacked when they taught us spatial disorientation in UPT. But I'm sure a believer in that stuff now." He grinned at Rusty briefly before gluing his eyes back on the instruments.

"Boy, I can understand that. I've never seen anything as black as that out there," Rusty pointed out his window. "I'll take it now if you want."

"Yeah, I'm ready. You fly and I'll pour some of that coffee. I couldn't risk letting go before to get some for myself."

"You haven't even poured any coffee? Man, how in hell did you do it?"

"Like I said, I was fine until just the past few minutes. Could sure use some java now, though. You fly. I'll pour."

"I have the aircraft, for sure. Pour away. You gonna sleep any?"

Craig unscrewed the cap of the thermos bottle and dribbled coal-black coffee into its cup. He handed it to Rusty. "You first and then I'll have some. Yeah, I'll grab a few winks, I guess. I have the cabin heat on, that okay with you?"

"Yeah, it feels good. Funny to need heat in the tropics though."

"Yeah. Combination of altitude and changing seasons, I guess. I wonder what autumn and winter are like here."

"I don't guess there's any color in the leaves. I don't suppose any of that ever gets bare," Craig gestured to the invisible jungle below.

"Guess not. It's been as green as can be as long as I've been in-country. Gazillions of mosquitoes, too. I got eaten alive my first night at Cam Rahn. It's absolutely thaumaturgic that I didn't get malaria."

"Thaw who?

"Miraculous. You ready for some brew?" Rusty handed him the emptied cup.

"Umm...sure. Was that a real word? That thaw thing?"

"Thaumaturgic? Oh yeah. It means miraculous."

"So why didn't you just say miraculous?"

"Oh, I just like words. I majored in English, so it's natural, I guess."

"You mean you majored in verbs and stuff?"

"No, in English literature: novels, plays, poems. You know, Chaucer, Shakespeare, Browning, Hawthorn...stuff like that," Rusty shrugged in the blackness.

"Man, I could never handle that. I majored in electrical engineering. Was never good at words or writing."

"It's the opposite for me. I can't understand numbers. Well, that's not quite true. I can add and multiply and like that. But I almost flunked trig and anything past that is just a complete mystery. Unfathomable."

"You're kidding. Trig is as easy as boiling water. Hell, differential calculus is as clear as...I don't know. I can't put it in words." He laughed, "See? I told you."

"As clear and crisply seen as the fluttering gold of Colorado aspen against the cobalt dome of October?"

His jaw dropped. "Uh, yeah. Like that. Geez, was that from something? A poem or..."

"Nope. Made it up right then. It comes naturally to me. But don't ask me what a logarithm is." Rusty rapped his helmet with his knuckles. "Nobody home for that."

Danny shook his head slowly. "Geez." He drained the little coffee cup and pointed at it. Rusty nodded, and Craig refilled it for him. Without another word, Craig stowed the thermos where Rusty could reach it, then crossed his arms and closed his eyes.

Conversation and coffee had revived Rusty, and he allowed his mind to wander from topic to topic. Eyes and hands flew the plane by themselves, with no conscious input needed. Around and around a huge aerial racetrack he droned, following invisible radio beams through the blackness.

A few moments before four, the radio squawked and Craig jolted upright.

"Mike 58, 51."

"Mike 51, 58. Go ahead."

"At the fence. What's it like out there?"

"Blacker than the bottom of hell's coal bin. And just as quiet."

"Copy that. Weather at the home drome is overcast and patchy rain. It might be a little dicey."

That got Danny's full attention. Rusty's, too.

"Uh, any recommendations, 51?"

"Nope, y'all just give her a whirl. There's ladies on the dance floor and the punch bowl's full."

"What the hell does he mean by that?" Danny asked.

"Beats hell outta me. That impenetrable Texas humor. He probably means that the jeeps are in place and the beer's cold. Or something."

"Copy, 51. Give me a flash."

Rusty stared eastwards and saw a white blink as Bridgewater flipped his landing lights on and off.

"58 has the flash, and you have the world. Good luck."

"51 has it. Good luck to you, too. You might need it."

Oh good. Why did he have to add that? Overcast and rain with no airport or runway lights at all. Terrific.

In moments, they saw his navigation lights. Rusty turned his on as the two planes approached, and saw the other turn his off. That confirmed the handoff. Craig and he were off duty. But not off the hook. They still had to land.

Rusty homed on the Ban Me Thuot TACAN station and when he was approximately over the border, called the TOC.

"Mike 50, 58."

"50 has you loud and clear, copy all previous."

"Roger 50, say weather and status."

"Weather is low clouds and rain, 58. Mike 52 is wet but ready. Say ETA"

"Estimate ten mike on the ETA, 50." Ten minutes to landing…if they could land at all. "And be advised we have 30 mike of fuel." If they had to divert to Cam Rahn or Pleiku, they'd arrive with nothing but fumes.

"Copy that, 58."

They droned along, descending slowly as they felt for the cloud bottoms. Gradually, a faint glow suffused the air around then, and then, with no warning, they could see lights directly below: Ban Me Thuot city.

Rusty changed the radio to the FM set and made sure the right frequency was dialed in. "Mike 52, 58. Five west."

"Copy 58, say when."

"52, how's the weather?"

"Dog shit, 58. Rain and wind. You'll be downwind."

Great. Not only poor visibility, but he'd be landing with the wind instead of against it. Not what any pilot wants.

"You recommend change of direction?"

"Negative, 58. Stick with the procedure."

He'd timed and practiced the landing from the west to take advantage of the few known lights and landmarks. The approach from the east had no landmarks or lights whatever. But wind from the west would make the timing different. Worse, it would make their touchdown speed much higher. This would be tricky.

"You feel comfortable with this?" Danny asked. It was clear he didn't.

"Sorta. At least I know the lights and stuff. Visibility isn't that bad right now. If I can just get aligned with the runway, it should be okay." Rusty didn't feel as confident as he tried to sound, but he planned to give it one pass and then...well, he'd cross that bridge if he had to.

Rusty lined up over a cluster of lights that he knew were almost aligned with the runway and dropped the landing gear and flaps. He started a descent, planning to come down to the limits of the instrument approach. "Stand by, 52."

There was nothing out front but a black pit. Rusty had now lost every visual reference from outside, and he was only a hundred feet or so above the ground. There was no choice.

"NOW!"

Two feeble sets of lights snapped on. Rusty saw them. They were almost underneath him, but off to his left.

"Shit!" Rusty said aloud as he stomped on the left rudder and dumped the nose. They skidded sickeningly to their left and down, but the cross-controlled maneuver kept the wings level. Rusty shot barely over one set of lights, still sliding left and dropping. He flared the nose reflexively as the other headlights glared in his peripheral vision. Then he hit. It wasn't a landing, it was an impact. They bounced crazily, and Rusty felt Craig go stiff as he clenched his hands into his thighs. There was a single shrill squeak from the back seat.

As they hit, they had already shot past the jeep headlights, and had lurched wildly into blackness. Rusty chopped the engines to idle and slammed on the brakes, hoping to steer straight ahead by the compass. The O-2 hopped and shuddered, its wheels locked up and skittering on wet asphalt, the nose swinging from side to side as Rusty fought to stay on the invisible runway.

Somehow, they did. The O-2 shuddered to a stop with the brakes squalling and the tires squeaking eeek, eek, eek as they skipped along the bumpy, pitted asphalt. But it stopped. And still on the runway, too. Rusty exhaled.

"Jesus Christ," Craig said. Rusty felt his seat back sag backwards. The robin's face appeared elf-like between Rusty and Craig's shoulders as he pulled himself forward. "Numba one, Daiwee! Numba one!"

"No, Nguyen, numba ten. Numba ten job. No good."

Rain hissed on the windscreen as they taxied up to the gate, where a sodden Lopez managed a smile and a salute as he pinned their flares and rockets. They taxied in. Rusty had no sooner shut down the engines when a jeep pulled up, and he saw a figure jump out. He strode up to the plane's door and pulled it open. In the reflection of the instrument lights, Rusty beheld McGuire, mud from chin to knees.

"Sir, I've been shot at, mortared, bombed and even stabbed. But until tonight, I'd never been attacked by an airplane. You owe me a drink." He wheeled and strode off.

Sanderson took his place.

"What was that all about, Dave?" Rusty asked, perplexed.

"Well, Sergeant McGuire was standing in the back of the jeep. On guard, you know?"

Rusty nodded.

"And the moment we flicked on our lights, you came over us so low that he was either blown off or he dove…right into the mud. I was looking the other way, but I *felt* you pass over. That was close. Damn close."

"Whew. I knew I was low, but I thought I was farther out. That tailwind must've blown us in a lot closer than I thought. When your lights came on, I sideslipped for all I was worth. But I had no depth perception at all until too late. I thought I was going to hit your jeep. That's when I flared, but it was purely a self-defense reaction. I hit hard anyway and I have no clue how we stayed on the runway long enough to stop."

Craig said, "Me neither. But I had my eyes closed from the instant he stomped on the rudder. I never did see the jeeps at all. When we hit, I opened 'em; but it was just pure blackness by then. Remind me not to fly left seat on a mission like this, willya?"

"I can almost guarantee that," Sanderson said.

Almost? Rusty thought. But he dismissed it in the business of shutting down and climbing out. He needed to pee, really bad.

"She looks okay, sir," Lopez said, as Rusty zipped his pants in the corner of the revetment and turned around. "No wrinkles in the skin or anything. We'll go over her better in daylight. But I think she's okay."

He meant his plane, of course. In the air, it might be Rusty's. But now that it was back on the ground, Lopez owned it. Or her.

"I hope so, Mike. I'm really sorry if I bent it. I'll come out and help you check it over first thing in the morning. Better make that when I wake up," Rusty corrected himself. It was damn near morning already: 0445. By the time he debriefed and got out of his sweaty clothes, the chow hall would be open for breakfast.

Debrief was mercifully short. Sanderson was the duty officer while Bridgewater was airborne, and he already knew almost all Craig and Rusty could tell him. It had been an uneventful mission until the final twenty seconds, and Sanderson had been witness to that. Danny and Rusty were dismissed immediately.

Rusty decided against food. He peeled off his flight suit and flopped into bed. Through the window, he noticed that the sky was the lightest possible shade of pearl gray, the cloud bottoms appearing like a vast inverted tub of bubble bath.

When he opened his eyes again, there were bright blue patches between floating cotton balls. It was almost noon.

Rusty showered, threw on clean fatigues and almost jogged to the mess hall. He was starving. There, he learned that Bridgewater had landed safely just after dawn, Batman had gone out and collected the team as quietly as if it had been a training mission, and that everyone would stand down for a day to regroup and plan new strategy.

Bridgewater called for an all-pilots meeting at 1600. In the meantime, Rusty went out to the flightline to see if he could help with inspecting 082, the plane he'd pranged last night. Lopez was off, but Cramer greeted him warmly.

"Oh, no, sir. She's fine. Nothing to worry about. No wrinkles, no stretch marks, ha ha! You can treat the old girl rougher than that before she cries rape."

"No damage at all? I thought I hit pretty hard."

"Well, maybe the tires are a bit rough. They were almost due for a change anyway. I'll have 'em replaced before you need her again."

"Anything I can do to help? Anything at all?"

"Nah. Never mind, sir. It's a snap. Damn good of you to ask, though."

"It's the least I can do, Cramer. You sure I can't help at all?"

"Truly, sir, no. But if you insist, I'll save something really nasty for you. If you feel you need to make it up to us, I mean. But you don't."

"You do that, Cramer. You do that. I'd be happy to atone for my sins." Rusty smiled and threw him a smart salute. Cramer almost dropped a wrench trying to return it, his grin as broad as Rusty's.

In the meeting, Bridgewater announced that the all-night cover missions would cease and they'd go back to daylight-only operations for the most part.

"Getting those Vietnamese tower controllers to go along with the plan is like pulling boots outta gumbo mud," he said. "Pulling one loose jist drives the t'uther one deeper in the muck. I give up."

They all laughed, and he went on, "Captain Dinh agrees – and he blames the Vietnamese t'ahr guys fer it, not y'all. We'll go back to the old way with the teams. There was nuthin' much we coulda done fer 'em at naht no way… 'cept listen to 'em on the radio as they died." His voice tailed off as he finished.

Sanderson spoke, "You all will be happy to know that the Major has made arrangements for another kind of mission. We'll be ferrying our planes one at a time to Ubon for inspection and routine overhaul. While the plane is there, the crew will RON." He let that sink in.

Kit was the first to reply. His face lit up, "Ubon? Ubon Royal Thai Air Base? Remain overnight? Holy shit! It's a mini R&R! How you arrange that, Major?"

"Never you mind. There's more to being an ALO than eating French food in Dalat. But you may have misheard the Captain: it's not an overnight deal."

"Not overnight? But I thought…"

"It's TWO nights, Bridgewater interrupted, triumphantly. He beamed at them, and the place erupted. "Yee haw!" "Wahoo!"

"When do we start?" Flip asked.

"Right away," Sanderson answered. "Batman is still the senior Mike FAC, so he gets first go. Now here's the deal…Ubon city has some great hotels, restaurants and a zillion places to buy tailored clothes, jewelry, gold and such. But it takes a few days to get custom-fitted things made. So if any of you buy anything like that, tell the shopkeeper to hold your purchases for pickup. Then the next guy over can get it and place his own orders. Make darn sure you get the right store addresses, though, or the next guy may never find your stuff. Copy?"

"Shit hot! Hell yes we copy! Hey Batman, what you gonna get?" Kit yelled, pounding Batman on the back.

"Uh, I have no idea. Some jewelry, probably. I guess I'll have to wait and see. I know I'd enjoy a night in a fine hotel and a good meal."

"Be sure to try the Kobe steak. I'll give you the name of the hotel I stayed in. They have the best Kobe steak in Thailand, they claim. It sure was good..." Bridgewater's eyes closed in reverent memory.

"What's Kobe steak?" Craig wanted to know. He beat them all to the question by a half second.

"It's special Japanese beef. Ah'm told the steers are raised on nothing but beer, and they are kept in small enclosures by themselves so they never get bruised or injured. The meat is tender beyond belief, and has a flavor that..."

"Oh, stop! You're killing me! Just stop! I don't even want to think about it. I'm so sick of monkey soup and water buffalo that I could scream," Flip said.

"Me, too," Sandy added.

Buchenhardt, staring off abstractedly, murmured, "Jewelry...and tailored clothes. You said there are good shops?"

"Oh, yeah. Custom shoe and boot stalls, too. Any kind of leather you can name: kangaroo, elephant, buffalo, snake, crocodile. Anything," Bridgewater shrugged and smiled. "And the jewelry shops all use 18-carat gold, too. Not the more diluted 14 or even 10-carat stuff in American jewelry. It's softer, but worth a whole lot more back in the world. Cheap here, though. A helluva good investment even if you don't like jewelry."

"Sounds right up my alley," Buchenhardt said, beaming.

From as far across the room as he could get from Buchenhardt, Kit muttered in Rusty's ear, "If somebody would just stick something sharp up his alley, I'd be happy."

Buchenhardt glared at Kit, but Rusty doubted he'd heard the comment. Rusty merely nodded, trying to keep any smug looks off his face. But he had to slap a hand over his tightly pressed lips. Buchenhardt widened his glare to cover both of them. Despite this exchange, the revelry and excitement flowed around the room.

"Well, that's about it, except for the boring stuff like work," Bridgewater said after they'd all calmed down a bit. "Here's the drill for future missions: we'll go back to operating day only over the teams. Both the SF and the ARVN people agree with that decision, by the way. And there are some special missions coming up, too. Some of them will be individual missions, and the people selected for those will be briefed one on one. But that's not all. There will be a few *other* jobs, too. Some of them might be interesting."

He let his eyes drift around the room, making contact with each of them in turn, then slid smoothly into his devilish drawl, "Course, when Ah say 'interestin' Ah reyally mean they'll be kinda like stuffin' a 60-pound bobcat inta a burlap sack." He grinned impishly. "What say we all adjourn to the bar now, boys. First round's on me!"

Every one of them knew it was the old "good news, bad news, good news" sandwich. Management technique 101 in practice. Oh well, Rusty thought, at least they'd get to enjoy the bread, even if the meat in that sandwich proved to be both tough and bitter.

They all jostled through the door of the club, and Rusty was glad to see Sgt McGuire already there. He did owe the man a drink for almost killing him. As Rusty walked up to him, he noticed the sour look on McGuire's face. "What's got you down, Sergeant? I'll buy you a round to make it better, whatever it is," Rusty said as he offered him his hand.

McGuire grasped it with a paw as rough and powerful as a vise with sandpaper jaws, but his scowl deepened even more. "That's just the problem, Lieutenant."

"What do you mean?"

"Just order that round and you'll see."

Rusty waved to the bar maid, who slithered her usual way over between the tightly packed little tables and groping hands.

"Two CC seven," Rusty said, holding up his fingers in emphasis.

"No hab," she said.

"No have what? No CC? No Seven-Up?" Rusty replied.

"No hab CC. No hab seben. No hab," she emphasized with a small pout on her face. "Numba ten. No hab."

"You have any bourbon?

She shook her head.

"Gin? Vodka? Anything?" Rusty asked. She merely shook her head nonstop.

"What do you have?"

"Onny hab scot. Scot roobee."

"Scott Ruby?" Rusty turned to McGuire for help in translation.

"They have scotch, sir. And root beer. That's all. If you want a mixed drink tonight, it'll be scotch and root beer or nothing at all. That's why I'm so glum. I hate scotch, but not as much as I hate root beer."

"Jesus Christ. Scotch and root beer. Hey guys, you all hear that? There's nothing in the place but scotch and root beer." Rusty shouted the last for everyone to hear.

There was a chorus of moans. Then Kit said, "I'll have one. Real men can drink anything. And Mike FACs are tougher than most other men, right?"

McGuire bristled a little, visibly clenching his jaw. "Make that two. If I have to uphold the honor of Army Special Forces, so be it."

"Three," someone said. Then Bridgewater raised his hand, "Scotch and root beer all round. The new official Mike FAC drink has now been created!"

When the bartender had mixed the dozen or so drinks, the barmaid passed them out. They all held their glasses, peering at the fizzy dark brown contents dubiously. Bridgewater again raised his glass, "Gentlemen, I present to you, the 'Mike FAC'. May it last in memory along with the brave souls who fly the Mike mission."

Steeling themselves with a hearty "Hear, Hear!" they all took a sip. It was dreadful. It was vile. It was…well, it was alcoholic, and by the third round of it, the taste didn't matter.

Rusty had just remembered that the official official Mike FAC drink was supposed to be the frozen daiquiri when he turned to see Batman smiling in the corner, a glass of straight root beer in his hand. Rusty made his way over.

"You lucky bastard," he said. "You don't have to enjoy this stuff."

"Amen to that," Batman said, tinking his glass against Rusty's. "I keep telling you there are advantages to being Mormon."

"Well, this one time, I might agree," Rusty said, sitting down. "But I don't think I'd live long without my morning coffee. Or a good cold beer in the afternoon, for that matter. Tobacco I can live without. Is one out of three okay?"

"Not really," Batman grinned back. "But we have our share of Jack Mormons who enjoy the same things you do. That line about never taking one Mormon fishing is true."

"What line's that?"

"You should never take one Mormon fishing. He'll drink all your beer. Take two, and they'll watch each other like hawks to make sure the other one never touches it."

Rusty guffawed so hard his guts hurt. When he finally could breathe again, he tinked his glass against Batman's and wandered back to McGuire's table. Rusty assured him the debt hadn't been settled, and he'd buy a double of his choice as soon as some came in. McGuire nodded. "Seagram's 7, Lieutenant. Got a taste for it in Korea. 'Bout all I drink now." He squinted at the foul mix in his glass. "Except on very rare occasions…like when a college puke, blue-suiter shave tail is buying."

He winked.

Rusty saluted.

CHAPTER TEN

T he extra missions Bridgewater had mentioned came down before Rusty's chance at Ubon. Sanderson told him to report to the SF bunker. There, a different SF Intelligence Officer took him to the same small briefing room he'd been to his first day at BMT and closed the door.

"We have an interest in an old walled compound located in Cambodia. It is reported to have been a prison, and we'd like to know if it is still being used as one. Your job is to fly over it and take a picture."

"I understand. Sounds like an easy job."

"Not so fast. To get the information we need, you'll have to approach and get directly over the compound unannounced. A surprise arrival. Can you do that?"

Rusty thought for a second.

"Yeah, I think so. Most of what I've seen out there is pretty flat terrain. But I think maybe I could come in really low and pop up right over it. I might be able to get in undetected, but it depends on if there are sentries on duty, and how watchful they are."

"Chances are, any sentries would be watching inward, not outward."

"True. That is, if it's in use as a prison. Who do you think are the prisoners?"

"I'm not at liberty to say."

That told Rusty what he'd suspected from the moment the man had said "prison." Somebody thought there were US POWs being held there.

Ever since the failed raid on the Son Tay prison camp a year or so before, there had been a concerted and single-minded search for other American POW camps suitable for a rescue attempt. If this was one of them, Rusty wanted desperately to be among those who helped in the effort.

"I see. No matter, I'm your man. Just say when you want it done."

"Immediately, of course. But I have a few restrictions for you to understand first."

Uh huh, Rusty thought. Here comes the filling for my mud sandwich.

The SF man went on, "First, you may not discuss any details of this mission with any person whatsoever except me personally. You may not reveal the target, the objective or the results, or even that you have any kind of special mission. Is that clear?"

"Perfectly. What else? You said 'first' so what's second?"

"Second, before you take off, your crypto radio will be given new codes, different from that day's code set. You will report via that radio only, and on a frequency you will be given, immediately after departing the target area. If you are able to get any photographs, you will deliver the undeveloped film to my hand immediately after landing. Are those points clear?"

"Yup. Hush hush all the way."

He looked hard at Rusty, not happy with the flippant replies, then went on in a flat, impersonal voice, "And finally…this is most important…if for any reason you are shot down or are forced to crash land, you will destroy both the radios and the camera before you are rescued." He laced his fingers together, hands on the table ahead of him and looked right into Rusty's eyes. "Or you will not be rescued."

That came as no surprise. Rusty had been living with that proscription since his first flight as a Mike FAC. "I copy all: No bragging. Talk to the mystery spook, and don't come home without the goodies. Now where exactly is this place?"

"It's just outside the city of Kratie."

"Kratie? Kratie on the Mekong? Kratie the known beehive of enemy river traffic? Kratie the NVA regimental headquarters? That Kratie? Jesus H Christ."

"The same," the spook smiled smugly. He pulled open the desk drawer and brought out a map. "Here is Kratie, and right…here…is the compound of interest." He held a pencil point on an open square figure nestled amid a few hundred tiny dots that represented buildings.

"Is that what it actually looks like? How tall is it?"

"Those are good questions. Here," he said as he reached into the drawer again. This time, he pulled out a somewhat grainy black and white 8x10 photograph. Almost in the center could be seen an open compound surrounded by high walls. There seemed to be a row of small roofs along the insides of the walls on two sides. The picture had been taken from high altitude, maybe really high altitude, Rusty thought, and from enough of an angle off the vertical that it gave some idea of height. Those walls were twice as tall as any other structure nearby. It'd be easy to spot from on the deck.

"So if you have this, why do you need me to fling my pink young ass over it to get another one?"

Again, the spook's smug smile dissolved into a hard stare. "We'd like one from a bit lower. With more detail. And using your pink ass is the best – no, the cheapest – way to get one." The smug smile came back.

You bastard, Rusty thought. But if that was a prison, and if there were some of our guys in it, then the spook was right. Rusty was the most expendable and easiest path to solid intelligence.

"Fair enough," Rusty shrugged. "At least you're honest about it." Or about some part of it, he thought. Rusty already knew enough about spooks to realize that they never reveal even a third of what they know – good news or bad.

"One final thing," the anonymous spook said as he put the map and photo back in the drawer, "When you do your immediate radio report, you'll probably have to climb quite a ways to achieve contact. And you may experience a longer than usual delay between send and reply."

"Why is that?"

"The altitude is because of line of sight from you to the receiver. The other is…not important for you to know."

"Ahh…that again. Okey doke. I think I can work it out for myself." Rusty winked at him as they both stood up. "If that's all, I just need to know when to do it."

"Tomorrow will be fine." The spook didn't smile.

Today, Rusty was scheduled to do an infil survey flight. The mission was called Butter Bucket, another wonderfully evocative code name from the code chimp. It would be another road-watch mission, and the five-man team was the usual pairing of Montagnards and an ARVN team leader. Sometimes these pairings didn't work out well, the Montagnards and the Vietnamese having a mutual hatred for one another. But more often than not, the reality of being under fire together and the need to trust each other with their lives forced the two to at least cooperate – if not amiably then at least professionally. And both of them hated the Northern invaders more than they did each other, as well.

At any rate, Rusty flew out to the mission box and began searching for a decent infil site. He hadn't orbited at high altitude long when he spotted a great looking spot with his binoculars. It was textbook. There was thick jungle all around, with no high terrain from which bad guys could see the insert. The actual clearing he was looking at was about two kilometers from the mission objective, on level terrain. It also was covered with thick grass. Probably elephant grass, which could be anywhere from six to ten feet tall, Rusty knew.

The helicopter downwash would flatten it enough to get the team on the ground safely, but then they could instantly disappear into it and hide. Perfect.

Rusty plotted the clearing's coordinates on his map, then flew a few miles away and completed two more large orbits there, solely to disguise his real area of interest. He then made a few low passes over a spot he'd used as an infil site weeks earlier – another ruse. Feeling euphoric at his excellent find, he fired two rockets for target practice, using a long-dead cargo truck as his target. To add to his glee, Rusty actually hit the damned thing on his second pass. He quit then, happy to stay ahead of the game.

The actual team insertion was scheduled for two days later. He could fly the secret photo flight in between. Rusty could even conceal the real reason for the flight by saying he needed to find a different or backup insertion site. Rusty grinned to himself as he droned back to BMT. A spook amid spooks am I, he mused. Heck, even the weather was cooperating. The monsoons were petering out more rapidly than usual, the weather guys said. That may be bad news for the rice growers, but it was good news for the Mikes. Good news for those guys below him on the Trail, too, Rusty realized. Which was actually bad news for everyone else... It reminded him of that great cowboy song where every other line changed bad news to good: "The bar's only one foot wide, boys... Booo! But it's a mile long...Yay! You're only allowed one drink, boys... Boooo! But it's a bucket-full...Yay! The bar girls are locked in their rooms, boys...Boooo! But here are the keys...Yay! And on and on the song goes, back and forth. Great fun, and closer to real life truth than some would guess.

After Rusty landed, he passed along the infil site coordinates to Capt Dinh, who bowed and smiled his gratitude as effusively as usual. You'd think Rusty had just won the war single-handedly. But it did make him feel special. Maybe this Asian sense of exaggerated politeness had something going for it, Rusty thought as he walked back to his room. But the thought of a cold beer pushed that one aside. Even with the approach of autumn's cooler air, the post-monsoon humidity seemed to cry out for cold beer. It was a cry Rusty was delighted to answer.

That evening, there was still no hard booze in the club except for scotch, and no mixer except root beer. So everyone crowded into the big room instead. It was a semi-quiet night and everyone talked quietly one on one or sat and read a paperback.

Then Major Bridgewater stuck his head in the door and asked, "Hey Batman, how short are you, anyway?"

"A month. Thirty-three days to be exact."

Of course, Batman could reply without thinking. Everyone in Vietnam started counting the days to his DEROS from the first day he was in country, and that magic number was never far beneath consciousness.

"Wanna bet?" Bridgewater asked, with an odd, innocent grin forming as he turned his eyes to the ceiling.

"Why? Don't tell me I've been extended…"

"Nope. Not extended. You're going home in ten days, pardner. Here's your orders." He pulled his hand from where he'd held it out of sight behind the doorjamb. "Boys, you're looking at the Air Force's next C-141 driver. I hope that makes you happy, Batman."

"Yee-ha! You bet it does, sir. Hot damn! Assigned to Travis! That's close enough to Hill that I can get to Utah and visit my family pretty often. Oh, man that DOES make me happy. Ten days! Yaaaaa HOOOOOO!" He screamed.

"Well, it means you won't be saying goodbye to Vietnam forever. Travis means the Ton San Nhut shuttle once a week, hauling beans and bullets out, and body bags back," Bridgewater shouted over the babble of congratulations and comments that filled the place. "But I see it's welcome news anyway."

"Hey, boss, does that mean I'm senior FAC now?" Flip asked. "Does that mean I'm first for Ubon R&R?"

Bridgewater reverted to his comedic drawl, "Wayal, that there's a yup and a nope. Yup, that makes you the prime bull in this leetle herd. But nope, it means you still ain't first in line to breed the cute cow. Them there massage parlors in Ubon still get Batman's business afore yore'n. If'n he goes fer that kinda thang," Bridgewater leered lasciviously at Batman.

Batman blushed a deep red. "Uh, no. Sir. I think Flip may be the first in line for that after all. Assuming he likes cows."

Kit whooped and pushed Flip over sideways on his rack. "Ha! Flip gets himself a heifer. You have any of 'em stump broke, Flip?" He hooted and laughed so hard he almost choked himself.

Everyone convulsed as well, and the laughter and hooting took several minutes to run down. Finally, Bridgewater was able to make himself heard again. "Dave, y'all are off combat status, effective raht now. But ah still want ya to saddle up and head for Ubon tomorra, ya hear? When ya gits back in two days, yer grounded. That'll give ya plenny a tahm to pack yore stuff and hitch a ride to Cam Rahn fer yore out-processing and yore final piss in the bottle test."

"You mean, I'm done? I made it? Oh, thank God!"

"Wall, damn near. If ya kin find yore way to and from Ubon without getting yore ass riddled, then yeah, yore done. Oh," he added, seemingly as an afterthought, "it's that-a-way." He pointed to the northwest.

Sandy clapped Batman on the back and said, "Good for you, my friend. Good for you. Nobody here deserves an early DEROS more than you. You're the best roommate I've ever had, a good teacher and a fine man. I'll miss you." For Sandy, it was practically a commencement speech. They all applauded.

In the morning, they all gathered to see Batman off on his adventure. Bridgewater handed him a leather briefcase and said, "Give this to the ALO at the 23rd TASS. It's technically the reason these flights are authorized. The maintenance guys for the Rustic FACs there will take a look at the plane and give it a 100-hour inspection. That'll take them at least a day, so you can spend tomorrow doing whatever you like. There's a set of enroute charts and a list of hotels and such in this folder. Enjoy. Oh, one more thing…climb steadily as you cruise. You want to be at least ten grand over the bottom end of Laos. There's a few big guns there. No sweat if you're high." He started to close the plane door, then leaned back in and cupped his hand next to Batman's helmet. Then he leaned back out and slammed the door.

Batman cranked up and taxied out. After the blast of his prop wash had passed over, Rusty sauntered over to Bridgewater, grinning slyly. "What was that last little thing you told him, boss?" Rusty looked at him out of the corner of his eye and saw him looking back, equally askance. "Jist one last leetle address. Jist in case…" He pursed his lips and whistled in complete innocence.

Rusty grinned. It was hard not to like this guy.

Rusty was still grinning a bit five minutes later when the spook gave him his own final instructions. Rusty's had none of the pleasant potential that Batman's had, though.

"Here is the frequency you are to report on. Memorize it. The code box in your plane is being changed to the special codes now. You will not use normal flight following with your control room after you cross the fence. Here is a new map of the Kratie area. There are no added pencil markings on it, as you observe. Do not make any of your own. Do not carry any other maps or charts with you. Here is the camera you will use. It is sealed. Do not tamper with the seal, and hand it to me personally immediately after you land. Is that all clear?"

"Yup," Rusty replied to this lengthy diatribe.

The spook glared, and Rusty could almost read his mind. It said "Smart ass."

"Repeat the frequency back to me." He had crumpled the slip of paper in his hand. Rusty recited the numbers. "Good. I'll be waiting on the ramp when you return."

Rusty walked out to the ramp, where he quickly found Sgt Cramer. "Sir, this one is yours. One of the SF guys just came out and re-coded your crypto radio. Is that something you know about?"

"Yes, it is. Thanks, Mike. It's nothing important."

"Sure. You got a one-off, didn't you sir?"

"Nothing much gets by you, does it Cramer?"

"Not much, sir. I've been here a while. You aren't the first pilot to get something a little...different...in the line of work." He held up both hands. "I know, I know, not a word. Candy bombs or funny stuff, I'm bullet proof in both directions."

Rusty grinned. "Thanks, I appreciate it. Both ways."

The plane was set up in the usual way: all four tanks filled, two rocket pods with seven white phosphorous marking rockets each. Rusty was outfitted in the usual way: unmarked fatigues, red Mike FAC bandanna around the throat, no dog tags or ID card, parachute, survival vest with .38 revolver, two radios, first aid kit, smoke flares, signal mirror, extra .38 ammo, ballistic helmet, CAR-15 carbine and extra ammo, canteen, binoculars and the camera. But no map case this time, no charts. The one sheet of virgin map he'd been given was folded in his pocket, and everything else he'd need was memorized.

Once airborne, Rusty headed west and called the fence to the TOC. Now he was on his own. He headed west southwest, climbing a little but allowing the slope of the land to give him most of his altitude. His plan was simple. He'd head generally west until he came to the Mekong – a little over 130 miles past the border. He'd determine exactly where he was and then turn south. Ten miles or so north of Kratie, he'd dive down right to the deck. He'd skim along as low as he could go until he saw those high walls, and then head almost straight for them. At the last second, he'd haul back on the yoke in a climbing left turn and try to snap a picture while he was directly overhead the compound in a 90-degree bank. He'd already set the camera for exposure and focus. If he simply pressed the lens flat against the window, he'd get a shot of whatever was under the wingtip. He hoped. Rusty wouldn't try to look through the narrow rangefinder, but would instead aim the camera with the airplane itself. Meanwhile, he'd attempt to memorize what he was seeing with his naked eye. Two views for the price of one, sort of. If he found what he thought he'd find, there'd be only one chance to observe it.

Rusty checked the camera and found the exposure setting on zero. Hmmm. Since he hadn't loaded it, how could he be sure it was loaded properly? He didn't dare break the seal to check, so he carefully wound the film crank until he felt pressure, then tripped the shutter. When he worked the film advance lever, he saw the rewind crank turn. Yup, there was film in it. To be doubly sure, Rusty snapped the shutter twice more. The exposure counter said "3." Good to go.

There was probably a light headwind: it took almost a full hour to get to the Mekong. When Rusty saw it, he was thunderstruck. The Asian Mississippi roiled along far outside its banks, an angry brown swath both turgid and turbid. Rusty could see immense trees not just floating but tumbling along end over end in that monstrous current. Debris of all kinds bobbed and raced in huge whirlpools. He'd intersected the giant just where he'd planned, just about at 13 degrees north, a spot where numerous sinuous side channels created a hundred elongated islands. Or would have at low water. Now, the Mekong was one immensely broad channel several miles wide. Only from boils of turbulence could he guess where islands would normally be. He gaped at the aqueous power below him for a few seconds, then shook himself and dutifully turned due south. Rusty started a slight descent and his airspeed began to creep up. Fifteen miles north of Kratie was supposed to be a small, unusable airfield just where the mighty Mekong narrowed again to a half-mile channel.

Rusty tipped the wings and saw the spot where the airfield should be. No hint of it, but the more reliable river contour showed plain. He steepened the dive. Five miles and two minutes later he should cross a highway. Rusty looked at the map again: Highway 13 - at 13 degrees latitude. He hoped it wasn't a premonition of bad luck. The highway came down to the river from the east, turned and ran right along the east bank south to Kratie and then made another abrupt turn back to the east. The compound Rusty sought was right on that road two miles from the river.

When he looked out again, he saw the road. Ten miles to go. Rusty pushed over harder, trimming the plane for the extra airspeed as it built up. He dropped through one thousand feet and kept plummeting. Down, down until the windscreen was all green and then he smoothly pulled back on the yoke, pacing his pull to level off about ten feet off the deck. The airspeed began to unspool down to a normal 140 knots. Rusty checked the mixture and propeller controls without looking: all full forward. Without taking his eyes off the blur of trees and water zipping by, he double-checked the camera held snugly between his legs: ready.

In his peripheral vision, Rusty could see the Mekong sliding by off his right side. The highway was invisible now, directly underneath. When he sensed the Mekong taking a smooth bend away, he knew he was only three miles from Kratie. Rusty started scanning for the compound, never losing sight of the immediate zone in front lest he hit some tree or – God forbid – a wire. Suddenly, he began to see buildings flash by, rusty corrugated iron roofs and whitewashed walls. Close now. Then, there it was, a dark rectangular mass jutting above the trees, sticking up higher than he was flying, the details of its stonework invisible on this shaded north side. It was that shadowed blackness he'd seen first, and he was glad he'd chosen to approach it from the north. Rusty aimed just to the right of it and tried to calm himself.

When he was but a few seconds from it, Rusty shoved the throttles to their stops and reached for the camera with his right hand. Without looking, he raised it and pressed its lens against the Plexiglas, and then took one final inbreath.

By instinct, he pulled smoothly back on the yoke and turned it, feeding in a little left rudder. The maneuver was almost like a chandelle, but Rusty kept rolling until he was at ninety degrees of bank. Suddenly, he was looking almost straight down into the square courtyard inside the compound. Rusty eased in a little more roll as he tried to memorize what he saw: three, no...four brown faces staring up from the walls. Green uniforms, whitish pith helmets, rifles slung on shoulders. And in the courtyard itself...a half dozen other figures in filthy bluish gray rags, black chains on their wrists, no hats – and pallid white faces. Rusty snapped the shutter.

Rusty held the vertical bank but allowed the nose to drop back down to the horizon, then kicked rudder and turned the yoke to roll level again. Rusty craned his neck and looked back. The courtyard was invisible behind the walls now, but he could see the sparkle of muzzle flashes and green tracers from atop those walls.

Holy Mother of God. It was true.

As Rusty high-tailed it eastwards again, he remembered his instructions and started a climb. He dialed in the frequency he'd memorized and switched the UHF radio to function through the crypto unit. As he climbed, a realization hit him: now that they'd been discovered, what would become of those poor souls down there? Had he just condemned them to something far worse than they'd already endured? He prayed not. Rusty did pray, in fact. As an agnostic, he simply didn't know if there were a God or not. He wouldn't be hypocritical enough to pray for his own behalf, but those poor wretches down there were another matter. Besides, like the rabbi says, "It couldn't hoit." So he prayed for those men, earnestly and devoutly enough to make proud all the nuns and priests who had taught him through sixteen years of Catholic school.

Rusty had made several contact attempts to no avail, but as he climbed he also flew eastward. When he'd topped ten thousand feet, Rusty squeezed the microphone switch again. The crypto unit whined its rapid way up through the scales and clicked.

"Relay, Mike 58."

A short pause. Then, "Mike 58, Relay has you loud and clear. How me?"

"Five by also, Relay."

"Do you have a report?"

"Affirmative. Are you ready to copy?"

"Negative. Stand by for a patch, 58. Repeat, stand by."

Rusty waited. Two minutes went by. He had almost decided to call again when his earphones clicked again. A different voice said, "Mike 58, this is Bedpost. Do you copy?"

"Loud and clear, Bedpost. How me?"

A pause. Just like the Intel guy said. Rusty thought he knew why, and it sobered him almost as much as those faces he'd seen.

"Loud and clear also. Go ahead with your report."

"Roger. The compound is guarded by sentries on the walls. Small arms only. Perhaps six guards on the walls and inside the compound were visible. All Asian in military uniforms. Bright green with white pith helmets. Break. I also observed as many as six non-Asian men with wrist shackles. Grayish blue uniforms, very dirty. No hats. One photograph taken, quality unknown. Over."

Another pause, longer this time. Rusty hoped they were as stunned as he had been.

"Mike 58, we copy. Bedpost out."

That was all? No amazement, no congratulations? Not even a 'good job' offered? The bastards. Rusty saw red and pounded the dash with his fist. Those unrepentant dildo-licking, shit-eating piss garglers! How could anyone hear that report and just sign off without even a sympathetic comment?

Rusty stayed angry until he landed. The Intel major was right there, arms crossed and fidgety when he pulled in through the gate and parked. He pulled open the door. "You get any pictures?"

"One. No time for more. I want to tell you…" But the spook snatched the camera and ran off, yelling to Rusty over his shoulder as he went, "Report for debrief in ten minutes." Rusty stared at his receding back, even madder now.

Cramer poked his head in. "Trouble with the plane, sir?"

"No, Mike, none. The plane's perfect. Thanks. I'm just steamed about… something else."

"Uh huh. I get ya. Those spooks'll get to ya every time. Not that there are any spooks around here, right sir?" He made a little-boy-with-a-secret face.

"You got it. None at all. Or maybe one less than none when I'm done with him."

Rusty took his time filling in the aircraft forms and hanging up his vest and such, trying to calm himself down, but the delay just made him angrier. When he got to the bunker, he was hot-faced.

"Reporting, Major," Rusty said viciously.

The spook recoiled a fraction of an inch and said, "Please sit down. Proceed. In your own words."

"I sure as shit will." Rusty summarized the flight, describing his approach on the map – which the spook demanded back and then examined to make sure it remained unmarked. Rusty was fairly calm until he got to the actual crux of the mission. He managed to describe what he'd seen almost word for word the way he'd reported it to Bedpost. But then he choked up. "Goddamn it, I saw US POWs in that damn prison, and those shit-eating fuck weeds in the Pentagon couldn't even bother to say thank you or 'those poor guys' before they coldly signed off. That's what has me pissed."

The spook major looked at Rusty coldly. "First of all, Lieutenant, I caution you to not make any unsupported observations, guesses or conclusions about what you saw or who you reported it to. That's not your job. Your job ended when you snapped the shutter. That's all you were sent there to do, and all you were expected to do. Analysis of intelligence data is beyond both your scope of authority and – if I may say so – your probable ability. And I see that look in your eye. Don't even think about any rash comments to me now."

"Oh they aren't rash. I've had an hour and more to get this much heat up. And now you're gonna feel some of it." Rusty raised a fist, and the major drew back slightly, but Rusty merely counted points with his fingers, "One, I'm no dummy. I'd compare my IQ with yours any time, buster. So don't you ever impugn my abilities again, you hear? Two, the next time you only want a shutter snapper, you send a drone or a U-2 or something, you hear? If you want a down in the weeds, eyeball-to-eyeball *intelligent* observer, you might ask me or any other Mike FAC, but you DAMN well will take advantage of what those trained eyeballs tell you. Three, when I do tell you what I've seen and what I think it means, you'd better listen and you'd better show some sign of having a soul when that involves good American soldiers in trouble. Because that IS what I saw out there, and that IS what I reported to those heartless, sterile, fucking bean counters in the Pentagon."

The spook started to say something, but Rusty cut him off. "Yeah, yeah, don't give me that crap about surmising things in a vacuum. I know what that long delay in transmission meant: I was talking either by submarine cable or by satellite link, or some combination of both. It even takes electrons some time to get from Kratie to Washington DC and back."

The spook closed his mouth and looked at Rusty, expressionless. "Thank you, Lieutenant. You are dismissed."

As Rusty walked back to the hootch, he wondered if he'd just gotten himself fired. Well, if he did, there's nothing they could do to him as bad as what was probably now happening to those poor guys whose haunted eyes he'd looked into. As long as he lived, Rusty knew he would never forget those eyes.

In his room, he stripped out of his sweaty fatigues and went to the shower. He didn't even mind the giggles from the hootch maids as he stood under the hot water. He stood there until the salty water stopped mingling with the fresh as it rolled down his cheeks.

Rusty skipped both his supper and the nightly drink fest at the club. Flip knocked on his door once, asking if he was okay. Rusty mumbled something about a headache, to which Flip jokingly answered, "I bet you wish you were where Batman is right now, don't ya?"

"Hmm? Oh. You know, Flip, I do. I really do. I wish to hell I were anywhere but here. Anywhere at all."

"Uh, okay. I see. Well, I hope you feel better tomorrow. You have an insert don't you?"

"Yeah. I'll be fine, honest. Thanks. Good night, okay?"

"Yeah, if you say so. G'night. Don't let the bed bugs bite."

Rusty stared at the springs above. Richard's bunk. And in the pattern of wire diamonds and splotchy mattress stains, he started to see faces. Crazy Eddie's then Richard's, and then the much fresher, vivid and excruciatingly pitiful faces of today. Faces wearing equal parts exhilaration, fear and pleading desperation. They swam into and out of Rusty's vision until he woke just before dawn, soaked with sweat again and twisted into his sheets like one of the flies he'd once fed to a spider in its web. Where and when had he done that? He couldn't remember.

Rusty showered again and then dressed and wandered down the dew-soaked dirt street to the mess hall. It was a little too early for breakfast, but there was always coffee to be had. By the time he'd finished two steaming cups, the breakfast line was open. The smells coming from the kitchen reminded Rusty he was famished. He ate a double portion of bacon, a heap of the terrible powdered scrambled eggs, and toast. Square slices of white bread toast, he suddenly realized. Where the hell had that come from?

Some of the others walked in as he was finishing up. They expressed surprise at seeing him, as Rusty usually was a late sleeper unless he had the dawn patrol. "Feeling better?" Flip asked.

"Uh huh. Much better," Rusty lied. "A pillow is man's best medicine, you know."

"Anything good?" Sandy jerked a thumb toward the doors to the chow line.

"You'll see," Rusty said as he pushed out of the entrance.

At the TOC, Brookside, Dinh and Rusty ran through the details of Butter Bucket once again. The Kingbees were ready, the weather looked good and the team was in good spirits and eager to go. That last was probably a bit of an exaggeration, Rusty thought to himself, but no harm to throw it in, as Dinh had done. Rusty almost laughed when he thought that: Dinh done. It sounded like a church bell. In the midst of this pleasant woolgathering, he almost missed a question from Brookside.

"Uh, Yessir. Yes, the site is grass-covered. I couldn't risk getting a closer look at it, but I don't think it is high enough to entangle a Kingbee's rotors. The downdraft alone should prevent that. And it will make excellent cover, of course." Always end with a positive, he'd learned.

Rusty turned to see the robin, sitting mutely in the back of the room, as always. It was Hua. Rusty had flown with him once before, and thought he was more than a little self-centered. Hua didn't seem to be overly concerned with what happened to the team; as long as Hua was safe and comfortable, that's what mattered.

When the briefing ended, Rusty went straight to the latrine, and hoped that Hua did also. Four and a half hours is a long time to hold anything. They met again at the plane, got strapped in and cranked up when Rusty heard the Kingbees takeoff. A broken deck of building cumulus clouds foretold more thunderstorms for later in the day, but the morning would be glorious. A picturebook day and a textbook infil, what could lift Rusty's seriously battered spirits more? He took a deep breath and focused on the immediate present...

hhhhhhh…HAAAAA. Hua looked over and grinned, pleased with himself as always.

Rusty took off and climbed smartly, the cool dense air of morning adding power to the twin Continentals and lift to the wings. It really was a glorious day to be flying. Crossing the fence, they caught up with the Kingbees and slid smoothly in ahead of them. Easing back to 90 knots and dropping the flaps to takeoff setting kept Rusty neatly in position. He took up the heading that would take them all a few miles south of the insert site. By the time they got there, he'd led them down to the deck. When Rusty turned for the run-in, he looked back to be damn sure both Kingbees were rock solid behind him – at least he'd never make that mistake again. The final few miles passed directly over triple canopy jungle, and they were as invisible from the ground as the ground was from them. Just like tooling down a broad green interstate with not a care in the world, Rusty mused.

Up ahead, Rusty soon saw the clearing basking blissfully in the moving patches of sun and shadow under the puffy clouds. He clicked his mic twice, and the lead Kingbee replied in kind. Hua sat up, straining to look over the dash, and he gave a big thumb's up when Rusty kicked a touch of rudder so he could see the clearing.

Rusty didn't even have to dive or maneuver. He simply keyed the mic and said "Three…two…one…Bingo, Bingo, Bingo!" when they droned across the clearing. But even that was hardly necessary: this was the only clearing in sight for miles around.

Seconds went by as Rusty flew smoothly on. Then Rusty's perfect insertion turned to absolute, unrefined dog shit.

Instead of fifteen minutes of silence while the team grouped up, there was an immediate cacophony of screams, shouts and shrill Vietnamese pouring in over the FM radio. Rusty heard multiple rifle shots, bursts of full-automatic fire and even the blasts of explosions. All coming from *very* near the microphone of whoever was screaming that supersonic stream of words. Hua almost leapt out of his seat harness as he snapped to rigid attention. Rusty had already shoved in full power and started to claw his way higher. He climbed and turned, zigzagging to avoid whatever part of that ground fire was aimed at him, and when he turned enough to look back, Rusty could see the clearing punctuated with puffs of dirty gray smoke. Both Kingbees had turned tight circles as well, preparing to either machine gun the enemy or make an immediate pickup of the team, if possible.

More shouts and automatic weapons fire came in over the radio, and Rusty looked to Hua for word of what was happening. But instead of writing on the window or even looking out of it, Hua had slid down almost to the point of sliding out of his seat belt. And he was clutching his sides; laughing his callous, self-indulgent, insensitive ass off. Rusty reached over and grabbed his shirt collar, jerking him upright with a tremendous shake. "Hua! How many NVA? How many team dead? Which way team run?"

Hua limply waved his hand and kept on laughing idiotically.

"Goddamn it, Hua! You bastard! How many team dead? How many NVA? You talk me now!" Rusty punched him in the ribs, hard.

Hua jerked. The pain calmed him down enough to gasp out between howls of laughter, "Dai-wee! No NVA...No team dead......Tiger!"

Rusty stared at him, then back down at the clearing, where the lead Kingbee was already on the ground. The firing had stopped. Nothing came over the radio as the Kingbee sat there...and sat. A full minute went by, then another. Finally, it lifted off, and Rusty heard the highly amused and gleeful voice of Chua Le Quang, "Kingbee go home now."

"Talk to me, Kingbee."

"Kingbee have team. Kingbee have tiger. Go home now...okay?"

The reason for the long delay on the ground was suddenly clear. Rusty laughed. "Okay, Kingbee. Go home now."

Rusty started to climb until he could make radio contact. When he could, he called the TOC and had them go crypto. That was usually a very bad omen, and when Rusty heard Hannah's voice again, it was full of trepidation. "Okay, 58, 50 on crypto. Uh, go ahead."

"50, tell 51 that Butter Bucket has gone rancid. The insert failed."

Even more trepidation in Hannah's voice now, "Okay, 58, I copy. Say casualties."

"Only one casualty, 50. He'll probably weigh three hundred pounds and has black and orange stripes."

"Uh, say that again, 58? Come back?"

"We inserted the team right onto a tiger, 50 – a real, live, no-shit tiger. And the team filled him with all the lead they were carrying. That kinda killed the insert as well as the tiger. We're bringing the team and the surprise guest home."

Rusty could hear the relief and the laughter even over the distorted, flat sound of the crypto set, "Oh, ha ha ha! Holy shit! Uh, I mean, I copy, 58. I'll pass it along. Oh, indeed I will! 50 is crypto out."

"58 crypto out" Rusty reset the radio to standard transmission, and chuckled. Boy, would Hannah enjoy giving *that* report!

By the time Rusty landed, the whole camp had heard. Cramer and Lopez both met him with huge grins and wild waving. When Rusty handed him the rocket pins, Lopez leaned in and said, "Hey Sahib Naille! Or is it Bwana? How'd the safari go?"

Rusty yelled back, "Just call me Ramar of the Jungle!"

He was still filling in the aircraft forms when the Kingbees landed. Hua sprinted off to join the huge crowd that had already assembled around their helipad. Sanderson was waiting in a jeep for an immediate TOC debrief, so Rusty never did get to see the dead tiger. By nightfall, it was downtown being skinned.

That night, there was booze again. A truck convoy had gotten in, and the camp was flush with supplies. That also explains the white bread toast, Rusty thought, as he shared his second double Seagram's with McGuire. Rusty bought the one he'd promised, and McGuire returned the favor. "You put new meaning to the term 'tiger team' Lieutenant. Maybe we could mount a big game safari just for shits and giggles sometime. You think a door-mounted M-60 is enough gun for those Cambodian beasties?"

"Oh, we could always take along a few 40-mm grenade launchers, just in case," Rusty replied, somewhat slurred. He was already over his booze intake limit. That might be why the idea of a helicopter safari sounded like fun.

"Good plan. I'll arrange it."

They tinked glasses to the idea.

The next day, Rusty awoke with something of a hangover. He hadn't barfed, but his head pounded and his muscles were all shaky. Powdered eggs were the farthest thing from his mind, even if there might still be some of that exotic white bread toast left. Rusty consoled his senses with coffee and aspirin. Thank God they had no teams out: Rusty wasn't on the flying schedule.

About noon, Batman swooped in from his Thai vacation. His arrival created almost as big a stir among the FACs as the tiger corpse had among the 'yards. Sporting a huge grin, Batman produced a seemingly endless supply of boxes, brown paper-wrapped packages and shopping bags from the rear seat of his plane. The rest of them eyed each one, shifting from foot to foot as excited as six-year-olds at Christmas.

Back at the hootch, Batman sat amid a pile of these mysterious objects and regally unwrapped each one for their inspection.

"First, that Hotel Ubon is a must. I even enjoyed the night club and the dancing – purely as an observer, of course. But the rest of you pagan heathens will love the drinking and the womanizing. And that Kobe steak…well, it defies description. My mouth is watering even now. Wow. Oh, and there's a magnificent Buddhist temple almost across the street from the hotel. It's called the Wat Sri Ratta-something or other. 'Wat' means temple, I gather, because there are zillions of 'Wat-this's and 'Wat-that's' everywhere. And 30-foot tall golden Buddhas, too. The most amazing one…"

"Yeah, yeah, Batman. Enough of that. Get to opening those goodies, willya?" Kit interrupted. "Geez!"

"Oh. Oh yeah. Sorry, it's just that the sights are so incredible, that I…"

"ENOUGH of the tourist guide spiel, already! Get on with the packages!" Kit again.

Batman abruptly pressed his lips tightly together and ceremoniously reached for an oddly-shaped, almost triangular package. He peeled off the string and brown paper wrapping to reveal a carving. Warm brown wood crafted into delicate details revealed a Buddha wearing a pointed headdress, poised serenely in the lotus position. "Like this, but 30 honest feet tall and all gilded with pure gold leaf, glowing in the sun," he said. Just the mental image of it staggered Rusty. It quieted the whole room, in fact.

Now that Batman had everyone's rapt attention, he continued to unwrap treasure after glorious treasure. Magnificent dark gold jewelry alight with brilliant rubies and sapphires; bolts of lustrous silk in pinks, blues and shimmering white; wooden carvings of elephants; wallets and purses of exotic leathers and more. When he finally finished, it made a cascading mound of wonder around his feet.

Sandy Hubert broke the dam of silence at last, "Wow." All heads nodded in agreement with his simple eloquence. It was a wow indeed.

"You look like Aladdin after he opened the cave," Danny said.

"Holy Moolah, Batman! How much did that pile cost?" Kit blurted.

"What, no duds for yourself?" Buchenhardt asked simultaneously.

Batman sat there with a Cheshire cat grin. "Guys, it's all dirt cheap over there. And I didn't buy any clothes for myself because it wouldn't be ready before I DEROS.

"Heck, we'd have sent it home after ya," Kit said.

"Yup, we could've done that easily," Sanderson agreed. "But even without clothes, you'd say your last flight was a good one?"

"Oh my gosh," Batman paled. "I completely forgot about that. Was that truly my last flight?"

"Afraid so, big guy. No more combat flying after you get your orders. It's the rule. A good one, too. Too many guys get killed on their last flight."

"Why is that, sir?" Craig wondered.

"Because you suddenly do things differently. Or your mind is on home, or you just get overly cautious. Whatever. But it's a fairly well-documented thing. So once you know you're done, you are done. If we'd thought it through a bit, we wouldn't have told you about your orders the other day. You'd be hearing it for the first time right now. We goofed, but we didn't want our foul-up to deprive you of this opportunity, either. So we bent that standing rule a little. It wasn't a combat mission, after all."

Everyone nodded at the wisdom in that. Rusty also caught the fact that Sanderson had said 'we goofed' when he might've said 'Bridgewater goofed.' Once again, he was so glad to have these two men as his bosses.

"Hey Batman," Rusty said, "It seems to me we have lots of reasons to celebrate. How about one last daiquiri party at the FAC hootch tonight?"

"Yaay! Blender bash! Blender bash!" everyone yelled. The party was on.

Dave Bates pulled out all the stops for his finale as Mike FAC bartender. They started with pineapple daiquiris, then pried open a can of pears. Somebody tossed in a jar of kumquats they'd gotten in a Care Package from home. By then it was far too late for any judgment whatever, and Batman concocted one round of after dinner mint daiquiris. He dumped a box of the chalky candies into the glass jar, added rum and ice and hit the switch. But within a few seconds, there was a loud buzz, smoke poured from the base of the blender like evil blue tongues, and the lights dimmed.

Batman jerked the cord from the socket, and they all cheered lustily and heartily. Those few who could still stand, not including Rusty, bellied up, and Batman dispensed the chunky remainder to those who had long since lost mobility.

"Here's to the last daiquiri," Kit toasted, weaving and slurry but upright. "The very last fucking one."

"The absofuckinglutely last daiquiri," Craig echoed, even more slurred. They raised their dinner mint drinks to the stars. Batman had lived up to his reputation at last. Not a soul among them could walk. Several couldn't even crawl. One or two had long since gone to the land of Nod. Only Batman was left standing: rock steady, stone cold sober and supremely happy.

They were a colorful lot the next morning – provided you consider ash grey, bilious yellow and an odd green as colorful. The ramp was decorated with more than a few puddles of recycled rum, and the whole area reeked of piss, puke and the electrically fried blender. No one flew that day, or was capable of it.

By late afternoon, Rusty's neurons had slackened their play of the Anvil Chorus, and his guts had stopped contracting in time with his pounding heart. He had improved almost to being extremely critical. Batman peeked in and said, softly, "Now don't you wish you were Mormon?"

"That's a trick question. I can't safely answer yes or no. If you want a duel of wits, I'm unarmed."

Batman peaked his eyebrows. "That'd be another first. Hey, why didn't you tell me about your tiger? That story is a hoot. I'm almost sorry I wasn't here."

"Thanks," Rusty said, turning over and groaning with the effort. The room still hadn't quite stopped its autorotation. "But yesterday was your party. Oooh. Even that word hurts."

"And now I'm cleaning up. Anything I can get you? Alka-Seltzer? Coffee? Toast? You should get some fluids back into you. That's the real trouble, you know."

"It must be. I ralphed every molecule of liquid above my toenails. They'd have to boil me to make me a mummy."

"Okay. Juice sound good?" Rusty nodded. "Juice it is. Instant Mike FAC, just add water." He disappeared, but came back a few minutes later with aspirin, a tall glass of bug juice and a handful of saltines. "Get these down. You'll be fine."

He was right. Before long, Rusty had stopped shaking and could stand without getting faint. His stomach even rumbled a short time later. Rusty wandered out to the shower and latrine, passing Flip, who was stretched out in one of the chairs he'd made. Rusty grunted a greeting. Flip cautiously lifted one eyelid. "Hmmph."

On the way back, Rusty slid slowly into the other chair. "Helluva party."

"Uh huh. You were something else."

"What do you mean?"

"You called Buchenhardt some name. Or some word. Had to be ninety-seven syballel...sillyba...sillabubble...you know what I mean. Long SOB."

"You're kidding. What was it?"

The right eyelid lifted again. "Fuck, if I could say it, I would have."

"Huh. I don't remember that."

"No fucking kidding. I've never seen you that drunk."

"Never been that drunk, I guess." Suddenly a crystal clear image of those prison faces flashed through Rusty's brain. "Maybe I needed it."

Flip lifted his head. "What's that mean?"

"Uh, nothing. Never mind. I can't say."

"That mission the other day? There's a rumor that you punched the SF Intel guy out for something. Sure surprised me to hear that. True?"

"Not that part. I can't say more."

He looked at Rusty, knowingly. "Ahh. A...umm...singular kind of thing?"

"Yeah."

"Say no more. Believe me, I understand." He lowered his head and closed his eyes again.

Rusty joined him. The sun felt good, and so did the intermittent shadows under the drifting clouds. Warm. Cool. Warm. Cool. The light coming through his eyelids went from orange to blue and back with each cycle. Beautiful.

A jab on the shoulder, "Hey Rusty, you alive enough to eat?"

Rusty pried his eyes open. It was Kit. The other chair was empty. "Umm...Yeah, I guess so."

Again, Rusty discovered he was ravenous. As he gulped down chow, he realized he hadn't eaten solid food except a few crackers since yesterday's lunch, and he'd blown the remains of that all over the ramp.

Nobody drank a drop that night. But they did have the traditional SF ceremony in the Club, maybe the only "dry" one ever. The SF guys, represented by Capt Brookside and MSgt McGuire, gave a little speech about how much they'd depended on Batman and how he'd fulfilled their expectations to the fullest. Then, while they played a cassette of the theme music from the TV show Batman, they ritually cut off Batman's fatigues, dressed him in new Tiger-Stripe cammies and then fitted him with a Green Beret sporting the MACV/SOG Death's Head patch. They gave him a plaque, shook his hand as the newest honorary Special Forces troop: emphasis on "honor." It was.

With Butter Bucket trashed, there were no teams on the ground, but the powers that be couldn't have that, so they hurriedly put the same team back in to watch a different part of the Trail. The new mission was called Rusty Deck, and Craig did the infil. This time, they got in without a hitch and the usual routine of all-day radio cap missions resumed.

Batman packed. His baggage was over the weight limit with all the Thai goodies he'd bought, so he did the logical thing: he abandoned every scrap of his military stuff except for two changes of fatigues. He'd wear one to out-process at Cam Rahn. On the morning of his Freedom Bird, he'd toss it and wear the other one home.

"The only thing I'll keep for my trip to the Land of the Big BX will be my Mike FAC bandanna and my new green beret," he said. "Those are irreplaceable. Those, my pictures and my memories will be enough to remind me of the best pilots and soldiers between heaven and earth."

As Batman's roommate, Sandy claimed the honors of flying him to Cam Rahn. The rest stood and watched them strap in and crank up. As they were taxiing out, Kit said, "Oh crap! I just realized Batman never got hosed down. He never really had a fini flight."

Bridgewater turned to him and replied, "That's all right, Kit. I think he's been baptized."

"That reminds me," Rusty said, "Derlin spent his last night in the big room. Did he ever get his SF sendoff? It'd be a damn shame if he didn't."

Sanderson turned to him, "Yeah, he did. He had it done quietly – said he wanted to spend the last night quietly with you guys. Kinda surprised me."

"It shouldn't. A genuine class act, that Derlin," Rusty said.

Sandy took off and made a wide circle of the compound so Batman could take pictures. Then they turned and headed southeast, disappearing in moments.

Buchenhardt took off on radio cap, but the rest of them gathered together in the big room. They all felt the normal depression of losing a friend, a brother. "Who's senior now Kit, you or Flip?" Sandy asked.

"Flip is, but I'm shorter than he is, so I guess I'm the next to DEROS."

"How short are you?"

"Short enough to walk under doors, brother. I'm a two-digit midget: 94 days."

"I'm right behind you, buster. I'm 102," Flip said.

"You got in country a week after I did? I don't remember seeing you at Cam Rahn."

"That's because I was originally assigned to 20th TASS. I did my in-country checkout stuff at Danang."

"Rocket City? No shit. Was it as bad as they say?" Rusty asked.

"Worse. The base took something like 9,000 rockets or mortar hits a year. I can't remember a single night we didn't spend some or all the time in a bunker."

"Nine thousand? Jesus. That's, what…250 a day? Holy shit. They ever hit anything?" Kit stared at him.

"Did they ever! They hit the BX…twice. They hit aircraft on the ramp. They hit latrines with people crapping inside. They hit the fuel dump. They hit bomb storage revetments. One of those left a crater fifty feet deep and a hundred yards across – bigger than an Olympic pool. They hit barracks. Christ, there wasn't anything they *didn't* hit, as far as I know."

"I can't imagine that. Cam Rahn had a rocket attack my first night there, but it was only a half dozen or so. It was over in ten minutes. But 250 of them every single night…man oh man," Rusty said.

"Rusty, why do you think I took the first job they offered me? Even if it was to some cloak and dagger, secret place nobody ever heard of? That's how I became a Mike."

"So BMT is a place of blissful quiet, huh? You know, I can't recall even a single round of incoming since I've been here. I wonder why not."

"Because big bases are big targets. Those huge bomb and fuel dumps are juicy bulls eyes. So are all those Yankee Imperialists running around. Ban Me Thuot? Sheeyit. We're not even a flea big enough to swat. Or even scratch," Flip said.

"Well, that sure puts a new light on where we stand in the pecking order," Craig laughed. "As well as how important this job is."

"That's an interesting point," Rusty said. "Flip, as senior Mike FAC, can you tell me just what the hell we ARE doing here?"

"Nope. That's not because I know something I can't talk about. I really haven't a clue. That's the part I hate the most about being here. We gather – or at least help to gather – information about the enemy. But we never, ever find out what the hell we gathered, or what it means, or even if it was worth a damn. Have any of you ever seen even one of the photographs you've taken?"

They all shook their heads.

"Has anyone ever come to you and said 'That river forge you found helped us kill 75 trucks'? Has anyone ever been told what his teams saw or did? No. Not one single scrap of feedback. Now, I don't expect a medal, or even thanks for any of this. But I sure as heck would like to know IF I've made a difference."

Rusty desperately wanted to tell them what he'd seen only a few days ago. And how he'd been told that they weren't even considered capable of coming to a conclusion about anything; that conclusions weren't even part of the job. But he couldn't. It fell under the same banner of honor he'd tried to explain to Mary Beth.

Under this added pall of gloom, they all drifted back to their rooms. Rusty suddenly realized that when he had arrived months ago, only Kit roomed alone, but now everyone except Kit roomed alone. How odd. It also meant the Mike force was shrinking. Maybe their nebulous job was close to being finished - or simply ended in the usual abrupt military way.

Dave Sanderson must be psychic, Rusty thought an hour later. He came by and knocked on everybody's door, cheerfully calling out, "Everybody out! Rocket party!"

For a few seconds, images of Danang and incoming rounds flashed through Rusty's mind, but the cheerful note in Dave's voice soon dispelled that. But what the heck was a rocket party?

One by one, the doors opened and FACs stepped out until everyone was standing on the narrow sidewalk between the hootch and the dirt-filled barrels of the shrapnel barrier. Everyone was there except Craig, who by now had taken Buchenhardt's place on radio cap.

"All hands who wish to volunteer for the rocket party, follow me!" Sanderson chirped. It sounded suspicious, but anything was better than brooding the afternoon away in their bunks. Out of sheer curiosity, everybody fell in line behind Dave - except Buchenhardt, who professed fatigue after his flight.

Sanderson led them to the southern edge of the aircraft ramp, where they saw a man-high stack of wooden crates. Cramer, Lopez. Corso and the newest enlisted guy, A1C Fleming were all there, smiling. Anytime enlisted guys smile at officers, something is up, Rusty thought.

"Ok, volunteers, here's the drill. Our esteemed maintenance folks will now teach you yoke yankers how to properly assemble and store 2.75-inch Folding Fin Aerial Rockets. Enjoy!" He started to turn away.

"Whoa there, Captain!" Kit brazenly said. "Is this not a time when 'leadership by example' might be profitably demonstrated?"

Sanderson at first glared, then slowly started to grin. "Yes. Yes, it is as a matter of fact." He took off his fatigue shirt, then cupped his hand next to his mouth and said in a stage whisper, "Besides, this'll get me away from that damn desk and paperwork." They all laughed.

Cramer stepped forward. "Thank you, sir. It's an honor to have you join us. Sirs, here is the drill…" And the four of them demonstrated how to properly take a rocket motor and warhead from their containers, screw them together, and then store the complete rocket in an electrically grounded storage rack.

They formed a conga line of sorts and started work. In the 100% humidity of the monsoon season, even the slightly cooler air couldn't prevent them from becoming sweat-soaked within minutes. The 25-pound rockets soon seemed to weigh a ton each, and before long they were all nearly exhausted. But they worked on until every last crate had been emptied and the rocket rack had almost every single pigeonhole filled with a completed rocket.

Sanderson took his leave and the rest of them sprawled down in the grass to rest. Lopez said, "Thanks for the help, sirs. That'll keep us in rockets for a few weeks."

Rusty asked him, "If that amount of rockets only lasts a few weeks, how come this is the first rocket party we've had since I got here?"

"Well, actually, sir, we didn't used to need this many. But ever since a certain pilot arrived, we've gone through them all at double time."

"And that certain pilot would be the only one who isn't here, right?"

"You got it, sir. Oh. Not the good Lt Craig. He's not the person in question."

"How is it that this one… umm, pilot… alters the situation?" Kit asked.

"Because he never ever brings a rocket back, sir. Full pods when he takes off, and empty ones when he lands. Every flight. The rest of you use none or one or two when you need to, and that's fine. No sweat, and we don't mind that a bit. But fourteen rockets used every single day…well…"

"And said individual is now too 'tired' to help replenish the stores. It figures," Kit growled. "It just fucking figures."

"It's not our place to complain, sir. But may I just say that it's a real pleasure and honor to work with every pilot here…almost," Cramer hurried to say.

"That cuts both ways, Mike," Flip said. "You guys and Hannah and Young are the best. Hands down.

Kit agreed, "Not only that, but we share your views on that 'almost'. Or at least I sure do. Wholeheartedly."

"Have you made this observation to Sanderson or Bridgewater?" Rusty asked.

"You should," Sandy said.

"I think that's how this party came to be," Cramer said. "I brought it up at this morning's maintenance brief with Sanderson. I said we were out of rockets, and he asked why, and well..." He shrugged.

"Ahh. Good. And now he also knows who leapt at the chance to help." Kit smiled smugly. "And who didn't. Beautiful."

"What's that noise?" Flip said, holding his hand to his ear. "Why...I do believe...yes... YES! It's the sound of chickens coming to roost."

All of them laughed, rolling in the grass, until their sides hurt.

CHAPTER ELEVEN

T rue to expectations, they began to see signs of increased enemy activity as the monsoon downpours abated. Corduroy strips of cut logs appeared where two-track roads dipped through low spots. Rusty-colored shallows suddenly developed where roads crossed deep brown streams – manmade truck fords. Ruts showed up where none had been the day before. All were obvious signs of increased night traffic.

Below Rusty, the sinuous trace of a road wound through single-canopy jungle. Seldom could the actual road be seen, but the telltale line where the treetops didn't quite meet could be followed from above. Follow it he did, flying with one hand while looking straight down through binoculars held in the other. It was a tactic that quickly left a FAC dizzy and a bit nauseated, and so Rusty had to put the field glasses down often. If nothing else, it was very difficult to fly the plane while looking through them. It was while he was resting his eyes thus that he saw a tiny metallic reflection pulsing below.

Intrigued, he stared at it. It was neither the reflection of sunlight on water drops, which would have kept pace with his shadow, nor was it the very rapid flash of gunfire, but rather a steady *tick tick tick tick* of light coming from the edge of the road. Rusty raised the glasses again and was astounded to see two bicycles being pushed along by two black-pajama-clad figures, sunlight repeatedly reflecting from the spokes of the lead bike. Across each bike were slung two enormous white sacks.

Neither figure so much as looked up at the sound of his engines. Rusty checked the position of his radio selector by feel, and keyed his mic, "Mike 50, 58."

"Go ahead 58"

"I have two enemy troops in the open, pushing bicycles apparently loaded with rice. Do we have any assets available?"

While he waited for an answer, Rusty quickly scanned his map to get a rough set of coordinates. He had calculated it down to one kilometer from true when the TOC came back.

"Uh, 58, we have nothing airborne, but can scramble two Hornets from pad alert. You want 'em?"

"Most affirmative, 50. Launch the Hornets. I'll need a gun and a slick, I think. Have a Cobra stand by."

"Copy, 58. One gun and one slick turning now. Say position."

"Uh, 50, go crypto." They both did. "I'm between the Toe and Disneyland. Rough coordinates are…" he read the two-letter plus four-digit fix he'd worked out so far. "That'll do until they get here. I should have it to six digits by then."

"Copy the fix, 58. 50 standing by and back off crypto."

Rusty deliberately flew off, trying to give the impression that he'd seen nothing, but every time he S-turned, he had the glasses up again. His two figures plodded on, heads down. Please, please let them stay oblivious to me, Rusty fervently wished.

Ten minutes went by, and he was beginning to despair that the two VC would suddenly panic, but they trudged on. They were now plainly visible, crossing a broad green meadow of fresh grass.

"Mike 58, Hornet 33."

"Hornet 33, good to hear you. Orville and Wilbur are still down there, and still unaware of me, I think."

"Hot damn, 58. The party is about to commence. Give me a hold down."

Rusty held down his mic switch for ten seconds, transmitting but not talking.

The instant he released it, he heard, "Gotcha on DF, 58. Heading your way right now."

"Make that beeline a hornetline, 33. They're crossing a meadow and we can catch them flat-footed if we hurry. If they make it to the trees…"

"I bic that, 58. How far do they have to go?"

"Couple hundred meters, 33. But they're pushing a helluva load. Five minutes, maybe."

"Duck soup, 58. I have you in sight. Be there in two."

Rusty turned and saw them. They were hauling ass, noses down and rotors churning. "Tally Ho on you too, 33. When you're ready, I'll buzz them and get their heads down. I don't want to use a rocket and panic them."

"Good idea, 58. I'm ready now. Two, you have the Mike in sight?"

"Two's tally and ready."

"Go for it, 58, 33 is guns hot."

"Copy, 33, I'm in." Rusty shoved the engines levers to the firewall and rolled hard. He had the two figures in the center of his windscreen for two whole seconds before he saw their faces snap up. Rusty started his pull-up just as they dropped their bikes and dove off the road. "Bingo bingo, 33," he said as he zoomed right over the two VC. As soon as he could, Rusty looked back.

Whatever plans the two might have had to shoot or run ended as the gunship stitched a tight circle of bullet holes around the pair with its door-mounted mini-gun. One hundred bullets a second hitting all around you like a picket fence is a powerful suggestion: don't run. They didn't.

As the gunship hovered, door gun staring down at the two with the promise of instant death, the slick landed nearby. Its crew quickly took the two and their bikes into custody. Everything was loaded and airborne in less than five minutes.

"Hornet 33, Hornet 34. We got 'em. Two gooks, two bikes, and four bags of rice. One of the gooks has a stack of papers and some kind of black book. Might be a good haul. Break. Mike 58, you copy?"

"Oh yeah, 34. I copy. Great job. And good shooting, 33. That's an A-plus."

"33 copies and dittoes on the good job. 34, let's head for the barn."

"34."

"Mike 50, 58."

"58, we only heard part of that. Please repeat."

"50, the Hornets have both enemy troops, both bikes and the rice aboard and inbound. They report some papers captured, also. Oh, and no casualties."

"Roger all that, 58. Sounds like you get an attaboy." It was Bridgewater's voice. "Come on home for debrief."

"Thanks. 58 is inbound."

If these had been ancient piston-engined Kingbees, Rusty would have beaten the choppers back, but the Green Hornets flew powerful twin-turbine Hueys, the very advanced "N" models. They could cruise almost as fast as he could, so Rusty throttled back and kept pace with them. It was odd to be following choppers rather than leading them, and he learned what a powerful downwash they created when he drifted lazily behind them. When Rusty hit their invisible wash, he flipped almost upside down in an eye blink. All his maps, the binoculars and his camera flew around the cabin like missiles. Something whacked hard into Rusty's helmet as he fought the controls. When he finally got upright and stable again, he moved well out to the side and decided to stay there.

While his heart rate slowed, Rusty wondered if anyone on the Hornets had even noticed his wild gyrations or would have seen it if he had crashed. Probably not. The crew in the slick would have their eyes glued to their captives, just in case, and the gunship crew would be scanning mostly ahead.

With the excitement their arrival would generate, how long would it be before anybody realized Rusty hadn't arrived? A sobering thought.

Both Hornets landed directly on the Mike ramp while Rusty used the runway. By the time he reached the gate, the ramp was the center of the camp's collective attention. The new guy, A1C Fleming, apparently got the short straw and met Rusty at the gate to de-arm. Rusty opened the right-side window and Fleming leaned in for the rocket pins, then did a double take. "Jeez, sir, what happened in here, a hurricane?"

Maps and papers were everywhere, strewn behind the seats, under the rear jump seat and in the radio rack. Rusty had no idea where the camera and field glasses had gone, but he remembered that whack on the head. As he sat there with both hands raised in clear sight while Fleming pinned the pods, he felt around until he found a deep chip in his helmet. Hmmmm.

By the time Rusty shut down, the two prisoners were long gone, but the two bicycles and rice sacks were still sitting on the ramp. Both Mike and Hornet people were standing there looking at them. Presiding over them like an African hunter with his trophy was the gunship's door gunner. Ironically, his nametag said Livingston.

Somebody yelled, "Hey Mule, you ride one of those home?" The crowd laughed.

Livingston grinned back, "Yeah. Tied it to the skid and pedaled the rotors the whole way!" More laughs. Then he saw Rusty walking up. "Hey, are you 58?"

Rusty nodded. "You must be 33. Shit hot work out there, guys. Tell me what it was like."

"Hey, it wouldn't have happened without you, sir. We just hauled the trash home." Realizing that he had the floor with an eager audience, the gunner went on.

"Well, when we got there, the Mike FAC here already had 'em spotted. When he buzzed them so low he damn near blew their coolie hats off, they dove for the ditches. We gave them a little demo of the mini-gun and they just went hands up. The slick scooped 'em in." He shrugged. "Simple."

"I'd have surrendered too if I saw that thing," Rusty said, pointing to a wicked weapon hanging from the gunner's belt. It was one of the Army's M-79 40-mm grenade launchers, but this one had been cut down and sawed off into a humongous pistol with a six-inch barrel. It swung from his belt on a wire clip and looked just plain evil.

"Oh, this?" Livingston said, touching it. "That's just for fun. Baby here is my real toy. He patted the copter's mini-gun with his other hand. "She absolutely pukes bullets, but she never jams, and she lays 'em right in there. You oughta try her sometime, sir."

"Hey, I'd like that," Rusty said. "It's a deal." In the excitement of checking out the two bikes, Rusty immediately forgot about the offer. The bikes were both piles of junk, completely worn out. Neither had a seat or pedals, and it was clear they'd been modified to be pushed rather than ridden. Where the seat should be, an upright steel shaft had been welded to serve as a push handle. A three-foot piece of bamboo had been tied to each handlebar so that it pointed to the rear. The bamboo allowed the pusher to steer no matter how bulky was the cargo strapped over the crossbars. It was a clever arrangement. Rusty looked at the rice sacks. They must weigh a hundred pounds each, and each bike carried two. How many trips down the Ho Chi Minh Trail had these bikes made; through rivers, along footpaths, up and down mountain roads and through the jungle? No wonder they were falling apart. But still going, he realized. Just like the VC.

Rusty glanced at the rice sacks. He had no idea what the printed words said, but the clearly stenciled '50k' confirmed what he'd estimated: fifty kilos is 110 pounds, and each bike carried two bags. Not an easy load to push. Hell, it was twice the weight of each pusher. Then a funny thought crossed his mind: if these two gomers were pushing their own rations, would they arrive at the end of the Trail with empty sacks? If so, why go? Rusty chuckled to himself. Maybe these guys' job was as pointless as his own seemed to be.

Rusty went in to be debriefed, and as he was answering questions from Brookside, Bridgewater and Dihn, he heard one of the Kingbees take off. Dihn grinned as he looked in the direction of the sound. "Your brief very easy, not like VC."

Rusty shot a querulous glance to Brookside, not understanding. Brookside smiled, "That would be the ARVN intel team taking off with the prisoners for a short talk."

Rusty still looked blank. Brookside went on.

"They take uncooperative prisoners up – two of them is ideal – blindfolded and strapped into harnesses. Neither of them has ever flown before today, almost certainly, so the noise and everything is both frightening and disorienting. Anyway, they get them up to about a thousand feet, sit them in the doorway and then rip off the blindfolds. They usually shit their pants right then. The interrogator asks one of them some pertinent questions. If he doesn't answer, he gets kicked out the door."

Rusty blanched. "What!"

"I'm not kidding, but there's more to it. Of course, he's clipped to a cable, and so he just drops out of sight and hangs there, but his buddy doesn't know that. Usually, you can't shut the second guy up after that. After he sings for a while, they haul the first guy up, sit him on the step again and make a big deal out of unsnapping the cable from his harness. He starts singing, too. Works every time."

"Jesus, I guess. Isn't that against the Geneva Accords or something?"

"Probably. You remember what the NVA claims? That the Geneva Accord doesn't apply to them because they never signed it? Well..." He shrugged.

"Good for the goose, huh?" Rusty said. "Or a two-way street."

"Something like that. Anyway, these guys are ARVN prisoners, being interrogated by ARVN intel. Out of our hands, and we never heard anything about it, anyway. I'll just say this: I've *heard* that before our side started insisting, the ARVN didn't use a cable. But that's just a rumor, you understand."

Dihn's eyes narrowed, and his half-smile sent chills down Rusty's spine.

Bridgewater walked with Rusty after the debrief. When they were alone, he said "Rusty my boy, Ah don't want you to get the big head 'bout this, but y'all are a raht fahn FAC. Ah ain't jist talkin' 'bout yore flyin' neither. I hear that y'all been out thar helpin' with the wrench benders."

"You mean the rocket party? Hell, we all helped with that. Or almost all." Rusty watched his face from the corner of his eye.

"Yeah, that, but afore that, too. A leetle bird tells me you been gettin' grease under yore nails purdy often. Ah got one thang to say 'bout that..."

"Yessir?"

"Ah'm proud' a ya. That naht flyin we did had us busier'n a one-armed juggler, and there's more like it comin'. That's why we got Fleming, cause the maintainers do about two ahrs work for ever ahr we fly. And thar weren't but three wrench benders doin' it. Ah cain't say how much they 'preciate yore help, son."

"Shit, I got in the way more than I helped. About all I learned to do was safety wiring, and Cramer had to inspect that when I finished. He could've done it faster by himself."

"Tain't the point. Y'all were there, not pitchin' horseshoes or sun bathin'. That counts. Counts big with the guys wearin' stripes. In their ahs, you got the hat *and* the cattle."

Where the hell does he get these lines, Rusty wondered. "What can I say? Thanks. I actually learned that lesson from my old ops officer back at LZ Emerald, so I can't take credit. Besides, I really started doing it just because I don't like jogging or playing horseshoes."

He laughed. "Well, Ah reckon it don't matter why. Lissen, whal Ah got yore ear, how'd y'all like to do something a leetle different?"

Uh oh – the sandwich again. Rusty hated it when he did that. "Like what?"

"Ever heard of a thang called Igloo White?"

"Is that those sensors they drop along the Trail? The ones that have antennas that look like branches and leaves? They drop 'em and they bury themselves in the ground – all but the antenna? And then the thing sends back seismic or sound data so the spooks know when trucks are rolling by? They showed us some back at Hurlburt in FAC school."

"Sneaky little program, ain't it? Just tickles me plumb to death. Anyhow, you remember those tubes you dropped up by Lumphat?"

Rusty nodded. "Only too well. They damn near killed me as heavy as they were."

"Yup, that's them. Well, the powers that be up at...let's just say *somebody* got an ideer to plant some sensors up there by hand. Without sayin' more, let's now say the big thinkers have given up on that ideer. How'd you like to plant some trees?"

"With a winged shovel, I trust."

"There really warn't no 'Slow Children' signs in your neighborhood was there?"

Rusty couldn't help laughing. "I guess I'm volunteered – again. Just tell me when and how."

"There ya go. Ah knew Ah could count on ya. Ah'll tell ya when Ah hear maself." He slapped Rusty's shoulder.

They walked a few more steps towards the hootch.

"I have to ask, sir. You implied that the manual planting job didn't exactly result in a bumper crop. Did I screw up that drop?"

"Hell, son, yore drop was about the only thang in that plan that did come up roses. Don't y'all fret none 'bout that."

"It's just that I have this overwhelming fear that I'll screw up and get some good folks killed. You know about a thing that happened at LZ Emerald? Did anybody at 21st TASS tell you?"

Bridgewater stopped walking and turned to Rusty. His face and voice both went serious. "Yeah Rusty, they did. That was a bitch. From what I heard, you had no choice and actually saved a whole Special Ops squad. I understand how losing that whole helo crew might haunt you, but it made you a better FAC, I think. You know better than most what rides on your decisions. That's why I might tend to lean on you at times for tough jobs. You're a tougher tool than most."

"I wish I felt like one. I've wet more than one pillow - and not just about that one incident."

"That proves my point, son. I wouldn't trust somebody without a conscience, or a heart. Or somebody who fires rockets but couldn't be bothered to build any."

Rusty looked at him with raised eyebrows.

"No slow children where I lived, either."

"Bilingual ones, though. English and Texan."

He barked a single laugh, slapped Rusty on the back again, turned and walked back to the TOC.

The routine of visual reconnaissance flights and radio caps resumed. They'd put in two teams much farther south than before, probably because the NVA had caught so many teams farther north. But as usual, nobody told the pilots the why of what they were doing, or what they accomplished.

Where they were now putting the teams was a long way from BMT, and somebody must've thought that their response time to a team in trouble would be shorter if a couple FACs and Hornets could be positioned at a satellite field. Bridgewater picked Rushing, Sandy and Craig to be the satellite FACs. Every morning, they flew to a tiny airstrip at Quan Loi. From there, one FAC would fly a cap mission while the other two stood on alert, along with two Hornets. Each of them flew one cap each day, and in the evening they all flew back to BMT.

In the meantime, Flip, Jack and Rusty flew VR and worked a more northern team. Sanderson and Bridgewater helped out at both locations, mostly on radio cap flights when guys had their malaria pill 'sitdown' days. Everyone flew at least once a day. Twice, if there were infil locations to scout or parts and paperwork that needed delivery to Cam Rahn.

It was in this busy time that Bridgewater suddenly said, "Rusty, it's time to do a little gardening."

Buchenhardt and Rusty were lounging in the courtyard's mid-morning sun at the time, and Jack looked at one then the other of them with a quizzical expression.

"Never mind, Jack, it's an inside joke. Rusty knows what I mean, don't ya?"

"Yup, and ah'm ready to saddle up the old combine," Rusty said, mimicking Bridgewater's sometimes drawl.

"That'd be a seed drill, son. The combine is fer harvestin'"

Rusty knew that, having grown up on a farm of sorts, but he was surprised that Bridgewater did. Rusty nodded in appreciation. "As long as it isn't a manure spreader, I'm ready."

"Good. Can you be ready to brief now and takeoff in an hour?"

"Sure can. I have the cap after Jack's so that leaves almost six hours. It won't take that long, will it?"

"Not if'n y'all kin read a map. Hell, even if'n ya cain't, ya should be back here quicker'n two bunnies. And tain't nuthin quicker'n two bunnies," he winked.

When they were in the secure confines of the TOC, Bridgewater showed him a map. He pointed to a classic military chokepoint. "The place is right near where you've been many times, including that supply drop. The powers that be want some Igloo White sensors placed as close to this point as possible. Fast movers aren't accurate enough, so they want to see if an O-2 can place 'em. Your job is to put one here and one here."

He pointed to a spot near the Elbow where a major road paralleled the Prek Nam Lieou and crossed a smaller tributary that wiggled its way to the Nam Lieou through a sinuous canyon. The highway was large enough to have a number: it was Highway 1452 while still in Cambodia, changing to 493 where it entered Vietnam. A more obvious section of the Ho Chi Minh Trail could not be imagined. It was only about twenty miles southeast of where Rusty had dropped those four massive tubes.

Rusty nodded. "Yeah, that figures. There's a major hand-laid rock ford there. And there's almost always wetter dirt on the south bank than the north, so they're using it as an active crossing. Same at this smaller creek here," he pointed to yet another crossing just two miles farther southeast. "Except that this one has a bridge over the Prek Nam. A bridge that gets new tire boards regularly, by the way."

Bridgewater looked at him and smiled, "That's why I'm sending you. You discovered all that stuff. Hell, you might say your reports were behind this whole shebang." He patted Rusty's shoulder. "Anyway," he continued, "you'll have four sensors, two of each kind. They want a mixed pair on each side of this crossing."

"Why bracket the ford and not the bridge?" Rusty asked.

"Good question. I suspect they think it's less obvious to put them at the smaller crossing. Or they expect they'd get a better signature from the sensors there than at the bridge. Maybe the ground's too rocky at the bridge. I'm not sure. But they were very specific."

"How am I loaded? I need to know which two to drop each time. Do I drop both left and then both right, or outboards then inboards?"

"That's another astute question. But I don't know. Cramer is the load chief, and he'll tell you. But make sure you drop one of each together. Oh, and they say you need to be at least 300 feet up so the sensors hit both vertically and fast enough to fully implant; and get them as close to the road as you can without hitting the road itself. Or dropped into the water, obviously. Try to get them exactly one kilometer apart, if you can. That's it."

"Okay, sounds simple. I'll go out right now and do it."

"Oh, one last thing, don't report on the drop. Just routine position reports. Make it seem like a regular VR mission, just in case the bad guys have us dialed in again today."

"I get it. Boring radio. Why do you say 'again'?"

"Uh, I reckon I done dumped the frijoles inta the fahr that time. Well, there was a curious spike in enemy radio traffic the other day when you caught those two rice carriers. Not afterwards, but *during* the capture." He looked at Rusty to see if that had sunken in.

Rusty nodded, and said, "So they obviously were listening in and had a real-time confab." Then he added, "But why would four measly bags of rice cause them to get their knickers in a twist?"

"See? I knew you'd get it! That little black book was…well, I'll just say VERY interesting to certain people."

"Ahh-haaa! I see now. Hot damn, that's good news. But it also means they know we have it. Because the Hornets radioed that they had it, and I repeated that when I relayed their report. I wish now that I'd used crypto."

"Couldn't be helped. The Hornets don't have crypto gear, and as you said, they'd already transmitted the fact that they'd found a black book. But, and here's the heart of it…the bad guys may or may not have heard that.

Remember, the Hornets were at low altitude when they transmitted to you, so the signal didn't go far. We didn't hear their transmission here in the TOC, for example. But we have to assume the VC did. Incidentally, you didn't actually mention a black book when you radioed. You said 'some papers' and that might be all the bad guys know. For all they know, the gooks may have been able to ditch or destroy the book. 'Papers' might just be letters from home – which some of them were, by the way."

"We never know anything for sure in this business, do we?"

"Nope, it's like a chess game: we guess what they're thinking and they guess about us. But there's one thing I do know for sure."

What's that?"

"That you'd better get your ass in gear or you won't get back in time to relieve Jack on the team cap."

"Roger that!" Rusty saluted and headed for the door. Funny that Bridgewater hadn't used even a hint of his drawl, Rusty thought to himself as he walked to the ramp. Either he knew that Rusty had seen behind the wizard's curtain, or else he no longer saw the need to wear that mask in private. Or maybe he was just dog-tired. Rusty was just beginning to realize how many hours an ALO put in every day: about twenty.

He also realized that he'd *finally* been given a tiny peek at some of the results of his work. It felt really, really good.

Cramer saluted and grinned when he walked up. "You sure do get your share of weird missions, sir!" What are these things? The back end looks like a plastic Christmas tree!"

"If you don't know, Mike, I can't tell you. But I hope you do, because there's something about them that I have to ask and only you can answer."

"Yessir? What?"

"I know there are two types of these things, and that I have two of each. But which two are which? How are they loaded?"

"Oh, I see. Well, sir the standard load procedure with mixed ordnance is to load them symmetrically. So you have one A and one B on each wing."

"Hmm. Mike, are the weights similar for each?"

"They seemed about identical to me, sir. Maybe 30 pounds each. I hand loaded 'em easy. Why?"

"Well, for reasons of my own, how tough would it be to swap 'em so I have both A's on one side and both B's on the other?"

"No sweat at all, sir. Two minutes. Does it matter which is where?"

"Nope, not at all. I just want them split the other way."

"Can do, sir. For you, anything."

True to his word, in two minutes flat Cramer had swapped two sensors. Rusty examined the things while he worked. Each sensor was a three-foot dark green cylinder about four inches in diameter. The front end tapered to a sharp cone like a crayon. But it was the rear that was odd. Here, the cylindrical body was capped with a flat circular plate a foot wide. Sticking out of the center of this plate was a small bush, a plastic bush complete with leaves. But that bush was actually an antenna.

In use, the sensor falls vertically until it hits the ground. With luck, it buries itself up to the flat plate. On impact, a vial of acid inside breaks and the acid activates a long-life battery. As long as the battery lasts, the device transmits either sound or seismic information through the antenna. Any vehicle that passes will produce a vibration or noise, to be heard by a high-flying monitor aircraft. Clever ways of coding the information, the frequency or both tells the aircraft which sensor the vehicle is passing. With sensors spaced precisely, the speed of a passing vehicle can be calculated. It's an easy matter to kill the vehicles with air attack or artillery – if that's the desire.

In FAC school, the instructors told their students a highly humorous (and equally improbable) story of one acoustic sensor that supposedly relayed sounds of an amorous encounter between two VC who unknowingly laid down next to one of those spindly little bushes for their tryst. The truck convoy they were in was destroyed not long after. The price of sin is high, the instructors had joked. Rusty doubted the story, but smiled to himself as he examined these sensors.

Rusty headed northwest as soon as he got airborne. It was almost a straight shot to his target, and the terrain features on the ground couldn't be any clearer or easier to see. First, he'd fly up the long side of the Elbow, keeping the river off to his left in full view. The ford that he was to straddle with the sensors was about half way up that long arm. Then, all he had to do was drop a pair of sensors as he neared the tributary, count exactly 15 seconds and drop the other pair. At a ground speed of 120 knots, that would put the two pairs exactly one kilometer apart.

The reason Rusty wanted Cramer to switch the sensors was because of those plastic bush antennas. Rusty was afraid that they'd tangle as they fell if he dropped two from the same side. As it was, they touched as they hung from his pylons. Rusty watched them closely as he flew, but they didn't seem to flail about. Mounted this way, Rusty could drop one from each side and be sure to get one acoustic and one seismic planted about ten feet apart. If all went well, they didn't get caught in a tree, crash into a rock or fail in some other way, that is.

On the way, Rusty made a series of long, sweeping turns just as though he were on a routine VR flight. In a way, he was, for he kept his eyes open and scanned the ground closely for any hints of the enemy. You never knew...

But within minutes, he saw the long straight slice in the jungle that he was looking for: the Prek Nam Lieou. At its far end was the abrupt 90-degree turn the Mikes called the Elbow. Rusty descended to about 500 feet off the ground and set his airspeed at 120 knots. He could detect no sideways drift, and the treetops below weren't waving, so winds must be almost calm.

When he passed over the bridge, he set his two outboard armament switches to their drop setting. A minute later, Rusty saw the little unnamed tributary that was the target. When he was almost to it, he raised the guard cover over the Master Arm switch, flipped the switch "On" and pressed the firing button. Silently, the two outboard sensors fell away. Rusty started the plane's stopwatch, flipped the Master Arm back off, then turned the inboard pylon switches down. Holding straight and level, he glanced down just as he passed directly over the river ford. Once again, Rusty was pleased to see fresh drain marks on the south bank, where water had recently poured off trucks as they climbed that bank.

Master Arm back on, and Rusty watched the stopwatch. Fifteen seconds. He pressed the trigger again. This time, he didn't even see his little trees go. By the time he glanced up from the clock, the pylons were empty. Time to go home. Rusty started a long climbing turn to the west. As he flew, he passed almost directly over the little clearing where he'd dropped those four tubes, and he wondered who had been down there to receive them. He knew he'd never be told that.

By the time he'd topped 1,500 feet he was crossing the still-swollen Tonle Srepok. Mindful that the bad guys were probably listening, he called back to the TOC and reported his position as the Elbow. If they were watching as well as listening, that might confuse them: what the Mikes called the elbow was now 20 miles behind him, but an almost identical bend in the Srepok was below. More chess tricks, he grinned to himself.

It was also likely that several thousand enemy troops were below him, many of them probably licking their lips and wishing they could open fire. But such a breach of discipline was sure to bring severe punishment down on them. Savvy NVA officers strictly forbade shooting at FACs without provocation. They'd long learned what it meant to give away their position to a FAC – near suicide.

Back at the TOC, Rusty debriefed with Bridgewater.

"How'd it go?" He wanted to know.

"About as perfect as I could've hoped, I think. I dropped a pair just short of the ford, and the other fifteen seconds later on the other side. I was as near over the highway as I could get. Unless I planted one of those trees right on the dotted line, it was as easy as falling off a log."

"Good. Excellent. Uh, how far west did you get after the drop?"

"I made a wide loop down the Srepok, as if it were a VR mission. I got almost to Stung Treng before I turned southeast and came home."

"Excellent! Did you observe anything...unusual?"

What was this, a trick question?

"No, not really. The south bank of the ford was wet; recently wet by the way. Our little bushes might be well-watered by tomorrow. The bridge looked the same as always. I saw no signs of enemy troops at all, but that's standard in the daytime, isn't it?"

"Yup, that's standard. Nothing else? Anywhere?"

"Like what? Do I get a hint?"

"Uh, no. Sorry. Okay, if that's all you can report, that's all. Go take a break. Jack is up, and Flip says his flight was dead quiet. You just have time to catch lunch if you want."

Rusty left, wondering what that was all about. Bridgewater didn't seem disappointed, so maybe it wasn't some kind of test that Rusty had flunked. But what in blazes was it?

The next day, the Quan Loi Three departed at daybreak, joining up and forming a three-ship flight for the half-hour flight. Rusty envied them that, formation flying being so much fun. FACs almost always worked alone, and even when two worked together, it was never in formation.

The three of them left behind decided to stick to a regular rotation. Flip liked to jog in the early morning, and Jack claimed that his four years at the Citadel had made him into an early riser. So Jack took the dawn patrol, Rusty flew the midday flight, and Flip agreed to the late afternoon mission that put the team to bed.

This was Buchenhardt's team, and they were watching for traffic where Cambodia highway 144 crossed the Prek Rouet. The FACs surmised that the highest levels of military intelligence had suddenly discovered that bridges are important in war. Hence, there was increased emphasis on such places.

The team had been in for two days with no trouble at all. Except for their morning and evening radio checks, they'd been silent.

Rusty got airborne and relieved Jack. This robin was a twitchy, pockmarked, emaciated little guy named Xuan. Rusty got him to smile and nod when he pronounced it "Swan" so Rusty let it go at that. They'd been up for two hours, well into burning the auxiliary fuel tanks down, and had just finished some C-rations that Rusty had warmed up by balancing the can on the high-intensity bulb in the base of the rocket sight. Xuan was fast asleep, and Rusty was getting a case of the yawns himself.

Rusty was debating the wisdom of reaching across to open the window and throw the C-rat can away, arguing with himself whether the risk of having the can hit the rear propeller outweighed the cloying odor of heavy grease. He had just decided to risk the propeller when the radio broke squelch and rasped, then stopped.

Rusty stared at the stack of black dials and frequency windows, wondering which radio that had been, when the airwaves erupted again with a torrent of high-pitched syllables. Uh oh.

Xuan sprang bolt upright, staring out the window at the ground. He turned to Rusty wide-eyed while he fumbled for his grease pencil. He jabbed towards the ground with his left hand while he frantically scribbled numbers and words on the window. Rusty didn't need any stronger hints. He chopped the power, rolling off into a dive and turning towards the center of the team's target box.

Rusty turned the radio selector to FM so Xuan could transmit, and Xuan rattled off a long stream of Vietnamese. He and the voice on the ground talked back and forth a few times, not in code and not quietly. As Rusty listened, the ground voice become punctuated with panting. They were running.

When he could, he broke in. "Swan, where team? VC? Team go hot?"

Xuan nodded rapidly and resumed his rapid talking, then released his transmit button and turned to Rusty, "Team hot. Many VC. Team run this way..." He pointed to the map and dragged his inch-long pinkie fingernail to the north.

"Any team dead? Wounded?"

"No. Team okay, but run. Run fast. Want go home now."

No shit, Rusty thought to himself. "Okay. We get team home." He looked at the ground and the map in turn. They were about five miles from the team. He flipped the radio switch to UHF and transmitted, "Mike 50, Mike 58, Yellow Gate is hot, repeat Yellow Gate is hot. Scramble the alert birds."

No answer.

"Mike 50, Mike 58. Do you copy?"

Nothing. Shit, he was already too low to reach them. Goddamn it. Should he climb back up or get to the team as fast as he could? Climbing would take too long just now. He'd find the team first. In a well-practiced routine, Rusty twisted the fuel selectors to Main, set the left rocket pod to Fire and Master Arm Off, shoved props and mixtures to takeoff setting, and flipped the radio back to FM. Finally, he tossed the ration can over his shoulder, jerked his shoulder straps tight and stowed the map under his left leg. Now he could start looking for any sign of the team or the enemy.

Leveling off 500 feet above the ground, Rusty started weaving back and forth. As he looked, he tapped Xuan on the leg, "Swan, can team signal? Flash?"

Xuan rattled off a series of words. There was a long pause before Rusty heard a single word in answer. "Okay." Xuan said.

Rusty leveled off where he could see well, and swept his eyes across the scraggly trees below. From underneath them, he saw a single bright flash of sunlight. "Okay, I see team." Xuan transmitted another quick few words. Rusty turned towards the spot where he'd seen the flash – hopefully from the team's signal mirror and not the enemy's. When that spot was only a few hundred meters off his left side, Rusty saw figures scrambling through the trees. Now to figure out if those were the good guys or the bad.

Rusty counted as the figures wove their frantic way pell-mell through the trees. Probably five. Then he turned his attention to the trees behind them. There, moving a bit slower, but obviously looking attentively ahead of them, were more figures. Lots more. As Rusty looked, he saw the telltale sparkle of muzzle flashes. Well, that sorts things nicely, he said to himself.

He snapped the wings around, flipped the Master Arm "On" and triggered two rockets at the flashes. Take that, you little bastards. Twin balls of writhing white smoke blossomed out of the thin trees. As Rusty zoomed up, he saw more figures pull up short and aim their rifles at him. Hard left bank, then reverse to the right. Rusty bunted the nose over and then pulled it up, dodging and weaving. When he got clear of the immediate vicinity, he turned and looked back. The VC were regrouping, already starting to move toward the team again.

Mentally, Rusty cursed his good friend and mentor Dave Sanderson. As ops officer, he'd decided that FACs had no business carrying high-explosive or flechette rockets, saying attack was the job of the Hornets. So all Rusty had under his wings were fourteen marking rockets – now only twelve. They were great for marking but almost useless as weapons. Oh well, do what you gotta…

Rusty turned and triggered off two more rockets. Again the VC stopped and fired upwards in anger, and again Rusty pulled out twisting and yanking the controls erratically. If he could keep this up, the team might be able to add some distance between themselves and the enemy. They might even get away.

Rusty kept turning tight circles, firing rockets and weaving his way through the streams of tracers zipping through the air. By now he was down to his last two rockets, but seemed to have the VC temporarily buffaloed. Rusty could see them standing and scanning the openings between the trees, looking for him. But they were not chasing the team. That was the only good news. The rocketing and jinking had soon brought Rusty down almost to the treetops. He was not only almost out of rockets, but out of altitude and airspeed, too. It was time for him to regroup. Rusty shallowed his turn and clawed for altitude. He'd lost track of the team in the flurry of rocket passes, but so had the VC.

"Swan, see where team go now, okay? Then we call Kingbee."

"Good, good, Daiwee! Okay!" Xuan looked a little queasy from the violent maneuvering, but still talked game. He transmitted again, a bit cautiously this time, voice slow and subdued. Rusty could have yelled in glee when the response came back the same way, measured and quiet. They'd moved off enough to get back to covert radio discipline. Xuan wrote a few two-digit numbers on the window: the team was using code numbers again – an even better sign.

"Mike 50, 58 come in."

"Mike 58, I have you weak but readable, go ahead."

"50, Yellow Gate is hot, repeat hot. I need all assets immediately. Over."

"Have you loud and clear now, 58. Copy Yellow Gate is hot. Launching alert birds."

Rusty turned to Xuan. "Kingbees take off now, Swan." Rusty gave him thumbs up, and Xuan grinned like a maniac, nodding and bouncing in his seat. Rusty looked at the clock. Flip should already be airborne, also.

"Mike 54, 58."

Nothing.

"Mike 50, is 54 airborne yet?"

"58, affirmative. He checked in but his radio was scratchy. Nothing since. Break. Mike 54, Mike 50. Radio check."

Nothing.

Now what, Rusty wondered. Where the hell was Flip? He turned back to the team.

"Mike 50, 58 is descending again. Team is running. I'll try to get coordinates for the pickup. I'll radio back when possible, or relay through 54. Copy?"

"Got you, 58. 50 will advise 54 if possible. Say fuel."

Oh, shit. "Mike 50, 58 is..." He was already below minimum to get home, Rusty realized with a shock. "58 is past bingo. Critical fuel now."

"58 are you breaking off with the team?"

"Negative, 50. If I leave now, we lose them. They're outnumbered."

"Mike 50 copies. Will alert assets in case."

In case he and Xuan have to walk home, Rusty realized. Rusty turned back west just as the FM radio delivered bad news from the ground. Yelling...and panting again, the sounds of weapons firing transmitted with the words.

Xuan listened, then said, "Team stop in rocks. Fight now. Kingbee come now?"

"I hope so, Swan." Rusty didn't try to explain the realities of their fuel state to Xuan. He dug the map from under his leg. "Where team now?" Xuan shrugged, but spoke a few words into his mic. He turned. "Map gone. All gone. Hab smoke. You want team make smoke now?"

That would instantly condemn them. "No, no smoke. Wait for Kingbee. Tell team no smoke." Xuan did, while Rusty turned back to where he'd last seen the enemy. Half a kilometer north of the spot was a small outcropping of crumbled black lava. Rusty would bet that's where the team was now. As he stared at it, he saw a few sparkles of rifle fire. Yup. And less than two hundred meters from the team, he saw more flashes, many more. Cursing, Rusty bunted the nose over and fired his last two rockets. Again, the area lit up with muzzle flashes as the enemy's attention turned from the team to his plane. Good, but now Rusty was truly out of options.

All but one, he thought. All but the penultimate, desperate one. Again.

Instead of pulling off and wildly jinking, Rusty pushed the nose over. The flashes increased to a fury as he dove straight at them, a motionless target from their perspective. Somehow, tracers and bullets whizzed past and around, but not one hit. Rusty pulled up at the last second, buzzing the enemy only a few feet over their heads, and zoomed back up. Cartwheeling off the top of the climb, he dove again and zoomed again to a paroxysm of flashes.

But now he was low and slow again. Rusty gritted his teeth and flew across the enemy's position for a third time, 50 feet above the trees, slow and level.

As he had in almost identical circumstances months ago at LZ Emerald, Rusty braced for the sounds of bullets ripping through the paper-thin aluminum. This time, he steeled himself and looked out his window, where – for a fraction of a second – he glared straight into the wide eyes of a VC soldier over rifle sights. Reflexively, Rusty ducked, almost seeing the Golden BB coming straight for his forehead.

"Mike 58, 54, Hey, I saw Willey Petes a minute ago, was that you?"

"Flip! Jesus Christ where have you been the team's hotter than hell I'm bingo and Winchester bust ass to get here!" The words tumbled out.

"Huh? Oh, shit! I mean, um… 54 copies. On the way. What happened?"

"Just get here, Flip. Kingbees are on the way. The team's pinned down and surrounded. They're down to just guns, a radio and a smoke. Lots of VC. I'm outta here, but I may not make it home. Way past bingo."

"Jesus. I copy. okay, I have you in sight. I got it. Break, Mike 50 54, do you copy?"

"Mike 54, 50. Roger, I have you loud and clear now. I copy you have the transfer and 58 is inbound. Kingbees and Hornets enroute, ETA ten mike. Copy?"

"Copy all, 50. Be advised that 58 is way past bingo. He's still below radio range but I'm in contact with him. And I'm going to change push now."

"54, 50 copies. Will monitor."

Rusty heard Flip's robin talking to the team, and then the team's answer. Half his mind was relieved, but the other half was fixated on the fuel gauges in horror. Rusty had to climb to get home – Ban Me Thuot runway was higher than he was now. Plus, if he ran out of fuel, Rusty didn't intend to belly in, crypto radio or not. He'd parachute. That took even more altitude, so he pushed the power up and started a climb. At least he'd be closer to the base when the engines quit.

Rusty switched back to the auxiliary tank for the front engine. It showed empty, but he wanted to burn every drop it might hold. A few minutes later, the engine coughed and sputtered. He flipped the selector back to main and the engine surged to life again. He repeated the act with the other aux tank, and got a few minutes of burn before the rear engine faltered. Rusty switched back to the main tank for that engine. He could do nothing more.

In the gauges for his main tanks, both needles pointed to Empty, but both fluttered slightly. They weren't accurate at that level, but that tiny motion gave him hope. Rusty had now climbed to field elevation, and was almost high enough to bail out, so he pulled back the throttles. He set power and props for maximum endurance. Then he slowly pulled back on the mixture knobs, leaning the fuel-to-air mix until the cylinder head temperatures soared to their redlines. Operating them at that temperature would ruin them, but screw the engines, Rusty thought. A warehouse-full of new Continentals was nothing compared to the value of his pink ass.

Thank God for the prevailing westerly wind. Every foot it pushed him eastward was welcome. They crawled along. Maximum endurance power allowed the engine to run as long as possible, but at very low power. Rusty squirmed in his seat, torn between the desperate need to get there, and the knowledge that this tortoise-like speed was the best way to do that. Emotion versus intellect was agony.

Xuan sat there as calm as a Buddhist monk. It dawned on Rusty that he had no clue of their status. Rusty pointed to the fuel gauges and said, "No gas. Numba ten. Motor stop soon, we go down. Bail out."

Xuan looked back, shaking his head quizzically, "No bic."

"We jump."

"NO! Nononono! No jump." Xuan clutched at his straps convulsively.

Rusty wondered if – when - the engines died, would he have to shoot Xuan? The only way to bail out of the O-2 is to jettison the right-side door, then unstrap and crawl out. The robin completely blocked Rusty's way out. Screw it, Rusty thought. If he shot the miserable little bastard, he'd only be a worse blockage. But Rusty vowed that, if they crash landed, he'd haul Xuan's little brown ass out of the plane and then shoot him.

They droned slowly along. Finally, Rusty saw Ban Me Thuot field appear out of the haze.

"Mike 50, Mike 58. I might make it. I'm going to tower frequency."

"Copy, 58, I'll monitor that push. Just in case."

"Thanks 50. 58 gone." Rusty hit the preset frequency button. "Ban Me Thuot Tower, Mike 58 is three miles northwest for emergency landing."

"My Fy Ay, hab you in sigh. You clear lan runway zeoh nine. Win two seben zeoh at six."

"Negative, Ban Me Thuot. Mike 58 will land runway two seven. Emergency fuel."

"You clear lan, My Fi Ay. Pilot discretion." Strange that he could say *that* clearly, Rusty thought, disjointedly.

Rusty held his altitude until he was sure he had the field made, no matter what. All he had to do would be to turn about 45 degrees left. He flew directly towards the end of the runway. He held it...held it... ...held it... and at the last second, simultaneously slapped the landing gear handle down, dropped the flaps and started a descending turn. The moment the nose dropped, the rear engine quit. Rusty checked the landing gear lights – three green. Thank goodness the front engine powers the landing gear hydraulics.

They touched down, and as Rusty lowered the nose to the runway, the front engine coughed and died. They rolled a short way, the tires thrumming on the rough asphalt. Rusty marveled: he'd never heard that sound so clearly before. They came to a stop, and the red-hot engines began tinkling as they cooled. The gyroscopic instruments whirred softly.

"Uh, Ban Me Thuot Tower, Mike 58 cannot taxi. I need a tow truck."

Hours later, Master Sergeant Mike Cramer stood over Rusty in the Club, grinning mischievously. "Sir, the O-2 Dash-One manual says there are one point two gallons of unusable fuel in the main tanks. Guess how much we drained from yours."

"Beats me. How much?"

"Exactly one point *one* gallons each. Sir."

"So you are implying that I cut things a wee bit close, huh?"

"Yessir. A wee bit, as you say. Just a wee bit."

"How are the engines? I had them leaned out until the cylinder head temps were pegged."

"Won't know that until we do some tests, sir. More bloody knuckles for Lopez."

"I'll be out there with him, Mike. Tomorrow morning. It's only fair."

"No need, sir. He needs to give Fleming a little OJT on engines anyway, and there ain't room inside those cowlings for three heads. You're off the hook."

"In that case, this round is on me. Tarbender, hey tarbender! Pour 'em. This one's on me!" The tiny club was moderately full with Special Forces guys, Hornet pilots and ground crew, and of course most of the Mike FAC guys. All present cheered Rusty's offer and bellied up.

The barmaid slinked her way through the rowdy tables and poured herself into Rusty lap. "You buy me, too?"

Rusty laughed. "Well, I buy you drink, but not buy you." She looked at him confused and ready to get angry, so he whispered in her ear, "Drink okay, no buy nookie."

She squirmed and squealed, "Ha! You no nookie man!" Standing up, she deftly spun and shot her hand into his crotch, then proclaimed to onlookers, "No hab!" Another roar of laughter, and somebody began singing, "No Balls

At All." Rusty shook his head and grinned, reddening; then wandered over to where Flip and Bridgewater were sitting.

"Flip, what the heck happened to you today? Why couldn't I reach you?"

"Well, I got airborne, but the radio was scratchy and almost unreadable. Then I noticed that the wires going into my headset were frayed and loose. So I took my helmet off and spliced them all together with band aids. The moment I finished, I looked up and saw white smoke plumes right out where I was headed. You know the rest."

"Actually, I don't. I was so absorbed in trying to squeeze the last drop out of my fuel tanks that I have no idea what happened after I split the scene. Fill me in."

Bridgewater beat Flip to it. "Flip did a masterful job. He figured out where everybody was, then worked the Hornet guns through the bad guys like coyotes in a chicken pen. Meanwhile, he moved the team a couple hundred meters further north and dropped the Kingbee in. Got the whole team out slicker'n snot in a bathtub."

"All of them? Nobody killed? Holy smoke!" Rusty said.

Flip spread his permanent smile even wider. "The holy smoke was yours, bro. If I hadn't seen your rockets, I'd still be taping wires together with my headset in my lap."

"Flip, those were my last two rockets. Maybe they were holy. Something made me hold them back."

Bridgewater slapped his back, "Son, you're just lazy. You didn't want to be a part of another rocket party quite yet."

They laughed and tinked glasses together. "Here's to rocket parties!"

Then Rusty got serious. "Major, that brings up a point. If I had been carrying a few HE or flechette rockets, I could've done a much better job of slowing the VC down. They practically ignored my Willey Petes unless they actually got splashed with the phosphorous. One pod of something lethal would make it a whole lot safer for the teams. Just until the Hornets get there, not instead of the Hornets."

"Ah'll have a chin wag with Sanderson. It was his call to fly with smoke only, and Ah cain't pull the rug from under his boots."

The bartender came up and presented Rusty with the tab for the round: $17. Rusty looked around the room, calculated a bit and decided he was being diddled on the price, but he was in high spirits. He handed the man two ten-dollar pieces of MPC scrip and held his palm vertically. The bartender beamed. It may have been the biggest tip he'd ever received.

Bridgewater offered Rusty another silent toast in acknowledgement, then leaned in close, "You remember me asking you if you saw anything unusual out there the other day?" He tipped his head to the west.

"Yeah, why?"

"Well, tomorrow, since you won't be working a team or bending a wrench, I may send you out there to look again."

"What for?"

"Not here. See me in the TOC after breakfast."

Belching uncomfortably from greasy bacon and powdered eggs, Rusty found Bridgewater in the TOC radio room. Over the now extremely familiar strains of "Our House," Bridgewater motioned him to the briefing room.

Behind that closed door, he started without preamble, "Rusty, I need you to fly a dangerous mission. The unusual thing I asked about is a reported 37mm anti-aircraft gun supposedly sitting on a rooftop in Stung Treng. I need somebody to go see if it's there or not. You're it."

"A 37mm gun? On a rooftop? Why the hell would the bad guys bother to put one in that rat's asshole of a town?"

"Well, it is the provincial capitol, and it is kind of like the Memphis of the Mekong. Three big rivers meet there, and the barge traffic out of Laos is known to be huge. If there's something there valuable enough to defend with AA guns, then maybe it's also worthwhile looking into."

"But isn't it pretty damn dangerous to go eyeball one with an O-2? Christ, talk about a sitting duck."

"O-2s face 37mm guns all the time up in the Mu Gia pass. And even bigger guns. It's not a suicide mission. I did say it was dangerous, but I expect you to come back. I wouldn't send you —or anybody else- if I thought otherwise."

"Yeah, I know. Okay. Where and when? I say that even though you just said where, and I can guess the when."

He grinned that wide-as-Texas grin. "Son, when all this is over, and Ah'm selling insurance, Ah'm gonna look you up. You're easy!"

"I'm also a cornered rat. Does this gun rumor extend down to a particular building, or do I have to loaf around in range until I spot it one shot too late?"

"Um, no. The report just says a rooftop. Sorry. But Stung Treng's not Houston. There can't be but a dozen buildings big enough to hold a 37mm gun."

Rusty thought about it. "I'd bet on it being right on the waterfront, where the cargo would be unloaded and stored. Or at that half-ass airport east of town. But that's less likely."

"Now yore gettin' the brain in gear. By the time you get there, you'll have it tied tighter'n a calf next to the brandin' fahr."

"Uh huh. I think I'll get right to it. So the Rescue guys can still find me before dark. Me or the smoking hole."

"That's what I like: confidence!"

Rusty changed into a standard flight suit – they were more fire resistant than cotton fatigues. Corso looked at him a bit funny when he came out of the parachute Conex on the flight line. Rusty was wearing a flak vest, then his regular survival vest, and a parachute over that. Plus, he was carrying another flak vest, which he folded up and put atop the left seat cushion. By the time he crammed himself into the seat and got his heavy ballistic helmet on, Rusty was bumping the roof window. Even with the seat full back, the yoke still touched his armored cocoon when he pulled it.

"You a little worried about ground fire this time, sir? That last mission leave you shook up or somethin'?"

"That would be a yes and a no, Corso. I'm off to get my ass shot at, but it wasn't that last mission that's got me feeling a little pale. It's the thought of this one."

Corso shook his head in sympathy. "Sir, there are days when I wish I could fly these things instead of just fixin' them. But today isn't one of those days. Good luck, sir."

He stood by with the fire extinguisher while Rusty started, then raced to the gate to pull the rocket pins. The standing orders hadn't changed yet, and all Rusty carried were smoke rockets. He got airborne and headed to the northwest. Rusty checked the binoculars and Nikon camera he had stowed on the right seat, got to altitude and got the props synchronized for cruise. Nothing to do now but sweat and hyperventilate for the better part of an hour, he joked to himself. Rusty set about finding a way to spot this hypothetical gun before it could blast him out of the sky. If this thing is designed to shoot at planes, he asked himself, would it be capable of shooting horizontal, or nearly so? Maybe not. If he could stay right on the deck while he got close enough to see it, maybe it couldn't traverse sideways fast enough, either. On the other hand, that tactic would put him in range of every other weapon from crossbows up. But he'd gladly gamble with those.

Rusty nodded to himself. Plan A would be to come in at low altitude, make one circle just outside the center of town, and then, if he saw the gun, bug out. Plan B would take over if he didn't see a 37mm gun on the first circle. In that case, he'd circle again, but from further away, checking things out with the binos. He wouldn't fly over the same place twice, and he'd stay as low as he could, turning constantly.

Now for Plan C. The map showed no bridges over any of the rivers. If he did get shot down, he'd try to get to the far side of running water first. It'd take pursuers a bit longer to come looking for him – he hoped.

Rusty tried to take his mind off deadly AA guns by looking at the map. Stung Treng was shown as a tiny town, hardly more than a village, despite being the provincial capitol. It sat at the confluence of the Mekong and the Tonle Sap. But just east of the town, the Tonle Kong and Rusty's old friend the Tonle Srepok joined to become the Sap. Why anybody would bother to rename a river for a measly ten mile stretch was beyond guess.

The rivers themselves were a study in opposites. The south-flowing Mekong meandered out of Laos through numerous small channels, wandering serenely among its collection of islands, sand bars and marshes: most of the year a broad, slumbering, umber giant. The westerly rushing Tonle torrents however, were different creatures. They plunged out of the highlands of Vietnam, cutting their way through rock beds that formed rapids after stepped rapids. Dropping more than a thousand feet in only a hundred miles, the Srepok's black waters sluiced along, sweeping all before them. Deep, turbulent and swift all year, they'd be suicide to navigate with any type of cargo craft. But they disappeared into the placid Mekong with the timidity and reserve of an initiate piously donning the saffron robes of a Buddhist monk.

Navigation was simplicity itself. All he had to do was follow the Tonle Srepok and it would lead him to Stung Treng. Not straight there, of course, rivers being Nature's vagabonds: always moving but always taking the path of least resistance. Airplanes also must always keep moving, but Rusty could cut across some of the huge loops and arcs of river, boring straight ahead to rejoin it later.

Twenty miles east of Stung Treng, Rusty took a deep breath, stowed the map and made sure everything inside the plane was set correctly. Then he pulled off some power, dropped the nose and prepared to merge with the river.

He dove down until he was less than 50 feet above the water. He shot downstream level with the treetops, following every curve of the stream.

Rapids after rapids shot beneath. When he passed the mouth of the Tonle Kong, he thought to himself, "Hey Kong, you looking for me? Or for Fay Wray?" Rusty laughed aloud to ease his own tension. Hootches began to appear on the banks, at first isolated and then more numerous. Rusty was ready when the left bank abruptly turned into a set of scalloped stone steps. He was suddenly looking at the tops of two- and three-story buildings: Stung Treng. Flicking his eyes rapidly front and left, he tried to scan for suspended wires. Shabby and dilapidated building after building flashed by, rusty iron corrugated roofs that he could ignore and the occasional flat mansard that drew his momentary but intense inspection. Nothing. When he had flown almost all the way to the Mekong, and the buildings had been replaced by more hootches, he hung a tight left turn.

Climbing only a few feet, Rusty made his second run past the ominous ghost town of Stung Treng. He'd seen not a soul, but the intense antipathy of many eyes made his neck hairs tingle. Muddy streets, collapsed hootches and the forgotten remnants of human-made things flashed beneath him. Looking ahead, he zigged slightly to the right to fly just outside the limits of downtown. He looked hard at every building with a flat roof, every cleared lot. He tried to ignore the remnants of lurid red and yellow signs hanging akimbo from store fronts, forcing himself to search for camouflaged things, the menacing hard angles and lines of military equipment.

He saw none.

Stung Treng moldered in the humidity and sun. Strips of corrugated roofing hung listlessly from the eaves of buildings. Objects cluttered what had been side streets. Puddles of rain sat clear and undisturbed in the main drag, right down the length of the levee. Stung Treng was dead.

Rusty held course until he'd flown over the airport. There, a half-dozen buildings were silently collapsing and surrendering to the irresistible jungle. What had been a paved runway was a maze of crazy cracks filled with grass. He briefly toyed with the idea of making a touch-and-go landing, just so he could cackle giddily as he lifted off again. But rational thought returned. He turned southeast and started a climb.

"Major, whoever told or sold you that rumor about an anti-aircraft gun at Stung Treng is as reliable as a politician a week after election." Bridgewater and Rusty were in the TOC briefing room again.

"None there, huh?"

"There isn't even a hobo village there any more. If there ever was. No, forget that. Stung Treng was once a decent little town. It had stores, maybe even hotels; and an airport. But now…well, it's just dead. Not a soul - or everything but a soul. Take your pick. It sure as hell doesn't have a 37mm anti-aircraft gun."

"You think it's abandoned? Completely?"

"Probably not. Something made the hair on my neck stand up when I flew through downtown. Like I was being watched, you know? But as hard as I looked, I didn't see any sign of enemy troops or equipment."

"I see." Bridgewater stared at the wall for a few seconds. "Any sampans or tracks from vehicles? Anything like that?"

"Nope. The puddles on the main street were clear – undisturbed. There were bits of broken furniture and stuff in the streets, just where they'd been thrown down by looters. I didn't see any boats at all in Stung Treng proper, just a few tiny dugouts a mile or so up the Srepok. Native stuff and too small for carrying military supplies."

"You might have said that about a bicycle not long ago," Bridgewater said, wagging a finger.

"True. Very true. But I just didn't get a feel for anything…threatening. Not when I looked at those hootches and boats…" Rusty shrugged. "That's all I can say: no gun, no obvious enemy masses, and no signs of anything but fungal decay."

"That's good enough for me. Okay, go get lunch and take the rest of the day off. You deserve one."

"Thanks, I appreciate that a lot." He did. And he needed to compose himself a bit, too. Rusty really had thought that he might not come back alive.

CHAPTER TWELVE

S tung Treng passed beneath him again, but this time 10,000 feet below. Still, Rusty kept a wary eye on it, just in case there really was a nasty but hidden 37mm gun there. He watched the rooftops until they'd slid behind him a comfortable way, but no red tennis balls rose toward him. He allowed his thoughts to drift to the more pleasant things that lay ahead.

Rusty was skirting the lower border of Laos, on the way to Ubon Royal Thai Air Force Base, it being his turn for the mini-vacation Major Bridgewater had somehow finagled for them. It felt almost weird to be speaking to regulation air traffic controllers again after almost two hundred covert missions where he'd spoken to no one but the Mike TOC and the semi-competent guys in the titty-pink control tower, but he managed to avoid disgracing himself.

On the ground, Rusty taxied to the transient aircraft ramp, where an airman first looked dubiously at the unmarked, plain grey O-2 but finally shrugged and placed chocks around the wheels. He stared again when Rusty emerged in a sterile flightsuit – no nametag or rank visible and a bright red Mike FAC bandanna tied at the throat. But he'd seen strange planes and aircrews before, and he made no comment.

Rusty delivered the brown leather briefcase – locked – to the 23rd TASS, and they arranged for his plane to get a minor checkout and inspection. With the official rigmarole done, Rusty was free to leave the base.

As lizard-like F-4 Phantoms roared off the runway laden with bombs, Rusty hopped into what Batman had called a samlor, a curious contraption half miniature bus and half motor scooter. The grinning Thai driver just said "Hotel?" and Rusty nodded. Still grinning at Rusty, the driver gunned the thing into a blue-cloud departure. Soon, Rusty could see his destination, a concrete building of seven stories, girdled by tiny balconies.

Above the covered entry, a sign proclaimed "Ubol Hotel" in English and at least one other strange script. Inside, the lobby was a magnificent and comfortable glen of carved mahogany, the staff spoke a smiling and competent English, and his room was comfortable if a bit Spartan by American standards. It was far beyond Ban Me Thuot standards, however, and Rusty ran his hand over the deliciously crisp ironed sheets on the bed. This was luxury he hadn't experienced since Hawaii, half a world and seemingly ages ago.

But there was little time for luxury. He changed into civvies and went right back down to the lobby. Rusty simply showed the tailor shop's business card to the doorman, and he instantly had another odd form of transport at hand – a hybrid of a wheelchair and a bike.

The Singh Tailor shop was stacked to the ceiling with thousands of bolts of material. Silks, tweeds, cottons and who knows what else tumbled in profusion towards the low tables and easy chairs that occupied the central aisle. On those tables were hundreds of men's magazines: Esquire, Playboy, Gentlemen's Quarterly and more were stacked or laid open to pages of elegant suits, fashionable shirts and haute couture of every stripe. Rusty immediately grasped the concept: language was superfluous. One merely had to point to a suit in a magazine, then to a roll of cloth. Immediately, a troop of brown-skinned, black-haired and white-toothed youngsters swarmed over him with tape measures.

Between measurement sessions, and while he perused more magazines, the man who apparently owned the place appeared. The turbaned Sikh, whose face was composed of a huge black tangle of beard, a wide curve of white teeth and two dancing, sparkling black eyes, supplied Rusty with endless glasses of cold Thai beer. Whether the beer came from Indian hospitality or merely as a means to lubricate additional purchases, the experience was a novel one. When shown the receipt showing Kit Rushing's recent purchases, the Sikh bowed deeply and wordlessly excused himself. In moments, he reappeared with a cascade of suits, shirts and pants draped across both arms. Kit must have really liked the beer, Rusty thought wryly.

If Kit's order was any indication, Mike FACs alone might be providing this man's living, or at least a daughter's dowry. As Rusty surreptitiously inspected the clothes in Kit's order, he marveled at how anyone could make a living at the paltry prices being charged. Even at that, Americans were probably paying three times what a local might pay for the same suit.

"How am I going to get this pile back to the hotel?" Rusty wondered aloud.

The smiling Sikh clapped his hands and a miniature, beardless copy of himself materialized. "My son Nahran will assist you, sahib." He spoke to the lad in a baritone singsong, and the boy nodded, took the entire stack of clothes into his arms and walked to the door. The senior Sikh handed Rusty a receipt for the clothes he'd ordered, and Rusty stood up. The youngster had already hailed yet another of the scooter hybrid baht buses. The driver tore off two postage-stamp-sized tickets, then punched them with the inch-long pinkie fingernail of his left hand. The fare was one half baht – about two cents – and Rusty happily paid the lad's fare and his own. They roared away amid throngs of other baht buses, motor scooters and bicycles, careened around a few corners and puttered to a squealing halt in front of the Ubol, where a doorman adamantly refused to allow the Sikh lad to enter the building, calling for a Thai bellman instead. Rusty thanked the boy, shook his hand and watched the lad bound off again on foot. The bellman carried the pile to Rusty's room and fastidiously hung them up. After he left with his tip, Rusty lay down on the bed just to check it out. He luxuriated in the cool crispness of the ironed pillow cover; the next thing he knew, golden-red light was streaming in through the window.

Rusty rose and wandered up to the top floor, where a nightclub blared. He ordered another of those curiously strong but smooth Singha beers and a Kobe steak. The Thai band played current US hits, singing the lyrics phonetically - and loudly: concentric ripples reverberated across the water in Rusty's glass. But the famed Kobe steak made up for it when it came. About three inches thick, it was about the diameter of a tuna can, deep pink inside shading to a deep brown crispy exterior. Whether the animal had been raised exclusively on beer as he'd been told or not, it was fork-tender and with a nut-like flavor that he'd never experienced before. Rusty devoured it.

In the morning, Rusty wandered out onto the exterior balcony and gazed across rusty iron rooftops between the hotel and the Moon River. Past that, jungle stretched to the horizon beyond. He breakfasted on a street vendor's bowl of noodle soup, joining a small crowd of head-bobbing Thais who grinned and jabbered to each other in appreciation of Rusty's skill with chopsticks.

Rusty finally found the shoe and boot store where Kit had ordered boots. Here, the sales technique was identical to that of the tailor's: magazines and pictures showed shoes and boots, and the non-Thai customer had merely to point and then select from stacks of deliciously aromatic leathers. As he sipped the apparently obligatory cold beer, a clerk traced a line around his bare right foot. Finally, he accepted his own receipt and handed over Kit Rushing's. The trade resulted in a woven straw bag with two pairs of boots inside it.

Wandering from shop to shop, Rusty bought a beautifully carved Thai Buddha like the one Batman had, and an impossibly delicate riverine scene carved completely out of cork and ensconced in a bottle. Then he spotted a delightful jade ring in a shop window and bought that for Mary Beth. He toyed with the idea of buying a heavy gold four seasons bracelet as an investment, but was running short of cash after he ordered his own Mike FAC ring.

As he wandered, he marveled at how comfortable and safe he felt at all times, as if the war were but a half remembered nightmare. He mingled unconcerned amid crowds of Thais, Sikhs and who knows how many other cultures and nationalities. In downtown Ban Me Thuot, one felt the persistent prickle of wariness, the half-held breath of constant suspicion, hostile eyes upon one's neck. But here, there was not the vaguest hint of enmity.

The next morning, Rusty hired a baht bus to haul all of Kit's clothes and boots plus Rusty's bags to the main gate. There, the Security Police phoned up a jeep, obviously accustomed to officers arriving with armloads of goods from the Ubon shops.

Rusty changed into a flightsuit at the TASS building, took repossession of the locked briefcase and was driven to the flightline. He managed to get the mountain of clothes stowed in the back of his plane, but by the time he finished, suits and shirts were festooned from the radio racks, bags of boots and carvings were belted into the third seat and plastic-wrapped airplane parts – his official cargo - were tied to the floor. The plane itself had been given a routine inspection, the oil changed in both engines and a few minor parts replaced, according to annotations in its forms. He'd arrived with empty rocket pods, but both were filled with marking rockets now. That'd make the enlisted guys happy, he thought: fourteen less they'd have to build up.

Cruising southeastwards just north of Stung Treng and almost over the triple border of Thailand, Laos and Cambodia, Rusty daydreamed, reliving his Ubon experiences when he became aware of a small but insistent buzzing sound in his earphones: zzzzzt...zzzzt...zzzzzt.

Suddenly, ice water poured into his veins. Tracking radar! Missile radar!

The O-2 had no such thing as sophisticated as radar threat warning receivers, but FACs had been told that under certain circumstances, the enemy's powerful search radars could sometimes be heard in the FM radio. Rusty's heart skipped when he realized that was what he was now hearing. Every time the beam of that powerful radar swept past, it created a tiny buzz in the radio: zzzzt…zzzzt…zzzzt. If that sound changed to a rapid zt zt zt zt zt, it meant that they'd detected him and had changed from search to targeting radar. And that in turn meant that they were about to fire a surface to air missile at him.

Frantically looking around – he had no idea where the radar might be – Rusty pushed the nose over and started a rapid descent. If he could get low enough, he'd disappear into low-level radar clutter and be invisible - and safe. If only they didn't spot him first. Diving, Rusty imagined what the pointy end of a 2,000 mile an hour missile would look like as it zeroed in on his 140 mile an hour box kite, and the very thought fairly stopped his heart. In his mind's eye he could see that telephone pole-sized thing trailing smoke, the nose of it twitching and seeking him like the head of an angry rattlesnake. And as he imagined that terrifyingly mindless thing ramming into him and exploding, that rattlesnake buzz went zzzzt…zzzt…zzt…

And then, silence.

Rusty breathed again, but kept descending another few hundred feet before he pulled back the yoke to level off at half his original altitude. He'd have descended all the way to the treetops if he had to, but here he was a comfortable thousand feet over the jungle, down where he'd flown so much that he felt comfortable there.

Comfortable, he thought to himself wryly. Over Cambodia? Where he'd be instantly shot as a spy if he were to go down? Over a luridly green jungle that he'd once had nightmares about? Where he'd laugh out loud if he were at this very moment to see muzzle flashes of the enemy shooting machine guns at him? Yes…comfortable. How things do change, he wondered to himself. Or perhaps how we change, he amended.

Landing at BMT was uneventful, except for the fact that Kit was waiting in a jeep, practically squirming with excitement to see the clothes he'd ordered. With him in the jeep was a strange face.

"Hey Rusty, meet your new roomie. Jim, Rusty Naille. This is Jim Getz. He got in yesterday and he's been briefed and had his Mike FAC wet Willie initiation already. Sanderson booked him in with you, if that's okay."

"Yeah, I guess so. Pleased to meet you, roomie," Rusty said, sticking out a hand.

Gripping it was a fellow about Kit's build, sturdy without being heavy. But unlike Kit's coal-black hair, Getz was a wavy blond with ice-blue eyes. Thoroughly Übermensch in a modern kind of way, except for his clothes. Unlike a rigidly uniformed Wehrmacht soldier, Getz wore tiger-stripe pants under a screaming blue and yellow Hawaiian shirt and his recently-awarded red neck bandanna: a disconcerting look to say the least.

"Howdy," he said, his face split into a broad, winning smile while Rusty took all this in.

"He's nuts," Kit said, deadpan. "Should make a perfect roomie for you."

"Which one of us are you talking to, Kit?" Getz asked.

"Yeah," Rusty added, immediately taking a liking to the way Getz thought, "Who do you mean is the nut? Getz or me?"

"Yes," Kit said, unable to hold the deadpan look any longer. All three of them broke into gales of laughter as they loaded Kit's haul into the jeep.

Over the next few days, Kit flew with Getz as his mentor, just as Rusty had done with Danny Craig. The routine of the Mike mission settled in again: scout a site, insert a team, fly dawn to dusk cover and extract the team when the mission was over or they had enemy contact. Rusty had thought night operations were a thankfully forgotten experiment when Bridgewater called for Flip and Rusty to fly one special mission.

"I won't even try to put any positive spin on this. Some numbskull somewhere has decided to airdrop a team over the fence at night. The same numbskull wants somebody to fly cover for them, and that would be you two," Bridgewater said, spreading his hands apologetically.

"Air drop as in parachutes? You gotta be shitting me," Flip said while Rusty just stared at Bridgewater.

"Uh huh. Ah know. It's dumber'n a shit sandwich," Bridgewater said, lapsing into his drawl. "Specially at the ass end of the monsoon. S'posed to rain tonight like a cow pissin' on a flat rock. But tonight's the night." He shrugged.

"Who are the poor bastards doing the jumping?" Rusty asked, "Or is that too secret for us peons?"

Bridgewater winked to agree, but added, "Po' bastards is raht. I wouldn't give 'em as much chance as an armadiller crossing I-35."

"Assuming they aren't killed outright by the jump, what kind of help will we be able to provide to them at night?" Flip asked.

"Beats hell outta me," Bridgewater admitted. "Read to 'em from the first aid manual, Ah guess. Like Ah said, this ain't my ideer."

"Sounds like a complete FUBAR trick to me, too, boss," Rusty said. "But what's new, huh? When and where do we do this?"

"T'naht, like Ah said. Ah'll brief y'all aftah suppah."

Flip and Rusty dutifully skipped happy hour and left the chow hall with Major Bridgewater after dinner. The skies were leaden and a few large drops of rain spattered as they walked. In the TOC, he brought out a map and a short list of radio frequencies and code phrases.

"Raht here's where the drop is s'posed to happen," Bridgewater said, pointing to a section of the map that portrayed open country laced with trails.

"That map's 30 years old. The whole area's heavily jungled now. Putting paratroopers in there at night is tantamount to murder," Rusty protested. "Does anybody in charge of this know that?"

"Like Ah said, son. This is outta our hands. But yeah, I did make that observation known."

"And the drop is still on, regardless?" Flip stared at him, incredulous.

His drawl disappeared. "Fraid so, boys. It's gonna happen. You two'll be there, either as support or as witnesses. But it'll happen."

"Can you just confirm that the poor bastards aren't Americans?" Flip asked.

Bridgewater shrugged. "Don't take this as racist, but I'm just glad they aren't GIs. Which reminds me; you'll have a robin. He's not one of our regulars, but a guy they brought in just for this mission. His name's Nguyen."

"Is that Vietnamese for Mr. Smith?" Rusty asked snidely.

"Probably. Anyway, his job's the usual: listen for the team to check in and pass whatever needs to be done to you. If the team checks in." He shrugged again. "Your job's a bit different, though."

Flip and Rusty perked up, bracing themselves for something truly awful.

"You'll be carrying a full load of ordnance. One pod of Willey Pete, two racks of parachute flares and a rack of log flares. What you're supposed to do is place two log flares down to serve as aim points for the drop. The drop plane will come in from south to north, so that's how you should place the logs. Try to get them as close to here as you can." He pointed to a spot a few miles north of Chbar, the supposedly abandoned city they called Disneyland.

"Then what? Orbit as usual?"

"Yup, Flip, that's it. Orbit to the east of that spot. I'd be well east if I were you. Hitting some poor bastard hanging in a parachute would spoil your evening."

"No shit. His too, although that might be the best thing to happen to him. Better than being impaled with a tree limb up his ass."

Rusty shivered in horror. "Jesus, Flip, don't say things like that. I'll have nightmares."

"You mean more nightmares, don't ya?"

"Whattaya mean?"

"I'll let Getz tell you. He'll know soon enough."

"Let's keep this to the business at hand," Bridgewater interrupted. "They'll drop from 1500 AGL. The drop is set for 0100 hours. Log flares burn for about 40 minutes, so you should place them ten to fifteen minutes before that. They need to be a bit apart...half a click or so. Just before the drop, the drop plane will check in with you on UHF. Here's the frequency for them and the FM push for the team. If possible, stick to these code phrases for everything transmitted in the open."

Flip and Rusty glanced at the list. The drop aircraft's call sign would be Tepee 16, and all the code phrases were names of Indian tribes or chiefs. The term for "ready to drop" was Arapaho. The word to abort the drop was Cherokee. Predictably, the word chosen to announce the drop had occurred was Geronimo.

"What's this Buffalo call sign?" Flip asked.

"That's you," Bridgewater said. "For this flight, you'll be Buffalo 22. Use that for all transmissions on the mission push. You can revert to your Mike 54 call sign on our regular frequencies. Try to not get them confused. That reminds me. Flip, you're in command for this one. No slight intended to you, Rusty, but Flip is senior FAC."

"I understand. No sweat. I don't mind flying right seat."

"Okay. That brings us to the nitty gritty. There's still no control tower support, so the runway is blacked out again. Go ahead and use your landing lights for visual cues on takeoff. Go blacked out at the fence, of course. With three of you and full tanks, you're going to be over max weight, so use every inch of runway available. When you get back, we'll do the jeep trick. Any questions?"

"Any weather reports?" Flip asked.

"Shitty would be optimistic," Bridgewater admitted. "Broken decks at 1,000 and 2,000, overcast at four, visibility a mile or less in rain to heavy rain. Winds 250 at 12 knots. Not much improvement expected all night."

"And we're still going to do this? Are you serious?"

"Serious as a heart attack, boys." Bridgewater scraped his chair back and they all stood. "Now go get some rest and I'll come roust you out at 11 or so. Takeoff at midnight."

Nguyen showed up as they pre-flighted in a driving rain. He gave a curt bow and climbed in to the plane's third seat without a word. By the time they got strapped in all three were soaked to the skin and chilled. So was Mike Cramer, who stood hunched under the right wing while the FACs completed their checklist items.

"Hey Mike, just how heavy are we tonight? Is it worse than that time I carried the four sewer pipes?"

"Uh, no sir. I put it at somewhere near 5,400, depending on how many burritos you had for supper. Those friggin pipes were worse. But I don't know how much worse, the goddamn spooks would never tell me what they actually weighed."

"Okay. But if there's a big fireball at the west end of the runway, you'll know what happened."

"Yeah, the bean burrito farts ignited," he grinned, water streaming his blond hair down his forehead.

"God, I wish he hadn't said that," Flip moaned after Rusty closed and locked the right-side window, "I haven't had a burrito in eight months. I'll be dreaming about them for a week. Unless we do pile up in the weeds, of course."

"Uh huh. I'd kill for a good burrito myself, not to mention a plate of cabrito with rice and beans and tortillas. God, I think I miss American food more than roundeyes."

"You haven't missed much, bud," Flip said, poking Rusty in the ribs. "You're porking up pretty good on fish heads and rice."

"Yeah, yeah. Just get us cranked and airborne, willya? Poor Cramer's about to drown out there."

"Starting number one." Flip opened his small storm window – appropriately named on a night like this – and yelled, "Clear one!"

"One's clear," Cramer replied, and dashed out to the fire extinguisher bottle.

The routine of engine start, radio checks and getting all four racks of ordnance armed for flight kept conversation to strictly business for the next few minutes. When they were at the end of the runway and about to roll, Rusty turned to Flip.

"Just let this mother roll, Flip. Don't even think of raising the nose until we're at flight speed or the added drag will keep us on the ground until we roll off the other end."

"Uh huh. I copy. Besides, I don't want to lose sight of the runway under the nose. Just as bad to roll off the side, I'd guess."

With that, he shoved the throttles all the way to the wall and released the brakes. As Rusty expected, even at full power the tires hardly rolled. On the rough asphalt, he could hear them: thrum…..thrum…thrum..thrum thrum thrumthrumthrum.

As their speed slowly increased, the drumming of the rain on the aluminum wings quickly drowned out the thrumming of the tires, and the drops on the windscreen changed direction from running down to streaming up.

"I can hardly see, Rusty. I'll keep my eyes outside and you call off speeds for me."

"At 55 now…60. Engines good."

Flip was staring ahead, his neck as high as he could stretch it, straining to keep the faded and worn white centerline in sight against the pure black of the runway and deeper black of the storm. That dashed line seemed the only thing in the universe worthy of his attention, and it truly was at that moment. More than rain streamed from under his helmet and down his brow.

"Sixty-five, Flip, but don't rotate." Takeoff speed was 85, but the runway was mostly all behind them now. "Too late to abort now, Flip. Pour it on!"

Flip's arm straightened as he leaned on the throttles even harder.

"Eighty! Almost there, Flip." Rusty snapped a look out the window and blanched when the end of the runway flashed past. Immediately, the plane bucked and bounced as the tires hit the much rougher overrun. "Eighty-five! Rotate, Flip!"

The nose came up just as they hit something with a huge banging jolt. The impact threw them upwards and they hung sagging in the air for a second before Rusty felt the wings grab and they gained a few feet of altitude.

"Shit, there's a tree out here somewhere," Flip shouted.

"Just hold it steady. I missed it once, and we will again. Probably have already, actually. Holding 90 knots, Flip. Engines good and positive rate of climb. Just hold it steady, bud. Leave everything hanging until we get some air under us."

"Yeah, I know. You touch that gear handle and I'll break your arm. I'm on the gauges. Back me up on them, but look outside, too, can you?"

"Can do. Climb straight ahead, we're clear of anything I can see."

By the time they got to the city, they'd climbed to five hundred feet and gotten the gear and flaps up. They checked in with the TOC, changed to the mission frequency and blacked out their exterior lights. Now in solid clouds, the ride got bumpy in turbulence.

"Yee haw," Flip said as they lurched first up and then down. He started to grin, but then wrinkled his nose. He turned around and looked over his shoulder. "Hey Nguyen, you okay back there?"

"Boo coo sick," came the miserable, plaintive reply.

"Yeah, I thought so. You have enough bags?"

"Okay"

The sour, pungent smell of vomit hit them, carried forward on the suffering man's breath. Rusty asked Flip, "You want me to take it while you reach back and check for sick sacks?"

"Yeah, good idea. Okay, you have it."

Rusty took the yoke and flew, looking across the cockpit at the flight instruments. Flip turned as far as he could and rummaged in the pocket behind Rusty's seat. He pulled out a wad of white plastic bags. "Uh, looks like five bags. That should be enough." He handed one over his shoulder and then put the others back into the seat pocket. "Nguyen, where's the first bag?"

"What mean?"

Flip scrunched around again. "Oh, crap. Nguyen, here - use this." He demonstrated opening the bag and holding it to his mouth. "Hand me that. Rusty, get the window open quick."

Rusty unlatched the window and looked back just in time to see Flip handing him a dripping wet boonie hat folded closed. The smell made him gag, but Rusty took the thing and managed to get it out the window without sloshing any of the vile contents on himself.

They left the window open for a few minutes, but they soon started shivering from the cold wind on wet clothes, and closed it again. The air inside had cleared a little, but Rusty knew that not all of Nguyen's supper had gone out the window. Some of it was in the rear cabin area.

They droned westward, staying below the clouds both for a smoother ride and to try to see something below. Both hopes were more or less futile; the storm was turbulent at all altitudes, and both sky and ground were impenetrably black. They navigated by TACAN, getting to the place where the drop was supposed to occur with about twenty minutes to spare.

"You really think they'll drop parachutists on a night like this?" Rusty asked aloud.

"No chance in hell unless they are deliberately trying to kill the whole stick of jumpers. I bet we hear them abort it any minute now."

Rusty double-checked the radio frequency against the slip of paper Major Bridgewater had given them. Both the drop plane and ground team numbers were set correctly.

"You think we ought to wait until they check in or just go ahead and drop two log flares now?" Rusty asked Flip, pointing to the clock. It was ten minutes to one.

"Oh hell, let's drop two. We'll keep the other two for backup in case they show up late," Flip said, sensibly.

Flip quickly maneuvered to the correct TACAN coordinates, descended and got lined up on a south-to-north run. "Get the rack set up, Rusty. Remember to set it for 'Fire' and not 'Drop' or we'll pickle off the rack instead of the flares."

"Uh huh, I do remember." Rusty remembered the story of an accidentally dropped flare rack miraculously hitting a VC soldier at LZ Emerald, and smiled to himself. "Inboard right, set to fire, Master Arm OFF. Ready for you to lay 'em in. You want me to time between them?"

"Nah. I'll just count off ten seconds to myself. I don't think the placement is critical." He paused for a few seconds, then, "Okay, on the DME reading, at altitude, the 255 radial coming up.....stand by." He reached over and flipped the Master Arm switch's protective cover, then raised the switch itself. "Switches hot. And...Drop!" He squeezed the trigger on his yoke.

Rusty had turned to watch the dim reflection of the cabin lights on the pylon, and caught just a momentary aluminum glint as something fell away. "One away."

"Holding heading. Holding altitude. Wish I were in my rack holding my dick instead of here, but...Drop!"

Rusty chuckled, but stared at the pylon rack. Again the momentary tumbling glint. "Two away." By the time he looked back in, Flip had slapped the Master Arm switch cover back down. "And switches safe," Rusty confirmed, resetting the pylon switch as well.

"Okay, let's climb and turn east. See if you can see the logs burning when we get around to the south again."

"I will, Flip. But I doubt I'll see anything if they hit in jungle. How the hell the team's supposed to see them is beyond me."

Flip held a standard rate turn, and they were back on a southerly heading two minutes later, climbing to get above the supposed jump plane's altitude. When Flip rolled out, they were scudding in and out of clouds, but Rusty saw two ghostly spots of diffuse red light below and to the right.

"I'll be damned, Flip. I can see both of those log flares. They're under tree cover, but there's a red glow that's visible anyway. Must be because there's no other light whatsoever. How about that?"

"Yeah, I can see them, too," Flip said, rocking the wing down a bit and craning his neck. "Fat lot of good they'll do. It's almost one."

Rusty looked at the clock: five minutes to go. The drop plane hadn't checked in.

"What do we do now, boss?" Rusty asked.

"Drone around and wait, I guess. If they don't check in, we'll just assume they aborted and forgot to tell us. That'd be typical, huh?"

"Yeah, probably aborted hours ago when they saw the weather report. We could be warm and cozy in our racks right now if they'd remembered to tell us."

"Fuck that, we could be crispy critters in our own little smoking hole," Flip snorted angrily. "It'd be just fucking typical if we'd died trying to take off to cover a mission somebody was too fucking lazy or incompetent to tell us had already been cancelled."

"Uh huh. Kinda sums up this whole damn war, doesn't it? All the decisions made by some bastard in wingtip shoes back in Washington, with no fucking clue about how his brain fart affects guys way over here. Worse, the dildo wouldn't care if he did know."

"I heard that the Thud drivers going downtown Hanoi have to fly exactly the same route, same altitudes and same time of day for every raid just because some dickhead in Washington decided it should be that way. And then they can't figure out why the poor bastards get shot down left and right – when their arrival over the triple A and SAM sites is as regular as Flight 875 into LaGuardia. Stupid bastards."

"Murderous bastards, you mean," Rusty said. "I'd rather be in a roomful of stinking antiwar hippies than with one goddamn politician. At least the stupid hippies are trying to save lives in their drug-addled way. The politicians don't care. Not one whit, they don't."

"The hippies would rather save the Commies' lives than ours, brother. We're the baby burners, while those infected with the Marxist virus are the world's saviors. At least according to those syphilitics with the flowers in their lice-ridden hair. They'd as soon exterminate anybody in a US uniform as light up a bong."

Why Flip, you've revealed a literary side. Those words were inspired."

"Oh shut up. Look, you fly while we wait for the drop plane to come up on push – if ever. Hold this altitude, fly inbound on the 255 radial for ten minutes, then racetrack right until you get back here. If they don't check in, make two circuits and wake me up." He looked over his shoulder. "Nguyen's alright. He's asleep. Don't you nod off, okay?"

"No sweat, GI," Rusty said, vividly recalling the afternoon he had nodded off and left nobody at the controls. "I got it. Two orbits will just about be when those logs burn out, too. Good time to decide what to do."

"Mpph," Flip said, already snuggled down with his chin on his chest.

Rusty straightened in his seat and settled into the monotonous and almost hypnotic routine of instrument flying, his eyes scanning the critical instruments in a constant pattern: Attitude indicator, heading. Attitude, altitude. Attitude, airspeed. Attitude, navigation display. Over and over again, his eyes moving in a "T" pattern among the four instruments, but occasionally flicking to the engine gauges or other less critical items. The soft red glow of the instruments became his whole universe. The drone of the engines and those red circles were his only sensory inputs. Only the slowly decreasing DME reading of the distance to the navigation station broke the monotony of the pattern, and when it had decreased by ten miles, Rusty started a slow turn to the right. When he'd turned to a heading of 255 degrees he rolled out. Another ten miles and another right turn would put them back exactly where they'd started. One.

Towards the end of the second circuit, Rusty began to look for the two faint pools of leaf-diffused red light put out by the log flares. Either they'd already burned out or he wasn't close to them, because only stygian blackness met his eyes. He completed the turn, and elbowed Flip. "Hey boss, that's twice around the racetrack with no winners."

Flip shook the cobwebs out of his head. "No contact at all, huh? Well, screw it. Let's call home and see what happened." He changed the UHF radio to their home frequency and when it clicked, hit his transmit button, "Mike 50, Mike 54."

A second or two passed, and Rusty envisioned Sgt Hannah or Young shaking his head awake as he scrambled to the microphone. "Mike 54, go ahead." It was Young and he did sound groggy.

"Um, better go crypto, Mike 50."

"Going"

When the scrambler whined into operation and clicked, Flip said, "Hey, what happened? Did the Indians fold their tepee and go home? We had negative contact on the other push."

"Uh, 54, understand you had negative contact? On either the air or ground push?"

"That's affirm, 50. Nada on nada."

"Uh, 54, be advised that according to our intel, the drop took place. Repeat did take place. You've had no contact?"

"Negative, 50. We put down flares, but never heard a peep from either the drop plane or the team. Negative contact on either push."

"Uh, copy that, 54. Stand by while I report to higher. Remain on crypto."

"Copy. 54 standing by on crypto."

A few minutes later, Bridgewater came up on the radio and asked again if they'd heard anything. Again, Flip said no. Bridgewater confirmed that the drop had indeed happened.

"You gotta be shitting me," Flip said when he'd gone off crypto and turned back towards the drop area. "They dropped without checking in with us? Without knowing where we were at the time? That just confirms what I said: stupid incompetent bastards."

"Now what do we do?" Rusty asked.

"You heard the major. Fly over the drop site and see if the team contacts us. Double check that FM freq, will ya?"

Rusty dug out the slip of paper and checked each digit of the frequency one by one. "It's exactly what's written here, Flip. So was the UHF. If somebody's got the frequencies screwed up, it isn't us." Rusty was already thinking along the lines of defending themselves if the shit hit the fan and there was an official inquiry.

"And we were in the right place, right?"

"Absofuckinglutely. The coordinates matched where Bridgewater pointed on the map, about five miles north of Chbar, and I double-checked the TACAN position for it myself. I can swear we were in the right place at the right time and on the frequencies we were given."

"Okay. Let's do this: we'll swing down south of Chbar and let down to minimum enroute altitude. Then we'll troll north and listen to the FM. Let's run a good twenty miles either side of the place we dropped the flares - just in case. That sound good?"

"Yeah. That should cover it. If the team's down there and they hear us fly over, maybe they'll check in. Hey Nguyen, you awake back there?" Rusty said.

"Here. Say what we do?"

"Okay. Team jump, but we no hear team. Go look one time. You listen and maybe team talk. You bic?"

"Yeah yeah. Numba one. Look one time, go home. Sick."

Flip changed the intercom switch so Nguyen couldn't hear. "Caring little fucker ain't he? Makes me glad he's not looking out for my pink ass."

"Uh huh," Rusty agreed. "He'd make a fine Democrat Senator, maybe even Secretary of Defense."

Flip laughed, "Yeah. Robert MacNguyen, whiz kid. Mostly good at whizzing on everyone under him." He changed the switch back. "Okay, we go look now."

Flip made a long turn and descended. Well south of Chbar, he leveled off and headed north, flying slowly in the pitch blackness and rain. "Keep your eyes outside, Rusty. Maybe their radios are busted. Maybe they'll pop a flare or something."

"Most likely it's their asses that are busted, but I'm looking with both hands and feet." Rusty hadn't stared into the utter blackness for long when he nudged Flip. "Looks like Disneyland isn't as abandoned as we thought, bud. Those tracers coming up ain't the midnight fireworks show."

Flip glanced down for a second but stayed on the instruments. "Firing at our sound, I'd guess. Way off. Let me unsynch the props a little and make it a bit tougher." He pushed the propeller control for the rear engine forward a fraction of an inch, and the smooth drone of the engines changed to a discordant wahwahwah wahwah wah wahwah wahwahwah wail. On the ground, the sound would seem to come from several places in the sky, hopefully not the one they were actually in.

"It must be catching, like a yawn. Now there are six or seven of 'em emptying their clips at us. All AK's, looks like. Oops, nope. Now there's a . 51-cal, too: slow fire and red tracers, all wide of us by a mile."

"Yeah, they know there's no chance of us running an airstrike at night in this shit. So they might as well take out their frustrations on us. Nothing else though? Nothing that might be the team?"

"Not unless it's the team doing the shooting. In their place, I'd be pissed enough to shoot at the morons who dropped me here, too. Couldn't blame them."

"You have a point there. Nothing on the radio, though?"

Rusty turned the volume up all the way. "Not even a whisper."

A short time later, they'd completed their twenty-mile search and climbed back up to an altitude where they could receive the TOC.

"Mike 51, 54," Flip said on crypto. "We made a long low troll past the drop area – or at least what was supposed to be the drop area. Nothing there but some sporadic small arms fire. Negative radio, negative visual. What are your instructions?"

"54, what's your fuel?"

"Uh, we've got maybe an hour more before bingo. But that would be pressing it if we have to divert. Say weather there."

"Good point, Flip. The weather's just like when you left. Estimate one thousand overcast, winds 250 at ten and visibility poor in rain. You guys did your best. Bring it home."

"Copy that, sir. We'll stay on this push now and call at the fence. Breaking crypto."

"51 off crypto, too. Call the fence."

"Nguyen, we go home now. You okay?"

"Boo coo sick. No like fly. Very bad." He tapped Rusty's shoulder and handed forward two filled sick sacks. Rusty dropped them out of the window, wondering how much the man had in him. One more bag, as it turned out. Rusty dropped it and closed the window.

The rain actually got heavier as they got closer to BMT. At the fence, Flip called in and learned that two jeeps were ready to rush out and give him some light. They'd be at the east end of the field because of the winds.

"Well, what we'll do is circle in from the south side. That way, we'll see the camp lights, and I'll be able to have some visual reference out my side in the turn. Surely there won't be any bad guys out on a night like this, right?" Flip brushed his mustache with his fingertip, a gesture that meant he was nervous, Rusty knew.

"Nah, even Charlie's smart enough to come in out of the rain. Unlike us," Rusty said. "I wonder who the poor boogers in the jeeps will be."

"Probably Cramer in one. He's the hardest worker I've ever seen."

"Yup. But then these are really his planes. We just borrow them once in a while. As long as we don't bend 'em, he's happy."

"Speaking of which, do you think the gear's okay? We had a pretty good knock just as we lifted off, you remember," Flip said.

"Well, they came up okay. So they can't be bent too much. I'd guess they're fine. Hope so anyway. That's why I'm allowing you to land...I don't want to get the blame again."

"Oh, thanks, Rusty. You're too kind." He elbowed Rusty in the ribs. "This mission is like an Agatha Christie book."

"How do you mean?"

"Well, it's hard at both ends like the covers, and it's a complete mystery in between."

"More like a horror story than a mystery, if you ask me. If what happened to that team is what I suspect, anyway."

"You too? What do you suspect?"

"Flip, I think they all died on landing. Impaled, caught and shot, drowned or something. Whatever. But all dead."

"Yeah, me too. Or else the stupid drop plane shoved them out miles from where they were supposed to be, and out of the range of our radio. Either way, we'll never find them."

"I'm afraid not. The only good part would be if Charlie never finds the radio. But they have dozens of those already, so what difference does it make?"

"I'm sure it matters to their families, and I don't mean the frigging radio."

"No, I don't either. Jesus, Flip, I hope whoever ordered this circle jerk fries in hell for it. Twice. No, seven times."

"I just hope it isn't ten times. There's still three pink asses on this mission."

"Amen, brother. Amen."

Flip simply held altitude as the ground slowly rose to meet them. They passed over Ban Me Thuot city, its scattered lights visible through the murk as a faint yellow glow.

"Mike 50, we're five miles out. Release the hounds."

"Roger, 54. Jeeps on the way. Weather is low overcast, visibility maybe a half mile in rain, winds 250 at ten gusting to fourteen. Altimeter is 2885. Call final to the jeeps."

"Copy all, 50. Who's in the jeep?"

"That'd be 57."

"Think we should tell him about the gear?" Rusty asked Flip on intercom.

"Nah. There's nothing they could do about it. The field crash truck isn't manned at night, either. Why worry them?"

"I guess you're right. Well then; home, Jeeves."

Flip double-checked the pre-landing checklist items, dropped flaps and then both of them involuntarily stared at the landing gear indicators when Rusty lowered the handle. With no fuss, all three green lights came on.

"Whew. Well, that's one good thing, anyway," Rusty said.

"Uh huh. I can see the field. You have the FM dialed?"

"Ready to go."

"Mike 57, 54 is overhead."

"We hear ya 54. Ready for ya wet and willing."

"Man, I don't need thoughts like that," Flip nervously joked as he maneuvered to make a broad final turn.

"He's not the only one who hears us, Flip. I have tracers out my side. I can even hear 'em."

"Mike 54, you're taking fire."

"Roger, 57, we see it. Keep your own head down. Stand by," Flip let go of the mic switch. "I have fire out my side too now. They're just firing straight up. I don't think they see us…yet. I'm going in blacked out. If we don't get down on the first pass, we'll go missed approach and divert."

"I agree. Don't bother with a smooth touchdown. Just set up a smooth descent and let this mother hit. I'll drop full flaps when we do and you get on the binders. Nguyen, be ready to get out of this thing quick if we have to."

"Okay."

As Flip rolled out on final, there were two streams of tracers coming up and crossing like a neon green St Louis arch. "Just aim between 'em, Flip. The runway's gotta be right in the middle."

"Now 57, NOW!" Flip transmitted, and two weak yellow beams from the jeeps' headlights came on – right in the bottom center of that deadly arch. Flip shoved in a bit of rudder to align them, and then they sunk between and past the beams into sheer blackness. They hit with a bang and a lurch, bounced into the air again and then hit again. The first shock drove Rusty's hand down as it was poised over the flap switch, and they hummed down to add drag. Flip already had the brakes on, and the locked tires squealed when they hit the second time. Completely blind, Flip just held them until the plane stopped. Somehow, they were still on the runway.

"Give me the landing lights for two seconds, just so I know which way to turn," Flip said, and Rusty fumbled the switch on, squinting his eyes tightly as he did so to avoid being light blind when he turned them off. "Got it. Lights off."

Flip gunned the engines and stomped hard on the right brake as he spun them around until they faced the jeeps again. "Run for it 57. Go!" Flip transmitted as the tracer arcs swooped down to horizontal – towards the jeeps and him. The headlights snapped off.

Flip taxied at a fast run until he'd gone a couple hundred yards. "Flip, there's the taxiway! I can see the glint of the camp lights on it. Turn!" Flip stomped on the right rudder, and they waddled onto the faintly glinting aluminum path. Ahead of them, red brake lights bloomed as the jeeps stopped at the gate. They eased through it seconds later as two wet black figures shoved the protesting gate closed behind them. From both watch towers, Rusty could hear the heavy thud of the .50-caliber machine guns and the faster bark of the thirties. Then, silence.

As their heart rates slowed, Flip handed the arming pins through his storm window. Corso safed all the remaining ordnance then ran to the first empty revetment. In the chocks, Corso pulled their door open as Cramer, Fleming and Sandy climbed out of their jeeps.

"Whew! Smells like you guys need a washout. Who lost their cookies?"

Rusty had almost forgotten Nguyen's back seat barforama. "Uh, the back seat, Andy. I'm sorry about that. I'll come back after we debrief and clean it up," Rusty said.

"Nah, no sweat, sir. I'll have it done by then. Besides, you look like you've had enough for one night. Talk about white guys! You two look like ghosts!"

Rusty looked over and wondered if his own face was as pale as Flip's. Probably. They unstrapped and climbed out on legs just a little wobbly. Nguyen crawled out looking even paler and wobblier, mumbled an embarrassed "Xin loi" then walked off into the rain, head down and without another word.

In the TOC, Bridgewater and Sanderson were waiting. So were two brimming tumblers of Scotch, neat.

"Before we start, let me say that we're not gonna be doing anything like this again. Ever," Bridgewater said, drawl-free and very earnestly. "Now tell us all about it."

CHAPTER THIRTEEN

When Rusty woke, it was mid-morning. Jim Getz, his new roomie, was gone. Rusty was delighted to note that he seemed to be a neat man. His upper bunk was made and there were no dirty clothes or towels thrown on the floor. With a sudden pang, Rusty noticed Richard's old steel helmet and flak vest hanging on the corner of the bunk again, but the guilty memory of how he had rejoiced in Richard's death had long ago dimmed. This small new pang passed quickly.

It had stopped raining but the skies were still pregnant with more, clouds scudding low overhead and a chill wind blowing. If you could call temperatures in the upper 60s chilly, that is. Certainly the Vietnamese could. Rusty opened the door and saw some of the hootch maids scurrying between rooms in the other hootch, their arms crossed under their tiny breasts for warmth and their loose black silk pajama bottoms billowing in the breeze. Baby-fat little Mai Lin waddled down the sidewalk on Rusty's side of the compound and pushed her way past him into the room.

"Are you cold, Mai Lin? Cold?" Rusty shivered and crossed his arms as sign language.

"Berry coal," she said in her usual way.

"Don't you own a coat or something?"

She wrinkled her brow, clearly in the dark about what a coat was. But how would she know what the English word 'coat' meant, Rusty corrected himself, just as he hadn't the slightest idea what the Vietnamese for coat might be. Nor did he have anything in his locker to point to as an example. He gave up. If she had one, she'd be wearing it: *ipso facto.*

Rusty left, still not comfortable with being in a room alone with such a young girl. He remembered the sensation that Airman Fleming had caused when the hootch maids first saw him and his flaming red hair. Rusty had seen them sneak into his room one at a time and stay for an hour. That boy either had the cleanest room on base or the hootch maids were learning if his head was the only place he had red hair.

In the radio room, Sgt Hannah lounged back in his chair, blowing smoke rings at the ceiling in time to 'Marrakesh Express' until he saw Rusty, then he sat up straight and crushed out his cigarette. "Uh, Yessir. Anything I can do for you?"

"My God, Hannah, don't you have a home other than this place?"

"Not really, sir. It's just Young and I as radio operators, so one or the other of us has to be here. And he's a little under the weather right now, so I pretty much am it."

"Young is sick? I didn't know that. What's he got?"

"Well, sir, it's a case of the clap, actually. The drips, to be precise. He's on penicillin and confined to quarters."

"How'd he get that? No, I mean - I know *how* he got it," seeing the sly smirk form on Hannah's face. "But where. Or maybe I shouldn't ask. It's not really my business, I was just taken by surprise."

"Oh, no problem, sir. He's spreading the story around himself. It's the Bakery again. He and some of the other guys went downtown last week and got a little tipsy. On the way home, they sorted made a wrong turn, accidental like. He got a steam and cream but didn't think to put on a rubber. He's kinda red about it now."

"More than just his face is red, I bet. Seems to me that being confined to quarters now is a little late. Locking the barn door, huh?"

Hannah grinned. "Yessir! I bic that. Anyway, what brings you in here this fine morning?"

"I'd argue the fine morning, Sergeant. It's sullen and chilly."

Young looked speculatively at the ceiling of the windowless room, "Really? Looks just the same as always to me."

Rusty laughed. "Okay, you got me. No, I didn't want anything in particular. I just dropped in to check the flight schedule and see who's doing what while I slept."

"That was a bastard last night, wasn't it, sir?" He'd been on duty then, too. When did the man sleep?

"Yeah. A complete cluster fuck. How much do you know about it?"

"Only as much as I need to, sir," he said, covering his butt perfectly. "But enough."

"I thought so. Well, as you probably heard us report, the drop plane never checked in with us at all. Hell, they may have dropped those guys on top of us for all I know. But we never heard a peep from plane or team. It was blacker than the inside of a cow out there, Hannah. If they jumped at the right place – and that's a big if – they never had a chance. If they dropped somewhere else…well, no difference. They're tiger shit by now."

"Ooh. That's an ugly image."

"It's probably a true one, though."

"Well sir, I may know about something that'll look a little better."

"What's that?"

"I'm supposed to keep it under my hat until the Major springs it, but we're getting a Doughnut Dollie visit."

"You're kidding. The Red Cross? Way out here in the middle of nowhere? I thought they stayed where it's nice and comfy, like Saigon or Vung Tau."

"Nope, they travel around bringing sweetness and light to the sad and oppressed. Well, they bring doughnuts and razors to soldiers, anyway."

"Sergeant Hannah, you astound me. There's a bit of the poet in you."

"That sweetness and light thing? Nah, I read that someplace. I guess the thought of seeing a roundeye just brought it back to me."

"Oh God, yes. Roundeyes. Women from the world; actual, real women who don't squat on their heels in black pajamas. I almost forgot they exist." Rusty's eyes unfocussed as he experienced a flash fantasy of making love to one of them.

"Oh, yeah. Real white women with smooth, shaved legs and lipstick and..." Hannah stared off dreamily, also. "Oh, sorry sir. I got carried away there."

They grinned at each other like guilty schoolboys for a second while each enjoyed his own fantasy.

"When?" Rusty finally broke the silence.

"Hm? Oh. Day after tomorrow, sir. Major Bridgewater's gonna tell us tonight. Don't tell anyone else, willya sir? I'm dead meat if it gets out, 'cause I'm the only one besides the Major who knows."

"No sweat, GI. That's just one more thing around here that's secret."

Rusty was walking back across the street when a voice hailed. "Hey, Lieutenant! There you are. I been looking for you."

Rusty turned to see Mule, the door gunner who'd helped capture the two VC bicycle guys. "Oh yeah, I remember you. Why do you need me?"

"You remember when you said you'd like to go on a hop with us, sir?"

Rusty nodded.

"Well, I'm back here on rotation, and we have a scouting mission this afternoon. You wanna go?"

"As it happens, I just checked the board and I'm not scheduled to fly today. If it's okay with my boss, I'd love to."

"Shit hot. I'll see ya after lunch." He trotted back to the Green Hornet hootches, which were on the back side of the Mike pilots' building.

Rusty knocked on Dave Sanderson' door. "Hey, sir. I've just been invited to ride along with the Green Hornets on a scouting mission this afternoon. I'm not scheduled to fly a mission. Any objections if I go?"

He thought for a second. "No, not really. I'll talk it over with the major, but I don't think he'd object. It's a good idea, actually. You might learn a little bit about how they operate. This is approved on their side, I presume?"

"Uh, I can't say for sure. It was their door gunner who invited me. I didn't think to ask if his bosses approve."

"Well, I'll check with them. But I'll encourage them to approve. When is this flight?"

"After lunch is all I know."

"Okay. No sweat. I'll get back with you, Rusty."

"Thanks, Dave!"

At lunch, Rusty sat with Flip and Sandy. Craig and Buchenhardt had flown the dawn patrol, and were sitting together at the next table. Sanderson came in and sat down next to Rusty. "Well, Rusty, your ride is on. The Hornets look forward to scaring the shit out of a Duck driver," his teeth flashed beneath his black mustache.

"What ride is this?" Flip asked.

Dave waved at Craig and Buchenhardt to join them. "Rusty's been invited to ride along with the Green Hornets this afternoon: a scouting mission on this side of the fence. Kind of an orientation ride to give him a better feel of their techniques and such. There's room for two, actually. Anybody else want to go?"

Sandy said, "I'm out. This is still my shitter day, and I wouldn't want to embarrass myself."

"Fair enough," Dave said. "Let's see, Flip, you're too short to apply anything you might learn. Jack?"

Buchenhardt just shook his head, disdain showing on his face.

"Well, that leaves you, Dan. You up for a little mixmaster action?"

Danny beamed, "Hell yeah! I've never been in a helicopter. Do we get to fly?"

"At the controls? No, sorry. This is a ride in back, observing kind of deal. But you might get to fire the door gun, they tell me."

Danny first deflated and then brightened again at the last half of Dave's words. "Oh, cool! Are we flying in a gunship or a slick?"

"Gun. With miniguns in both doors."

"Outstanding!"

"Okay, it's settled then. You two report to the flightline at 1330. Wear flight suits and your flak vest. Survival vest and helmet, too. Oh, and bring your CAR-15 and three or four spare clips, they say. Just in case."

"How'd you swing this?" Danny asked as they walked back from the mess hall.

"I'm not sure I did. You remember when the Green Hornets captured those two rice-hauling VC bikes I spotted?"

"Uh huh."

"Well, after they landed, the wacko-looking door gunner – the one they call Mule – asked me if I'd like a ride sometime. That same crew just rotated back here yesterday, and Mule buttonholed me. He invited me up for a ride today. I checked with Sanderson, and the thing snowballed. You heard the rest just now."

"I'll be jiggered. You have any idea what this ride is supposed to be?"

"Nope, just that it was a previously-scheduled scouting mission and somehow we're going along. I guess we'll be the first to know."

The two changed into flight suits and picked up their carbines and flak vests. Rusty stuck four full ammo magazines into his leg pockets, making sure the rifle itself was empty. They grabbed their survival vests and helmets from the equipment Conex, then walked across the ramp to where two of the powerful twin-engine Hueys were being pre-flighted.

As they walked up, Rusty immediately saw the guy called Mule. He was dressed in fatigue pants and a ragged OD tee shirt. He had a black silk scarf tied tightly over his head like a Negro brother but the most unnerving thing about his outfit was a bandolier of 40mm grenades across his chest and that wicked sawed-off M-79 grenade launcher clipped to his belt. He looked for all the world like a B-movie pirate.

When he jumped to the ground, Rusty was startled to see that he stood only about five feet five, but he was powerfully muscled and had bottomless black eyes. As Rusty got closer, he also noticed Mule was wearing five or six brass bracelets from Montagnard nam pei parties. The word "pirate" flashed into Rusty's mind again.

The aircraft commander looked up and saw them approaching, and waved them over to his cockpit window. His nametag said Rooney. "Hi, I'm Brett Rooney. You must be our riders. One of you goes with me and the other with Bob Bridger over there. You been briefed?"

They introduced themselves, then Rusty said "No, we haven't. Our boss just said to show up. I'll ride with you, I guess. It was Mule who started all this by inviting me."

"Oh! Are you the guy who captured the two bicycles? Mule still talks about that! I hope you bring us luck today." He looked from Rusty to Danny, "We'll be flying a typical high/low scout mission. No slicks, just these two gunships. We'll swap positions halfway through the mission. Get yourselves strapped in, and keep your own guns unloaded until one of the gunners tells you otherwise. If we have to ditch or anything, do exactly what the gunners say. Any questions?"

They shook their heads.

"Okay, climb in and hang on!" Rooney grinned.

Rusty turned to Danny, "See you later, bud. I think we're in for something interesting. Have fun!" Craig trotted off to the other chopper.

Mule yelled, "Yeeha! Come on, Lieutenant! I'll get you strapped in on my side. Put this harness on under your flak vest."

Rusty eyed it dubiously. It was a harness just like the Vietnamese used to interrogate prisoners by shoving them out of the helicopter on a wire. Rusty got into it and his other gear, and then climbed up into the wide side door of the copter. Mule sat him down and clipped him to a cable – just as Rusty had feared. When the intercom came on he said, "There ya go. Now you can move around once we get airborne with no worries about falling out." Mule clipped himself to a similar cable, and in the other door, the other gunner did the same, which allayed most of Rusty's fears.

Brett came up on intercom and said, "Ok, crew. Our rider is Lt Rusty Naille. If you lose him, it'll come out of your pay. That means you, Mule. Rusty, they call this crew Rooney and the looney. Again, that means Mule." Mule whooped and slapped his thigh. "I've already told Rusty to obey you gunners and hang on. Let's get this thing cranked."

Rusty heard him check in with the other helo on radio, and then begin his starting checklist. With a rapidly growing whine and a dull whump, each engine spooled up and ignited. The whole craft rocked and shook as the main rotor began to turn, but the rocking rapidly became an all-pervasive heavy vibration as rotor speed increased. When Rusty touched his helmet to the metal bulkhead behind him, he felt it as a deep hum in his back teeth. Rusty wondered how much more vibration there must be in a Kingbee with its massive piston engine. Those things must be like rock crushers inside.

Before long, the copter lifted slightly and slid sideways out of its revetment, the two gunners leaning out and verifying clearance all around them as it did. Rusty heard the other helo get takeoff clearance, and saw him lift vertically, then dip his nose to move out. Rooney followed instantly. As their forward speed increased, the noise and vibration seemed to abate a bit, but it was still very loud and the metal seat thrummed against Rusty's tailbone. They took up a position behind and slightly above the other helo, about 45 degrees off to one side. Formation flying, Rusty realized.

Brett came on the intercom again. "We'll be high bird first. You know what that is, Rusty?"

Rusty fingered his transmit button, "Yup, like an Army pink team except their low bird is usually unarmed."

"Very good. Well, the way we do it, the low bird pokes around and finds what it can. If things get hot, they use their door guns and we cover with our rockets. We swap roles when fuel gets to half or the high bird gets low on rockets."

"Sounds good to me," Rusty said.

As they flew to wherever it was they were going to do the actual scouting – northwest of BMT, Rusty could see – he watched Mule prepare his beloved mini-gun. These General Electric wonders were the 20th century version of the cavalry's old Gatling gun. Equipped with six barrels and powered by a powerful electric motor, they could churn out more than 6,000 shots per minute. Mule moved the gun through its full length of travel, first fore and aft and then up and down. Rusty noted that it could be pointed almost straight down, but would go no higher than level. He made hand motions to Mule to question that, and Mule laughed and twirled his finger over his head. Of course! It wouldn't do to hit the rotors with all those bullets. They both laughed as Rusty slapped his forehead with a palm.

Then he saw Mule reach for his intercom switch. "Starboard gun requests firing test."

Rooney answered, "Stand by. Port, you ready, too?"

"Affirmative, port's ready," said the other door gunner, whose name Rusty still hadn't seen or heard.

"Hornet 21, 22."

"Go ahead, 22."

"We'd like a gun check, both sides."

"Uh, roger, one sec." There was a short pause. "Hornet 22, we're over a friendly plantation. Negative on the gun check. Stay cold for now."

"Copy cold for now." There was a click. "Hang loose for now, guys. Do not fire until we're cleared by lead."

Rusty saw Mule mouth an expletive, but he did flip the gun's arming switch back to safe.

A few minutes later, Rusty looked down. The geometrically ordered rows of the rubber trees had passed behind them, to be replaced by thick jungle. He was just starting to wonder where they were headed, when the intercom hissed again, "Hornet 22, this is 21. We're entering the search box. Free fire approved on any target. Check your guns and we'll initiate the mission."

"Hornet 22 copies. Gun check in five seconds." Another click as Rooney switched from transmit to intercom. "Okay Mule and Homer, one burst approved to check guns. Try to miss the other bird this time."

Mule cackled, but unheard over the roar of the rotors and windblast. He already had the safety off, and he pointed the wicked-looking gun aft and down. There was an immediate ripping roar and a yard-wide ball of white-hot flame from the muzzle. Rusty jumped in his seat, startled by the violence of it, then jumped again as another half-second blast came from the left-side gun. He hadn't even had time to wonder at the name he'd heard. Homer?

"Starboard gun okay." "Port gun okay, too." The gunners reported.

Rooney transmitted again, "Hornet 22 guns good and safed. Rockets safe and ready. Ready to go high."

"Copy 22. Hornet 21 is guns hot and rockets cold. Going low now."

Rooney immediately banked left and started to climb, and Rusty saw the other helo drop down and to the right. When there was about a half-mile between them, Rooney banked back around and said, "22 is in."

"21's working."

Rooney now said, "Okay, crew. Intercom is hot. Keep your eyes peeled and call out anything urgent, otherwise silence. You too, Rusty."

"Port." "Starboard." "Rusty."

As the lower bird banked and wheeled just over the treetops, searching for any sign of the enemy, the higher one flew huge S-turns at about 1,000 feet, never losing sight of the other bird. It was mesmerizing and Rusty found himself leaning right out the side door following the other helicopter's moves intently, his helmet visor locked down against the windblast. He looked back and saw Mule leaning out even farther.

Suddenly, the radio crackled, and a voice just slightly high-pitched and faster than before said, "Taking fire starboard." Rusty saw the right side of the low bird erupt in white flame – their mini-gun. "One hundred, now my five.

One gun. Stay cold." The low bird didn't want Rooney to fire any rockets — not worth it for one gook rapidly falling behind him off to their right.

"22 copies cold. Crew?"

"Negative," Mule said. He hadn't seen anything. Neither had Rusty, so he stayed silent.

Rooney turned right and Rusty lost sight of the low bird just as he heard "Fire now left. Multiple flashes!" Their mini-gun roared in the background of the radio call.

Rooney replied, "Tally! Break right! Two's in hot!" The nose slewed left and plunged, then steadied at a steep downward angle. From beneath Rusty's feet erupted loud whooshing roars as rockets fired and fired again. Rusty slumped in his seat under the "G" forces as Rooney pulled up hard. Then, "Two's off left."

As they turned and climbed, Rusty saw Homer pivot his gun down and aft. "Multiple flashes eight o clock, Port engaging." His muzzles blazed in a long burst. "Port's cold."

They reversed the turn, and Rusty saw Mule's stare intensify like a falcon's.

"Lead, two is in position. Hold your turn."

"Copy."

Rusty saw the low bird again, circling back to where they'd taken fire, where a slim column of gray smoke now rose from the jungle. "Lead has a vehicle in sight. Stand by...Bingo!"

"Tally the bingo, lead. Two's in hot. Break left."

Rooney plunged again and fired four more rockets. He pulled up and turned hard right. Mule pivoted his gun but didn't fire. "Shack, boss! Shit hot!" Mule reported: Rooney had hit whatever it was.

They swooped hard left as Rooney again transmitted, "Two's up." He was back in position above and behind the low bird, ready for more action. But nothing more happened. Lead continued his snake-like S-turns and Rooney mirrored them.

Soon, Rusty heard Rooney transmit, "Halftime, lead."

"Lead's coming up." The other bird replied, and Rusty saw them start a climbing turn.

As they climbed, Rooney said to his crew, "Great job, guys. Super! Okay, we're getting ready to switch and be low bird. Rusty, you belt in good, wouldn't want to lose you."

The other bird climbed to altitude and Rooney again took up station as wingman. Then, in response to hand signals from Rooney, they drifted back and Rooney became lead. Just like fighter pilots, Rooney mused.

As Rooney and the other copter exchanged fuel states and other information, Mule tapped Rusty's shoulder. He motioned to the carbine and mimed inserting a magazine. Rusty nodded, unstrapped the gun from where he'd stowed it and slapped a magazine into place, charged the chamber and double-checked the safety on. Mule nodded approvingly. Then he leaned in close and yelled, "If you get a chance to shoot, turn it on its side." He laid his right hand over, palm up. "Keeps the hot empties outta my face. And never shoot above here." He waved his palm level with Rusty's eyes, then pointed to where the rotors whirled invisibly.

Rusty nodded back and gave him a thumbs up.

Rooney soon dove down to the treetops, and when he began that snake track search, Rusty's stomach leapt into his throat. When they turned right, the treetops whizzed past his eyes only feet away, and when they turned left, Rusty could see almost nothing but sky. Back and forth, back and forth they wove. If it hadn't been so exhilarating and frightening, Rusty might've gotten ill. Before long, Rusty learned to crane his head back or down so he could look about halfway to the horizon. That helped with the disorienting motion and helped him see better, too.

They were turning hard right, with Rusty staring down between the trees whooshing by when he heard. "Fire from port, engaging!" Homer's gun let out a long blast. They held the hard turn and Rooney said, "Lead's breaking right!"

"Tally and Two's in hot!" came over the radio. Rusty heard and saw nothing until, "Two's off left!" But as Rooney continued his turn, Rusty saw gray smoke pluming up. Rooney roared toward it, and Mule whooped aloud, "Fuckin' A! My turn!"

Rusty snapped his rifle's safety to Full Auto and, remembering, turned it onto its right side. They zoomed past the smoke and Rusty glimpsed running men and muzzle flashes just as Mule's mini-gun roared. Reflexively, Rusty pulled his own trigger and the little carbine spit its tiny bullets out. Every fifth cartridge was a tracer, and Rusty aimed by simply playing the stream of red dashes like a garden hose. Suddenly, the dashes stopped and he looked down. The bolt had locked open on an empty magazine. Rusty ejected it and was fishing around in his leg pocket for another when Rooney whipped them hard over again. Rusty looked up just in time to see Mule shove that ridiculous but terrifying pistol out through the door. It bucked silently in his hand, its muzzle blast lost in the maelstrom of noise. Rusty didn't see the grenade hit, but Mule let out another crazed hoot and pumped his fist in the air.

"Yes! Busted the motherfucker!" he yelled to Rusty, off the intercom, "Hey, you did good. Get up here. You shoot Baby on the next run!"

Excited, Rusty safed and stowed the rifle. He struggled against the heavy G forces of yet another wrenching turn, but managed to unbelt and wriggle to a spot behind the wicked mini-gun. Mule yelled in his ear again. "Hold these two handles. There are two triggers for slow and fast, but only use the right one," he tapped it with a finger. "Keep your bursts to no more than two seconds. If anything breaks, tap my arm."

Rusty braced, grabbed the handles and looked forward just as they began another run. Mule snapped a fresh grenade into his pistol and flashed a maniacal, murderous grin.

The still-smoking clearing created by the high bird's rocket blasts flashed beneath them. Rusty was startled to be looking straight at a green-clad soldier from only 20 feet away. His black eye was plainly visible right over a set of rifle sights, and just as Rusty braced himself for the bullet that would hit him between the eyes, he heard a strange little "poop" sound, and then everything disappeared in an explosion of white light...

...the ground flowed past in glacial slowness and there was a sudden, inexplicable and eerie silence. Rusty could see individual flashes of light in front of his face. Between flashes, the enemy soldier jerked and exploded into a red spray. His whole body seemed to disintegrate as Rusty watched, spellbound. Rusty could see pieces of the soldier's rifle spin off in slow, elegant cartwheels...

...Like a thunderclap, all his senses came back. Noise, wind and G forces struck him like a giant fist. Rusty made a convulsive jerk as the edge of the jungle clearing rushed past, the bright dark green of trees whizzing by only feet away and then lurching downwards as blue sky and patchy gray clouds whirled.

Mule shook his elbow and screeched unintelligibly. He pried Rusty's left hand from the mini-gun's handle, and Rusty suddenly let go of the right one as if it were red hot. Mule pushed him toward his seat, where Rusty collapsed just in time, his legs shaking violently and the muscles giving way as if they'd been cut. Blurry blackness swirled into his vision from all sides.

Dimly, as if from a hundred miles away, Rusty heard voices, nonsensical at first and then resolving themselves like a figure emerging from a fog...

"...clear and safe. Negative damage. Lead's off left...Crew? Report!"

"Port is clear and safe. Gun cold."

"We whumped 'em over here, sir. Slammed their yellow asses!" Mule's voice brayed and broke, and then in a more soldierly tone, reported "Starboard is cold again."

"How's Rusty?" It was Rooney's voice.

Rusty was numb for a heartbeat, but then he panicked.

Rusty began sliding his hands under his flak vest, dreading yet unable to avoid probing for the hot sticky blood pouring from his guts.

"Christ, he's the one who whumped 'em! Cut that little fucker in two with Baby. Just pounded him into a steel pyramid. Sheeeyit hot!"

Rusty looked up. As he tended to his Baby, his face smeared with sweat and black streaks of gun smoke, Mule grinned down at Rusty. He made no motion towards the first aid kit mounted to the bulkhead behind him. Rusty looked down at himself and saw...no blood. With a start, Rusty felt his flight suit again. It was wet and cold, not hot and sticky. Sweat. He wasn't hit.

The rotors stopped with a squall as Rooney engaged their brake. The silence of the ramp was almost deafening, as Rusty's ears rang. He unstrapped slowly and edged his butt off the seat, testing his legs. They still felt rubbery, but he could stand. Danny trotted over from his helo.

"Wow, that was cool! I had no idea they flew missions like that – or that way. Did you believe how low they got? Man, I thought sure the rotors would hit the trees sometimes! And those mini-guns! Man, are those things nasty. And loud, ha ha! I got to shoot one, did you?" His words tumbled out in a blue streak.

Mule answered for Rusty. "He damn sure did. Christ, he's one bad-assed mother. Good shot, too. Cut one of the bastards in half. That gook was almost IN the muzzle when Rusty burned him. I'm surprised we don't have guts sprayed all over the side of our bird. Yeowee!"

Rusty's knees almost buckled again as the image flashed through his mind.

"You're kidding me! He did? Holy smoke! We creamed a car out there, but nothing like that. You know what it was? You'll never guess."

Rusty shook his head, stunned by the excited rush of Danny's words. Craig's eyes bulged slightly and his skin was flushed; he was standing still, but skipping from foot to foot and flashing his hands around at random.

"It was a goddamned Citroen. One of those long, tapered things that look like a French turd. It was purple, so help me. Was. It's black as bear crap right now. We hit it with the mini, and then you guys blasted it with a rocket. The roof flew a hundred yards. Man!" Craig finally wound down.

Then he seemed to see Rusty for the first time. "Hey. You alright? You look funny."

"It's just the adrenaline. I'll be fine." Rusty started to walk to the equipment Conex, but Mule tapped him on the shoulder.

"You might need this, killer!" he said, still with a trace of that maniacal grin showing through the grime. He handed Rusty the forgotten carbine. "Uh...sir."

On the short walk back to the hootch, Danny suddenly said, "Whew! Now I feel it, too. Man, my knees are wobbly and I feel like I might barf. Wow." He'd gone pale and looked like Rusty felt. "I think I better lay down."

"Yeah," was all Rusty could manage.

Rusty dropped his flak vest on the floor and leaned the carbine in the corner, then flopped into his bunk. His head swam in the aftermath of violent motion, extreme noise and vibration – and the precipice-edge of near death. Rusty felt his ribs again, still half-expecting to find spurting blood. The image of that NVA soldier's black eyes whirled in and out of his mind, and he relived the weird slow-motion play of it as it happened.

As if from a camera, he watched himself from above. Rusty could see the trees as they crept past, the individual rotor blades sweeping slowly through the edges of his vision in a stately whirl. As he watched, a figure uncoiled up from behind a bush, mouth open in a silent yell, an automatic rifle coming up to his shoulder until the sights settle just below his coal-black eye. His equally black hair is unkempt, and in slow motion it waves in the air like undersea grass.

Rusty sees his own shoulders hunch as he tenses, and his right thumb clenches down. The barrels of the mini-gun turn, not in a blur, but with the smooth rotation of a carriage wheel. A tongue of white flame puffs out of the lowest barrel, and as the next barrel reaches that point, it also belches a spurt of fire. Then the next and the next and the next... The ball of flame builds upon itself with each shot until it is a yard wide by the time the first barrel makes its way around to the firing position again.

Rusty looks to the soldier again, and he seems frozen, until his shirt puffs once, then again and again in perfect time with the spurts of flame from the mini-gun. The puffs of fabric turn to widening holes and the holes march across his chest, then down towards his belly. They hesitate there a moment and finally turn and march upwards again through a thickening red fog-like spray. Pieces of his rifle suddenly start to flake off amid sparks, and then the holes reach the man's face. His hair flies again, but this time as a fountain of black feathery wisps now unconnected to his head. As the holes drift down again like a string of round footprints, the enemy's whole body slowly crumples and bends as if it were hinged in the middle, but sideways; and his shoulders and chest tumble languidly free of his midsection.

Rusty jolted upright in his bunk, skinning his head on the springs of the upper bunk. He heard himself yelp, and then realized it was the second syllable of a much longer, louder and hoarser sound.

Rusty sat stock still but with heart and lungs racing, sweat pouring from icy armpits and groin. He expected to hear footsteps racing to the sound of that hoarse yell, but nobody came. Gradually, his panting subsided and his heartbeat slowed. Rusty found that he could stand. He took down a towel and walked to the showers still dressed. There, he stood under the hot water until the stink of fear and sweat was gone, and then he stripped off his clothes and soaped down.

As he walked back, Flip stuck his head out of the big room. "Hey Rusty, I know the laundry service sucks, but I didn't think it was bad enough for you to do your own."

"Not now, Flip. Please."

"Oh. Bad dream?"

"Uh huh."

"Those midday naps'll get ya, bud. Why don't you get yourself a stiff drink before supper?"

"I think it'll be booze for supper tonight, Flip."

"Ooch. Don't miss the pilots' meeting at seven, though. Right here in the glamorous Waldorf Astoria ballroom."

"Uh huh."

Rusty blew his two-drinks per night rule and did miss supper altogether, but he managed to stagger into the big room for the meeting. Bridgewater looked at him sternly when he banged into the doorframe and belched wetly. He announced the Doughnut Dollie visit and everybody except Rusty cheered and laughed. When Kit whistled on two fingers, the shrill blast just about decapitated Rusty with pain. He staggered outside and vomited, collapsing to hands and knees in the muddy courtyard. Somehow, Rusty got to bed and passed out.

In the morning, he awoke to see Dave Sanderson framed in his doorway. "Good thing today's your shitter day. Looks like you're gonna be in there all day anyway. Come talk to me when you feel better."

He left just as Rusty felt his guts go all liquid and squirmy. Rusty ran to the shitter, doubled over with cramps, nausea and a splitting skull.

Much later, after lots of coffee and some cold cereal he managed to cadge from the chow hall between official breakfast and lunch hours, Rusty knocked on Dave's door. He motioned Rusty in to a chair. "You okay? You don't usually drink like that."

Rusty shrugged. "Yeah, I'm fine now. Still a bit wobbly, but I'll live."

"What set it off?"

"That helo ride yesterday. Dave, I never killed somebody before then. I mean, not face-to-face. I guess I've killed hundreds in air strikes and maybe even with my own rockets, but that's somehow...I don't know...remote? Disconnected? This time, I actually was looking at this guy's face. He was only a few feet away, and I blew him apart. And then I dreamed about it all again, but in weird slow motion. And I could see myself doing it, but kind of from above and behind myself, you know?"

"God's eye view."

"Huh?"

"From God's viewpoint."

"Uh, yeah, I guess so. Yeah. That's weird."

"No it isn't. You were judging yourself. Like God would. How'd you come out?"

Rusty stared. "I don't know. That's a new one on me."

"Maybe it is, but you do know. You've already tried and judged yourself, if you just think about it. You feel any guilt?"

"Um...no. You know what, I don't. It was horrible, and I don't think I'll ever forget the images, but no. I don't feel any guilt at all."

"There ya go. Not guilty."

"By reason of insanity?" Rusty half laughed.

"Doesn't matter. By insanity, or by self-defense or even by accident. But not guilty nonetheless." He looked deeply into Rusty's eyes, "Good thing, too. Guilt can eat you alive from the inside, and self-assigned guilt is the strongest poison there is. Before long you'd be second-guessing yourself, trying to assuage that guilt. Maybe even sacrificing yourself to achieve what you see as balance."

"You mean suicide? No way."

"It does happen. They call it survivor's syndrome. You ever hear of something where a guy is the sole survivor of an accident where all his friends are killed? Or he gets replaced on a crew at the last minute and they never come back?"

"Yeah, I saw that in a movie once."

"Ever had it happen in real life?"

"To me? No. But now that I think about it, there was a guy in college who was supposed to go on a fishing trip but begged off at the last minute. The boat sank. The other three guys drowned. He was a wreck after that."

"Bingo. What happened to him?"

"I don't know for sure, he just went downhill. Dropped out of college the next year. Maybe he got drafted, but he was an acid head by then."

Sanderson looked at him, eyebrows raised expectantly.

"Oh. I see. Survivor syndrome, huh?

"That's it," he said, then leaned back and relaxed. "Do me a favor?"

"Sure, what is it?"

"It's two favors, actually. First, I don't want you to dwell on this thing, but if it keeps popping back up on you, come see me again. Promise me."

"Um, yeah, I can do that. I promise. And...?"

"No more drinking your supper. You're a lousy drunk."

To make sure, Dave gave Rusty the dawn patrol the next day. Rusty abstained from any booze at all that night, sipping Seven-Up in the big room while Kit played the guitar and Jack told them all for the umpteenth time how glorious it was to be a Citadel grad. To keep his mind off Jack's egomania, Flip puttered around, putting paperbacks in order on their shelves and humming along with Kit's music. Rusty happened to be watching him when Flip picked up his own CAR-15 and went to hang it on a nail. Somehow, he managed to let it slip through his fingers, and it dropped butt first onto the concrete floor.

BABABAM three shots blasted out, and in the closed room, the blast was louder than the world's end. Blue smoke eddied, and everyone froze for a split second: Jack in mid-word, Kit's fingers on his guitar strings, and Flip standing there, arm extended and with an astonished look on his face. Sandy Hubert sat staring, mouth agape, as did Jim Getz, sitting next to Kit. Then all hell broke loose.

Half of them flinched and threw their arms up protectively, the other half dove for the floor.

"Jesus Christ, what happened?" Jack bellowed. Flip stared at his hand.

From next door, Danny Craig ran in, followed a second later by Dave Sanderson.

"What happened?" Sanderson said, almost as Jack's echo. "Is anybody hit?"

They all snapped their eyes to Flip, who stood rooted, still staring at his hand. Rusty's stomach sank.

"Uh, no. I don't think so," Flip finally said. He looked stupidly at both sides of his hand, then blanched when he looked at his locker. Three ragged holes dug long, trough-like gouges in the sheet steel, their shiny edges gleaming like knives. Three more holes had appeared in the ceiling above the locker, and tan wood dust swirled with blue smoke in the air.

By now, the sounds of many other feet approached, and soon the door was filled with faces of our own enlisted guys and unknown ones from the Green Hornets.

Sanderson walked over and gingerly picked up the carbine. He turned it in his hand. "Safety is set on Full Auto. Flip? How long has it been like this?"

Flip blanched doubly pale. "Oh shit! I haven't touched it since we went target shooting a couple of weeks ago."

"Hmm. I'm having second thoughts about the wisdom of allowing you guys to keep your weapons in your rooms. I'm not at all sure I shouldn't confiscate them all right this minute and lock 'em up."

"But we all have assigned positions on the perimeter if we get attacked. How would we do that with our guns locked up?" Craig practically squeaked.

"Hmmm," Dave repeated. "Well, that is a point. All right. But I'm going to make an inspection right this minute, and if I find any other weapons in an unsafe condition, that'll settle it and I'll confiscate them all. Everybody out in the courtyard. Now!"

As they filed out, Rusty had a horrible thought. He remembered leaning his own carbine in the corner formed by the locker and wall after the helo flight. But had he remembered to unload it? Had he even remembered to put it on safe after he'd fired it in the helo? He recalled snapping in a fresh magazine, but…Oh crap, was it ready to fire, too? Jesus, to screw that up…and being a lifelong shooter, besides.

Dave went to every room and asked where the guns were. Most were unloaded. Kit's had a full magazine in it, but the chamber empty. Buchenhardt's had a magazine inserted and a live round in the chamber, but the safety on. "An unloaded gun is just a poor club," he said, trying to be both superior and flippant. Dave glared at him until Jack's innocent simper sagged. Dave emptied the chamber before he set the gun down again.

Dave went to Rusty's room. Rusty could only watch, knees shaking. Getz's carbine was completely empty, but Rusty's clearly had a magazine inserted. Rusty braced himself for the awful castigation he was sure was on the way. "Chamber empty, safety on. Good," Dave said.

Rusty let out a long-held breath, and Dave looked at him suspiciously. Good old Mule, Rusty thought to himself. Oh, good and efficient Mule. A looney he is for sure, and a pothead, too, maybe; but he's damn good with guns. Rusty thought pleasantly of Mule as Dave left, and suddenly, Rusty knew what that odd little "poop" sound that he'd heard on the chopper actually was: Mule's wicked pirate pistol slash grenade launcher being fired right next to Rusty. No wonder they called M-79s bloopers! And he suddenly also knew who had really killed that soldier.

He slept very well.

The dawn patrol was another four hours spent boring holes in the sky, and Rusty's robin slept the whole time. Buchenhardt relieved him, and Rusty chuckled to himself knowing that Jack would probably miss the Doughnut Dollie visit. Couldn't happen to a better guy, Rusty thought to himself. Could Bridgewater, that sly devil, have arranged that little bit of crew scheduling for rocket-wasting Buchenhardt? Rusty grinned to himself.

After Rusty landed, he showered and shaved, primping unabashedly. He wasn't the only one. Kit was busy waxing his mustache at the next mirror and when Flip walked in to take a leak, he was wearing his best flight suit. All of them had their red bandannas on. It was almost comical.

Finally, they got word that the Red Cross had arrived and were in the mess hall. They all pretended to be unconcerned, but everybody in earshot walked there at the fastest pace they could manage without actually breaking into a run. The effect was like a rumor of free meat in Gdansk.

In the center of the chow hall were two genuine American roundeyed women and a tall, tough man. The women were dressed in modest Red Cross uniforms: dark blue slacks and a pastel blue jumper/apron over a clean white blouse – opaque and buttoned all the way to the throat. And they were two of the plainest, commonest, just-this-side-of-homely women that could possibly have been recruited for the job.

It didn't matter. They were already surrounded by a phalanx of simpering idiots, men so desperate for the sight of a roundeye that they practically slobbered. One of the women handed Mike Cramer a doughnut, and Rusty could have sworn he saw Cramer's eyes glisten when she spoke to him.

Every single man on the place tried his level best to impress one or the other of the two women, even the normally ironbound SF guys. But it was the smiling, deeply tanned and Latin face of Miguel "Mike" Lopez who proved to be their favorite. Both women foisted cookies, doughnuts and razors on him, enough so that the women's burly and square-jawed escort – and obvious chaperone – stared hard at Lopez. He got the message and backed out of the ring of would-be flirts, both hands filled with goodies.

As Rusty watched, he had the strangest mental image of his own mother, a Special Services sergeant back in World War II, handing out doughnuts and coffee to another man with wavy black hair; a truck driving corporal who would someday be Rusty's Dad. It was unnerving, but he beamed at the two women with a genuine warm spot in his heart.

When the visit finally ended an hour later, the three climbed into a jeep and were driven back to the civilian airfield terminal where their dedicated C-7 Caribou transport waited. They left behind a stash of cookies, some razors and small toiletries – and an ephemeral waft of perfume.

"Christ, Lopez, what have you got that I don't?" Airman Fleming whined as they walked back toward the hootch. "How come they came on to you and nobody else could even get a handshake?"

"Yeah. Explain that," Cramer said. "Lt Rushing and Captain Sanderson are just as dark, and maybe even more handsome besides being officers. Lt Hubert, Getz and Fillipini are all blond and good looking, Fleming's a boyish, freckled redhead and, well heck, all of us are just plain woman-slayers." All of them guffawed before he could finish, but he eventually went on, "And yet those two roundeyes glom onto you like…well, like stink on shit is hardly what I mean, but…"

"Like kittens on catnip?" Craig injected.

"Yeah, perfect. Like that. Explain that, willya?"

"Well, they probably sense that I'm the only really safe bastard here," Lopez said.

"Huh? Whattaya mean?"

"Don't you remember? I had a vasectomy last month. I'm the only horny guy here shooting blanks!"

More guffaws. Rusty had forgotten. The month before, Lopez had gone to the camp clinic and gotten his tubes trimmed. He'd walked bowlegged for almost a week, and claimed that he was purple from bellybutton to thighs –

nobody volunteered to verify the claim – but had long since returned to normal.

"That's it?" Cramer went on, "How could they know that?"

"Well, like the doc said: it's a small operation, but it makes a vas deferens," Lopez said, struggling to keep his face straight.

Rusty laughed so hard he tripped and fell down in the mud.

Later that day, Major Bridgewater returned from another of his perpetual ALO conferences. He called everyone available into the big room. "Guys, I hear you had a nice visit this morning," he began, smiling.

"The Dollies were really nice, sir. Not what you'd call gorgeous, but they were wonderful," Craig said.

"Sorry I missed them. What did you like best about 'em if they weren't stunners?"

"Well sir, it's kinda hard to pin down. They were roundeyes, of course, and maybe that's enough, but there's something else I can't put my finger on."

"Or in," Kit said with a lascivious sneer. Flip hit him with a perfectly thrown pillow.

"Their voices," Sandy said, almost too quietly to be heard over the raucous laughing.

When it died down, Bridgewater turned to Sandy, "Their voices? How do you mean?"

"They weren't Vietnamese voices. We get pictures in Playboy, we get letters, but female American voices..." he trailed off.

"You know, I think he's right," Flip said.

"Me too," Rusty said, "Throaty, mellifluous voices with no screeching, no yammer and no supersonic syllables. It was like hearing music versus fingernails on a blackboard – like Mama San."

"I'll be damned. These guys are right. Seeing them was nice, don't get me wrong; but what I remember was that everybody tried to *talk* with them. Somehow, that was nicer than jumping their bones," Jack said.

Bridgewater smiled and nodded to himself. "Well, whatever you enjoyed most, I'm glad it was a welcome change." He paused dramatically, "And now I hate to cast a pall over the day, but I have important news."

The mood in the room turned instantly chill. 'Important' always meant bad.

"Intelligence thinks that this whole sector is due for some increased enemy activity. They're picking up signs of heavy infiltration and coercing of locals. Our recent experiences with night landings and team losses back that up."

They all nodded.

"And we've also had a change in the behavior of some of the mercenary 'yards we use as night guards," Bridgewater went on.

"What does that mean, sir. Excuse me," Getz injected.

"Ah, maybe you're not aware. We use a small cadre of mercenaries as night watch guards here. They typically report for duty in late afternoon, just about the time the hootch maids leave and we close the gates. We hire some of them more or less permanently, but others of them come and go from month to month. Clear?"

Getz nodded.

"Well, lately, a few of the temporary ones have been found to be or suspected to be VC agents. So have a few of the hootch maids. Not many, but we've definitely been compromised to some extent. Nor is there enough hard evidence to come down on anybody and maybe let out that we know something's cooking. So the word is to quietly button up and expect things to get a little warmer around here."

"So what does that mean to us?" Kit asked.

"Good question, Kit. First of all, it means that trips off base are hereby halted. Nobody goes downtown without specific approval from me personally. No more Bakery, Young," he reached over and poked Young playfully in the arm. Young instantly went beet red, grinning sheepishly.

"Second, it means we stop all night flying and we'll have to start doing sweeps of the runway before the first takeoff in the morning. The word is that the bad guys may try mining or booby-trapping the runway."

That got their attention. Several of them blurted out questions, but Bridgewater held up his hands for silence.

"I'll get to the details in a minute, but let me finish summarizing first. Alright, where was I? Oh yeah. We can maybe expect some security probes, maybe some incoming mortar rounds or rockets and possibly even some sabotage attempts. Emphasis here on the maybes. None of this is certain, but the indications are troubling."

He went on, "Okay, now a few specifics. I want Capt Sanderson to go over our security assignments and make sure that everybody knows what to do and where to go if the shit hits the fan. Keep your personal gear in shape and nearby, especially at night. Keep your rifles ready. But not too damn ready," he said, eyeing the still-shiny gouges in Flips locker but showing Flip a half-smile. Flip hung his head in mock mortification.

"The SF guys will begin searching the outgoing maids and incoming guards at the main gate, both morning and night. ID checks, too, not that it makes much difference. Where we come in is that there just aren't enough SF troops to work day and night. All of us may have to start pulling guard duty, too. If we do, and that's still an undecided if, we'll start pulling what you might call supervisory duty on the north berm and the main gate bunkers. Four-hour shifts at night only."

They all groaned.

Bridgewater looked at each of them in turn, and then started back again, the drawl kicking in now, "Tain't all, fellers. Ah'm savin' the worst fer the last. Seems downtown Ubon burned down naht fore last. So takin' one thang and t'uther, our leetle trips thar are on hold."

"What about the stuff I have on order, and paid for?" Rusty asked. He'd been the last one to go, two weeks ago, and Buchenhardt had been scheduled to go soon.

"Don't know, son. Yore stuff maht be thar, and it maht not. I cain't 'ford a plane or a body to go git it, even if'n it ain't all burned up. Not now, nohow. Mebbe in a few weeks. We'll see. That's all fer now, fellers."

The meeting dissolved into a babble of questions, half-hearted griping and wild speculation. Bridgewater stayed and answered what he could, reassured who he could and kidded as much as he could. As he was leaving, he turned back and called for silence.

"Sheeyit, Ah damn near fergot. Ah don't know how this happened," he made an exaggerated wink, "but summa the movies I brung back this time seem ta be a leetle bit...racy. Mebbe we can give 'em a look see tomorrow naht. Whatcha thank?"

Hoots and hollers followed him out the door.

The club that night was abuzz with rumor, both about the enemy and the purported porn films. As Rusty sat there nursing a drink, he watched the barmaid circulate. How much of this loose talk is she absorbing, he wondered. More to the point, how much of it does she pass along to – whomever? Rusty finished his drink and motioned for her. She wove her way through the tables, smiling at him with unusual intensity. I must have tipped her pretty well the other night, Rusty thought.

"Scot wat, sweetie." Before she could turn away, Rusty touched her arm. "Hey sweetie, you VC?"

"Choi oi!" She spun back and slapped his hand away. "Me VC? No way! You dinky dau GI for sure. You numba ten, you boo coo dinky dau! VC!" She mumbled the last as she walked away, huffily.

Well, he'd hardly expect her to puff up with pride and say, "You bet! Me numba one VC." Still, the amount of real, valuable intelligence an enemy agent might gather in a room of drunken GIs was incalculable. Rusty wondered how many teams they'd lost as the result of such tidbits, and he looked hard again at her and the bartender. Then he thought back to conversations he'd participated in sitting right here and wondered if any such deadly pearls had dropped from his own lips. No way to take them back if they had, he realized, but he could sure put a clamp on his own lips from now on. He resolved to bring it up in the big room the next time they were all together. Maybe he'd even mention it to Bridgewater.

Rusty turned to Flip at the table behind him, "Hey Flip, what the hell is the barmaid's name? I've somehow never managed to catch it."

Flip looked back, blankly. "You know what, I don't know either. I just order drinks from her. I've never heard her name either. Hang on a tick." He slid back his chair and walked over to where SF sergeant McGuire was standing. Rusty saw them talk for a few seconds and then Flip came back. "When in doubt, go to the fountain of knowledge," Flip said as he sat. "Her name's Xuan. Chi Li Xuan."

"Shyly? You gotta be shitting me. Shyly Swan might be the most singularly oxymoronic name I could compose for that little hellion. You ever have her pinch you? Man!"

Flip grinned back, looking over Rusty's shoulder, "Careful, she's coming your way, and she ain't smiling!"

She stumped haughtily up to Rusty's table and pointedly dropped his drink the last two inches to the table, spilling half of it, "Bah moui nam!"

Rusty peeled off thirty-five cents in paper scrip, then peeled off another quarter's worth and handed it to her. "Xin loi," Rusty said, pronouncing it as well as he could and hoping his inflection didn't change it from 'sorry' to something completely insulting.

Her face softened a bit but she didn't say anything. As she turned to go, though, she managed to dig two fingernails of her left hand into the skin over Rusty's collarbone.

"Ow! Jesus Christ!"

She eyed him over her shoulder as she wiggled her little butt away from him. The corners of her mouth curled up minutely.

Rusty was scheduled for a routine solo VR mission the next morning, and a radio cap mission in the afternoon, but when he went to the TOC to brief the morning flight, the guy they called No Name was waiting for him instead of the usual SF Captain Brookside. He motioned Rusty into a side office and closed the door. "You recall that little personal mission you flew a number of weeks ago? The very personal one?"

Rusty's shoulders slumped. "Yeah. Again?"

He nodded. "Here is the frequency and call sign for today's report. Memorize it." He showed Rusty a scrap of paper without letting go of it. "Your plane is already set to a special crypto group, just like before. Here's your sealed camera. Get more than one shot if you can, from different angles. Ideally, we'd like shots showing the interior courtyard from all four cardinal directions with mid-morning sun angle."

He didn't ask if Rusty had any questions, but Rusty had to try. "Tell me what you learned from my last visit. I have to know. Were they who I think they were?"

He looked into Rusty's eyes, softening a fraction, almost as if he were considering telling him; but then his face blanked into stone again. Silence.

Rusty looked back at him, and said with all the bitterness he could muster, "All due respect...if any is...but fuck you."

There was no visible reaction. "Report directly back to me after landing. Good morning, Lieutenant."

Rusty slammed the door hard enough to bring a cloud of dust wafting down. Sgt Young stared at him in surprise as he stormed through the radio room on the way out.

Corso was acting as crew chief, and he shied away a bit as Rusty made a quick and silent pre-flight, slamming the forms closed and banging access panels shut. As Rusty strapped in, Corso meekly asked, "Are you mad at me, sir? Have I done something wrong?"

Rusty stopped dead and turned to him, "Oh, I'm sorry, Andy. No, it's not you. You're fine. As always," Rusty added. "How's the plane?"

"Just fine, sir. She's a bit of a dog, as you probably already know, and they had to reset the scrambler twice, but she's fueled, armed and in the green." He visibly relaxed as he summarized the plane's status.

"Yeah, 686 is a dog alright. But I'm solo, so it should be fine." Rusty had a sudden thought as he glanced into the next revetment. "Andy, can you do me a favor?"

"You bet, sir."

Rusty asked what he wanted, and Corso grinned. A few minutes later, it was done and Rusty climbed in. "You pulling my pins?" Corso nodded. "Okay, button her up and I'll see you in a couple hours."

Corso shoved the door closed while Rusty finished strapping in. He ran through the checklist from memory, got the engines started and got taxi clearance from the tower. Corso pulled the chocks on signal, and then he jumped into a jeep to meet Rusty again at the rocket arming area outside the gate.

Rusty got airborne after rolling an extra hundred yards or so. The engines on this bird might have been spunky and strong when they were new, but that was a long time ago, and now they were tired and sluggish. "Come on squirrels," Rusty said aloud to the plane, "spin that cage for me." Purchased only as an interim FAC machine, the overloaded O-2 was a dog even at the best of times, loaded down as they flew it. On a good day, one might gain 300 feet of altitude per minute. But this old pig was giving Rusty only about two-thirds that at full power.

Still, Rusty's humor improved as he flew westward. It was hard to hold a black mood when flying, especially on a day as nice as this. The monsoons were definitely ending; more and more the autumnal days brought cerulean skies swept by brilliantly white horsetail clouds, crisply clean air and a freshly laundered look to a landscape that continually astounded Rusty with its beauty.

He called his position at the fence, headed southwest and leveled off at 6,000 feet. As he cruised, Rusty re-studied the unmarked map of the Kratie area he'd again been given. Rusty decided that his best tactic would be to come in very low again, popping up to achieve some surprise to take the critical first picture from the north. He'd fly past the prison a ways, make a sharp turn and barrel past again on the south side, ready to take another picture if he weren't drawing a lot of ground fire, or shearing off to the south if he were. For the sake of a few pictures, he wasn't about to get hosed bad enough to get shot down and maybe join those poor bastards inside.

Rusty held his altitude until he was about ten miles east of Kratie, the broad latté swath of the Mekong having been in sight for several minutes already. As soon as he could clearly see highway 13, he set the power, got the camera ready in his lap, and nosed over in a long shallow dive. He didn't want too much airspeed when he made the first popup or he wouldn't have time to aim the camera properly. When he got down to about 50 feet above the road, he started watching out to his left. The road, as he fully expected, was empty in daylight. When he passed the deserted airport he started his pull-up and immediately spotted the old prison sticking up above the structures around it. Deciding to look through the camera viewfinder this time, he flew by feel as he climbed and turned slightly.

This camera had a power film advance, and all Rusty had to do was hold down the shutter release to take multiple pictures. As he popped up just north of the awful place, he squeezed the button. The image in the viewfinder winked black every time the shutter tripped, and what Rusty saw was like watching individual frames of a movie, but even with this distracting, disorienting, interrupted view, one thing was plain: the place was now empty – abandoned.

Rusty lowered the camera and looked back down and behind as he flashed past. The central courtyard was littered with junk, what clearly had been cell doors hung open and broken, and there wasn't a soul in sight. Obviously, the place had been emptied, then looted for anything that could be carried off. Whoever had been interred there was long gone.

Rusty cursed, shouting every expletive he knew as he continued his climbing turn out over the Mekong. As he started a turn back, his predatory eyes were drawn to a flicker of motion. A solitary figure, dressed head to toe in black, was clambering up the stone steps that served as river wharf. As Rusty watched, the figure turned, looked up and saw his plane, then broke into a frantic run up the steps. Without a thought, Rusty reached up, armed the left rocket pod and flipped the master arm on. He kicked the rudder, rolled and pulled his way through a crooked split-S: the classic rocket attack. There was no time to turn on the gun sight, but he wouldn't need it. When the black-pajama-clad man was in the center of the windscreen, Rusty touched the firing button once. With a PWHOOSH, the rocket zipped out ahead.

What he'd fired was not a marking rocket. It carried a warhead packed with flechettes. It worked like a shotgun, sending thousands of razor-sharp, finned nails into a dense pattern. When the rocket had accelerated to maximum speed and burned out, the warhead burst with a puff of red smoke. For a fraction of a second, nothing seemed to happen, and then a wide circle of white dust spurted from those stone steps. Near the edge of that dust cloud, but well inside it, ran the VC. Still in his dive, Rusty saw the figure take one more faltering step, then keel over and lay still.

"Yes!" Rusty shouted, pulling on the yoke just enough to bottom out at a hundred feet, heading east again. "Take that you son of a bitch!"

He leveled and got the camera up again. When he got to the prison, Rusty made a lazy turn completely around it, taking pictures from all sides. Not a sign of occupation, not a shot fired at him, and not another person visible. But again, he felt that sixth sense of being stared at, and he zig-zagged away to foil the aim of anyone he hadn't seen but might be shooting anyway.

As Rusty climbed and headed east, he looked out at his left rocket pod. There was one empty hole, five light green marking warheads sticking out the front of it – and one longer, chocolate-colored warhead, the second of two flechette rockets he'd had Corso steal from the Cobra gunship parked in the next revetment. Andy said he would replace them undetected, and Rusty knew he'd succeed. Rusty would have to fire the second one before he landed – Sanderson still hadn't approved carrying anything except marking rockets – and he fervently hoped he'd see something else worth ventilating.

As Rusty searched for something to kill, he made his scrambled report to whoever it was, and the disembodied voice on the far side of the globe once again accepted it laconically, as if Rusty had been submitting an inventory of toilet paper.

It occurred to him that he really had killed somebody now, personally and not by airstrike proxy. There was no doubt about it. This time, though, it felt good. Rusty was proud of the skill it took and hoped that somehow it might avenge whatever had happened to the guys in that prison. All he wanted now was a chance to do it again, as soon as possible.

But nothing else appeared on the trip home, and nearing the fence again Rusty prepared to fire the remaining flechette round. He dove, pointing the nose down at a broad expanse of triple canopy jungle and fired the flechette rocket. Except for the puff of red smoke, he saw not the slightest sign of impact. As he pulled the nose up again, the front engine suddenly roared. Rusty shot a look at the RPM gauge as the needle flashed up past the red line maximum. He jerked the throttle back to idle and the needle fell again, along with the scream and roar of the engine.

The engine stabilized at idle, and seemed normal, but when Rusty experimentally added a little power, the prop revolutions raced up the scale again, and he immediately pulled it back to idle. He tried moving the prop lever, but nothing happened; he'd lost propeller control on that engine.

"Mike 50, Mike 58."

"Go ahead, 58"

"Uh 50, I'm declaring an emergency. I've just had a runaway propeller on the front engine. It's in idle and stable, no apparent damage, but I'm pretty sure I oversped the engine before I got it pulled back."

"Copy all that 58, say position and fuel."

"Um, I'm at the fence inbound with two hours fuel, but I'm below field altitude and I'm unable to climb with the rear engine only. I'm in a slight descent, and that's as good as I can do."

"Stand by 58." There was only a moment's delay, and then he heard Sanderson, "Mike 58, this is 52. Copy you had a runaway prop, are now in a controlled descent and are unable to climb back to field altitude?"

"That's affirmative 52. I still have both pods. Request permission to jettison them."

"Say position, 58"

"I'm just inside the fence, east of the Toe and over triple canopy."

"Permission granted. Jettison both pods immediately. Report what happens."

Rusty set the pylon switches to drop and hit the firing button. Both pods immediately plummeted away. Rusty felt the plane jump with the 400-pound weight loss, and the vertical velocity indicator jiggled, paused and crept to 100 feet per minute of climb. Yahhoooo!

"Mike 52, the pods are gone and I now have about a hundred feet per minute positive rate. I intend to press in and see if I can clear the terrain. I'll edge north of BMT to avoid the radio towers, and if I have to, I'll make a wide 360 to get a bit more altitude."

"Sounds like a good plan, 58. We'll alert the tower. Um, winds are about 240 at ten. You could possibly make a downwind landing, but it'd be better if you could make it around to land on 27."

"Uh huh, I copy. I'll try for 27. I don't think I'll have a go-around ability with the gear down."

"Roger that. Okay, 58, we have the tower on landline now. We've declared your emergency, and they say they have no traffic in the area. The runway is clear, and winds are 250 at eight, altimeter 3003. The field is yours. What's your ETA?"

"I'm at best climb speed - 90 knots, boss. Uh, maybe 15 to 20 mike. But I still have a few hundred feet to climb before I even get to runway altitude, so I may have to dink around a while until I climb high enough to land." The oddity of what he'd just said struck him and he chuckled to himself.

"Copy, 58. Do you have enough altitude now to bail out?"

That let the air out of Rusty's laugh balloon. He looked at the altimeter, checked the map and took a squinty-eyed look at the jungle below. "Um, I don't think so. According to the chart, I should be about 800 AGL, but the trees look closer than that. I wouldn't want to bet on getting a full chute from here."

"Copy, 58. Press on. But if you get below 100 feet AGL, turn west again and we'll re-evaluate."

"I copy, 52. Headed your way."

Rusty churned east. He had plenty of time to get everything set up, adjusted, tweaked and double-checked as the ground crept by underneath, but the terrain rose faster than he could climb. Even though he was slowly climbing, the tops of the trees steadily got nearer and nearer.

He was getting a bit apprehensive about taking any ground fire because he was almost a stationary target and couldn't possibly do any jinking without dropping still lower. When he got down to what looked like 200 feet above the trees, but still below field altitude, Rusty rolled in just a few degrees of left bank and started a very wide, very slow turn back west. Too much bank would cancel out his climb rate.

"Mike 50, 58. I'm turning west. I need more time and distance to climb. Rear engine still looks good at full power." But how long would that be, Rusty wondered. Engines weren't designed to be run at absolute full power for long, and this plane's engines were already old and worn.

"We copy 58," it was Young again. "We are launching the alert Hornets and 52 is taking off now to escort you. Say position."

"I'm due west of the city, 50. Maybe five miles and I'm now in a shallow left turn, just passing through 050 heading for 270."

"Are you still climbing, 58?"

"Just barely, 50. With wings level I can get maybe 100 feet a minute, but in any bank at all, it's less."

Rusty looked at the camera, wondering if he should take the film out and then chuck the thing overboard. Nah. A couple pounds wouldn't help, he thought. And with his luck so far, the damn thing would hit the rear prop – not a happy thought.

What if he milked down a few degrees of flaps, he thought? Rusty bumped the switch down just barely out of its detent, and saw the flap indicator move slightly out of the full up position. He waited, and a few seconds later, thought he saw the VVI –vertical velocity indicator- nudge up almost a needle-width. Well! He nudged the flaps another tiny amount and again the VVI moved, a bit more enthusiastically this time. Rusty had adjusted the flaps down to about ten percent extended when he looked up and saw Sanderson slide into position on his wing.

"Two's in, 58!"

"I see ya there 52. Nice to have company."

"You look good, 58. I don't see anything leaking." So he was worried about that tired old rear engine, too, huh? "Are your flaps extended a bit?"

"Affirmative, 52. I've just been experimenting with them. I'm at about ten degrees extension and the VVI is up to maybe 150 positive. That's better than when they were full up. So I'm leaving them right there." Rusty checked his heading and altitude: 240 and 4,700. "Uh, I think I'll continue this slow turn back east and see what happens. I'm almost up to field altitude. By the time I get around and cover the last few miles, I should be high enough to circle and make 27."

"Sounds good, 58. I'll fly a loose wing. You also have a pair of Hornets about a klick in trail."

Well, if Rusty had to bail out or skid this pig in, at least help would be at hand. It'd be the world's record for quickest survivor pickup, he smiled to himself. Good old Horny Greenits. Rusty wondered if Mule was aboard and watching. That'd be ironic.

By the time he rolled out eastbound again, Rusty had climbed all the way to runway altitude – 4,750 feet. He kept climbing. He knew he'd start losing height again the instant he put the gear down, and the turn to final wouldn't help, either. He couldn't help watching the ground go by right underneath his wings. He droned across asphalt roads and dark green rubber plantations. Thatched and tin-roofed hootches passed below, and he even saw a few little Vietnamese kids looking up at him from their bare red dirt yards. Naked except for dingy once-white little tee shirts, they stared at him expressionless.

He was actually climbing better now, probably the result of the fuel he'd burned off. But he'd also been at maximum takeoff power now for almost half an hour, and the engine temperature was getting close to red line.

"Uh, 52, the rear engine is still fine, except that the cylinder head temp is getting up there. Almost red line, but I don't dare open the cowling to cool it."

"I agree, 58. Let it cook. You don't need the drag. I suggest you continue on past the field a bit and make your turn to final as wide and level as you can. Hold the gear until you have the field made and leave the power up on final. Use the flaps to add drag if you have to. Oh, and don't be afraid to use the front engine if you get low. But it's your call."

"Ahh, good ideas, 52. Thanks. I'll try it just that way. I'm going to tower push now."

"52's going, too."

Rusty contacted the tower, gave them his position and confirmed that he was indeed the emergency traffic. They said they had him and his escorts in sight and that he was cleared to land and maneuver anywhere he needed to.

As Rusty flew along just north of the runway, he looked down and saw dozens of people on the ramp, watching. If they wanted excitement, he sure hoped he'd disappoint them.

He'd managed to claw his way almost 200 feet above the field, and as Dave had suggested, he kept flying eastwards a mile or so, still greedy for every foot of altitude he could get. Finally, he could stand it no more and banked right. Rusty watched the runway pirouette under his right wingtip during the turn, and he was actually able to shallow out his bank a bit. He'd lost a few feet in the turn, but the shallower bank allowed him to almost hold level. The ground whizzed by hardly more than a hundred feet below. Rusty rolled out aligned with the runway. He didn't know where Sanderson had gone, but there was no time to worry about him. Rusty concentrated on the runway. The end of the pavement crept under the nose but he held the nose up in level flight another few seconds. The last thing he wanted to do after all this effort was crash short of the runway.

Finally, Rusty couldn't stand it any longer and pulled the landing gear handle out and down. Instantly, with the tremendous drag of the main gear doors opening, the nose pitched down. The runway shot up towards him, and he knew he'd hit before the gear could get down. Rusty slammed the front engine throttle forward. It hesitated, then roared in protest, the propeller RPMs screaming up through the red line. But he felt the surge of power it added, even with the propeller almost flat, and he pulled the yoke back even as he hunched his shoulders for the impact. The nose had rotated sluggishly up, but was just above the horizon when BANG, the main wheels slammed down.

Rusty instantly yanked both throttles to idle, dancing on the rudders to keep the nose straight and lowering the nose wheel to the runway. He let it roll a bit to stabilize his directional control before he got gingerly on the brakes. He was down.

"Uh, Ban Me Two tower, Mike 58 is down. I'll taxi back to clear the runway."

"Okay okay, My Fi Ay. You clear to My FAC ramp."

Rusty looked up and saw Sanderson flash past, then turn and climb away. "Ban Me Thuot tower, Mike 52 will loiter until the runway is clear, then land full stop. Break. Good job, 58."

"Okay, Fi Tu."

Rusty didn't reply. He'd have time to do that later. He taxied back down their snaky ramp and stopped outside the gate. Corso was standing there, and on a whim, Rusty opened his little storm window and dangled the rocket safety pins outside. Corso reflexively started to dash in for get them, them skidded to a stop looking at the bare pylons. He playfully shot Rusty one raised finger, and Rusty saluted him.

In the revetment, Rusty finally shut both engines down. Mike Lopez, their prop and engine tech, immediately rushed in and started looking at the front propeller hub. Rusty saw him shake his head sadly, then he moved around to the rear engine, now pinging away in a metallic paroxysm as it cooled down from near red heat.

Rusty climbed out just as Dave Sanderson taxied in through the gate, and then the ramp erupted in a swirl of dust and noise as the two Green Hornet gunships landed. The turmoil allowed Rusty to lean in next to Lopez, who had moved again to the front engine. Lopez pointed, "See that little clevis, sir?"

"Uh huh."

That's your propeller pitch control cable end. The other end attaches to your prop control handle."

"This end doesn't appear to be attached to anything, Sergeant Lopez."

"Bingo, sir. Some of you pilot types are smarter than you look, you know that?"

Rusty punched his shoulder playfully.

Lopez went on, "Looks like the cotter pin, nut and bolt are gone. The prop is designed to go to full fine pitch if the cable comes off. Did it?"

"I'll say. It went way past 2850 RPM, though - probably past 3000. I was pulling up from a dive at the time, and had the throttles in."

"That explains the oil streaks on the prop. You blew the oil seal when it slammed to full fine. The hub's probably toast." He shrugged. "There's only one horribly bad thing about it..." He trailed off.

"What's that?"

"There's no way I can pin this on 'Pilot error'."

Rusty punched him again, harder this time, but Lopez just rubbed his shoulder and grinned.

CHAPTER FOURTEEN

The mess hall was filled to brimming with Mikes, Green Hornets, SF people, ARVN soldiers and Montagnards. The latter two groups sat themselves along opposite sides of the room, by virtue of their mutual dislike, with all the rest arranged in small groups between. Seated front center were the ARVN camp commander, the SF commander, Major Bridgewater, the ranking Green Hornet pilot and a tribal chief of the Jarais, specially invited for the occasion. Tubs of iced beer had been placed every few feet in the aisles, and the merriment had been suitably lubricated when the SF commander nudged Major Bridgewater to his feet.

He raised his hand, and the noise gradually subsided. The ribaldry had almost ended when Mule yelled, "If you can't hover, you ain't shit!" The hoots and boos erupted again. Over them, Jim Getz stood up in his loudest, wildest Hawaiian shirt and bellowed, "Does that mean if you *can* hover, you *are* shit?" But he was smiling and he saluted Mule to show he was joking; their guffaws showed that even the Green Hornets loved the line.

Bridgewater finally recaptured the attention of most. "Whale, if'n Ah kin git an edge in word wise..." The last murmurs subsided. "Ah bin tole that these here movies is kinda racy..." He paused for the inevitable hoots and catcalls.

"So Ah figgered - afore Ah pass 'em along ta some innocent gyrenes or somethin' - who's better ta judge 'em than the fightin' troops of Ban Me Thuot?" He waited again for the last bout of rowdiness to subside.

"Ya'll crowd up front here and watch close, now! Let 'er rip!"

He motioned to Sgt Young, who stood next to the club's 16mm projector, mounted atop a stack of rocket boxes on a mess table in the middle of the room. As the machine clattered to a start, those in the back of the room did indeed edge forward.

The lights snapped out, and on the stretched sheet that served as a screen bloomed a black and white, ancient and horrible porn film featuring a chubby, stringy blonde who cavorted carnally in turn with a German Shepherd and a bored-looking pony. Even the animals needed extra encouragement to get interested in her. The Jarai chief laughed uncontrollably through the whole thing.

But it was porn, and for a crowd of men so collectively horny they could probably be aroused by a tree's knothole, it was spellbinding. The silent movie ground on, accompanied by filthy comments, critical judgments of the dog's performance and some ribald envy of the pony's reproductive equipment.

Then, with no warning, machine gun fire blasted out overhead, bits of the ceiling rained down and bullets began ricocheting off the hall's concrete floor. Two hundred men shouted, dove for cover under tables or sprinted for the exits. Shouts and screams in three languages pierced the semi-dark. Surreally, the only light came from the flickering image of the movie that played on. Then, with an almost bell-like 'whang' the projector took a bullet and crashed to the floor amid a blue-white shower of electrical sparks. Total darkness descended on the panicking room. Within seconds, over the staccato of the light machine gun came the heavy thud of five or six shots from a .50 caliber Browning. Then, abrupt silence.

For a full second, everything seemed suspended in time, and then everyone scuttled and shoved for the exits. Outside, the first illumination flares from the heavy mortars were popping, bathing the whole compound in weird, pulsing orange light.

"Everyone get to your posts," someone ordered at a bellow. Rusty didn't recognize the voice, but it seemed like a good plan. He ran back to the hootch, but almost everyone else had beaten him there. Rusty snatched up his carbine, ammo, steel helmet and flak vest, then ran back outside. His assigned post was on the northern dirt berm, near the laundry building. Rusty scrambled up it and flopped down on his belly, looking out towards the runway and through the field of barbed wire, razor wire and flagged mounds that hid claymore mines inside. Nothing moved in the glare of the descending parachute flares, but Rusty's heart did flip-flops in his chest nonetheless.

Except for the wailing camp siren and some sporadic shouts, Rusty heard nothing: no further shots, no ripping air of incoming rounds, nothing that sounded like an attack. Eventually, even the siren and the regular thump of outgoing mortar flares stopped. The camp's streetlights came back on one by one. A final, short burst of the siren signaled it was over. Whatever it had been.

But something or somebody sure as hell had fired into the mess hall. Rusty double-checked that his carbine was safe and walked back to the hootch. Even as everyone drifted back in, the rumors had already begun. We'd been probed by sappers, one said. We'd been strafed by some plane, said another. Bullshit, cried another: we'd obviously been fired on from the guard tower.

In the morning, after a long and fitful night spent fully garbed in combat gear, they learned that the latter supposition had been the truth. Whether the miscreant had been a VC plant or just a Vietnamese who saw a chance to gun down a whole crowd of Montagnards – or maybe just a religious fanatic who objected to the porn film - they'd never know. But the guard in the west tower had dismounted his M-60 machine gun, pointed it down at the roof of the mess hall and let fly.

Either through his misjudgment or everyone else's dumb luck, he'd concentrated his fire on the center of the roof. Dozens of holes were found there, but due to the angle of fire, most of those rounds had impacted the floor towards the western end of the hall – while everyone inside had been crowded close to the screen in the east end. Miraculously, the only casualty was the miscreant himself, thoroughly and terminally perforated by the massive slugs fired from the east tower's .50-caliber heavy gun. Well, he was the only casualty if you don't count the movie projector and the porn film, both of which were destroyed.

Poor Sandy Hubert had the dawn patrol, and he trudged off with red eyes while the rest of them stowed gear and assembled in the big room. Sanderson came in and briefed them.

"Here's the scoop. You all know it was the west tower guard who hosed us, and that there were no casualties except for him."

"And the movie," Getz interjected.

"Fuck the porn flick," Kit said, to general guffaws, "The projector died. No more nightly movies."

"And screw that, too," Rusty said. "How about the mess hall? And breakfast?"

"Oh, Christ yeah," Flip said. "Where we gonna eat now?"

Sanderson held up his hands for quiet. "You're right about the projector. It's dead. But the chow hall is open right now for breakfast. Nothing got hit except for some tables and chairs. There are a bunch of gouges in the floor, and the roof is gonna need patching, but all the kitchen stuff is fine."

"Whew! Let's go eat!" Craig said.

"Not so fast, junior. Let's thrash out a few things first. Number one, did everybody remember where to go last night?"

Guys looked at each other sheepishly. Rusty broke the silence. "Yup, north berm, center. Nothing to see there; but there I was, protecting the strategically vital laundry." Flip's deadly accurate pillow smacked into Rusty's head.

"Good. Now who forgot?" Sanderson pressed.

Getz raised his hand, guiltily. "I guess I did. I ended up just tagging along with Kit and hoofing it to the east berm by the fuel truck."

"Is that your post, Kit?" Sanderson turned to him.

"Uh, I think so. Maybe. Oh, alright, no. I didn't remember until it was all over. I'm assigned to the TOC."

"That's correct. Nobody is assigned to guard the fuel truck. Because of what would happen to you if it took a hit while you were defending it."

Kit's jaw dropped, and he hung his head in shame.

"Okay, enough recriminations. Let's have a remedial 'what if' session later today. I'll post the security response assignments one more time. I expect all of you to get them down pat this time. For now, let's grab some chow. Then try to get some rest. There's just the one team active so we'll scrub everything but two Quan Loi guys and local radio cap flights today. We're short one plane anyway," he said, looking toward Rusty.

Rusty almost made a remark, knowing he was not only blameless for the broken plane, but that he'd also gone to the correct place last night. But he buttoned his lip. Best not to quibble. He had cost them two perfectly good rocket pods and a dozen rockets, after all.

Kit and Craig saddled up and took off for Quan Loi, as usual. Jack relieved Sandy on the local cap, and the rest of them racked out. Rusty and Getz were soundly asleep when Sanderson banged on the door.

"I hate to break this to you, sport, but there's a Chico bird at the gate and they're asking for Lieutenant Naille."

"Huh? A who? What's a Chico bird?" Rusty rubbed his eyes and sat up.

"Unfortunately, the millstones of Air Force chickenshittery grind on, even in a war zone. Somebody somewhere discovered that you never received a formal in-country checkride at Cam Rahn. The Chico FACs are the 21st TASS Stan-Eval guys, and they're here to give you a no-notice checkride."

"You are absofuckinglutely shitting me. A checkride? During a war?"

"Yeah," Sanderson said, holding his palms out, "I know, I know. And I agree. It's idiocy. But these are steel-core REMFs. The closest thing to combat they've seen is an occasional VC rocket landing a mile or so away from them at Cam Rahn. They think the Air Force should be run the same no matter where it is; the dickheads. Major Bridgewater is out there talking to them. Get a regulation flight suit on and get out there."

When Rusty walked up to the still-closed and locked gate, he saw Major Bridgewater standing there, hands on hips, talking to another major through the barbed wire.

"Here's your victim," he said as Rusty approached.

Rusty reported, and Bridgewater turned his back on the other major. "This here's Major Barcum, Rusty. He's a Stan-Eval weenie and he says he's here to give you a no-notice check ride. But there's a leetle problem," he said, discretely winking at Rusty. "See, the major here hasn't been briefed in, so Ah cain't allow him or his plane through the fence," he winked again.

Rusty kept a straight face, but he was beginning to catch on to Bridgewater's dirty trick. Rusty nodded to let him know, and Bridgewater winked a third time.

"Y'all go grab your gone and checklist. We'll open the gate a crack to let ya out. See ya real soon. Oh, your map bag has sensitive materials, so leave it." Bridgewater grinned but composed his face to a blank before he turned around again. "Lt Naille will be with you in a moment, major. I trust he'll do well for you in what little airtime you'll have."

"What do mean by little airtime?" the stranger asked.

As Rusty walked away, he heard Bridgewater say, "Well, the only fuel here is inside the compound, and since you can't enter..." Back turned, Rusty grinned to himself. If the REMF had to get back to Cam Rahn unrefueled, this would have to be a very abbreviated checkride, especially if the weather was bad enough that the REMF had to allow for a significant reserve of diversion fuel.

Rusty grabbed every bit of flight gear he'd been issued and lugged it back to the gate. Even though he seldom used much of it, the Stan-Eval guy would write him up if he didn't pretend that he faithfully used it on every flight. Likewise, he read every single item in the checklist aloud before he performed it. It took forever that way, but they finally got airborne. The moment the wheels were in the well, the major said, "Alright, take me out to your operating area and we'll try to find a target for an air strike."

"Uh, I regret that I can't do that, sir."

"What do you mean you can't do that?" He was clearly pissed already by Bridgewater's outrageous but unassailable restrictions.

"As Major Bridgewater explained, sir, you have not been briefed on my mission. Therefore, I can't take you to my operating area. Besides, I don't have my maps with me, under Major Bridgewater's direct orders. I'm sorry." Rusty feigned anguish at being unable to comply.

"Then you will fly us to the nearest free fire zone and we will work there."

"Um, again, sir, I regret that I cannot do that. I'm not cleared to operate anywhere near here. You could go where you are cleared to operate, or I can go to where I operate, but we can't go to either place together."

"And why in hell is that, Lieutenant?"

Rusty pulled the trump card. "I'm afraid that I can't tell you that, sir. You have neither the clearance nor the need to know."

The Stan Eval REMF smacked the glare shield so hard with his fist that Rusty thought he heard it crack. Well, it was his plane, not Rusty's. "Just what exactly can you do by way of a checkride?"

Rusty shrugged and wrinkled his brow as if he were thinking hard. "Sir, the only thing I believe might be acceptable is the traffic pattern. You want to see me land?"

"Goddamn it. Yes. If that's all the goddamn cooperation I'm going to get from you, then yes, I want to see you land. See if you can handle this," he said pulling the front engine to idle. "You just lost the front engine. See if you can…"

But before he could even finish the sentence, Rusty had run the rear engine to maximum power, closed the cowl vents and then reached over and set the flaps at about ten degrees down. Rusty hesitated and then announced, "Rear engine to takeoff power, everything clean and we have level flight. If this were real, I'd jettison the rocket pods, also. I'll turn back now and enter the downwind." Rusty rolled in five degrees of bank and told the tower he'd be landing immediately with a simulated emergency. Finally, Rusty flipped the checklist open to the correct page and ran his finger down the list for loss of an engine.

Barcum said triumphantly, "Got you. Nowhere in the checklist does it call for adding flaps, especially to an intermediate position."

"That's correct, sir. But it is necessary to maintain level flight. If I were solo, I could even climb a bit in this configuration – but not if I were either flaps full up or flaps in takeoff position." Rusty said, smugly.

"Lieutenant, how in the living hell do you think you know more than the checklist? More even than the qualified test pilots who developed the checklist?"

"Actually sir, I learned it yesterday…in a real single engine landing."

"Yesterday? Why hasn't some report of this been forwarded to the TASS?"

"I couldn't say, sir. Neither do I have the time right now to divert my attention. Will this be a touch and go?"

"Fuck it. No. Full stop."

Rusty was yip yip yahooing inside, but kept a straight face. "Ban Me Thuot tower, Mike 58, base, full stop, taxi back."

"You clear lan, Mi Fi Ay"

As he had done the day before, Rusty held as much altitude as he could until the runway was well assured, then dropped the gear. Keeping the rear engine at full power, he held his speed by dropping the nose, lowered flaps to takeoff and started his flare just a touch early. They touched down almost normally and Rusty slowed to a stop before making a careful U-turn.

"Hmmmph. Acceptable." Barcum snorted. He silently began filling out a sheaf of forms, not finishing until after Rusty had shut down the engines in front of the gate. When he finished, he stowed all the forms, unstrapped and climbed out. "That will be all, Lieutenant." Rusty climbed out after him. Before he walked as far as the gate, the major had already climbed back in and was strapping in.

Bridgewater was waiting, one corner of his mouth curled up. "Mighty short ride."

"Uh huh. Seems there wasn't much we had in common, mission-wise."

"You caught on raht good, Ah'd say."

"That was pretty devious. Especially the fueling part."

"Whah? Ah' was jist holding to the letter 'a the law, s'all. Same's them Stan-Eval types make us do. Good for the goose, ya know." But he was working hard to suppress a face-splitting laugh as he turned away. "'Sides, if he don't know there's fuel available at the civilian terminal, ain't no skin off'n my nose. Ah assume ya passed?"

"I suppose. He didn't say much after we landed. But he didn't say that I hadn't passed either," Rusty said.

"Naow yore talkin'!"

"Why do you think he's such a jerk? I mean why come out here to give me a chicken-shit checkride six months late?"

"Oh, he's jist got his boxers in a bunch 'cause they're finally closing Cam Rahn."

"Cripes, that was in the rumor mill almost year ago when I was at Emerald. I thought the idea had been scrapped when I got back and found it still open."

"Well, Ah reckon them thangs take tahm is all. Movin' the whole kit and caboodle to Saigon. Hell, son, they'll be closin' all the bases afore long. This nag is on her way to the glue factory."

"Yeah, that's what everybody says. When? Closing Cam Rahn, I mean."

"Hell, they been sayin' it fer a year now. I cain't imagine they'll git around to actually leavin' fer months yet."

"So if they're closing a place with two-mile runways, a deep-water port, a hospital and all that, how long before they close a shithole like this?"

"Sorry, Rusty. The batteries in my crystal ball are dead. Beats me. But if I were the commissary officer for this dump, I wouldn't be buying any green bananas. I'm just kidding. I haven't even heard a rumor about us closing. Hell, the way the Air Force works, they'd close down a paradise and leave a shithole open until last. *If* they even remember to tell us that everybody else done left!"

"Ain't that the truth? Based on that, the commissary guy could plant a walnut tree tomorrow because he someday wants to serve Waldorf salad here."

Bridgewater chuckled all the way back to the TOC. "Waldorf salad. Sheeyit!"

Within hours, it seemed like the very foundation of Ban Me Thuot had crumbled: Mike Cramer got orders for an immediate DEROS.

They threw him a helluva party in the club that night. The Special Forces guys made him an honorary Green Beret, a tradition normally reserved for pilots.

"Where ya headed, Mike?" Kit said, his arm angled up around the lanky sergeant's shoulders.

"Reese. T-37 maintenance. I guess the Cessna company likes me. Or hates me, one or the other."

"I love ya, too, bud," said Kit, planting his tongue firmly in Cramer's ear. Cramer hunched his shoulders and squirmed away, "Well, I sure hate THAT!"

The room erupted in gales of laughter at Cramer's plight. "Hey Kit! It looked like you enjoyed that a little too much," Craig shouted the expected jibe.

"Let's see how you like it then," Kit said, lunging at him. But Craig spun and dodged Kit's attack, knocking a chair over and bumping into Chi Li in the process. She let out a long screech of what had to be bluest Vietnamese, smacking Craig over the head with her round tin barmaid tray.

As the evening wore on, man after man pressed drink after drink on Cramer in tribute. At last, even as Flip told yet another funny Cramer story, the object of the tale slid smoothly out of his chair onto the floor as though someone had cut the wire holding him up.

"Well, that was a party he'll never forget," Buchenhardt said.

"More likely one he'll never remember," Rusty corrected, chuckling as four others tried to carry Cramer's wet-rag body to his bed.

"How short are you now?" Buchenhardt said.

"I just turned two-digit midget. A mere 98 days and a wakeup and I hope to be feted just as our good crew chief has been."

"I can't wait," Buchenhardt said, icily.

What a plastic prick, Rusty thought, as Buchenhardt stood up and left. What an absolute runs-on-two-batteries-can-be-used-with-creams-or-oils dildo he is.

In the morning, Cramer looked much better than anyone expected, but nowhere near his usual sunny self. Somehow, he must have gotten packed, because he was standing on the ramp with two duffel bags when Major Bridgewater showed up to ferry him to Cam Rahn. Cramer solemnly shook hands all round, gave Mike Lopez a big hug and then took a long, slow, final look around the ramp.

"It probably looks better than Reese will," Getz said in a hoarse stage whisper. "Jesus. Lubbock fucking Texas." He shuddered in mock horror.

"I went through Laredo myself," Rusty said. "They said it was the nearest thing to a foreign assignment you could get. And they were just about right. I actually saw signs in some downtown Laredo stores that said 'English Spoken Here' and at first I thought it was a joke. It wasn't. There were retail stores in that city where nobody spoke English…in the US of A!"

"Damn," Getz said. "Of course, you might say nobody spoke English in Selma, Alabama, either."

"Craig?"

"What?" Danny said.

"Yup," Getz said simultaneously.

"No, sorry, Danny. I was asking Jim if he went through pilot training at Craig AFB. Hey, where'd you go? They didn't send a Craig to Craig did they?"

"Nah. I went to Williams."

"Ooh! Lah de dah…Phoenix! The jewel of jewels! How'd you rate a slot to Willy?"

"Oh, you might not say that if you've ever sat under a closed Tweet canopy when it's 130 degrees, Getz. Especially in full flight regalia."

"Hmm, he has a point, Jim. I damn near baked to death at Laredo, and it seldom topped 105 there. Another 25 degrees woulda killed me, I think," Rusty said, wiping his brow reflexively at the mere thought of that sun-blasted flightline.

Comparing and contrasting their flight training bases went on while Bridgewater and Cramer strapped in and cranked up.

"Hey, wait! I have an idea. C'mon!" Flip said, running off toward the gate. There, he quickly outlined his idea, and they split up and stood by both sides of the taxiway at attention. When Bridgewater stopped there, all of them walked solemnly to the rocket pods, pulled the pins, and then handed them through the window to Cramer. The two men in the plane saluted them smartly, and Rusty saw Cramer's eyes welling.

"Great idea, buddy," Kit said as Bridgewater taxied off with a burst of propeller blast. "He sure pulled 'em or stuck 'em often enough for us. Helluva crew chief, that boy."

"Amen to that."

Lopez pulled up in a jeep. "Everybody grab a smoke grenade. Let's give him a sendoff. I'm sure the major will give him a low pass."

They jogged a short distance down the taxiway and waited. Bridgewater took off to the west, and they saw him make a turn, then another as he lined himself up with the runway again. "Now!" Lopez said, and they all pulled the pins and tossed their smoke grenades. Plumes of red, yellow, orange, green and purple smoke blossomed into a drifting rainbow. The O-2 came low over their heads, wings rocking furiously, one smiling face showing out the near window. They watched in silence as that face dwindled into the southeast.

The last smoke grenade sputtered out with a wheezy hiss. Lopez turned and started walking back to the gate.

"Well, now what?" Kit asked to the air.

Nobody answered. Strange how a lowly enlisted man can mean so much to a bunch of exalted jet jockeys, Rusty thought. No, he corrected himself. No, it isn't strange at all.

In the big room, they all sat around and stared at the floor. Kit finally broke the fugue, "Did any of you hear the rumor that they're closing Cam Rahn?"

"Oh bullshit," Flip said. "Really?" added Sandy.

"That's what Bridgewater told me this morning. I think it's true. He said it's why that Chico weenie was here: because while they were closing out records, they'd stumbled onto the fact that I'd never had an in-country checkride," Rusty said. "The 21ˢᵗ TASS is relocating to Saigon."

"No shit?" Buchenhardt stared at them agog, seemingly having forgotten his aversion to Rusty and Kit. "The whole fucking base is closing?"

"That's what Bridgewater said. He thinks they all will pretty soon. According to him, the war's essentially over."

"Who won?" Craig joked.

"We didn't," Kit said with not a trace of laughter on his face or in his voice.

"Oh come on. The VC haven't had a major success since Tet in '68, and they actually lost that in terms of battles and bodies. Nah, we haven't lost," Craig asserted.

"Maybe not in the field or in our own minds, Danny boy, but in the next century's history books, I bet we did," Rusty said.

"How's that possible?" Getz asked.

"Because you don't really win a war until the other guy is belly up and begging," Flip contributed. "And the NVA aren't. They have the support of China, Russia and all the other Commie countries. Look at who makes all their gear, delivers their gear, maybe even operates some of their more sophisticated gear like missile sites. Who supports the South Vietnamese like that? Just us, and we're leaving. Then what? You can guess."

"But the VC and the NVA aren't doing anything. It's quiet everywhere. Well, except for what Bridgewater told us about activity around here, but that's nothing. And they're talking peace again in Paris."

"They may be Commies, but they ain't stupid, Dan. Why should they do anything now? We're packing up and leaving on our own. All they have to do is nod politely in Paris, and wait until the last guard turns out the last light at the last base open. Then they can just walk in and take this place without a shot," Kit said, nodding to Flip as if to bolster his comments.

"Not all that fucking quiet, either," Buchenhardt said. "You've all seen the truck tracks and stuff out there on the trail. They're moving shit by the fucking ton every night."

"That's what worries me about this local activity," Rusty agreed. "All that shit they're moving is coming either near here or through here. It could get really interesting really fast - just like it did during Tet, by the way."

"Like what?" Jack asked, seemingly genuinely curious.

"Well, from what I read, about a bazillion NVA completely overran Ban Me Thuot during Tet. The mighty 23ʳᵈ ARVN and the worthless Ruff Puffs just turned tail. The NVA butchered some nurses and doctors at the leprosarium in BMT. White American nurses, by the way. It wasn't just Saigon that got hit, but many of the province capitals: BMT, Hue, Pleiku and more. They came within a red cunt hair of winning outright. I think that next time, they will."

"Son of a bitch," Buchenhardt said. "Wait a minute. Did you say a leprosarium? A leper colony? Here in Ban Me Thuot?"

"Uh huh. It might even still be there. Leprosy is common in Vietnam, like malaria or TB. Why?"

"Jesus Christ," Buchenhardt shuddered in real disgust. "Now I know I want to get out of this fucking place."

"Make you think twice about the Bakery, Jack?" Flip teased.

"Oh, Christ!" Buchenhardt said, grabbing his crotch and running from the room.

They all laughed, and then Kit said, "That really scared him. I wonder…" More laughter, but some of it was a bit forced, Rusty noticed. He thought of Sgt Young and his recent case of the clap. Hmmm. The unbidden mental image of his own dick turning black and falling off gave him a bit of a shudder, too. Maybe there are worse things than death.

Rusty wrote to Mary Beth that night, chatting lightly all about Cramer and the abbreviated checkride. He even talked a bit about the leprosarium, but he didn't mention the Bakery.

"I have a little job for you," said Bridgewater a few days later. "Kind of a taxi service."

Rusty shrugged, recalling the Army guys he'd taken to Qui Nhon. "Okay. Teeny Weeny Airlines at your service. Who, when and where?"

"A little guy. You don't know him. I need to deliver his little brown butt to Duc Lap this morning. You're the taxi driver."

"An just where in hell is Duc Lap?" Rusty had never heard of the place, but at least it sounded Vietnamese and not Cambodian or Laotian.

"Oh, just a good spit from here. Twenty, thirty miles, maybe - southwest. Just a small strip, but plenty for an Oscar Duck. Just drop him off and come back. Piece of cake."

"Uh huh. Do you have the tower freqs or should I look them up?"

"Well, you won't need to. There aren't any. The field's abandoned."

"Abandoned as in 'nobody home' or abandoned as in 'bad guy real estate'?"

"Nobody home, far as I know," he shrugged and half-grinned. "But you won't be there long. Just land, let out our little friend and take off. You'll be back here in twenty minutes."

"Or twenty years if there's a reception committee."

"I wouldn't send you if I thought it was impossible, you know."

"Yeah, I know that. But I can't help thinking how I felt when I flew past those so-called abandoned airstrips in Kratie and Stung Treng. The hair on my neck stood straight out I was being watched so hard."

"You do need a haircut," Bridgewater said, leaning sideways to look behind Rusty's ear.

"Don't change the subject. When does this passenger need to be there?"

"No rush. An hour from now more or less is fine. He'll meet you on the ramp."

"Does he speak English?"

"Yup. He should. You don't need to ask him any questions, though. Copy?"

"Ahh. I see. Yeah, I do. Okey doke. One anonymous warm body to scenic downtown Duc Lap. I'm on my way."

Rusty got to the ramp after pulling out his maps and checking the place. One runway, supposedly paved but abandoned. No facilities, naturally. Fifteen hundred feet long, which was enough, but it left no cushion in case one end of it was bad.

Corso was there to act as crew chief, and a middle-aged Vietnamese stood against the revetment wall waiting. He looked deferentially down, revealing a thinning head of oily black hair, a face marked with early wrinkles and ancient pox scars, wearing clean but worn black pants and a white short-sleeved shirt. Anonymous is right, Rusty thought. Damn near invisible he was so unremarkable. When he looked up and smiled briefly, he revealed a picket fence of brown, decayed teeth in a non-threatening face.

"Andy, after I get around the bird and strap in, would you help my passenger here climb in? He may need help with the straps and headset."

"Sure thing, sir. Where you two headed?"

"Oh, it's just a taxi ride for him. I'll be back before the linguini is al dente."

"Oh, you hurt me when you talk like that, sir. Jesus, I miss real pasta. The Boyardee shit in the chow hall is enough to make a maggot gag."

"Me too, brother, me too. Anyway, see ya soon."

Corso got the man in after Rusty, fastened his lap and shoulder belts, then got his headset on and plugged in. Rusty wondered what to call him, then gave up the idea of using any name at all. When the battery was on he asked, "Can you hear me alright?"

The man turned to Rusty with a broad smile and bowed his head rapidly several times.

"Have you ever flown before?"

More silent smiles and polite nodding. Rusty began to suspect his English wasn't as good as Bridgewater had implied.

"And your name is Mister Yrious?" Nods and smiles.

"You like hypersonic weasel clamps for breakfast?" Enthusiastic nods and smiles. Well, that settled that.

The smile disappeared abruptly when they broke ground, and Rusty saw the man's fingers tighten to whiteness on his own thighs, his pointed, lacquered nails almost punching through his pants legs. Just keep those hooks to yourself my man, and we'll be fine, Rusty thought. Rusty reached behind the seat and found a sick sack, tucking it under his own leg just in case.

It was a beautiful day with not a hint of bumpiness, and they headed southwest. The man gradually began to relax, and even look outside. He turned and smiled again, but weakly. Rusty hoped he felt a whole lot better before they had to land.

Duc Lap was easy to find. Rusty simply followed a paved highway from Ban Me Thuot right to the place. Why in hell couldn't they have driven the booger down here in a jeep, he wondered? Oh well, he was Rusty's bag of rice now.

The runway was asphalt, Rusty saw as he circled down from overhead, but cracked and broken. There was a wide pink-brown line of dust diagonally across it, too: a well-used path of some kind. Rusty turned to the man, "I hate to do this to your tummy, but I'm going to have to do a low pass along the runway to check it out and maybe scare off any animals," or worse, he thought to himself. One nod and a weak smile was the reply. Was his yellowish-brown skin turning the least bit green? God, Rusty hoped not.

Rusty let down and made a low pass at a slower airspeed than he would have liked, scanning carefully. He saw no rocks or potholes he couldn't avoid. No large animals, either. But he also saw not a hint of a welcome party for his passenger. Not a car or even a cart awaited him. Oh well, that wasn't Rusty's worry.

Rusty climbed up to a sort of downwind leg, dropped gear and flaps and slid around onto final. He cast worried glances at that now-plainly green face, afraid he'd see the first convulsive heave any second. But nothing happened, and they touched down perfectly. Rusty turned around, taxied rapidly back to the approach end, and stopped, keenly aware of that being-watched feeling again. With no further ado, he popped the man's harness, lifted his headset off and reached past him to open the door. Rusty had to shove it out hard against the blast of the front engine prop, which he had no intention of shutting off, and nudged the man's left knee with his left hand.

"Thanks for flying Teeny Weeny Airlines," Rusty shouted. 'Mister Yrious' smiled broader now, nodded once again and hopped out. Rusty had a momentary panicky thought of him running straight into one of the invisibly-whirling propellers, but he walked straight away from the plane towards the tall grass. Rusty saw nobody there at all, but wasted no time trying to, either. He slammed the door and goosed the engines to turn around. As soon as the now-empty shoulder harness straps in the right seat were fastened, he shoved the power in for takeoff.

Rusty couldn't shake that neck hair feeling, but he was busy dancing on the rudders in order to miss holes and loose chucks of asphalt. Nearing the end of the pavement, he pulled the plane off the ground and let it skim along gathering speed. From there on, Rusty's neck hairs relaxed a bit with every foot of altitude gained. By the time he got the gear up and turned back, there was no sign whatever of Mister Yrious. Spooky in more ways than one, Rusty thought.

"You really were quick," Corso said after he'd shut down in the chocks.

"Such is my wife's constant complaint," Rusty joked.

"Ha ha, oh that's good," Corso laughed.

"That's what I always say to her."

Corso laughed even harder. "I wish we had some of that linguini right now. I'd love to share some with you, sir."

"You prefer the marinara, carbonara or maybe a simple clam with garlic and butter sauce?"

"Oh God. The clam with garlic, every time. With butter and olive oil, and just a pinch of fresh parsley. Jesus."

"Me, too, Andy. Just exactly like that. And a Romaine salad with pan-browned croutons and crumbled Asiago cheese, balsamic vinegar and olive oil dressing, a glass of table wine and a chunk of crusty bread. Heaven, isn't it?"

"Almost, but you quit too soon. A canolli for dessert?"

"Not for me. I'm not a sweet tooth guy. Give me another glass of wine with a ripe peach sliced into it, and maybe a *biscotti de regina.*"

Corso shook his head ruefully. "We could be brothers, you know?"

"No, not me. I'm adopted - by my wife. I'm Slavic. My wife's the Italian, but she's also a teacher, and I learned the food part of her life quick."

"Man, you sure did. I'd have thought you were born to it. What do Slavs eat?"

"Unfortunately, not much, if you read the history of the last half-century. But they're famous for their baked goods. Pastries and cakes and such. I don't know many of the right names for them, but my mother delighted in baking. She'd make four or five dozen chocolate cream-puffs at a time. I damn near exploded eating them. Man."

"That's not a sweet tooth guy? Right."

"Maybe that's what burned me out on sweets. But I just don't crave 'em any more except for an occasional Snickers bar. Those I do like."

Corso nodded wistfully for the unobtainable treats.

"Well, I have to go debrief with the major, so I'd better be truckin'. I'll see ya later."

As he turned away, Rusty remembered the line he'd used on Captain Blake back at Emerald. "Hey, Andy, you know why Slavs are so unpopular?"

"No, why?"

"Because no matter where they go, they're out-of-town Czechs." Rusty walked away, leaving Corso laughing hysterically.

Back in the TOC, Bridgewater asked, "How'd it go?"

"One more mission, one more combat hour, three percent of an Air Medal," Rusty shrugged. "There didn't seem to be anybody there to meet him, and he just disappeared into the grass. I saw him walking away from the plane, and when I looked again he was just gone."

"How was the field?"

"Oh, pretty badly cracked, and there's a well-used footpath across the middle, but no serious obstacles or potholes. No water buffaloes dozing on it, at least."

"If we had to send somebody else there, would you say it's safe?"

"Well, the runway is usable, if that's what you mean. But it's not secure by any means. The tall grass around it could hide anything, and if I were the VC, I'd have it pre-sighted for mortar fire. You wouldn't operate there for long before you got a nasty reception. But for a rare one-time landing like mine? Yeah, it's probably less risky than landing here at night."

"Okay. That's what I wanted to hear. I don't have anything planned, I just like to have something in my back pocket. Any other observations?"

"Nope. Well, just that your friend doesn't understand much English if any, and he'd never been off the ground before. The parts of him that weren't clenched white were a pale green."

"He blow lunch?"

"No, but it was a short flight. He was fine in level flight, but when I swooped down and did a low pass to check out the runway, I thought he was gonna climb right out through the upper window. I think he was too paralyzed to puke."

"Hmmm. Okay. That doesn't square with what I'd heard, but I believe you. How do you know he didn't speak English?"

"Well, he'd just nod and smile whatever I said. I know that's pretty standard, but he did it even when I spoke utter nonsense words. Not a sign of confusion on his face."

"We ought to make you an interrogator. What'd you say that was nonsense?"

"Oh, I don't know. I think I asked him if he liked supersonic weasel clamps for breakfast or something. He nodded and smiled even more."

"Uh huh. I think I'd agree with you. Well, okay. Enough of that. I have good news and bad news for all of us."

"Oh, groan. Now what?"

"Well, the good news is that I managed to get a whole ton of prime steaks delivered here," Bridgewater said without a hint of a smile.

"And the bad?"

"The chow hall freezer went tits up this morning. We have to eat steak twice a day before it spoils."

"How is that bad news?" I asked.

"It came up on a truck, and it took two days."

"Let me guess: it wasn't a refrigerated truck, was it?"

"Uh, no. Some of it's already a bit off. We'll be eating the ones that are farthest gone. At least until the vet says to stop."

"What do you mean by the vet?" Rusty was really confused now.

"Didn't you know the Army has a veterinarian assigned to most field units?"

"No. What the hell for?"

"In Army logic – probably since the Cavalry days – they assume that the person best qualified to judge animal flesh would be a vet. So that's who inspects and approves Army chow."

Rusty shook his head. In a very weird kind of way, it almost did make sense. Well, Army sense, he amended - if you were eating horses.

"Tell all the guys to enjoy their steak lunch, will you? Tell 'em to have seconds. Thirds, even."

"Oh, sure. Should I give them the bad news half of that, too?"

"They'll learn it soon enough, anyway. Go ahead. What a day for our new crew chief to show up."

"New crew chief? What new crew chief?" Rusty asked, stopping halfway to the door.

"Guy named Dick Schields. Tech Sergeant. He got in a few minutes ago and he's unpacking now. Might as well get Cramer's room if he's filling his shoes, huh?"

"Yeah, that makes sense. You don't do that with us pilots, though, do you?"

"No. I told Sanderson to rotate people around. I don't want a guy to be the mentor for his own roommate. So he pairs guys and rooms separately. Like when Derlin was your mentor, and you were Craig's, and Kit taught Getz. I don't even like roomies to fly missions together."

"Why?"

"Oh, call it a superstitious eccentricity. I just believe it's better that way," this time Bridgewater shrugged. He turned away and Rusty left.

When he got to the hootch, Rusty yelled, "Hey everybody! Steaks for lunch! Steak for everybody! Belly up."

Heads popped out of doors, including one Rusty didn't know. He wore tech sergeant's stripes on his regular green fatigues. He had brown hair a bit long for regulations, a Roman nose and bright friendly brown eyes. A cigarette dangled from the corner of his upturned lips. Tanned skin and a chiseled jaw completed the package. He looked almost like he had just stepped off a movie set. Any Doughnut Dollie would love him.

A small crowd walked to the chow hall, the conversation split about equally between the steaks awaiting them and introductions all round.

"I sure hope there's enough left over for Kit and Danny," Getz said as they walked. "And Flip, too." Flip was on the midday cap flight.

"Oh, I think you can count on that," Rusty said. And then he told them what Bridgewater had said.

"You mean we'll be eating steak every day, but they'll be rotten?" Buchenhardt asked.

"Not rotten, Jack. Just a bit well aged, let's say. Hey, it's steak. When was the last beef steak you've had? Look at the bright side."

"Fuck your bright side, Naille. We get steak here pretty often."

"That's water buffalo, Jack. Not beef. And the soup is monkey. Surely you know that, don't you? You've been here for months." Rusty saw the blank look on his face. Blank turning to red. He stopped in his tracks and the group did, too.

"*WHAT!* You can eat shit for all I care, but I'm not eating any fucking monkey or buffalo. Unless you're just picking my ass with your stupid humor. In which case, I've had enough of it."

"Look, Buchenhardt, I'm not picking your ass, and it isn't me that's feeding you. We all eat buffalo and monkey here because that's what they serve. Hell, we've even joked about it. If you weren't so stuck up that you have to eat by yourself, you'd have heard. If you refuse to eat it, that's fine. There's plenty of nuoc mam and rice. Or you can wait for a care package or just starve. I don't care one bit what you do, and that is no joke."

Buchenhardt turned and stormed off towards the TOC.

Sandy said to Schields, "I'm sorry about that, Dick. Buchenhardt is just kinda…well, proud of himself. He has a hair trigger. I hope you don't get a bad first impression of this place."

"Oh, I've been around officers and other superior beings before," Schields said with a twinkle in his eye. "Buffalo? And monkey? You're shitting me."

"Nope," Hannah piped up. "But it's not bad. Just don't eat the lettuce or the shit part will be all too real."

The two sergeants talked together as they walked. Sandy turned to Rusty, "Did nobody ever tell Jack about the meat? Really? They told me right away. I thought everybody knew."

"Me, too. Sanderson was his mentor. I wonder if he forgot to mention it," or maybe he just chose not to, Rusty realized. Maybe he thought it'd be better that way, or maybe he'd gotten as sick of Buchenhardt's haughty demeanor as they had. Ol' Dave was a deeper puddle of water than he seemed, Rusty had learned long ago. "Of course, who talks to Buchenhardt for long about anything?"

"There is that," Sandy chuckled. "He doesn't talk about much unless he's the subject. Oh, you can *listen* to Jack all you like. But talk? Nah."

Despite their fears, the steaks were pretty good, discounting the chow hall cook's way of leaving them on the grill until they turned to leather. Almost everybody had two of them. Schields asked questions about the little people in the chow hall, and they whispered what they could. It soon became obvious that enlisted guys like Schields didn't get the full SOG briefing.

Well, they probably didn't need to, Rusty thought, but it seemed both silly and counterproductive to try to keep them in the dark about the mission. They did see the pilots launch with little guys strapped in, and they did work to carefully sanitize the planes by stripping off all the USAF and national emblems. They weren't stupid, and they certainly figured out every detail of what was going on. The radio operators certainly had to know. They kept position reports on the map of Cambodia, and they certainly passed that along to their fellow enlisteds. It was just another example of how stupid any bureaucracy can become.

Sandy filled a canteen with bug juice for the late afternoon cap, and they all walked back to their hootches. Schields lit up another cigarette as soon as he stepped out of the building and said he wanted to check out the maintenance shed and the spare parts bins. "Gotta let the other guys get some steak, too. I'll hold down the fort while they go to chow."

Rusty nodded appreciatively. The guy was already thinking about his job and his crew: a good sign. He'd fit in very well, indeed.

A little while later, Rusty was sitting in the courtyard reading.

"Hey Rusty, come quick! You gotta see this." It was Getz, shouting from around the edge of the long pilot's hootch.

Rusty jumped up and sprinted to the flight line after him. He saw a crowd of guys clustered in front of an O-2 in the middle of the ramp. When he got closer, Rusty saw that the whole lower half of the front engine compartment - from just below the propeller to the nose gear – was missing. Fibers from torn fiberglass and bent sheet metal edges framed the exposed engine bottom. Flip stood there, staring at it ashen-faced.

Rusty overheard Schields say, "Is this how you guys welcome all your new crew chiefs?" He laughed, and then asked, "How did it happen, sir?"

"Uh, I don't know. I didn't even know it was missing until I pulled up to the gate to be disarmed. Fleming here got real bug-eyed when he saw it."

Schields bent down and looked closer. "Weird, just plain weird. It looks like something whacked the cowl pretty good, but there's no stains from a tree, no sign of enemy fire and absolutely no damage to the propeller. Not even any blood or feathers. I can't figure out what happened."

Bridgewater and Sanderson pulled up in a jeep and repeated all the same questions. Flip still proclaimed ignorance and innocence, but neither man looked as though they believed him completely. They asked Schields and Lopez what they thought. Both said it was a mystery to them.

"Can you fix it here at BMT?" Bridgewater asked Schields.

"I think so. That's just a first look, mind. But if Lopez can give the prop and engine a pass, it looks like just some simple sheet metal work and a new lower cowl half. Just a bolt-on. But for the life of me..." Schields shook his head in wonderment.

It was two weeks later when they learned the truth.

Flip called them all into the big room, including Bridgewater and Sanderson. "Time to fess up," he said turning red-faced. "Watch."

He turned on a tiny 8mm movie projector. Projected on the wall, they saw a view out the front of an O-2. In silence, blue sky disappeared as green jungle slid into view and then a broad brown river appeared from the left. The O-2 leveled out just a few feet over the river. Black boulders surrounded by caramel waves flashed beneath. A gray-white trail of rocket smoke flashed out and smacked into the far bank in a silent blossom of white marking smoke. Then another rocket whooshed out, but instead of flying straight off into the jungle, it lurched into a wild corkscrew spiral, impacting the river just yards in front of the nose. Instantly, a huge geyser of white water fountained upwards, looking just like one of those WWII depth charge explosions...right in front of the plane. The film view went instantly and completely white.

"So that's why there were no green stains and no damage to the prop!" Sanderson said, slapping his leg. "You hit that water column!"

"Ah bet there was a stain alright, but in yore drawers," Bridgewater drawled.

"I'll say," Flip admitted. "I did just about crap my pants. It felt like I hit a wall. I jerked back on the yoke, scared to death I'd pitch right into the damn river. But somehow, it kept flying and I came straight home. I really didn't know that I'd lost the cowl until Fleming saw it. Musta lost a fin on the rocket or something."

"And your reason for being that low over the river? More to the point, the reason for the movie camera?" Sanderson asked pointedly.

"Oh. Well, there's no point in denying it. I was just goofing around and trying to get some interesting film to take home with me. I taped the camera to the gun sight and just turned it on."

"So whah're ya showin' it ta us?" Bridgewater had that twinkle in his eye and that half-smile on.

"Shit, sir, it came out way too cool to keep it a secret from you guys!"

CHAPTER FIFTEEN

R usty jerked bolt upright to a tremendous explosion. Getz flew out of his bunk from above, and his bare feet splatted on the floor. Rain was roaring down and the echoes of the tremendous thunder blast rolled away through the skies.

"Jesus Christ! What a way to wake up. Wonder where that hit?" Rusty said, rubbing his eyes as his heart hammered.

"As long as it missed me, I guess I'm happy, but it was damn close. Inside the compound, anyway. Let's go find out," Jim said, peering out the window.

"If you're afraid of lightning, better stay away from me, bub. Remind me to tell you how many times I've been hit sometime. You really want to go out in this? You'd drown before you got twenty feet."

Getz looked at Rusty suspiciously, the lightning remark sinking in. Then he looked out at the water cascading off the roof in a solid, curving sheet. "Uh…maybe we can wait until it tapers off a might. Not too long, though. I have to whiz."

"Me too. Sometimes a big lightning blast like that is the beginning of the end and the storm stops real soon after that. I hope so."

They stood there looking out the head-high window at the just-barely-dawn charcoal sky. The torrent continued unabated for minute after minute.

"Crap, it's raining even harder now," Rusty said, shifting from foot to foot with the urgency of his bladder. "Probably wouldn't hurt if we just stood in the door and peed. What difference would it make?"

"Amen to that. Ah, screw it." Getz took three steps to the door, pulled it open a few inches and stood there, feet spread, his belly pressed against the opening. "Ahhh."

Between his legs, Rusty saw a dark shadow pass from left to right. "Jim, did somebody just walk past the door? Did you just piss on somebody?"

"Huh? I don't know. I had my eyes closed in blessed relief. Did somebody walk by for real?"

"That's what I asked you. I saw a shadow go past, but you're blocking the view. Peek out and see."

"I can't just yet. Wait. Arrrgh, gotta waggle the lizard." He jiggled a little, then poked his head out. "Oh shit, that's Sanderson going into the shitter. I must've pissed on him when he walked past. Had to have. Do you think he didn't even notice?"

"Too late to worry about that now. But if you don't say anything, I won't."

"Deal. What are you doing?"

"I'm getting dressed so I can go pee in the shitter," Rusty said, pulling on pants and boots before tugging a poncho over his head. "Be back in a bit. You going for breakfast?"

"Green steak and powdered eggs? I think not. I'll just brew up a cup of coffee here." He'd brought an immersion heater, a coil of heavy wire that he'd plug in and stick into a cup of water. It would boil in a few minutes and he'd stir in powdered coffee.

"How can you drink that godawful stuff?" Rusty had tried a sip of it once at Jim's invitation. "It's worse than the crap they put into combat rations. I'd rather walk through lightning, hail and plummeting pitchforks than drink that."

"I hope so, because you have two out of three right now." Getz gestured with his head toward the door. Marble-sized balls of ice were splatting into the mud or bouncing with a crack off of anything hard.

"I can't wait. I'm gonna make a dash for the shitter." Rusty hugged the wall of the hootch, amazed at the solid sheet of shining water pouring off the edge of the tin roof in an arch that took it just over the lips of the dirt-filled blast barrels. He turned and yelled back to Getz, who came from southern California, "Hey Jim, look! I'm ironing the curl!" Rusty struck a pose like a rubber-draped surfer.

"That's shooting the curl, you flatlander."

Next door, Flip pulled open his door. "What's all the ruckus?"

"Oh, did I wake you up, Flip? Sorry."

"After that thunder? No way. Where you going, to the john?"

"Yup, nature calls."

"Nature goddamn near bellowed. Wonder where the lightning hit?"

"So did we. Had to be inside the wire somewhere. Maybe it hit the wire. That'd be no surprise."

"Hmmm. No, it wouldn't. I guess I'll join you." He stepped out in his underwear and flip flops.

"You going to put something on first?"

"Why? I wouldn't stay any drier and whatever I wore would be wet, too. I'm not gonna melt."

"Well, I can't wait either way. I'm about to bust. Dam," Rusty chortled at his own pun. He and Flip took off at a near-run, turning at the end of the blast barrels and then dashing the last few yards through the deluge to the door. Inside, Rusty heard a stall flush. Sanderson came out as the two stood at the piss trough.

"Hey boss, what the heck got hit?" Flip said.

Sanderson looked at Flip's streaming near-nakedness but ignored the sight. "The big tree outside the TOC. Split the north half of it clean off. It must've hit one of the antennas too, because the backup UHF radio is fried. It smells like the second parking garage of hell in there with all that awful electrical smoke and stuff. Young just about shit. He said the earphones flew off his head like they'd been snatched. He's not hurt, though."

"Cripes," Flip said. "There was a fire?"

"Just briefly. Young got it with the extinguisher. There's carbon tet everywhere – he sprayed everything. We've got all the radios down until we can dry 'em, check the wiring and power 'em back up one at a time. The SF guys are monitoring our freqs with their radios until we're back up."

"How do you know all this already? It hit just a few minutes ago," Rusty asked, amazed.

Sanderson smiled. "I was already up and reworking the schedule...it's obviously a weather day. When it hit, I looked out and saw the tree down. Just then, Young threw open the radio room door and smoke came out. I deedeemau-ed over there really ricky-tick, but it was all over except the shouting." He grinned broadly, "Then I came here, but don't you go saying I had the crap scared out of me."

They both smiled back. "And after the crap there's the paperwork, right?"

"Always," Sanderson laughed. "Just to clean everything up."

As Sanderson left, Rusty stole a look down at his legs But Sanderson was soaked to the skin and Rusty couldn't tell anything.

"What are you looking at?" Flip whispered as Sanderson went through the door.

"Oh, nothing. Never mind. Just something Getz wanted to know."

Flip looked at him dubiously, his brows knitted. "Ooookay."

The thunderstorm passed soon after, and within minutes practically the whole camp was standing in the roadway looking at the remains of what had been the only big tree in the compound. Once shaped like a giant slingshot, the north arm was now ripped off right at the fork, leaving a huge gaping wound in the wood. Vietnamese team members stood pointing at it, gabbling and laughing nervously, while small groups of Montagnards stood and looked silently. Every few seconds, one of the Vietnamese would dash forward and touch one of the small limbs, then jerk his hand back and run back to his small group laughing.

"What's that all about?" Schields asked.

"Beats me," Kit said. "Maybe they think it's still electrified and they're daring each other to go find out."

"Yeah, that's exactly what it looks like. But how come those other guys aren't acting like that at all?"

"Ah, those are Montagnards," Kit explained. "They probably know better. They've seen the results of lightning a lot more often, I'd bet. They're just smarter about some things than the Vietnamese."

"Does it work both ways?" Schields asked, intelligently.

"I'd bet on it. I can't come up with an example, but I bet it would if you plunked both groups down in Saigon."

"The 'yards would probably stand there gaping at the buildings and get run over by a bus," Rusty suggested.

"Yeah, that's a good one. I can almost see that happening."

"Me too," said Schields. "They're not so different are they?"

"From us you mean? Well, except for the holding hands thing, no. And the beef. You notice how empty the chow hall is lately?"

"Now that you mention it, yeah," I said. "You think they don't like the smell of the beef?"

"No more than you'd enjoy chowing down in one of their fish markets," Kit said.

Rusty thought back to the times he'd been to the market in Ban Me Thuot. The place reeked of rotting fish and worse. He almost gagged just from the remembered smell. He couldn't imagine eating anything there and keeping it down. "That's a point, Kit. The smell of that beef is getting to me, even. It's going downhill fast. Hey, do you know that an Army veterinarian is the one who passes on all chow?"

"Yeah, I forget where I heard that, but I did know. I didn't know we had one here, though."

"We must have. Bridgewater told me one would stop them from serving the steaks when they got too ripe."

"Then there's no vet here, 'cause I think it's about three days too late," Schields said. "I can't face it any more."

"Yeah, it's already to the point where not even those yellow peppers can drown out the taste. I'll be happy to get back to some fresh water buffalo or monkey or rat or whatever," Rusty said. "And I never in all my days thought I'd ever hear myself say *that*!"

Bridgewater came up behind them, "Boys, we're dead in the water."

Rusty looked at him expecting a pun or joke of some kind.

"The radio room is toast. Every time we turn the breakers back on, they blow again. The wiring, we think. It'll take a couple of days to get it back up because we have to get a civil engineer in from somewhere and rewire the whole place. I'm going to send Flip out to pick up his team if the clouds break a little. I've already called around on landline and cancelled the Quan Loi ops. In the meantime, you're all on vacation."

"What's that?" Kit joked.

"What I'm about to offer is what," Bridgewater said. "There's a black C-130 on the ramp at the terminal. Just landed. It's a 'company' bird." He paused to see if that registered with them. It did. "And they're going to Taipei for three days. They'll take one guy along. Now before you all go volunteering, here are my thoughts: Kit, you're too short. You'll be home in a few weeks. Flip has to pick up that team he's running. Sandy and Rusty are next in seniority around here. Rusty, do you want the trip?"

"Me? What about Sandy?"

"I'm asking you right now. Yes or no?"

"Uh, yeah, I'd like to, I think. But only if Sandy says no."

"He already did. Beats me why, but he did. All right, go pack a bag. Take all civvies except for the fatigues you're wearing now. Take your time, but if you're not on that bird in ten minutes, they're leaving anyway. Scoot!"

Rusty did. He ran back, grabbed a bag and threw in civvies, shoes and underwear for three days, tossed in his shaving kit and a towel, then rushed out to the jeep. Bridgewater drove him to the terminal, spinning the tires and throwing red mud everywhere.

As they slid to a stop, he said, "You fixed for cash?"

"Oh my god." Rusty fished out his wallet. "No, I only have thirty bucks!"

Bridgewater flashed out his own. "Here, I only have twenty myself. Maybe you can cash a check somewhere. Go! They're waving at you from the ramp."

Rusty ran, jamming the scrip into his pocket as he went. The prop blast of the plane's engines almost knocked him over as he ran to the rear ramp and scrambled up. A loadmaster in jeans and yellow golf shirt pointed to the fold-down strap seat along one wall and took Rusty's bag. By the time he had his seat belt snapped, the loadmaster had closed the ramp and plunged the plane's interior into almost complete blackness. Only a sparse row of tiny bulbs burned up along the ceiling Rusty could make out a row of dim figures seated in the seats opposite him, but they were only shapes. He looked over his shoulder as the engines roared even louder, and discovered that the round porthole window behind him had been painted over. In fact, they all seemed to be.

The plane slewed around a few turns, then the engines roared and they were soon airborne. Rusty could feel them climbing but after that the turbulence was such that he couldn't tell anything else and he couldn't see outside at all. Suddenly the lights came on brightly, and Rusty's eyes bugged out in surprise. Seated across from him were ten North Vietnamese soldiers in full battle gear and loaded AK-47 rifles. He must have stared, because they looked back at him stonily until he tore his eyes away and looked pointedly at his own lap. What the hell had he gotten himself into now, he wondered.

A few minutes later, Rusty heard the landing gear go down, felt the flaps follow, and moments later they banged down hard. The props screamed in full reverse thrust and the brakes squealed in protest. Rusty had to brace his left arm to keep from slamming sideways, but it was over in a few seconds. The loadmaster ran back down the cargo bay and lowered the ramp. As Rusty strained to see what was outside or where he might be, the ten NVA stood up and jogged down the ramp and out. The ramp closed, the loadmaster went back up to the flight deck, and Rusty was completely alone.

They were airborne again when another figure backed down the ladder from the flight deck. This man was burly but powerful. He was dressed in combat boots, very old and tattered green fatigue pants cut off into shorts and a positively glowing red and green Hawaiian shirt that would have made even Getz gag. At the bottom of the ladder he turned to face Rusty. He was Chinese, and he was wearing a .45 automatic in a shoulder holster.

He strode up to Rusty, his face split into a smile so wide his slanted eyes all but disappeared. He shouted over the engine roar, "You wanna go Taipei, eh?"

"Uh, yeah. I guess," Rusty stammered.

"Okay! Good deal. We go."

"Now? Direct?"

"Oh, no. No, no, no," The Chinese laughed as if it were the funniest joke ever told. "First go Saigon. Safe house. Change all new. You go Taipei tomorrow."

Safe house? Change all new? What the hell does that mean? But before he could ask, the man had turned to go forward again. "Wait!" Rusty yelled. "Who are you?"

He grinned back and turned his hands as though driving. The pilot. Oh, Christ.

Rusty contemplated his own stupidity for what seemed like an hour, and then came the changes that signaled another landing. This one was much gentler and smoother, and Rusty mentally complimented the burly Chinese guy – if it had been him doing the flying. They taxied for a long time, and the sticky heat in the back rose steadily as they did. Eventually, the engines shut down with a pop and a rapidly descending whine. Rusty's ears rang in the aftermath of the deafening noise, and nothing happened for several minutes. He was drenched with sweat when the Chinese pilot, the Caucasian loadmaster and another man who looked to be vaguely Middle Eastern came down the ladder and walked aft. The ramp dropped and Rusty saw a bus parked right at its foot. The bus too was painted all black – even the windows. Heavy wire mesh had been welded over the windows, like a prison bus.

The four of them carried their own bags onto the bus. Rusty was able to look out the windshield, and this was clearly a huge airbase. If this was indeed Saigon, it had to be Ton San Nhut. He said as much to the loadmaster, seated just in front of me.

"Sure," he said, and looked at Rusty as though the latter might be mentally defective.

They went through a gate and clearly were off the base.

The windows had been painted over, but the paint was scratched enough that Rusty could see a sliver of what they passed. By dividing his attention out the front and through his scratched window, he saw that they wound their way through several bustling main streets, then into slightly quieter streets and finally into a tree-lined lane that seemed almost serene. Out the front, Rusty could see a massive iron gate that opened as they eased through. The bus engine stopped and Rusty could hear the gate creaking together and banging closed behind. When he stepped down, he stared up at a somewhat rundown but still elegant villa, three stories tall and surrounded by a solid whitewashed stone wall almost as high as the villa.

The villa itself was also whitewashed stone with red clay tiles on the roof and a prominent portico. Rusty could hear the voices of many children playing outside the wall. A school? But the only people in sight were themselves and a man attending or guarding the front door. The flight crew walked in with no ceremony, the pilots going up one stairway and the bus driver and loadmaster headed down another off the other side of a small lobby. Rusty stood there flummoxed. The guard's voice behind him said, "Go on up and find yourself a room for the night. Any will do. There's a common shower and bathroom on each floor. The bar's downstairs."

"Uh, okay. Thanks." Rusty wandered up the stairs to the next floor. There were six doors along each side. All but two were locked, and those two had bags on the single beds within. Rusty climbed again. Here, he found a tiny vacant room from among four and the bath. He dropped his bag, went down to the bath and washed his face. Still somewhat stunned and disoriented by the whirl of strange happenings, he wandered back to his room and pulled aside the drapes that covered the tiny window. From here, he could see the top of the surrounding wall: recently installed razor wire had been strung above hundreds of broken bottles embedded in the cement. Somebody wanted to keep everybody else out.

Across the wall he saw the source of all the young gaiety. The next walled villa appeared to be a boarding school of some kind. Vietnamese children in clean white dresses or white shirts and dark trousers played in complete mirth. As he watched, a bell chimed and they all trooped solemnly inside. Recess? Rusty's mind reeled with nostalgia. Rusty dropped the drapes when the last young girl skipped inside, her satin-black hair swaying in the sun.

Rusty went down to the lobby and found the stairs to the basement. He followed his ears to the bar. It was a small but comfy little nook, lined with dark wood paneling, the chairs padded with green leather and brass tacks, an oak bar backed with softly lit glass shelves and dozens of liquor bottles. On the main wall was a Communist rocket-propelled grenade launcher, obviously a war trophy; it had been buffed and cleaned into a kind of sinister sculpture. He was bending to read the tiny engraved plaque when the bartender said, "Your pleasure, sir?"

Rusty read something about Dien Bien Phu, but turned away and said, "A martini if you have the makin's. It's been a long time between good ones." The man smiled and bowed his head slightly at the implied compliment, and Rusty was rewarded with what had to be a triple: ice cold, perfectly dry and – glory of glories! – adorned with a huge stuffed olive. He sipped. "Oh yeah. Oh, Lord yeah."

Rusty fished out a dollar and laid it on the bar. "Oh, we don't take scrip here," The bartender said, and Rusty almost jumped in surprise. "You can change it, though. Two doors down on the left. And you really ought to change clothes, too. Civvies."

"Oh. Oh sure. You want me to leave the drink here?"

"Nah, you'll come back. You'd have to. Ain't nowhere else to go," he smiled at his own joke.

On the way back up the stairs, Rusty recalled that massive gate and those walls. The man was right: he wasn't going anywhere.

Rusty changed and then made his way back down. He went straight to the room the bartender had mentioned. Inside was a red-faced, balding man whose demeanor spelled out his job as clearly as a placard: a pay sergeant. A very senior one, and maybe not even a military one, but he was a pay sergeant nonetheless.

"You the guest going along to Taipei?"

"Yes." Rusty almost added 'sergeant' but bit it back.

"How much you want to change," the clerk said as he brought a steel money box up from a drawer of the desk.

"Uh, fifty."

"Not just for tonight, mister. Total. For the trip."

"Well, fifty dollars is all I have with me."

"Fifty dollars? That's all? You're going to Taipei with only fifty bucks total on you?" He rocked back and stared as if Rusty had just scuttled out of a flying saucer with eight legs and sixteen eyes.

In the stunned silence, Rusty felt compelled to say, "I only had five minutes warning. It's all I could get my hands on. Maybe I could write a check?" At that moment, Rusty remembered: he hadn't brought a checkbook, either. Oh shit, he said to himself, maybe he'd better forget the whole, thing and see if they'd just take him back to Ban Me Thuot.

"No. No checks. Fifty dollars," the man said in a hoarsely whispered monotone. He continued to stare while his hands counted money autonomously. Four tens and two fives in US dollars lay fanned out on the table. Rusty opened his wallet and pulled out the bills of multi-colored military scrip.

He methodically counted them onto the table. "And thirty-five cents."

The genuine US currency looked funny after all this time. Rusty loved the feel of it between his fingers. But he stuffed it into his wallet in embarrassment, then scooped up the quarter and the dime as well.

Rusty nursed the martini in the bar until a gong rang for supper. He was immensely relieved to learn that there was no charge for the food, but he was equally dismayed when he found he simply couldn't eat it. It was steak, and the mere smell of it gave his stomach a small heave. Rusty left the room, and the six or seven others there inclined their heads towards him and whispered behind their hands. I must really be an odd duck, Rusty thought. They'll talk for weeks about that dumb dork who wanted to go to Taipei with only fifty bucks in his pocket. The one who wouldn't eat prime, aged steak.

He slept fitfully, partly because he was hungry but also because he felt so inadequate, so…he couldn't think of the word for it. Typical, Rusty thought: can't even do that right.

In the pink-gray of dawn Rusty stumbled out and showered, dressed and went down for coffee. He hadn't made it to the second floor when the wonderful odors of real bacon, fresh coffee and real eggs reached his nose. Rusty practically ran down the steps and into the dining room he'd slunk out of the evening before. He tore into a heaping platter of that manna, to the astonished stares (again) of the others. He stuffed himself and was having a third cup of that delicious black brew when a tall black man walked up and said. "Time to get on the bus. Have you gotten your ID yet?"

"My ID? Yeah, it's right here, why?"

"No, your new ID. Your alias?"

"My what?"

"This is your first time at this, isn't it? Well, come with me. You can't go under your own name, you see. We'll hold your ID card here and give you another."

He led the way into another first-floor room, an office. The man slid behind the desk. "Where are you from originally?"

"Illinois."

"Okay, let's see…" He ruffled through a box of cards. "No, none of those. Kansas is close enough. Stand there." He pointed to a white cross on the floor near the wall. Rusty went over and stood on it. The man took Rusty's picture with a Polaroid camera, then sat down at a typewriter while the print cured. He looked at Rusty a bit slyly and smiled secretly to himself. "Grant. You are now…Ron Grant of Kansas City, Kansas. You got that?"

"Yeah, I guess." Rusty watched as the other man snipped out his picture, then laminated it onto a regular military ID card.

"You're assigned to MACV. You're a covan."

"A what?"

"An advisor. Pick a field you know a little about. Agriculture or construction or something." He handed Rusty the just-typed ID still warm from the laminator. "Just give this one back when you return. You'll be brought back here and then you'll catch a hop back to your base. They'll tell you all you need to know on the plane. Grab your bag and go now. You're almost late."

Five men were already on the bus, none of whom he'd seen last night. As they rode, Rusty was examining the fake ID and missed the view, but they wound up parked next to a black C-130. It seemed to be a different plane, but it was hard to tell. They all piled off, bags in hand and walked straight up the ramp.

This flight crew was composed of all US-looking men in casual civilian clothes. The loadmaster, a portly black man, balding and with two gold front teeth that flashed against his deep mahogany skin, bustled about tying down all their bags. He stopped in front of Rusty. "You de new one?"

"Yeah. Just along for the ride, I guess."

"Dat's what dey all say, suh!" He laughed and shook his head.

"No, really. I'm from up country. Yesterday my boss asked me if I wanted to spend three days in Taipei and I said yes. Here I am. And I'm pretty damned confused about it all, too."

The gold teeth disappeared as his laugh melted to a look of avuncular concern. "Ah kin see dat. Lemme git done here and ah'll sit down wit ya. Mebbe ah kin fill in some blanks."

After the plane started up and eventually taxied out, Rusty wondered if his Uncle Remos accent was real or just a put-on like Bridgewater's. Either way, it was a relief from the arrogant, perpetually pissed-off manner of most of the black soldiers he'd seen in Vietnam. Their intricate and artificial 'dapping' routines every time they met seemed to be deliberately designed to irritate anyone and everyone in authority. Some of the elaborate routines took so long that it became impossible to get anyone to move anywhere. Every two black soldiers who met went through their dap, tapping fists, slapping palms and carrying on. If any officer tried to interrupt, they bawled racial prejudice and harassment.

They got airborne and the other passengers stretched out on the strap seats to sleep. Rusty was about to join them when the loadmaster motioned for him to come up to the flight deck. Rusty climbed the ladder and automatically scanned the flight instruments as they came into view. Out the window, he could see nothing but sapphire water.

"Charley here says you're an FNG," said a voice from just behind him. Rusty turned and saw a man in his late forties with graying temples and a distinct paunch sitting at the navigator's console.

"Well, yes and no. I've been in-country for almost ten months total, but I'm sure new to this." Rusty waved his hand to indicate the plane and all it implied.

"What do you do?"

"Um," Rusty tried to remember his instructions. "I'm a covan. MACV advisor, and I..."

"No, no," the man waved a hand amiably. "We don't need your fake cover story. We all have those. No, your real self."

"Oh. Well, I'm a FAC. A Mike FAC at Ban Me Thuot. That's where I got picked up yesterday. For a quick few days off, they said. I'm not sure what I'm in for, quite frankly."

"Yeah, that's the rumor. Do you really have only fifty bucks on you?"

"Yeah, that's all. It's all I could grab up with five minutes notice. Am I in trouble?"

"Well, no. Not any legal trouble. But that's not gonna go far. Everything in Taipei is dirt cheap – I may even retire there – but I don't see how you could get by for less than about twenty bucks a day. Ten of that will be for your room. You won't be able to hire a bar girl at all unless you don't eat."

"What do you mean?"

"The bar girls? Didn't you know that prostitution is legal in Taipei?"

Rusty shook his head.

"Oh shit, that's the main reason most of these guys go there. Good clean healthy girls for fifteen bucks a day, all legal."

"Did you say fifteen dollars a *day*? Not a throw?"

"No, all day. For 24 hours. Hell, a good one will save you more than that in the shops. She'll do the bargaining for you, get everything delivered to your hotel or even shipped home. Argue on your behalf like a rabid raccoon. Not to mention the sex, which can be unbelievable. You can't afford not to hire one. Well," he stopped and reconsidered, "*you* can't afford *to* hire one, but for anybody with two shekels to rub together, they're a routine expense." He shrugged, a bit apologetic.

"I'm astounded. Completely. I mean I never would've dreamed of such a thing. What did you mean about buying stuff?"

"Oh Jesus, you really are green. Taiwan is the world headquarters of piracy. Not pirates as in 'Ho Ho Ho, me hearties,' but piracy as in copying stuff. Rip-offs. You can buy anything and everything there, all direct and damn near perfect copies of the real thing. Yamaha guitars, Rolex watches, hell even the Encyclopedia Britannica. Right down to the copyright marks," he chuckled. "And at a tenth the price. It's good stuff, too. I bought a fake Yamaha guitar there myself, and it's a honey. Why do you think we go there in a cargo plane?" He laughed so hard that his nose dripped.

"Why exactly do you go there?" Rusty asked.

Charley the loadmaster took over from the laughter-disabled navvie, "We go dere ta get dese planes overhauled. Dere's a contract maintenance depot dere and dey do de work cheap. We drop one off and pick up anudder one."

The Mike FAC Ubon scam done large, Rusty realized. Things never change. "Does the idea of flying with rip-off parts bother you any?"

Charley's gold grin disappeared and he looked around as if he expected to see smoke curling up all round, "Damn! You know, I nebber did tink of dat!" He relaxed after a few seconds. "No, dis one's fine. It ain't been dere yet. But you sho got me all goosy about dat one we gonna bring back! Lordy!"

"Sorry, Charley," Rusty said and immediately grimaced at the cliché. "Oops, I bet you've heard that a lot. One time too many, maybe."

"Dat I have. But I don' mind none. I'm almost famous wit dat." He smiled again, his dental carats flashing. "What else you need ta know?"

"I'll think of more later. I'm kinda stunned with what I've heard so far. Let me recover a bit." Rusty turned to the navvie again, "What's our ETA?"

"Three hundred knots, eighteen hundred miles," was his answer. "Thatta way," he stretched his arm straight out between the two pilots.

"Damn, I can see why they have you here," Rusty said shaking his head in mock amazement. "Why, we'd all be lost without you."

The co-pilot jiggled with laughter, "Yeah, and only one of us is lost when he is here!"

"Hey, I always know exactly where I am," the navvie answered. "Right here at this console."

When the laughing died out, the command pilot turned in his seat. "What you fly?"

"O-2," I said.

"Ruptured duck, huh? Not the B model, I hope."

"No, not a Bullshit Bomber. Regular old FAC."

"Not quite, if you were at BMT East. Or if you got invited here, for that matter. You're SOG, right?"

"Yeah. Just like you guys, I guess."

"Oh, we're pure Company. You'd never see old farts and reprobates like those two in SOG," he waved generally in the direction of Charley and the nav. "We're kinda the lower left-hand corner, behind the filing cabinet part of Air America, but without the fame and glory."

"Or the pay," the co-pilot added.

"Is that why their planes are mostly all silver and yours is..."

"Flat-ass black," he finished before Rusty could. "Yup. We have been known to fly at night. Occasionally." He smirked.

"Is that why the windows are painted over? So the cargo bay lights won't show?"

"Contrary to rumor, you are not altogether a sluggard in the thought department, are you?" The left-seater appraised Rusty closer. "You ever think of changing jobs?"

"It's been said there were no Slow Children signs in my neighborhood, but no to the question. I'm happy where I am."

The copilot nodded and held up his hand to change the topic.

"But I do have a question about painted windows."

"Shoot."

"Why the ones on the bus, and why also the grillwork over them?"

"Ah, well, mainly it's to keep from having the bus riders identified and associated with the planes. But the real benefit is that people outside won't know if the bus is empty or full."

"What does that matter?"

"Well, the answer to that also explains the mesh: grenades."

"Of course!" Rusty slapped his forehead. "That makes perfect sense."

"Yeah, fragging is pretty common in Saigon. How about where you are?"

"Which kind of fragging? If you mean ten-year-old waifs dropping grenades into your jeep, then no, it's not all that common. It's happened, but not recently. Back at a unit where I used to work, there were half a dozen or so lieutenants that got fragged by their own platoon. Nasty shit."

"Where was that?"

"LZ Emerald, up by Bong Son pass on Highway One."

"That whacko wannabe general still there then? The one with the goddamn duck pond?"

Rusty looked at the back of his head in utter amazement. "How in hell did you hear about that?" Rusty sputtered.

"Oh, hell. Trash haulers go everywhere and hear everything. Wanna know what we just heard about Bang My Twat?"

"Yeah, what?"

"That one of your own guards hosed the mess hall one night while you were all watching a suck and fuck flick. That true?"

"You have it pretty straight. I'm dumbfounded. That's around already? It just happened!"

"Oh yeah, the fresh ones always travel fastest. Here's another one: up at Pleiku they've been catching the hootch maids smuggling mortar rounds out the gate under their skirts."

"You know, our boss says that things only seem quiet right now, but that weird little things like that are happening all over. That your impression?"

The co-pilot nodded, and the left-seater said, "Pretty much. The natives are getting restless. If we keep drawing down our forces, at some point the scales are gonna shift. When they do, it's gonna be Tet all over again, but bigger."

"That's not the first time somebody's told me that," Rusty said. "And nobody's said anything to the contrary, either. I hope I'm gone when the fireworks start."

"Lost your zeal to help out a beleaguered country, huh?"

"I think so. I'm not sure when the last drop dripped, or if it has, but my fervor tank is damn low. I do feel for some of the real Vietnamese fighters, though; mostly for the Montagnards. Those poor bastards are gonna take it in the ass no matter who wins."

"Tell us about it. You oughta see what's happening in Laos. Hey, there's an idea. You ever hear of a program called Steve Canyon?"

"Maybe a whisper. Why?"

"Well, if you wanted to, we might be able to offer your name up for it. It's a lot like the stuff you do, but even deeper in the dark: more Company and less Air Force. A goodly amount more money too, but that's all I can say."

"I'd have to get the 'Mission Impossible' brief for that, huh?"

"You got it right down the middle, brother. How much time you have left in-country?"

"Just over 90 days."

"Oh, well, you'd have to extend to get into Steve Canyon. You crazy enough to do that?" He turned to look at Rusty again.

"Uh, no." And then he realized what the pilot was talking about and Rusty added, "I'm not a Raven lunatic." Rusty winked.

The pilot's eyebrows went up. "No, it doesn't seem you are. Even for a guy who'd go to Taipei with only a Grant...Mr. Grant."

Rusty smiled, but didn't admit that he hadn't gotten the pay sergeant's joke until just that moment. Fifty bucks. Mr. Grant. Oh, brother.

Two hours later, Charley woke up the sleepers and passed out in-flight lunches. Marvels of food service, the white shoe-box cartons were absolutely stuffed with food. Rusty's contained two pieces of fried chicken, two cartons of real milk, an apple and an orange, two sandwiches (one peanut butter and jelly, the other sliced turkey with mayo and lettuce) and – will wonders never cease! – a genuine Snickers bar. Rusty practically inhaled the fried chicken and the cartons of milk, finished the turkey sandwich and then slowly, reverently nibbled the Snickers bar. He even licked the wrapper. The other things would keep without spoiling, so he set them aside.

Filled with good food, Rusty napped and didn't wake until landing. They were picked up by a Customs bus and taken to a hangar. "Just stay near the middle of the line and do what we do," the co-pilot whispered to him. Rusty looked at him with alarm. "No, no. There's no problem. It's a set routine, and they know ours."

They were escorted by a carbine-carrying Taiwanese soldier and made to line up in front of a seated officer. Rusty listened to the perfunctory exchange of those ahead of him and relaxed a little. When it was his turn, he stepped up to the desk.

"Name and ID," the officer said, not even looking up from his papers.

"Grant. Ron Grant. From Kansas," Rusty added as he handed him the ID card.

The man peered at Rusty over his reading glasses without tipping his head up. "Sure. How long will you be in our country?"

"Three days."

"Business or pleasure?"

"Pleasure. Um, just a short visit."

The officer peered over his glasses again and sighed slightly. He handed the ID card back without even examining it. "Next."

Rusty walked quickly over to the ones who'd been ahead of him. The navigator was chuckling a little. "Don't put in for a James Bond job, Ron."

"Why?"

"That was the worst acting job I've ever seen. You practically broke down and sobbed a confession. If you'd been any more nervous, I think you might've been shaking."

"I was…a little. I thought he'd hear my knees knocking."

"He might have. That's what saved you."

"What do you mean?"

"Heck, you were so transparent, you have to be a snow-pure innocent. I'm sure he passed you because of it. That and the fact that he's seen every single one of us a few times each, but never twice with the same names."

The last of the other passengers finished with the official, who stood and left without a backward glance. They boarded yet a different bus and drove downtown. The country was exquisitely beautiful, rolling country land, scrupulously tilled and not a speck of junk or litter anywhere. Snow-capped mountains shimmered in the distance. The sky was clean and blue, and it was calm and deliciously balmy. Best of all, the countryside smelled of turned earth and flowers.

Taipei itself was sparkling clean even though it thrummed with people and traffic. Bicycles and motor scooters far outnumbered autos, but pedestrians outnumbered both. They pulled up in front of a modest, medium-sized hotel a bit separate from the smaller buildings around it.

"Here's where we always stay, Ron. It's discrete as well as inexpensive. You're on your own from here on, but be damn sure to be here in the lobby the day after tomorrow, oh-seven hundred sharp. Got it?"

Rusty was gratified to note that the whole crew booked in without a qualm, even Charley, who the others in the flight crew treated as an absolute equal. What a change from the LZ Emerald bunch of bigots, Rusty thought.

Rusty handed the clerk his ID and twenty dollars for two nights, just as the others had done. This time, he resolved not to blurt out extraneous information. But the clerk neither asked a single question nor looked up. He scribbled Chinese characters in a large book, dropped the money into a drawer and handed Rusty a key with a numbered tag attached.

It was only mid-afternoon, and so Rusty decided to wander around the city. He was afraid of getting lost, so kept pretty much to the street the hotel was on. Everywhere he went, people bustled past, but nodded and smiled to him as if they were overjoyed to see him. It was heartwarming. He turned a corner at random and within a few blocks, had found a school or orphanage. Beautiful, immaculate children played and ran up and down the street, ducking in and out of the institution's open gate. Some stared at him openly, others peeked slyly and giggled, while still others came right up and jabbered openly and happily with him. All he could do was smile and laugh at their lilting words, which were much more musical and melodious than the sharp, screeching sounds of Vietnamese. He fell instantly in love with every one of them.

When the shadows grew long, Rusty started back, his stomach growling. Thankfully, many signs on stores and restaurants were in English. As he tried to find a restaurant, he was bemused by the fact that he couldn't find a Chinese restaurant anywhere – but Italian restaurants were chockablock! On the other had, Rusty thought, how many places in the US are labeled "American Restaurant?" Finally, only a block from the hotel, he settled on one of the Italian ones. It couldn't be worse than rancid steak, no matter what.

He had to point to a menu item (again, miraculously with English sub-titles), but the waiter was all smiles. When it came, it wasn't exactly what he thought he'd ordered, but it was surprisingly good. It was a pasta casserole with marinara sauce. He ate every scrap and devoured a whole loaf of delicately crusty garlic bread. Maybe the Chinese did teach Marco Polo all about pasta, he mused. The bill came to two dollars. Rusty was unsure of how to tip, or even if he should. He left the quarter and dime he had in his pocket, and hoped it was acceptable.

It had been an exciting day, and Rusty wanted a nightcap before he went to bed. He stepped into what was clearly a bar, right next door to the restaurant. The bartender gave him one look and said, "Yes, sir?"

Emboldened by this, Rusty said, "Martini?" But the man's face was blank. "Beer?" The barman brightened and nodded, then asked a question that could only be "What kind?" but in Chinese. Rusty shrugged and opened his palms to the sky. The bartender understood and uncapped a bottle, pouring it into a glass with a flourish. Rusty had taken exactly one sip when two very pretty girls sat down on either side of him. Uh oh.

"I be your friend?" They both spoke simultaneously: stereo bar girl. Rusty laughed and shook his head, "No, not tonight." The bartender handed him a clipboard with multi-copy forms on it. Curious, Rusty had to see what it was. The lines were in English and Chinese: Name, Date, Hotel and a two-paragraph agreement. It was a contract for a bar girl slash escort. Damn! That pilot wasn't kidding!

Rusty handed it back to him, shaking his head. The man looked as astounded as if Rusty were a street beggar refusing a fiver. The girl on his right went all huffy and left, but the one on the left stayed and talked incomprehensibly but pleasantly. Rusty took a closer look at her. She was stunning: delicate features with a flawless light mocha skin that glowed even in the bar's dim lights. Her hair glistened like an ebony waterfall, but Rusty's eyes were drawn magnetically to her truly magnificent pair of breasts. He could feel his resolve melting. Rusty could imagine those luscious, full, honey-gold breasts rubbing against him, and he almost quivered with the reaction it caused. Who'd know, he rationalized? Here he was not only ten thousand miles from home, but two thousand from where he's assumed to be - and with a fake name. Nobody on this earth would ever know if he…

Except that he would.

Rusty pushed the stool back, laid a dollar on the bar and left, not daring to look back at that girl for a final and probable pillar-of-salt glimpse. That night's sleep was even more fitful than the last, and there was only one release possible. The brown soap in the shower was nowhere near as nice as that brown girl, but he had taken no vows about soap.

The C-130 pilot had been right about another thing: Taipei was a pirate market gone to extremes. The streets were crowded with shops, and every shop was crowded with the best possible brand name merchandise at implausibly low prices. Hawkers stood in every doorway and beseeched passers by with promises of undreamt-of bargains. Rusty wandered into several and looked over some of the offerings. Yes, even the copyright notices had been... copied. Blatantly stolen would be a better description. Acquire one book and reprint millions just like it. But printing books was one thing, how did they manage to duplicate the quality of, say, a guitar? They couldn't be photocopied, they had to be physically made. That aspect of the scam mystified him.

The only possible explanation involved cheap wood, cheap glue and cheap finish assembled by pennies-a-day labor and finally slapped with a genuine-looking label, he finally decided. Maybe a guitar would sound good in the store, and maybe even for a while afterwards. But let it get too damp or too dry, or handle it too much, and... Rusty wondered how many Taipei specials were returned to legitimate manufacturers under "warranty" for repair? And what would those companies do about it? Do they dare send back a letter saying, "We regret, Sir or Madam, this item is not genuine?" Could they afford the reputation they'd soon have of not only selling shoddy things but refusing to admit ownership of them? Would their reputation be worth the cost of destroying the bogus items and sending the customer a genuine one as replacement? What a dilemma this piracy thing creates, he realized. What a cost! Because the genuine company has to make back the losses of dealing with the fake items somehow, and the only way is to raise their prices – which in turn almost assures more cut-rate pirated junk!

Rusty resolved not to contribute to the problem, even though some of the stuff he saw really was tempting. Not as tempting as that bar girl, though. Rusty went back to the orphanage. Here at least was unfeigned innocence and honest, genuine pleasure.

By evening, he was beginning to feel a little bit blue. He'd spent two days in one of the most bustling, vibrant and exciting cities in the world; but he'd been forced to spend them almost like a vagrant, walking the streets and watching six-year-olds play to while away the hours. The most exotic delight he'd been able to sample was Italian food. It was too late now to even succumb to temptation and hire a girl: he didn't have fifteen dollars left. Rusty bought a bowl of soup from a street vendor and went back to his room just as the sun was setting. There, he re-discovered the fruit and peanut butter sandwich he'd saved from the box lunch and ate those, too. The bread was stale and dry, which matched his mood.

Rusty was in the lobby early, waiting for the others to stagger down, which they did at intervals. The last one down was the command pilot, and he belched as he approached them, "Good thing you can't leave without me! Let's boogie." Rusty had doubts he was actually sober, but suppressed any comments.

There was even less examination of their papers as they prepared to board. Just a casual tick off name by name: Arrived – Departed. Everybody back in the cargo compartment slept most of the way. Rusty read the one pirated book he'd bought against his better judgment. Not until they were actually on the black bus heading back to the safe house did the tales of revelry begin. First, one of the guys would tell a tale of improbable sexual adventure, then another would try to top it with even more exaggerated claims. "My girl did this…" "Oh yeah, well mine…" It soon surpassed the farthest limits of even physical possibility; but none of it was intended to be believed anyway.

"How about you, Grant. You get your clock cleaned?" one of them asked.

"Nope. Couldn't afford the price."

"You couldn't afford fifteen dollars?"

"I couldn't afford the alimony."

They all roared. Rusty just let it stay there.

The red-faced pay official was speechless – probably dumbfounded - when Rusty handed him back a five-dollar bill. He exchanged the currency for MPC scrip and re-traded ID cards. MACV covan Mr. Ron Grant of Kansas ceased to exist.

In the morning, Rusty learned that there was a civilian flight leaving almost immediately with a stop at Ban Me Thuot. On the ramp, he was almost bowled over at the sight of the plane; an absolutely ancient C-46. This pointy-nosed competition to the justly famous C-47 Gooney Bird could actually haul almost twice as much cargo as its better-known rival. But it somehow never really caught on. Maybe that's because it had a somewhat vexing tendency *to* catch on…fire.

Rusty climbed up the short boarding ladder. "Mornin, guys!" He was in fatigues again, and the crew gave him a welcome smile. "Wow, I've never flown in a Curtis Comet before."

"That's Curtis Commando," the copilot said.

"Not with my luck. These things as bad as they say for turning into flamers?"

"Well, this one hasn't...yet." He gave a fatalistic smile. "And it doesn't have to last much longer to avoid the reputation."

"Why's that?"

"This is almost the last one in-country. The Air Force quit flying them almost four years ago and sold them to Air Vietnam. The Vietnamese crashed or cannibalized all but this one and then sold it to us. The two of us own it, maintain it and we haul stuff for whoever needs it hauled."

"So why do you sound like it won't be flying much longer?"

"Because this whole war gig is about over, that's why. And we ain't gonna be the last white faces here when the curtain comes down. When the time comes, we'll either fly this thing out, or just walk away from it and boogie ourselves. It's paid for itself but it wouldn't bring us much even if we managed to get it somewhere it could be sold."

Rusty couldn't get over their audacity, "You guys are independent? A one-plane airline? Really? How the hell do you manage that? I mean, how'd you wind up here...doing this?"

"Oh, we were Army. Flew Caribous together. When we both DEROS'd, our enlistments were up. We decided to separate here, pooled our separation bonuses to buy this crate, and *voila*: the world's smallest airline," the co-pilot said

"Yup," added the pilot. "We're independent alright, but we aren't an official, on-paper airline. We're more of a 'greased palm' airline, you see? Somebody needs something hauled, we haul it. Today it's a few warm bodies, a pallet of mixed supplies and some sacks of mail. Yesterday we hauled drums of cooking oil, tomorrow it might be a dozen goats or pigs. We rope it down beforehand and hose it out after."

"You ever haul any, um...recreational substances? High profit items?"

The copilot's face lost its friendly openness. "Better find a seat, bud."

As they talked, the plane had filled with a crowd of Vietnamese, from very young to very old. Some carried little bamboo cages of chickens. All sat mute and apprehensive on the aluminum benches along the walls. Rusty wedged himself in next to the cockpit bulkhead.

Two landings later, they arrived at Ban Me Thuot. It felt like home. Rusty phoned the TOC to let them know he was back.

Bridgewater came for him in a jeep. "Welcome back. You have a good time?"

"Well, it was something I won't forget," Rusty said honestly. "Anything new happen here?"

"You remember last week when I said you needed a haircut?"

"Yeah," Rusty said, taken off balance by the abrupt change in conversation and the equally quick change in Bridgewater's face – from welcoming joy to something darker.

Rusty was about to offer the excuse that he hadn't had time to get one before his surprise departure, but Bridgewater waved his hand to stop him. "Be damn glad you didn't get one."

"What are you talking about?"

"Well, the day you left, one of the Green Hornet enlisted guys – not that Mule guy, one of their ground maintenance troops – went missing. Just disappeared. That was Friday. Then Monday another weird thing happened... the barber never showed up for work. Well, one thing and another and we ended up breaking into the barber shop. There was our missing Green Hornet, right there in the chair with his throat cut."

"Oh my God, you're not serious."

"Serious as a heart attack, son. That barber bastard was VC. Been working here for two years. No telling what he learned just chit-chatting while he cut hair. But on Friday afternoon, we suppose that the Green Hornet guy was his last customer of the day, and he just killed him, locked the shop and walked off."

"But why did he suddenly cut somebody's throat? I mean, what the hell triggered that if he hadn't been discovered?" Rusty said, horrified. How many haircuts had that guy given him? How many times had his straight razor been at Rusty's throat? A dozen times or more. Jesus.

"We have no idea. Maybe he thought he was about to be found out. Maybe he just panicked. Or maybe his bosses just told him to do it. Maybe the Green Hornet guy said something that pissed him off. Hell, we'll never know unless we find the barber, and that ain't bloody likely. Oh. Sorry."

Rusty couldn't help staring at the barber shop as they drove past. It was a tiny room at the back of the canteen/BX. It had its own door, was right next to the main gate and was off every natural walkway. You had to be going there to go past it. It was a natural place to stage the perfect murder. Now it was a murder scene, the door crisscrossed with yellow tape.

They pulled up and stopped in front of the TOC. "Anyway," Bridgewater said after he'd shut off the engine, "I got this real bad feelin' about it. I think we're in for somethin' - and soon. You know what else we found? One of the hootch maids was waddling a little when she left the compound the other day. They searched her and found..."

"Let me guess," Rusty put a hand on his arm. "Two mortar rounds slung under her skirt."

"How the hell did you guess that?" Bridgewater turned quizzically.

"I heard they're catching them doing the same thing up at Pleiku. The C-130 guys told me."

"I'll be go to hell. Shit, that's even worse. It means it's a concerted plan. I gotta go tell the SF guys that little tidbit. Thanks, that could be *very* valuable info. You just might have made that trip pay off, Rusty. Goddamn," he said as he swung out of the jeep and trotted off.

Rusty hadn't gotten to his room when Danny Craig assailed him, "Rusty, hey man, have you heard the news?"

"About the barber? Yeah, and about the hootch maids, too."

"Man, you shoulda been here. The place turned into a beehive. The SF guys sent in a team of cops and all to investigate it, and then a team of Air Force cops showed up, too. They stopped all the hootch maids from coming in, and doubled the guards at night. No flying except for Jack – he went to Ubon. Oh, he got your clothes and stuff. And Kit and Flip *both* got DEROS orders. And, oh yeah, we're gonna have a rat race!"

"Calm down, Dan. You're gonna blow a gasket. Say all again, willya? At half speed."

Danny looked at Rusty and said, "Oh, sorry. But it's been so exciting. Okay. Well...The green Hornet guy got killed, right? And the Army and Air Force both sent in teams to investigate it like a murder. Well, it *was* a murder, right? And until they get it sorted out, there aren't any hootch maids or mercenary guards. And that's why we're not flying, either. But Buchenhardt did get to go to Ubon – just one night – and he brought back your clothes. Bridgewater told him he probably shouldn't order any for himself, because we might not be going back. Boy, was Jack pissed! Let me see...what else? Oh, and they got the radio room rewired and the freezer fixed again, but the steaks all went bad first. Boy, they were bad, too. Whew! They stank. Had to bury them with a bulldozer."

"Uh huh. I think I have all that. Been busy huh? You said something before about Flip and Kit? They have orders? And there was another thing, too. A rat race?"

"Oh, yeah. Flip and Kit have their DEROS parties tomorrow night. Their orders came in. Today we're going to have a flaming rat race and a barbecue."

Rusty shook his head, still disbelieving his ears. "A flaming rat race *and* a barbecue? You don't mean to tell me that…"

Craig laughed. "Oh! No, not together! I mean they will be both today, but the rats won't be at the barbecue! I mean…the Green Hornets went on a mission and shot a big deer. That's what we're cookin' at the barbecue!"

"I think I'm getting closer. Maybe I'll get it all sorted out later. I want to unpack."

"Oh yeah. Jeez. How was it? Your trip, I mean?"

"Well, it was different. I'll tell you all about it later."

"Okay! I'll see ya later," and he disappeared at a run.

What has him so high strung, Rusty wondered? Getz was in his bunk when Rusty pushed the door open. "Jim, poor Craig is wound up tighter than an eight-day clock. Can you tell me what the hell's going on around here? I know about the barber, but Craig ran on like a blue streak about eight or nine other things besides."

"He's been like that for two days. Maybe it's the tension of the murder or something, but he gets talking so fast he almost wets himself, I swear. Okay, where do I start? You know about the barber. And the hootch maids?"

Rusty nodded. "And the radio room and the freezer."

Getz swung his legs over the bunk edge and sat there looking down at Rusty. "Okay. Important stuff first. Kit and Flip are leaving day after tomorrow. Kit got a Tweet to Columbus and Flip got a KC-135 to Barksdale."

"Columbus? Where's that? And how's Flip taking it? I mean SAC and a gas bag and all?"

"Columbus is an ATC base in Mississippi. Kit asked for it. So did Flip. A tanker, that is. He says he's gonna parley the multi-engine time into an airline job after three years. They're both happy. Their SOG party is tomorrow night, and tonight the maintenance guys are throwing them a barbecue."

"Oh, that's nice of them. What great guys. Go on."

"Yeah. Well, we're still standing down like we were when you left…how was Taipei by the way?"

"Later; keep going."

"Oh, okay. Killjoy! Well, Jack got his Ubon trip, but it was the last one and he didn't get to order any clothes for himself. Man, did he throw a hissy fit! Your clothes are in your locker, by the way. Bridgewater's been flying all over hell and gone talking with other ALOs and the SF weenies. From what he gathers, there's evil afoot all over. So they're battening the chickens and counting hatches."

"You mean they're locking the horses before they leap."

"Huh?"

"Never mind. Sorry. Go on."

"Uh...oh, yeah. So we're pulling gate watch at night instead of paid guards. That's it, I guess."

"So what does all this have to do with flaming rats, for Chrissake?"

"Shhhh!" Getz went on at a conspiratorial whisper, "Nothing, except that with all the little guys idle, they spend their time catching rats. And they're going to hold a rat race. To make it interesting, they dip 'em in diesel fuel and light 'em first. We're all gonna watch, but we don't want Sanderson or Bridgewater to hear about it. They might object."

"On the grounds of cruelty? They'd kill the rats anyway, wouldn't they? How do they usually do it?"

"Club 'em to death, I guess. I dunno. We just thought it'd be better if the brass didn't know."

"Maybe you're right. But if it's the little guys doing it, what difference does it make?"

"I don't know. Maybe we've all just gone paranoid nutso. But it just seemed like..." He shrugged.

"I can bic that. You said my Ubon clothes are in here? I can't wait to see them."

Rusty had hardly opened the locker door and glanced in when Craig tapped on the door and whispered, "It's time! Race time!" He scurried along to the next room.

"Shit! Just when I'm getting a look at my new clothes."

"Oh, you'll have forever to look at those. How often do you get to see a flaming rat race?" Getz said as he jumped down from the top bunk. "Come on!"

Everyone went out to the road, and Rusty was surprised at how different everything looked with half the big tree gone. There was a noisy, excited crowd of Vietnamese wearing a mix of uniform items and a smaller, quieter crowd of Montagnards in their own tribal dress standing just apart from the others.

In the center of the street, they'd built a tiny fire in the center of a circle perhaps ten feet in diameter scuffed into the dirt. Several woven bamboo cages sat on the ground, and inside them Rusty could see gray forms bouncing madly about in panic or rage.

"What's all this?" Rusty asked Kit, who walked up and stood next to him.

"The First Annual Ban Me Thuot Flaming Rat Race, brother! The event of the season."

"Forgive me for being a jerk, Kit, but that's one of my all-time pet peeves."

"What? Flaming rats?"

"No. First annual. There can't be any such thing. If it's the first of something, it can't possibly be annual yet, and if it's celebrated annually, it can't possibly be the first one. It's nonsense, an oxymoron."

"It's gonna be outrageous, is what it's gonna be. Look! They're getting the first one ready."

The rest of the FACs and most of the Green Hornets were present by now, forming a third group standing in a distinct segment of a circle surrounding the little fire. One of the Vietnamese guys took a bamboo cage and poured a few ounces of liquid into it, then stepped to the fire, opened the end of the cage and dumped out a rat. It fell, twisting and writhing in midair, right onto the fire, where it burst into flame with a disturbing *whup* sound. Then it ran. Fast and straight at first, but quickly wobbling, turning aimlessly and finally falling over on its side almost on the scratched circle. It quivered briefly, still aflame, before going still.

The Vietnamese screamed, laughed and jumped in the air in glee. Most of the 'yards stared stonily but several of them grinned and chattered among themselves. The Americans, unsure of how to react at first, finally burst into yells and hoots of laughter. The next cage was already being doused, and Rusty could see money changing hands amid excited gabbling in both groups of little people.

"Hey, a buck on the next rat!" Lopez yelled.

"To do what?" Hannah asked.

"Hell I don't know. Go farther? A buck says he gets outside the circle."

"You're on," Fleming said.

"Me, too. I'm in." One of the Green Hornet guys said. "And me!" said Flip.

"You're covered. Any more? Quick, here we go!"

There were no more takers before the second rat was dumped onto the fire. This one squealed and shrieked, ran in a tight circle and just fell over, almost in the fire again.

"Ha! Pay up, Lopez! You lose!"

"Not as much as the rat lost," Rusty mumbled to Kit.

"Oh, who gives a fuck about the rat? This is fun."

"Two bucks says the next one beats the first one! I'll take five bets," said Mule.

"Here," said Kit. In seconds, the five bets were laid. "Here, hold the pot," Mule handed Rusty a wad of scrip. It looked odd again after the real US currency he'd had in Taipei.

The next rat ran hard and straight, causing some of the jostling Vietnamese to leap back from its flaming rush. The rat collapsed outside the circle, but only by a body length. The Vietnamese argued and yelled until somebody got a string and measured from the edge of the fire to both still-smoking rats. The last one had indeed gone farther. Rusty handed the pot to Mule.

"You did good, Killer! You're my good luck charm!"

"No, I think you're mine, Mule. You killed that VC I was shooting at with Baby. He might've killed me otherwise."

"What are you talking about? You mean the gook who jumped up right in front of you? Hell, I didn't kill him. He was too close for the grenade to arm up. They have to fly a hundred feet before they arm. I was shooting at another gook. You nailed that close one good. You wanna bet on the next rat? No, wait. I don't want to take your money. You're my good luck charm!"

Rusty heart sank. He saw that VC again in his mind, and not even the cheers and hoots around him made it into his consciousness. He turned and walked back to the room, his mind numbed and stomach churning.

Flip followed, "Hey. Hey Rusty! What's wrong? You all right?"

"Huh? Oh, Flip. Yeah. Um, yeah. Hey, congrats on your airline job."

Flip stopped short, staring. Rusty stumbled on.

In the room, Rusty went to his locker and numbly tried on the boots he'd ordered. The Thai boot makers had measured his right foot and he'd ordered three pairs of boots. The right one of all three fit perfectly. All the left ones were a half-size too small. Rusty rolled onto his bunk and stared at the springs above until Getz came back.

"Hey Rusty, you shoulda seen…Hey, what's wrong. Hey, bud," Getz shook a shoulder. "What is it? You sick? Should I call the Doc?"

"No. I'm…I'll be okay in a bit. It's just that everything just kinda hit me at once. I can't explain. Just leave me alone, okay? Really."

"No, man. Something's wrong, and has been for some time, if those regular nightmares you have mean anything – and they do. Talk to me."

"I really have those? Flip said…well…" Rusty rolled over and looked at him, wiping his eyes with the backs of his hands. "Look. It's just been rough lately. I've been shoving things under the rug, kinda, ever since LZ Emerald. And it all…I don't know. Just hit bottom. I'll talk to Sanderson. Later. I promise. Just forget about it, okay?"

"I don't know, man. You're not gonna go Section Eight on me are ya?"

"No. I'm not crazy. I'm not gonna attack you while you sleep or anything, Jim. I'm gonna be fine."

"Oh, thanks. Just another nice thought for me. You shoving a bayonet up through my mattress tonight. Fucking wonderful ideas you plant."

Rusty laughed despite himself. "Jim, that might have been just the medicine I needed. No, no fear. I'm sane. Maybe too sane. But I'm beginning to understand what they mean when they say a guy's first three months and his last three months in Vietnam are the worst. I'm under 90 days short, and I'm just so fucking scared that when I do go home, I'm going to be…I don't know. Not really human. Does that make sense?"

"No. But then, I have six months to go. Ask me again later. If I don't die of terminal horniness before then."

Rusty laughed again. "No. I don't think horniness is fatal. On the other hand, let me tell you about a certain Taiwan bar girl some time."

"Ah ha! There's a streak of manliness in you after all, is there?"

"Huh? What do you mean 'after all'?"

"Well, from what I hear, you're about the only one here who never diddles a hootch maid, never goes to the Bakery. Hell, you never even cop a feel of the barmaid. You're either light in the loafers or you're a goddamn saint. And I hope to hell it's the latter, or that might not be a bayonet I feel sticking up through my mattress!" He chuckled.

Rusty did, too. "I assure you, I'm as straight as the lines on a Mercator projection chart, Jim. Hell, maybe that's my problem. I don't know."

"Well, speaking from my own point of view, having an arrow-straight hetero roomie is not a problem," he laughed for a second. "But I think I know what you mean. You've been in a pressure cooker for almost a year. Hell, you've *been* a pressure cooker. No release, is what I mean."

Rusty cocked his head in thought. "Go on."

"You're afraid your personal geyser is gonna blow."

"Well, that may be a mixed analogy, but I see what you mean. So?"

"So you're afraid that when you go home to that bride of yours, she'll see you as some kind of freak. Worse, some kind of monster. And even worse than that, you're afraid she might be right. Right?"

"Yeah. That's about it."

"Uh huh. She's a great, warm, loving and…oh, let's say motherly – not to suggest anything Oedipus-like – but someone you want to be a mother. Right?"

"Yeah. She sure is."

"And you're afraid she'll be repulsed by this baby-burning, psychopathic cannibal that comes home to her with enough bottled up inside him that he could turn into an axe-murderer any second. Tell me that's wrong."

"It's not wrong. How do you…"

"Psych major. Now shut up and listen. You weren't like that when she married you, were you? No. You weren't like that when you got here, were you? No. So what in the flying fantod makes you think you'll be like that when you get home to her? Huh?"

"But the war…"

"Oh, for Pete's sake. War is shitty. It's awful. It affects people forever. I'll stipulate that. But it doesn't make people into something they aren't. Guys who come over here nuts go home even worse nuts. Guys who come over here boozers or druggies go home completely whacked. But guys who come here with a solid head on solid shoulders – like you, you dickhead – go home with a new and deeper appreciation of life, of beauty, of the people they love."

"What do you mean?"

"I mean, pull up your fucking socks. You're a pilot. A good one, from what I hear. More important, you're a decent guy. You're a man. With all that being a real man means. Even I can see that. So, do your job here. And when you finish that job, leave the fucking job here. All of it. Close that door. Go home. Take what you've learned, of course." He paused to think for a moment. "Look, you like food. Use what this hellhole has given you as if it were food. Digest it and build yourself up with it. But leave the bad parts behind you like a turd."

Rusty looked at him for a long minute. "And what do I do now, right now, to get through it all until I do leave?"

"Now? Right now you wash your face, put on a fresh shirt and go to the barbecue."

"How come we haven't talked this way before, Jim?"

"You know Rusty, you don't talk to people much at all. When you're 'on' you're as lively as a standup comedian; but when you're not performing, you're like the man who wasn't there."

"Well, I do know that much about myself. I'm an overcompensating introvert."

Getz laughed, "Yeah, right."

"No, I am. That's the truth. That's what I am. I'd much rather be alone than with anybody. To a point, I guess. And then I overcompensate and turn 'on' as you say."

"Overcompensating introvert, huh? That'd be a new psychological category. I'll have to mull that over. Right now, just go to the party hootch and try not to bawl, okay?"

"I can handle that."

There were cases of second-rate but cold beer, as always. The zebras – guys wearing stripes – had rigged up a barbecue grill made from fuel drums cut in half lengthwise and welded to legs. They'd bought charcoal from the locals and were busily searing thick slabs of a rich dark meat. It was some of the Asian red deer the Horny Greenits had killed from their choppers. Rusty allowed himself to turn 'on' – self-consciously so after Jim's comments – and had a thoroughly good time on Kit and Flip's behalf. It was their party, and he could safely hang near the edges of it as he preferred. Buchenhardt tried to steal as much of the limelight as he could with his never-ending tales of his alma mater. But Kit and Flip were ultimate extroverts. Firmly established as the center of the party's mass, they regaled all with ribald jokes, war stories, brags about how soon they'd be engaged in round-the-clock sex and the musings about first things they'd buy when they got to the Land of the Big BX.

It lasted until dark, when Major Bridgewater announced an end. "Time to hobble this pony, boys. Ah don't want nobody a-noddin' off on guard duty. Rusty, as your official welcome back from sunny Taiwan, you git the first watch. You take the main gate. Jack? You take t'uther. Relief at midnight. The rest of y'all turn in and git ready fer the second shift - Getz and Craig. Ya'll pick who goes whar, y'hear?"

As everyone wandered away, Rusty buttonholed Sanderson. "Dave? What's this guard duty stuff? What do I do and how do I do it?"

"Oh, that's right. You were gone and haven't had the briefing. Well, no matter. Get your flak vest, steel pot and your CAR-15. It wouldn't hurt to take a flashlight and some extra ammo, either. Go to the main gate and you'll find either an SF guy or a trusted ARVN troop there already. You watch the approach road and stay awake. If you see, hear or even suspect something's not right, crank up the field phone in there and report to the SF TOC. If worst come to worst, there are Claymores, a .50-cal and your own rifle to use. But I don't expect that'll ever be necessary."

"Who's in charge? The other guy or me?"

"Technically, you'd outrank him, but as far as ground combat's concerned, all of us FACs are babes in the woods. Use your best judgment before you start bellowing orders."

"Makes sense. Okay, I have the plane. Or the bunker, or whatever."

"Good goin'."

"Uh, Dave? One more thing."

"Yeah, what's that?"

"I think I finally have my head around that chopper thing a bit better. Maybe a lot better."

"What made this change?"

"Getz, actually. He said some things this afternoon that made sense. Helped a lot. I think I'm fine now."

"Good. You and I have come a long way together. We'll probably be going separate ways from here on. I'm glad to know you'll be okay."

"Thanks, Dave. Can I say something?"

"Sure."

In the deepening dark, Rusty didn't worry about the glisten in his eyes, but the words choked up on their way out, "I uh, think you're the best. The best IP I had in UPT, and the...best boss I've had...since. Well, one of the best. Thanks."

Sanderson squeezed the back of his neck. "That's good to know. You weren't half bad yourself...usually. Now get to that bunker and stay awake, okay?"

"Yessir!" Rusty said cheerily. He saluted - and meant the salute from the bottom of his being.

CHAPTER SIXTEEN

The damp, chilly bunker smelt of mildew, urine and the particular sweetly chemical odor of synthetic sandbags. Tall enough for his ARVN compatriot to stand upright, Rusty had to bend his head sideways or hunch forward to clear the corrugated steel ceiling.

Across the outward-facing wall were several long wood-framed slits, one sandbag layer tall. In the center of the bunker stood the heavy tripod on which swiveled the oiled menace of the Browning .50-cal machine gun, its muzzle poking out through the center slit. Through each end slit draped several sets of wires and at the end of each pair hung a peculiar device called a "clacker" by the Army – the firing trigger for the Claymore mine at the other end of each wire.

Rusty pondered all this lethal equipment now at his disposal while the ARVN soldier wordlessly unrolled and hung a net-like device. It was a hammock, and he soon crawled into it and unabashedly prepared to sleep.

As Rusty stared at this blatant goldbrick, his emotions tumbled swiftly from disbelief through anger and finally into numb acceptance. This one ARVN summed up how the vast majority of how these people seemed to deal with their war: they didn't really care. Or maybe they'd been at war so long that the daily act of living with it had devolved into the mundane. Death, ironically, was their life.

Through the slit, Rusty watched the barbed wire-draped steel fence posts become moon dials. The hours crept by, measured by the slow sweep of the ink-blue shadows. Rusty thought about what Getz had said. Maybe he was his own pressure cooker, letting the day-to-day events and emotions stew themselves into angst.

Rusty debated it with himself, bending uncomfortably over and staring through the plastic-smelling slit. Mary Beth's letters and forwarded newspapers talked about returned Vietnam vets who'd gone berserk or quietly crazy. They already had a clinical-sounding name for it: post traumatic stress.

In World War II they called it combat fatigue, and before that it was shell shock. What had they called it in the Civil War, or during the Crusades, he wondered? Those wars were certainly bloodier, more physical, more intimately, personally violent than this one – at least for a pilot. Were those soldier's nightmares worse? Or were those warriors of sterner stuff? He doubted it. What bullets and explosives did to bodies was certainly far ghastlier than arrows and swords. Maybe it's the contrasts of aerial war. Pilots have a roof over our heads at night, hot food, even flush toilets and maid service, for crying out loud. But they also step from that almost comfortable situation and within minutes are plunged into the noise, smoke and horror of blood-soaked battle. And then, abruptly, they're back again. Is that it? Would he be more inured to the death – or even the daily frustrations - if he were cold, wet, hungry and exhausted around the clock? Was the old cliché that a complaining soldier was also a happy soldier really a truism?

"Bang, you're dead."

Rusty leapt convulsively and banged his head, "Ow! Jesus Christ you scared me shitless!" It was Getz, his body filling the single opening in the back wall.

"Midnight, brother. My shift. Go get some sleep."

The ARVN's snuffling breathing changed and he squirmed in his netting. "There's your help," Rusty said caustically.

"So what else is new? That's standard procedure for them, according to Bridgewater, or didn't you hear? No, maybe you didn't. The word is, consider yourself alone out here, because you are."

"That's damn straight."

"You sound torqued at something. Are you just processing your earlier depression into anger? That's normal. By morning, you'll be over it – the cold clear light of morning damps a lot of fires. So I repeat, go to bed."

"Yeah. Maybe you're right. Psych major, huh? You remind me of a Stan Eval guy at 21ˢᵗ TASS when I got in-country...McKenzie. He almost wet himself when I mentioned a dream I'd had about war. Turns out he's a psychologist in real life."

"And?"

"And what? You mean the dream?"

Getz nodded in the faint moonlight.

"Oh, it was nothing. I dreamt about flying over the jungle and being shot at, but I wasn't hit. I thought it was an omen that I'd come home safe. I have to say, it was damned accurate as far as how everything actually looks and feels. But essentially meaningless."

"What makes you say that?"

"Well, dreams can't really predict the future, right? I mean, there must be millions of dead guys who dreamed they'd go home safe. And vice versa. Like that William Bendix movie. It's silly."

"I wouldn't say that a dream controls the future, but it might control how you control yourself."

"Now what are you saying?" Rusty half-raised his arms in frustration.

"Sometimes there is such a thing as self-fulfilling prophecy. I think that's what that first and last few months in country thing means. The first few months, a guy isn't experienced enough to really protect himself. By the end of the tour, he is, but he starts to worry so much about screwing up and getting killed that he starts to dwell on that. In his preoccupation with it, he *does* screw up. That's why we don't tell guys they're going home while they still have flights left. You know how Kit and Flip found out about their orders?"

"No, they didn't say."

"When they taxied in, we met them with a fire hose and doused them down. Their orders had been in for two days, but neither Bridgewater nor Sanderson even hinted to them. Just met them with the hose, first one and then the other. Sanderson scheduled them so they'd land within minutes of each other."

"He's quite a guy, that Sanderson."

"Yeah. Hey, therapy session over. Go to bed and let me ponder the universe. Stop off at the TOC and report all's well on the western gate, willya?"

"Yeah, yeah. Alright. See ya in the morning. Thanks, Jim."

"Wait'll you get my bill!"

Getz was right about the light of dawn: Rusty did feel better in the morning. At breakfast, Sanderson announced that they'd be ramping back up to normal flight ops starting immediately. He scheduled Rusty for a mid-morning reconnaissance flight combined with an insert site survey. Rusty would be running yet another team up near Lumphat, the nominally abandoned provincial capital about halfway to Stung Treng. Abandoned only by friendlies was closer to the truth.

A few hours flying alone on a gorgeous day is enough to evict the boogiemen from even the most infested head. Rusty headed out northwest, following a weaving, almost random course as he watched for signs of enemy activity below. The NVA were extremely good at camouflage. Their trucks, wagons and other vehicles were impossible to spot while they laid up in hiding during the day. But they had never learned – or bothered – to hide their tracks. Sections of dirt roads stretched between areas of solid tree canopy, and those sections had clearly been chewed up by recent and heavy traffic.

Rusty took pictures of many of those places from several angles so that photo interpreters could analyze the depth of the ruts. From there, a rough guess of the number of trucks and tonnage could be worked out. Or he supposed that it could. Like virtually all the other information he gathered and pushed up the intelligence pipe, no hint of results ever came back down.

Rusty finally meandered his way to the bridge and river crossing where he'd dropped the Igloo White sensors. The bridge looked different to him, somehow. Rusty spiraled down to get a better look and closer pictures. Through binoculars, he could see what seemed to be faint parallel lines a few inches apart and aligned side to side on the bridge like the lines on ruled paper. But only at the edges: there were none down the center of the bridge. As he turned and descended, he got down almost level with the bridge on the downstream side, and as Rusty flew past, he thought he saw a surprising thing – the underside of the bridge had been reinforced with steel girders. It had been all wooden at one time. He knew because a Mike FAC had once hit it with a white phosphorous rocket and the bridge had burned completely away. Since then, it had 'magically' reappeared. Rusty knew better than to make another circle and try for a picture. If the enemy thought enough of this small bridge to conceal major structural additions, they'd care enough to shoot at anybody who discovered their work. Rusty turned and climbed out of there immediately.

His curiosity over those faint parallel lines was settled within minutes. When he checked out the river ford, there were similar but much deeper and clearer marks on both the dry and the muddy banks. They were made by caterpillar treads – something big and heavy had passed here not long ago. The idea of the enemy getting brazen enough to bring heavy road-building equipment into Cambodia was bad enough, but the thought that they might be bringing battle tanks down the Ho Chi Minh trail was paralyzing.

Rusty continued looking, and even found a decent infil site in the target box for the team he'd run soon, but his mind was on those tread marks. Rusty flew back to base as soon as he could. He debriefed with Capt Brookside, handing him the 35mm film.

"This could be big. I'm positive I saw tread marks out there, both on a bridge and at a river crossing that leads to the bridge. It's the same place where I placed those sensors a while back. I shot pictures of them."

"That's rather unlikely. None of those bridges out there could support tracked vehicles. Perhaps you were just seeing travel ruts, like those that appear on gravel roads."

"The bridge isn't gravel, it's wood. That's the other thing. This bridge isn't all wooden any more. It has steel supports added underneath."

"How exactly did you manage to see the underside of a bridge?" Brookside looked at him skeptically.

"I managed to get down level with it by flying across the downstream side. I only got a quick look, but I'm sure I saw the profile of girders, not the truss shapes of wooden beams. But I didn't get pictures because it caught me by surprise and I was not about to make a second pass. Maybe if I waited a few days and made another surprise run at it…"

Brookside shook his head. "No, I'm sure it was just a trick of the light or something. There have never been reports of any tracked vehicles or reinforced bridgework in our sector. At most, they might have a small road grader or something in action. Nothing worse."

"I disagree. I'm making a report of both things right now. You didn't see what I saw. If you want, I'll take you out there and you can put your own Mark One eyeball on it. We could go right now."

"That is not my job."

"It isn't?"

"No. I do not gather raw intelligence, you do. Furthermore, you do not analyze or interpret raw data. That *is* my job…Lieutenant."

Rusty considered asking him if his green beret wasn't turning the slightest bit yellow, but bit his lip. "I understand completely…Captain."

Jim awoke when Rusty opened the door. He sat up and rubbed his eyes. Rusty apologized, "Oh, I'm sorry. I forgot that you'd probably still be asleep after the second shift in the bunker. How was it?"

"Fine. Boring as hell, which is good, I guess. I solved all the world's problems, but now I can't remember the solution," he chuckled to himself. "It's time for me to be up anyway. Wouldn't want to scandalize the hootch maid." He climbed down from the bunk. "How are you? Did a dose of morning sun perk you up?"

"Huh? Oh you mean from last night? Yeah, I guess so. Flying probably had more to do with it. Wait'll I tell you what I think I found out there."

"Whatever the medicine was, I'm glad it worked. Listen, here's something you'll like, seeing as how you're so addicted to puns and stuff. While I had all that time to cogitate, I created a new term for your mental state."

"Oh yeah, what?" Rusty said, warily.

"You have osteomorosis. It's the state of being sad all the way to your bones."

Rusty brightened up immediately. "Osteo – morose – is? Oh, I do like that! That's excellent. In fact, if a diagnosis could ever serve as a cure, that almost does it. That's gonna make my whole day. Osteomorosis…" Rusty let it slide off his tongue. "Yeah, that even feels good to say!"

"What's all the unauthorized hilarity in there? I'm the only one allowed to be happy today!" Kit poked his head in the door. "You two long-timers aren't allowed to be cheerful, not while I have one and a wakeup until DEROS."

"What's that?" Rusty cupped a hand next to his ear. "Could that be Kit? You're so short I'd have to get down on the floor just to hear you. Besides, you'd laugh too if you'd heard it. Listen…" Rusty told him the line, and Kit laughed aloud.

"That's better. I wouldn't want to think you're glad 'cause the Kit man is leaving."

Rusty's smile deflated. "I'm not, Kit. After you and Flip, there's nobody of the old crowd left except Sanderson. Sandy and I got here the same day. I never thought we'd be the old heads, but now we are."

"Hell, Rusty, that's how I've felt for weeks. When Flip and I came aboard, Larry Jensen and Gary Dickerson were the old heads. Then, suddenly, Flip and I were the last of that crowd, and all of you guys were the newbies. Now it's you and Sandy's turn. Before he knows it, Getz here will be senior FAC. But neither you nor I will care, cause *we'll be outta here!*" He shouted the last few words joyously.

"That raises a question, Kit," Rusty said. "Cramer's gone, but all the other enlisted guys are still here, and most of them were here when I arrived. Why is that?"

"Well, they come here directly and spend their whole tour here. All of us FACs were recruited into the job. Except for Danny, we all had at least a few months somewhere else. Lopez, Hannah and Young all came in either just before I arrived or at almost the same time, so they'll all be due to rotate out soon. They just happened to span your time is all."

"Ahhh. Of course. I just didn't make the connection that they got here directly. They seem like fixtures. Boy, what will Mike 50 be without Crosby Stills and Nash playing in the background, huh?"

"You write and tell me, okay? Cause it ain't gonna happen on my watch."

The three of them had lunch, sitting with Major Bridgewater. He told them that the investigation teams had finished with the obvious conclusion: the barber was an enemy agent, as were some of the hootch maids. The ARVNs had arrested the maids but had little hope of catching the barber. Trusted mercenaries and maids were being allowed into the camp again. As a result, the pilots' stint as night guards was over.

"Hell, ain't hardly 'nuff of ya left even to fly, no how," he concluded.

"Are we gonna get replacements for Kit and Flip?" Rusty asked.

"Nobody will ever fill my shoes," Kit grinned and puffed his chest.

"Or your ego," Getz jibed him.

"Oh no, ego is Buckandfart's department," Kit said. "And he holds the majority share of that stock. Tell me, sir, how'd we really get that guy?"

Bridgewater looked around furtively, and leaned his head in towards us. "Y'all were right all along. Kinda the runt 'a the litter."

Getz arched his eyebrows, while Kit and Rusty shot each other quick looks and nodded.

Bridgewater sat back again and changed the subject. "Whar's that Flip at? He's gonna miss his last gourmet lunch here."

"He went for a run as usual and was gonna pack, but now the laundry's lost his clothes. He's over there arguing with 'em," Kit said.

"Why?" Getz asked. "I mean who the hell would want to take any of it home anyway? I think they wash clothes in battery acid and red mud. It comes out orange and falling apart."

He had a point. Even Rusty's nominally sage green, indestructible Nomex flight suits had become paper-thin, threadbare shells dyed to a putrid gray-orange.

"Like Batman did, I tossed all of mine," Kit said. "I'm not going home to my wife in pink underwear."

It was a good thing there was no more guard duty, because the blowout for Kit and Flip that evening was a double humdinger. The Special Forces presented both of them with plaques and green berets, and even Daiwee Dinh told a few surprisingly funny anecdotes about them. Rusty was once again impressed at the man's command of English, which was acute enough to be subtly biting.

The guests of honor got suitably lubricated. Rusty shook his head with a mix of humor and mild concern as he watched Flip teeter. "I hope your hangover isn't too big a problem for you to DEROS, old buddy," Rusty said to him.

Flip refocused his eyes on Rusty, then slapped an arm around his shoulders and slurred, "Rusty old duck, there is no such thing as a problem."

"Yeah, yeah, Flip."

"No really, old buddy. Not. Look," he took his arm back and held up one finger. "If it kills you, your problems are over." He extended a second finger and tapped it in emphasis, "And if it doesn't kill you…it wasn't a problem. See? No problems."

Without any warning, he grabbed Rusty's head, turned it and stuck his tongue in one ear. Rusty squirmed away, "Jeez, Flip, what was that for?"

"That's how I said hello to you, Rusty, and that's how I wanna say g'bye."

Rusty laughed as that idea visibly took hold of Flip's fogged mind. He wobbled off to tongue every ear in sight, joined by Kit. They even managed to get Bridgewater, surprising him from behind. Flip was right; it was certainly a memorable way to say goodbye.

In the morning, both of them a pale greenish white, they crammed their bags and selves into an O-2 with Dave Sanderson, waved at the small crowd and were gone. Those seeing them off smoked them with a dozen grenades at the end of the runway. Sanderson made a low pass just inches off the ground and swooped up into almost a victory roll. Another chapter in the Mike FAC story had ended in a rush. The story, however, crawled on.

Within minutes, Rusty was preparing to take off to insert his team. The new team mission was called Bare Wheel. He took off with his favorite robin Truong and they rendezvoused with the Kingbees as usual. The flight out to the insert site was smooth under sparsely scattered puffy clouds, and Rusty diverted far from the bridge that he suspected was carrying tracked vehicles.

He approached the drop site by crossing the Tonle Srepok at a long island, then heading northeast for two miles. He could see the bare, gently rolling field almost from the time he crossed the river. No sweat, he thought to himself. Truong was relaxed and peering out his window as they neared the edge of the jungle. Rusty clicked the mic and said "Kingbee, stand by…3…2…"

Truong slapped his leg hard, "Daiwee, VC shoot! Many VC!"

Out his own window, the entire edge of the clearing blinked to life with muzzle flashes. Rusty could even hear some of the muzzle blasts as guns fired at him. "Kingbee abort, abort, abort!" he yelled into the mic, and broke left as hard as his barely-flying airspeed would allow.

It seemed to take forever as they practically hung there just a hundred feet above the ground at only 90 knots, but they crawled toward the edge of the clearing. Nearing it, Rusty was startled by a sudden trail of gray-white smoke that streaked past the windscreen so close that he had flown through it almost the instant he saw it. Rusty reflexively glanced down and saw a man with a black tube on his shoulder – a rocket-propelled grenade launcher like the one he'd seen in the CIA safe house. But this one was no trophy to be admired. That little bastard had come within an eyelash of blowing Rusty out of the sky.

"Kingbee see. Kingbee no go down. Okay!" The unflappable Chau Le Quang in the lead Kingbee answered. Over the radio, Rusty heard the blast of the Kingbee door gunner returning fire, and also the awful metallic banging of rounds hitting the helicopter.

Excited words told him that the second Kingbee was talking to Chau. Rusty dreaded what it meant, "Truong, what other Kingbee say?"

"Hit, Daiwee. Many hits. One man hit."

Rusty waited for Chau's report. All three planes had flown clear of the enemy fire by now, and they were above protective jungle. Rusty turned to shape a course for home. The mission was obviously busted. After a minute he heard, "Mike? Kingbee go home?"

"Yes. Affirmative. Kingbee go home. Kingbee hit?"

"Kingbee one hit tee-tee. Okay. Kingbee gun have many hits. One hurt."

"Kingbee fly okay?"

"Uh…One okay, gun ok maybe."

He meant he wasn't sure for how long. "Okay. Go home. Mike go up."

Rusty started climbing: he was too low for radio contact. As he climbed, he called repeatedly on the radio until he got the first possible contact. Over the encrypted radio, he reported that they'd been ambushed at the infil site, had aborted the mission and were coming straight home with two damaged helicopters and at least one wounded man, condition unknown. He requested launch of a rescue team, just in case.

Halfway home, Rusty heard more excited chatter on the Kingbee frequency. Truong turned to him. "No good. Kingbee gun land now."

"Kingbee, Mike copies." Rusty told Chau. "Pickup come now."

"Numba one, Mike. Okay." Chau's favorite English word.

Within thirty minutes, the sky was full of helicopters. Both standby Kingbees, two Green Hornet gunships and two Cobra attack helicopters had launched to help their wounded flingwing fellow. Rusty had Chau continue on his own way as soon as the others came into sight, and he gladly peeled off. With the full team still aboard, Chau had no room for the other crew anyway, and he'd taken hits, too.

The stricken Kingbee had made it to the open grasslands and had set down in the center of a big rolling meadow. The rescue birds set up a wide circle around the crashed bird as protection while the pickup Kingbee went in and landed nearby. Rusty could see two of the downed crew carrying one limping man between them as they hurried to the rescue bird. In minutes, the rescue bird was airborne again, escorted by the other standby Kingbee. That left the abandoned bird as the only loose end.

"Mike 50, 58. Pickup clean and cold. No activity noted near the downed bird. Do we guard it or what?"

"Stand by, 58"

Rusty had the Green Hornets stand by. They knew what was going on and they were eager to shoot at something, either bad guys or the dead Kingbee.

"58, we have conflicting thoughts one up." It was Bridgewater. At least two higher headquarters couldn't agree what to do. Most likely it was a pissing contest between the ARVN and US commands. All the active players at this end could do was wait - and burn fuel while they orbited over Indian country.

"You up, Hornets?"

"We copy, Mike."

Thirty more minutes went by. "Say status, Hornets."

"Mike, we're fine but the snakes ought to be about ten minutes to bingo."

There were two clicks on the frequency: the Cobras agreed.

Just what Rusty had thought. The heavily-laden Cobras were near the time when they'd have to turn for home. "Mike 50, 58. Any word? We're about to go bingo fuel on some of the assets."

"Copy, 58. Stand by and we'll try to expedite."

More minutes drug by. Rusty was about to release the Cobras to fly home when the TOC finally called, "Mike 58, this is 51. You are authorized to go Flash Gordon. Acknowledge."

"Uh, 51, Mike 58 acknowledges Flash Gordon." Except that Rusty had no clue what that meant. He dug frantically through the code phrases for this mission. Nothing. Giving up, Rusty asked to go crypto.

"Mike 50, I can't find Flash Gordon."

"Sorry, Rusty," it was Bridgewater again, "I was being cute. Use the disintegrator ray. Bust the Kingbee. Destroy it."

Back on regular radio, Rusty said, "Hornets, you are cleared to expend on the downed bird. Use random attack headings. Attack at your discretion. Cleared hot."

Rusty could hear the mixed emotions in the Green Hornet leader's voice as he cleared the Cobras to shoot first due to their fuel state. Hornet Lead knew there wouldn't be much left for his two birds to shoot at. He was right. The lead Cobra rolled in and ripple-fired his entire load of 64 high explosive rockets, and then his wingman did the same. The result was a huge cloud of brown smoke and dust surrounding a boiling red core. In minutes, there was nothing left but a column of black smoke.

On the ground again, Rusty debriefed with both Dinh and Brookside. "I think Bare Wheel is more of a Square Wheel" he began. Dinh chuckled silently, but Brookside was stony.

Rusty went on. "We were obviously expected. There was a pre-positioned force of NVA soldiers arranged all around that clearing when we arrived. They all opened fire simultaneously, so I don't think we just surprised them. They knew we were coming and had us in their sights when we showed up."

"That, again, is an assumption on your part," Brookside said.

"Based on the results, I believe it is a warranted one," Rusty answered, just as levelly.

Dinh looked at both of them and interjected, "No matter. The mission failed. Our losses were small. No problem," he said, looking at Rusty with twinkling eyes.

"How bad is the wounded man?" Rusty asked him.

"You are gracious to ask, Daiwee. Leg. No problem," Dinh flipped his hand to dismiss the thought.

"Any other astute observations?" Brookside asked after Rusty filled them in on the details of the destroyed Kingbee.

"Well, just that I believe I was fired on by an RPG," Rusty added, remembering the rocket-propelled grenade.

Brookside suddenly perked up and leaned toward him, head cocked. "Describe exactly what you saw. As much detail as you can recall."

Rusty wondered at his sudden shift from acid to intense interest. He went through what he'd seen, emphasizing that he had but fractions of a second to see anything.

"Let me be sure. There was a column of whitish smoke? A thick column or just a faint trail?"

"Pretty thick…maybe a bit more than from one of our Willey Pete's. Why?"

"That's very interesting," Brookside evaded. "Thank you. That will be all for now."

They found themselves suddenly too undermanned to resume the Quan Loi operation, so Bridgewater turned it over to FACs from another base. Sandy, Jack, Danny, Jim and Rusty soldiered on, putting in teams and flying cover for them – even Sanderson flew regularly.

With Kit gone, Buchenhardt seemed to mellow a bit, even towards Rusty. They were functioning like a sports team, not altogether friends, but willing to run plays successfully. It was odd to have the big room empty. Only Getz and Rusty shared a room. A few days after Kit and Flip left, Bridgewater told them that they'd be getting a new guy. The five of them voted before he arrived and the result was that they'd keep the big room empty. It'd be the day room, library and briefing room.

When the new guy came and was briefed in, he bunked in with Danny. Lt. Ed King was from Indianapolis, and he came to BMT from a base in Thailand where he'd been killing trucks along the Trail in Laos until the defenses there got to be too intense for O-2s and all the Duck pilots were rotated out in favor of faster, better armed OV-10s.

Sanderson made Jack his mentor, a move that surprised Rusty, as he would have expected Sandy or himself to be the natural choice. Two days later, it did make sense. Rusty was in one of Flip's lawn chairs reading and wondering what they'd do now if they needed any more carpentry done. Jack and Ed were up learning the territory over the fence, and Sandy was flying cap over a team that Danny had put in. Jim came up to Rusty excitedly.

"Hey, Rusty, come on. We have to wet Sandy down. Sanderson just told me his DEROS came through. He's going home tomorrow, and he's about to land on his fini flight!"

They ran to the flight line, where Mike Lopez and the other maintenance guys were already getting ready. Sanderson strolled up just as Sandy taxied in through the gate. He saw the crowd and stopped in the middle of the ramp. They could see his grin widen as he figured out what was going on. His robin clambered out and scurried to the side, then Sandy came out, shucking his vest and parachute as he did. He rushed Lopez, but not fast enough. Lopez opened the fire hose nozzle and soaked Sandy instantly. Braving the blast, Sandy wrestled the hose away and turned it on all of them. Whooping and cheering, they all ended up soaked to the skin, laughing and wrestling for the hose until everyone simply stopped, out of breath.

"Sandy, you know what?" Rusty said when they'd all calmed down a little, "If all goes well, you'll be home for Thanksgiving."

He looked at Rusty, and then brightened. "Hey, yeah! You're right. Today's Sunday, right?"

Rusty nodded.

"So if I get out of here tomorrow, out-process on Tuesday and get a flight Wednesday, I might just make it."

"You will," Sanderson chimed in. "Remember the International Date Line. You'll actually get two Wednesdays. Have some turkey for all of us, okay?"

"I promise!"

Only later did Sandy remember to ask Sanderson what assignment he'd gotten. He'd been assigned to a B-52, which was not what Sandy had bid for – and emphatically didn't want. "Well, it's better than a missile silo, I guess. Maybe I can get it changed. If not, well…"

"Hey, Flip's rule, Sandy. There are no problems," Rusty said without thinking.

Rusty took the sunset flight after Danny, who had relieved Sandy. As he orbited, he thought about Flip's drunken ramble. The more Rusty thought about it, the more sense it made. Distilled to a single sentence, Flip's Rule was crystal clear: Anything that doesn't kill you isn't a problem. Rusty wished that he'd learned that a year ago. He resolved to repeat it like a mantra the next time something unpleasant happened to him.

They took the opportunity to initiate Ed at the same time they said goodbye to Sandy. When the moment came, Sandy stepped up and planted his tongue in Ed's left ear while Rusty did his right side. Sandy had rarely done it before, being a little squeamish about it. But now, just slightly red-faced, he bent to the task with a will. When they tied Ed's red bandanna around his neck, the room cheered as much for Sandy as for Ed.

As the SF guys were presenting Sandy's plaque and beret, Rusty sidled up to Sanderson. "How do they get those things engraved so fast? Sandy only heard about his DEROS today."

"*He* heard today," Dave said out of the corner of his mouth, "But I knew three days ago."

"Ah! I see! And you withheld that little nugget until the last minute so he wouldn't get overcautious on his last few flights, right?"

"Yeah, I learned better after my goof with Batman."

"I thought as much. Nice to know even IPs screw up," Rusty shot him a lopsided grin. "But who'll tell you about yours? You must be leaving soon; you've been here even longer than Sandy and I."

"Yeah, I expect so. All you guys had other in-country assignments before you came here, but I came almost directly here. Still, it's about over for all of us.

"*ALL* of us? You know something about BMT?"

"Let me rephrase that. It's about over for all of us senior Mike FACs."

"Not for two months or so for me, though. Right?" Rusty studied Sanderson's profile as intently as the booze allowed and saw a bemused look. "Or do you know something else?"

"No, I don't, Rusty. Truly. But with this rapid drawdown... Kit, Flip and Sandy all got early releases, so... Anyway, I was just thinking about home. Wishful thinking, I guess. Thanksgiving and all."

"Oh. Yeah, I had almost forgotten about it myself. Holidays don't seem to mean much here. Like Sundays, they're just another work day."

"That might be a blessing come Christmas. Maybe it'll just slide by and we won't get too depressed," Sanderson said, wistfully.

Bridgewater stood up and began roasting Sandy with anecdote after anecdote, all in that wonderfully corny, put-on Texas drawl.

Rusty suddenly realized he didn't know something about Sanderson. "Dave, do you and Judy have any kids?"

"Boy and a girl. It's an occupational disease in ATC. Almost everybody has kids during UPT, IPs and married students alike. Don't you remember?"

"I was a little busy trying to avoid pink slip rides. But yeah, now that you mention it, I do."

"More like too busy over on Padre Island, you mean," Dave prodded. "You got married right at the end of UPT didn't you?"

"Yeah. Married, graduated and went to Cannon for fighter lead-in - all within two weeks."

"Have you put in for your next assignment yet? If not, you ought to start thinking about it before they hand you something you'd hate – like Sandy. ATC isn't a bad life, and I think you'd be a good IP. I told you that before, when Danny got here. Have you thought about it?"

"Not a lot. Maybe I should. I'd hate to get a B-52 or KC-135. Fighters are hard to come by, though."

"And it'd mean coming right back to Vietnam."

"I hadn't thought of that. True, though, isn't it?"

Sanderson nodded. "Not the best way to start a marriage, Rusty. Back to back combat tours, unaccompanied. Either SAC or ATC would allow you to start a life together. Making a preemptive phone call to Officer Assignments might be smart."

"Hmmm. Maybe you're right. I couldn't stomach SAC. I saw how they live when I went to ROTC summer camp at Plattsburgh. My God, the crews have to brief the wing commander in person before every flight. And they act like robots." Rusty shivered for effect. "Not for me, brother."

"Well then, maybe you ought to start campaigning for an IP slot."

"Yeah, maybe I should."

Sandy's ceremony came to an end and everyone refilled his drink.

"Hey, Dave, can I ask a favor?"

"Again? Well, you can sure ask," he smiled.

"I'd like to be the one to ferry Sandy out tomorrow. I know that you or the major usually do, but I'd like to."

"Why?"

"Well, Sandy and I go back all the way to Cam Rahn. We flew in here together, and he's always been sort of a soul brother to me, I guess. I'd like to close it out by being the one to ferry him back to Cam Rahn."

Dave smiled wider and nodded. "That's a nice touch. Yeah, I think I can swing that. I'll take your cap flight tomorrow as a straight swap. Take him to Cam Rahn and they'll take care of his out-processing."

Right after breakfast, Rusty helped pile Sandy's bags into a plane. They took off, flew a low pass over a rainbow of smoke plumes and then made a wide circle over the field as Sandy snapped pictures of the place. Aside from a long, yodeled "Yeeeeha!" during the smoke pass, Sandy was even quieter than usual. When they were almost to Cam Rahn, Rusty asked him about it.

"It's just starting to sink in, Rusty. It's over. I'm going home. *Home.*"

"You're single, I know, but is there somebody special?"

"Sorta. Maybe…if I'm lucky. A B-52, though…" He shrugged.

"Hey, I didn't mean to bring you down. Your chances are a helluva lot better than while you're here, ya know. At least you'll be on the same continent."

He brightened. "No problems, huh?"

"Exactly! Old Flip was a lot smarter than he seemed, and that's saying something. 'No problems' isn't a bad philosophy of life. Flip's Rule, I'm gonna call it."

They landed and taxied to the 21st TASS ramp by following a jeep with checkered flags flying. As soon as they had shut down, a sergeant ran up and asked which of them was the DEROS. Sandy barely had time to turn and shake Rusty's hand before he was hustled off. Rusty had to shout at his back, "Bye, Sandy…and welcome home!"

The ground crew refueled and armed the plane with rockets – they'd flown down with empty pods just to replenish the inventory – then Rusty took off again. The trip back to Ban Me Thuot was bittersweet. Rusty was now senior

FAC, but senior to a crowd of strangers. He felt oddly lonely, almost an alien emotion for a man who relished being alone.

Over the next few days of trying, Rusty managed to get an official phone call through to Officer Assignments. The person working his file – Rusty was surprised it was already in work – confirmed the pattern Rusty had been seeing. The choices for a returning FAC were slim. He could expect a B-52 or an assignment to Air Training Command. Rusty immediately and fervently told him that he fairly lusted to be a T-38 instructor, gushing with such exuberance that he actually started to believe it himself. Nope, the voice said, no T-38 slots open. Those went to returning high-performance pilots. He might be able to find a T-37 slot.

"You have any right there at Randolph? I love San Antonio."

Again, the oily voice professed regret. Rusty could tell the jerk was yanking his chain. The man probably already had Rusty's assignment picked and was just enjoying his feeble bit of power and leverage against pilots. Probably a resentful UPT washout, or some dorky guy with acres of acne pimples and Coke-bottle glasses, Rusty imagined.

"What do you have?"

"A T-37 to Columbus," the voice tried to make it sound like a plum assignment.

Rusty suddenly remembered that was exactly what Kit Rushing had drawn. He may have surprised the Personnel officer off his stool when he said, "I'll take it."

Rusty hung up and went to see Sanderson. "Well, I seem to have sealed my fate."

"How so?"

"I think I just agreed to be a T-37 IP."

Sanderson grinned and stuck out his hand. "No shit? Good. That's really good. Where to? Williams? Randolph?"

"No such luck. Columbus, probably."

"Oh. Well, at least it's not a Buff, right?"

"Yup. No problems," Rusty grinned. It was beginning to work, that philosophy.

The chow hall had ham and turkey for Thanksgiving. Buchenhardt ate three times as much as anyone else, sighing and moaning that this was finally food fit for a real American. Rusty had to grin. It almost made Buckandfart seem human.

Afterwards, they were all lying around the big room, trying to digest the huge meal. Ed King was telling them what it was like to FAC up on the border of North Vietnam and Laos. "We faced big guns, not just 51-calibers and 14.5s but those damn four-barrel 23mms that fire so fast it looks like a golden hose of bullets. There were clusters of 37, 57 and even 85-millimeter guns guarding the Mu Gia pass. We busted more AAA guns than trucks, until it got to be so dangerous that we simply couldn't risk sending O-2s in there any more."

Rusty stared at him, embarrassed to admit that he had been petrified at the thought of facing a single 37mm gun. They faced down *clusters* of 37s - and even bigger guns? My God, how had they survived?

"What finally made them pull you guys out? Radar?" Getz asked.

"No, not altogether, although radar-controlled guns were starting to show up. What pulled the plug was the SA-7. It's a nasty little sonofabitch, a shoulder-fired heat-seeking missile. Kinda like a bazooka but the bastard guides on you. Damn near suicide to face one in an O-2. If you're high enough to evade the guns, you can't outmaneuver the missile. Drop down to get out of that Strella envelope – that's what they call the SA-7, the Strella – and the guns hose the shit outta you."

"No shit! A shoulder fired SAM? Jesus!" Jack spurted, forgetting for a moment to project an invincible, godlike image. "What do they look like?"

"Just like an RPG, until they fire it. It leaves a big white smoke donut behind when it launches, and that's how you first detect it. Then it climbs on a column of white smoke."

Rusty almost fainted. "Holy shit," he wheezed. "I think I had one of those fired at me!"

Every eye in the room turned to him.

"Last week, when I tried to put that team in up by Lumphat. I was down at a hundred feet and 90 knots when the whole fucking NVA army started shooting at me and the Kingbees. Then there was a flash and a column of smoke that passed right in front of me. I swear it came by between me and the front prop, it just appeared there and then I flew through it – whoosh. I thought it was an RPG."

"A white smoke column? Was there a donut or mushroom of white smoke on the ground?" Ed leaned toward him and asked.

"Yeah. Yeah there was. It looked like the smoke from a Willey Pete."

"That was no RPG. RPGs burn clean with a big bang and a big dust plume behind, but the motor burns out before it leaves the launch tube. They don't trail any column of smoke," Ed said with authority. "Where was this again?"

"Lumphat. It's a former provincial capital, maybe 20 or 30 miles south of the Laotian border. There's been a shitload of truck traffic and more through there recently. The guys that fired at me were regular NVA, in uniform and all."

"Hmmm. It's possible. That sounds like it's just a few dozen miles farther down the trail from where we worked. Maybe they're bringing portable anti-aircraft defenses along with them. The bastards," he added with a spit of contempt. "You were doubly lucky, Rusty."

"How so?"

"Well, you were too low for the thing to have armed up. By the time it did, and then started looking for a heat source, it had already passed you. And second, that must've been a one-level gunner on that thing. If he were better trained, he'd have waited until you had flown past him a half-mile or so before he fired. And then...well let's just say you'd have gotten a Strella suppository."

The room was silent for a full minute as that image chilled them all. King started again, "Strellas this far south. Man, what else?"

"Hell, I think they have tanks," Rusty added. "There are tread marks out there on one trail I watch."

"Tanks! Are you shitting me?" Danny Craig spurted, forgetting himself.

"Well, Brookside didn't want to believe me either, but I know what I saw. I think one of the bridges out there has been reinforced with steel girders underneath, too."

"Now how the hell could you have seen that?" Jack said, reverting back into character.

"Funny, that's almost exactly what Brookside said. I got down low on the downstream side and looked is how. Those aren't logs under there. They're I-beams, I say. And it does not portend anything good."

"No fucking shit," Getz said. "Tanks. Holy mother of pearl." He said the last few words in a perfect rendition of WC Fields.

They all laughed at him. The tense mood loosened by orders of magnitude immediately.

The six of them – counting Sanderson – fell back into a regular routine of missions. King quickly became a seasoned veteran. He said it was almost like being on autopilot after dueling with the big guns on the North Vietnam border. Rusty believed him. Suddenly, the whole Mike FAC experience started to seem like a quiet backwater of the war to Rusty, not the dangerous, exotic business he'd assumed all along. The cloak and dagger war had lost its glitter. Rusty began to consider what that C-130 crew had said about the Steve Canyon program.

He cornered Dave Sanderson. "Dave, what's this I hear about Steve Canyon? I'm thinking about being a Raven."

"No. Forget it. Why would you even consider that? Do you have any idea…?"

"No, I don't. That's why I'm asking."

"Rusty, I don't know what triggered this, but forget it. First, you're too short. You'd have to extend at least another six moths. Second, it's…I don't want to say beyond your abilities, because it isn't. But, almost half of those guys go home in a body bag. I've met Mary Beth, and I couldn't face her if you… Let's just say that if you did volunteer for it, I'd recommend against you being accepted. Let's let it go at that, okay?"

"But what is it? Why would you do that?"

"I'm not at liberty to say what the Raven program is. That's not a cop out; it's really all I'm allowed to say. Maybe it's even a bit beyond what I can say. No. Go home. Be a T-37 IP and push this stupid thought out of your mind. That's an order. Okay?"

"But I don't understand. I've been talking with Ed; and what the Nail FACs do seems so much more…I don't know…important. I feel like I should volunteer for something bigger. I thought this job was important and dangerous, but when I hear him talk…well, he seems to think this SOG thing is a walk in the park. Hell, even Buchenhardt said that way back when. Maybe I haven't paid my dues or something."

"Do you think you haven't done enough if you don't get killed?"

"No. That's not it, but…"

"Then shut up right now. You've done a good job here as a Mike. And before you got here as well, or you wouldn't have been hired in here. Yes, I'll admit that there are more dangerous FAC jobs than this one. That doesn't mean that anyone who didn't do those jobs isn't worthy of respect or honor. Let me ask you…do you think that Cramer, or Lopez, or Hannah or anybody else around here who isn't a pilot doesn't deserve respect for the job they do?"

"Of course not. Those guys work their asses off."

"Then put yourself in the same perspective. Just because you don't face SA-2 missiles or big AAA guns on every single flight doesn't mean that you haven't faced danger, or that you aren't worthy of respect. You did your job. It wasn't easy. You might have been killed on any one of your missions. You weren't. So don't feel as though you have to stick your dick into every knothole in the fence until it gets bitten off by a rabid dog, okay?"

Rusty thought about it. As always, Sanderson was right. "I paid my dues, huh?"

"In spades. Go home. Be a good IP. Hell, be as good an IP as you imagine I was."

"What does *that* mean?"

"Just that nobody's perfect. I have warts, just like everyone else. So do you. If somebody asks you if you have warts, you'd admit to it. There's nothing shameful about it. The point is that you don't run down the street screaming that you have warts."

All Rusty could do was laugh.

Rusty inserted a team a few days later, well clear of the Lumphat danger. Almost miraculously, the team got in safely and stayed cold for its entire five-day mission, and he extracted them just as cleanly. It was almost like the first days at BMT, when one could almost count on a team going in and out like commuters.

To their surprise, a package arrived for Sandy Hubert the next day. It was heavy and clunked dully when shaken. It was clearly a "care" package, and from the condition of the wrapping, it had also been in transit for a long time. After discussion, it seemed silly to send it back to the States. There was nothing in this box that Sandy wasn't already enjoying to his heart's content. They opened it.

Inside was a whole Hickory Farms beef stick salami, now green with mold; a jar of homemade sweet pickles, miraculously unbroken because it was swaddled in socks, new underwear and T-shirts; and a tin of fruitcake, as naturally indestructible as all its kind. They reluctantly disposed of the moldy salami, divvied up the underwear and enjoyed the pickles immensely with their beer that evening. Even the hootch maids turned their noses up at the fruitcake.

Rusty landed after a routine look-see mission and wandered into the big room for a beer. He was startled to see a monkey perched on the bookshelves, tethered there by a red silk ribbon tied around its neck. The creature eyed him warily at first and then leapt over to him when he sat down. It sat on Rusty's knee looking cautiously into his face for a few seconds, then scrambled onto his shoulder. Rusty was enjoying the attention of this exotic pet when, without warning, the cussed thing bit his ear hard enough to draw blood. Rusty yelped and swatted it across the room. It landed with a thud, then scrambled back up onto the same shelf it had occupied when Rusty came in. It sat there and scratched itself as though nothing had happened, except that it glared doubly hard at Rusty.

Getz wandered in. "I see you've met Ham," he said as Rusty dabbed at his bleeding ear with a handkerchief. "Count yourself lucky. He seems to have an ear fixation, and he'll either bite one, piss in one or fuck one. Of the three, biting may be best."

"I doubt it. Do these damn things get rabies? It'd be just my luck to die from rabies given to me by some fucking VC monkey."

"I don't think so. And in your case, it's a biting monkey. Buchenhardt got the fucking monkey. He was even less happy. He wondered about syphilis."

Rusty had to laugh, despite the pain. "Just the same, if that critter jumps up on me again, I'm gonna grab him by the tail and bash his brains out. They make better soup than they do pets, in my opinion. Where'd he come from, anyway?"

"One of the little guys brought him by as a gift."

"Uh huh. He probably got tired of having his ears bitten or screwed and just dumped the thing."

"Don't forget pissed in. Trust me, that's no picnic, either."

"There's only one way you could know," Rusty laughed again.

"Uh huh," Getz grinned.

A week later, the monkey vanished. It had been in the big room, contentedly scratching its scrotum when Rusty went out for a morning flight, and it was gone when Rusty landed. Nobody had seen where it went. Nobody cried to see it gone, either. When they went to lunch, Buchenhardt warily asked, as he had begun to do, what they were eating. "Ham and noodle soup," Getz said with a straight face.

They all managed to keep quiet until Buchenhardt had almost finished a brimming bowl, but then they broke down and guffawed so hard they could hardly stand. Jack looked at them mystified until he suddenly got it, then shoved the bowl back across the table so hard it slopped all over the place.

The comfortable routine went on. With one FAC off every day to handle the aftereffects of his malaria pill, that left four to fly cap missions, do some VR or scout out the next infil site. Bridgewater flew to ALO meetings or elsewhere, and Sanderson filled in as needed or to ferry airplanes on maintenance or parts runs. Days drifted by in this predictable, almost somnolent routine.

Rusty was airborne on a morning cap, reveling in the crisp clear air of the winter calm and starting to think a bit about Christmas. His robin was Truong, and Truong was dozing contentedly. It was almost time to be relieved, and Rusty was starting to put his maps away.

"Mike 58, Mike 50." Rusty turned down the music from AFVN. "Bring it home, 58. You're done."

"Copy, 50. Uh, I haven't heard from 54 yet."

"He'll be there shortly. Mike 58, you DEROS tomorrow. Repeat, you're done."

Rusty stared at the radio as if he were in a dream, then he yelled, "YEEEEHAW!" Poor Truong almost leapt out of his harness. Rusty slammed the throttles to the stops, dove steeply and then zoomed up, twisting in full yoke and some rudder to swoop through one barrel roll and then another. Finally, he leveled out, heading east. Truong wasn't sure what had happened, but he grinned at Rusty nonetheless.

"Truong, I go home now. Go home...real home."

Truong nodded and smiled, but with an oddly rueful look.

"Truong no go home...ever."

Rusty looked at him and remembered Truong had been a Chieu Hoi. His home was in North Vietnam and he certainly would never live to see it again. How selfish it must seem to Truong for Rusty to be this happy – or to have a home free from war. But even that guilty reflection couldn't dampen Rusty's spirits.

Back at the field, Rusty flew the downwind leg of his landing pattern right over the compound, and he could see the fire hoses already being laid out. Grinning, he turned final. Only as he told the tower, "Mike 58, base for full stop," did he realize that it was indeed a full stop. It would be his very last landing in an O-2. Trying too hard to make it a good one, Rusty managed to bump it down rather than grease it on, but he didn't care. He taxied in and Andy Corso pinned his rockets, grinning ear to ear. Rusty parked in the center of the ramp just as Sandy had done, Truong jumped out and Lopez tried to drown Rusty the moment he stepped away from the plane's door. Lopez eluded Rusty's attempts to wrest the hose away, but in the scuffle, everybody got pretty wet anyway.

The rest of the day was a complete blur for Rusty. He decided to keep his Ubon clothes, even the ill-fitting boots and the too-tight shirts. He wrapped the lovely Thai Buddha and the cork carving in layers of clothes, hoping beyond hope that they'd survive shipment home. And when the duffel was nearly full, he took the rest of his red, threadbare fatigues and flight suits and tossed them into the trash.

As he worked, Sanderson appeared in the doorway. "Forget something, Spike?" he said, using the mildly derogatory term he'd always used for his students so long ago in UPT. He waved a sheaf of papers.

"My orders! Tell me – what did I get?"

"Just what you asked for: a Tweet to Columbus. Congratulations. I mean that."

Rusty shook his hand and beamed at him. "I know. Thanks to you, too."

Before he knew it, they were all in the Club, and one of the Special Forces officers was saying things about him. All Rusty heard was the sound of his own blood roaring in his ears, but felt immense pride when the green beret settled on his head – and at Sergeant McGuire's crisp salute. There was much hooting and cheering. Rusty remembered having drinks, but felt not the least tinge of a buzz. Chi Li came up to him and he cringed, anticipating another cruel pinch, but felt a demure peck on his cheek instead. In a great whirl of noise and laughter, tinged with a whiff of the Club's remnant CS gas, the night somehow ended.

Rusty lay in his bunk, but looked around the room in an almost maudlin attempt to memorize every detail of it, from the rusty window screens to the Playmate of the Month pinned to his locker. He tried to remember the squeak of Getz's bed springs, the predictable quadruple bang of the night's outgoing mortar rounds, the faint rumble of the diesel generators in the far corner of this 400-yard square prison that had been and still was – for oh so short a time yet – his home.

And then it was morning. Rusty was one and a wakeup: just today and the morning he'd leave Vietnam forever. He laid there, heart thudding with excitement as he realized that, like Sandy, he'd be home for the holidays. He was going home almost seven weeks early. And then, Rusty panicked. Mary Beth didn't know! He had to try to call her.

"I'm sorry sir,' Hannah said, hanging up the phone. "There's no MARS line available at all." He was disconsolate, as if he'd had to tell Rusty his DEROS had been canceled after all.

Rusty started to protest, but then stopped and patted him fondly on the shoulder. "That's okay, my old friend. There's no problem. None at all."

Before Rusty realized it, he was strapping into the right seat, Sanderson in the left. They took off, zooming through the now-traditional smoke sendoff, and not until that moment did Rusty remember to try to take some pictures. By the time he'd squirmed his camera out, they were almost too far from BMT to get a good shot. Rusty watched it dwindle, and then turned his eyes away from it forever.

As they were landing, Rusty realized that he'd been even quieter than Sandy had. He laughed, "Is everyone this quiet on their DEROS flight?"

"Pretty much. Overwhelmed?"

"Completely. I still can't believe it, that it's over; that I'm not going back there ever again. Mostly that I *am* going home…alive."

"Uh huh. But you are. Really." He waited a few seconds, then asked, "You know what's going to happen now?"

"Um, out-process, right?"

"Yeah. You'll turn in all your gear. You do still have the same guns you were issued, right? No mix-up, because they check the serial numbers of everything."

Rusty nodded, but secretly had a panic attack that somehow he had the wrong one or something.

"Then you'll have a drug test. Assuming you pass," he paused to snicker, "only then will they issue you a plane ticket for the Freedom Bird. If that all gets finished today, they'll pop you down to Ton San Nhut and you'll be airborne tomorrow. Got it?"

"I guess so." Rusty sounded as muddled as he felt.

"Just go where they point you, Spike."

Sanderson was busy with approach control and the tower next, and they didn't get to talk until they'd stopped behind that same flagged truck.

"Goodbye, Rusty. Say hello to Mary Beth for me, and look me up if you ever need to. For anything, you hear?"

"I do, Dave. But I don't think I'll have to, now." They shook hands, and Rusty turned away to follow a sergeant who already was tossing his duffel into a jeep.

To his relief, all Rusty's gear matched the numbers written on the issue sheets. As the supply clerk took it from him, Rusty had a pang of regret to lose the Smith & Wesson revolver. It had been with him on every flight, and he suddenly wanted it as a souvenir — but with no hope of getting it home, he dismissed the thought.

The drug test was humiliating. Along with seven or eight other guys, Rusty had to stand at a standard urinal trough and fill a bottle. The humiliating part was the one-way mirror wall. Behind it had to be someone watching to make sure one of them didn't try to fill his bottle with someone else's urine. Guys on drugs had been known to stash a condom or balloon in their sleeve and use it to dribble drug-free urine into their sample bottle.

Next, he went to the TASS headquarters to pick up his records and sign out. They issued him a sizable advance on his travel money. While he was there, the drug result came in – negative of course. With an envious smile, the sergeant handed him the last, most precious bit of paper: a one-way ticket aboard Pan American Airways from Saigon to San Francisco. Rusty's were not the only glistening eyes the sergeant had ever seen.

Rusty was bundled aboard a painfully loud C-123 for the short flight to Saigon, and then to an isolated set of quarters surrounded by razor wire. He asked the desk clerk about it, and learned that these were secure quarters only for those DEROSing the next day. The security was to prevent anyone from changing places with someone not supposed to go. As if.

A meal was delivered, and Rusty ate it, but he was too overwhelmed to notice what it was. He showered and crawled into bed, only to be tormented by a vivid and terrifying scene in his head. He imagined a Russian 122-mm rocket slamming into this very building, killing him hours before he was to finally depart. He tossed and turned much of the night, unable to get the frightening vision out of his head. At last, head swimming with fatigue, he heard others arising and clambered out of bed. Not even another shower helped, but he shaved and put on his least scruffy uniform. Rusty hadn't worn this khaki uniform since he gotten back in-country, but it was now battered and reddish nonetheless. Stained and damaged like everything else that ever went to Vietnam, he sneered.

He and others were bused to a hangar and locked inside a huge wire cage like criminals, although Rusty now knew the point was to keep others out, not them in. At a long table, a phalanx of grim-faced soldiers methodically emptied and searched every single bag and parcel. Large signs listed items prohibited from being taken back to the US, and underneath it a red barrel was labeled "Amnesty Barrel. No questions asked." Rusty peeked inside and was astonished to see guns, hand grenades, explosives, a bag of what had to be drugs, two bottles of liquor, a Montagnard crossbow and at least a dozen wicked knives. As a humorless drone picked through his bag, Rusty mused

≈ 418 ≈

aloud that it might be dangerous to leave that barrel sitting there full like that all the time.

The man answered without looking up, "That's all from this morning, sir." Rusty turned to look at it again, even more astonished. When he turned back, the soldier had closed his duffel and was sliding it back. "Go through that gate, sir. You cannot come back this way for any reason. There's a latrine in there."

As men cleared the bag inspection, they came into this claustrophobic, intimidating space, which was double-walled and double-roofed with chain-link fence. There was a space five feet wide between the inner and outer walls, and Rusty realized that was to prevent anything from being passed through the wire. Were drugs that big a problem, he wondered? But such a thing wouldn't have been built unless experience showed it was needed. Finally, they counted and exchanged everyone's scrip for real US currency. Again, Rusty luxuriated in the supple feel of it.

At last, buses pulled up, two armed guards unlocked a gate that led down a chain link tunnel right to the doors of the bus, and they all clambered aboard. As the first bus filled, another pulled up until four were crammed with men and their bags. As if to serve as a final, stunning contrast between Vietnam and the World, the peeling, smoky, rancid-smelling buses disgorged them at the boarding stairs of a gleaming, pristine, blue and white jet with Pan Am on the side. Their bags were taken and they filed aboard like automatons in eerie silence. Not one man spoke. On the plane, they sat and wordlessly buckled in. Not even the sight of pert roundeyed stewardesses broke the spell. It was if the entire 200 of them were holding one collective breath. As if one tiny disturbance would burst the bubble and the whole thing would evaporate like a dream.

Rusty's heart began to hammer when the door closed and the engines started. By the time the brakes released for takeoff, it was racing. The instant the plane broke ground, most of the men erupted in wild, joyously frantic cheers, but Rusty still dug his nails into the armrest. He knew takeoff was the most dangerous time of flight, but he also stared at the ground, almost paralyzed with the fear that he'd see a white donut blossom into a racing column of white smoke. Oh, God, not now, he fervently wished among the cheers. And then, finally, the ugly brown sewer of the Mekong passed behind, magically becoming the sapphire of the South China Sea; and Rusty knew he was, finally, safe.

The flight droned endlessly across the Pacific, refueling twice, and Rusty remained largely sleepless. He thought about all that he'd so suddenly left behind, and what would become of the men he'd known. When the collapse came, as he knew it would, what would happen to men like Truong, Hua, Xuan, Dinh? To Y-Monh? He grieved now for their future. By the time they landed in San Francisco, he'd been cramped into his seat for almost sixteen hours. He was sweaty, rumpled, stinky and crusty-eyed. It was barely dawn as they landed.

There were greeters lined up at the jetway gate, but they weren't family or friends. Arranged in two jeering lines was a troop of scruffy, long-haired, obscenity-shouting war protesters bedecked in peace symbols and reeking of marijuana smoke. As the men passed through this gauntlet of filth, the protesters spat on them. "Don't even touch 'em, guys," a kindly airport gate worker warned, "Or they'll prefer charges and you'll go to jail."

Rusty had been hit several times with gobs of spit and mucous, but he was nearing the end of the gauntlet with his pride intact when one particularly smelly and ugly bastard stepped out to block his path. He screamed at Rusty, pointing to his wings and calling him a baby bomber. Rusty was too exhausted to have either a quick wit or temper, but could feel a red heat building inside. He leaned his nose to within an inch of the scumbag's and rasped with all the venom he could muster, "And you, you mangy little fag fucker, are NOT A PROBLEM." The hairball recoiled back in astonishment, and Rusty strode away.

Rusty had a voucher for any connecting flight he wanted, but it was so early in the day most of the ticket counters weren't open yet. He staggered to one that was, and pleaded for the next possible flight to Chicago. The sight of his phlegm-spattered uniform, red eyes and the obvious point of his departure must have melted the ticket agent's heart, because he found a seat on a flight leaving almost immediately. Rusty just had time to dab some of the filth from his uniform in a men's room.

He finally did fall asleep, or more accurately unconscious, on that flight. He was awakened by a touch at his shoulder as they were landing. He collected his bag, hailed a cab and said "9938 South Claremont, just off 95th and Western" to the cabbie.

"Where you coming in from, soldier? Vietnam?"

"How'd you know?"

"Hell, man. This is Chicago – on December 19th. It's a thousand degrees below zero and you sit there in a short-sleeve shirt. It don't take no Einstein." He shook his head and chuckled, then turned around to look at Rusty. "Hey, buddy, I ain't one'a them hippie types, but is it as bad as they say over there?"

"You'll never know. But it's worse."

Rusty paid him and walked up the frost-heaved, ice-armored concrete steps leading to Mary Beth's parents' house. He never did get a chance to call and warn her, even from San Francisco. He simply rang the bell, and the door opened. She screamed, "Rusty! Oh my God, oh my God, you're home!"

Rusty crushed her to him and whispered into Mary Beth's ear, "I am home. Just like I promised. And I always keep a promise."

For a long time, they compulsively touched and held hands as they talked. Rusty told her about Columbus and his – their - assignment, how they'd be stable there for three years or so. She was excited to learn that she'd get to meet Kit there, too.

Later, Rusty started to unpack. As soon as he opened the duffel, he knew. His prized green beret was gone. The son of a bitch bag inspector back in Saigon must have filched it while his back was turned. Rusty muttered a curse, and Mary Beth rushed to his side, "What's wrong? What's the problem?"

Rusty took a deep, calm breath. "Honey," he smiled broadly, "It may sound Flip when I say this, but; there is not now, nor will there ever again be another problem."

The End